W9-BRH-160

THE HUNCHBACK OF NOTRE-DAME
(NOTRE-DAME DE PARIS)

THE GOLDEN HERITAGE SERIES

THE HUNCHBACK OF NOTRE-DAME (NOTRE-DAME DE PARIS)

VICTOR HUGO

Galley Press

Published in this edition by Galley Press, an imprint of
W. H. Smith Limited, Registered No. 237811 England.
Trading as W. H. Smith Distributors, St John's House
East Street, Leicester, LE1 6NE.

ISBN 0 86136 602 6

Production services by
Book Production Consultants, Cambridge

Printed and bound in Yugoslavia by Mladinska Knjiga

CONTENTS

BOOK I

BOOK II

BOOK III

BOOK IV

BOOK V

BOOK VI

BOOK VII

BOOK VIII

BOOK IX

BOOK X

BOOK XI

NOTRE-DAME

BOOK I

CHAPTER I

THE GRAND' SALLE

ON the 6th of January 1482 the Parisians were awakened by the noise of all the bells within the triple circuit of the City, the University, and the Town ringing in full peal. Yet this is not a day of which history has preserved any remembrance. There was nothing remarkable in the event which thus put in agitation so early in the morning the bells and the good people of Paris. It was neither an assault of Picards or of Burgundians; nor a shrine carried in procession; nor a revolt of scholars in *la vigne de Laas;* nor an entry of *notre dit très-redouté seigneur Monsieur le Roi*—that is, in plain English, of their most dread lord the King; nor yet a good hanging up of thieves, male and female, at the Justice de Paris (justice and gibbet having been synonymous in the good old feudal times). Neither was it the sudden arrival, so frequent in the fifteenth century, of some ambassador and his train, all covered with lace and plumes. Scarcely two days had elapsed since the last cavalcade of this sort, that of the Flemish envoys commissioned to conclude the marriage treaty between the Dauphin and Margaret of Flanders, had made its entry into Paris, to the great annoyance of Monsieur le Cardinal de Bourbon, who to please the King had been obliged to give a gracious reception to that rude train of Flemish burgomasters, and entertain them, at his Hôtel de Bourbon, with one of the rude dramatic exhibitions of the time, while a beating rain drenched the magnificent tapestry at his door.

But on the 6th of January that which set in motion the whole *populaire* of Paris, as old Jean de Troyes phrases it, was the double holiday, united since time immemorial, of the *Jour des Rois*, or Day of the Kings (being the day on which the Eastern king, or *magi*, came to worship the new-born Saviour at Bethlehem, known amongst us as the Epiphany or Twelfth Day), and the *Fête des Fous*, or Feast of Fools.

This same Feast of Fools, strange a figure as it makes among Christian festivals, was once universally celebrated throughout Christendom, though on different days of the year, in different places. But when the Church of Rome was alarmed by the progress of the early champions of the Reformation, this annual exhibition of licentiousness and buffoonery, as being one of the most conspicuous occasions of scandal, fell under her censure. It was formally condemned by several councils; and a circular in disapproval of it was sent to all the clergy of France by the Paris University, dated the 11th of March 1444. From this letter, which is printed at the end of the works of Peter of Blois, we find that this feast had been, in the eyes of the clergy, so well imagined and so Christian that those who sought to suppress it were looked upon as excommunicate and cursed; and the Sorbonne doctor, Jean des Lyons, in his discourse against the *Roi-boit,* one of the popular remnants of paganism, informs us that a doctor of divinity publicly maintained at Auxerre, about the close of the fifteenth century, "that the Feast of Fools was no less pleasing to God than the Feast of the Immaculate Conception of the Blessed Virgin; besides, that it was of much higher antiquity in the Church." Nor, for a number of years, could the denunciations issued from the highest ecclesiastical authority even so much as put an end to the participation of the clergy themselves in these indecent saturnalia, since we find those of Dijon, according to their own registers, running about the streets with the precentor of the Fools in 1521; and the parliament of that city found it necessary, by a decree of the 19th of January 1552, to forbid the celebration of this feast.

Seeing, then, that the ecclesiastics themselves were so loath to part with their share in the enjoyment of this disorderly revel, it is little to be wondered at that the people, ever tenacious of their holidays, should in many places, and in Paris amongst others, in an age in which they experienced enough of iron constraint in the ordinary course of their existence, have clung to the delight of this one day of uncontrolled licence in the year—for which that very constraint gave them an eager and unhealthy appetite; an appetite, however, which, for some time longer, it was found politic to indulge.

On that day then, the last of the Christmas holidays in 1482, a bonfire was to be made in the Place de Grève, a maypole planted at the Chapelle de Braque, and a mystery performed at the Palais de Justice. Proclamation to that effect had been made the day before, by sound of trumpet, at the crossings of the streets, by the provost's men, dressed in fine hacquetons, or sleeveless frocks, of violet-coloured camlet, with large white crosses on the breast.

The crowd of people accordingly took their way in the morning from all quarters of the town, leaving their houses and shops shut up, towards one of the three places appointed. Each one had made his choice, for the bonfire, the maypole, or the mystery. It must be said, however, to the praise of the ancient good sense of the Parisian cockneys, that the greater part of the multitude directed their steps towards the bonfire, which was perfectly seasonable, or towards the mystery, which was to be performed in the *Grand' Salle*, or great hall of the Palais de Justice, well roofed and windowed; judiciously leaving the poor ill-dressed maypole to shiver all alone, under a January sky, in the cemetery of the Chapelle de Braque.

The people flocked chiefly into the approaches of the Palais de Justice, because it was known that the Flemish ambassadors, who had arrived the day but one before, intended to be present at the performance of the mystery and the election of the Fools' Pope, which was likewise to take place in the Grand' Salle.

It may be as well here to observe that in France the Palais de Justice and the Grand' Salle held the same place, not only in history and tradition, but in modern associations, as is occupied in England by the ancient palace and hall of Westminster. In this oldest metropolitan residence of the French kings, as once at Westminster, the monarchs administered justice, or what passed for such, in person; until, in either country the immense accumulation of judicial proceedings keeping pace with, if not outstripping, the increase of population and artificial wealth, the discharge of the judicial functions of royalty was finally altered from an actual exercise into a constant delegation. The supreme courts of judicature, however, remained in each country where they were originally established. The Grand' Salle of the Palais at Paris, like Westminster Hall in England, ceasing to be the resort of royalty, except on certain great public occasions, took the almost exclusive character in the popular mind of the great seat and centre of the administration of the law; and what we in England should term legal phrases were universally denominated in France *termes de Palais*, so intimately were law and the Palais associated in the public imagination; and although the Palais, including the Grand' Salle, was destroyed by fire in 1618 (of which more anon), and its architectural existence consequently underwent a metamorphosis, its character as the principal seat of judicature, like that of the Westminster palace itself, has subsisted to the present time; and the Court of Cassation, the Cour Royale, the civil courts, and that of Exchequer are still held within its precincts.

It was no easy matter, on the day with which our narrative opens, for a person to make his way into that great hall, although it was then reputed to be the largest single apartment in the world—whence its popular designation as *La Grande Salle*, the great hall *par excellence*. It is true, observes our author, that Sauval had not yet measured the great hall of the castle of Montargis; nor, we may add, is it probable that the Parisian public were exactly acquainted with the dimensions of that of Westminster.

The open space in front of the Palais, thronged with people, presented to the gazers from the windows the appearance of a sea, into which five or six streets, like the mouths of so many rivers, were every moment discharging fresh floods of human heads. The waves of this multitude, incessantly swelling, broke against the angles of the houses, which projected here and there, like so many promontories, into the irregularly-shaped basin of the Place, or, as we should perhaps term it in England, the Palace yard—the word Place being used by our neighbours to express almost any open space in a town, whatever its form or dimensions. In the centre of the high Gothic [1] front of the Palais the great steps, incessantly ascended and descended by a double stream, which, after being broken by the intermediate *perron* or staircase leading from the basement story, spread in broad waves over its too lateral declivities—the great steps, we say, poured their stream incessantly into the Place, like a cascade into a lake. The shouts, the peals of laughter, the clattering of those thousands of feet, made altogether a great noise and clamour. From time to time this noise and clamour were redoubled; the stream which carried all this multitude towards the steps of entrance was checked, disturbed, and

[1] The word Gothic, in the sense in which it is generally employed, though quite improper, is perfectly established. It is, therefore, adopted by the author, as by everybody else, to denote the architecture of the latter half of the Middle Ages, that of which the pointed arch is the characteristic—immediately succeeding the architecture of the former period, of which the circular arch is the principle.

thrown into an eddy. This was occasioned by the thrust of some archer, or the horse of some one of the provost's sergeants prancing about to restore order—" which admirable expedient," observes our author, " the *prévôté* handed down to the *connétablie*, the *connétablie* to the *maréchaussée*, and the *maréchaussée* to our gendarmerie of Paris."

At the doors, at the windows, at the *lucarnes*, or small round attic windows, and on the roofs swarmed thousands of goodly *bourgeois* faces, looking calmly and soberly at the Palais or at the crowd, and exhibiting a most perfect satisfaction; for many of the good people of Paris are quite content with the spectacle of the spectators—nay, even a wall behind which something is going on is to them an object of no small interest.

If it could be given to us men of 1833 to mingle, in imagination, among those Parisians of the fifteenth century, and to enter along with them, all thrust about, squeezed, and elbowed by the crowd, into that immense hall of the Palais, which was found so small on the 6th of January 1482, the spectacle would have both interest and attraction for us, for we should find around us the most striking kind of novelty—that of great antiquity brought suddenly before the eye.

With the reader's permission, we will endeavour to retrace in idea the impression which he would have received in crossing with us the threshold of that great hall, amidst that motley throng in surcoat, hacqueton, and *cotte-hardie;* for while the two former terms denoted the ordinary upper garments of the men, the latter daring name was given to the upper skirt worn by Frenchwomen of that day.

And first of all our ears are filled with the buzzing of the multitude, and our eyes dazzled by the objects around us. Over our heads is a double vault of Gothic groining, lined with carved wainscoting, painted azure, and sprinkled with golden fleurs-de-lis; under our feet, a pavement of black and white marble in alternate squares; a few paces from us, an enormous pillar—then another—then another—making in all seven pillars in the length of the hall, supporting, in a central line, the internal extremities of the double vaulting. Around the four first pillars are little shops or stalls, all glittering with glass and trinkets; and around the three last are oaken benches, worn and polished by the breeches of the pleaders and the gowns of the *procureurs.* Around the hall, along its lofty walls, between the doors, between the windows, between the pillars, we behold the interminable range of the statues of all the French kings, from Pharamond downwards; the *rois fainéans*, or do-nothing kings, with their eyes upon the ground and their arms hanging down; the valiant and battling kings, with their faces and hands boldly lifted up to heaven. Then, in the long pointed windows, glows painted glass of a thousand colours; at the large entrances of the hall are rich doors, finely carved; and the whole—vaults, pillars, walls, cornices, and door-cases; wainscoting, doors, and statues—are splendidly illuminated, from top to bottom, with blue and gold, which, already a little tarnished at the period to which we have carried ourselves back, had almost entirely disappeared under dust and cobwebs in the year of grace 1549, in which the early Parisian antiquary, Du Breuil, still admired it by tradition.

Let the reader now figure to himself that immense oblong hall, made visible by the wan light of a January day, and entered by a motley and noisy crowd, pouring along by the walls and circling round the pillars; and he will at once have a general idea of the scene, of which we will endeavour to point out more precisely the curious particulars.

It is certain that if Ravaillac had not assassinated Henry IV., there would have been no documents relative to the trial of Ravaillac deposited in the registry of the Palais de Justice; no accomplices interested in causing the disappearance of the said documents, and therefore no incendiaries obliged, for want of any better expedient, to burn the registry for the sake of burning the documents, and to burn the Palais de Justice for the sake of burning the registry—in short, no fire of 1618. The whole Palais would have been still standing, with its old Grand' Salle; we might have said to the reader, " You have only to go to Paris and see it;" and so neither we should have been under the necessity of writing, nor he of reading, any description of it whatever. All which proves this very novel truth—that great events have incalculable consequences.

It is indeed very possible that Ravaillac's accomplices had nothing at all to do with the fire of 1618. We have two other very plausible explanations of it. The first is the great fiery star, a foot broad and half a yard high, which, as every Parisian knows, fell from the sky right upon the Palais, on the 7th of March, just after midnight.

The other is this noble quatrain of the old humorist Theophile:—

> " Certes, ce fut un triste jeu
> Quand à Paris dame Justice,
> Pour avoir mangé trop d'épice,
> Se mit tout le palais en feu "—

which, unluckily, is quite unsusceptible of translation, on account of the pun upon the word *épice*, which signifies fees as well as spices.

Whatever may be thought of this triple explanation—political, physical, and poetical—of the conflagration of the Palais de Justice in 1618, the fact of which, unfortunately, there is no doubt is the conflagration itself. Owing to that catastrophe, and above all to the divers successive restorations which have made away with what it had spared, there now remains very little of that original residence of the kings of France, of that palace the elder sister of the Louvre, and so ancient, even in the time of Philippe le Bel, that it was sought to discover the traces of the magnificent buildings erected there by King Robert and described by Helgaldus. Nearly all has disappeared. What has become of the Chancery chamber? What of the garden in which St. Louis administered justice, "clad in a *cotte* of camlet, a surcoat of *tiretaine* without sleeves, and over it a mantle of black sendal, lying upon carpets with Joinville?" Where is the chamber of the Emperor Sigismund?—that of Charles IV.?—that of Jean sans Terre? Where is the staircase from which Charles IV. promulgated his edict of pardon?—the flagstone on which Marcel, in the presence of the Dauphin, murdered Robert de Clermont and the Marshal de Champagne?—the wicket at which the bulls of the anti-pope Benedict were torn, and through which the bearers of them set out on their return coped and mitred in derision, and thus making the *amende honorable* through all Paris?—and the great hall itself, with its gilding, its azure, its pointed arches, its statues, its pillars, its immense vaults all variegated with carving?—and the gilded chamber?—and the stone lion which knelt at its door, with his head bowed down and his tail between his legs, like the lions of Solomon's throne, in the posture of humiliation appropriate to Strength in the presence of Justice?—and the rich doors?—and the beautiful stained glass?—and the carved iron-work, the perfection of which discouraged Biscornette?—and the delicate cabinet-work of Du Hancy? "What has time, what has man done with all those wonders?" asks our author. "What has been given us in exchange for all this—for all that Gaulish history, for all that Gothic art? In art we have the heavy, lowering arches of M. de Brosse, the awkward architect of the Portail Saint-Gervais; and as for history, we have the gabbling reminiscences of the great pillar, still resounding with the prattle of the *Patrus*. Here is not much to boast of. Let us go back to the real Grand' Salle of the real old Palais."

The two extremities of that vast parallelogram were occupied —the one by the famous marble table of a single piece, so long, so broad, and so thick that, say the old court-rolls in a style which might have given an appetite to Rabelais's Gargantua, "never was there such a slice of marble seen in the world;" the other by the chapel in which the reigning king, Louis XI., had caused his own figure to be sculptured kneeling before the Virgin, and into which he had conveyed, regardless that he was leaving two niches empty in the file of the royal statues, those of Charlemagne and St. Louis, two saints whom, as kings of France, he supposed to be very influential in heaven. This chapel, which was still quite new, having scarcely been built six years, was all in that charming state of delicate architecture, miraculous sculpture, and bold and exquisite carving which characterises the close of the Gothic era, and which we find perpetuated through the first half of the sixteenth century in the fantastic fairy-work of the period of the revival. The little pierced *rosace*, or rose-shaped window, above the entrance of the chapel, was in particular a masterpiece of grace and lightness; it had almost the airiness of lace. In the middle of the hall, opposite to the great door, an *estrade*, or short projecting gallery, covered with gold brocade, fixed against the wall, and a private entrance to which had been contrived by means of a funnel window of the gilded chamber, had been erected for the Flemish envoys and the other personages invited to the performance of the mystery.

It was upon the marble table that, according to custom, this exhibition was to take place. It had been prepared for that purpose early in the morning; and the rich slab of marble, scrawled all over by the heels of the lawyers' clerks, supported a high wooden framework, the upper surface of which, visible from every part of the hall, was to form the stage, while its interior, hidden by drapery, was to serve the actors as a dressing-room. A ladder, placed with great simplicity, outside, established a communication between the stage and the dressing-room, serving alike for entrance and for exit. No character ever so unexpected, no turn of events, no stroke of stage effect, but had to ascend this ladder. Innocent and venerable infancy of the art and of machinery!

Four sergeants of the bailiff of the Palais, the appointed guardians of all the popular pleasures, whether on holidays or on execution days, stood on duty at the four corners of the marble table.

The piece was not to commence until the twelfth stroke of noon from the great clock of the Palais. This was undoubtedly thought very late for a theatrical performance; but it had been necessary to consult the convenience of the ambassadors.

Now, all this multitude had been waiting since the early morning. A good many of these worthy people, in the greatness of their curiosity, had stood shivering since daybreak before the great steps of the Palais; some even affirmed that they had lain all night against the great door, to be sure of getting in first. The crowd was growing denser every moment, and, like a body of water overflowing its borders, began to ascend the walls, to squeeze round the pillars, to inundate the architraves, the cornices, the window-cases, every architectural or sculptural projection. The general impatience and uncomfortableness, the freedom allowed by a licentious holiday, the quarrels incessantly produced by the pressure of some sharp elbow or iron heel, and the wearisomeness of long expectation, infused, long before the hour at which the ambassadors were to arrive, a tone of sourness and bitterness into the clamours of this shut-up, squeezed, trodden, and stifled multitude. Nothing was heard but complaints and imprecations against the Flemings—the *prévôt des marchands*—the Cardinal de Bourbon—the Bailiff of the Palais—the Lady Marguerite d'Autriche—the sergeants of the wand—the cold—the heat—the bad weather—the Bishop of Paris—the Fool's Pope—the pillars—the statues—a door shut here—a window open there—all to the great amusement of the tribes of scholars from the University, and of lackeys from all quarters, scattered among the crowd, who mingled up with this mass of dissatisfaction all their mischievous tricks and jests, thus goading, as it were, the general ill-humour.

Amongst others, there was a group of these merry devils, who, after bursting out the glass of a window, had boldly seated themselves upon the entablature, and from thence cast their looks and their railleries by turns within and without the hall, upon the internal and the external crowd. By their mimic gestures, their peals of laughter, and the jocoseness with which they exchanged calls with their comrades the whole length of the hall, it was evident enough that those young clerks did not share the weariness and exhaustion of the rest of the assemblage, and that they very well knew how, for their own particular enjoyment, to extract from what was already under their eyes an entertainment which enabled them to wait patiently for the other.

"Upon my soul, it's you, Joannes Frollo de Molendino," shouted one of them to a little light-complexioned fellow, with a pretty, roguish face, clinging to the foliage of one of the capitals. "Rightly are you called John of the Mill, for your arms and legs look very much like the sails. How long have you been here?"

"By the devil's mercy," answered Jehan Frollo, commonly called *Du Moulin*, or *of the Mill*, "above four hours; and I'm in good hopes that they'll be deducted from my time in purgatory. I heard the King of Sicily's eight chanters strike up the first verse of the high mass of seven hours in the Sainte Chapelle."

"Fine chanters, truly," returned the other, "with voices still sharper than the points of their caps. Before founding a mass in honour of St. John, it would have been as well if the King had inquired whether St. John be fond of hearing Latin droned out with a Provençal accent."

"It was all for the sake of employing those cursed chanters of the King of Sicily that he did it," screamed an old woman in the crowd beneath the window. "What think you of a thousand livres parisis for a mass, and charged, too, upon the farm of the salt-water fish of the fish-market of Paris!"

"Peace, old woman!" replied a portly personage who was stopping his nose at the side of the fish-seller; "it was quite necessary to found a mass. Would you have had the King fall sick again?"

"Bravely spoken, Sire Giles Lecornu, master-furrier to the King's wardrobe!" cried the little scholar clinging to the capital.

A burst of laughter from the whole tribe of the scholars greeted the unlucky name of the poor furrier to the king's wardrobe.

"Lecornu—Giles Lecornu!" said some.

"*Cornutus et hirsutus*," answered another.

"Oh, to be sure," continued the little imp at the top of the pillar; "what have they to laugh at? Is not worthy Giles Lecornu brother to Maître Jehan Lecornu, provost of the king's household, son of Maître Mahiet Lecornu, first porter of the Bois de Vincennes—all citizens of Paris—all married, from father to son?"

This grave appeal redoubled their gaiety. The fat furrier, without answering a word, strove to escape the looks fixed upon him from all sides; but he exerted himself in vain, for all his efforts served only to wedge more solidly between the shoulders of his neighbours his great apoplectic face, purple with anger and vexation.

One of these neighbours, however, fat, short, and reverend-looking like himself, at length raised his voice on his behalf.

"Abominable," he exclaimed, "that scholars should talk thus to a townsman. In my time they would have been first beaten with a fagot and then burned with it."

At this the whole tribe burst out afresh.

"Hollo! who sings that stave? who's that ill-boding screech-owl?"

"Oh! I see who it is," said one: "it's Maître Andry Musnier."

"Because he's one of the four sworn booksellers to the University," said the other.

"All goes by fours in that shop," cried a third: "there are the four nations, the four faculties, the four attorneys, and the four booksellers."

"Well, then," resumed Jehan Frollo, "we must play four hundred devils with them all."

"Musnier, we'll burn thy books."

"Musnier, we'll beat thy lackey."

"Musnier, we'll kiss thy wife——"

"The good fat Mademoiselle Oudarde——"

"Who's as fresh and buxom as if she were a widow."

"The devil take you!" muttered Maître Andry Musnier.

"Maître Andry," said Jehan, still hanging by the capital, "hold your tongue, or I'll drop upon your head."

Maître Andry looked up, seemed to calculate for a moment the height of the pillar and the weight of the young rogue, multiplied in his mind that height by the square of the velocity, and was silent.

Jehan, being thus master of the field, continued triumphantly,—

"Yes, I would do it, though I am brother to an archdeacon."

"Fine fellows, in truth, are our gentlemen of the University, not even to have taken care that our privileges were respected on a day like this: for here are a maypole and a bonfire in the Town; a mystery, a fool's pope, and Flemish ambassadors in the City; and in the University, nothing at all!"

"And yet the Place Maubert is large enough," observed one of the young clerks posted in the recess of the window.

"Down with the rector, the electors, and the attorneys!" cried Joannes.

"We must make a bonfire to-night in the Champ-Gaillard," continued the other, "with Maître Andry's books."

"And the desks of the scribes," said his neighbour.

"And the wands of the beadles."

"And the spitting-boxes of the deans."

"And the buffets of the attorneys."

"And the tubs of the electors."

"And the rector's stools."

"Down, then," said little Jehan, winding up the stave; "down with Maître Andry, the beadles, and the scribes—the theologians, the physicians, and the decretists—the attorneys, the electors, and the rector!"

"Ah! then the world is at an end," muttered Maître Andry, stopping his ears.

"Apropos! the rector himself! here he comes through the Place!" cried one of those in the window-case.

They all now strove to turn themselves towards the Place.

"Is it really our venerable rector, Maître Thibaut?" asked Jehan Frollo du Moulin, who, as he was clinging to one of the internal pillars, could not see what was passing outside.

"Yes, yes," answered all the rest, "it is he—he himself—Maître Thibaut, the rector."

It was, in fact, the rector and all the dignitaries going in procession to meet the ambassadors, and crossing at that moment the Place of the Palais. The scholars, all crowded together at the window, greeted them as they passed by with sarcasms and ironical plaudits. The rector, marching at the head of his band, received the first broadside, and it was a rough one.

"Good-day, Monsieur le Recteur! Hollo! good-day to you!"

"How has the old gambler contrived to be here? Has he really quitted his dice?"

"How he goes trotting along on his mule! its ears are not so long as his."

"Hollo! good-day to you, Monsieur le Recteur Thibaut! *Tybalde Aleator!* Ah, you old noodle, you old gamester!"

"God preserve you! did you often throw twelve last night?"

"Oh, what a scarecrow countenance! all blue and battered through his love of dice and gaming."

"Where are you going to now, Thibaut, *Tybalde ad dados*—turning your back on the University, and trotting towards the Town?"

"No doubt he's going to seek a lodging in the Rue Thibautodé," cried Jehan du Moulin.

The whole gang repeated the pun with a voice of thunder and a furious clapping of hands.

"You're going to seek lodgings in the Rue Thibautodé, aren't you, Monsieur le Recteur, the devil's own gamester?"

Then came the turn of the other dignitaries.

"Down with the beadles! down with the mace-bearers!"

"Tell me, Robin Poussepain, who's that man there?"

"It's Gilbert de Suilly, *Gilbertus de Soliaco*, chancellor of the college of Autun."

"Here, take my shoe—you're better placed than I am—throw it in his face."

"*Saturnalitias, mittimus ecce nuces.*"

"Down with the six theologians with their white surplices!"

"Are those the theologians? I thought they were the six white geese that Ste. Geneviève gave to the Town for the fief of Roogny."

"Down with the physicians!"

"Down with the disputations, cardinal, and quadlibetary!"

"Here goes my cap at yon chancellor of St. Geneviève; I owe him a grudge."

"True; and he gave my place in the nation of Normandy to little Ascanio Falzaspada, belonging to the province of Bourges, because he's an Italian."

"It's an injustice!" exclaimed all the scholars.

"Ho there, Maître Joachim de Ladehors! Ho, Louis Dalmille! Ho, Lambert Hoctement!"

"The devil smother the attorney of the nation of Germany!"

"And the chaplains of the Sainte Chapelle, with their grey amices, *cum tunicis grisis!*"

"*Sue de pellibus grisis fourratis.*"

"Hollo, the masters of arts! All the fine black copes! all the fine red copes!"

"That makes the rector a fine tail!"

"It might be a Doge of Venice going to marry the sea."

"Now again, Jehan—the canons of St. Geneviève!"

"The devil take all the canons together!"

"Abbé Claude Choart—Doctor Claude Choart—are you seeking Marie la Giffarde?"

"She's in the Rue de Glatigny."

"She's making the bed for the king of the ribalds."

"She's paying her four deniers, *quatuor denarios.*"

"*Aut unum bombum.*"

"Would you have her pay you in the nose?"

"Comrades, there goes Maître Simon Sanguin, elector of Picardy, with his wife mounted behind him."

"*Post equitem sedet atra cura.*"

"Courage, Maître Simon!"

"Good-day to you, Monsieur l'Electeur."

"Good-night, Madame l'Electrice."

"Now, aren't they happy, to be seeing all that?" said Johannes de Molendino, with a sigh, from his perch on the capital.

Meanwhile the sworn bookseller to the university, Maître Andry Musnier, whispered in the ear of the king's furrier, Maître Giles Lecornu,—

"I tell you, monsieur, the world's at an end. Never were there such breakings-out of the scholars! It's the accursed inventions of the age that are ruining everything—the artillery—the serpentines—the bombards—and, above all, the printing press, that German pest! No more manuscripts—no more books! Printing puts an end to bookselling—the end of the world is coming!"

"I see it is, by velvet's coming so much into fashion!" sighed the furrier.

At that moment it struck twelve.

"Ha!" exclaimed the whole crowd with one voice of satisfaction.

The scholars held their peace.

Then there was a great shuffling about, a great movement of feet and heads, a general detonation of coughing and blowing of noses, each one striving to place himself to the best advantage for the spectacle. Then there was a deep silence, every neck remaining outstretched, every mouth open, every eye turned towards the marble table; but nothing appeared. The bailiff's four sergeants still kept their posts, as stiff and motionless as if they had been four painted statues. All eyes then turned towards the gallery reserved for the Flemish envoys. The door remained shut, and the gallery empty. The multitude had been waiting since the early morning for three things—that is to say, for the hour of noon, for the Flemish embassy, and for the mystery—but only the first of the three had kept its time.

This was rather too bad.

They waited one—two—three—five minutes—a quarter of an hour, but nothing came. The *estrade* remained solitary, the stage mute. Meanwhile impatience was succeeded by displeasure. Angry words circulated about, though as yet only in whispers. "The mystery! the mystery!" was muttered in an undertone. The heads of the multitude began to ferment. A storm, which as yet only growled, was agitating the surface of that human sea. It was our friend Jehan du Moulin that elicited the first explosion.

"The mystery! and the devil take the Flemings!" cried he with the whole force of his lungs, twisting himself like a serpent about his pillar.

The multitude clapped their hands. "The mystery!" they all shouted, "and let Flanders go to all the devils!"

"We must have the mystery!" immediately resumed the scholar; "else, for my part, I would have us hang up the bailiff of the Palais by way of play and morality."

"Well said!" exclaimed the people; "and let us begin the hanging with his sergeants."

A great acclamation followed. The four poor devils of sergeants began to turn pale and look anxiously at each other. The multitude pressed towards them, and they already saw the slight wooden balustrade which separated them from the crowd bending inwards under their pressure.

The moment was critical.

"Bag them! bag them!" was shouted from all sides.

At that instant the hangings of the dressing-room, which we have described above, were lifted up to make way for the advance of a personage, the first sight of whom sufficed to stop the eager multitude, and changed their anger into curiosity as if by enchantment.

"Silence! silence!" was now the cry.

This personage, but little reassured, and trembling in every limb, came forward to the edge of the marble table, making a profusion of bows, which, the nearer he approached, approximated more and more to genuflections.

Tranquillity, however, was almost restored. Only that slight murmur was heard which is always exhaled from the silence of a great crowd.

"Messieurs les Bourgeois," said he, "and Mesdemoiselles les Bourgeoises, we shall have the honour of declaiming and performing before his Eminence Monsieur le Cardinal a very fine morality, entitled "The Good Award of our Lady the Virgin Mary." I play Jupiter. His eminence is at this moment accompanying the most honourable embassy from Monsieur the Duke of Austria, which is just now detained by hearing the harangue of Monsieur the Rector of the University at the Bandets gate. As soon as the most eminent Cardinal is arrived we shall begin."

It is certain that nothing less than the intervention of Jupiter was necessary to save the four unhappy sergeants of the bailiff of the Palais. If we had had the happiness of inventing this very true and veritable history, and had consequently been responsible for it before Our Lady of Criticism, it is not in this place, at all events, that we should have incurred any citation against us of the classical precept, *Nec Deus intersit*, etc. Besides, the costume of Seigneur Jupiter was a very fine one, and had contributed not a little to calm the irritated assemblage by attracting all their attention. Jupiter was clad in a brigandine covered with black velvet and gilt nails; his head-dress was a *bicoquet* decorated with silver gilt buttons; and but for the rouge and the great beard which covered each one-half of his face—but for the scroll of gilt pasteboard strewed with *passequilles* and stuck all over with shreds of tinsel, which he carried in his hand, and in which experienced eyes easily recognised his thunderbolts—and but for his flesh-coloured feet, sandal-bound with ribbons *à la Grecque*—he might have borne a comparison, for the severity of his aspect, with a Breton archer of that day, of Monsieur de Berry's corps.

CHAPTER II

GRINGOIRE

HOWEVER, while Jupiter was delivering his speech, the satisfaction, the admiration unanimously excited by his costume, were dissipated by his words; and when he arrived at that unlucky conclusion, "as soon as the most eminent Cardinal is arrived we shall begin," his voice was lost in a thunder of hooting.

"Begin directly! The mystery! the mystery directly!" cried the people. And above all the other voices was heard that of Joannes de Molendino, piercing through the general uproar, like the sound of the fife in a *charivari* at Nimes. "Begin directly!" squeaked the scholar.

"Down with Jupiter and the Cardinal de Bourbon!' vociferated Robin Poussepain and the other young clerks nestling in the window.

"The morality directly!" repeated the crowd immediately;

"begin, begin! The sack and the rope for the players and the Cardinal!"

Poor Jupiter, all haggard, aghast, pale under his rouge, let fall his thunderbolts, took his *bicoquet* in his hand; then, bowing and trembling, he stammered out, "His Eminence . . . the ambassadors . . . the Lady Margaret of Flanders . . ."—he knew not what to say. But the fact was he was afraid he should be hanged—hanged by the populace for waiting, or hanged by the Cardinal for not having waited; on either hand he beheld an abyss.

Happily, some one came forward to extricate him and take the responsibility upon himself.

An individual who stood within the balustrade in the space which it left clear around the marble table, and whom no one had yet perceived, so completely was his long and slender person sheltered from every visual ray by the diameter of the pillar against which he had set his back—this individual, we say, tall, thin, pale, light-complexioned—still young, though wrinkles were already visible in his forehead and his cheeks—with sparkling eyes and a smiling mouth—clad in a garment of black serge, threadbare with age—approached the marble table, and made a sign to the poor sufferer. But the other, in his perturbation, did not observe it.

The newcomer advanced another step forward.

"Jupiter," said he, "my dear Jupiter!"

The other did not hear him.

At last the tall fair man, losing all patience, shouted in his ear, "Michel Giborne!"

"Who calls me?" said Jupiter, as if starting from a trance.

"I do," answered the other personage.

"Ah!" exclaimed Jupiter.

"Begin directly," returned the other; "satisfy the people, and I take upon myself to appease Monsieur the Bailiff, who will appease Monsieur the Cardinal."

Jupiter now took breath. "Messeigneurs les Bourgeois," cried he, at the utmost stretch of his lungs, to the multitude who continued to hoot him, "we are going to begin directly."

"*Evoe! Jupiter! plaudite, cives!*" cried the scholars.

"Noël! Noël!" cried the people—that cry being the burden of a canticle sung in the churches at Christmas in honour of the Nativity, whence apparently it was adopted by the populace as a general mark of approbation and jubilation as long as the season lasted.

Then followed a deafening clapping of hands, and the hall still shook with acclamations when Jupiter had withdrawn behind his tapestry.

Meanwhile the unknown, who had so magically changed the tempest into a calm, had modestly retired under the penumbra of his pillar, and would no doubt have remained there, invisible, motionless, and mute as before, if he had not been drawn from it by two young women, who, being in the first line of the spectators, had remarked his colloquy with Michel Giborne Jupiter.

"Maître," said one of them, beckoning to him to approach.

"Hush, my dear Liénarde," said her fair neighbour, pretty, blooming, and quite courageous by virtue of her holiday attire. "It is not a clerk; it is a layman. You should not say Maître, but Messire."

"Messire!" then said Liénarde.

The unknown then approached the balustrade.

"What is your pleasure with me, mesdemoiselles?" asked he with an air of complaisance.

"Oh, nothing," said Liénarde, all confused. "It's my neighbour here, Gisquette-la-Gencienne, that wants to speak to you."

"No, no," rejoined Gisquette, blushing; "it was Liénarde that said 'maître' to you—I only told her that she ought to say 'messire.'"

The two girls cast down their eyes. The gentleman, who felt quite disposed to enter into conversation with them, looked at them smiling. "You have nothing to say to me then, mesdemoiselles?"

"Oh no, nothing at all," answered Gisquette.

"No, nothing," said Liénarde.

The tall fair young man now made a step to retire; but the two curious damsels were not inclined to let him go so soon.

"Messire," said Gisquette, with the impetuosity of water escaping through a sluice or a woman taking a resolution, "then you're acquainted with that soldier that's going to play Our Lady the Virgin in the mystery?"

"You mean the part of Jupiter," returned the unknown.

"Oh dear, yes!" said Liénarde. "Is she stupid? You're acquainted with Jupiter then?"

"With Michel Giborne," answered the unknown; "yes, madame."

"He has a fierce-looking beard," answered Liénarde.

"Will it be very fine what they are all going to say?" asked Gisquette timidly.

"Very fine indeed, mademoiselle," answered their informant without the least hesitation.

"What will it be?" said Liénarde.

"The good Award of our Lady the Virgin—a morality, if it please you, mademoiselle."

"Ah, that's different!" returned Liénarde.

A short silence followed, which was broken by the stranger. "It is a morality entirely new," said he, "which has never yet been played."

"Then it's not the same," said Gisquette, "as what was played two years ago, on the day of the entry of Monsieur the Legate, and in which three beautiful girls performed——"

"As sirens," interrupted Liénarde.

"And quite naked," added the young man.

Liénarde modestly cast down her eyes. Gisquette looked at her, and did likewise. The other continued, smiling, "It was a very pretty thing to see. But to-day it is a morality made on purpose for the lady of Flanders."

"Will they sing bergerettes?" asked Gisquette.

"Oh, fie!" said the unknown. "What! in a morality? We must not confound one kind of pieces with another. In a *sottie*, indeed, it would be quite right."

"That's a pity," rejoined Gisquette. "That day there were, at the Fountain du Ponceau, savage men and women fighting, and making different motions, singing little motets and bergerettes all the while."

"That which is suitable for a legate," said the stranger very dryly, "is not suitable for a princess."

"And near them," continued Liénarde, "was playing a number of base instruments that gave out wonderful melodies."

"And to refresh the passengers," resumed Gisquette, "the fountain threw out, by three mouths, wine, milk, and hippocrass, and everybody drank that liked."

"And a little below the Ponceau Fountain," continued Liénarde, "at the Trinity Fountain, there was a Passion performed without any speaking."

"Oh yes; don't I remember it!" exclaimed Gisquettte: "God on the cross, and the two thieves on each side of Him."

Here the young gossips, getting warm in the recollection of the legate's entry, began to talk both at once.

"And farther on, at the Porte-aux-Peintres, there were other characters, very richly dressed—"

"And do you remember, at St. Innocent's Fountain, that huntsman following a hind, with a great noise of dogs and hunting-trumpets—"

"And then, at the Boucherie de Paris, those scaffolds that presented the Bastille of Dieppe—"

"And when the legate was going by, you know, Gisquette, they gave the assault, and the English all had their throats cut—"

"And what fine characters there were against the Châtelet Gate—"

"And on the Pont-au-Change, which was all covered with carpeting from one end to the other—"

"And when the legate went over it they let fly from the bridge above two hundred dozen of all kinds of birds.—Wasn't that a fine sight, Liénarde?"

"There will be a finer to-day," at length interrupted their interlocutor, who seemed to listen to them with impatience.

"You promise us that this mystery shall be a fine one," said Gisquette.

"Assuredly," returned he. And then he added, with peculiar emphasis, "Mesdemoiselles, 'tis I who am the author of it."

"Really!" said the young women, all amazed.

"Yes, really," answered the poet, bridling up a little; "that is to say, there are two of us—Jehan Marchand, who has sawn the planks and put together the wood-work of the theatre; and myself, who have written the piece. My name is Pierre Gringoire."

The author of the Cid himself could not have said with a loftier air, "My name is Pierre Corneille."

Our readers may have observed that some time must already have elapsed since the moment at which Jupiter retired behind the drapery and that at which the author of the new morality revealed himself thus abruptly to the simple admiration of Gisquette and Liénarde. It is worthy of remark that all that multitude, who a few minutes before had been so tumultuous, now waited quietly on the faith of the player's promise—an evidence of this everlasting truth, still daily experienced in our theatres, that the best means of making the audience wait patiently is to assure them that the performance will commence immediately.

However, the scholar Joannes was not asleep. "Hollo!"

shouted he suddenly, amidst the peaceful expectation which had succeeded the disturbance. "Jupiter—Madame the Virgin—you rowers of the devil's boat! are you joking to one another? The piece! the piece! Begin, or we'll begin again!"

This was enough. A music of high and low keyed instruments now struck up in the apartment underneath the stage; the hangings were lifted up; and four characters in motley attire, with painted faces, came out, clambered up the steep ladder already mentioned, arrived safe upon the upper platform, and drew up in line before the audience, whom they saluted with a profound obeisance; whereupon the symphony was silent, for the mystery was now really commencing.

The four characters, after receiving abundant payment for their obeisances in the plaudits of the multitude, commenced, amidst a profound silence, the delivery of a prologue, which we willingly spare the reader. However, as still happens in our time, the audience paid more attention to the dresses they wore than to the parts they were enacting; and, in truth, they did right. They were all four dressed in gowns half yellow and half white, different from each other only in the nature of the material—the first being of gold and silver brocade, the second of silk, the third of wool, and the fourth of linen. The first character carried in the right hand a sword, the second two golden keys, the third a pair of scales, and the fourth a spade. And in order to assist such indolent understandings as might not have seen clearly through the transparency of these attributes, there might be read in large black letters worked at the bottom of the brocade dress, *Je m'appelle Noblesse* (my name is Nobility); at the bottom of the silk dress, *Je m'appelle Clergé* (my name is Clergy); at the bottom of the woollen dress, *Je m'appelle Marchandise* (my name is Trade); and at the bottom of the linen garment, *Je m'appelle Labour* (my name is Tillage). The sex of the two male characters, Clergé and Labour, was clearly indicated to every judicious spectator by the comparative shortness of their garments, and the *cramignole* which they wore upon their heads; while the two female ones, besides that their robes were of ampler length, were distinguished by their hoods.

It would also have argued great perverseness not to have discovered, through the poetic drapery of the prologue, that Labour was married to Marchandise and Clergé to Noblesse, and that these two happy couples possessed in common a magnificent golden dolphin, which they intended to adjudge only to the most beautiful damsel. Accordingly, they were going all over the world in search of this beauty; and after successfully rejecting the Queen of Golconda, the Princess of Trebizond, the daughter of the Cham of Tartary, etc., etc., Labour and Clergé, Noblesse and Marchandise, were come to rest themselves upon the marble table of the Palais de Justice, and deliver at the same time to the worthy auditory as many moral sentences and maxims as might in that day be expended upon the members of the faculty of arts, at the examinations, sophisms, determinances, figures, and acts, at which the masters took their degrees.

All this was, in truth, very fine.

Meanwhile, in all that assemblage upon which the four allegorical personages seemed to be striving which could pour out the most copious floods of metaphor, no ear was so attentive, no heart so palpitating, no eye so eager, no neck so outstretched, as were the eye, ear, neck, and heart of the author, the poet, the brave Pierre Gringoire, who a moment before had been unable to forego the satisfaction of telling his name to two pretty girls.

He had returned to the distance of a few paces from them, behind his pillar; and there it was that he listened, looked, and enjoyed. The benevolent plaudits which had greeted the opening of his prologue were still resounding in his breast; and he was completely absorbed in that species of ecstatic contemplation with which a dramatic author marks his ideas dropping one by one from the lips of the actor, amid the silence of a crowded auditory. Happy Pierre Gringoire!

It pains us to relate it, but this first ecstasy was very soon disturbed. Scarcely had the lips of Gringoire approached this intoxicating cup of joy and triumph before a drop of bitterness was cruelly mingled in it.

A tattered mendicant, who, lost as he was among the crowd, could receive no contributions, and who, we may suppose, had not found sufficient indemnity in the pockets of his neighbours, had bethought himself of finding some conspicuous perch from which to attract the attention and the alms of the good people. Accordingly, while the first lines of the prologue were delivering, he had hoisted himself up, by means of the pillars that supported the reserved estrade, to the cornice which ran along the bottom of its balustrade; and there he had seated himself, soliciting the attention and the pity of the multitude by the display of his rags, and of a hideous sore that covered his right arm. However, he did not utter a word.

The silence which he kept allowed the prologue to proceed without any distraction; and no sensible disorder would have occurred, but that, as ill luck would have it, the scholar Joannes espied, from his own perch upon one of the great pillars, the beggar and his grimaces. The young wag was seized with an immoderate fit of laughter; and regardless of the interruption to the performance, and the disturbance to the general attention, he cried out in a tone of gaiety. "Look at that sham leper there asking alms!"

Any one that has ever thrown a stone into a pond full of frogs, or fired a gun amongst a flock of birds, may form an idea of the effect produced by these unseasonable words dropped in the midst of the universal attention fixed upon the heroes of the mystery. Gringoire started as if he had felt an electric shock. The prologue was cut short; and all heads were turned tumultuously towards the mendicant, who, far from being disconcerted, found in this incident a good opportunity of making a harvest, and began to cry out, with a doleful look, half shutting his eyes, "Charity, if you please!"

"Why, on my soul," cried Joannes, "it's Clopin Trouillefou. Hollo, friend!—so thy sore wasn't comfortable on thy leg, that thou'st put it on thy arm."

So saying he threw, with the dexterity of a monkey, a small white coin into the old greasy hat which the beggar held out with his diseased limb. The beggar received without flinching both the alms and the sarcasm, and continued in a piteous tone, "Charity, if you please!"

This episode had considerably distracted the auditory, and a good many of the spectators, with Robin Poussepain and all the clerks at their head, merrily applauded this whimsical duet which had been struck up thus unexpectedly in the middle of the prologue, between the scholar with his shrill clamorous voice and the beggar with his imperturbable drone.

Gringoire was grievously dissatisfied. Having recovered from his first stupefaction he was tearing his lungs with crying out to the four characters on the stage, "Go on!—what the devil?—go on!" without even deigning to cast a look of disdain upon the two interrupters.

At that moment he felt some one pulling at the skirt of his coat. He turned round, not without some little ill-humour, and had much ado to smile. Nevertheless he found it necessary to do so, for it was the pretty arm of Gisquette-la-Gencienne, which, extended through the balustrade, thus solicited his attention.

"Monsieur," said the girl, "will they go on?"

"To be sure," answered Gringoire, much shocked at the question.

"Oh, then, messire," she resumed, "would you just have the courtesy to explain to me . . ."

"What they are going to say?" interrupted Gringoire. "Well—listen."

"No," said Gisquette, "but what they have said already."

Gringoire started as if touched to the quick. "A plague on the little, stupid, witless wench!" muttered he, and from that moment Gisquette was utterly ruined in his estimation.

Meanwhile the actors had obeyed his injunction; and the audience, observing that they were once more trying to make themselves heard, had again set themselves to listen—not, however, without the loss of many a poetic beauty, in the sort of soldering that had been made of the two parts of the piece which had been so abruptly cut short. Gringoire whispered to himself this bitter reflection. However, tranquillity had been gradually restored; the scholar held his tongue, the beggar was counting some coin in his hat, and the piece had resumed its ascendency.

It was really a very fine composition, and we really think it might be turned to some account, even now, by means of a few modifications. The exposition, rather long indeed, and rather dry, was simple; and Gringoire, in the candid sanctuary of his own judgment, admired its clearness. As may well be supposed, the four allegorical personages were a little fatigued with travelling over the three known quarters of the world without finding an opportunity of suitably disposing of their golden dolphin. Hence a long eulogy upon the marvellous fish, with numberless delicate allusions to the young prince betrothed to Margaret of Flanders—which young prince was at that time in very dismal seclusion at Amboise, without the slightest suspicion that Labour and Clergé, Noblesse and Marchandise, had just been making the tour of the world on his account. The dolphin aforesaid, then, was young, was handsome, was vigorous, and above all (magnificent origin of all the royal virtues!) was son of the lion of France. "Now, I declare," says our author, "that this bold metaphor is admirable, and that dramatic natural history, on a day of allegory and of a royal epithalamium, finds nothing at all shocking in a dolphin the son of a lion. On the contrary, it is precisely those rare and pindaric mixtures that prove the poet's enthusiasm. However, to have disarmed criticism altogether, the poet might have developed this fine idea in less than two hundred lines. It is true that the mystery was to last, according to the order of Monsieur the Provost, from noon till four o'clock, and that it was necessary to say something. Besides, it was very patiently listened to."

All at once, just in the middle of a fine quarrel between Mademoiselle Marchandise, and Madame Noblesse, at the moment when Maître Labour was pronouncing this wondrous line,

> Beast more triumphant ne'er in woods I've seen,

the door of the reserved gallery, which had until then been so unseasonably shut, opened more unseasonably still, and the stentorian voice of the *huissier*, doorkeeper, or usher, abruptly announced, "Son Eminence Monseigneur le Cardinal de Bourbon!"

CHAPTER III

THE CARDINAL

Poor Gringoire! The noise of all the great double petards let off on St. John's day—the discharge of a score of cracking arquebusses—the report of that famous serpentine of the Tour de Billy, which, at the time of the siege of Paris, on Sunday, the 29th of September 1465, killed seven Burgundians at a shot—the explosion of all the gunpowder stored up at the Temple Gate—would have split his ears less violently at that solemn and dramatic moment, than those few words from the lips of an usher, "Son Eminence Monseigneur le Cardinal de Bourbon."

Not that Pierre Gringoire either feared the Cardinal or despised him; he was neither weak enough to do the one, nor self-sufficient enough to do the other. A true *eclectic*, as he would nowadays be called among Parisian philosophers, Gringoire was one of those firm and elevated spirits, calm and temperate, who can preserve their composure under all circumstances—*stare in dimidio rerum*—and who are full of reason and of a liberal philosophy even while making some account of cardinals. Invaluable and uninterrupted line of philosophers, to whom wisdom, like another Ariana, seems to have given a clue, which they have gone on unwinding from the beginning of the world through the labyrinth of human affairs. They are to be found in all times, and ever the same—that is to say, ever conforming themselves to the time. And, not to mention our Pierre Gringoire, who would be their representative of the fifteenth century if we could succeed in obtaining for him the distinction which he deserves, it was certainly their spirit which animated Father du Breul in the sixteenth, when writing these words of sublime simplicity, worthy of any age: " I am a Parisian by my birthplace, and a *parrhisian* by my speech; for *parrhisia* in Greek signifies liberty of speech, which liberty I have used even to messeigneurs the cardinals, uncle and brother to Monseigneur the Prince of Conti, albeit with respect for their greatness, and without offending any one of their train, and that is a great deal to say."

So there was neither hatred for the Cardinal, nor contempt of his presence, in the disagreeable impression which it made upon Pierre Gringoire. On the contrary, our poet had too much good sense and too threadbare a frock not to attach a particular value to the circumstance that many an allusion in his prologue, and in particular the glorification of the dolphin, son of the lion of France, would fall upon the ear of *éminentissime*. But interest is not the ruling motive in the noble nature of poets. Supposing the entity of a poet to be represented by the number ten, it is certain that a chemist, on analysing and pharmacopolising it, as Rabelais says, would find it to be composed of one part of self-interest with nine parts of self-esteem. Now, at the moment that the door opened for the entrance of his eminence, Gringoire's nine parts of self-esteem, inflated and expanded by the breath of popular admiration, were in a state of prodigious enlargement, quite overwhelming and smothering that imperceptible particle of self-interest which we just now discriminated in the constitution of poets—an invaluable ingredient, by the way, a ballast of reality and humanity, without which they would never touch the earth. It was enjoyment for Gringoire to see and feel that an entire assemblage (of poor creatures, it is true, but what then?) were stupefied, petrified, and asphyxiated by the immeasurable tirades which burst from every part of his epithalamium. We affirm that he himself shared the general beatitude; and that, quite the reverse of La Fontaine, who, at the performance of his play of *The Florentine*, asked, " What poor wretch has written that rhapsody? " Gringoire would willingly have asked the person nearest to him, " Whose masterpiece is this? " Hence it may be supposed what sort of effect was produced upon him by the sudden and untimely arrival of the Cardinal.

All his fears were but too fully realised. His eminence's entrance threw the whole auditory into motion. All eyes were turned towards the estrade, and there was a general buzz. "The Cardinal! the Cardinal!" repeated every tongue. The unfortunate prologue was cut short a second time.

The Cardinal stopped a moment upon the threshold of the gallery; and while casting his eyes with great indifference over the assemblage, the tumult redoubled. Everybody wanted to obtain a better view of him, each one stretching his neck over his neighbour's shoulder.

He was in truth an exalted personage, the sight of whom was worth almost any other spectacle. Charles, Cardinal de Bourbon, Archbishop and Count of Lyons, and Primate of Gaul, was allied both to Louis XI., through his brother Pierre, Seigneur of Beaujeu, who had espoused the King's eldest daughter, and at the same time to the Burgundian Duke Charles-le-Téméraire, through his mother, Agnes of Burgundy. Now the ruling, the characteristic, the distinctive feature in the character of the Primate of Gaul, was his courtier-like spirit and his devotedness to power. Hence, it may well be supposed in what numberless perplexities this double relationship had involved him, and amongst how many temporal shoals his spiritual bark must have tacked about, to have escaped foundering either upon Louis or upon Charles, the Charybdis and the Scylla which had swallowed up the Duke of Nemours and the Constable of Saint-Pol. However, Heaven be praised! he had got happily through his voyage, and had reached Rome without any cross accident. But although he was now in port—and indeed precisely because he was in port—he never recollected without a feeling of uneasiness the various chances of his political life, which had so long been perilous and laborious. So also, he used to say, that the year 1746 had been to him both a black and a white year—meaning thereby that he had lost in that one year his mother, the Duchess of Bourbonnais, and his cousin, the Duke of Burgundy, and that one mourning had consoled him for the other.

However, he was a very worthy man; he led a joyous cardinal's life; was wont to make merry with wine of the royal vintage of Challuau; had no dislike to Richarde-la-Gamoise and Thomasse-la-Saillarde; gave alms to pretty girls in preference to old women; and for all these reasons was in great favour with the good people of Paris. He always went surrounded by a little court of bishops and abbots of high lineage, gallant, jovial, and fond of good eating; and more than once had the good devotees of Saint-Germain d'Auxerre, in passing at night under the windows of the Hôtel de Bourbon, all blazing with light, been scandalised by hearing the same voices which had been singing vespers to them in the daytime, striking up, to the sound of glasses, the bacchanalian sentiment of Benedict XII., the Pope who had added a third crown to the tiara—*Bibamus papaliter*.

No doubt it was this popularity, so justly acquired, which preserved him at his entrance from anything like ill reception on the part of the crowd, who a few moments before had been so dissatisfied, and so little disposed to pay respect to a cardinal, even on the day when they were going to elect a pope. But the Parisians bear little malice; and besides, by making the performance begin of their own authority, the good citizens had had the better of the Cardinal, and this triumph satisfied them. Moreover, Monsieur le Cardinal de Bourbon was a handsome man—he had on a very handsome scarlet gown, which he wore in excellent style—which is as much as to say that he had in his favour all the women, and consequently the better part of the audience. Certainly it would be both injustice and bad taste to hoot a cardinal for being too late at the play, when he is a handsome man, and wears handsomely his scarlet robe.

He entered, then; saluted the company with that hereditary smile which the great have always in readiness for the people; and stepped slowly towards the *fauteuil* or state chair of scarlet velvet placed for his reception, looking as if some other matter occupied his mind. His train—what a Frenchman might now call his staff—of bishops and abbots issued after him upon the estrade, not without exciting redoubled tumult and curiosity among the spectators below. All were busy in pointing them out, or in telling their names, each one striving to show that he knew at least some one of them; some pointing to the Bishop of Marseilles (Alaudet, if we remember right), some to the *Primicier* or Dean of St. Denis, others to Robert de Lespinasse, abbot of the great neighbouring monastery of Saint-Germain-des-Près, the libertine brother of a mistress of Louis XI.—all their names being repeated with a thousand mistakes and mispronunciations. As for the scholars, they swore. It was their own day—their feast of fools—their saturnalia—the annual orgies of the *basoche* and the *école*. No turpitude but was a matter of right to be held sacred that day. And then there were mad gossips among the crowd—Simone Quatre-livres, Agnès-la-Gadine, Robine Piédebou. Was it not the least that could be expected that they should swear at their ease, and profane God's name a little, on such a day as that, in such good company with churchmen and courtesans? And accordingly they made no mincing of the matter, but amidst the uproarious applause a frightful din of blasphemies and enormities proceeded from all those tongues let loose—those tongues of clerks and scholars, tied up all the rest of the year by the fear of St. Louis's branding-iron. Poor St. Louis! how did they banter him in his own Palais de Justice! Each one of them had singled out among the newly-arrived company some one of the cassocks, black, grey, white, or violet. As for Joannes Frollo de Molendino, and his being brother to an archdeacon, it was the red robe that he audaciously assailed, singing out as loud as he could bawl, and fixing his shameless eyes upon the Cardinal, "*Cappa repleta mero!*"

All these particulars, which are thus clearly detailed for the reader's edification, were so completely drowned in the general hum of the multitude, that they were lost before they could reach the reserved gallery; though indeed the Cardinal would have been little moved by them, so intimately did the licence of the day belong to the manners of the age. He had something else to think of, which preoccupation appeared in his countenance—another cause of solicitude, which followed closely behind him, and made its appearance in the gallery almost at the same time as himself. This was the Flemish embassy.

Not that he was a profound politician, or concerned himself about the possible consequences of the marriage of madame his cousin, Margaret of Burgundy, with monsieur his cousin, Charles, Dauphin of Vienne; nor how long the patched-up reconciliation between the Duke of Austria and the French King might endure; nor how the King of England would receive this slight towards his daughter. All that gave him little anxiety; and he did honour every night to the wine of the royal vineyard of Chaillot without ever suspecting that a few flasks of that same wine, revised and corrected a little by the physician Coictier, and cordially presented to Edward IV. by Louis XI., might possibly, some fine morning, rid Louis XI. of Edward IV. *La moult honorée ambassade de Monsieur le Duc d'Autriche* brought none of these cares to the Cardinal's mind, but annoyed him in another respect. It was, in truth, rather too bad, and we have already said a word or two about it in the first page of this volume, that he should be obliged to give good reception and entertainment—he, Charles de Bourbon, to obscure burghers—

he, a cardinal, to a pack of scurvy *échevins* [1]—he, a Frenchman and a connoisseur in good living, to Flemish beer-drinkers—and in public too! Certes, it was one of the most irksome parts he had ever gone through for the *bon plaisir* of the King.

However, he had so perfectly studied it that he turned towards the door with the best grace in the world, when the usher announced in a sonorous voice, "*Messieurs les envoyés de Monsieur le Duc d'Autriche!*" It is needless to say that the whole hall did likewise.

Then appeared, two by two, with a gravity which strongly contrasted with the flippant air of the Cardinal's ecclesiastical train, the forty-eight ambassadors from Maximilian of Austria, having at their head the reverend father in God, Jehan, Abbot of Saint-Bertin, Chancellor of the Golden Fleece, and Jacques de Goy, Sieur Dauby, High Bailiff of Ghent. A deep silence now took place in the assemblage, a general titter being suppressed in order to listen to all the uncouth names and mercantile additions which each one of these personages transmitted with imperturbable gravity to the usher, who then gave out their names and callings, pell-mell and with all sorts of mutilations, to the crowd below. There were Maître Loys Roelof, échevin of the town of Louvain; Messire Clays d'Etuelde, échevin of Brussels; Messire Paul de Baeust, sieur of Voirmizelle, president of Flanders; Maître Jehan Cologhens, burgomaster of the city of Antwerp; Maître George de la Moere, principal échevin of the *kuere* of the city of Ghent; Maître Gheldolf van der Hage, principal échevin of the *parchons* of the said city; and the sieur de Bierbecque, and Jehan Pinnock, and Jehan Dimaerzelle, etc., etc., etc., bailiffs, échevins, and burgomasters—burgomasters, échevins, and bailiffs—all stiff, sturdy, drawn-up figures, dressed out in velvet and damask, and hooded with black velvet *cramignoles* decorated with great tufts of gold thread of Cyprus —good Flemish heads after all, with severe and respectable countenances, akin to those which Rembrandt has made stand out with such force and gravity from the dark background of his picture of "Going the Rounds at Night"—personages on every one of whose foreheads it was written that Maximilian of

[1] The elective magistrates of the communes which erected themselves in many of the cities and great towns in the Middle Ages took, in the north of France and in Flanders, in which that ancient Germanic people, the Franks, had established themselves, this name of *échevin*, from *skepen*, which in the Frankish tongue signified a judge. (See Thierry's *Lettres sur l'Histoire de France*, 3me édition, pp. 257, 258.) It answers very nearly to the English title of alderman, as applied in later ages; though the substitution of the latter term in the text would be manifestly improper.

Austria had done right in "confiding to the full," as his manifesto expressed it, "in their sense, valour, experience, loyalty, and good endowments."

There was one exception, however, to this description: it was a subtle, intelligent, crafty-looking face—a sort of mixture of the monkey and the diplomatist—to whom the Cardinal made three steps in advance and a low bow, but who, nevertheless, was called simply Guillaume or William Rym, counsellor and pensionary of the town of Ghent.

Few persons at that time knew anything about Guillaume Rym—a rare genius, who, in a time of revolution, would have appeared with *éclat* on the surface of events, but who, in the fifteenth century, was confined to the practice of covert intrigue, and "to live in the mines," as the Duke de Saint-Simon expresses it. However, he was appreciated by the first miner in Europe—he was familiarly associated in the secret operations of Louis XI.; all which was perfectly unknown to this multitude, who were amazed at the Cardinal's politeness to that sorry-looking Flemish bailiff.

CHAPTER IV

JACQUES COPPENOLE

While the pensionary of Ghent and his eminence were exchanging a very low bow, and a few words in a tone still lower, a man of lofty stature, large-featured and broad-shouldered, presented himself to enter abreast with Guillaume Rym, looking something like a mastiff dog by the side of a fox. His bicoquet of felt and his leathern jerkin were oddly conspicuous amidst the velvet and silk that surrounded him. Presuming it to be some groom who knew not where he was going, the usher stopped him with, "Hollo, friend! you can't pass here."

The man of the leathern jerkin shouldered him aside. "What would this fellow with me?" said he in a thundering voice, which drew the attention of the whole hall to this colloquy. "Seest thou not I'm one of them?"

"Your name?" demanded the usher.

"Jacques Coppenole."

"Your description?"

"A hosier, at the sign of the Three Chains at Ghent."

The usher shrunk back. To announce échevins and burgomasters might indeed be endured—but a hosier!—it was rather too bad. The Cardinal was upon thorns. All the people were looking and listening. For two days his eminence had been doing his utmost to lick these Flemish bears into rather more presentable shape, and this freak was too much for him. Meanwhile Guillaume Rym, with his cunning smile, went up to the usher. "Announce Maître Jacques Coppenole, clerk to the échevins of the city of Ghent," said he to the officer in a very low whisper.

"Usher," then said the Cardinal aloud, "announce Maître Jacques Coppenole, clerk to the échevins of the illustrious city of Ghent."

This was an error. Guillaume Rym, by himself, would have snatched the difficulty out of the way; but Coppenole had heard the Cardinal's direction. "No! *Croix-Dieu!*" he cried, with his voice of thunder: "Jacques Coppenole, hosier. Dost thou hear, usher? Neither more or less.—*Croix-Dieu!* a hosier—that's fine enough. Monsieur the Archduke has more than once looked for his *gant* in my hose."

This play upon the word *gant*, a glove, pronounced exactly like *Gand* or *Ghent*, the great manufacturing town in Flanders, occasioned a burst of laughter and applause from the people below. A pun is immediately understood at Paris, and consequently is always applauded.

We must add that Coppenole was one of the people, and that the auditory around him were of the people also; so that the communication between them and him had been quick, electric, and, as it were, on equal footing. This lofty air which the Flemish hosier gave himself, by humbling the courtiers, had stirred in the plebeian breasts a certain latent feeling of dignity, which, in the fifteenth century, was as yet vague and undefined. They beheld one of their equals in this hosier, who had just borne himself so sturdily before the Cardinal—a welcome reflection to poor devils accustomed to pay respect and obedience to the servants of the sergeants of the bailiff of the Abbot of Sainte-Geneviève, the Cardinal's train-bearer.

Coppenole made a stiff bow to his eminence, who returned the salute of the all-powerful burgher, formidable to Louis XI. Then, while Guillaume Rym, *sage homme et malicieux*, as Philippe de Comines expresses it, followed them both with a smile of raillery and superiority, they moved each to his place—the Cardinal thoughtful and out of countenance—Coppenole quite at his ease, thinking, no doubt, that after all his title of hosier was as good as any other, and that Mary of Burgundy, mother of that Margaret for whose marriage he was now treating, would have feared him less as a cardinal than as a hosier; for no cardinal would have stirred up the people of Ghent against the favourites of the daughter of Charles the Rash; nor could any cardinal, by a single word, have fortified the multitude against her tears and prayers when the Lady of Flanders came and supplicated her people on their behalf, even to the foot of their scaffold, while the hosier had only had to raise his leathern elbow to cause both your heads to be struck off, most illustrious seigneurs, Guy d'Hymbercourt and Chancellor Guillaume Hugonet.

Yet the poor Cardinal had not gone through all his penance; he was doomed to drain the cup of being in such bad company even to the dregs.

The reader has probably not forgotten the audacious mendicant who, at the time of the commencement of the prologue, had climbed up to the fringes of the gallery reserved for the Cardinal. The arrival of the illustrious guests had not in the least disturbed him; and while the prelates and the ambassadors were barrelling themselves up like real Flemish herrings within the narrow compass of the gallery, he had put himself quite at his ease, with his legs bravely crossed upon the architrave. This piece of insolence was extraordinary; yet nobody had remarked it at the first moment, every one's attention being fixed elsewhere. He, for his part, took notice of nothing in the hall; he was moving his head backwards and forwards with the unconcern of a Neapolitan, repeating from time to time, amidst the general hum, and as if by a mechanical habit, "Charity, if you please!" and indeed, amongst all present, he was probably the only one who would not have deigned to turn his head on hearing the altercation between Coppenole and the usher. Now it so chanced that his hosiership of Ghent, with whom the people already so warmly sympathised, and upon whom all eyes were fixed, went and seated himself in the front line of the gallery, just over the place where the beggar was sitting; and it excited no small astonishment to see the Flemish ambassador, after scrutinising the fellow beneath him, give him a friendly slap on his ragged shoulder. The beggar turned round. Surprise, mutual recognition, and kindly gratulation were visible in both faces. Then, without giving themselves the slightest concern about the spectators, the hosier and the leper fell into conversation in a low voice, holding each other by the hand; while the tattered arm of Clopin Trouillefou, displayed at length upon the cloth of gold that decorated the gallery, had somewhat the appearance of a caterpillar upon an orange.

The novelty of this singular scene excited such noisy mirth among the crowd, that the Cardinal quickly remarked it. He leaned gently aside; and as, from the point where he was situated, he caught only an imperfect glimpse of Trouillefou's ignominious garment, he very naturally imagined that the beggar was asking alms, and indignant at his audacity he exclaimed, "Monsieur the Bailiff of the Palais, throw me that fellow into the river."

"*Croix-Dieu!* Monseigneur le Cardinal," said Coppenole, without leaving hold of Clopin's hand, "this is one of my friends."

"Noël! noël!" cried the mob. And from that moment Maître Coppenole was at Paris, as at Ghent, "in great favour with the people; for men of great stature are so," says Phillippe de Comines, "when they are thus disorderly."

The Cardinal bit his lip. He leaned towards the Abbot of Sainte-Geneviève, who sat next him, and said, in a half-whisper, "Pretty ambassadors, truly, Monsieur the Archduke sends us to announce the Lady Margaret."

"Your Eminence's politeness," returned the abbot, "is thrown away upon these Flemish grunters—*margaritas ante porcos*."

"Say rather," rejoined the Cardinal, smiling, "*porcos ante Margaritam*."

The whole of the little court of churchmen were in ecstasy at this *jeu de mots*. The Cardinal felt a little relieved. He was now even with Coppenole, for he too had had his pun applauded.

And now such of our readers as have the power of generalising an image or an idea, as we say nowadays, will permit us to ask them whether they figure to themselves quite clearly the spectacle presented at the moment at which we give this pause to their attention, by the vast parallelogram of the great hall of the Palais.

In the middle of the western side is a spacious and magnificent gallery, with drapery of gold brocade, which is entered, in procession, through a small Gothic doorway, by a series of grave-looking personages, announced successively by the clamorous voice of an usher; while on the first benches are already seated a number of reverend figures, wrapped in velvet, ermine, and scarlet cloth. Below and all about this gallery, which remains still and stately—below, in front, and around, are a great multitude and a great hum of voices. A thousand looks are cast from the crowd upon every face in the gallery—a thousand muttered repetitions are made of every name. The spectacle is indeed curious and well worthy the attention of the spectators. But, at the same time, what is that down there, quite at the extremity of the hall—that sort of mountebank stage, with four puppets in motley upon it, and four others below? And at one side of the stage who is that white-faced man in a long black coat? Alas! dear reader, it is Pierre Gringoire with his prologue.

We had all utterly forgotten him; and that is just what he had apprehended.

From the moment at which the Cardinal entered, Gringoire had been incessantly exerting himself for the salvation of his prologue. He had first of all enjoined the actors to proceed, and elevate their voices; then, finding that no one listened, he had stopped them, and for nearly a quarter of an hour, during which the interruption had continued, he had been constantly beating with his foot and gesticulating, calling upon Gisquette and Liénarde, and urging those near him to have the prologue proceeded with, but all in vain. No one could be turned aside from the Cardinal, the embassy, and the gallery—the sole centre of that vast circle of visual rays. It is also credible, we regret to say it, that the prologue was beginning to be a little tiresome to the auditory at the moment that his eminence's arrival had made so terrible a distraction. And after all, in the gallery itself, as on the marble table, it was still in fact the same spectacle—the conflict of Labour with Clergé, of Noblesse with Marchandise; and many people liked better to see them in downright reality, living, breathing, acting, elbowing one another in plain flesh and blood, in that Flemish embassy, in that episcopal court, under the Cardinal's robe, under Coppenole's jerkin, than tricked out, painted, talking in verse, and packed up, as it were, in straw, under the yellow and white gowns in which Gringoire had muffled them.

Nevertheless, when our poet saw tranquillity a little restored, he bethought himself of a stratagem which might have saved the performance.

"Monsieur," said he, turning to one of the persons nearest him, of fair round figure, with a patient-looking countenance, "suppose they were to begin again?"

"Begin what?" said the man.

"Why, the mystery," said Gringoire.

"Just as you please," returned the other.

This demi-approbation was enough for Gringoire, and, taking the affair into his own hands, he began to call out, confounding himself at the same time as much as possible with the multitude, "Begin the mystery again! begin again!"

"The devil!" said Joannes de Molendino; "what is it they're singing out at yon end?" (for Gringoire made as much noise as four people). "Tell me, comrades, isn't the mystery finished? They want to begin it again—that's not fair."

"No, no!" cried all the scholars together; "down with the mystery! down with it!"

But Gringoire only multiplied himself the more, and cried out the louder, "Begin again! begin again!"

These clamours attracted the attention of the Cardinal. "Monsieur the Bailiff of the Palais," said he to a tall dark man standing a few paces from him, "what possesses those fellows that they make that infernal noise?"

The bailiff of the Palais was a kind of amphibious magistrate, a sort of bat of the judicial order, a sort of compound of the rat and the bird, of the judge and the soldier. He approached his eminence, and with no small apprehension of his displeasure; he stammered out to him an explanation of the people's refractoriness—that noon had arrived before his eminence, and that the players had been forced to begin without waiting for his eminence.

The Cardinal laughed aloud. "I'faith," said he, "Monsieur the Rector of the University should e'en have done likewise. What say you, Maître Guillaume Rym?"

"Monseigneur," answered Rym, "let us be satisfied with having escaped one-half of the play. 'Tis so much gained, at any rate."

"May those rogues go on with their farce?" asked the bailiff.

"Go on, go on," said the Cardinal, "'tis all the same to me; I will be reading my breviary the while."

The bailiff advanced to the edge of the gallery, and called out, after procuring silence by a motion of his hand—"Townsmen! householders! and inhabitants!—to satisfy those who desire that the play should begin again, and those who desire it should finish, his eminence orders that it shall go on."

Thus both parties were obliged to yield, although both the author and the auditors long bore a grudge on this score against the Cardinal. The characters on the stage accordingly took up their text where they had laid it down, and Gringoire hoped that at least the remainder of his composition would be listened to. This hope, however, was soon dispelled, like the rest of his illusions. Silence had indeed been somehow or other restored in the auditory; but Gringoire had not observed that, at the moment when the Cardinal had given his order for the continuance of the play, the gallery was far from being full, and that subsequently to the arrival of the Flemish envoys there were come other persons forming part of the Cardinal's train, whose names and description, thrown out in the midst of his dialogue by the intermitted bawling of the usher, made considerable ravage in it. Only imagine, indeed, in the midst of a dramatic piece, the yelp of a doorkeeper, throwing in between the two lines of a couplet, and often between the first half of a line and the last, such parentheses as these:—

"Maître Jacques Charmolue, King's Attorney in the Ecclesiastical Court!"

"Jehan de Harlay, Esquire, Keeper of the Office of Horseman of the Night-watch of the town of Paris!"

"Messire Galiot de Genoilhac, Knight, Seigneur of Brussac, Master of the King's Artillery!"

"Maître Dreux-Raguier, Commissioner of our Lord the King's Waters and Forests in the Dominions of France, Champagne, and Brie!"

"Messire Louis de Graville, Knight, Councillor and Chamberlain to the King, Admiral of France, Keeper of the Bois de Vincennes!"

"Maître Denis le Mercier, Keeper of the House of the Blind at Paris!"

Etc., etc., etc.

This became insupportable. All this strange accompaniment, which made it difficult to follow the tenor of the piece, was the more provoking to Gringoire, as he could not disguise from himself that the interest was going on increasing, and that nothing was wanting to his composition but to be listened to. It was, indeed, difficult to imagine a plot more ingeniously or dramatically woven. While the four personages of the prologue were bewailing their hopeless perplexity, Venus in person—*vera incessu patuit dea*—had presented herself before them, clad in a fine *cotte-hardie*, having blazoned fair upon its front the ship displayed on the old city escutcheon of Paris. She was come to claim for herself the dolphin promised to the most beautiful. She was supported by Jupiter, whose thunder was heard to rumble in the dressing-room; and the goddess was about to bear away the prize—that is, in plain terms, to espouse Monsieur the Dauphin—when a little girl, dressed in white damask, and carrying a *marguerite* or daisy in her hand, lucid personification of the Lady of Flanders, had come to contend with Venus. Here were at once *coup-de-théâtre* and preparation for the catastrophe. After a proper dispute, Venus, Margaret, and those beneath the scene had agreed to refer the matter to the award of the holy Virgin. There was another fine part, that of Don Pedro, King of Mesopotamia; but amidst so many interruptions it was difficult to discover what was his share of the action. All these personages climbed up the ladder to the stage.

But it was all over with the play; not one of these beauties was felt or understood. It seemed as if, at the Cardinal's entrance, some invisible and magical thread had suddenly drawn away every look from the marble table to the gallery, from the southern extremity of the hall to its western side. Nothing could disenchant the auditory; all eyes remained fixed in that direction; and the persons who successively arrived on that side, with their cursed names and their faces and their dresses, made a continual diversion. The case was desperate. Except Gisquette and Liénarde, who turned aside from time to time when Gringoire pulled them by the sleeve—except the lusty, patient man that stood near him—no one listened to, no one looked at the poor abandoned morality. Gringoire could see in the faces of the auditory nothing but profiles.

With what bitterness did he see all his fabric of poetry and of glory thus falling to pieces! Only to think that this multitude had been on the point of rebelling against monsieur the bailiff through their impatience to hear his composition; and now that they had it, they cared nothing about it—that same performance which had begun amid such unanimous acclamation! Everlasting ebb and flow of the popular favour! Only to think that they had been near hanging the bailiff's sergeants!—what would he not have given to have recalled that blissful moment! However, the usher's brutal monologue ceased at length—everybody had arrived; so that Gringoire took breath, and the actors were going on bravely, when all at once Maître Coppenole, the hosier, got upon his legs, and Gringoire heard him deliver, in the midst of the universal attention to his piece, this abominable harangue:—

" Messieurs the *bourgeois* and *hobereaux* of Paris—Croix-Dieu! I know not what we're doing here. I do indeed see, down in that corner, upon that stage, some people who look as if they wanted to fight. I know not whether that be what you call a mystery; but I do know it's not amusing. They belabour one another with their tongues, but that's all. For this quarter of an hour I've been waiting to see the first blow; but nothing comes: they're cowards, and maul one another only with foul words. You should have had boxers from London or Rotterdam; and then indeed we should have hard knocks, which you might have heard the length of this hall. But those creatures there are quite pitiful. They should at least give us a morris-dance, or some other piece of mummery. This is not what I was told it was to be: I'd been promised a feast of fools, with an election of a pope. We at Ghent, too, have our fools' pope; and in that, Croix-Dieu! we're behind nobody. But we do thus:—a mob gets together, as here for instance; then each in his turn goes and puts his head through a hole and makes faces at the other: he that makes the ugliest face, according to general acclamation, is chosen pope. That's our way, and it's very diverting. Shall we make your pope after the fashion of my country? At any rate it will not be so tiresome as listening to those babblers. If they've a mind to come and try their hands at face-making, they shall have their turn. What say you, my masters? Here's a droll sample enough of both sexes to give us a right hearty Flemish laugh, and we can show ugly phizzes enow to give us hopes of a fine grinning-match."

Gringoire would fain have replied, but amazement, resentment, and indignation deprived him of utterance. Besides, the motion made by the popular hosier was received with such enthusiasm by those townsfolk, flattered at being called *hobereaux* (a term in that day somewhat approaching to gentlemen as now used in England in addressing a mixed multitude, though in this day it is no longer used complimentarily), that all resistance would have been unavailing. All that could now be done was to go with the stream. Gringoire hid his face with both his hands, not being so fortunate as to possess a mantle wherewith to veil his countenance like the Agamemnon of Timanthes.

CHAPTER V

QUASIMODO

In the twinkling of an eye everything was ready for putting Coppenole's idea into execution. Townspeople, scholars, and *basochians* had all set themselves to work. The small chapel, situated opposite to the marble table, was fixed upon to be the scene of the grinning-match. The glass being broken out of one of the divisions of the pretty, rose-shaped window over the doorway, left open a circle of stone through which it was agreed that the candidates should pass their heads. To get up to it they had only to climb upon two casks which had been laid hold of somewhere or other, and set upon one another just as it happened. It was settled that each candidate, whether man or woman (for they might make a *she*-pope), in order to leave fresh and entire the impression of their grin, should cover their face and keep themselves unseen in the chapel until the moment of making their appearance at the hole. In a moment the chapel was filled with competitors, and the door was closed upon them.

Coppenole, from his place in the gallery, ordered everything, directed everything, arranged everything. During the noisy applause that followed his proposal, the Cardinal, no less out of countenance than Gringoire himself, had, on pretext of business and of the hour of vespers, retired with all his suite; while the crowd, amongst whom his arrival had caused so strong a sensation, seemed not to be in the slightest degree interested by his departure. Guillaume Rym was the only one who remarked the discomfiture of his eminence. The popular attention, like the sun, pursued its revolution: after setting out at one end of the hall, it had stayed for a while in the middle of it, and was now at the other end. The marble table, the brocaded gallery, had each had its season of interest; and it was now the turn of Louis XI.'s chapel. The field was henceforward clear for every sort of extravagance; the Flemings and the mob had it all to themselves.

The grinning commenced. The first face that appeared at the hole, with eyelids turned up with red, a mouth gaping like the swallow of an ox, and a forehead wrinkled in large folds like our hussar boots in the time of the Empire, excited such an inextinguishable burst of laughter that Homer would have taken all those boors for gods. Nevertheless, the Grand' Salle was anything but an Olympus, as no one could better testify than Gringoire's own poor Jupiter. A second face and a third succeeded—then another—then another—the spectators each time laughing and stamping with their feet with redoubled violence. There was in this spectacle a certain peculiar whirling of the brain—a certain power of intoxication and fascination—of which it is difficult to give an idea to the reader of the present day, and the frequenter of our modern drawing-room. Imagine a series of visages, presenting in succession every geometrical figure, from the triangle to the trapezium, from the cone to the polyhedron—every human expression, from that of anger to that of lust—every age, from the wrinkles of the new-born infant to those of extreme old age—every religious phantasm, from Faunus to Beelzebub—every animal profile, from the jowl to the beak, from the snout to the muzzle. Figure to yourself all the grotesque heads carved on the Pont-Neuf, those nightmares petrified under the hand of Germain Pilon, taking life and breath, and coming one after another to look you in the face with flaming eyes—all the masks of a Venetian carnival passing successively before your eye-glass—in short, a sort of human kaleidoscope.

The orgie became more and more Flemish. Teniers himself would have given but a very imperfect idea of it. Imagine, if you can, the "battle" of Salvator Rosa bacchanalised. There was no longer any distinction of scholars, ambassadors, townspeople, men, or women. There was now neither Clopin Trouillefou, nor Giles Lecornu, nor Marie Quatre-Livres, nor Robin Poussepain. All was confounded in the common licence. The Grand' Salle had become, as it were, one vast furnace of audacity and joviality, in which every mouth was a shout, every eye a flash, every face a grin, every figure a gesticulation—all was bellowing and roaring. The strange visages that came one after another to grind their teeth at the broken window were like so many fresh brands cast upon the fire; and from all that effervescent multitude there escaped, as the exhalation of the furnace, a humming noise, like the buzzing of the wings of ten thousand gnats.

"Curse me," cries one, "if ever I saw anything like that."

"Only look at that phiz," cries another.

"It's good for nothing."

"Let's have another."

"Guillemette Maugerepuis, just look at that pretty bull's head; it wants nothing but horns. It can't be thy husband."

"Here comes another."

"Bless the pope! what sort of a grin's that?"

"Hollo! that's not fair. You must show nothing but your face."

"That devil, Perette Callebotte! That must be one of her tricks."

"Noël! noël!"

"Oh! I'm smothered!"

"There's one that can't get his ears through,"—etc., etc.

We must, however, do justice to our friend Jehan. In the midst of this infernal revel he was still to be seen at the top of his pillar like a ship-boy on the topsail. He was exerting himself with incredible fury. His mouth was wide open, and there issued from it a cry which, however, was not audible: not that it was drowned by the general clamour, all intense as that was, but because, no doubt, it attained the utmost limit of perceptible sharp sounds, of the twelve thousand vibrations of Sauveur or the eight thousand of Biot.

As for Gringoire, as soon as the first moment of depression was over, he had resumed his self-possession. He had hardened himself against adversity. "Go on," he had said for the third time to his players—"go on, you talking machines." Then pacing with great strides before the marble table, he felt some temptation to go and take his turn at the hole in the chapel window, if only to have the pleasure of making faces at the ungrateful people. "But no—that would be unworthy of us—no revenge—let us struggle to the last," muttered he to himself. "The power of poetry over the people is great—I will bring them back. We will see which of the two shall prevail—grinning, or the belles lettres."

Alas! he was left the sole spectator of his piece.

This was much worse than before, for instead of profiles he now saw nothing but backs.

We mistake. The big, patient man whom he had already consulted at one critical moment had remained with his face towards the stage. As for Gisquette and Liénarde, they had deserted long ago.

Gringoire was touched to the soul by the fidelity of his only remaining spectator. He went up to and accosted him, giving him, at the same time, a slight shake of the arm, for the good man had leaned himself against the balustrade, and was taking a gentle nap.

"Monsieur," said Gringoire, "I thank you."

"Monsieur," answered the big man with a yawn, "what for?"

"I see what annoys you," returned the poet; "all that noise prevents you from hearing as you could wish. But make yourself easy; your name shall go down to posterity. Will you please to favour me with your name?"

"Renauld Château, Seal-Keeper of the Châtelet of Paris, at your service."

"Monsieur," said Gringoire, "you are here the sole representative of the Muses."

"You are too polite, monsieur," answered the seal-keeper of the Châtelet.

"You are the only one," continued Gringoire, "who has given suitable attention to the piece. What do you think of it?"

"Why—why—" returned the portly magistrate, but half awake, "it's very diverting indeed."

Gringoire was obliged to content himself with this eulogy, for a thunder of applause, mingled with a prodigious acclamation, cut short their conversation. The fools' pope was at last elected.

"Noël! noël! noël!" cried the people from all sides.

It was indeed a miraculous grin that now beamed through the circular aperture. After all the figures, pentagonal, hexagonal, and heteroclite which had succeeded each other at the round hole, without realising that idea of the grotesque which had formed itself in the imaginations of the people excited by the orgie, it required nothing less to gain their suffrages than the sublime grin which had just dazzled the assemblage. Maître Coppenole himself applauded; and Clopin Trouillefou, who had been a candidate (and God knows his visage could attain an intensity of ugliness), acknowledged himself to be outdone. We shall do likewise. We shall not attempt to give the reader an idea of that tetrahedron nose—that horse-shoe mouth—that small left eye over-shadowed by a red bushy brow, while the right eye disappeared entirely under an enormous wart—of those straggling teeth with breaches here and there like the battlements of a fortress—of that horny lip, over which one of those teeth projected like the tusk of an elephant—of that forked chin—and, above all, of the expression diffused over the whole—that mixture of malice, astonishment, and melancholy. Let the reader, if he can, figure to himself this combination.

The acclamation was unanimous. The crowd rushed towards the chapel, and the blessed pope of the fools was led out in triumph. And now the surprise and admiration of the people rose still higher, for they found the wondrous grin to be nothing but his ordinary face.

Or rather, his whole person was a grimace. His large head, all bristling with red hair—between his shoulders an enormous hump, to which he had a corresponding projection in front—a framework of thighs and legs, so strangely gone astray that they could touch one another only at the knees, and, when viewed in front, looked like two pairs of sickles brought together at the handles—sprawling feet—monstrous hands—and yet, with all that deformity, a certain gait denoting vigour, agility, and courage—a strange exception to the everlasting rule which prescribes that strength, like beauty, shall result from harmony. Such was the pope whom the fools had just chosen. He looked like a giant that had been broken and awkwardly mended.

When this sort of Cyclop appeared on the threshold of the chapel, motionless, squat, and almost as broad as he was high—squared by the base, as a great man has expressed it—the populace, by his coat half red and half violet, figured over with little silver bells, and still more by the perfection of his ugliness—the populace recognised him at once, and exclaimed with one voice, "It's Quasimodo the ringer! It's Quasimodo the hunchback of Notre-Dame! Quasimodo the one-eyed! Quasimodo the bandy-legged! Noël! noël!" The poor devil, it seems, had a choice of surnames.

"All ye pregnant women, get out of the way!" cried the scholars.

"And all that want to be so," added Joannes.

The women, in fact, hid their faces.

"Oh, the horrid baboon!" said one.

"As mischievous as he's ugly," added another.

"It's the devil!" cried a third.

"I've the misfortune to live near Notre-Dame, and at night I hear him scrambling in the gutter."

"With the cats."

"He's constantly upon our roofs."

"He casts spells at us down the chimneys."

"The other night he came and grinned at me through my attic window—I thought it was a man. I was in such a fright!"

"I'm sure he goes to meet the witches—he once left a broomstick on my leads."

"Oh, the shocking face of the hunchback!"

"Oh, the horrid creature!"

The men, on the contrary, were delighted, and made great applause.

Quasimodo, the object of the tumult, kept standing in the doorway of the chapel, gloomy and grave, letting himself be admired.

One of the scholars (Robin Poussepain, we believe) came and laughed in his face, rather too near him. Quasimodo quietly took him by the waist, and threw him half a score yards off among the crowd, without uttering a word.

Maître Coppenole, wondering, now went up to him. "Croix-Dieu! holy Father! why, thou hast the prettiest ugliness I ever saw in my life! Thou wouldst deserve to be Pope at Rome as well as at Paris."

So saying, he clapped his hand merrily upon the other's shoulder. Quasimodo stirred not an inch. Coppenole continued: "Thou art a fellow whom I long to feast with, though it should cost me a new *douzain* of twelve livres tournois. What say'st thou to it?"

Quasimodo made no answer.

"Croix-Dieu!" cried the hosier, "art thou deaf?"

He was indeed deaf.

However, he began to be impatient at Coppenole's motions, and he all at once turned towards him with so formidable a grinding of his teeth that the Flemish giant recoiled like a bull-dog before a cat.

A circle of terror and respect was then made round the strange personage, the radius of which was at least fifteen geometrical paces; and an old woman explained to Maître Coppenole that Quasimodo was deaf.

"Deaf!" cried the hosier, with his boisterous Flemish laugh, "Croix-Dieu! then he's a pope complete!"

"Ha! I know him," cried Jehan, who was at last come down from his capital to have a nearer look at the new pope; "it's my brother the archdeacon's ringer. Good-day to you, Quasimodo."

"What a devil of a man!" said Robin Poussepain, who was all bruised with his fall. "He shows himself—and you see he's a hunchback. He walks—and you see he's bow-legged. He looks at you—and you see he's short of an eye. You talk to him—and you find he's deaf. Why, what does the Polyphemus do with his tongue?"

"He talks when he likes," said the old woman. "He's lost his hearing with ringing the bells. He's not dumb."

"No—he's that perfection short," observed Jehan.

"And he's an eye too many," added Robin Poussepain.

"No, no," said Jehan judiciously; "a one-eyed man is much more incomplete than a blind man, for he knows what it is that's wanting."

Meanwhile all the beggars, all the lackeys, all the cut-purses, together with the scholars, had gone in procession to fetch from the wardrobe of the *basoche* the pasteboard tiara and the mock robe appropriated to the fools' pope. Quasimodo allowed himself to be arrayed in them, without a frown, and with a sort of proud docility. They then seated him upon a parti-coloured chair. Twelve officers of the brotherhood of fools, laying hold of the poles that were attached to it, hoisted him upon their shoulders; and a sort of bitter and disdainful joy seemed to spread itself over the sullen face of the Cyclop when he beheld under his deformed feet all those heads of good-looking and well-shaped men. Then the whole bawling and tattered procession set out, to make, according to custom, the internal circuit of the galleries of the Palais before parading through the streets.

CHAPTER VI

ESMERALDA

We are delighted to have to inform our readers that during all this scene Gringoire and his piece had held out. His actors, goaded on by himself, had not discontinued the enacting of his play, nor had he ceased to listen to it; he had taken his part in the uproar, and was determined to go to the end, not despairing of a return of public attention. This gleam of hope revived when he saw Quasimodo, Coppenole, and the deafening train of the fool's pope march with great clamour out of the hall, while the rest of the crowd rushed eagerly after them. "Good!" said he to himself; "there go all the disturbers at last!" But, unfortunately, all the disturbers made the whole assemblage, and in a twinkling the great hall was empty.

It is true there still remained a few spectators, some scattered about, and others grouped around the pillars—women, old men, and children—weary and exhausted with the squeezing and the clamour. A few of the scholars, too, still remained, mounted on the entablature of the windows, and looking out into the Place.

"Well," thought Gringoire, "here are still enow of them to hear the end of my mystery. They are few, but they are a chosen, a lettered audience."

But a moment afterwards a symphony which was to have had the greatest effect at the arrival of the Holy Virgin was missing. Gringoire discovered that his music had been carried off by the procession of the fools' pope. "Pass it over," said he stoically.

He approached a group of townspeople who seemed to him to be talking about his piece, and caught the following fragment of their conversation:—

"Maître Cheneteau, you know the Hôtel de Navarre, which belonged to Monsieur de Nemours?"

"Oh yes—opposite to the Chapelle de Braque."

"Well, the government have just let it to Guillaume Alixandre, heraldry-painter, for six livres eight sols parisis a year."

"How rents are rising!"

"So!" said Gringoire with a sigh; "but the others are listening."

"Comrades!" suddenly cried one of the young fellows at the windows, "La Esmeralda! La Esmeralda in the Place!"

This word produced a magical effect. All who remained in the hall rushed towards the windows, climbing up the walls to see, and repeating, "La Esmeralda! La Esmeralda!" At the same time was heard a great noise of applauses outside.

"What is the meaning of La Esmeralda?" said Gringoire, clasping his hands in despair. "Ah, my God! it seems to be the turn of the windows now!"

He returned towards the marble table, and saw that the performance was interrupted. It was precisely the moment at which Jupiter was to enter with his thunder. But Jupiter remained motionless at the foot of the stage.

"Michel Giborne!" cried the irritated poet, "what are you doing there? Is that your part? Go up, I say."

"Alas!" exclaimed Jupiter, "one of the scholars has just taken away the ladder."

Gringoire looked. It was but too true. All communication between his plot and his catastrophe was cut off. "The fellow!" muttered he; "and why did he take *that* ladder?"

"To go and see La Esmeralda," cried Jupiter in a piteous tone. "He came and said, 'Here's a ladder that nobody's using;' and away he went with it."

This was the finishing blow. Gringoire received it with resignation. "The devil take you all!" said he to the players; "and if they pay *me*, I'll pay *you*."

Then he made his retreat, hanging his head indeed, but still the last in the field, like a general who has fought well. And as he descended the winding stairs of the Palais—"What a fine drove of asses and dolts are these Parisians!" grumbled he. "They come to hear a mystery, and pay no attention to it. They've attended to everybody else—to Clopin Trouillefou—to the Cardinal—to Coppenole—to Quasimodo—to the Devil! but to our Lady the Virgin not at all. If I'd known it, I'd have given you Virgin Maries, I dare say, you wretched cockneys! And then, for me to come here to see faces, and see nothing but backs!—to be a poet, and have the success of an apothecary! True it is that Homerus begged his bread through the villages of Greece, and that Naso died in exile among the Muscovites. But the devil flay me if I understand what they mean with their Esmeralda. Of what language can that word be?—it must be Egyptian!"

BOOK II

CHAPTER I

FROM CHARYBDIS INTO SCYLLA

THE night comes on early in January. The streets were already growing dark when Gringoire quitted the Palais. This nightfall pleased him: he longed to reach some obscure and solitary alley, that he might there meditate at his ease, and that the philosopher might lay the first unction to the wound of the poet. Besides, philosophy was now his only refuge; for he knew not where to find a lodging for the night. After the signal miscarriage of his first dramatic attempt, he dared not return to that which he occupied in the Rue Grenier-sur-l'Eau, opposite to the Port-au-Foin, having relied upon what the provost was to give him for his epithalamium to enable him to pay to Maître Guillaume Doulx-Sire, farmer of the duty upon cloven-footed beasts brought into Paris, the six months' rent which he owed him—that is to say, twelve sols parisis, twelve times the value of all he possessed in the world, including his breeches, his shirt, and his *bicoquet* hat. After considering, then, for a moment, provisionally sheltered under the wicket-gate of the prison belonging to the treasurer of the Sainte-Chapelle, as to what place of lodging he should select for the night, all the pavements of Paris being at his service, he recollected having espied, the week before, in the Rue de la Savaterie, at the door of a councillor to the parliament, a foot-stone for mounting on mule-back, and having said to himself that this stone might serve upon occasion as an excellent pillar for a beggar or a poet. He thanked Providence for having sent him this happy idea; but as he was preparing to cross the Place du Palais in order to reach the tortuous labyrinth of the city, formed by the windings of all those sister streets, the Rue de la Barillerie, Rue de la Vieille-Draperie, Rue de la Savaterie, Rue de la Juiverie, etc., which are yet standing, with their houses of nine stories, he saw the procession of the fools' pope, which was also issuing from the Palais, and rushing across the Place with loud cries, with great glare of torches, and with Gringoire's own band of music. This sight revived his anguish, and he fled away rrom it. In the bitterness of his dramatic misadventure everything which recalled to mind the festival of the day irritated his wound and made it bleed afresh.

He turned to cross the Pont-Saint-Michel, but found boys running up and down it with squibs and crackers.

"A plague on the fireworks!" said Gringoire; and he turned back on the Pont-au-Change. There were attached to the front of the houses at the entrance of the bridge three *dradels* or pieces of painted cloth, representing the King, the Dauphin, and Margaret of Flanders; and six smaller pieces or *drapelets*, on which were portrayed the Duke of Austria, and the Cardinal de Bourbon, and Monsieur de Beaujeu, and Madame Jeanne of France, and Monsieur the Bastard of Bourbon, and we know not who besides, all lighted by torches, and a crowd admiring them.

"Happy painter, Jehan Fourbault!" said Gringoire with a heavy sigh; and he turned his back upon the *drapels* and *drapelets*. A street lay before him; and it seemed so dark and forsaken that he hoped there to forget all his mental sufferings by escaping every ray of the illuminations, and he plunged down it accordingly. He had not gone far before he struck his foot against some obstacle; he stumbled and fell. It was the bundle of may which the clerks of the *basoche* had placed in the morning at the door of a president of the parliament, in honour of the day. Gringoire bore this new accident heroically: he arose, and reached the water-side. After leaving behind him the Tournelle Civile and the Tour Criminelle, and passing along by the great wall of the king's gardens, on that unpaved strand in which he sank to the ankles in mud, he arrived at the western point of the city, and gazed for some time upon the small island of the Passeur-aux-Vaches, or ferryman of the cows, which has since disappeared under the brazen horse and the esplanade of the Pont-Neuf. The islet appeared to his eyes in the darkness as a black mass beyond the narrow stream of whitish water which separated him from it. He could discern upon it, by the rays of a small glimmering light, a sort of hut in the form of a bee-hive, in which the ferryman sheltered himself during the night.

"Happy ferryman!" thought Gringoire, "thou dreamest not of glory, thou writest not epithalamiums! What are royal marriages or Duchesses of Burgundy to thee? Thou know'st no Marguerites but the daisies which thy April greensward gives thy cows to crop; while I, a poet, am hooted—and shiver —and owe twelve sous—and my shoe-sole is so transparent that thou might'st use it to glaze thy lantern! I thank thee, ferryman. Thy cabin gives rest to my eyes, and makes me forget Paris!"

He was awakened from his almost lyric ecstasy by a great double St. John's rocket (so called from the custom of discharging it on St. John's Day) which suddenly issued from the blessed cabin. It was the ferryman himself, taking his share in the festivities of the day, and letting off his firework.

This rocket made Gringoire's hair stand on end.

"O cursed holiday!" cried he, "wilt thou follow me everywhere—O my God! even to the ferryman's hut?"

Then he looked upon the Seine at his feet, and felt a horrible temptation.

"Oh!" said he, "how gladly would I drown myself—if the water were not so cold!"

Then he took a desperate resolution. It was—since he found that he could not escape the fools' pope, Jehan Fourbault's paintings, the bundles of may, the squibs and the rockets—to plunge boldly into the very heart of the illumination, and go to the Place de Grève.

"At least," thought he, "I shall perhaps get a brand there to warm my fingers; and I shall manage to sup on some morsel from the three great chests of sugar plumbs that will have been set out there on the public sideboard of the town."

CHAPTER II

THE PLACE DE GRÈVE

THE Place de Grève, so long and so dismally conspicuous in Parisian history, derives its name from the simple circumstance of its being situated close upon the northern shore or strand of the Seine, with which latter term the French word *grève* is perfectly synonymous. There now remains but a very small and scarcely perceptible vestige of this square, such as it existed formerly, and that is the charming turret which occupies the northern angle of the Place, and which, already buried under the ignoble washing which encrusts the delicate lines of its carving, will soon, perhaps, have totally disappeared, under that increase of new houses which is so rapidly consuming all the old fronts in Paris.

Such Frenchmen as, like our author, never pass over the Place de Grève without casting a look of pity and sympathy at this poor turret, squeezed between two paltry houses of the time of Louis XV., can easily reconstruct in their mind's eye the assemblage of edifices to which it belonged, and thus imagine themselves in the old Gothic Place of the fifteenth century.

It was then, as now, an irregular square, bounded on one side by the quay, and on the three others by a series of lofty houses, narrow and gloomy. In the daytime you might admire the variety of these buildings, all carved in stone or in wood, and already presenting complete specimens of the various kinds of domestic architecture of the Middle Ages, going back from the fifteenth to the eleventh century—from the Perpendicular window which was beginning to supersede the Gothic, to the circular arch which the Gothic had supplanted, and which still occupied underneath it the first story of that ancient house of the Tour-Rolland, or Roland's Tower, at the angle of the Place adjoining to the Seine, on the side of the Rue de la Tannerie. By night nothing was distinguishable of that mass of buildings but the black indentation of their line of gables, extending its range of acute angles round three sides of the Place. For it is one of the essential differences between the towns of that day and those of the present that now it is the fronts of the houses that look to the squares and streets, but then it was the backs. For two centuries past they have been turned fairly round.

In the centre of the eastern side of the Place rose a heavy and heterogeneous pile formed by three masses of buildings in juxtaposition. The whole was called by three several names, expressing its history, its purpose, and its architecture. It was called the Maison-aux-Dauphin, or Dauphin's House, because Charles V., when dauphin, had lived in it; the Marchandise, because it was used as the Hôtel-de-Ville, or Town House; and the Maison-aux-Piliers (*domus ad piloria*) or Pillared House, on account of a series of large pillars which supported its three stories. The town had there all that a good town like Paris wants—a chapel to pray in; a *plaidoyer*, or court-room, for holding magisterial sittings, and, on occasion, reprimanding the king's officers; and, at the top of all, a magazine stored with artillery and ammunition. For the good people of Paris, well knowing that it was not sufficient, in every emergency, to plead and to pray for the franchises of their city, had always in reserve, in the garrets of the Hôtel-de-Ville, some few good rusty arquebusses or other.

La Grève (as the ancient square was familiarly and elliptically called) had then that sinister aspect which it still derives from the execrable ideas which it awakens, and from the gloomy-looking Hôtel-de-Ville of Dominique Bocador's erection, which has taken the place of the Maison-aux-Piliers. It must be observed that a permanent gibbet and pillory, a *justice* and an *échelle*, as they were then called, erected side by side in the middle of the square, contributed not a little to make the passenger avert his eyes from this fatal spot, where so many beings in full life and health had suffered their last agony, and which was to give birth, fifty years later, to that St. Valliere's fever, as it was called, that terror of the scaffold, the most monstrous of all maladies, because it is inflicted not by the hand of God, but by that of man.

"It is consolatory," here observes our author, "to reflect that the punishment of death, which, three centuries back, still encumbered with its iron wheels, with its stone gibbets, with all its apparatus for execution permanently fixed in the ground, the Grève, the Halles, the Place Dauphine, the Croix du Trahoir, the Marché aux Pourceaux, or Hog-Market, the hideous Montfaucon, the Barrière des Sergens, the Place aux Chats, the Ports Sainte-Denis, Champeaux, the Porte Baudets, the Porte Saint-Jacques—not to mention the innumerable *échelles* of the provosts, of the bishop, of the chapters, of the abbots, of the priors having justice—not to mention the judicial drownings in the river Seine,—it is consolatory to reflect that now, after losing, one after another, every piece of her panoply—her profusion of executions, her refined and fanciful torments, her torture, for applying which she made afresh every five years a bed of leather, in the Grand-Châtelet—this old queen of feudal society, nearly thrust out of our laws and of our towns, tracked from code to code, driven from place to place, now possesses, in our vast metropolis of Paris, but one dishonoured corner of the Grève—but one miserable guillotine—stealthy, anxious, ashamed—which seems always afraid of being taken in the fact, so quickly does it disappear after giving its blow."

CHAPTER III

THE GIPSIES

When Pierre Gringoire arrived at the Place de Grève he was in a shiver. He had gone over the Pont-aux-Meuniers, or Millers' Bridge, to avoid the crowd on the Pont-aux-Change and Jehan Fourbault's drapelets; but the wheels of all the bishop's mills had splashed him as he went by, so that his coat was wet through; and he thought that the fate of his piece had rendered him yet more chilly. Accordingly, he hastened towards the bonfire which was burning magnificently in the middle of the Place; but a considerable crowd encircled it.

"You damned Parisians!" said he to himself (for Gringoire, like a true dramatic poet, was subject to monologues), "so, now you keep me from the fire!—and yet I've some occasion for a chimney-corner. My shoes let in wet, and then all those cursed mills have been raining upon me. The devil take the Bishop of Paris with his mills! I wonder what a bishop can do with a mill! Does he expect, from being a bishop, to turn miller? If he only wants my malediction to do so, I heartily give it him, and his cathedral, and his mills! Let us see, now, if any of those cockneys will stand aside. What are they doing there all this while? Warming themselves—a fine pleasure, truly! Looking at a hundred logs burning—a fine sight, to be sure!"

On looking nearer, however, he perceived that the circle was much wider than was requisite to warm themselves comfortably at the bonfire, and that this concourse of specators were not attracted solely by the beauty of a hundred blazing logs.

In a wide space left clear between the fire and the crowd, a young girl was dancing. Whether she was a human being, a fairy, or an angel, was what Gringoire, sceptical philosopher and ironical poet as he was, could not at the first moment decide, so much was he fascinated by this dazzling vision.

She was not tall, but the elasticity of her slender shape made her appear so. She was brown; but it was evident that in the daylight her complexion would have that golden glow seen upon the women of Andalusia and of the Roman States. Her small foot, too, was Andalusian; for it was at once tight and easy in its light and graceful shoe. She was dancing, turning, whirling upon an old Persian carpet spread negligently under her feet; and each time that in turning round her radiant countenance passed before you, her large black eyes seemed to flash upon you.

Around, every look was fixed upon her, every mouth was open; and, indeed, while she was dancing thus to the sound of a tambourine which her two round and delicate arms lifted above her head—slender, fragile, brisk as a wasp in the sunshine, with her golden corset without a plait, her parti-coloured skirt swelling out below her slender waist, her bare shoulders, her fine-formed legs of which her dress gave momentary glimpses, her black hair and her sparkling eyes—she looked like something more than human.

"Truly," thought Gringoire, "'tis a salamander—a nymph—a goddess—a bacchante of Mount Mænalus!"

At that moment one of the braids of the salamander's hair came undone, and a small piece of brass that had been attached to it rolled upon the ground.

"Oh no!" said he; "it's a gipsy." All the illusion had disappeared.

She resumed her dance. She took up from the ground two swords, the points of which she supported upon her forehead, making them turn in one direction while she turned in the other. It was indeed no other than a gipsy. Yet, disenchanted as Gringoire found himself, the scene, taken altogether, was not without its charm, not without its magic. The bonfire cast upon her a red flaring light, which flickered brightly upon the circle of faces of the crowd and the brown forehead of the girl, and, at the extremities of the Place, threw a pale reflection, mingled with the wavering of their shadows—on one side, upon the old dark wrinkled front of the Maison-aux-Piliers; on the other, upon the stone arms of the gibbet.

Among the thousand visages which this light tinged with scarlet, there was one which seemed to be more than all the rest absorbed in the contemplation of the dancer. It was the face of a man, austere, calm, and sombre. This man, whose dress was hidden by the crowd that surrounded him, seemed to be not more than thirty-five years of age; yet he was bald, having only a few thin tufts of hair about his temples, which were already grey. His broad and high forehead was beginning to be furrowed with wrinkles; but in his deep-sunken eyes there shone an extraordinary youth, an ardent animation, a depth of passion. He kept them constantly fixed upon the gipsy; and while the sportive girl of sixteen was dancing and bounding to the delight of all, his reverie seemed to grow more and more gloomy. From time to time a smile and a sigh encountered each other on his lips, but the smile was yet more dismal than the sigh.

The girl, having at length danced herself quite out of breath, stopped, and the people applauded with fondness.

"Djali!" cried the gipsy.

Gringoire then saw come up to her a little white she-goat, lively, brisk, and glossy, with gilt horns, gilt feet, and a gilt collar, which he had not before observed; as, until that moment, it had been lying squat upon one corner of the carpet, looking at his mistress dance.

"Djali," said the dancer, "it's your turn now;" and, sitting down, she gracefully held out her tambourine to the goat. "Djali," she continued, "what month of the year is this?"

The animal lifted its fore-foot and struck one stroke upon the tambourine. It was, in fact, the first month of the year. The crowd applauded.

"Djali," resumed the girl, turning her tambourine another way, "what day of the month is it?"

Djali lifted her little golden foot and struck six times upon the tambourine.

"Djali!" said the gipsy, each time altering the position of the tambourine, "what hour of the day is it?"

Djali struck seven strokes, and at that very moment the clock of the Maison-aux-Piliers struck seven. The people were wonder-struck.

"There is witchcraft in all that," said a sinister voice in the crowd. It was that of the bald man who had his eyes constantly upon the gipsy.

She shuddered and turned away. But the plaudits burst forth and smothered the sullen exclamation. Indeed they so completely effaced it from her mind that she continued to interrogate her goat.

"Djali!" said she, "how does Maître Guichard Grand-Remy, captain of the town pistoliers, go in the procession at Candlemas?"

Djali reared up on her hind-legs, and began to bleat, marching at the same time with so seemly a gravity that the whole circle of spectators burst out into a laugh at this mimicry of the self-interested devotion of the captain of pistoliers.

"Djali!" resumed the girl, emboldened by this increasing

success, "how does Maître Jacques Charmolue, the king's attorney in the ecclesiastical court—how does he preach?"

The goat sat down upon its posteriors and began to bleat, shaking its fore-paws after so strange a fashion that, with the exception of the bad French and worse Latin of the preacher, it was Jacques Charmolue to the life, gesture, accent, and attitude; and the crowd applauded with all their might.

"Sacrilege! profanation!" cried the voice of the bald-headed man.

The gipsy turned away once more. "Ah," said she, "it's that odious man!" Then putting out her lower lip beyond her upper, she made a little pouting grimace which seemed familiar to her, turned upon her heel, and began to collect in her tambourine the contributions of the multitude.

All sorts of small coins—*grands, blancs, petits blancs, targes, liards à l'aigle*—were now showered upon her. In taking her round she all at once came before Gringoire, and as he, in perfect absence of mind, put his hand into his pocket, she stopped, expecting something. "*Diable!*" exclaimed the poet, finding at the bottom of his pocket the reality—that is to say, nothing at all—the pretty girl standing before him all the while, looking at him with her large eyes, holding out her tambourine, and waiting. Gringoire perspired profusely. Had all Peru been in his pocket, he would assuredly have given it to the dancer; but Gringoire had not Peru in his pocket—nor, indeed, was America yet discovered.

Fortunately an unexpected incident came to his relief. "Wilt thou be gone, thou Egyptian locust?" cried a harsh voice from the darkest corner of the Place. The girl turned away affrighted. This was not the voice of the bald-headed man; it was the voice of a woman—one, too, of dèvotion and of malice.

However, this cry, which frightened the gipsy, highly delighted a troop of children that were rambling about there. "It's the recluse of the Tour-Rolland," cried they with inordinate bursts of laughter—"it's the *sachette* that's scolding. Hasn't she had her supper? Let's carry her something from the town sideboard." And they all ran towards the Maison-aux-Piliers.

Meanwhile Gringoire availed himself of this disturbance of the dancer to disappear among the crowd. The shouts of the children reminded him that he too had not supped. He therefore hastened to the public *buffet*, or sideboard. But the little rogues had better legs than he, and when he arrived they had cleared the table. They had not even left one wretched *camichon* at five sous the pound. There was nothing now against the wall but the light fleurs-de-lis intermingled with rose-trees, painted there in 1434 by Mathieu Biterne; and they offered but a meagre supper.

'Tis an unpleasant thing, after going without one's dinner, to go to bed supperless. 'Tis less gratifying still to go without one's supper and not know where to go to bed. Yet so it was with Gringoire. Without food, without lodging, he found himself pressed by Necessity on every side, and he thought Necessity very ungracious. He had long discovered this truth—that Jupiter had created man in a fit of misanthropy, and that throughout the life of the wisest man his destiny keeps his philosophy in a state of siege. For his own part, he had never found the blockade so complete. He heard his stomach sound a parley, and he thought it very ill-ordained that his evil destiny should reduce his philosophy by simple starvation. He was sinking more and more deeply into this melancholy reverie, when he was suddenly startled from it by the sound of a fantastically warbling voice. It was the young gipsy singing.

Her voice had the same character as her dance and as her beauty. It had an undefinable charm—something clear, sonorous, aërial—winged, as it were. There was a continued succession of swells, of melodies, of unexpected falls—then simple strains, interspersed with sharp and whistling notes—then a running over the gamut that would have bewildered a nightingale, yet ever harmonious—then soft octave undulations, which rose and fell like the bosom of the youthful songstress. The expression of her fine countenance followed with singular flexibility every capricious variation of her song, from the wildest inspiration to the most chastened dignity. She seemed now all frolic and now all majesty.

The words that she sang were in Spanish, a language unintelligible to Gringoire, and which seemed to be unknown to herself, so little did the expression which she gave in singing correspond with the sense of the words. For instance, she gave these four lines, from an old ballad of the time of the Moors, with the most sportive gaiety:—

"Un cofre de gran riqueza
Hallaron dentro un pilar;
Dentro del, nuevas banderas
Con figuras de espantar."

And then, a moment after, at the tone which she gave to this stanza—

"Alarabes de cavallo
Sin poderse menear,
Con espadas, y a los cuellos
Ballestas de buen echar"—

Gringoire felt the tears come to his eyes. Yet joyfulness predominated in her tones, and she seemed to warble like a bird, from pure lightness of heart. The gipsy's song had disturbed Gringoire's reverie, but it was as the swan disturbs the water. He listened to it with a sort of ravishment and forgetfulness of everything else. It was the first moment for several hours in which he felt no suffering.

The moment was a short one. The same female voice which had interrupted the gipsy's dance now interrupted her song. "Wilt thou be silent, thou hell-cricket?" it cried, still from the same dark corner of the Place.

The poor cricket stopped short, and Gringoire stopped his ears. "Oh," he cried, "thou cursed broken-toothed saw, that comest to break the lyre!"

The rest of the bystanders murmured like himself. "The devil take the *sachette!*" cried some of them. And the old invisible disturber might have found cause to repent of her attacks upon the gipsy, had not their attention been diverted at that moment by the procession of the Fool's Pope, which, after traversing many a street, was now debouching upon the Place de Grève, with all its torches and all its clamours.

This procession, which our readers have seen take its departure from the Palais, had organised itself on the way, and been recruited with all the ragamuffins, the unemployed thieves and disposable vagabonds in Paris, so that when it reached the Grève it presented a most respectable aspect.

A history of vagabondism, beggary, and thievery, could it be faithfully and sagaciously written, would form neither one of the least entertaining nor least instructive chapters in the great history of mankind, and especially in that of all such old governments as have been established originally by violence and brigandage (commonly called conquest), and for the benefit of the invading and armed minority and their descendants, at the expense of the unarmed, peaceful, and laborious majority—of such governments, in short, as that of France before the revolution of 1789, and that of England before the grand Norman plunder and ravage of our country, and butchery of the best and bravest of our free Anglo-Saxon forefathers, to the present day—where the system of aristocratical tyranny and hereditary legislation, originally set up by that great bad man, Duke William the bastard, and his copartners in iniquity, having borne its full fruits, in these two naturally favoured but so long politically cursed islands, is now on the point of being washed away by the ocean waves of public opinion, swelled by the terrific tide of general distress. Who can help exclaiming with the mariner in *The Tempest,*—

> "What care these roarers for the name of king?"

Who can help deploring that the fortunes of the united people of Great Britain and Ireland should be in the hands of a Prime Minister, who, less discreet than Canute of old, is blindly and childishly bent on saying to this political sea, "Thus far shalt thou go, and no farther, and here shall thy proud waves be stayed!"

The reader must pardon this burst of political feeling; but we write in no ordinary times—we write in the vicinity of the British metropolis—and cold indeed must be the heart of that man who, placed in such a locality, does not, when the word beggary meets his ear or his eye, reflect with mingled grief and indignation upon that flood of mendicity which he now encounters at every turn, among the most industrious people, possessing the richest resources, on the face of the globe—a flood which sets magistrates and policemen alike at defiance—reminding him daily and hourly that a *régime* is yet standing which says to such a people as that of these islands, not "Work or starve," but "Starve, for you shall not work."[1]

Having thus vented in some degree our uncontrollable feelings on this point, we return to the consideration of that description of beggary which, for the sake of distinction, we may denominate the comic species, and which, though not springing so immediately, as the tragic and revolutionary species just now alluded to, from political iniquity or mismanagement, yet owes its toleration, if not its existence, to the same cause as the former—the establishment over a nation of

[1] To this effect it is that our "government" has spoken, and still speaks by its acts—coupled with which acts its words are intolerably insulting. In Earl Grey's speech from the Throne on the assembling of the first reformed Parliament, it has been gravely announced to the "lords and gentlemen" that it would be their "anxious but grateful duty to promote, by all practicable means, habits of industry and good order among the labouring classes of the community." Well might Mr. Attwood of Birmingham, in the debate on the Address, after observing that "within the last twelve months millions of these industrious people had been going from door to door seeking employment to obtain food," exclaim, as he did, "Surely this cold insult might have been spared!"

a system of plunder, fraud, and coercion miscalled government, in which the self-styled governors are utterly regardless of the morals and happiness of the great mass of the community—a system which makes up for lack of prevention by profusion of punishment, and for neglect of moral culture by alacrity with the halter.

This it is which creates one species of vagrancy and encourages the other. The Beggar's Opera has generally passed for a very good joke, but it conveys an awful moral to those who look a little below the surface of things. The identity of principle between wholesale and petty robbery, between murder of hundreds by thousands and murder of an individual by two or three; the fact that robbery consists in taking the property of others without their own consent, by whatever number of men, upon whatever number committed; and that the destruction of life in executing that robbery is murder, whether perpetrated by few or many upon few or many—are moral maxims as evident as any mathematical axioms, when once clearly presented to the mind.

> "The statesman, because he's so great,
> Thinks his trade is as honest as mine,"

sings Peachum; and assuredly, the statesman who volunteers his services to prosecute and uphold a system which extorts the money of the majority of a people by intimidation, and uses cannon and bayonets if they resist, is not a whit more honest, though less adventurous, than the robber on the highway—nay, if the number of persons injured affect the weight of crime, he is immeasurably the more guilty of the two. And in those cases where his ends may be gained not by open force, but by simple fraud, he must be content to be placed on exactly the the same moral ground as the race of petty impostors, whom his example encourages in a vastly greater degree than his judicial terrors deter—with this difference only, that in the case of fraud, as in that of violence, he practises on a larger scale.

This latter class of vagrants, the "sturdy beggars" of our old laws and popular ballads, and the "rogues and vagabonds" of our modern statutes, are ever found abundant in large and populous countries in which a vicious government is too much occupied in duping and plundering the society by wholesale to care for the moral habits of the individuals composing it. Where is vagabondism now found to thrive? In the British Islands, in Germany, above all, in Italy and Spain, where such frames of government still subsist. Where is it nearly banished from the soil? In the United States of America and in France; in the former of which countries nothing, and in the latter but little, of such system remains.

The sources of vagabondism in general, existing amidst a great civilised society, are then, we think, pretty clearly traceable in misgovernment, or, more properly, false government; but there is one variety of it the origin of which has never been, and perhaps never can be, distinctly made out—we mean the mixture in the general tide of vagrancy of that peculiar stream the race of gipsies, whose source, like that of the great Egyptian river itself, has so long been wrapped in mystery. They share this distinction with the Jews—that they form a nation without a country; but here every shadow of resemblance ends. They seem to have something of the Ishmaelite, but certainly nothing at all of the Israelite. The Jews are a people of ancient literature, with a regular history the most ancient that has obtained any currency in Europe, an attachment to their ancient civil and religious dispensation unexampled for its persevering resistance to the operation of time, place, and persecution, and cherishing through a long succession of ages—if they do not cherish it still—the hope of being finally restored to the occupation of a particular territory, endeared to them, not indeed by natural beauty or fertility, but by those ancient traditions of liberty, glory, and Divine favour, which seemed to grow the dearer to them as they softened under the mellowing hand of Time. The gipsies, on the contrary, are a people without letters, without religion, and, which is most surprising of all, without superstition (indeed it may fairly be said that, without either religion or superstition of their own, they live in a great measure upon the heathenish superstitions of persons professing the Christian religion); and it is quite certain that, so far from their enjoying the promise of a residence in such a country as Palestine, the severest punishment that could be devised for them would be to compel them to take up their abode finally in any tract upon the face of the earth, though it were the most paradisal or elysian that could be found or imagined—so essentially migratory is their Arab nature.

As to the clime from which they originally sprung, the English word *gipsy*, the Spanish *gitano*, and the French *égyptien*, seem to point to it much more truly than the more ordinary French term *bohemien*, which can denote nothing more than that they came or were popularly supposed to have come into France from Bohemia, their complexion and form sufficiently denoting a southern as well as an eastern origin. Now, it seems most likely that in the Middle Ages the ancient fame of Egypt for sorcery, which in Egypt itself must have been confined to the real students and adepts in pretended necromancy, became inseparably attached in the vulgar imagination, among the nations of the west, to the name Egyptian itself; and that while the real Egyptian sorcerers would certainly practise at home, the more roving of the Egyptian vagabonds, originally, perhaps, from the other side of the Red Sea, thinking that a harvest might be made and their wandering habits indulged among these western nations of Europe, rambled off in that direction, and set up for necromancers themselves, their native cunning, and the hints they had picked up from practitioners of more solid pretension, furnishing them with quite enough of the science to impose upon the general ignorance and credulity of the people upon whom they were going to practise, and whose imaginations were also excited by the (to them) singular habits of these rovers, and their affection for haunting woods, caves, and wildernesses, for holding themselves in close communication, as it were, with all the elemental agencies—with the winds and the waters, the light and the darkness, the mist and the sunshine, the lightning and the tempest.

At any rate, until a better solution can be given, this may perhaps be allowed to pass.[1] And in the meantime we may also note this indubitable phenomenon in the moral constitution of these people, for the contemplation of the believers in the universality of natural religion—that the true gipsies themselves have no notion of a Supreme Being whatever, nor apparently of any supernatural agency.

We must now return to the vagabonds of France in the fifteenth century, who will be found to make no inconsiderable figure in this narrative.

And here we must confess we feel rather at a loss for want of the labours of some French Captain Grose to give us a classical dictionary of their vulgar tongue. Had we more leisure than is just now at our command to reperuse the valuable collections in this way of our late venerable countryman just now mentioned, the highly authentic biography of the illustrious Bamfylde Moore Carew (interesting also to us politicians, as having been

[1] Since writing this paragraph our attention has been called to some recent researches into the origin of these people by a German investigator, Rienzi, which strikingly countenance our conjecture as to their having come from beyond the Red Sea, and our contemplating them in the light of a dispersed nation.

an elective sovereign), and the classic pages of that living ornament to our literature, Pierce Egan, it is probable that this course of study, together with a few weeks' personal research, under some ingenious disguise or other, first in the Holy Land, and then in Epping Forest or Maidenhead Thicket (for Norwood is no longer the classic region of gipsydom), might enrich our vocabulary to such a degree as to leave the reader, in the sense intended by the encouraging French-English advertisements of the French hotel-keepers, "nothing to hope for."

However, we shall make the best we can of it in the course of our story; and we solicit the reader's indulgence for such deficiency of illustration as may arise from our being of the uninitiated.

And, in the first place, we will offer an explanation of two general denominations, the understanding of which is essential to that of the succeeding part of our narrative. The word *argot* denotes in French, or rather it once denoted, the whole tribe of vagabonds by profession; and at the same time was used to denote that part of their speech which was peculiar to themselves—their cant language, as we should phrase it. Every member of the nation of Argot, as they termed it, was consequently an Argotier; but there was another term synonymous with vagabond, and which seems to have been yet more popularly familiar—namely, the word *truand* or *truant*.

This ancient and venerable word has, with slight variations of orthography, been in very general use on this western side of Europe; and the curious in etymologies will find in Ducange two folio columns of gratification under this head. The English word *truant*, apparently one of the Norman introductions, though now confined to denote the vagabond schoolboy, had once, no doubt, a more extended signification; and the Spanish *truhan*, though it, again, is limited in its application to one particular species of vagabond, the buffoon or jester, evidently comes from the same etymological root, whatever that was. But as the English word *truant*, corresponding with one of the old French orthographies of the word, is by no means associated with the compound idea of beggar, thief, and impostor, which attached to the French term, we prefer *truand*, which indeed seems to have been in most general use formerly, and is the present form of the word: then we shall say *truandess*, for a *truande* or female truand; and *truandry*, for *truanderie*, the state or profession of a truand, as also the whole community of truands collectively.

On the state of the Parisian truandry at the period in question, we cannot help remarking that it does not exactly correspond with the intimation in one of the lyrical effusions given us by King Bamfylde's biographer and laureate,—

> "Where's the nation lives so free
> And so merrily as we?"

nor yet with Béranger's song in praise of modern beggarhood,

> "Les gueux, les gueux,
> Sont les gens heureux."

Poetry and history, it seems, must always be a little at variance. Besides that, at the period of our story, truandism partook of the general savageness of the age; and the violent criminal was more frequently associated in the same person with the mendicant than in later times.

But to return to the fools' pope, whom we left rather unceremoniously, in the midst of his triumphal progress, and whose procession we must now endeavour to describe.

First of all marched the tribes of Egypt. The Duke of Egypt was at their head, with his counts on foot, holding his bridle and stirrup; behind them came the Egyptian men and women, pell-mell, with their little children squalling upon their shoulders; all of them, duke, counts, and people, covered with rags and tinsel. Then followed the kingdom of Argot—that is, all the rest of the vagabond community—arranged in bands according to the order of their dignities, the *moines* or monks walking first. Thus marched on, four abreast, with the different insignia of their degrees in that strange faculty, most of them crippled in some way or other—some limping, others with only one hand—the *courtaux de boutanche*, the *coquillarts*, the *hubins*, the *sabouleux*, the *calots*, the *franc-mitoux*, the *polissons*, the *piètres*, the *capons*, the *malingreux*, the *rifodés*, the *marcandiers*, the *narquois*, the *orphelins*, the *archisuppôts*, the *cagoux*—denominations enough to have wearied Homer himself to enumerate, and some explanation of which will occur as we proceed. It was with some difficulty that you could discern, in the centre of the band of *cagoux* and *archisuppôts*, the king of Argot himself, the *grand-coësre*, as he was called, sitting squat in a little waggon drawn by two large dogs. After the nation of the Argotiers came the empire of Galilee. Guillaume Rousseau, emperor of the empire of Galilee, walked majestically in his robe of purple stained with wine, preceded by mummers dancing warlike dances, and surrounded by his mace-bearers, his *suppôts,* and the clerks of the *chambre des comptes.* Lastly came the members of the *basoche,*[1] with their garlanded maypoles, their black gowns, their music, worthy of a witches' meeting, and their great candles of yellow wax. In the centre of this latter crowd, the great officers of the brotherhood of fools bore upon their shoulders a *brancard,* or chair carried upon poles, more loaded with wax tapers than was the shrine of Sainte-Geneviève in time of pestilence; and upon this chair shone, crosiered, coped, and mitred, the new fools' pope, the ringer of Notre-Dame, Quasimodo the hunchback.

Each division of this grotesque procession had its particular music. The Egyptians sounded their *balafos* and their African tambourines. The Argotiers, a very unmusical race, had advanced no farther than the viol, the bugle-horn, and the Gothic *rubebbe* of the twelfth century. The empire of Galilee had not made much greater progress. You could but just distinguish in its music some wretched rebeck of the infancy of the art, still confined to the *re, la, mi.* But it was around the fools' pope that were displayed, in magnificent discordance, all the musical riches of the age: there were rebeck trebles, rebeck tenors, and rebeck counter-tenors—not to mention the flutes and the *cuivres.* Alas! our readers will recollect that it was poor Gringoire's orchestra.

It is not easy to give an idea of the expression of proud and beatific satisfaction to which the melancholy and hideous visage of Quasimodo had attained in the journey from the Palais to the Grève. It was the first feeling of self-love that he had ever enjoyed. He had hitherto experienced nothing but humiliation, disdain for his condition, disgust for his person. So that, deaf as he was, he nevertheless relished, like a true pope, the acclamations of that crowd whom he hated because he felt himself hated by them. What though his people were a people of fools, an assemblage of cripples, thieves, and beggars! still they were a people, and he was a sovereign. And he took in earnest all the

[1] This was originally the denomination of the jurisdiction formerly exercised by the clerks to the *procureurs* or attorneys in the court of the Parisian parliament, for the decision of differences arising among the clerks themselves, or complaints brought against clerks by tradesmen or artisans. There was a *chancellerie* or Chancery of the Basoche; and that one of the clerks who presided over the rest was called the *Roi de la Basoche* (King of the Basoche). But the word *basoche,* by extension, seems to have come to signify the whole tribe of clerks and writers of all degrees, employed in the offices of the legal profession at Paris, and consequently haunting the Palais de Justice; and in that signification it is used in the text.

ironical applause and mock reverence which they gave him; with which, at the same time, we must not forget to observe that there mingled, in the minds of the crowd, a degree of fear perfectly real: for the hunchback was strong; though bow-legged, he was active; though deaf, he was malicious—three qualities which have the effect of moderating ridicule.

However, that the new pope of the fools himself at all analysed the feelings which he experienced and those which he inspired we by no means imagine. The spirit that was lodged in that misshapen body was necessarily itself incomplete and dull of hearing, so that what it felt at that moment was to itself absolutely vague, indistinct, and confused. Only joy beamed through, and pride predominated. Around that dismal and unhappy countenance there was a perfect radiance.

It was, therefore, not without surprise and dread that all at once, at the moment when Quasimodo, in that state of demi-intoxication, was passing triumphantly before the Maison-aux-Piliers, a man was seen to issue from the crowd, and, with an angry gesture, snatch from his hands his crosier of gilt wood, the ensign of his mock papacy.

The person who had this temerity was the man with the bald forehead, who the moment before, standing in the crowd that encircled the gipsy, had chilled the poor girl's blood with his words of menace and hatred. He was in an ecclesiastical dress. The moment he stepped forth from the crowd he was recognised by Gringoire, who had not before observed him. "What!" said he with a cry of astonishment. "Why, 'tis my master in Hermes, Dom Claude Frollo, the archdeacon! What the devil can he want with that one-eyed brute? He's going to get himself devoured!"

Indeed, a cry of terror proceeded from the multitude. The formidable Quasimodo had leaped down from his chair; and the women turned away their eyes, that they might not see him tear the archdeacon to pieces.

He made one bound up to the priest, looked in his face, and then fell upon his knees before him. The priest snatched his tiara from his head, broke his crosier, and rent his tinsel cope. Quasimodo remained upon his knees, bowed down his head, and clasped his hands. They then entered into a strange dialogue of signs and gestures, for neither of them uttered a word—the priest erect, angry, threatening, imperious; Quasimodo prostrate, humble, suppliant. And yet it is certain that Quasimodo could have crushed the priest with a single gripe,

At last the priest, roughly shaking Quasimodo's powerful shoulder, made him a sign to rise and follow him; and Quasimodo rose accordingly.

Then the brotherhood of fools, their first amazement being over, offered to defend their pope, thus abruptly dethroned. The Egyptians, the Argotiers, and all the Basoche came yelping round the priest. But Quasimodo, placing himself before the priest, put the muscles of his athletic fists in play, and faced the assailants, gnashing his teeth like an enraged tiger. The priest resumed his sombre gravity, made a sign to Quasimodo, and withdrew in silence. Quasimodo walked before him, scattering the crowd as he passed along.

When they had made their way through the populace and across the Place, the mob of the curious and the idle offered to follow them. Quasimodo then placed himself in the rear, and followed the archdeacon backwards, looking squat, snarling, monstrous, shaggy, gathering up his limbs, licking his tusks, growling like a wild beast, and impressing immense vibrations on the crowd by mere look or gesture.

At length they both plunged down a dark narrow street, into which no one ventured after them, so effectually was its entrance barred by the mere image of Quasimodo gnashing his teeth.

"All this is wonderful enough," said Gringoire to himself, "but where the devil shall I find a supper?"

CHAPTER IV

THE INCONVENIENCES OF AN EVENING CHASE

Gringoire, at a venture, had set himself to follow the gipsy girl. He had seen her, with her goat, turn down the Rue de la Contellerie, and accordingly he turned into the Rue de la Contellerie likewise. "Why not?" said he to himself.

A practical philosopher of the streets of Paris, Gringoire had remarked that nothing is more favourable to a state of reverie than to follow a pretty woman without knowing whither she is going. In this voluntary abdication of one's free will—in this fancy subjecting itself to the fancy of another, while that other is totally unconscious of it—there is a mixture of fantastic independence with blind obedience, a something intermediate between slavery and freedom, which was pleasing to the mind of Gringoire, a mind essentially mixed, undecided, and complex —holding the medium between all extremes, in constant suspense amongst all human propensities, and neutralising one of them by another. He likened himself with satisfaction to the tomb of Mohammed, attracted by the two lodestones in opposite directions, and hesitating eternally between the top and the bottom, between the roof and the pavement, between fall and ascension, between the zenith and the nadir.

Had Gringoire been living in our time, what a fine medium, what a *juste milieu* he would have kept between the classic and the romantic! But he was not primitive enough to live three hundred years, and 'tis really a pity. His absence leaves a void which, in these days of ours, is but too sensibly felt.

However, for thus following the passengers through the streets, especially the female ones, which Gringoire readily did, there is nothing that better disposes a man than to know where to go to bed.

He walked along, therefore, all pensive, behind the young girl, who quickened her step, making her pretty little four-footed companion trot beside her, as she saw the townspeople reaching home and the taverns shutting up—the only shops that had been opened that day. "After all," he half thought to himself, "she must have a lodging somewhere—the gipsy women have good hearts—who knows?" And there were some points of suspension about which he went on weaving this web in his mind—certainly very flattering ideas, or shadows of ideas.

Meanwhile, at intervals, as he passed by the last groups of *bourgeois* closing their doors, he caught some fragment of their conversation which snapped the thread of his pleasing hypotheses.

Now it was two old men accosting each other.

"Maître Thibaut Fernicle, do you know, it's very cold."

(Gringoire had known it ever since the winter had set in.)

"Yes, indeed, Maître Boniface Disome. Are we going to have such a winter as we had three years ago, in the year '80, when wood rose to eight sols a load, think you?"

"Bah! it's nothing at all, Maître Thibaut, to the winter of 1407, when it froze from Martinmas to Candlemas, and so sharp that the ink in the pen in the parliament's registrar's hand froze, in the Grand' Chambre, at every three words—which interrupted the registering of the judgments!"

Then farther on there were two good female neighbours,

talking to each other through their windows, with candles in their hands that glimmered through the fog.

"Has your husband told you of the mishap, Mademoiselle La Boudraque?"

"No, Mademoiselle Turquant; what is it?"

"The horse of Monsieur Gilles Godin, notary at the Châtelet, took fright at the Flemings and their procession, and ran over Maître Philippot Avrillot, lay brother of the Celestines."

"Did it indeed?"

"Yes, indeed."

"A paltry hack-horse too! That was rather too bad: had it been a cavalry horse, now, it would not have been so much amiss."

And the windows were shut again. But Gringoire had completely lost the thread of his ideas.

Luckily he soon found it again, and easily pieced it together at the sight of the gipsy girl and of Djali, who were still trotting on before him—two slender, delicate, and charming creatures, whose small feet, pretty figures, and graceful motions he gazed at with admiration, almost confounding them together in his contemplation; their common intelligence and mutual affection seeming those of two young girls; while, for their light, quick, graceful step, they might have been both young hinds.

Meanwhile the streets were every moment becoming darker and more solitary. The curfew had long ceased to ring, and now it was only at long intervals that a person passed you on the pavement, or a light was to be seen at a window. Gringoire, in following the gipsy, had involved himself in that inextricable labyrinth of alleys, courts, and crossings which surrounds the ancient sepulchre of the Holy Innocents, and may be compared to a skein of thread ravelled by the playing of a kitten. "Very *illogical* streets, in truth!" muttered Gringoire, quite lost in the thousand windings which seemed to be everlastingly turning back upon themselves, but through which the girl followed a track that seemed to be well known to her, and with a pace of increasing rapidity. For his own part, he would have been perfectly ignorant as to his "whereabout" had he not observed, at a bend of a street, the octagonal mass of the pillory of the *Halles*, the perforated top of which traced its dark outline upon a solitary patch of light yet visible in a window of the Rue Verdelet.

A few minutes before his step had attracted the girl's attention: she had several times turned her head towards him, as if with uneasiness; once, too, she had stopped short—had availed herself of a ray of light that escaped from a half-open bake-house to survey him steadily from head to foot; then, when she had taken that glance, Gringoire had observed her make that little mow which he had already remarked, and she had gone on without more ado.

This same little mow furnished Gringoire with a subject of reflection. There certainly was disdain and mockery in that pretty little grimace. So that he was beginning to hang down his head, to count the paving-stones, and to follow the girl at a rather greater distance, when, just after she had made a turn into a street which took her for a moment out of his sight, he heard her utter a piercing shriek.

He quickened his pace. The street was quite dark. However, a twist of tow steeped in oil, which was burning in a sort of iron cage, at the foot of a statue of the Virgin at the corner of the street, enabled Gringoire to discern the gipsy struggling in the arms of two men, who were endeavouring to stifle her cries, while the poor little goat, all wild with affright, hung down its head, bleating.

"Hither, hither, gentlemen of the watch!" cried Gringoire, and he advanced bravely. One of the men who laid hold of the girl turned towards him. It was the formidable visage of Quasimodo. Gringoire did not fly, but he did not advance another step.

Quasimodo came up to him, threw him four paces off upon the pavement with a back stroke of his hand, and plunged rapidly into the darkness, bearing off the girl, her figure drooping over his arm almost as flexibly as a silken scarf. His companion followed him, and the poor goat ran behind with its plaintive bleat.

"Murder! murder!" cried the unfortunate gipsy.

"Stand, there, you scoundrels, and let that wench go!" was all at once heard in a voice of thunder from a horseman, who suddenly made his appearance from the neighbouring crossway.

It was a captain of that description of household troops which were still called archers (from the crossbows which they carried before the invention of firearms), armed *cap-à-pie,* with his *espadon,* or great two-edged sword, in his hand. He snatched the gipsy from the grasp of the amazed Quasimodo, laid her across his saddle, and at the moment when the redoubtable hunchback, having recovered from his surprise, was rushing upon him to seize his prey a second time, fifteen or sixteen archers who followed close upon their captain made their appearance, each brandishing his broadsword. They were a detachment going the counterwatch, by order of Messire Robert d'Estouteville, keeper of the provostry of Paris.

Quasimodo was surrounded, seized, and bound. He roared, he foamed, he bit; and had it been daylight, no doubt his visage alone, rendered yet more hideous by rage, would have put the whole detachment to flight. But being in the dark, he was disarmed of his most formidable weapon, his ugliness. His companion had disappeared during the struggle.

The gipsy girl gracefully gained her seat upon the officer's saddle, leaned both her hands upon the young man's shoulders, and looked fixedly at him for a few seconds, as if delighted with his fine countenance and the effectual succour he had rendered her. Then speaking first, and making her sweet voice still sweeter, she said to him, "Monsieur le Gendarme, what is your name?"

"Captain Phœbus de Chateaupers, at your service, my fair one," said the officer, drawing himself up.

"Thank you," said she.

And while Captain Phœbus was curling his moustache *à la Bourguignonne* she glided down from the horse like an arrow falling to the ground, and fled with the speed of lightning.

"*Nombril du Pape!*" exclaimed the captain, while he made them tighten the bands upon the limbs of Quasimodo, "I'd rather have kept the wench."

"Why, captain," said one of the gendarmes, "what would you have? The linnet is flown; we've made sure of the bat."

CHAPTER V

CONSEQUENCES OF THE CHASE

Gringoire, quite stunned with his fall, had remained stretched upon the pavement before the good Virgin of the corner of the street. By degrees, however, he recovered his senses. At first he was for some minutes in a sort of half-somnolent reverie, which was not altogether disagreeable, and in which the airy figures of the gipsy and the goat were confounded in his imagination with the weight of Quasimodo's fist. This state of his feelings, however, was of short duration. A very lively impression of cold upon that part of his body which was in contact with the ground suddenly awoke him, and brought back his mind to the surface. "Whence is this coolness that I feel?" said he hastily to himself. He then perceived that he lay somewhere about the middle of the gutter.

"The devil take the humpbacked cyclop!" grumbled he, and he strove to get up. But he was too much stunned and too much bruised; so that he was forced to remain where he was. Having, however, the free use of his hand, he stopped his nose and resigned himself to his situation.

"The mud of Paris," thought he (for he now believed it to be decided that the kennel was to be his lodging,

Et que faire en un gîte à moins que l'on ne songe?)—

"the mud of Paris is particularly offensive. It must contain a large proportion of volatile and nitrous salts. Such, too, is the opinion of Maître Nicolas Flamel and the hermetics."

This word hermetics reminded him of the Archdeacon Claude Frollo. He reflected on the scene of violence of which he had just before had a glimpse; that he had seen the gipsy struggling between two men; that Quasimodo had a companion with him; and the sullen and haughty countenance of the archdeacon floated confusedly in his recollection. "That would be strange," thought he; and then, with this datum and upon this basis, he began to rear the fantastic framework of hypothesis, that house of cards of the philosophers; then suddenly returning once more to reality, "Oh, I freeze!" he cried.

The position was, in fact, becoming less and less tenable. Each particle of water in the channel carried off a particle of caloric from the loins of Gringoire, and an equality of temperature between his body and the fluid that ran under it was beginning to establish itself without mercy.

All at once he was assailed by an annoyance of quite a different nature. A troop of children, of those little barefooted savages that have in all times run about the streets of Paris, with the everlasting name of *gamins*, "and who," says our author, "when we were children also, used to throw stones at us all as we were leaving school in the evening, because our trousers were not torn"—a swarm of these young rogues ran to the crossway where Gringoire was lying, laughing and shouting in a manner that showed very little concern about the sleep of the neighbours. They were dragging after them some sort of a shapeless pack, and the noise of their wooden shoes alone was enough to waken the dead. Gringoire, who was not quite dead yet, half raised himself up.

"Hollo, Hennequin Dandèche!—Hollo, Jehan Pincebourde!" cried they as loud as they could bawl. "Old Eustache Moubon, the old iron-seller at the corner, is just dead. We've got his straw mattress, and we're going to make à bonfire with it. This is the *Flamings'* day."

And so saying, they threw down the mattress precisely upon Gringoire, whom they had come up to without perceiving him. At the same time one of them took a handful of straw, and went to light it at the Blessed Virgin's torch.

"*Mort-Christ!*" muttered Gringoire, "am I now going to be too hot?"

The moment was critical. He was about to be fixed between fire and water. He made a supernatural effort, such as a coiner might have made in trying to escape when they were going to boil him to death. He rose up, threw back the mattress upon the *gamins,* and took to his heels.

"Holy Virgin!" cried the boys, "it's the old iron-seller's ghost!" And they too ran away.

The mattress remained master of the field. Those judicious historians, Belleforêt, Father le Juge, and Corrozet, assure us that the next morning it was taken up with great solemnity by the clergy of that part of the town, and carried in great pomp to the treasury of Sainte-Opportune's church, where, until the year 1789, the sacristan drew a very handsome income from the great miracle worked by the statue of the Virgin at the corner of the Rue Mauconseil, which, by its presence alone, in the memorable night between the 6th and 7th of January 1482, had exorcised the deceased Jehan Moubon, who, to cheat the devil, had, when dying, slyly hidden his soul within his mattress.

CHAPTER VI

THE COURT OF MIRACLES

AFTER running for some time as fast as his legs would carry him, without knowing whither, whisking round many a corner, striding over many a gutter, traversing many a court and alley, seeking flight and passage through all the meanders of the old pavement of the Halles, exploring what are called in the elegant Latin of the charters *tota via, cheminum et viaria,* our poet all at once made a halt—first because he was out of breath, and then because a dilemma had suddenly arisen in his mind. "It seems to me, Maître Pierre Gringoire," said he to himself, applying his finger to his forehead, "that you're running all this while like a brainless fellow that you are. The little rogues were no less afraid of you than you of them. It seems to me, I say, that you heard the clatter of their wooden shoes running away southward while you were running away northward. Now one of two things must have taken place: either they have run away, and then the mattress, which they must have forgotten in their fright, is precisely that hospitable couch after which you have been hunting ever since the morning, and which the Lady Virgin miraculously sends you to reward you for having composed in honour of her a morality, accompanied with triumphs and mummeries; or the boys have not run away, and in that case they will have set a light to the mattress, and that will be exactly the excellent fire that you're in want of, to comfort, warm, and dry you. In either case—good bed or good fire—the mattress is a present from Heaven. The ever-blessed Virgin Mary that stands at the corner of the Rue Mauconseil perhaps caused Jehan Moubon to die for the very purpose; and 'tis folly in you to scamper away at such a rate, like a Picard running from a Frenchman, leaving behind you what you are running forward to seek, blockhead that you are!"

Then he began to retrace his steps, and ferreting about to discover where he was—snuffing the wind and laying down his ears—he strove to find his way back to the blessed mattress; but in vain. All was intersections of houses, courts, and clustering streets, amongst which he incessantly doubted and hesitated, more entangled in that strange network of dark alleys than he would have been in the labyrinth of the Hôtel des Tournelles itself. At length he lost patience, and vehemently exclaimed, "A curse upon the crossings! The devil himself has made them after the image of his pitchfork!"

This exclamation relieved him a little, and a sort of reddish reflection, which he at that moment discovered at the end of a long and very narrow street, completed the restoration of his courage. "God be praised," said he, "there it is! There is my blazing mattress!" And likening himself to the pilot foundering in the night-time, "*Salve*," added he piously, "*salve, maris stella!*"

Did he address this fragment of a litany to the Holy Virgin or to the straw mattress? We really cannot say.

He had no sooner advanced a few paces down the long street or lane, which was on a declivity, unpaved, descending quicker and becoming more miry the farther he proceeded, than he observed something very singular. The street was not quite solitary, for here and there were to be seen crawling in it certain vague, shapeless masses, all moving towards the light which was flickering at the end of the street; like those heavy insects which drag themselves along at night, from one blade of grass to another, towards a shepherd's fire.

Nothing makes a man so adventurous as an empty stomach. Gringoire went forward, and soon came up with that one of the *larvæ* which seemed to be dragging itself along most indolently after the others. On approaching it he found that it was nothing other than a miserable stump of a man, without legs or thighs, jumping along upon his two hands, like a mutilated father-longlegs, with only two of its feet remaining. The moment he came up to this sort of spider with a human face, it lifted up to him a lamentable voice: "*La buona mancia, signor! la buona mancia!*"

"The devil take thee," said Gringoire, "and me along with thee, if I know what you mean." And he passed on.

He came up to another of these ambulatory masses, and examined it. It was a cripple, both legless and armless, after such a manner that the complicated machinery of crutches and wooden legs that supported him made him look for all the world like a mason's scaffolding walking along. Gringoire, being fond of noble and classical similes, compared him in his mind to the living tripod of Vulcan.

This living tripod saluted him as he went by, but staying his hat just at the height of Gringoire's chin, after the manner of a shaving-dish, and shouting in his ears, "*Senor cabarellero, par comprar un pedaso de pan!*"

"It appears," said Gringoire, "that this one talks too; but it's a barbarous language, and he's more lucky than I am if he understands it." Then striking his forehead through a sudden transition of idea—"Apropos! what the devil did they mean this morning with their Esmeralda?"

He resolved to double his pace; but for the third time something blocked up the way. This something, or rather this somebody, was a blind man, a little blind man, with a bearded Jewish face, who, rowing in the space about him with a great stick, and towed along by a great dog, snuffled out to him with a Hungarian accent, "*Facitote caritatem!*"

"Oh, come," said Pierre Gringoire, "here is one at last that talks a Christian language. Truly I must have a most almsgiving mien that they should thus ask charity of me in the present extenuated state of my purse. "My friend," said he, turning to the blind man, "last week I sold my last shirt; that is to say, as you understand no language but that of Cicero, *Vendidi hebdomade nuper transitâ meam ultimam chemisam.*"

Then turning his back upon the blind man, he went forward on his way. But the blind man quickened his pace at the same time; and now also the cripple and the stump came up in great haste, with great clatter of the platter that carried one of them, and the crutches that carried the other. Then all three, shoving one another aside at the heels of poor Gringoire, began to sing him their several staves,—

"*Caritatem!*" sang the blind man.

"*La buona mancia!*" sang the stump.

And the man of the wooden legs took up the stave with "*Un pedaso de pan!*"

Gringoire stopped his ears. "O tower of Babel!" he cried.

He began to run. The blind man ran. The wooden-legs ran. The stump ran.

And then, as he advanced still further down the street, stump men, wooden-legged men, and blind men came swarming around him; and one-handed men, and one-eyed men, and lepers with their sores—some coming out of the houses, some from the little adjacent streets, some from the cellar-holes—howling, bellowing, yelping—all hobbling along, making their way towards the light, and wallowing in the mire, like so many slugs after the rain.

Gringoire, still followed by his three persecutors, and not well knowing what was to come of all this, walked on affrighted among the others, turning aside the limpers, striding over the stumpies, his feet entangled in that anthill of cripples, like the English captain who found himself beset by a legion of crabs.

The idea just occurred to him of trying to retrace his steps. But it was too late: all this army had closed upon his rear, and his three beggars were still upon him. He went on, therefore, urged forward at once by that irresistible flood, by fear, and by a dizziness which made it all seem to him like a sort of horrible dream.

At last he reached the extremity of the street. It opened into an extensive place, into which a thousand scattered lights were wavering in the thick gloom of the night. Gringoire threw himself into it, hoping to escape by the speed of his legs from the three deformed spectres that had fixed themselves upon him.

"*Onde vas, hombre?*" cried the wooden-legs, throwing aside his scaffolding, and running after him with as good a pair of legs as ever measured a geometrical pace upon the pavement of Paris. Meanwhile the stump-man, erect upon his feet, clapped his heavy iron-sheathed platter upon his head, while the blind man stared him in the face with great flaming eyes.

"Where am I?" said the terrified poet.

"In the Court of Miracles," answered a fourth spectre who had accosted them.

"On my soul," returned Gringoire, "I do indeed find here that the blind see and the lame walk; but where is the Saviour?"

They answered him with a burst of laughter of a sinister kind.

The poor poet cast his eyes around him. He was, in fact, in that same terrible *Cour des Miracles*, or Court of Miracles, into which no honest man had ever penetrated at such an hour—a magic circle, in which the officers of the Châtelet and the sergeants of the provostry, when they ventured thither, disappeared in morsels—the city of the thieves—a hideous wen on the face of Paris—a sink from whence escaped every morning, and to which returned to stagnate every night, that stream of vice, mendicity, and vagrancy which ever flows through the streets of a capital—a monstrous hive, into which all the petty hornets of society returned each evening with their booty—a lying hospital, in which the gipsy, the unfrocked monk, the abandoned scholar—the worthless of every nation, Spaniards, Italians, Germans—of every religion, Jews, Christians, Mohammedans, idolaters—covered with simulated sores, beggars in the daytime, transformed themselves at night into robbers—an immense dressing-room, in short, in which dressed and undressed at that period all the actors in that everlasting drama which robbery, prostitution, and murder enacted upon the pavements of Paris.

It was a large open space, irregular and ill-paved, as was at that time every place in Paris. Fires, around which strange groups were gathered, were gleaming here and there. All was motion and clamour. There were shrieks of laughter, squalling of children, and screaming of women. The arms and heads of this crowd cast a thousand fantastic gestures in dark outline upon the luminous background. Now and then upon the ground, over which the light of the fires was wavering, intermingled with great undefined shadows, was seen to pass a dog resembling a man, or a man resembling a dog. The limits of the different races and species seemed to be effaced in this commonwealth as in a pandemonium. Men, women, beasts; age, sex; health, sickness—all seemed to be in common amongst this people; all went together, mingled, confounded, placed one upon another, each one participating in all.

The weak and wavering rays that streamed from the fires enabled Gringoire, amidst his perturbation, to distinguish all round the extensive enclosure a hideous range of old houses, the decayed, shrivelled, and stooping fronts of which, each perforated by one or two circular attic windows with lights behind them, seemed to him, in the dark, like enormous old women's heads, ranged in a circle, looking monstrous and crabbed, and winking upon the diabolical revel.

It was like a new world, unknown, unheard of, deformed, creeping, swarming, fantastic.

Gringoire, growing wilder and wilder with affright, held by the three mendicants as by three pairs of pincers, and deafened by a crowd of other vagrants that flocked barking round him—the unlucky Gringoire strove to muster presence of mind enough to recollect whether he was really at a witches' sabbath or not; but his efforts were vain. The thread of his memory and his thoughts were broken; and doubting of everything—floating between what he saw and what he felt—he put the insoluble question to himself, "Am I really in being? Do I really exist?"

At that moment a distinct shout was raised from the buzzing crowd that surrounded him of "Let's take him to the king! let's take him to the king!"

"Holy Virgin!" muttered Gringoire; "the king of this place must surely be a he-goat!"

"To the king! to the king!" repeated every voice.

They dragged him along, each striving to fix his talons upon him. But the three beggars kept their hold, and tore him away from the others, vociferating, "He is ours!"

The poet's poor doublet, already in piteous plight, gave up the ghost in this struggle.

In crossing the horrible place his dizziness left him. After proceeding a few paces the feeling of reality had returned to him. His apprehension began to adapt itself to the atmosphere of the place. At the first moment, from his poet's head, or perhaps, indeed, quite simply and prosaically, from his empty stomach, there had risen a fume, a vapour as it were, which, spreading itself between him and the surrounding objects, had allowed him to survey them only in the incoherent mist of a nightmare, in that dark shrouding of our dreams which distorts every outline, and clusters the objects together in disproportioned groups, dilating things into chimeras, and human figures into phantoms. By degrees this hallucination gave way to a less bewildered and less magnifying state of vision. The *real* made its way to his organs, struck upon his eyes, struck against his feet, and demolished piece by piece all the frightful poetry with which he had at first thought himself surrounded. He could not but perceive at last that he was walking, not in the Styx, but in the mud; that he was elbowed, not by demons, but by thieves; that not his soul, but, in simple sooth, his life, was in danger, seeing that he was unaccompanied by that invaluable conciliator who places himself so effectually between the robber and the honest man—the purse. In short, on examining the orgy more closely and more coolly, he found that he descended from the witches' revel to the pothouse.

The Court of Miracles was, in truth, no other than one great public-house; but it was a public-house, a *cabaret*, of brigands, in which blood flowed almost as frequently as wine.

The spectacle which presented itself to him when his tattered escort at length deposited him at the term of its march was little adapted to bring back his mind to poetry, though it were the poetry of hell. It was more than ever the prosaic and brutal reality of the tavern. Were we not writing of the fifteenth century, we should say that Gringoire had descended from Michael Angelo to Callot.

Round a great fire, which was burning upon a large round flagstone, and the blaze of which had heated red-hot the legs of an iron trivet which was empty for the moment, some worm-eaten tables were set out here and there, as if by chance, without the smallest geometrician of a waiter having condescended to adjust their parallelism, or mind that at least they should not meet at too unaccustomed angles. Upon these tables shone some pots flowing with wine and beer, around which were grouped a number of bacchanalian visages, reddened by the fire and the wine. There was one man with a fair round belly and a jovial face, noisily throwing his arms round a girl of the town, thick-set and brawny. Then there was a sort of false soldier, a *narquois,* as he was called in the Argotian tongue, who whistled away while he was undoing the bandages of his false wound, and unstiffening his sound and vigorous knee, which had been bound up since the morning in a thousand ligatures. On the other hand, there was a *malingreux* preparing, with celandine and ox-blood, his *jambe de Dieu,* or sore leg, for the morrow. Two tables higher up, a *coquillart,* with his complete pilgrim's habit (from the *coquilles* or shells of which this denomination arose), was conning a spiritual song, the Complaint of Sainte-Reine, the psalmody and the nasal drone included. In another place a young *hubin* was taking a lesson in epilepsy from an old *sabouleux,* or hustler, who was teaching him the art of foaming at the mouth by chewing a piece of soap; while four or five women, thieves, just by them, were contending at the same table for the possession of a child stolen in the course of the evening. All which circumstances, two centuries later, "seemed so laughable at court," says Sauval, "that they furnished pastime to the king, and an opening to the royal ballet entitled 'Night,' which was divided into four parts, and danced upon the stage of the Petit-Bourbon." And "never," adds an eyewitness, in the year 1653, "were the sudden metamorphoses of the Court of Miracles more happily represented. Benserade prepared us for them by some very pleasant verses."

The loud laugh everywhere burst forth, and the obscene song. Each one let off his own exclamation, passing his remark, and swearing, without attending to his neighbour. The pots rattled, and quarrels were struck out of their collision, the smashing of pots thus leading to the tearing of rags.

A large dog, sitting on his tail, was looking at the fire. There were some children mingled in this orgy. The stolen child was crying; another, a bouncing boy of four years old, seated with his legs dangling upon a bench which was too high for him, with his chin just above the table, said not a word; a third was gravely spreading over the table with his finger the melted tallow running from a candle; and a fourth, a very little one, squatting in the mud, was almost lost in a great iron pot which he was scraping with a tile, drawing from it a sound enough certainly to have agonised the most obdurate nerves.

There was a barrel near the fire, and upon the barrel was seated one of the beggars. This was the king upon his throne.

The three who had possession of Gringoire brought him before this cask, and the whole bacchanalia were silent for a moment, excepting the cauldron tenanted by the child.

Gringoire was afraid to breathe or lift up his eyes.

"*Hombre, quita tu sombrero!*" said one of the three fellows who had hold of him; and before he could understand what that meant, another of them had taken off his hat—a wretched covering, it is true, but still of use on a day of sunshine or a day of rain. Gringoire heaved a sigh.

Meanwhile the king from the top of his barrel put the interrogatory, "What is this rascal?"

Gringoire started. This voice, though speaking in a tone of menace, reminded him of another voice which that very morning had struck the first blow at his mystery by droning out in the midst of the audience, "Charity, if you please!" He raised his eyes: it was indeed Clopin Trouillefou.

Clopin Trouillefou, arrayed in his regal ensigns, had not one rag more or less upon him. His sore on the arm had indeed disappeared. He held in his hand one of those whips with lashes of whitleather which were at that time used by the sergeants of the wand to drive back the crowd, and were called *boullayes.* He had upon his head a sort of *coiffure* formed into a circle and closed at the top; but it was difficult to distinguish whether it was a child's cushion or a king's crown, the two things are so much alike.

However, Gringoire, without knowing why, had felt some revival of hope on recognising in the King of the Court of Miracles his cursed beggar of the Grand' Salle. "Maître," stammered he, "——Monseigneur——Sire—— How must I call you?" said he at last, having mounted to his utmost stretch of ascent, and neither knowing how to mount higher nor how to come down again.

"Monseigneur—your Majesty—or Comrade—call me what you like—only dispatch. What hast thou to say in thy defence?"

"In my defence!" thought Gringoire; "I don't like that." He replied, hesitating, "I am he—he who this morning——"

"By the devil's claws," interrupted Clopin, "thy name,

rascal, and nothing more. Hark ye! thou art before three mighty sovereigns—me, Clopin Trouillefou, King of Tunis, successor to the *Grand-Coësre,* supreme sovereign of the kingdom of Argot; Mathias Hungadi Spicali, Duke of Egypt and Bohemia, that yellow old fellow that thou seest there with a clout round his head; and Guillaume Rousseau, Emperor of Galilee, that fat fellow that's not attending to us, but to that wench. We are thy judges. Thou hast entered into the kingdom of Argot without being an Argotier—thou hast violated the privileges of our city. Thou must be punished, unless thou art either a *capon,* a *francmitou,* or a *rifodé*—that is to say, in the *argot* of the honest man, either a thief, a beggar, or a vagrant. Art thou anything of that sort? Justify thyself; tell over thy qualifications."

"Alas!" said Gringoire, "I have not that honour. I am the author——"

"That's enough," interrupted Trouillefou; "thou shalt be hanged. It's a matter of course, messieurs the honest townsfolk. Just as you treat our people amongst you, so we treat yours amongst us. Such law as you give to the Truands the Truands give to you. If it's bad law, it's your own fault. It's quite necessary that an honest man or two should now and then grin through the hempen collar; that makes the thing honourable. Come, my friend, merrily share thy tatters among these young ladies. I'll have thee hanged for the amusement of the Truands, and thou shalt give them thy purse to drink thy health. If thou hast any mumming to do first, there is down there, in that mortar, a very good stone God the Father that we stole from Saint-Pierre-aux-Bœufs. Thou hast just four minutes' time to throw thy soul at his head."

This was a formidable harangue.

"Well said, upon my soul! Clopin Trouillefou preaches like a holy father the Pope!" cried the Emperor of Galilee, breaking his pot at the same time to prop his table leg.

"Messeigneurs the emperors and kings," said Gringoire coolly, for his resolution had somehow or other returned to him, and he spoke quite firmly, "you do not consider. My name is Pierre Gringoire; I am the poet whose morality was performed this morning in the Grand' Salle of the Palais."

"Ah! it's you, master, is it?" said Clopin. "I was there, *par la tête-Dieu.* Well, comrade, is it any reason, because thou tiredst us to death this morning, that thou shouldst not be hanged to-night?"

"I shall not so easily get off," thought Gringoire. However, he made another effort.

"I don't very well see," said he, "why the poets are not classed among the Truands. A vagrant forsooth! why, Æsopus was a vagrant. A beggar! well, Homerus was a beggar. A thief! was not Mercurius a thief?"

Clopin interrupted him. "Methinks," said he, "thou'st a mind to *matagrabolise* us with thy gibberish. *Pardieu!* Be hanged quietly, man; and don't make so much ado about nothing."

"Pardon me, Monseigneur the King of Tunis," replied Gringoire, disputing the ground inch by inch; "it's really worth your while. Only one moment—hear me. You'll not condemn me without hearing me."

His unfortunate voice was, in fact, drowned by the uproar that was made around him. The little boy was scraping his kettle with more alacrity than ever; and, as the climax, an old woman had just come and set upon the red-hot trivet a frying-pan full of fat, which yelped over the fire with a noise like the shouts of a flock of children running after a mask in carnival-time.

Meanwhile Clopin Trouillefou seemed to confer a moment with the Duke of Egypt and with the Emperor of Galilee, who was completely drunk. Then he called out sharply, "Silence!" and as the pot and the frying-pan paid no attention to him, but continued their duet, he jumped down from his barrel, gave the cauldron a kick which rolled it and the child half a score yards off; gave the frying-pan another, which upset all the fat into the fire; and then gravely reascended his throne, regardless of the smothered cries of the child and of the grunting of the old woman, whose supper was evaporating in a beautiful white flame.

Trouillefou made a sign; whereupon the duke and the emperor, and the *archisuppôts* and the *cagoux*, came and ranged themselves about him in the form of a horse-shoe, of which Gringoire, upon whom they still kept rough hands, occupied the centre. It was a semicircle of rags, tatters, and tinsel—of pitchforks and hatchets—of reeling legs and great naked arms—of sordid, dull, and sottish faces. In the midst of this Round Table of beggarhood Clopin Trouillefou, as the doge of this senate, the king of this peerage, the pope of this conclave, predominated—in the first place by the whole height of his cask, and then by a certain lofty, fierce, and formidable air which made his eyeballs flash, and corrected in his savage profile the bestial type of the Truand race. He might be compared to a wild boar among swine.

"Hark ye," said he to Gringoire, at the same time stroking his shapeless chin with his horny hand, "I don't see why thou shouldst not be hanged. To be sure thou dost not seem to like it, and that's but natural—you *bourgeois* aren't used to it. You think it very shocking. After all, we don't wish thee any harm. There's one way of getting off for the moment. Wilt thou be one of us?"

It may be supposed what an effect this proposal produced upon Gringoire, who saw life just about to escape him, and felt his grasp of it beginning to fail. He caught at it energetically. "That I will—certainly, assuredly," said he.

"You consent," said Clopin, "to enlist yourself among the men of the *petite flambe?*"

"Of the *petite flambe*—exactly so," responded Gringoire.

"You acknowledge yourself a member of the *franche-bourgeoisie?*" added the King of Tunis.

"Of the *franche-bourgeoisie.*"

"A subject of the kingdom of Argot?"

"Of the kingdom of Argot."

"A Truand?"

"A Truand."

"In your soul?"

"In my soul."

"I will just observe to thee," resumed the king, "that thou wilt be none the less hanged for all that."

"The devil!" cxclaimed the poet.

"Only," continued Clopin, quite imperturbable, "thou wilt be hanged later, with more ceremony, at the expense of the good town of Paris, upon a good stone gibbet, and by honest men. That's some consolation."

"Just so," answered Gringoire.

"There are other advantages. As being a *franc-bourgeois*, a free burgess, thou wilt have to pay neither towards the pavements, the lamps, nor the poor—to which the burgesses of Paris are subject."

"Be it so," said the poet; "I consent. I am a Truand, an Argotier, a *franc-bourgeois*, a *petite-flambe*, whatever you please. And indeed I was all that beforehand, Monsieur the King of Tunis; for I am a philosopher, and, as you know, *Omnia in philosophiâ, omnes in philosopho continentur*——"

The King of Tunis knit his brows. "What dost thou take me for, friend? What Jew of Hungary's cant art thou singing us now? I don't understand Hebrew: because a man's a robber, he's not obliged to be a Jew. Nay, I don't even rob now—I'm above all that; a cutthroat, if you like, but no cutpurse."

Gringoire strove to slip in some sort of an excuse between these brief ejaculations, of which each succeeding one came bouncing out with increased momentum. "I ask your pardon, monseigneur—it's not Hebrew, it's Latin."

"I tell thee," rejoined Clopin, in a rage, "that I'm no Jew, and that I'll have thee hanged, *ventre de synagogue*, as well as that little *marcandier* of Judea that stands by thee, and whom I hope to see, one of these days, nailed to a counter like a piece of bad coin as he is!"

So saying, he pointed with his finger to the little bearded Hungarian Jew that had accosted Gringoire with his *Facitote caritatem!* and who, understanding no other language, was surprised to see the ill-humour of the King of Tunis vent itself upon him.

At length Monseigneur Clopin's passion subsided. "Rascal," said he to our poet, "then thou'rt willing to be a Truand?"

"Undoubtedly," answered the poet.

"Willing isn't all," said Clopin surlily. "Good will doesn't put one onion more into the soup, and's of no use at all but for going to heaven—and there's a difference between heaven and Argot. To be received in Argot thou must prove that thou art good for something, and to do that thou must feel the *mannequin*."

"I'll feel anything you like," said Gringoire.

Clopin made a sign; whereupon some Argotiers detached themselves from the circle, and returned in a minute. They brought two posts, terminated at the lower extremity by two broad feet which made them stand firm on the ground. To the upper extremities of these two posts they applied a cross beam; and the whole formed a very pretty portable gallows, which Gringoire had the satisfaction of seeing erected before him in the twinkling of an eye. Everything was there, including the rope, which gracefully depended from the transverse beam.

"What can be their meaning?" thought Gringoire to himself with some uneasiness. But a noise of little bells which he heard at that moment put an end to his anxiety, for it proceeded from a stuffed figure of a man which the Traunds were suspending by the neck to the rope—a sort of scarecrow, clothed in red, and so completely covered with little bells and hollow, jingling brasses that there were enow to have harnessed thirty Castilian mules. These thousand miniature bells jingled for a time under the vibrations of the rope, their sound dying away gradually into a profound silence, which resulted from the state of perfect rest into which the body of the mannequin was speedily brought by that law of the pendulum which has superseded the use of the hour-glass.

Then Clopin, pointing to an old tottering joint-stool placed underneath the mannequin, said to Gringoire, "Get upon that."

"*Mort-diable!*" objected Gringoire, "I shall break my neck. Your stool halts like one of Martial's distichs—it has one hexameter leg, and one pentameter."

"Get up!" repeated Clopin.

Gringoire mounted upon the stool, and succeeded, not without some oscillations of his head and his arms, in recovering his centre of gravity.

"Now," proceeded the King of Tunis, "turn thy right foot round thy left leg, and spring up on the toe of thy left foot."

"Monseigneur," said Gringoire, "you are then absolutely determined that I shall break some of my limbs."

Clopin shook his head. "Hark ye, friend," said he, "you talk too much. It all amounts to this: you're to spring up on your toe; you'll then just be able to reach up to the mannequin's pocket; you'll put your hand into it—pull out a purse that's in it; and if you do all that without jingling one of the bells, well and good—thou shalt be a Truand. We shall then have nothing more to do but to belabour thee soundly for a week."

"*Ventre-Dieu!* I shall not care to do it," said Gringoire. "And suppose I make the bells jingle?"

"Then thou shalt be hanged. Dost thou understand?"

"No, I don't understand it at all," answered Gringoire.

"Hark ye once more. You're to put your hand in the mannequin's pocket and take out his purse. If one single bell stirs while you're doing it, you shall be hanged. Now do you understand?"

"Well," said Gringoire, "I understand that. What next?"

"If you manage to draw out the purse without making any jingle at all, you're a Truand, and will be soundly belaboured for eight days together. You understand now, I dare say."

"No, monseigneur, I don't understand this time. Where is

my advantage? To be hanged in one case, or beaten in the other!"

"And to be a Truand into the bargain," rejoined Clopin —"to be a Truand! Is that nothing? It's for thy own advantage we shall beat thee, to harden thee against stripes."

"I'm greatly obliged to you," answered the poet.

"Come! quick!" said the king, striking his barrel with his foot and making it ring. "Pick the mannequin's pocket, and let's have done with it. I tell thee once for all, that if I hear the smallest tinkle, thou shalt take the mannequin's place."

The whole company of Argotiers applauded the words of Clopin, and ranged themselves in a circle round the gallows, with so pitiless a laugh that Gringoire saw plainly enough that he gave them too much amusement not to have everything to fear from them. He had therefore no hope left but in the faint chance of succeeding in the terrible operation which was imposed upon him. He resolved to risk it; but he first addressed a fervent prayer to the man of straw from whose person he was going to do his best to steal, and whose heart was even more likely to be softened than those of the Truands. That myriad of bells, with their little brazen tongues, looked like so many asps with their mouths open, ready to hiss and to sting.

"Oh!" said he in a low voice, "and can it be that my life depends upon the smallest vibration of the smallest of those bits of metal? Oh!" he added, clasping his hands, "ye bells, tinkle not—ye balls, jingle not!"

He made one more effort with Trouillefou. "And if there come a breath of wind!" said he.

"Thou shalt be hanged," replied the other without hesitation.

Finding that there was no respite, delay, or subterfuge whatsoever, he bravely set about the feat. He turned his right foot about his left leg, sprang up on the toe of his left foot and stretched out his arm; but the moment that he touched the mannequin, his body, which was now supported only by one foot, tottered upon the stool, which had only three, he mechanically caught at the mannequin, lost his balance, and fell heavily to the ground, quite deafened by the violent vibration of the scarecrow's thousand bells; while the figure, yielding to the impulse which his hand had given it, first revolved on his own axis, and then swung majestically backwards and forwards between the two posts.

"*Malédiction!*" he exclaimed as he fell; and he lay with his face to the ground as if he was dead.

However, he heard the awful chime above him, and the diabolical laughter of the Truands, and the voice of Trouillefou, saying, "Lift the fellow up, and hang him in a trice."

He rose of himself. They had already unhooked the mannequin to make room for him. The Argotiers made him get upon the stool again. Clopin came up to him, passed the rope round his neck, and, slapping him on the shoulder, "Good-bye, friend," said he; "thou'lt not get away now, though thou should'st be as clever as the Pope himself."

The word "Mercy!" expired on Gringoire's lips; he cast his eyes round, but saw no gleam of hope—all were laughing.

"Bellevigne de l'Etoile," said the King of Tunis to an enormous Truand who stepped out of the ranks, "do you get upon the cross-beam."

Bellevigne de l'Etoile climbed nimbly up to the transverse bar; and an instant after, Gringoire, looking up, saw him with terror squatted just above his head.

"Now," continued Clopin Trouillefou, "as soon as I clap my hands, do you, Andry-le-Rouge, push down the stool with your knee; you, François Chante-Pruen, hang at the rascal's feet; and you, Bellevigne, drop upon his shoulders; and all three at the same time—do you hear?"

Gringoire shuddered.

"Are you ready?" said Clopin Trouillefou to the three Argotiers about to throw themselves upon the post. The poor sufferer had a moment of horrible expectation, while Clopin was quietly pushing into the fire with the point of his shoe some twigs which the flame had not reached. "Are you ready?" he repeated, and he held his hands ready to give the signal. A second more, and all would have been over.

But he stopped as if something suddenly occurred to him. "Wait a moment," said he; "I'd forgotten. It's customary for us not to hang a man without first asking if there be a woman that'll have anything to say to him. Comrade, it's thy last chance; thou must marry either a she-Truand or the halter."

Gringoire took breath. This was the second time he had come to life again within half an hour, so that he could not venture to rely very much upon it.

"Hollo!" shouted Clopin, who had reascended his cask; "hollo, there, women, females! is there among you all, from the witch to her cat, ever a jade that'll have anything to say to this rogue? Hollo! Collette la Charonne! Elisabeth Trouvain! Simone Jodouyne! Marie Piédebou! Thonnela-la-Longue!

Bérarde Fanouel! Michelle Genaille! Claude Rouge-Oreille! Mathurine Girorou! Hollo! Isabeau-la-Thierrye! Come and see! A man for nothing! Who'll have him?"

Gringoire, in this miserable plight, was, it may be supposed, not over-inviting. The Truandesses displayed no great enthusiasm at the proposal. The unhappy fellow heard them answer, "No, no—hang him!—it'll please us all!"

Three of them, however, stepped out of the crowd, and came to reconnoitre him. The first was a large, square-faced young woman. She carefully examined the philosopher's deplorable doublet. The coat was threadbare, and had more holes in it than a chestnut-roaster. The woman made a wry face at it. "An old rag!" muttered she; and then, addressing Gringoire, "Let's see thy cope."

"I've lost it," said Gringoire.

"Thy hat?"

"They've taken it from me."

"Thy shoes?"

"They've hardly a bit of sole left."

"Thy purse?"

"Alas!" stammered Gringoire, "I've not a single denier parisis."

"Let them hang thee, and be thankful," replied the Truandess, turning her back upon him.

The second woman, old, dark, wrinkled, of an ugliness conspicuous even in the Court of Miracles, now made the circuit of Gringoire. He almost trembled lest she should want to have him. But she only muttered, "He's too lean," and went her way.

The third that came was a young girl, fresh-complexioned, and not very ill-looking. "Save me!" whispered the poor devil. She looked at him for a moment with an air of pity, then cast down her eyes, made a plait in her skirt, and remained undecided. He watched her every motion—it was his last gleam of hope. "No," said the girl at last—"no; Guillaume Longue-joue would beat me." And she returned into the crowd.

"Comrade," said Clopin, "thou'rt unlucky." Then, standing up on his barrel, "So nobody bids?" cried he, mimicking the tone of an auctioneer, to the great diversion of them all—"so nobody bids? Going—going—going——" then, turning towards the gallows with a motion of his head, "gone."

Bellevigne de l'Etoile, Andry-le-Rouge, and François Chante-pruen again approached Gringoire. At that moment a cry was heard among the Argotiers of "La Esmeralda! la Esmeralda!"

Gringoire started and turned towards the side from which the shout proceeded. The crowd opened and made way for a clear and dazzling countenance. It was that of the gipsy girl.

"La Esmeralda!" said Gringoire, amazed in the midst of his emotions by the instantaneousness with which that magic word linked together all his recollections of that day.

This fascinating creature seemed to exercise, even over the Court of Miracles, her sway of grace and beauty. Argotiers, male and female, drew up gently to let her pass by; and their brutal countenances grew kindly at her look.

She approached the sufferer with her elastic step, her pretty Djali following her. Gringoire was more dead than alive. She gazed at him for a moment in silence.

"So you're going to hang that man," said she gravely to Clopin.

"Yes, sister," answered the King of Tunis, "unless thou wilt take him for thy husband."

She made her pretty little grimace with the under lip. "I take him," she said.

And now Gringoire was firmly persuaded that he must have been in a dream ever since the morning, and that this was but a continuation of it. In fact, the turn of events, though gratifying, was a violent one. They undid the noose, and let the poet descend from the stool. The violence of his emotion obliged him to sit down.

The Duke of Egypt, without uttering a word, brought forth a clay pitcher. The gipsy girl presented it to Gringoire. "Throw it on the ground," said she. The pitcher broke in four pieces. "Brother," then said the Duke of Egypt, laying his hands upon their foreheads, "she is thy wife.—Sister, he is thy husband—for four years. Go your way."

CHAPTER VII

A WEDDING NIGHT

In a few minutes our poet found himself in a little chamber with a Gothic-vaulted ceiling, the windows and doors well closed, and comfortably warm, seated before a table which seemed quite ready to borrow a few articles from a sort of small pantry or safe suspended just by, having a good bed in prospect, and *tête-à-tête* with a pretty girl. The adventure had something of enchantment. He began seriously to take himself to be a personage of the fairy-tales; and now and then he cast his eyes around him, as if to see whether the fiery chariot drawn by two hippogriffs, which alone could have conveyed him so rapidly from Tartarus to Paradise, were still there. At intervals, too, he fixed his eyes steadfastly upon the holes in his coat, by way of clinging to reality, so as not to let the earth altogether slip from under him. His reason, tossed to and fro in imaginative space, had only that thread left to hold by.

The girl seemed to pay no attention to him. She was going backwards and forwards, shifting first one article and then another, talking to her goat, making her little mow here and there. At length she came and sat down near the table, and Gringoire could contemplate her at leisure.

"You have been a boy, reader," our author here exclaims, "and perhaps you have the happiness to be so still. It is quite certain, then, that you have more than once (and for my own part I can say that I have passed whole days in that manner, the best-spent days of my life), that you have followed from brier to brier, on the brink of a rivulet, on a sunshiny day, some pretty *demoiselle* fly,[1] green or blue, checking its flight at acute angles, and kissing the extremity of every spray. You recollect with what amorous curiosity your thoughts and your looks were fixed upon that little whirl of whiz and hum, of wings of purple and azure, in the midst of which floated a form which your eyes could not seize, veiled as it was by the very rapidity of its motion. The aërial being confusedly perceptible through all that fluttering of wings, appeared chimerical, imaginary, impossible to touch, impossible to see. But when, at last, the demoiselle settled on the point of a reed, and you could examine, holding

[1] The same, we believe, as the English dragon-fly, the French having named it from its beauty, the English from its voracity.

in your breath all the while, the long gauze pinions, the long enamel robe, the two globes of crystal, what astonishment did you not experience, and what fear lest you should again see the form go off in shadow and the being in chimera! Recall to your mind those impressions, and then you will easily understand what were the feelings of Gringoire in contemplating, under her visible and palpable form, that Esmeralda, of whom until then he had only caught a glimpse amid a whirl of dance, song, and flutter."

Sinking deeper and deeper into his reverie, "So then," said he to himself, as his eyes wandered over, "I now see what this Esmeralda really is—a heavenly creature, a dancer in the streets—so much, and yet so little! She it was who gave the finishing blow to my mystery this morning—she it is who saves my life to-night. My evil genius, my good angel! A pretty woman, upon my word—and who must love me to distraction, to have taken me as she has done. By-the-bye," said he, suddenly rising up from his seat, with that feeling of the real which formed the substance of his character and of his philosophy, "I don't very well know how it happens, but I'm her husband!"

With this idea in his head and in his eyes, he approached the young girl in so military and gallant a manner that she drew back. "What do you want with me?" said she.

"Can you ask me such a question, adorable Esmeralda?" returned Gringoire in so impassioned a tone that he himself was astonished to hear himself utter it.

The gipsy opened her large eyes. "I don't know what you mean."

"What!" rejoined Gringoire, growing warmer and warmer, and reflecting that, after all, he had only to do with a virtue of the Court of Miracles; "am I not thine, my sweet friend?—art thou not mine?" And without more ado he threw his arm round her waist.

The gipsy's corset slipped through his hands like the skin of an eel. She sprang from one end of the cell to the other, stooped down, and rose again with a small poniard in her hand, and all before Gringoire had even time to observe whence the poniard came, looking irritated and indignant, her lips puffed out, her nostrils distended, her cheeks all scarlet, and her eyeballs flashing. At the same time the little white goat placed itself before her, and presented a hostile front to Gringoire, lowering its two pretty gilt and very sharp horns. All this was done in the twinkling of an eye. The demoiselle turned *wasp*, and had every disposition to sting.

Our philosopher stood quite confused, looking sheepishly first at the goat and then at its mistress. "Holy Virgin!" he exclaimed at last, as soon as his surprise permitted him to speak, "here are a pair of originals!"

The gipsy girl now broke silence. "You must be a very bold fellow!" she said.

"I ask your pardon, mademoiselle," said Gringoire with a smile; "but why, then, did you take me for your husband?"

"Was I to let you be hanged?"

"So, then," rejoined the poet, a little disappointed in his amorous expectations, "you had no other intention in marrying me but to save me from the gallows?"

"Why, what other intention should I have had?"

Gringoire bit his lip. "Humph!" said he, "I'm not yet quite so triumphant in Cupido as I thought. But then, what was the use of breaking that poor pitcher?"

Meanwhile the poniard of Esmeralda and the horns of the goat were still in a posture of defence.

"Mademoiselle Esmeralda," said the poet, "let us make a capitulation. As I am not registering-clerk at the Châtelet, I shall not quibble with you about your thus carrying a dagger in Paris in the teeth of Monsieur the Provost's ordinances and prohibitions. You are aware, however, that Noël Lescrivain was condemned, only a week ago, to pay a fine of ten sous parisis for carrying a braquemard.[1] But that's no business of mine; and so, to come to the point, I swear to you, by my chance of salvation, that I will not approach you without your leave and permission. But pray, give me my supper."

The truth is that Gringoire, like Despréaux, was "very little voluptuous." He was not of that *cavalier* and *mousquetaire* species who carry girls by assault. In a love affair, as in every other affair, he willingly resigned himself to temporising and to middle terms; and a good supper, in comfortable *tête-à-tête*, appeared to him, especially when he was hungry, to be a very good interlude between the opening and the catastrophe of an amatory adventure.

The gipsy gave him no answer. She made her little disdainful mow, drew up her head like a bird, then burst into a laugh; and the little dagger disappeared, as it had come forth, without

[1] A sort of short cutlass which was worn hanging down by the thighs.

Gringoire's being able to discover whereabouts the wasp concealed its sting.

In a minute there were upon the table a loaf of rye bread, a slice of bacon, some withered apples, and a jug of beer. Gringoire set to with perfect violence. To hear the furious clatter of his iron fork upon his earthenware plate, it seemed as if all his love had turned to hunger.

The girl, seated before him, witnessed his operations in silence, being evidently preoccupied by some other reflection, at which she smiled from time to time, while her delicate hand caressed the intelligent head of the goat, pressed softly between her knees.

A candle of yellow wax lighted this scene of voracity and of musing.

And now, the first cravings of an empty stomach being appeased, Gringoire felt a twinge of false shame at seeing that there was only an apple left.

"Mademoiselle Esmeralda," said he, "you don't eat."

She answered by a negative motion of the head, and then her pensive look seemed to fix itself upon the vault of the chamber.

"What the devil is she attending to?" thought Gringoire; "it can't be that grinning dwarf's face carved upon that keystone that attracts her so mightily. The devil's in it if I can't bear *that* comparison, at any rate."

He spoke louder—"Mademoiselle!"

She seemed not to hear him.

He repeated, louder still, "Mademoiselle Esmeralda!" It was all in vain. The girl's mind was wandering elsewhere, and Gringoire's voice was unable to bring it back. Luckily the goat interfered. It began to pull its mistress gently by the sleeve. "What do you want, Djali?" said the gipsy sharply, as if starting out of her sleep.

"It's hungry," said Gringoire, delighted at an opportunity of entering into conversation.

La Esmeralda began to crumble some bread, which Djali gracefully ate out of the hollow of her hand.

Gringoire, however, allowed her no time to resume her reverie. He ventured upon a delicate question: "You won't have me for your husband, then?"

The girl looked steadily at him, and answered, "No."

"For your lover?" proceeded Gringoire.

She thrust out her lip, and again answered, "No."

"For your friend?" then demanded the poet.

Again she looked at him steadily; and after a moment's reflection she said, "Perhaps."

This perhaps, so dear to philosophers, encouraged Gringoire. "Do you know what friendship is?" he asked.

"Yes," answered the gipsy; "it is to be like brother and sister—two souls meeting without mingling—two fingers on the same hand."

"And love?" proceeded Gringoire.

"Oh, *love!*" said she, and her voice trembled, and her eye beamed—"that is to be two and yet but one—a man and a woman mingled into an angel; it is heaven!"

The street dancing-girl, while saying this, had a character of beauty which singularly struck Gringoire, and seemed to him to be in perfect harmony with the almost Oriental exultation of her words. Her pure and roseate lips were half smiling. Her clear, calm forehead was momentarily ruffled by her thoughts, like the mirror dimmed by a passing breath. And from her long, dark, drooping lashes there emanated a kind of ineffable light, giving her profile that ideal suavity which Raphael afterwards found at the mystic point of intersection of virginity, maternity, and divinity.

Gringoire, nevertheless, continued. "What must a man be, then, to please you?"

"He must be a man."

"And what am I, then?"

"A man has a helmet on his head, a sword in his hand, and gilt spurs at his heels."

"Good!" said Gringoire; "the horse makes the man. Do you love anybody?"

"As a lover?"

"Yes—as a lover."

She remained thoughtful for a moment. Then she said with a peculiar expression, "I shall know that soon."

"Why not to-night?" rejoined the poet in a tender tone. "Why not me?"

She gave him a grave look, and said, "I can never love a man who cannot protect me."

Gringoire coloured, and took the reflection to himself. The girl evidently alluded to the feeble assistance he had lent her in the critical situation in which she had found herself two hours before. This recollection, effaced by his other adventures of the evening, now returned to him. He struck his forehead. "Apropos, mademoiselle," said he, "I ought to have begun with that. Pardon my foolish distractions. How did you contrive to escape from the clutches of Quasimodo?"

At this queston the gipsy started. "Oh, the horrid hunchback!" said she, hiding her face with her hands and shivering violently.

"Horrid indeed!" said Gringoire, still pursuing his idea. "But how did you manage to get away from him?"

La Esmeralda smiled, sighed, and was silent.

"Do you know why he had followed you?" asked Gringoire, striving to come round again to the object of his inquiry.

"I don't know," said the girl. Then she added sharply, "But you were following me too. Why did you follow me?"

"To speak honestly," replied Gringoire, "I don't know that either."

There was a pause. Gringoire was marking the table with his knife. The girl smiled, and seemed as if she had been looking at something through the wall. All at once she began to sing in a voice scarcely audible,—

> "Quando las pintadas aves
> Mudas estan, y la tierra. . . ."

She suddenly stopped short, and fell to caressing Djali.

"You've got a pretty animal there," said Gringoire.

"It's my sister," answered she.

"Why do they call you La Esmeralda?" asked the poet.

"I don't know at all."

"But why do they though?"

She drew from her bosom a sort of small oblong bag, suspended from her neck by a chain of grains of adrezarach. A strong smell of camphor exhaled from the bag; it was covered with green silk, and had in the centre a large boss of green glass, in imitation of an emerald. "Perhaps it's on account of that," said she. Gringoire offered to take the bag, but she drew back. "Touch it not," she said; "it's an amulet. You would do mischief to the charm, or the charm to you."

The poet's curiosity was more and more awakened. "Who gave it you?" said he.

She placed her finger on her lip, and hid the amulet again in her bosom. He tried a few more questions, but could hardly obtain any answer.

"What's the meaning of that word, La Esmeralda?"

"I don't know," she replied.

"What language does it belong to?"

"I think it's Egyptian."

"I suspected so," said Gringoire; "you're not a native of France?"

"I don't know."

"Are your parents living?"

She began to sing to an old tune,—

> "A bird was my mother;
> My father, another;
> Over the water I pass without ferry;
> Over the water I pass without wherry.
> A bird was my mother;
> My father, another."

"Very good," said Gringoire. "At what age did you come to France?"

"A very little girl."

"And when to Paris?"

"Last year. At the moment we were coming in by the Porte Papale, I saw the red linnet scud through the air—it was at the end of August. I said, It'll be a hard winter."

"It has been so," said Gringoire, delighted at this commencement of conversation. "I've done nothing but blow my fingers. So you've the gift of prophecy?"

She fell into her laconics again. "No," she answered dryly.

"That man whom you call the Duke of Egypt is the chief of your tribe?"

"Yes."

"It was he, however, that married us," observed the poet timidly.

She made that pretty little habitual grimace of hers. "I don't know so much as your name."

"My name? If you wish to know it, it is this — Pierre Gringoire."

"I know a finer one," said she.

"Naughty girl!" rejoined the poet. "No matter—you shall not provoke me. Nay, you will perhaps love me when you know me better; and then, you have told me your history with such unreserved confidence that I am bound to give you some account of myself. You must know, then, that my name is Pierre Gringoire, and that I am the son of a farmer of the *tabellionage* of Gonesse—that is to say, of the office of notary in that seigneurial jurisdiction. My father was hanged by the Burgundians, and my mother ripped open by the Picards, at the time of the siege of Paris twenty years ago. At six years of age, then, I was an orphan, without any other sole to my foot than the pavement of Paris. How I got over the time from six years old to sixteen I hardly know. Here a fruit-woman used to give me a plum, and there a baker used to throw me a crust. At night I used to get myself picked up by the *Onze-vingts*, who put me in prison, and there I found a bundle of straw. All this did not prevent my growing tall and thin, as you see. In winter I warmed myself in the sun, under the porch of the Hôtel de Sens; and I thought it very ridiculous that the great fire on the Feast of St. John should be reserved for the dog-days. At sixteen I wished to choose a calling. I tried everything in succession. I turned soldier, but was not brave enough. I then turned monk, but was not devout enough; and besides, I'm a poor drinker. In despair, I apprenticed myself among the carpenters of the *grande coignée;* but I was not strong enough. I had more inclination to be a schoolmaster: to be sure, I couldn't read; but that needn't have hindered me. I perceived, at the end of a certain time, that I was in want of some requisite for everything; and so, finding that I was good for nothing, I, of my own free will and pleasure, turned poet and rhymester. 'Tis a calling that a man can always embrace when he's a vagabond; and it's better than robbing, as I was advised to do by some young plunderers of my acquaintance. Fortunately, I met one fine day with Dom Claude Frollo, the reverend Archdeacon of Notre-Dame. He took an interest in me; and to him I owe it that I am now a true man of letters, acquainted with Latin, from Cicero's Offices to the Mortuology of the Celestine fathers, and not absolutely barbarous either in scholastics, in poetics, or rhythmics, nor yet in hermetics, that science of sciences. I am the author of the mystery that was performed to-day, with great triumph and concourse of people, all in the Grand' Salle of the Palais. I've also written a book that will make six hundred pages, upon the prodigious comet of 1465, about which one man went mad. These are not the only successes I have had: being something of an artillery carver, I worked upon that great bombard of Jean Maugue, which, you know, burst at the bridge of Charenton the first time it was tried, and killed four-and-twenty of the spectators. You see that I'm not so indifferent a match. I know many sorts of very clever tricks, which I will teach your goat—for instance, to mimic the Bishop of Paris, that cursed Pharisee whose mill-wheels splash the passengers the whole length of the Pont-aux-Meuniers. And then my mystery will bring me a good lump of hard cash, if I get paid. In short, I'm at your service, I and my wit and my science and my letters—ready to live with you, damsel, as it shall please you, chastely or otherwise; as man and wife, if you think good; as brother and sister, if you like it better."

Here Gringoire was silent, awaiting the effect of his harangue upon the gipsy girl. Her eyes were fixed upon the ground.

"*Phœbus,*" said she, with an emphasis upon the word, though in a half whisper; then, turning to the poet, "*Phœbus,*" said she—"what does that mean?"

Gringoire, though not at all understanding what relation there could be between his address and this question, was not sorry to show off his erudition. He answered, bridling with dignity, "'Tis a Latin word that signifies the sun."

"The sun?" repeated she.

"'Tis the name of a certain handsome archer, who was a god," added Gringoire.

"A god!" ejaculated his companion; and there was something pensive and impassioned in her tone.

At that moment one of her bracelets came unfastened, and dropped on the floor. Gringoire eagerly stooped to pick it up; and when he rose again the girl and the goat had both disappeared. He heard the shoot of a bolt. It was a small door, communicating no doubt with an adjoining chamber, which some one was fastening outside.

"Has she, at any rate, left me a bed?" said our philosopher.

He made a tour of the chamber. There was no piece of furniture at all adapted to repose, except a very long wooden chest; and the lid of that was carved, so that it gave Gringoire, when he stretched himself upon it, a sensation much like that which the Micromegas of Voltaire's tale would experience lying all his length upon the Alps.

"Come!" said he, making the best he could of it, "there's nothing for it but resignation. And yet this is a strange wedding-night. 'Tis pity, too. That broken-pitcher marriage had something sweetly simple and antediluvian about it that quite pleased me."

BOOK III

CHAPTER I

NOTRE-DAME

ASSUREDLY, the church of Our Lady at Paris is still at this day a majestic and sublime edifice. Yet, noble an aspect as it has preserved in growing old, it is difficult to suppress feelings of sorrow and indignation at the numberless degradations and mutilations which the hand of Time and that of man have inflicted upon the venerable monument, regardless alike of Charlemagne, who laid the first stone of it, and of Philip-Augustus, who laid the last.

Upon the face of this old queen of the French cathedrals, beside each wrinkle we constantly find a scar. *Tempus edax, homo edacior.* Which we would willingly render thus: Time is blind, but man is stupid.

If we had leisure to examine one by one, with the reader, the traces of destruction imprinted on this ancient church, the work of Time would be found to form the lesser portion; the worst destruction has been perpetrated by men, especially by men of art. We are under the necessity of using the expression *men of art*, seeing that there have been individuals in France who have assumed the character of architects in the two last centuries.

And first of all—to cite only a few leading examples—there are, assuredly, few finer architectural pages than that front of the Parisian cathedral, in which, successively and at once, the three receding pointed gateways; the decorated and indented band of the twenty-eight royal niches; the vast central circular window, flanked by the two lateral ones, like the priest by the deacon and subdeacon; the lofty and slender gallery of trifoliated arcades, supporting a heavy platform upon its light and delicate columns; and the two dark and massive towers, with their eaves of slate—harmonious parts of one magnificent whole, rising one above another in five gigantic stories—unfold themselves to the eye, in combination unconfused, with their innumerable details of statuary, sculpture, and carving in powerful alliance with the tranquil grandeur of the whole—a vast symphony in stone, if we may so express it—the colossal work of a man and of a nation—combining unity with complexity, like the Iliads and the Romanceros, to which it is a sister production—the prodigious result of a draught upon the whole resources of an era—in which, upon every stone, is seen displayed in a hundred varieties the fancy of the workman disciplined by the genius of the artist—a sort of human Creation; in short, mighty and prolific as the Divine Creation, of which it seems to have caught the double character—variety and eternity.

And what is here said of the front must be said of the whole church, and what we say of the cathedral church of Paris, must be said of all the churches of Christendom in the Middle Ages. Everything is in its place in that art—self-created, logical, and well-proportioned. By measuring the toe we estimate the giant.

But to return to the front of Notre-Dame as it still appears to us when we go to gaze in pious admiration upon the solemn and mighty cathedral, looking terrible, as its chroniclers express it—*quæ mole suâ terrorem incutit spectantibus*.

Three things of importance are now wanting to this front: first, the flight of eleven steps by which it formerly rose above the level of the ground; then the lower range of statues, which occupied the niches of the three portals; and, lastly, the upper series, of the twenty-eight more ancient kings of France, which filled the gallery on the first story, beginning with Childebert and ending with Philip-Augustus, each holding in his hand the imperial ball.

As for the flight of steps, it is Time that has made it disappear, by raising, with slow but resistless progress, the level of the ground in the city. But while thus swallowing up, one after another, in this mounting tide of the pavement of Paris, the eleven steps which added to the majestic elevation of the structure, Time has given to the church, perhaps, yet more than he has taken from it; for it is he who has spread over its face that dark-grey tint of centuries which makes of the old age of architectural monuments their season of beauty.

But who has thrown down the two ranges of statues? who has left the niches empty? who has cut in the middle of the central portal that new and bastard pointed arch? who has dared to hang in it that heavy unmeaning wooden gate, carved *à la* Louis XV., besides the arabesques of Biscornette? The men, the architects, the artists of our times.

And—if we enter the interior of the edifice—who has overturned that colossal St. Christopher, proverbial for his magnitude among statues, as the Grand' Salle of the Palais was among halls, as the spire of Strasburg among steeples? And those myriads of statues which thronged all the intercolumniations of the nave and the choir—kneeling, standing, equestrian—men, women, children—kings, bishops, warriors—in stone, in marble, in gold, in silver, in brass, and even in wax—who has brutally swept them out? It is not Time that has done it.

And who has substituted for the old Gothic altar, splendidly loaded with shrines and reliquaries, that heavy sarcophagus of marble, with angels' heads and clouds, which looks like an unmatched specimen from the Val-de-Grâce or the Invalides! Who has stupidly fixed that heavy anachronism of stone into the Carlovingian pavement of Hercandus? Was it not Louis XIV. fulfilling the vow of Louis XIII.?

And who has put cold white glass in place of those deep-tinctured panes which made the wondering eyes of our forefathers hesitate between the round window over the grand doorway and the pointed ones of the chancel? And what would a subchanter of the sixteenth century say could he see that fine yellow-washing with which the Vandal archbishops have besmeared their cathedral? He would remember that it was the colour with which the hangman brushed over such buildings as were adjudged to be infamous; he would recollect the *hôtel* of the Petit-Bourbon, which had thus been washed all over yellow for the treason of the constable—"yellow, after all, so well mixed," says Sauval, "and so well applied, that the lapse of a century and more has not yet taken its colour." He would believe that the holy place had become infamous, and would flee away from it.

And then if we ascend the cathedral—not to mention a thousand other barbarisms of every kind—what have they done with that charming small steeple which rose from the intersection of the cross, and which, no less bold and light than its neighbour, the spire (destroyed also) of the Sainte-Chapelle, pierced into the sky yet farther than the towers—perforated, sharp, sonorous, airy? An architect *de bon goût* amputated it in 1787, and thought it was sufficient to hide the wound with that great plaster of lead which resembles the lid of a porridge-pot.

Thus it is that the wondrous art of the Middle Ages has been treated in almost every country, and especially in France. In its ruin three sorts of inroads are distinguishable, and have made breaches of different depths—first, time, which has gradually made deficiencies here and there, and has gnawed over its whole surface; then religious and political revolutions, which, blind and angry in their nature, have tumultuously wreaked their fury upon it, torn its rich garment of sculpture and carving, burst its rose-shaped windows, broken its bands of arabesques and miniature figures, torn down its statues, here for their mitre, there for their crown; and lastly, changes of fashion, growing more and more grotesque and stupid, which, commencing with the anarchical yet splendid deviations of the revival, have succeeded one another in the necessary decline of architecture. Fashion has done more mischief than revolutions. It has cut to the quick—it has attacked the very bone and framework of the art. It has mangled, dislocated, killed the edifice—in its form as well as in its meaning, in its consistency as well as in its beauty. And then it has remade, which, at least, neither Time nor revolutions had pretended to do. It has audaciously fitted into the wounds of Gothic architecture its wretched gewgaws of a day—its marble ribands—its metal pompoons—a very leprosy of ovolos, volutes, and *entournements,* of draperies, garlands, and fringes, of stone flames, brazen clouds, fleshy Cupids, and chubby cherubim, which we find beginning to devour the face of art in the oratory of Catherine de Médicis, and making it expire two centuries after, tortured and convulsed, in the boudoir of Madame Dubarry.

Thus, to sum up the points which we have here laid down, three kinds of ravages now disfigure Gothic architecture: wrinkles and knobs on the surface—these are the work of Time; violences, brutalities, contusions, fractures—these are the work of revolutions, from Luther down to Mirabeau; mutilations, amputations, dislocation of members, restorations—these are the labours, Grecian, Roman, and barbaric, of the professors according to Vitruvius and Vignola. That magnificent art which the Vandals had produced the academies have murdered. To the operations of ages and of revolutions, which, at all events, devastate with impartiality and grandeur, have been added those of the cloud of school-trained architects, licensed, privileged, and patented, degrading with all the discernment and selection of bad taste—substituting, for instance, the *chicorées* of Louis XV. for the Gothic lace-work, to the greater glory of the Parthenon. This is the kick of the ass at the expiring lion. 'Tis the old oak which, in the last stage of decay, is stung and gnawed by the caterpillars.

How remote is all this from the time when Robert Cenalis,

comparing Notre-Dame at Paris to the famous temple of Diana at Ephesus, "so much vaunted by the ancient pagans," which immortalised Erostratus, thought the Gaulish cathedral "more excellent in length, breadth, height, and structure." [1]

Notre-Dame, however, as an architectural monument, is not one of those which can be called complete, definite, belonging to a class. It is not a Roman church, nor is it a Gothic church. It is not a model of any individual order. It has not, like the abbey of Tournus, the solemn and massive squareness, the round broad vault, the icy bareness, the majestic simplicity, of the edifices which have the circular arch for their basis. Nor is it, like the cathedral of Bourges, the magnificent, airy, multiform, tufted, pinnacled, florid production of the pointed arch. It cannot be ranked among that antique family of churches, gloomy, mysterious, lowering, crushed, as it were, by the weight of the circular arch—almost Egyptian, even to their ceilings—all hieroglyphical, all sacerdotal, all symbolical—more abounding in their ornaments with lozenges and zigzags than with flowers—with flowers than with animals, with animals than with human figures—the work not so much of the architect as of the bishop—the first transformation of the art—all stamped with theocratical and military discipline—having its root in the Lower Empire, and stopping at the time of William the Conqueror. Nor can this cathedral be ranked in that other family of lofty, airy churches, rich in sculpture and painted windows, of pointed forms and bold disposition—as political symbols, communal and citizen—as works of art, free, capricious, licentious—the second transformation of ecclesiastical architecture—no longer hieroglyphical, immutable, and sacerdotal, but artistical, progressive, and popular—beginning at the return from the crusades and ending with Louis XI. Notre-Dame, then, is not of purely Roman race like the former, nor of purely Arabic race like the latter.

'Tis an edifice of the transition. The Saxon architect was just finishing off the first pillars of the nave when the pointed arch, arriving from the crusade, came and seated itself as a conqueror upon the broad Roman capitals which had been designed to support only circular arches. The pointed arch, thenceforward master of the field, constructed the remainder of the building. However, inexperienced and timid at its commencement, we find it widening its compass, and, as it were, restraining itself, as not yet daring to spring up into arrows and

[1] *Histoire Gallicane*, liv. ii., perioche 3, f. 130, p. 1.

lancets, as it afterwards did in so many wonderful cathedrals. It might be said to have been sensible of the neighbourhood of the heavy Roman pillars.

However, these edifices of the transition from the Roman to the Gothic are not less valuable studies than the pure models are. They express a gradation of the art which would be lost without them. It is the pointed species engrafted upon the circular.

Notre-Dame, in particular, is a curious specimen of this variety. Each face, each stone, of this venerable monument, is a page of the history, not only of the country, but of the science and the art. Thus, to point out here only some of the principal details, while the small Porte-Rouge attains almost to the limits of the Gothic delicacy of the fifteenth century, the pillars of the nave, in their amplitude and solemnity, go back almost as far as the Carlovingian abbey of St. Germain-des-Près. One would think there were six centuries between that door and those pillars. Not even the hermetics fail to find, in the emblematical devices of the great portal, a satisfactory compendium of their science, of which the church of St. Jacques-de-la-Boucherie was so complete a hieroglyphic. Thus the Roman abbey—the hermetical church—Gothic art—Saxon art—the heavy round pillar, which carries us back to Gregory VII.—the hermetical symbolism by which Nicolas Flamel anticipated Luther—papal unity, and schism—St. Germain-des-Près and St. Jacques-de-la-Boucherie—all are mingled, combined, and amalgamated in Notre-Dame. This central and maternal church is, among the other old churches of Paris, a sort of chimera: she has the head of one, the limbs of another, the back of a third—something of every one.

We repeat it, these compound fabrics are not the least interesting to the artist, the antiquary, and the historian. They make us feel in how great a degree architecture is a primitive matter—demonstrating (as the Cyclopean vestiges, the Egyptian pyramids, and the gigantic Hindu pagods likewise demonstrate) that the greatest productions of architecture are not so much the work of individuals as of society—the offspring rather of national efforts than of the conceptions of particular minds—a deposit left by a whole people—the accumulation of ages—the residue of the successive evaporations of human society—in short, a sort of formations. Each wave of time leaves its alluvion; each race deposits its stratum upon the monument; each individual contributes his stone. So do the beavers—so do the bees—so does man. The great symbol of Architecture, Babel, is a hive.

Great edifices, like great mountains, are the work of ages. Often the art undergoes a transformation while they are yet pending—*pendent opera interrupta*—they go on again quietly, in accordance with the change in the art. The altered art takes up the fabric, incrusts itself upon it, assimilates it to itself, develops it after its own fashion, and finishes it if it can. The thing is accomplished without disturbance, without effort, without reaction, according to a law natural and tranquil. It is a graft that shoots out, a sap that circulates, a vegetation that goes forward. Certainly there is matter for very large volumes, and often for the universal history of human nature, in those successive engraftings of several species of art at different elevations upon the same fabric. The man, the artist, the individual, are lost, and disappear upon those great masses, leaving no name of an author behind. Human nature is there to be traced only in its aggregate. Time is the architect, the nation is the builder.

To consider in this place only the architecture of Christian Europe, that younger sister of the great masonries of the East—it presents to us an immense formation, divided into three superincumbent zones clearly defined: the Roman [1] zone; the Gothic zone; and the zone of the Revival, which we would willingly entitle the Greco-Roman. The Roman stratum, the most ancient and the deepest, is occupied by the circular arch; which reappears, rising from the Grecian column, in the modern and upper stratum of the Revival. The pointed arch is found between the two. The edifices which belong to one or other of these three strata exclusively, are perfectly distinct, uniform, and complete. Such is the abbey of Jumièges; such is the cathedral of Rheims; such is the church of Sainte-Croix at Orleans. But the three zones mingle and combine at their borders, like the colours of the prism. And hence the complex fabrics—the edifices of gradation and transition. One is Roman in its feet, Gothic in the middle, and Greco-Roman in the head. This is when it has taken six hundred years to build it. This variety is rare: the donjon tower of Etampes is a specimen of

[1] The same which is also called, according to place, climate, and species, Lombard, Saxon, or Byzantine. These are four sister architectures, parallel to one another, having each its particular character, but all deriving from the same principle, the circular arch.

> " Facies non omnibus una,
> Non diversa tamen, qualem," etc.

it. But the fabrics of two formations are more frequent. Such is the Notre-Dame of Paris, an edifice of the pointed arch, which, in its earliest pillars, dips into that Roman zone in which the portal of St. Denis and the nave of St. Germain-des-Près are entirely immersed. Such is the charming semi-Gothic chapter-house of Bocherville, which the Roman layer mounts halfway up. Such is the cathedral of Rouen, which would have been entirely Gothic, had not the extremity of its central spire pierced into the zone of the Revival.[1]

However, all these gradations, all these differences, affect only the surface of the structures. It is only the art that has changed its coat: the conformation of the Christian temple itself has remained untouched. It is ever the same internal framework, the same logical disposition of parts. Whatever be the sculptured and decorated envelope of a cathedral, we constantly find underneath it at least the germ and rudiment of the Roman basilic. It eternally develops itself upon the ground according to the same law. There are invariably two naves crossing each other at right angles, the upper extremity of which cross is rounded into a chancel: there are constantly two low sides for the internal processions and for the chapels—a sort of lateral ambulatories communicating with the principal nave by the intercolumniations. This being once laid down, the number of the chapels, of the doorways, of the steeples, of the spires, is variable to infinity, according to the fancy of the age, of the nation, of the art. The performance of the worship being once provided for and ensured, Architecture is at liberty to do what she pleases. Statues, painted glass, rose-shaped windows, arabesques, indentations, capitals, and bas-reliefs—all these objects of imagination she combines in such arrangement as best suits her. Hence the prodigious external variety of these edifices, in the main structure of which dwells so much order and uniformity. The trunk of the tree is unchanging, the vegetation is capricious.

[1] This part of the spire, which was of timber, is precisely that which was consumed by lightning in 1823.

CHAPTER II

A BIRD'S-EYE VIEW OF PARIS

We have endeavoured to repair for the reader the admirable church of our Lady at Paris. We have briefly pointed out the greater part of the beauties which it possessed in the fifteenth century, and which are wanting to it now; but we have omitted the principal—the view of Paris as it then appeared from the summit of the towers.

Indeed, when, after feeling your way up the long spiral staircase that perpendicularly perforates the thick wall of the steeples, you at last emerged all at once upon one of the two elevated platforms inundated with light and air, it was a fine picture that opened upon you on every side, a spectacle *sui generis*, some idea of which may easily be formed by such of our readers as have had the good fortune to see a Gothic town, entire, complete, and homogeneous—of which description there are still a few remaining, as Nuremberg in Bavaria, and Vittoria in Spain—or even any smaller specimens, provided they be in good preservation, as Vitré in Brittany, and Nordhausen in Prussia.

The Paris of three hundred and fifty years ago, the Paris of the fifteenth century, was already a giant city. The Parisians in general are mistaken as to the ground which they think they have gained. Since the time of Louis XI., Paris has not increased much more than a third, and certainly it has lost much more in beauty than it has gained in size.

Paris took its birth in that anciently-inhabited island of the *Cité* or City, which has indeed the form of a cradle, lying about the centre of the present town, and embraced between the two channels of the Seine, which, dividing at its eastern, meet again at its western extremity. The strand of this island was its first enclosure, the Seine its first trench. And for several centuries Paris remained in its island state, with two bridges—one on the north, the other on the south—and two *têtes-de-ponts*, which were at once its gates and its fortresses—the *Grand Châtelet* on the right bank of the northern channel of the river, and the *Petit Châtelet* on the left bank of the southern channel.

In the next place, under the first line of French kings, being too much confined within the limits of its island, behind which it could never return, Paris crossed the water. Then, on each side, beyond either Châtelet, a first line of walls and towers began to cut into the country on both sides of the Seine. Of this ancient enclosure some vestiges were still remaining as late as the last century; but now there is nothing left but the memory of it, with here and there a local tradition, as the *Baude's* or *Baudoyer* gate—*porta Bagauda.*

By degrees, the flood of houses, constantly impelled from the heart of the town towards the exterior, overflowed and wore away this enclosure. Philip-Augustus drew a fresh line of circumvallation. He imprisoned Paris within a circular chain of great towers, lofty and massive. For upwards of a century the houses pressed upon one another, accumulated, and rose higher in this basin, like water in a reservoir. They began to deepen—to pile story upon story—to climb, as it were, one upon another. They shot out in height, like every growth that is compressed laterally, and strove each to lift its head above its neighbours, in order to get a breath of air. The streets became deeper and narrower, and every open space was overrun by buildings and disappeared. At last we find the houses overstepping the wall of Philip-Augustus, and spreading themselves merrily over the plain in all manner of positions, without plan or arrangement, taking their unrestricted ease, and slicing themselves gardens out of the surrounding fields.

In 1367 the suburbs were already so extensive that another enclosure became necessary, and one was built by Charles V. But a town like Paris is perpetually on the increase, and it is only such towns that become capitals. They are a sort of funnels, which receive all the drains, geographical, political, moral, and intellectual of a country—all the natural tendencies of a people—wells of civilisation, as it were; and also sinks, where commerce, manufactures, intelligence, population—all the vital juices of a state—filter and collect incessantly, drop by drop, and century after century.

The circumvallation of Charles V., then, had the same fate as that of Philip-Augustus. At the end of the fifteenth century a new suburb had collected beyond it, and in the sixteenth we find it rapidly receding and becoming buried deeper and deeper in the old town, so dense was the new town becoming outside it. Thus, in the fifteenth century—to stop there—Paris had already worn away the three concentric circles of walls which, in the time of Julian, falsely called the Apostate, may be said to have been in embryo in the two *castella,* since called the Grand Châtelet and the Petit Châtelet. The growing city had successively burst its four girdles of walls, like a child grown too large for its last year's clothes. In the reign of Louis XI. were to be seen rising here and there amid that sea of houses some groups of ruinous towers belonging to the ancient bulwarks, like *archipelagos* of the old Paris submerged under the inundation of the new.

Since then, Paris has undergone another transformation, unhappily for the eye of Taste; but it has overleaped only one boundary more—that of Louis XV.—the wretched mud-wall, worthy of the king who built it, and of the poet who sang in it this magnificent line, too ingenious to be translatable,—

"*Le mur murant* Paris rend Paris *murmurant*."

In the fifteenth century Paris was still divided into three towns quite distinct and separate, having each its peculiar features, manners, customs, privileges, and history—the City, the University, and the *Ville* or Town properly so called. The City, which occupied the island, was the most ancient, the smallest, and the mother of the other two—looking squeezed (if we may be allowed such a comparison), like a little old woman between two fine flourishing daughters. The University covered the left bank of the Seine, from the *Tournelle* to the *Tour de Nesle;* the points answering to which, in modern Paris, are—to the former the *Halle-aux-Vins* or Wine-mart, and to the latter the *Monnaie* or Mint. Its circuit included an ample slice of that tract in which Julian had constructed his baths, and comprised the hill of St. Geneviève. The apex of this curve of walls was the *Porte Papale* or Papal Gate—that is to say, very nearly, the site of the present Pantheon. The Town, which was the largest of the three portions of Paris, occupied the right bank. Its quay, in which there were several breaks and interruptions, ran along the Seine from the *Tour de Billy* to the *Tour du Bois*—that is, from the spot where the *Grenier d'Abondance* now stands, to that occupied by the Tuileries. These four points at which the Seine cut the circumference of the capital —on the left the Tournelle and the Tour de Nesle, and on the right the Tour de Billy and the Tour du Bois—were called, by distinction, the four towers of Paris. The Town projected yet more deeply into the territory bordering on the Seine than the University. The most salient points of its enclosure (the one constructed by Charles V.) were at the *Portes St. Denis* and *St. Martin,* the sites of which were precisely the same as those of the gates now so called.

As we have just before said, each one of these three great divisions of Paris was a town; but it was a town too peculiar to be complete in itself—a town which could not dispense with the vicinity of the other two. So, also, each had its characteristic aspect. In the City, the churches abounded; in the Town, the palaces; in the University, the colleges. Leaving apart the secondary original features of old Paris, and the capricious dispositions attaching to the *droit de voirie* or right of road—and noting only the great masses in the chaos of the communal jurisdictions—we may say in general that the island belonged to the bishop; the right bank to the *prevôt des merchands*, or provost of the traders; and the left bank to the rector of the University. The provost of Paris, a royal and not a municipal officer, had authority over all. Among the conspicuous edifices, the City had Notre-Dame; the Town, the Louvre and the Hôtel-de-Ville; and the University, the Sorbonne. Again, the Town had the Halles; the City, the Hôtel-Dieu; and the University, the Prè-aux-Clercs. Offences committed by the scholars on the left bank, in their Prè-aux-Clercs, they were tried for in the island at the Palais-de-Justice, and punished for on the right bank at Montfaucon—unless, indeed, the rector, feeling the University to be strong at that particular time, and the king weak, thought proper to interfere; for it was a privilege of the scholars to be hanged at home—that is to say, within the University precincts.

Most of these privileges, we may observe in passing—and there were some of greater value than this—had been extorted from the kings by revolts and disturbances. Such has been the course of things time out of mind. As the French proverb saith, *Le roi ne lache que quand le peuple arrache;* in plain English, the king never leaves hold until the people pull too hard for him. In one of the old French charters we find this popular fidelity defined with great simplicity—*Civibus fidelitas in reges, quæ tamen aliquoties seditionibus interrupta, multa peperit privilegia.*

In the fifteenth century, the Seine embraced five islands within the circuit of Paris—the *Ile Louviers*, on which there were then living trees, though there are now only piles of wood; the *Ile aux Vaches*, the *Ile Notre-Dame*, both uninhabited, excepting only one sorry tenement, both fiefs of the bishop's, which two islands, in the seventeenth century, were made into one, since built upon, and now called the Ile St. Louis; and the City, having, at its western extremity, the islet of the *Passeur-aux-Vaches*, since lost under the esplanade of the Pont-Neuf.

The City had at that time five bridges—three on the right (the *Pont Notre-Dame* and the *Pont-au-Change* of stone, and the *Pont-aux-Meuniers* of wood), and two on the left (the *Petit Pont* of stone, and the *Pont St. Michel* of wood)—all of them laden with houses. The University had six gates, built by Philip-Augustus; which, to set out from the Tournelle, occurred in the following order—the *Porte St. Victor,* the *Porte Bordelle,* the *Porte Papale,* the *Porte St. Jacques,* the *Porte St. Michel,* and the *Porte St. Germain.* The Town had also six gates, built by Charles V.; namely, setting out from the Tour de Billy, the *Porte St. Antoine,* the *Porte du Temple,* the *Porte St. Martin,* the *Porte St. Denis,* the *Porte Montmartre,* and the *Porte St. Honoré.* All these gates were strong and handsome withal—which latter attribute is by no means incompatible with strength. A wide and deep trench, having a running stream during the winter floods, washed the foot of the walls all round Paris, the Seine furnishing the water. At night the gates were shut, the river was barred at the two extremities of the town with massive iron chains, and Paris slept in tranquillity.

Seen in a bird's-eye view, these three great pieces of town, the City, the University, and the Ville, presented each an inextricable web of streets fantastically ravelled. Yet a glance was sufficient to show the spectator that those three portions of a city formed but one complete whole. You at once distinguished two long parallel streets, without interruption or deviation, running almost in a straight line, and intersecting all the three towns, from one extremity to the other, from the south to the north, at right angles with the Seine, connecting and mingling them, and incessantly pouring the people of each into the precincts of the other, making the three but one. One of these two lines of street ran from the Porte St. Jacques to the Porte St. Martin, and was called—in the University, *Rue St. Jacques;* in the City, *Rue de la Juiverie* (Anglicè, *Jewery* or *Jewry*); and in the Town, *Rue St. Martin.* It crossed the water twice under the names of Petit-Pont and Pont Notre-Dame. The other line—called, on the left bank, *Rue de la Harpe;* in the island, *Rue de la Barillerie;* on the right bank, *Rue St. Denis;* over one arm of the Seine, *Pont St. Michel,* and over the other, *Pont-au-Change*—ran from the Porte St. Michel in the University to the Porte St. Denis in the Town. However, though under so many different names, they were still, in fact, only two streets; but they were the two normal, the two mother streets—the two arteries of Paris, by which all the other veins of the triple city were fed, or into which they emptied themselves.

Independently of these two principal, diametrical streets, running quite across Paris, common to the entire capital, the Town and the University had each its own great street, running in the direction of their length, parallel to the Seine, and intersecting the two arterial streets at right angles. Thus, in the Town, you descended in a straight line from the Porte St. Antoine to the Porte St. Honoré; in the University, from the Porte St. Victor to the Porte St. Germain. These two great ways, crossing the two first mentioned, formed with them the frame or skeleton upon which was laid, knotted and drawn in every direction, the tangled network of the streets of Paris. In the unintelligible figure of this network you might, however, also discover, upon attentive observation, two bunches, as it were, of large streets, the one in the University, the other in the Town, which ran diverging from the bridges to the gates. Somewhat of the same geometrical disposition still exists.

Now, what aspect did all this present when viewed from the top of the towers of Notre-Dame in 1482? We will endeavour to describe it.

The spectator, on arriving, out of breath, upon this summit, was first of all struck by a dazzling confusion of roofs, chimneys, streets, bridges, squares, spires, steeples. All burst upon the eye at once—the formally-cut gable—the acute-angled roofing—the hanging turret at the angles of the walls—the stone pyramids of the eleventh century—the slate obelisk of the fifteenth—the donjon tower, round and bare—the church tower, square and decorated—the large and the small, the massive, and the airy. The gaze was for some time utterly bewildered by this labyrinth, in which there was nothing but proceeded from art—from the most inconsiderable carved and painted house-front, with external timbers, low doorway, and stories projecting each above each, up to the royal Louvre itself, which, at that time, had a colonnade of towers. But the following were the principal masses that were distinguishable when the eye became steady enough to examine this tumultuous assemblage of objects in detail.

First of all, the City. The island of the City, as is observed by Sauval, the most laborious of the old explorers of Parisian antiquity, who, amidst all his trashiness, has these occasional happinesses of expression—"The isle of the City is shaped like a great ship, sunk in the mud, and run aground lengthwise in the stream, about the middle of the Seine." We have already shown that, in the fifteenth century, this ship was moored to the two banks of the river by five bridges. This form of the hull of a vessel had also struck the heraldic scribes; for, from this circumstance, according to Favyn and Pasquier, and not from the siege by the Normans, came the ship emblazoned upon the old escutcheon of Paris. To him who can decipher it, heraldry is an emblematic language. The whole history of the latter half of the Middle Ages is written in heraldry, as that of the former half is in the symbolism of the churches of Roman architecture. 'Tis the hieroglyphics of feudality succeeding those of theocracy.

The City, then, first presented itself to the view with its stern to the east and its prow to the west. Looking towards the prow, you had before you an innumerable congregation of old roofs, with the lead-covered bolster of the Sainte-Chapelle rising above them, broad and round, like an elephant's back with the tower upon it. Only that here the place of the elephant's tower was occupied by the boldest, openest, airiest, most notched and ornamented spire that ever showed the sky through its lace-work cone. Close before Notre-Dame three streets terminated in the *parvis*, or part of the churchyard contiguous to the grand entrance—a fine square of old houses. The southern side of this *Place* was overhung by the furrowed and rugged front of the Hôtel-Dieu, and its roof, which looks as if covered with pimples and warts. And then, right and left, east and west, within that narrow circuit of the City, were ranged the steeples of its twenty-one churches, of all dates, forms, and sizes, from the low and decayed Roman campanile of St. Denis-du-Pas (*carcer Glaucini*) to the slender spires of St. Pierre-aux-Bœufs and St. Landry. Behind Notre-Dame extended, northward, the cloister, with its Gothic galleries; southward, the demi-Roman palace of the bishop; and eastward, the uninhabited point of the island, called the *Terrain*, or *ground*, by distinction. Amid that accumulation of houses the eye could also distinguish, by the high perforated mitres of stone which, at that period, placed aloft upon the roof itself, surmounted the highest range of palace windows, the mansion presented by the Parisians, in the reign of Charles VI., to Juvénal des Ursins; a little farther on, the black, pitch-covered market-sheds of the *Marché Palus*; and in another direction, the new chancel of St. Germain-le-Vieux, lengthened in 1458 by an encroachment upon one end of the *Rue-aux-Febves*; and then here and there were to be seen some cross-way crowded with people—some pillory erected at the corner of a street—some fine piece of the pavement of Philip-Augustus—a magnificent flagging, furrowed in the middle to prevent the horses from slipping, and so ill replaced in the sixteenth century by the wretched pebbling called *pavé de la Ligue*—some solitary backyard, with one of those transparent staircase turrets which they used to build in the fifteenth century, one of which is still to be seen in the Rue des Bourdonnais. And on the right of the Saint-Chapelle, to the westward, the Palais-de-Justice rested its group of towers upon the water's brink. The groves of the royal gardens, which occupied the western point of the island, hid from view the islet of the *Passeur*. As for the water itself, it was hardly visible from the towers of Notre-Dame, on either side of the City—the Seine disappearing under the bridges, and the bridges under the houses.

And when you looked beyond those bridges, the roofs upon which were tinged with green, having contracted untimely mouldiness from the vapours of the water, if you cast your eye on the left hand, towards the University, the first edifice that struck it was a large, low cluster of towers, the Petit Châtelet, the gaping porch of which seemed to devour the extremity of the Petit-Pont. Then, if your view ranged along the shore from east to west, from the Tournelle to the Tour de Nesle, you beheld a long line of houses exhibiting sculptured beams, coloured window-glass, each story overhanging that beneath it—an interminable zigzag of ordinary gables, cut at frequent intervals by the end of some street, and now and then also by the front or the corner of some great stone-built mansion, which seemed to stand at its ease, with its courtyards and gardens, its wings and its compartments, amid that rabble of houses crowding and pinching one another, like a *grand seigneur* amidst a mob of rustics. There were five or six of these mansions upon the quay, from the *Logis de Lorraine*, which shared with the house of the Bernardines the great neighbouring enclosure of the Tournelle, to the *Hôtel de Nesle*, the principal tower of which formed the limit of Paris on that side, and the pointed roofs of which were so situated as to cut with their dark triangles, during three months of the year, the scarlet disk of the setting sun.

That side of the Seine, however, was the least mercantile of the two: there was more noise and crowd of scholars than of artisans; and there was not, properly speaking, any quay, except from the Pont-St.-Michel to the Tour de Nesle. The rest of the margin of the river was either a bare strand, as was the case beyond the Bernardines, or a close range of houses with the water at their foot, as between the two bridges. There was a great clamour of washerwomen along the waterside, talking, shouting, singing, from morning till night, and beating away at their linen—as they do at this day, contributing their full share to the gaiety of Paris.

The University, from one end to the other, presented to the eye one dense mass forming a compact and homogeneous whole. Those thousand thick-set angular roofs, nearly all composed of the same geometrical element, when seen from above, looked almost like one crystallisation of the same substance. The capricious fissures formed by the streets did not cut this conglomeration of houses into slices too disproportionate. The forty-two colleges were distributed among them very equally, and were to be seen in every quarter. The amusingly varied summits of those fine buildings were a product of the same description of art as the ordinary roofs which they overtopped, being nothing more than a multiplication, into the square or the cube, of the same geometrical figure. Thus they complicated the whole without confusing it, completed without overloading it. Geometry itself is one kind of harmony. Several fine mansions, too, lifted their heads magnificently here and there above the picturesque attic stories of the left bank—as the *Logis de Nevers*, the *Logis de Rome*, the *Logis de Reims*, which have disappeared; and the *Hôtel de Cluny*, which still exists for the artist's consolation, but the tower of which was so stupidly shortened a few years ago. Near the Hôtel de Cluny, that Roman palace, with fine semicircular arches, were once the baths of Julian. There were also a number of abbeys, of a beauty more religious, of a grandeur more solemn, than the secular mansions, but not beautiful nor less grand. Those which first caught the attention were that of the Bernardines, with its three steeples; that of Sainte-Geneviève, the square tower of which, still existing, makes us so much regret the disappearance of the remainder; the Sorbonne, half college, half monastery, so admirable a nave of which yet survives; the fine quadrilateral cloister of the Mathurins, and, adjacent to it, the cloister of St. Benedict's; the house of the Cordeliers, with its three enormous and contiguous gables; that of the Augustines, the graceful spire of which formed, after the Tour de Nesle, the next lofty projection on that side of Paris, commencing from the westward. The colleges—which are, in fact, the intermediate link between the cloister and the world—held the medium in the architectural series between the great mansions and the abbeys, exhibiting a severe elegance, a sculpture less airy than that of the palaces, an architecture less stern than that of the convents. Unfortunately, scarcely anything remains of these structures, in which Gothic art held so just a balance between richness and economy. The churches—and they were numerous and splendid in the University, and of every architectural era, from the round arches of Saint-Julien to the Gothic ones of Saint-Severin—the churches, we say, rose above the whole; and, as one harmony more in that harmonious mass, they pierced in close succession the multifariously indented outline of the roofs, with boldly cut spires, with perforated steeples, and slender *aiguilles*, or needle spires, the lines of which were themselves but a magnificent exaggeration of the acute angle of the roofs.

The ground of the University was hilly. The *Montagne* Ste. Geneviève, on the south-east, made one grand swell; and it was curious to see, from the top of Notre-Dame, that crowd of narrow, winding streets (now the *pays Latin*), those clusters of houses which, scattered in every direction from the summit of that eminence, spread themselves in disorder, and almost precipitously down its sides to the water's edge—looking, some as if they were falling, others as if they were climbing up, and all as if hanging to one another; while the continual motion of a thousand dark points crossing one another upon the pavement gave the whole an appearance of life. These were the people in the streets, beheld thus from on high and at a distance.

And in the intervals between those roofs, those spires, those innumerable projections of buildings, which so fantastically bent, twisted, and indented the extreme line of the University, you distinguished here and there some great patch of moss-covered wall, some thick round tower, or some embattled, fortress-looking town-gate: this was the enclosure of Philip-Augustus. Beyond extended the green meadows, across which the roads were seen diverging, having along their sides, at quitting the body of the town, a number of *maisons de faubourg*, or houses without the walls, which were seen more thinly scattered the greater their distance from the barriers. Some of these *faubourgs* were considerable. First of all (to go round from the Tournelle) there was the *bourg St. Victor*, with its bridge of one arch over the Bièvre; its abbey, in which was to be read the epitaph of King Louis the Fat, *epitaphium Ludovici*

Grossi; and its church, with an octagonal spire flanked by four steeple turrets, of the eleventh century (such a one is still to be seen at Etampes). Then there was the *bourg St. Marceau,* which had already three churches and a convent. Then, leaving on the left the mill of the Gobelins and its four white walls, came the *faubourg St. Jacques,* with the fine sculptured cross in the middle of it; the church of St. Jacques du Haut-Pas, then a charming Gothic structure; that of St. Magloire, with its fine nave of the fourteenth century, which Napoleon turned into a hay-barn; and that of *Notre-Dame des Champs,* or Notre-Dame in the Fields, in which were to be seen some *byzantins.* And after leaving in the open country the monastery of the *Chartreux,* or Carthusians, a rich structure of the same period as the Palais de Justice, with its little compartmented gardens, and the haunted ruins of Vauvert, the eye fell, towards the west, upon the three Roman-built spires of *St. Germain-des-Près,* St. Germain, or Germanus in the Meadows. The *bourg St. Germain,* already a large commune, formed fifteen or twenty streets in the rear, the sharp steeple of St. Sulpice indicating one of its corners. Close by it was to be distinguished the quadrilateral enclosure of the *Foire St. Germain,* where is now the market; then the abbot's pillory, a pretty little round tower, well capped with a cone of lead: farther on was the *tuilerie,* or tile-kiln; and the Rue du Four, which led to the *four banal,* or manorial bakehouse, with the manorial mill perched upon its mound —a specimen of one of the most vexatiously tyrannical characteristics of "the good old times"—and the lazaretto, a small, detached, and half-seen building. But that which especially attracted the eye, and kept it long fixed upon this point, was the abbey itself. It is certain that this monastery, which had an aspect of grandeur both as a church and as a *seigneurie* or temporal lordship—that abbatial palace, in which the bishops of Paris deemed themselves happy to sleep a single night—that refectory, to which the architect had given the air, the beauty, and the splendid rose-shaped window of a cathedral —that elegant chapel of the Virgin—that monumental dormitory—those spacious gardens—that frowning portcullis and jealous drawbridge—that circuit of battlements which marked its indented outline upon the verdure of the meadows around— those courts in which the mail of men-at-arms shone mingled with golden copes—the whole grouped and rallied, as it were, about the three round-arched spires, solidly based upon a Gothic chancel—made a magnificent figure in the horizon.

When at length, after long contemplating the University, you turned towards the right bank, to the Town, properly so called, the character of the scene was suddenly changed. The Town was not only much larger than the University, but also less uniform. At first sight it appeared to be divided into several masses, singularly distinct from each other. First of all, on the east, in that part of the Town which still takes its name from the *marais*, or march, in which Camulogenes entangled Cæsar, there was a collection of palaces, the mass of which extended to the waterside. Four great mansions almost contiguous—the *hôtels De Jouy, De Sens*, and *De Barbeau*, and the *Logis de la Reine*—cast upon the Seine the reflection of their slated tops intersected by slender turrets. These four edifices occupied the space from the Rue des Nonaindières to the abbey of the Celestines, the small spire of which formed a graceful relief to their line of gables and battlements. Some sorry, greenish-looking houses overhanging the water did not conceal from view the fine angles of their fronts, their great square stone-framed windows, their Gothic porches loaded with statues, the boldly-cut borderings about their walls, and all those charming accidents of architecture which made Gothic art seem as if it recommended its combinations at every fresh structure. Behind those palaces ran in every direction, in some places cloven, palisaded, and embattled, like a citadel, in others veiled by large trees like a Carthusian monastery, the vast and multiform circuit of that wonderful *Hôtel de St. Pol*, in which the French King had room to lodge superbly twenty-two princes of the rank of the Dauphin and the Duke of Burgundy, with their trains and their domestics—besides the *grands seigneurs*, or superior nobles, and the Emperor when he came to visit Paris, and the lions, who had a mansion to themselves within the royal mansion. And we must here observe that a prince's lodgings then consisted of not less than eleven principal apartments, from the audience-room to the chamber appropriated to prayer; besides all the galleries, baths, stove-rooms, and other "superfluous places," with which each suite of apartments was provided; besides the private gardens of each one of the King's guests; besides the kitchens, cellars, pantries, and general refectories of the household; the *bassescours* or backyards, in which there were two-and-twenty general offices, from the *fourille*, or bakehouse, to the *échansonnerie*, or butlery; places for games of fifty different kinds, as mall, tennis, riding at the ring, etc.; aviaries, fish-ponds, menageries, stables, cattle-stalls, libraries, armouries, and foundries. Such was, at that day, a *palais de roi*—a Louvre—a Hôtel St. Pol: it was a city within a city.

From the tower upon which we have placed ourselves the Hôtel St. Pol, though almost half hidden from view by the four great mansions of which we have just spoken, was, nevertheless, very considerable and very wonderful to behold. You could clearly distinguish in it, although they had been skilfully joined to the main building by means of long-windowed and pillared galleries, the three several mansions which Charles V. had thrown into one together with his former palace; the Hôtel du Petit-Muce, with the airy balustrade which gracefully bordered its roof; the hôtel of the abbot of St. Maur, presenting the variety of an entrance regularly fortified, with a massive tower, machicolations, shot-holes, *moineaux de fer*, and, over the wide Saxon gateway, the abbot's escutcheon placed between the two notches for the drawbridge; the hôtel of the Count d'Etampes, the keep of which, being ruinous at the top, looked rounded and indented like the crest of a cock; here and there three or four old oaks, making together one great swelling tuft; haunts of swans amid the clear waters of the fish preserves, all wavering in light and shade; the picturesque corner of many a court; the Hôtel des Lions, or mansion of the lions, with its low, pointed arches upon short Saxon pillars, its iron portcullises, and its perpetual roaring; then, shooting up above this group of objects, the scaly spire of the Ave-Marïa; on the left the mansion of the Provost of Paris, flanked by four turrets delicately moulded and perforated; and, in the centre and heart of the whole, the Hôtel St. Pol itself, properly so called, with its multiplied fronts, its successive enrichments since the time of Charles V., the heterogeneous excrescences with which the fancy of the artists had loaded it in the course of two centuries; with all the chancels of its chapels, all the gables of its galleries, its thousand weathercocks, and its two contiguous towers, the conical roof of which, surrounded by battlements at its base, looked like a pointed hat with the brim turned up.

In continuing to ascend the steps of that amphitheatre of palaces which thus displayed itself at a distance, after crossing a deep fissure in the roofs of the Town, which marked the course of the Rue St. Antoine, the eye travelled on to the *Logis d'Angoulême*, a vast structure of several different periods, in which there were some parts quite new and almost white, scarcely better harmonising with the rest than a red waistcoat might with a blue doublet. However, the singularly sharp and elevated roof of the modern palace, bristling with carved spout ends, and covered with sheets of lead, over which ran sparkling incrustations of gilt copper in a thousand fantastic arabesques—that roof so curiously damaskened sprang gracefully up from amid the brown ruins of the ancient edifice, the old massive towers of which were bellying with age into the shape of casks, their height shrunk with decrepitude, and breaking asunder from top to bottom. Behind rose the forest of spires of the *Palais des Tournelles*. Nor was any assemblage of objects in the world—not even at Chambord nor at the Alhambra—more magical, more aërial, more captivating, than that grove of spires, turrets, chimneys, weathercocks, spiral staircases, airy lanterns, pavilions, spindle-shaped turrets, or *tournelles*, as they were then called—all differing in form, height, and position.

To the right of the Tournelles, that bundle of enormous towers perfectly black, growing, as it were, one into another, and looking as if bound together by their circular fosse; that donjon tower, looped much more with shot-holes than with windows; that drawbridge always lifted; that portcullis always down—those are the Bastille. Those objects like black beaks, projecting between the battlements, and which at this distance you would take for the mouths of spouts, are cannon. Under their fire, at the foot of the formidable structure, you may perceive the Port St. Antoine, almost buried between its two towers.

Beyond the Tournelles, as far as the wall of Charles V., extended, in rich compartments of verdure and of flowers, a tufted carpet of garden-grounds and royal parks, in the midst of which was distinguishable, by its labyrinth of groves and walks, the famous *Dædalus* garden which Louis XI. had given to Coictier. The doctor's observatory rose above the labyrinth, like a great isolated column with a small house for its capital; and in that study had been practised astrologies of terrible effect. That spot is now occupied by the Place Royale.

As we have already observed, the Palace and its precincts, of which we have endeavoured to give the reader some idea, though by specifying only its most prominent features, filled up the angle which Charles V.'s enclosure made with the Seine on the east. The centre of the Town was occupied by a heap of ordinary houses. Indeed, it was there that the three bridges of the City on the right bank discharged their stream of passengers; and bridges led to the building of houses before that of palaces.

This accumulation of common dwelling-houses, pressed against one another like the cells in a hive, was not without its beauty. In the roofs of a capital, as in the waves of a sea, there is at least grandeur of outline. In the first place, then, the streets crossed and intertwined, diversified the mass with a hundred amusing figures; around the *Halles* it was like a star with a thousand rays. The Rues St. Denis and St. Martin, with their innumerable ramifications, ascended one after the other like two great trees mingling their branches; and then there were tortuous lines, the Rue de le Plâtrerie, etc., winding about over the whole. There were also some fine edifices lifting their heads above the petrified undulation of this sea of gables. First, at the entrance of the Pont-aux-Changeurs, behind which the Seine was seen foaming under the mill-wheels at the Pont-aux-Meuniers, there was the Châtelet; no longer a Roman tower as under the Emperor Julian, but a feudal tower of the thirteenth century, and of a stone so hard that in three hours the pick did not remove it to the depth of a man's fist. Then there was the rich square steeple of St. Jacques-de-la-Boucherie, its angles all rounded with sculptures, and already worthy of admiration, although it was not finished in the fifteenth century. (It wanted in particular those four monsters which, still perched at the four corners of its roof, look like so many sphinxes giving to the modern Paris the enigma of the ancient to unriddle. Rault, the sculptor, placed them there, not until the year 1526; and had twenty francs for his trouble.) Then, again, there was the Maison-aux-Piliers, overlooking that Place de Grève, of which we have already given some description. There was the church of St. Gervais, which a doorway in good taste has since spoiled; that of St. Méry, the old pointed arches of which were almost approaching to the semi-circular; and that of St. Jean, the magnificent spire of which was proverbial; besides twenty other structures which disdained not to bury their attractions in that chaos of deep, dark, and narrow streets. Add to these the carved stone crosses, more abounding in the crossways even than the gibbets themselves; the cemetery of the Innocents, of which you discovered at a distance the architectural enclosure; the pillory of the Halles, the top of which was visible between the chimneys of the Rue de la Cossonnerie; the *échelle* of the Croix-du-Trahoir, in its *carrefour*, or opening, which was constantly darkened with people; the circular hovels of the *Halle-au-Blè*, or Corn Market; the broken fragments of the old wall of Philip-Augustus, distinguishable here and there, buried among the houses—ivy-mantled towers—ruinous gateways—crumbling and shapeless pieces of wall—the quay, with its thousand shops and its bloody-looking *écorcheries,* or skinning yards; the Seine covered with boats from the *Port-au-Foin* to the *For-l'Evéque,*—and you will have some general idea of the appearance presented in 1482 by the central trapezium or irregular quadrangle of the town.

Together with these two quarters—the one of palaces, the other of houses—the third great feature then observable in the Ville was a long zone or belt of abbeys which bordered it almost in its whole compass on the land side, from east to west, and, behind the line of fortification by which Paris was shut in, formed a second internal enclosure, consisting of convents and chapels. Thus, close to the park of the Tournelles, between the Rue St. Antoine and the old Rue du Temple, there was St. Catherine's, with its immense grounds, bounded only by the wall of Paris. Between the old and the new Rue du Temple there was the Temple itself, a frowning bundle of towers, lofty, erect, and isolated in the midst of an extensive embattled enclosure. Between the Rue Neuve du Temple and the Rue St. Martin, in the midst of its gardens, stood St. Martin's, a superb fortified church, whose girdle of towers, whose tiara of steeples, were second in strength and splendour only to St. Germain-des-Près. Between the two Rues, St. Martin and St. Denis, was displayed the circuit of the *Trinité,* or convert of the Trinity. And between the Rue St. Denis and the Rue Montorgueil was that of the Filles-Dieu. Close by the latter were to be distinguished the decayed roofs and unpaved enclosure of the *Cour des Miracles,* the only profane link that obtruded itself into that chain of religious houses.

Lastly, the fourth compartment which presented itself distinctly in the conglomeration of roofs upon the right bank, occupying the western angle of the great enclosure, and the waterside downwards, was a fresh knot of palaces and great mansions crowding at the foot of the Louvre. The old Louvre of Philip-Augustus, that immense structure—the great tower of which mustered around it twenty-three principal towers, besides all the smaller ones—seemed at a distance to be encased, as it were, within the Gothic summits of the Hotel d'Alençon and the Petit-Bourbon. This hydra of towers, the giant-keeper of Paris, with its four-and-twenty heads ever erect—with the monstrous ridges of its back, sheathed in lead or scaled with slates, and all variegated with glittering metallic streaks—

surprisingly terminated the configuration of the Town on the west.

Thus an immense *pâté*—what the Romans called an *insula* or *island*—of ordinary dwelling-houses, flanked on either side by two great clusters of palaces, crowned, the one by the Louvre, the other by the Tournelles, and bordered on the north by a long belt of abbeys and cultivated enclosures—the whole mingled and amalgamated in one view—and over those thousands of buildings, whose tiled and slated roofs ran in so many fantastic chains, the steeples, engraved, embroidered, and inlaid, of the forty-four churches on the right bank—myriads of cross-streets—the boundary on one side a line of lofty walls with square towers (those of the University wall being round), and on the other the Seine, intersected by bridges and crowded with numberless boats—such was the town of Paris in the fifteenth century.

Beyond the walls there were some *faubourgs* adjacent to the gates, but less numerous and more scattered than those of the University side. Thus behind the Bastille there were a score of mean houses clustered around the curious carvings of the cross called the *Croix-Faubin*, and the buttresses of the Abbey of St. Antoine-des-Champs, or St. Anthony's-in-the-Fields; then there was Popincourt, lost amid the cornfields; then La Courtille, a merry village of *cabarets*, or public-houses; the *bourg St. Laurent*, with its church, the steeple of which, at a distance, seemed in contact with the pointed towers of the Porte St. Martin; the *faubourg St. Denis*, with the extensive enclosure of St. Ladre; then out at the Porte Montmartre the Grange-Batelière, encircled with white walls; and behind it Montmartre itself, with its chalky declivities—Montmartre, which had then almost as many churches as windmills, but which has retained only the windmills, "for," observes our author, "society now seeks only bread for the *body*"—an observation which the reader may interpret in his own way. And then, beyond the Louvre, you saw, stretching into the meadows, the *faubourg St. Honoré*, even then of considerable extent; and, looking green, *La Petite-Bretagne*, or Little Britain; and, spreading itself out, the *Marché-aux-Pourceaux*, or Hog Market, in the centre of which heaved the horrible boiler used for executing those convicted of coining. Between La Courtille and St. Laurent your eye had already remarked, on the summit of a rising ground that swelled amidst a solitary plain, a sort of structure which looked at a distance like a ruinous colonnade standing upon a basement with its foundation laid bare. This, however, was neither a Parthenon nor a temple of the Olympian Jupiter; it was the dismal Montfaucon, already alluded to, and hereafter to be described.

Now, if the enumeration of so many edifices, brief as we have sought to make it, have not shattered in the reader's mind the general image of old Paris as fast as we have endeavoured to construct it, we will recapitulate it in a few words. In the centre was the island of the City, resembling in its form an enormous tortoise, extending on either side its bridges all scaly with tiles, like so many feet, from under its grey shell of roofs. On the left the close, dense, bristling, and homogeneous quadrangle of the University; and on the right the vast semicircle of the Town, much more interspersed with gardens, and great edifices. The three masses—City, University, and Town—are veined with innumerable streets. Across the whole runs the Seine, "the nursing Seine," as Father Du Breul calls it, obstructed with islands, bridges, and boats. All around is an immense plain, chequered with a thousand different sorts of cultivation, and strewed with beautiful villages; on the left Issy, Vanvres, Vaugirard, Montrouge, Gentilly, with its round tower and its square tower, etc.; and on the right twenty others, from Conflans to Ville l'Evêque. In the horizon a circle of hills formed, as it were, the rim of the vast basin. And in the distance, on the east, was Vincennes, with its seven quadrangular towers; on the south, the Bicêtre, with its pointed turrets; on the north, St. Denis and its spire; and on the west, St. Cloud and its donjon. Such was the Paris beheld from the summit of the towers of Notre-Dame by the crows who lived in 1482.

And yet it is of this city that Voltaire has said that "before the time of Louis XIV. it possessed only four fine pieces of architecture"—that is to say, the dome of the Sorbonne, the Val-de-Grâce, the modern Louvre, and—we have forgotten which was the fourth; perhaps it was the Luxembourg. Voltaire, however, was not the less the author of *Candide* for having made this observation; nor is he the less, among all the men who have succeeded one another in the long series of human characters, the one who has possessed in the greatest perfection the *rire diabolique*, the sardonic smile. This opinion of his only affords one evidence, among so many others, that a man may be a fine genius, and yet understand nothing of an art which he has not studied. Did not Molière think he was doing great honour to Raphael and Michael Angelo when he called them "those *Mignards* of their age"?

But to return to Paris and to the fifteenth century. It was

not then a fine town only, but it was a homogeneous town, an architectural and historical production of the Middle Ages—a chronicle in stone. It was a city composed of two architectural strata only—the Romanish and the Gothic layer: for the true Roman layer had long disappeared, except in the Baths of Julian, where it still pierced through the thick incrustation of the Middle Ages; and as for the Celtic stratum, no specimen of that was now to be found, even in sinking a well.

Half a century later, when the Revival came and broke into that consistency, so severe and yet so varied, with the dazzling profuseness of its systems and its fancies, rioting among Roman arches, Grecian columns, and Gothic depressions—its carving so delicate and so imaginative, its peculiar tastes for arabesques and foliage, its architectural paganism contemporary with Luther—Paris was perhaps more beautiful still, though less harmonious to the eye and to the mind. But that splendid period was of short duration. The Revival was not impartial. Not content with erecting, it thought proper to pull down; it must be acknowledged, too, that it wanted room. So the Gothic Paris was complete but for a moment. Scarcely was the tower of St. Jacques-de-la-Boucherie finished before the demolition of the old Louvre was begun.

Since then this great city has been daily sinking into deformity. The Gothic Paris, under which the Romanish Paris was disappearing, has disappeared in its turn; but what name shall we give to the Paris that has taken its place?

There is the Paris of Catherine de Médicis at the Tuileries,[1] the Paris of Henry II. at the Hôtel-de-Ville—two edifices which are still in fine taste; the Paris of Henry IV. at the Place Royale—a brick front, faced with stone, and roofed with slate—real tricoloured houses; the Paris of Louis XIII. at the Val-de-

[1] Our author has here subjoined the following note:—

"We have seen with mingled grief and indignation that there has been some intention of enlarging and remodelling—that is to say, of destroying—this admirable palace. The architects of our time have hands too heavy for handling these delicate works of the Revival. We still hope that they will not venture upon it. Besides, this demolition of the Tuileries would now be not only a brutal piece of violence which a drunken Vandal would have been ashamed of; it would be an act of treason. The Tuileries are no longer to be considered merely as a masterpiece of art of the sixteenth century; they form a page in the history of the nineteenth. This palace belongs not now to the king, but to the people. Let us leave it as it is. Our revolution has twice marked it on the forehead. Upon one of its two fronts it has the balls of the 10th of August; on the other, those of the 29th of July. It is sacred.

"Paris, 7th April 1831."

Grâce—of architecture crushed and squat, with basket-handle vaults, big-bellied columns, and a humpbacked dome; the Paris of Louis XIV. at the Invalides—great, rich, gilded, and cold; the Paris of Louis XV. at St. Sulpice—with volutes, knots of ribbons, clouds, vermicelli, and succory, all in stone; the Paris of Louis XVI. at the Pantheon—St. Peter's at Rome ill-copied, and the building has been awkwardly heightened, which has by no means rectified its lines; the Paris of the Republic at the School of Medicine, a poor Greek and Roman style, just as much to be compared to the Coliseum or the Parthenon as the constitution of the year III. is to the laws of Minos—the French denomination for which style in architecture is *le goût messidor ;* the Paris of Napoleon at the Place Vendôme—something sublime, a brazen column composed of melted cannon; the Paris of the Restoration at the *Bourse,* or exchange—a colonnade very white, supporting a frieze very smooth; the whole square, and costing twenty millions of francs.

To each of these characteristic structures is allied, by similarity of style, manner, and disposition of parts, a certain number of houses scattered over the different quarters of the town, which the eye of the connoisseur easily distinguishes and assigns to their respective dates. When a man understands the art of seeing, he can trace the spirit of an age and the features of a king even in the knocker on a door.

The present Paris has therefore no general physiognomy. It is a collection of specimens of several different ages, and the finest of all have disappeared. This capital is increasing in dwelling-houses only, and in what dwelling-houses? If it goes on as it is now doing, Paris will be renewed every fifty years. So also the historical meaning of its architecture is daily wearing away. Its great structures are becoming fewer and fewer, seeming to be swallowed up one after another by the flood of houses. "Our fathers," a Parisian of the present day might exclaim, "had a Paris of stone; our sons will have one of plaster."

As for the modern structures of the new Paris, we shall gladly decline enlarging upon them. Not, indeed, that we do not pay them all proper admiration. The Ste. Geneviève of M. Soufflot is certainly the finest Savoy cake that was ever made of stone. The Palace of the Legion of Honour is also a very distinguished piece of pastry. The *Halle-au-Blè,* or Corn Market, is an English jockey-cap on a magnificent scale. The towers of St. Sulpice are two great clarinets; now, nobody can deny that a clarinet shape *is* a shape, and then the telegraph, crooked and grinning, makes an admirable diversity upon the roof. The church of Saint-Roch has a doorway with whose magnificence only that of St. Thomas d'Aquin can compare; it has also a plum-pudding Mount Calvary down in a cellar, and a sun of gilt wood. These, it must be owned, are things positively marvellous. The lantern of the labyrinth at the Jardin des Plantes, too, is vastly ingenious. As for the *Palais de la Bourse*, or Exchange, which is Grecian in its colonnade, Roman by the circular arches of its doors and windows, and of the Revival by its great depressed ceiling, it is doubtless a structure in great correctness and purity of taste, one proof of which is that it is crowned by an attic story such as was never seen at Athens, a fine straight line, gracefully intersected here and there by stove pipes. We must add that if it be a rule that the architecture of a building should be so adapted to the purpose of the building itself as that the aspect of the edifice should at once declare that purpose, we cannot too much admire a structure which from its appearance might be either a royal palace, a chamber of deputies, a town hall, a college, a riding-house, an academy, a repository, a court of justice, a museum, a barrack, a mausoleum, a temple, or a theatre—and which all the while is an exchange. It has been thought too that an edifice should be made appropriate to the climate, and so this one has evidently been built on purpose for a cold and rainy sky. It has a roof almost flat, as they are in the East; and consequently in winter, when it snows, the roof has to be swept. And does any one doubt that roofs are intended to be swept? As for the purpose of which we have just now been speaking, the building fulfils it admirably. It is an exchange in France, as it would have been a temple in Greece. True it is that the architect has had much ado to conceal the clock-face, which would have destroyed the purity of the noble lines of the *façade*; but to make amends we have that colonnade running round the whole structure, under which, on the grand days of religious solemnity, may be magnificently developed the schemes of money-brokers and stock-jobbers.

These, doubtless, are very superb structures. Add to these many a pretty street, amusing and diversified, like the Rue de Rivoli, and we need not despair that Paris shall one day present, as seen in a balloon flight, that richness of outline and opulence of detail, that peculiar diversity of aspect, that something surpassingly grand in the simple and striking in the beautiful, which distinguishes a draughtboard.

However, admirable as you may think the present Paris,

reconstruct in your imagination the Paris of the fifteenth century; look at the sky through that surprising forest of spires, towers, and steeples—spread out amidst the vast city, tear asunder at the points of the islands, and fold round the piers of the bridges, the Seine, with its broad green and yellow flakes, more variegated than the skin of a serpent—project distinctly upon a horizon of azure the Gothic profile of that old Paris—make its outline float in a wintry mist clinging to its innumerable chimneys—plunge it in deep night, and observe the fantastic display of the darkness and the lights in that gloomy labyrinth of buildings—cast upon it a ray of moonlight, showing it in glimmering vagueness, with its towers lifting their great heads from that foggy sea—or draw that dark veil aside, cast into shade the thousand sharp angles of its spires and its gables, and exhibit it all fantastically indented upon the glowing western sky at sunset, and then compare.

And if you would receive from the old city an impression which the modern one is quite incapable of giving you, ascend, on the morning of some great holiday, at sunrise, on Easter or Whitsunday, to some elevated point from which your eye can command the whole capital, and attend the awakening of the chimes. Behold, at a signal from heaven—for it is the sun that gives it—those thousand churches starting from their sleep. At first you hear only scattered tinklings going from church to church, as when musicians are giving one another notice to begin. Then, all on a sudden, behold—for there are moments when the ear itself seems to see—behold, ascending at the same moment from every steeple a column of sound, as it were, a cloud of harmony. At first the vibration of each bell mounts up direct, clear, and, as it were, isolated from the rest into the splendid morning sky. Then by degrees as they expand they mingle, unite, are lost in each other, and confounded in one magnificent concert. Then it is all one mass of sonorous vibrations, incessantly sent forth from the innumerable steeples—floating, undulating, bounding, and eddying, over the town, and extending far beyond the horizon the deafening circle of its oscillations. Yet that sea of harmony is not a chaos. Wide and deep as it is, it has not lost its transparency: you perceive the winding of each group of notes that escapes from the several rings; you can follow the dialogue by turns grave and clamorous, of the *crecelle* and the *bourdon;* you perceive the octaves leaping from one steeple to another; you observe them springing aloft, winged, light, and whistling from the bell of silver, falling broken and limping from the bell of wood. You admire among them the rich gamut incessantly descending and reascending the seven bells of Sainte-Eustache; and you see clear and rapid notes running across, as it were, in three or four luminous zigzags, and vanishing like flashes of lightning. Down there you see Saint-Martin's Abbey, a shrill and broken-voiced songstress; here is the sinister and sullen voice of the Bastille; and at the other end is the great tower of the Louvre, with its counter-tenor. The royal chime of the Palais unceasingly casts on every side resplendent trillings, upon which fall at regular intervals the heavy strokes from the great bell of Notre-Dame, which strikes sparkles from them like the hammer upon the anvil. At intervals you perceive sounds pass by of every form from the triple peal of Saint-Germain-des-Près. Then, again, from time to time that mass of sublime sounds half opens, and gives passage to the *stretto* of the Ave-Maria, which glitters like an aigrette of stars. Below, in the deepest of the concert, you distinguish confusedly the internal music of the churches, exhaled through the vibrating pores of their vaulted roofs. Here, certainly, is an opera worth hearing. Ordinarily, the murmur that escapes from Paris in the daytime is the city talking; in the night it is the city breathing; but here it is the city singing. Listen, then, to this *tutti* of the steeples: diffuse over the whole the murmur of half a million of people—the everlasting plaint of the river—the boundless breathings of the wind—the grave and far *quartet* of the four forests placed upon the hills in the distance like so many vast organs, immersing in them, as in a demi-tint all in the central concert that would otherwise be too rugged or too sharp; and then say whether you know of anything in the world more rich, more joyous, more golden, more dazzling than this tumult of bells and chimes—this furnace of music—these thousand voices of brass, all singing together in flutes of stone three hundred feet high—this city which is all one orchestra—this symphony as loud as a tempest.

BOOK IV

CHAPTER I

GOOD FOLKS

It was sixteen years before the period of our story that on a fine morning of the first Sunday after Easter—called in England Low Sunday, and in France, *le dimanche de la Quasimodo*, or *Quasimodo Sunday*, from the word *Quasimodo*, which commences the Latin offertory appropriated to the mass of that day—that a young child had been deposited, after mass in the cathedral church of Notre-Dame, upon the bedstead fixed in the pavement on the left hand of the entrance, opposite to that great image of St. Christopher which the stone figure of Messire Antoine des Essarts, knight, had been contemplating on his knees since the year 1413, at the time that it was thought proper to throw down both the saint and his faithful adorer. Upon this bedstead it was customary to expose foundlings to the charity of the public. Any one took them that chose; and in the front of the bedstead was placed a copper basin for the reception of alms.

The sort of living creature that was found lying upon these planks on Low Sunday morning in the year of our Lord 1467 appeared to excite in a high degree the curiosity of a very considerable group of persons which had collected round the bedstead, and which consisted in great measure of individuals of the fair sex. Indeed, they were nearly all old women.

In the front line of the spectators, and stooping the most intently over the bedstead, were to be seen four of them, who, by their grey *cagoule* (a sort of cassock), appeared to be attached to some devout sisterhood. We know not why history should not hand down to posterity the names of these discreet and venerable demoiselles. They were Agnès la Herme, Jehanne de la Tarme, Henriette la Gaultière, and Gauchère la Violette—all four widows, all four *bonne femmes* of the *Chapelle Etienne Haudry*, who had come thus far from their house, with their mistress's leave and conformably to the statutes of Pierre d'Ailly, to hear the sermon.

However, if these good *Haudriettes* were observing for the moment the statutes of Pierre d'Ailly, assuredly they were violating, to their hearts' content, those of Michel de Brache and the Cardinal of Pisa, which so inhumanly prescribed silence to them.

"Whatever can that be, sister?" said Agnès to Gauchère, as she looked at the little exposed creature which lay screaming and twisting itself about upon the bedstead, frightened at being looked at by so many people.

"Bless me!" said Jehanne, "what's to become of us all if that's the way they make children now!"

"I'm no great judge of children," resumed Agnès, "but it must surely be a sin to look at such a one as this!"

"It's no child at all, Agnès——"

"It's a misshapen baboon," observed Gauchère.

"It's a miracle," said Henriette la Gaultière.

"Then," remarked Agnès, "this is the third since Lætare Sunday; for it's not a week since we had the miracle of the mocker of pilgrims divinely punished by Our Lady of Aubervilliers, and that was the second miracle of the month.

"This pretended foundling's a very monster of abomination," resumed Jehanne.

"He brawls loud enough to deafen a chanter," added Gauchère. —"Hold your tongue, you little bellower."

"To say that it's Monsieur of Reims that sends this monstrosity to Monsieur of Paris!" exclaimed La Gaultière, clasping her hands.

"I imagine," said Agnès la Herme, "that it's some strange animal—the offspring of some beastly Jew or other—something, at all events, that's not Christian, and so must be thrown into the water or into the fire."

"Surely," resumed La Gaultière, "nobody'll ask to have it!"

"Ah, my God!" exclaimed Agnès, "these poor nurses that live down there in the foundling-house at the bottom of the alley, going down to the river, close by the lord bishop's—suppose they were to go and take them this little monster to suckle! I'd rather give suck to a vampire."

"Is she a simpleton, that poor La Herme?" rejoined Jehanne. "Don't you see, my dear sister, that this little monster is at least four years old, and wouldn't have half so much appetite for your breast as for a piece of roast meat."

In fact the "little monster" (for we ourselves should be much puzzled to give it any other denomination) was not a new-born infant. It was a little angular, restless mass, imprisoned in a canvas bag marked with the cipher of Messire Guillaume Chartier, then Bishop of Paris, with a head peeping out at one end of it. This head was very deformed, exhibiting only a forest of red hair, one eye, a mouth, and some teeth. The eye was weeping; the mouth was crying; and the teeth seemed to desire, above all things, to bite. The whole lump was struggling violently in the bag, to the great wonderment of the increasing and incessantly renewing crowd around it.

Dame Aloïse de Gondelaurier, a wealthy and noble lady, holding by the hand a pretty little girl about six years of age, and drawing after her a long veil attached to the golden horn of her coif, stopped as she was passing before the bedstead, and looked for a moment at the unfortunate creature; while her charming little daughter, Fleur-de-Lys de Gondelaurier, all clad in silk and velvet, was spelling with her pretty finger, upon the permanent label attached to the bedstead, the words *Enfans Trouvés*.

"Really," said the lady, turning away with disgust, "I thought they exposed here nothing but children."

She turned her back, at the same time throwing into the basin a silver florin, which rang among the liards, and opened wide the eyes of the poor *bonnes femmes* of the Chapelle Etienne Haudry.

A moment afterwards the grave and learned Robert Mistricolle, king's prothonotary, passed by, with an enormous missal under one arm, and his wife under the other (Damoiselle Guillemette-la-Mairesse), having thus at his side his two regulators, the spiritual and the temporal.

"Foundling, indeed!" said he after examining the living lump; "yet—found, apparently, upon the parapet of the river Phlegethon!"

"It has but one eye visible," observed Damoiselle Guillemette; "it has a great wart upon the other."

"It's no wart," exclaimed Maître Robert Mistricolle; "it's an egg that contains just such another demon, which has upon its eye another little egg enclosing another devil, and so on."

"How do you know that?" asked Guillemette-la-Mairesse.

"I know it for very sufficient reasons," answered the prothonotary.

"Monsieur the Prothonotary," asked Gauchère, "what do you prognosticate from this pretended foundling?"

"The greatest calamities," answered Mistricolle.

"Ah, my God!" said an old woman among the bystanders, "withal that there was a considerable pestilence last year, and they say the English are going to land in great company at Harfleur!"

"Perhaps that'll prevent the Queen from coming to Paris in September," observed another; "and trade's so bad already!"

"I'm of opinion," cried Jehanne de la Tarme, "that it would be better for the inhabitants of Paris for that little conjurer there to be lying upon a fagot than upon a board."

"A fine flaming fagot!" added the old woman.

"It would be more prudent," said Mistricolle.

For some minutes a young priest had been listening to the argument of the *Haudriettes* and the oracular sentences of the prothonotary.

He had a severe countenance, with a broad forehead and a penetrating eye. He made way silently through the crowd, examining the little conjurer with his eye, and stretched out his hand over him. It was time, for all the devout old ladies were already regaling themselves with the anticipation of the fine flaming fagot.

"I adopt that child," said the priest. He wrapt it in his cassock and carried it away with him, the bystanders gazing after him with looks of affright. In a minute he had disappeared through the Porte-Rouge, or red door, which at that time led from the church into the cloisters.

When the first surprise was over Jehanne de la Tarme whispered in the ear of La Gaultière, "Did not I tell you, sister, that that young clerk, Monsieur Claude Frollo, is a sorcerer?"

CHAPTER II

CLAUDE FROLLO

Claude Frollo was in fact no vulgar person. He belonged to one of those families of middle rank which were called indifferently, in the impertinent language of the last century, *haute bourgeoisie* or *petite noblesse*—that is, high commoners or petty nobility. This family had inherited from the brothers Paclet the fief of Tirechappe, which was held of the Bishop of Paris, and the twenty-one houses of which had been, in the thirteenth century, the object of so many pleadings before the official. As possessor of this fief, Claude Frollo was one of the *sept-vingt-un,* or hundred and forty-one seigneurs claiming *censive,* or manorial dues, in Paris and its faubourgs; and in that capacity his name was long to be seen inscribed between that of the Hôtel de Tancarville, belonging to Maître François le Rez, and that of the college of Tours, in the chartulary deposited at Saint-Martin-des-Champs.

The parents of Claude Frollo had destined him, from his infancy, for the ecclesiastical state. He had been taught to read in Latin; and had been bred to cast down his eyes and to speak low. While yet a child, his father had cloistered him in the college of Torchi, in the University; and there it was that he had grown up, over the missal and the lexicon.

He was, moreover, a melancholy, grave, and serious boy, who studied ardently and learned with rapidity. He never shouted loud when at play; he mixed little in the bacchanalia of the Rue du Fouarre; knew not what it was to *dare alapas et capillos laniare;* nor had figured in that mutiny of 1463, which the annalists gravely record under the title of "Sixième Trouble de l'Université." It did not often happen to him to rally the poor scholars of Montaigu upon their *cappettes,* from which they derived their university nickname; nor the fellows of the college of Dormans upon their smooth tonsure and their tripartite frock, made of cloth blue grey, blue, and violet, *azurini coloris et bruni,* as the charter of the Cardinal des Quatre-Couronnes expresses it.

But, on the other hand, he was assiduous at the great and the little schools of the Rue Saint-Jean-de-Beauvais. The first scholar whom the Abbot of Saint-Pierre-de-Val, at the moment of commencing his reading in canon law, always observed intently fixed, opposite to his chair, against a pillar of the école Saint-Vendregesile, was Claude Frollo, armed with his inkhorn, chewing his pen, scrawling upon his much-worn knee, and in winter blowing his fingers. The first auditor that Messire Miles d'Isliers, *docteur en décret,* saw arrive every Monday morning, quite out of breath, at the opening of the doors of the school Du Chef Saint-Denis, was Claude Frollo. Thus at the age of sixteen the young clerk was a match, in mystical theology, for a father of the Church; in canonical theology for a father of the Council; and in scholastic theology, for a doctor of the Sorbonne.

Theology being passed through, he had then rushed into the *décret,* or study of the decretals. After the *Master of the Sentences,* he had fallen upon the Capitularies of Charlemagne; and had successively devoured, in his appetite for knowledge, decretals upon decretals—those of Theodore, Bishop of Hispalis; those of Bouchard, Bishop of Worms; those of Yves, Bishop of Chartres; then the *décret* of Gratian, which succeeded the capitularies of Charlemagne; then the collection by Gregory IX.; then the epistle *Super specula* of Honorius III. He made himself clearly familiar with that vast and tumultuous period of the civil and the canon law, in collision and at strife with each other in the chaos of the Middle Ages—a period which opens with Bishop Theodore in 618, and closes in 1227 with Pope Gregory.

Having digested the decretals, he plunged into medicine and the liberal arts. He studied the science of herbs, the science of unguents. He became expert in the treatment of fevers and of contusions, of wounds and of imposthumes. Jacques d'Espars would have admitted him as a physician, Richard Hellain as a surgeon. In like manner he ran through every degree in the faculty of arts. He studied the languages—Latin, Greek, Hebrew—a triple sanctuary then but very little frequented. He was possessed by an absolute fever of acquiring and storing up science. At eighteen he had made his way through the four faculties; it seemed to the young man that life had but one sole object, and that was to *know*.

It was just about this period that the excessive heat of the summer of 1466 gave birth to that great plague which carried off more than forty thousand souls within the viscounty of Paris, and amongst others, says John of Troyes, "Maître Arnoul, the king's astrologer, a man full honest, wise, and pleasant." It was rumoured in the university that the Rue Tirechappe was one of those especially devastated by the pestilence. It was there, in the midst of their fief, that the parents of Claude resided. The young scholar hastened in great alarm to his paternal roof. On entering he found that his father and his mother had both died the day before. A little brother, quite an infant, still in its swaddling-clothes, was yet living, and crying abandoned in his cradle. It was all that remained to Claude of his family. The young man took the child under his arm, and went away pensive. Hitherto he had lived only in science; he was now beginning to live in the world.

This catastrophe was a crisis in Claude's existence. An elder brother, an orphan, and the head of a family at nineteen, he felt himself rudely aroused from the reveries of the school to the realities of this life. Then, moved with pity, he was seized with passion and devotion for this infant brother; and strange at once and sweet was this human affection to him who had never yet loved anything but books.

This affection developed itself to a singular degree; in a soul so new to passion it was like a first love. Separated since his childhood from his parents, whom he had scarcely known—cloistered and walled up, as it were, in his books—eager above all things to study and to learn—exclusively attentive, until then, to his understanding, which dilated in science—to his indignation, which expanded in literature—the poor scholar had not yet had time to feel that he had a heart. This little brother, without father or mother—this infant which suddenly dropped, as it were, from heaven into his charge—made a new man of him. He discovered that there was something else in the world besides the speculations of the Sorbonne and the verses of Homerus—that man has need of affections—that life without tenderness and without love is but a piece of dry machinery, noisy and wearisome. Only he fancied—for he was still at that age when illusions are as yet replaced only by illusions—that the affections of blood and kindred were the only ones necessary, and that a little brother to love was sufficient to fill up his whole existence.

He threw himself, then, into the love of his little Jehan with all the warmth of a character which was already deep, ardent, concentrated. This poor helpless creature, pretty, fair-haired, rosy, and curly—this orphan with another orphan for its only support — moved him to the inmost soul; and, like a grave thinker as he was, he began to reflect upon Jehan with a feeling of the tenderest pity. He bestowed all his solicitude upon him, as upon something extremely fragile especially commended to his care. He was more than a brother to the infant—he became a mother to it.

Now little Jehan having lost his mother before he was weaned, Claude put him out to nurse. Besides the fief of Tirechappe, he inherited from his father that of Moulin, which was held of the square tower of Gentilly; it was a mill standing upon a hill near the Château de *Winchestre*, since corrupted into *Bicêtre*. The miller's wife was suckling a fine boy. It was not far from the university, and Claude carried his little Jehan to her in his own arms.

Thenceforward, feeling that he had a burden to bear, he began to look on life as a serious matter. The thought of his little brother became not only his recreation from study, but the object of his studies themselves. He resolved to devote himself entirely to the future life of the being for whom he thought himself answerable before God, and never to have any other spouse, any other offspring, than the happiness and the fortune of his brother. He attached himself, therefore, more devotedly than ever to his clerical vocation. His merit, his learning, his quality as an immediate vassal of the Bishop of Paris, opened wide to him the gates of the Church. At twenty years of age, by special dispensation from the Holy See, he was ordained priest, and performed the service, as the youngest of the chaplains of Notre-Dame, at the altar called, on account of the late mass that was said at it, *altare pigrorum*, the altar of the lazy.

There, more than ever immersed in his dear book; which he quitted only to hasten for an hour to the fief Du Moulin, this mixture of learning and austerity, so rare at his age, had speedily gained him the admiration and reverence of the cloister. From the cloister his reputation for learning had been communicated to the people, amongst whom it had been in some degree converted, as not unfrequently happened in that day, into renown for sorcery.

It was at the moment of returning, on the Quasimodo Sunday, from saying his mass of the slothful at their altar, which was at the side of that gate of the choir which opened into the nave, on the right hand, near the image of the Virgin, that his attention had been awakened by the group of old women screaming around the bed of the foundlings.

Then it was that he had approached the unfortunate little creature, the object of so much hatred and menace. That distress, that deformity, that abandonment, the thought of his little brother, the idea which suddenly crossed his mind that were he himself to die his dear little Jehan, too, might chance to be miserably cast upon those boards—all that had rushed upon his heart at once, a deep feeling of pity had taken possession of him, and he had borne off the child.

When he drew the infant out of the bag he found it to be very deformed indeed. The poor little imp had a great lump covering its left eye, the head compressed between the shoulders, the spine crooked, the breast-bone prominent, and the legs bowed. Yet it seemed to be full of life; and although it was impossible to discover what language it spluttered, yet its cry indicated a certain degree of health and strength. Claude's compassion was increased by this ugliness; and he vowed in his heart to bring up this child for the love of his brother, in order that, whatever might in future time be the faults of little Jehan, there might be placed to his credit this piece of charity performed on his account. It was a sort of putting out of good works at interest, which he transacted in his brother's name—an investment of good actions which he wished to make for him beforehand—to provide against the chance of the little fellow's one day finding himself short of that sort of specie, the only kind taken at the gate of heaven.

He baptized his adopted child by the name of Quasimodo; whether it was that he chose thereby to commemorate the day when he had found him, or that he meant to mark by that name how incomplete and imperfectly moulded the poor little creature was. Indeed, Quasimodo, one-eyed, hump-backed, and bow-legged, could hardly be considered as anything more than an *almost*.

CHAPTER III

THE RINGER-GENERAL OF NOTRE-DAME

Now in 1482 Quasimodo had grown up, and had been for several years ringer of the bells of Notre-Dame, by the grace of his adoptive father, Claude Frollo, who was become Archdeacon of Joas, by the grace of his suzerain, Messire Louis de Beaumont, who had become Bishop of Paris in 1472 on the death of Guillaume Chartier, by the grace of his patron Olivier le Daim, barber to Louis XI., king by the grace of God.

Quasimodo, then, was ringer-general at Notre-Dame.

With time a certain peculiar bond of intimacy had been contracted between the ringer and the church. Separated for ever from the world by the double fatality of his unknown birth and his natural deformity, imprisoned from his infancy within that double and impassioned circle, the poor unfortunate had been accustomed to see nothing on this earth beyond the religious walls which had received him into their shade. Notre-Dame had been to him successively, as he grew up, the egg, the nest, his house, his country, the world.

And certain it is, there was a sort of mysterious and pre-existing harmony between this creature and this edifice. When, while yet quite little, he used to drag himself along, tortuously and tumblingly, under the gloom of its arches, he seemed, with his human face and his bestial members, the native reptile of that damp dark floor, upon which the shadows of the Saxon capitals projected so many fantastic forms.

And afterwards, the first time that he clung mechanically to the bell-rope in the towers, hung himself upon it, and set the bell in motion, the effect upon Claude, his adoptive father, was that of a child finding its tongue and beginning to talk.

Thus it was that, gradually unfolding his being, which constantly took its mould from the cathedral, living in it, sleeping in it, scarcely ever going out of it, receiving every hour its mysterious impress, he came at length to resemble it, to be fashioned to it, as it were, to make an integral part of it. His salient angles fitted themselves (if we may be allowed the expression) into the re-entering angles of the structure, and he seemed to be not only its inhabitant, but even the natural tenant of it. He might almost be said to have taken its form as the snail takes that of its shell. It was his dwelling-place, his hole, his envelope. Between the old church and himself there was an instinctive sympathy so profound—so many affinities, magnetic as well as material—that he in some sort adhered to it, like the tortoise to its shell. The cathedral, with its time-roughened surface, was his carapace.

It is needless to hint to the reader that he is not to accept literally the figures that we are here obliged to employ in order to express that singular assimilation, symmetrical, immediate—consubstantial, almost—of a man to a building. Nor is it less evident to what a degree he must have familiarised himself with the whole cathedral during so long and so intimate a cohabitation. This was his own peculiar dwelling-place; it had no depth which Quasimodo had not penetrated, no height which he had not scaled. Many a time had he clambered up its front to one story after another, with no other help than the projections of its architecture and sculpture. The towers, over the external surface of which he was sometimes seen creeping, like a lizard gliding upon a perpendicular wall—those two giant cheeks of the building, so lofty, so threatening, so formidable—had for him neither giddiness, nor dizziness, nor terror. To see them so gentle under his hand, so easy to scale, one would have said that he had tamed them. By dint of leaping, climbing, sporting, amid the abysses of the gigantic cathedral, he was become in some sort both monkey and chamois — like the Calabrian child, which swims before it can run, and plays in its infancy with the sea.

Moreover, not only did his body seem to have fashioned itself according to the cathedral, but his mind also. In what state was that soul of his? What bend had it contracted, what form had it taken, under that close-drawn envelope, in that savage mode of life? This it would be difficult to determine. Quasimodo was born one-eyed, hump-backed, limping. It was with great difficulty and great patience that Claude Frollo had succeeded in teaching him to speak. But a fatality pursued the poor foundling. Made ringer of Notre-Dame at fourteen years of age, a fresh infirmity had come to complete his desolation—the bells had broken his tympanum, and he had become deaf. The only door that nature had left him open to the external world had been suddenly closed for ever.

And in closing, it intercepted the sole ray of joy and light that still penetrated to the soul of Quasimodo. That moonlight was veiled in deep night. The poor creature's melancholy became incurable and complete as his deformity; add to which, his deafness rendered him in some sort dumb. For, that he might not make himself laughed at by others, from the moment that he found himself deaf he resolutely determined to observe a silence which he scarcely ever broke except when he was alone. He tied up voluntarily that tongue which Claude Frollo had had so much trouble to untie. And hence it was that, when necessity compelled him to speak, his tongue moved stiffly and awkwardly, like a door of which the hinges have grown rusty.

Were we now to endeavour to penetrate to Quasimodo's soul through that thick, hard rind—could we sound the depths of that ill-formed organisation—were it possible for us to look, as it were, with a torch in our hands, behind the non-transparency of those organs—to explore the darksome interior of that opaque being—to elucidate its obscure corners and absurd no-thoroughfares, and throw all at once a strong light upon the Psyche chained down in that drear cavern—doubtless we should find the poor creature in some posture of decrepitude, stunted and rickety, like those prisoners that used to grow old in the low dungeons of Venice, bent double in a stone chest too low and too short for them either to stand or to lie at full length.

It is certain that the spirit pines in a misshapen body. Quasimodo scarcely felt, stirring blindly within him, a soul made after his own image. The impressions of external objects underwent a considerable refraction before they reached his apprehension. His brain was a peculiar medium; the ideas which passed through it issued forth completely distorted. The reflection which proceeded from that refraction was necessarily divergent and astray.

Hence he was subject to a thousand optical illusions, a thousand aberrations of judgment, a thousand wanderings of idea, sometimes foolish, sometimes idiotic.

The first effect of this fatal organisation was to disturb the look which he cast upon external objects. He received from them scarcely any immediate perception. The external world seemed to him much farther off than it does to us.

The second effect of his misfortune was to render him mischievous. He was mischievous, indeed, because he was savage; and he was savage because he was ugly. There was a consequentiality in his nature as well as in ours. His strength, too, developed in so extraordinary a degree, was another cause of mischievousness—*malus puer robustus*, says Hobbes.

Besides we must do him the justice to observe that mischievousness was perhaps not inherent in him. At his very first steps among mankind he had felt himself—and then he had seen himself—repulsed, branded, spit upon. Human speech had ever been to him a scoff or a malediction. As he grew up he had found naught around him but hatred. What wonder that he should have caught it! He had but contracted his share of malice—he had but picked up the weapon that had wounded him.

And, after all, he turned but reluctantly towards mankind—his cathedral was sufficient for him. It was peopled with figures in marble—with kings, saints, bishops—who at all events did not burst out a-laughing in his face, but looked upon him with uniform tranquillity and benevolence. The other figures, those of the monsters and demons, had no hatred for him, Quasimodo. He was too much like them for that. They seemed much rather to be scoffing at the rest of mankind. The saints were his friends, and blessed him; the monsters were his friends, and protected him. And accordingly he used to have long communings with them; he would sometimes pass whole hours squatted down before one of those statues, holding a solitary conversation with it, on which occasion, if any one happened to approach, he would fly like a lover surprised in his serenade.

And the cathedral was not only society to him—it was the world, it was all nature. He dreamt of no hedgerows but the stained windows ever in flower, no shades but the stone foliage which unfolds itself loaded with birds in the tufted Saxon capitals, no mountains but the colossal towers of the church, no ocean but Paris, murmuring at their feet.

That which he loved above all in his maternal edifice—that which awakened his soul, and made it stretch forth its poor pinions which it kept so miserably folded up within its cavern; that which sometimes made him happy—was the bells. He loved them, caressed them, talked to them, understood them. From the carillon in the central steeple to the great bell over the doorway they all shared his affections. The central steeple and the two towers were to him three great cages, the birds in which, taught by himself, sang for him alone. It was, however, those same bells that had made him deaf. But a mother is often the fondest of that child which has cost her the most suffering.

It is true that their voices were the only ones that he was still capable of hearing. On this account the great bell of all was his best-beloved. She it was whom he preferred among this family of noisy sisters that fluttered about him on festival days. This great bell was named Marie. She was placed in the southern tower, where she had no companion but her sister Jacqueline, a bell of smaller dimensions, shut up in a smaller cage by the side of her own.

This Jacqueline was so named after the wife of Jean Montagu, which Jean had given her to the church—a donation, however, which had not prevented him from going and figuring without his head at Montfaucon. In the northern tower were six other bells; while the six smallest inhabited the central steeple, over the choir, together with the wooden bell, which was rung only from the afternoon of Maundy Thursday until the morning of Holy Saturday or Easter Eve. Thus Quasimodo had fifteen bells in his seraglio; but the big Marie was his favourite.

It is not easy to give an idea of his delight on those days on which they rang in full peal. The moment the archdeacon had set him off with the word "Go," he ascended the spiral staircase of the steeple quicker than any other person would have descended it. He rushed, all breathless, into the aërial chamber of the large Marie. He gazed upon her for a moment intently and fondly; then he addressed her softly, patted her with his hand, like a good horse setting out on a long journey, expressing sorrow for the trouble he was going to give her. After these first caresses he called out to his assistants, placed in the lower story of the tower, to begin. The latter then hung their weight at the ropes, the capstan creaked, and the enormous round of metal swung slowly. Quasimodo, panting, followed it with his eye. The first stroke of the clapper against the brazen wall that encircled it shook the wood-work upon which he stood. Quasimodo vibrated with the bell. "Vah!" he would cry with a burst of insensate laughter. Meanwhile the motion of the bell became quicker; and as it went on, taking a wider and wider sweep, Quasimodo's eye, in like manner, opened wider and wider, and became more and more phosphoric and flaming. At length the great peal commenced, the whole tower trembled—wood, lead, stone, all shook together—from the piles of the foundation to the trifoliations at the summit. Quasimodo was now in a boiling perspiration, running to and fro and shaking with the tower from head to foot. The bell, now in full and furious swing, presented alternately to each wall of the tower its brazen throat, from whence escaped that tempest breath which was audible at four leagues' distance. Quasimodo placed himself before this gaping throat, squatted down and rose up again at each return of the bell, inhaled that furious breath, looked by turns down upon the Place which was swarming with people two hundred feet below him, and upon the enormous brazen tongue which came, second after second, and bellowed in his ear. It was the only speech that he understood—the only sound that broke to him the universal silence. His soul dilated in it, like a bird in the sunshine. All at once he would catch the frenzy of the bell; and then his look became extraordinary—he would wait the next coming of the vast mass of metal, as the spider waits for the fly, and then throw himself headlong upon it. Now, suspended over the abyss, borne to and fro by the formidable swinging of the bell, he seized the brazen monster by the ears, gripped it between his knees, spurred it with both his heels, and redoubled, with the whole shock and weight of his body, the fury of the peal. Meanwhile the tower trembled, while he shouted and ground his teeth, his red hair bristling up, his breath heaving like the blast of a forge, and his eye flaming, while his monstrous steed was neighing and palpitating under him. Then it was no longer either the great bell of Notre-Dame or Quasimodo the ringer—it was a dream, a whirl, a tempest, dizziness astride upon clamour, a strange centaur, half man, half bell—a sort of horrible Astolpho, carried along upon a prodigious hippogriff of living bronze.

The presence of this extraordinary being breathed, as it were, a breath of life through the whole cathedral. There seemed to escape from him—so at least said the exaggerating superstitions of the multitude—a mysterious emanation, which animated all the stones of Notre-Dame, and heaved the deep bosom of the ancient church. To know that he was there was enough to make you think you saw life and motion in the thousand statues of the galleries and doorways. The old cathedral did indeed seem a creature docile and obedient to his hand. She waited his will to lift up her loud voice; she was filled and possessed with Quasimodo, as with a familiar spirit. One would have said that he made the immense building breathe. He was to be seen all over it; he multiplied himself upon every point of the structure. Sometimes you beheld with dread at the very top of one of the towers a fantastic, dwarfish-looking figure, climbing, twisting, crawling about, descending outside over the abyss, leaping from projecting to projection, and then thrusting his arm into the throat of some sculptured gorgon; it was Quasimodo pulling the crows from their nests. Sometimes in a dark corner of the church you would stumble against a sort of living chimera, squatting and dogged-looking; it was Quasimodo musing. Sometimes you espied upon one of the steeples an enormous head and a parcel of deranged limbs swinging furiously at the end of a rope; it was Quasimodo ringing the vesper-bell or the Angelus. Often at night a hideous form was seen wandering upon the light, delicate balustrade which crowns the towers and borders the top of the chancel; it was still the hunchback of Notre-Dame. Then the good women of the neighbourhood would say something fantastic, supernatural, horrible, was to be seen in the whole church—eyes and mouths opened in it here and there; the stone dogs, griffins, and the rest that watch day and night, with outstretched neck and open jaws, around the monstrous cathedral were heard to bark. And if it was a Christmas night—while the great bell, that seemed to rattle in its throat, was calling the faithful to the blazing midnight mass, there was such an air spread over the gloomy front that the great doorway seemed to be devouring the multitude, while the round window above it was looking down upon them—and all this came from Quasimodo. Egypt would have taken him for the god of this temple—the Middle Ages believed him to be its demon—he was in fact its soul.

So much was this the case that to those who know that Quasimodo has existed, Notre-Dame is now solitary, inanimate, dead. They feel that something has disappeared. That vast body is empty—it is a skeleton—the spirit has quitted it—they see the place of its habitation, but that is all. It is like a skull, which still has holes for the eyes but no look shining through them.

CHAPTER IV

THE DOG AND HIS MASTER

THERE was, however, one human creature whom Quasimodo excepted from his malice and hatred for the rest, and whom he loved as much—perhaps more than his cathedral—this was Claude Frollo.

The case was simple enough. Claude Frollo had received him, adopted him, brought him up. While yet quite little, it was between Claude Frollo's knees that he had been accustomed to take refuge when the dogs and the children ran yelping after him. Claude Frollo had taught him to speak, to read, to write. Claude Frollo, in fine, had made him ringer of the bells—and to give the great bell in marriage to Quasimodo was giving Juliet to Romeo.

Accordingly Quasimodo's gratitude was deep, ardent, boundless; and although the countenance of his adoptive father was often clouded and severe—although his mode of speaking was habitually brief, harsh, imperious—never had that feeling of gratitude wavered for a single instant. The archdeacon had in Quasimodo the most submissive of slaves, the most tractable of servants, the most vigilant of watch-dogs. When the poor ringer had become deaf there was established between him and Claude Frollo a language of signs, mysterious, and intelligible only to themselves. So that the archdeacon was the only human being with whom Quasimodo had preserved a communication. There were only two existences in this world with which he had any intercourse—Notre-Dame and Claude Frollo.

Unexampled were the sway of the archdeacon over the ringer and the ringer's attachment to the archdeacon. One sign from Claude, and the idea of pleasing him would have sufficed to make Quasimodo throw himself from the top of the towers of Notre-Dame. There was something remarkable in all that physical strength, so extraordinarily developed in Quasimodo, and blindly placed by him at the disposal of another. In this there was undoubtedly filial devotion and domestic attachment; but there was also fascination of one mind by another mind,

There was a poor, weak, awkward organisation, hanging its head and casting down its eyes in the presence of a lofty and penetrating intellect, powerful and commanding. In fine, and above all the rest, there was gratitude—gratitude pushed to that extreme limit that we know not to what to compare it. This virtue not being one of those of which the finest examples are found amongst mankind, we must therefore say that Quasimodo loved the archdeacon as no dog, no horse, no elephant ever loved his master.

CHAPTER V

MORE ABOUT CLAUDE FROLLO

IN 1482 Quasimodo was about twenty years old, and Claude Frollo about thirty-six. The one had grown up; the other had grown old.

Claude Frollo was no longer the simple scholar of the Torchi College, the tender protector of a little boy, the young dreaming philosopher, who knew many things and was ignorant of many. He was a priest, austere, grave, morose—having cure of souls—Monsieur the Archdeacon of Joas—the second acolyte of the bishop—having charge of the two deaneries of Montlhéry and Châteaufort, and of a hundred and seventy-four *curés ruraux*, or country parochial clergy. He was an imposing and sombre personage, before whom trembled the chorister boys in *aube* and *jaquette*, the *machicos*, the brethren of St. Augustine, and the *cercles matutinels* of Notre-Dame, when he passed slowly under the lofty pointed arches of the choir, majestic, pensive, with his arms crossed, and his head so much inclined upon his breast that nothing could be seen of his face but his large bald forehead.

Dom Claude Frollo, however, had abandoned neither science nor the education of his brother, the two occupations of his life. But in the course of time some bitterness had been mingled with these things which he had found so sweet. Little Jehan Frollo, surnamed Du Moulin from the place where he had been nursed, had not grown up in the direction which Claude had been desirous of giving him. The elder brother had reckoned upon a pupil pious, docile, learned, creditable. But the younger brother, like those young plants which baffle the endeavours of the gardener, and turn obstinately towards that side alone from which they receive air and sunshine—the younger brother grew up, and shot forth full of luxuriant branches only on the side of idleness, ignorance, and debauchery. He was a very devil—extremely disorderly—which made Dom Claude knit his brows; but very droll and very cunning—which made the elder brother smile. Claude had consigned him to that same College de Torchi in which he himself had passed his earlier years in study and modest seclusion; and it grieved him that this sanctuary, once edified by the name of Frollo, should be scandalised by it now. He sometimes read Jehan very long and very severe lectures upon the subject, which the latter intrepidly sustained. After all the young rake had a good heart—as all our comedies take care to assure us on the like occasion. But when the lecture was over he did not the less quietly resume the course of his seditions and his enormities. Sometimes it was a *béjaune* or *yellow-beak*, as a newcomer at the university was called, whom he had plucked for his entrance-money—a precious tradition which has been carefully handed down to the present day. Sometimes he had set in motion a band of scholars, who had classically fallen upon a cabaret—*quasi classico excitati*—then had beaten the tavern-keeper *avec bâtons offensifs*, and merrily pillaged the tavern, even to the staving-in of the hogsheads of wine in the cellar. And then there was a fine report, drawn up in Latin, which the sub-monitor of the Torchi College brought piteously to Dom Claude, with this dolorous heading—*Rixa ; prima causa vinum optimum potatum.* And, in fine, it was said—a thing quite horrible in a boy of sixteen—that his raking oftentimes led him as far as the Rue de Glatigny.

Owing to all this, Claude, saddened and discouraged in his human affections, had thrown himself the more ardently into the arms of science, that sister who, at all events, does not laugh in your face, but ever repays you (albeit in coin sometimes rather light) for the attention you have bestowed upon her. He became, then, more and more learned, and at the same time, by a natural consequence, more and more rigid as a priest, more and more melancholy as a man. There are in each individual of us certain parallelisms between our understanding, our manners, and our character which develop themselves continuously, and interrupted only by the greater disturbances of life.

As Claude Frollo had in his youth gone through nearly the whole circle of positive human knowledge, external and lawful, he was under the absolute necessity, unless he was to stop *ubi defuit orbis*, of going further, and seeking other food for the insatiable activity of his intellect. The ancient symbol of the serpent biting his tail is especially appropriate to science, and it seems that Claude Frollo had experienced this. Many grave persons affirmed that after exhausting the *fas* of human knowledge he had ventured to penetrate into the *nefas*. He had, they said, successively tasted all the apples of the tree of knowledge; and, whether from hunger or disgust, he had ended with tasting of the forbidden fruit. He had taken his place by turns, as our readers had seen, at the conferences of the theologians at the Sorbonne; at the meetings of the faculty of arts at the image of St. Hilary; at the disputations of the decretists at the image of St. Martin; at the congregations of the physicians at the *bénitier* of Notre-Dame, *ad cupam nostræ dominæ*. All the viands, permitted and approved, which those four great *cuisines* called the four faculties could prepare and serve up to the understanding, he had devoured; and he had been satiated by them before his hunger was appeased. Then he had penetrated further—lower—underneath all that finite, material, limited science. He had perhaps risked his soul, and seated himself in the cavern, at that mysterious table of the alchemists, the astrologers, the hermetics, of which Averroës, Guillaume de Paris, and Nicolas Flamel occupy the lower extremity in the Middle Ages, and which extends in the East, under the light of the seven-branched candlestick, up to Solomon, Pythagoras, and Zoroaster. So, at least, it was supposed, whether rightly or not.

It is certain that the archdeacon often visited the cemetery of the Holy Innocents, in which, it is true, his father and mother had been buried, with the other victims of the plague of 1466; but that he testified much less devotion to the cross at the head of their grave then to the strange figures upon the tomb of Nicolas Flamel and his wife Claude Pernelle, which stood close by it.

It is certain that he had often been seen to pass along the Rue des Lombards, and enter stealthily into a small house at the corner of the two streets, the Rue des Ecrivains and the Rue Marivaux. It was the house which Nicolas Flamel had built, in which he had died about the year 1417, and which, uninhabited ever since, was beginning to fall into ruins, so much had the hermetics and the alchemists of all countries worn away its walls by simply engraving their names upon them. Some of the neighbours even affirmed that they had once seen, through an air-hole, the Archdeacon Claude digging and turning over the earth at the bottom of those two cellars, the buttresses in which had been scrawled over with innumerable verses and hieroglyphics by Nicolas Flamel himself. It was supposed that Flamel had buried the philosopher's stone in these cellars; and the alchemists for two centuries, from Magistry down to Father Pacifique, never ceased to turn about the ground, until the house itself, so mercilessly ransacked and turned inside out, had at last crumbled into dust under their feet.

It is certain, too, that the archdeacon had been seized with a singular passion for the symbolical doorway of Notre-Dame, that page of conjuration written in stone by Bishop William of Paris, who has undoubtedly been damned for attaching so infernal a frontispiece to the sacred poem eternally chanted by the rest of the structure. Archdeacon Claude had also the credit of having sounded the mysteries of the colossal St. Christopher, and of that long enigmatical statue which then stood at the entrance of the Parvis, and which the people had nicknamed *Monsieur Legris*. But what everybody might have remarked was the interminable hours which he would often spend, seated upon the parapet of the Parvis, in contemplating the sculptured figures of the portal—now examining the light maidens with their lamps turned upside down, and the prudent ones with their lamps the right end up; at other times calculating the angle of vision of that crow which clings to the left side of the doorway, casting its eye upon a mysterious point within the church, where the philosopher's stone is certainly hidden, if it be not in Nicolas Flamel's cellar.

It was a singular destiny (we may remark in passing) for the church of Notre-Dame, at that period, to be thus beloved in two different ways, and with so much devotion, by two beings so unlike as Claude and Quasimodo—loved by the one, a sort of half-human creature, instinctive and savage, for its beauty, for its stature, for the harmonies dwelling in the magnificent whole; loved by the other, a being of cultivated and ardent imagination, for its signification, its mystic meaning, the symbolic language lurking under the sculpture on its front, like the first text under the second in a *palimpsestus*—in short, for the enigma which it eternally proposes to the understanding.

And, furthermore, it is certain that the archdeacon had fitted himself up in that one of the two towers which looks upon the Grève, close by the cage of the bells, a little cell of great secrecy, into which no one entered—not even the bishop, it was said—without his leave. This cell had been constructed of old, almost at the top of the tower, among the crows' nests, by Bishop Hugo de Besançon,[1] who had played the necromancer there in his time. What this cell contained no one knew. But from the strand of the Terrain at night there was often seen to appear, disappear, and reappear, at short and regular intervals, at a small round window or luthern, that admitted light into it from the back of the tower, a certain red, intermittent, singular glow, seeming as if it followed the successive puffings of a pair of bellows, and as if it proceeded from a flame rather than from a light. In the dark, at that elevation, it had a very odd appearance; and the good women of the neighbourhood used to say, "There's the archdeacon blowing! Hell-fire's casting sparks up there!"

Not that there were, after all, any great proofs of sorcery; but still there was quite as much smoke as was necessary to make the good people suppose a flame, and the archdeacon had a reputation not a little formidable. We are bound to declare, however, that the sciences of Egypt—that necromancy—that magic—even the fairest and most innocent—had no more violent enemy, no more merciless denouncer before messieurs of the officialty of Notre-Dame, than himself. Whether it was a sincere abhorrence, or merely the trick of the robber who cries "Stop thief!" this did not prevent the archdeacon from being considered by the learned heads of the chapter as one who had risked his soul upon the threshold of hell—as one lost in the caverns of the Cabala—feeling his way in the darkness of the occult sciences. Neither were the people blinded to the real state of the case. To the mind of every one possessed of the smallest sagacity Quasimodo was the demon, and Claude Frollo the sorcerer: it was evident that the ringer was to serve the archdeacon for a given time, at the expiration of which he was to carry off his soul by way of payment. So that the archdeacon, despite the excessive austerity of his life, was in bad odour with all pious souls; and there was never a nose of a devotee, however inexperienced, but could smell him for a magician.

And if as he grew older he had formed to himself abysses in science, others had opened themselves in his heart. So, at least, they had reason to believe who narrowly observed that face of his, in which his soul shone forth only through a murky cloud. Whence that large bald forehead—that head constantly bent forward—that breast constantly heaved with sighs? What

[1] "Hugo de Bisuncio." 1326-1332.

secret thought wreathed that bitter smile about his lips, at the same moment that his lowering brows approached each other fierce as two encountering bulls? Why were his remaining hairs already grey? What internal fire was that which occasionally shone in his glance, to such a degree as to make his eye look like a hole pierced through the wall of a furnace?

These symptoms of a violent moral preoccupation had acquired an especially high degree of intensity at the period to which our narrative refers. More than once had a chorister boy fled affrighted at finding him alone in the church, so strange and fiery was his look. More than once in the choir, at service-time, the occupant of the stall next this own had heard him mingle, in the plain chant *ad omnem tonum*, unintelligible parentheses. More than once had the laundress of the Terrain, whose business it was "to wash the chapter," observed, not without dread, marks of finger nails and clenched fingers in the surplice of Monsieur the Archdeacon of Joas.

However, he became doubly rigid, and had never been more exemplary. By character as well as by calling, he had always kept at a distance from women; and now he seemed to hate them more than ever. The mere rustling of a silken *cotte-hardie* brought his hood down over his eyes. On this point so jealous were his austerity and reserve, that when the King's daughter, the Lady of Beaujeu, came in December 1481 to visit the cloister of Notre-Dame, he gravely opposed her entrance, reminding the bishop of the statute in the *Livre Noir*, or Black Book of the chapter, dated St. Bartholomew's Eve, 1344, forbidding access to the cloister to every woman "whatsoever, old or young, mistress or maid." Whereupon the bishop having been constrained to cite to him the ordinance of the legate Odo, which makes an exception in favour of certain ladies of high rank—*aliquæ magnates mulieres, quæ sine scandalo evitari non possunt*—the archdeacon still protested; objecting that the legate's ordinance being dated as far back as the year 1207, was a hundred and twenty-seven years anterior to the Livre Noir, and was consequently, to all intents and purposes, abrogated by it. And accordingly he had refused to make his appearance before the Princess.

It was, moreover, remarked that for some time past his abhorrence of gipsy women and zingari had been redoubled. He had solicited from the bishop an edict expressly forbidding the gipsies from coming to dance and play the tambourine in the Place du Parvis; and for the same length of time he had been rummaging among the mouldy archives of the official, in order to collect together all the cases of wizards and witches condemned to the flames or the halter for having been accomplices in sorcery with he-goats, she-goats, or sows.

CHAPTER VI

UNPOPULARITY

THE archdeacon and the bell-ringer, as we have already stated, were no favourites with either high or low among the dwellers around the cathedral. When, as often happened, Claude and Quasimodo left the building at the same time, and together, the man following the master, traversed the cool, narrow, dark streets that ran between the houses adjoining Notre-Dame, they were assailed with many injurious words, muttered innuendoes, and insulting jests, unless, as was rarely the case, Claude Frollo walked with head erect and awed the scoffers with his austere and almost commanding countenance.

Both men, in their own neighbourhood, were like the poets of whom Regnier writes:—

> " All kinds of people, like the lesser fowl,
> Pursue the poet, as these do the owl."

Now it was a sneaking little brat who risked skin and bones for the ineffable pleasure of sticking a pin into Quasimodo's hump; now a pretty young girl, somewhat livelier and bolder than was becoming, who brushed past the black-gowned priest, singing under his very nose the ironical refrain of " Hide, hide, the devil is caught; " sometimes it was a party of squalid old women squatting side by side on the steps of a shadowy porch, whose voices rose in loud grumblings as the archdeacon and bellringer passed, accosted by their curses and such encouraging remarks as " Hum! there goes one with a soul as misshapen as the other's body; " or it might be a group of students or soldiers playing at hop-scotch, who stood up in a body to give them a classic salutation, flinging some Latin gibe at them, as " *Eia! Eia! Claudius cum Claudo!* "

As a rule the insults passed unheeded by priest and bell-ringer. Quasimodo was too deaf, and Claude too deep in thought to take note of all these courteous greetings.

BOOK V

CHAPTER I

ABBAS BEATI MARTINI

Dom Claude's fame had travelled far. About the time when he refused to see Madame de Beaujeu it procured him a visit of which the remembrance remained with him long after.

It was evening. Service was over, and he had just returned to his canonical cell in the cloister of Notre-Dame. There was nothing unusual or mysterious about this cell, if we except certain glass phials put away in the corner, that were filled with a somewhat suspicious-looking powder, remarkably like powder of projection. There were, it is true, some inscriptions on the walls, but these were merely scientific phrases or pious quotations from well-known authors. The archdeacon had just taken his seat by the light of the copper lamp, with its triple burner, in front of a huge chest piled with manuscripts, his elbow was resting on the open pages of Honorius d'Autun's *De Prædestinatione et libero arbitrio*, and, plunged in thought, he was turning over the pages of a printed folio he had brought in with him, the sole product of the printing-press that stood in his cell. In the midst of his reverie a knock came to the door. "Who is there?" he called, in a tone not more gracious than that of a dog disturbed over his bone. A voice replied from outside, "Your friend, Jacques Coictier." He went to the door and opened it.

It was in fact the king's physician, a man of about fifty years of age, the harshness of whose countenance was only diversified by an expression of cunning. He was accompanied by another man. Both were clad in a long slate-coloured gown, closed down the front and fastened with a belt, their caps being of the same material and colour. Their hands were hidden under their sleeves, their feet under their gowns, and their eyes under their caps. "May God preserve me, gentlemen!" said the archdeacon as he ushered them in, "I did not expect such distinguished visitors at this hour," and as he uttered his courteous phrases his glance wandered anxiously and inquiringly from the physician to his companion.

"It is never too late to call upon so eminent a scholar as Dom Claude Frollo de Tirechappé," replied Doctor Coictier, whose drawling Franche-Comté accent caused his sentences to trail as majestically as a lady's train.

And then the physician and the archdeacon began to exchange the complimentary speeches which at that time were the usual prologue to conversation when two learned men came together, but which did not make them hate one another less cordially. As for that, however, it is just the same nowadays; the lips that utter the compliments of one scholar to another are as a cup of honeyed gall.

The congratulations addressed by Claude Frollo to Jacques Coictier had reference chiefly to the many temporal advantages which the physician in the course of his envied career, knowing how to turn each of the king's maladies to good account, had procured for himself, by means of an alchemy of higher virtue and more to be depended upon than the search for the philosopher's stone.

"In truth, Monsieur Coictier, I was delighted to hear of the bishopric that had fallen to your nephew, my reverend lord Pierre Versé. He is now, I believe, bishop of Amiens?"

"Even so, Archdeacon, by the favour and mercy of God."

"Well, I must confess, you looked a fine figure on Christmas Day at the head of your fellow-officers of the Exchequer, Monsieur President."

"Vice-president, Dom Claude. Alas! nothing more!"

"How is that superb mansion of yours in the Rue Saint André-des-Arcs getting on? It is quite a Louvre. I admire that apricot-tree carved over the door with the lively play of words *a l'abri cotier*."

"Alas, Master Claude, all that stone-work costs me a perfect fortune. As the house rises, I am gradually being ruined."

"But surely you have your fees from the gaol and the palace bailiwick, and the rents from all the houses, booths, stalls, and workshops within the boundary. That's a fine milch-cow."

"My domain of Poissy has brought me in nothing this year."

"But your tolls at Triel, Saint-James, and Saint Germain-en-Laye always pay well."

"A hundred and twenty pounds, and those not even of Paris."

"You have your post as King's Counsellor; that, doubtless, is a permanent one."

"Yes, friend Claude; but that wretched manor of Poligny, which people talk so much about, is not worth sixty gold crowns, taking the bad years with the good."

In the compliments addressed by Dom Claude to Jacques Coictier might be detected the bitter sardonic tone of underlying raillery, the soft cruel smile of the superior and less fortunate man, who finds a passing amusement in playing with the ponderous prosperity of the vulgar.

The other man, however, was quite unconscious of all this.

"On my soul," said Claude at last, pressing the physician's hand, "I am glad to see you in such robust health."

"Thank you, Master Claude."

"By the way," exclaimed Dom Claude, "how fares it with your royal patient?"

"He does not pay enough to his doctor," answered the physician, as he cast a sidelong glance towards his companion.

"Do you think so, friend Coictier?" said the latter.

The tone of surprise and reproach with which these words were uttered drew the attention of the archdeacon to his unknown visitor, although, if truth be told, it had not been wholly diverted from him for a single moment since he crossed the threshold of the cell. He had a thousand reasons for keeping friends with Jacques Coictier, the influential court physician, otherwise he would have been less ready to receive him in such company. He responded therefore with no great cordiality of manner when Jacques Coictier turned and said:—

"By the way, Dom Claude, I have brought a fellow-worker, who, hearing of your fame, wished to make further acquaintance with you."

"Monsieur is interested in science?" asked the archdeacon, fixing a penetrating glance upon Coictier's companion.

He was met by a look no less penetrating and suspicious than his own. As far as the archdeacon could judge by the feeble light of the lamp, the man before him was about sixty years of age, of middle height, and apparently ill and broken in health. The face, though far from aristocratic in outline, held something in it of power and severity; the deep-set eyes flashed out from under the overhanging brows, like a light from the depth of a cave, while under the cap that fell low over the face one was aware of the finely proportioned forehead of a man of genius.

He made answer himself to the archdeacon's question. "Reverend sir," he said gravely, "your fame reached me and

I was anxious to consult you. I am but a poor country gentleman who puts off his shoes before he enters the presence of a learned man. But I must not keep you in ignorance of my name. I am known as Friend Tourangeau."

"A curious name for a gentleman," thought the archdeacon. He was conscious, nevertheless, of a presence of gravity and importance. His own lofty intelligence made him instinctively aware of one not less lofty under the furred cap of Father Tourangeau, and as he looked at the serious figure, the ironical sneer which Coictier's presence had evoked gradually died away from his face, like the low evening light along the horizon. He had reseated himself, silent and melancholy, in his armchair, reassuming his accustomed attitude, his elbow resting on the table, his head on his hand. After remaining thus for some moments in thought, he made a sign to his two visitors to seat themselves, and then turning to Tourangeau:—

"You wish to consult me, sir," he said, "and on what matter of science?"

"Reverend sir," replied Tourangeau, "I am ill, very ill. You are renowned as an Æsculapius, and I have come to ask your advice as a man of medicine."

The archdeacon lifted his head. "Medicine!" he exclaimed. Then, after a minute or two of consideration he continued, "Friend Tourangeau, since that is your name, turn your head, you will find my answer written on the wall."

Friend Tourangeau obeyed, and read the following inscription engraved on the wall above him, "Medicine is the daughter of dreams.—Jamblique."

Doctor Jacques Coictier, meanwhile, had been listening with scorn to his friend's question and the doctor's reply. He now lent forward and whispered to his companion, so as not to be overheard by the archdeacon, "I warned you that the man was mad, but you would insist on seeing him."

"It is possible that this madman, Doctor Jacques, may be in the right after all," replied Tourangeau, in the same low voice, and with a bitter smile.

"Be it as you please," answered Coictier drily. Then turning to the archdeacon, "You are clever at your work, Dom Claude, and Hippocrates offers no more difficulty to you than a nut does to a monkey! Medicine a dream! The herbalists and masters of the profession would hardly be restrained from throwing a stone or two at you were they here. And so you deny the influence of drugs on the blood, and of unguents on the body! You deny the eternal pharmacy of flowers and metals—the world, in short, which has been prepared expressly for that eternal malady we call man!"

"I deny neither the pharmacy nor the malady," said Dom Claude calmly. "I deny the doctor."

"It is not true then," continued Coictier, his anger rising, "that gout is an internal eruption, that a gun wound may be cured by applying a roasted mouse, that age may be rejuvenated by the careful infusion of young blood; it is not true that two and two make four, and that emprostathonos succeeds to opistathanos?"

The archdeacon, who had retained his composure, replied, "There are certain things about which I have my own ideas."

Coictier grew red in the face with fury.

"There, then, my good Coictier, do not let us quarrel," said Tourangeau; "monsieur the archdeacon is our friend."

Coictier grew calmer, only muttering to himself, "After all, he is only a madman!"

"Pasquedieu, Master Claude," continued Tourangeau after a short silence, "you put me out of my reckoning. I came here to consult you on two matters—one was my health, the other my star."

"If that is what you came for, monsieur," replied the archdeacon, "you would have done well to save yourself the fatigue of mounting my stairs. I have no faith in medicine, and I do not believe in astrology."

"Do I hear you aright!" exclaimed Tourangeau in surprise.

Coictier gave a forced laugh.

"You see for yourself now that he is mad," he said in a low voice to his companion. "He does not believe in astrology!"

"The idea of imagining," continued Dom Claude, "that every ray of light from a star is a thread attached to a man's head."

"And what do you believe in then," exclaimed Tourangeau.

There was a moment's pause, then with a sombre smile that seemed to belie his words, the archdeacon replied, "*Credo in Deum.*"

"*Dominum nostrum,*" added Tourangeau, crossing himself.

"Amen," said Coictier.

"Reverend master," Tourangeau went on, "I am delighted at heart to find you so sound in your religion. But is it possible that, learned as you are, you have reached the point when you no longer believe in science?"

"No," said the archdeacon, and as he spoke he grasped Tourangeau's arm, while his sombre eye kindled with a flash of enthusiasm, "no, I do not deny science. I have not gone crawling so long with my face to earth and my nails digging the ground through the innumerable windings of the cave without catching a glimpse of a distant light, a flame, a something at the end of the dark maze, the reflection, no doubt, of that resplendent central laboratory where the patient and the wise have at last detected God."

"And what, then," interrupted Tourangeau, "do you hold as true and certain?"

"Alchemy."

At this Coictier exclaimed, "By my faith, Dom Claude, alchemy no doubt has its claims, but why should you blaspheme medicine and astrology?"

"It is naught, your science of man! Naught, your science of heaven!" said the archdeacon, in a tone of authority.

"You are unsparing towards Epidaurus and Chaldea," answered the doctor, with a sneer.

"Listen, Monsieur Jacques, I speak in all good faith. I am not the king's physician, and his Majesty has not given me the garden of Dædalus that I might have opportunity of studying the constellations—do not get angry but listen to me. What truth has been revealed to you, I do not say by medicine, which is too foolish to mention, but by astrology? Tell me what virtues reside in the vertical boustrophedon, and in the discovery of the numbers ziruph and zephirod?"

"Do you deny the sympathetic power of the clavicle," retorted Coictier, "and that the cabala is derived from it?"

"All a mistake, friend Jacques! None of your formulas lead to any real truth, whereas alchemy has achieved certain discoveries. For instance, can you dispute such results as these? Ice enclosed beneath the earth for a thousand years is transformed into rock crystal. Lead is the progenitor of all other metals, for gold is not a metal, gold is light. Lead passes successively first into the state of red arsenic, then into that of tin, then into that of silver, and that in the course only of four periods of two hundred years each. And these are facts, are they not? But to believe in the clavicle, and in aspects and stars, is as great a folly as to believe with the inhabitants of Grand Cathay that the oriole changes into a mole, and grains of wheat into fishes of the genus cyprinidæ."

"I have studied hermetics," exclaimed Coictier, "and I affirm—"

The impetuous archdeacon did not allow him to finish his sentence. "And I have also studied medicine, astrology, and hermetics. And here alone will you find truth," and as he spoke he took up a small bottle from the chest full of the powder to which we have already referred, "here alone is light! Hippocrates, a dream; Urania, a dream; Hermes, an idea! But gold, gold is the sun! To make gold is to become a god! It is the one sole science! I have probed the value of medicine and astrology, and I tell you it is naught—naught! The human body, a phantom; the stars, shadows!"

He fell back in his chair in an attitude of inspiration. Tourangeau watched him in silence. Coictier gave an obligatory sneer, and with a slight shrug of his shoulders repeated in an undertone, "A madman!"

"And have you attained to that marvellous goal?" broke in Tourangeau. "Have you succeeded in making gold?"

"If I had," replied Claude, bringing his words out slowly, like a man wrapped in thought, "the king of France would call himself Claude, not Louis."

Tourangeau frowned.

"But what am I saying?" continued Dom Claude, smiling disdainfully, "what should I care for the throne of France when I might rebuild the whole empire of the East?"

"What indeed!" said Tourangeau.

"Oh, the poor fool!" murmured Coictier.

But the archdeacon continued, as if making response to his own thoughts only, "But no, I am still crawling. I graze my face and knees against the stones in the subterranean way. I have a glimpse, but no full view! I cannot read, I only spell."

"And when you know how to read," asked the father, "will you then make gold?"

"Who can doubt it?"

"In that case, Notre-Dame knows that I am in great need of money, and I should like to study your books. Tell me, reverend master, is your science in no ways inimical or displeasing to Notre-Dame?"

To this question Dom Claude with quiet hauteur only replied, "Whom I serve as archdeacon?"

"That is true, my master. Well! would you be willing to initiate me into the secret? Let me spell with you."

Claude assumed the majestical and pontifical bearing of a Samuel.

"Old man, more years than remain to you are required for this voyage into the things of mystery. Your head is already grey! and although all leave the cave with whitened hairs, with black alone may one enter. Science knows too well how to furrow, wither, and discolour the human face, and has no need that age should bring her faces ready wrinkled. At the same time if you have so strong a desire to put yourself to school at your age and to learn the formidable alphabet of sages, come to me and I am willing to do my best. I do not tell you, you poor old man, to visit the sepulchral chambers of the Pyramids, of which Herodotus speaks, nor the brick tower of Babel, nor the immense white marble sanctuary of the Indian temple at Eklinga. I have not seen, any more than you have, the stone buildings constructed by the Chaldeans after the sacred model of the Sikra, or Solomon's temple which exists no longer, nor the stone doorways from the sepulchre of the Kings of Israel now broken in pieces. We will content ourselves with the fragments from the book of Hermes which I have here. I will explain to you the statue of S. Christopher, the symbol of the Sower, and that of the two angels that stand at the door of the Sainte-Chapelle, one with his hand in an urn and the other in a cloud—"

But now Jacques Coictier, who had felt baffled by the archdeacon's vehement replies, recovered himself, and with the triumphant tone of a learned man who has caught another tripping, interrupted, calling out, "*Erras, amice Claudi*, symbol is not number. You are mistaking Orpheus for Hermes."

"It is you who are in error," answered the archdeacon composedly. "Dædalus is the base, Orpheus the wall, Hermes the completed edifice—the whole. You can come when you please," he continued, turning to Tourangeau. "I will show you the particles of gold clinging to the bottom of Nicolas Flamel's crucible, and you will compare them with the gold of Guillaume de Paris. I will instruct you in the occult virtues of the Greek word *peristera*. But first of all, I shall make you read, one after the other, the marble letters of the alphabet, the granite pages of the book. We will go from the porch of Bishop William and of Saint-Jean to the Sainte-Chapelle, then to the house of Nicolas Flamel in the Rue Marivaulx, to his court in the Saints-Innocents, to the two hospitals in the Rue de la Ferronnerie. We will spell together the façades of Saint-Côme, of Sainte-Geneviève des Ardents, of Saint-Martin, of Saint-Jacques de la Boucherie—"

Tourangeau, although of so intelligent an aspect, had for some minutes past apparently been unable to follow Dom Claude. He now interrupted the latter:—

"Pasquedieu! and what kind of books are these you are talking about?"

"There is one of them," said the archdeacon. He threw open his cell window and pointed to the vast church of Notre-Dame, the dark outline of its towers, its stone walls, and immense hip-roof silhouetted against the starry sky, and looking like a gigantic sphinx seated in the middle of the town.

The archdeacon stood a while without speaking, contemplating the stupendous edifice. Then with a sigh he pointed with his right hand to the book lying open on the table, and with his left to Notre-Dame, and looking sorrowfully from one to the other, "Alas!" he said, "this will kill that!"

Coictier, who had come forward eagerly to look at the book, could not help an exclamation of surprise. "Well! what is there then so formidable in this? *Glossa in epistolas, D. Pauli. Norimbergae, Antonius Koburger*, 1474. It is not a new book. It is a work by Pierre Lombard, the Master of the Sentences. Is it on account of its being in print?"

"Just so," replied Claude, who was still standing, apparently lost in thought, with his forefinger on the folio from the famous printing-press at Nuremberg. Then he added the mysterious words: "Alas! alas! small things overmaster the great; a tooth destroys a whole body; the Nile-rat kills the crocodile, the sword-fish the whale, and the book will kill the church!"

The curfew rang out just as Doctor Jacques was repeating in a whisper to his companion his eternal refrain, "The man is mad." To which the other replied this time, "I think you are right."

No stranger was allowed to remain in the convent after this hour. The two strangers took their leave.

"Master," said Tourangeau as he bid farewell to the archdeacon, "I admire learning and intellect, and for you I have a particular esteem. Come to-morrow to the Palace des Tournelles and ask for the Abbé of Saint-Martin de Tours."

The archdeacon went back to his cell overcome with astonishment, realising as he now did whom he had been entertaining in the person of Friend Tourangeau, and he recalled the passage in the Cartulary of S. Martin de Tours: *Abbas beati Martini, Scilicet Rex Franciæ, est canonicus de consuetudine et habet parvam præbendam quam habet sanctus Venantius et debet sedere in sede thesaurarii.*

It is stated that from this time forth the archdeacon was frequently in conference with Louis XI. when his Majesty came to Paris, and that Dom Claude's credit threw that of Olivier Le Daim and of Jacques Coictier into the shade, the latter, as was his wont, rating the king soundly on this matter.

CHAPTER II

THIS WILL KILL THAT

OUR readers will pardon us if we pause a moment to discover, if possible, the underlying meaning of the enigmatical words uttered by the archdeacon: This will kill that! The book will kill the church!

To us it seems that the words bear two interpretations. First, there was the thought of the priest, a sacerdotal horror in face of this new factor of printing. It was the terror and amazement of the dweller in the sanctuary at the sight of Gutenberg's light-dispensing press. It was the pulpit and the manuscript, the spoken and the written word, in alarm at the printed word; something similar to the fear a sparrow might feel at beholding the angel Legion spreading his six million wings. It was the cry of the prophet who already detects the sound of the gathering troops of emancipated humanity, who foresees the time when knowledge will sap the foundations of faith, opinion dethrone belief, the world shake off the yoke of Rome. Presage of the philosopher who sees human thought, volatised by the press, and evaporating from the theocratic receiver. Terror of the soldier who inspects the battering-ram and exclaims, "The tower must fall." The words meant that one power was to be superseded by another. They signified, "The printing press will kill the church!"

But underlying this, doubtless the first and simplest idea, there was, we think, a secondary and later one, a corollary of the first, less easily detected and more easily contested, an equally philosophic point of view, but in this case not only that of the priest, but of the scholar and of the artist. It was a presentiment that human thought, in changing its form, would also change its method of expression, that the leading idea of each succeeding generation would no longer be inscribed with the same tools and in the same manner, that the book of stone, so solid and lasting, would give place to the book of paper, more solid and more lasting still. Looked at in this connection, the vague formula of the archdeacon had a further meaning; it signified that one art was on the eve of dethroning another. What it wished to say was, "Printing will kill architecture!"

From the beginning of time to the fifteenth century of the Christian era, architecture was, in truth, the great book of humanity, the chief expression of man in his various stages of development, whether as a physical or an intellectual power.

When the memory of the early races became overcharged, when the store of remembered things grew so weighty and confused that the bare, flying verbal record risked losing part of it upon the way, man began to transcribe his recollections in the manner that at the same time was the clearest, most durable and natural. Every tradition was sealed beneath a monument.

The earliest monuments were mere portions of rocks "which the iron had not touched," says Moses. Architecture began like all writing. There was first the alphabet. A stone was set up, and that was a letter, and every letter was a hieroglyph, and every hieroglyph supported a group of ideas, which were like the capital to the pillars. And similarly, and at the same moment, did all the early races over the whole surface of the world. The Celtic "Cromlech" is found in Asiatic Siberia and the pampas of America.

Later on words began to be formed. One stone was placed above another, the granite syllables were linked together, and the best attempted certain combinations. The Celtic dolmen and cromlech, the Etruscan tumulus, the Hebrew galgal, are words. Some of them, especially the tumulus, are proper names. Occasionally, when there was plenty of stone and a wide area, a whole sentence was constructed. The immense pile at Karnac is a complete formula.

At last we come to books. Old traditions had given birth to symbols, under which they themselves disappeared as the trunk of a tree behind its foliage; and all these symbols, in which men placed their faith, were continually growing and multiplying and crossing one another, becoming more and more complicated; the early monuments were no longer capable of holding them; they were overflowing in every direction; they were hardly equal to expressing even the primitive tradition, as simple, unadorned, and bound to the soil as they were themselves. It was imperative that symbolism should expand into an edifice. Architecture thus developed side by side with human thought, growing into a giant of a thousand heads and a thousand arms, and all this floating symbolism became fixed in an eternal, visible, and palpable form. While Dædalus, who stands for force, was measuring, while Orpheus, who stands for intellect, was singing, the pillar, representing the letter, the arcade, representing the syllable, and the pyramid, the word, simultaneously set in motion by a law of geometry and a law of poetry, were grouping, combining, and amalgamating with one another, descending, rising, meeting in juxtaposition on the ground, mounting in stages towards the sky, until, under the dictate of the ruling idea of the period, they had written those marvellous books which are equally marvellous edifices: the Pagoda of Eklinga, the Rhamseion of Egypt, the Temple of Solomon.

The word, the principal idea, not only served as a base for all these edifices, it was embodied in their form. The temple of Solomon, for instance, was not merely the binding of the Word of God, it was the Word of God itself. On each of its concentric walls the priests could read the translated Word set forth in plain letters before their eyes, and they followed its transformations from sanctuary to sanctuary until, having reached the last, they discerned it under its most concrete form—also an architectural one—the arch. The Word was thus enshrined in the building, but its image was seen on the surrounding walls, as the human figure on the case of a mummy.

And the site chosen for these edifices revealed the idea which they represented as truly as their form. According as the creed to be expressed was cheerful or gloomy, Greece crowned her mountains with gracefully proportioned temples, delightful to the eye, or India excavated her rocks in order to carve therein her monstrous subterranean pagodas, supported by gigantic rows of granite elephants.

During the first six thousand years of the world's existence, from the immemorial date of the earliest Hindoo pagoda to that of Cologne cathedral, architecture was therefore the chief writing of the human race. And so true is this, that not only every religious symbol, but every human thought finds a page in this vast monumental book.

Every civilisation starts with theocracy and ends in democracy. This law of liberty succeeding to unity is found written in architecture. And here let us pause to lay stress on this point, that the mason's work is not limited in power to the mere erection of the temple, to giving expression to myth and priestly symbolism, to transcribing the mysterious tables of the law in hieroglyphic language on the pages of stone. Were it so, then, as happens in all human society, when the moment came that some sacred creed was worn out and obliterated by free thought, that the man had escaped from the priest, or that the excrescences of philosophies and systems had eaten away the face of religion, architecture would be incapable of reproducing this new state of the human mind, and its leaves, written on the right side, would be blank at the back, the work would be mutilated, the book incomplete. But it is not so.

Let us take for example the Middle Ages, where, being nearer to us, we obtain a clearer view. During the earlier mediæval period, when theocracy was organising Europe, when the Vatican was rallying and reclassing around it the elements of a Rome built up from the Rome which lay in ruins around the Capitol, when Christianity was searching for relics of the past stages of society among the rubbish that remained of a former civilisation, and using these remnants for the erection of a new hierarchical universe of which sacerdotalism was to be the keystone of the arch, we hear the first trickling sound among the chaos, and then, little by little, under the inspiration of Christianity and by barbarian hands, we see arising from the ruined mass of Greek and Roman architectures that mysterious Roman architecture, the sister to the theocratic stonework of Egypt and India, the inalterable emblem of pure Catholicism, the immutable hieroglyph of papal unity. The dominant idea of that age is in truth written in that gloomy Roman style. One is conscious on all sides of authority, of unity, of the impenetrable, the absolute, of Gregory VII.; the priest everywhere, the man nowhere; everywhere a caste, the people nowhere. Then the Crusades are started. It is a grand popular movement, and a popular movement, whatever its cause or aim, frees the spirit of liberty from its final precipitate. New ideas come to the surface. The stormy period of the Jacqueries, the Pragueries, and Leagues. Authority is tottering, unity is bifurcated. Feudality insists on equal shares with theocracy, waiting for the people who will assuredly arrive unexpectedly upon the spot, and, as usual, will play the part of the lion: *quia nominor leo*. The nobles undermine the priesthood, and the commune the nobles. The face of Europe is changed. Look, and you will see the face of architecture changed also. In company with civilisation she has turned the page, and the newly-awakened spirit of the times finds her ready to write at its dictation. She has returned from the Crusades with the pointed arch, as the nations with their liberty. As Rome gradually becomes dismembered, Roman architecture decays. The hieroglyphs forsake the cathedral, and henceforth emblazon the dungeon in order to procure prestige for feudality. The cathedral itself, once so dogmatic an edifice, but now invaded by the citizens, by the populace, by liberty, escapes out of the hand of the priest and falls into the power of the artist. The artist builds according to his taste. Good-bye to mystery, to myth, to law. Now we have fancy and caprice. Provided that the priest has his basilica and his altar, he can say nothing. The four walls belong to the artist. The architectural book is no longer the property of the priest, of religion, of Rome; its owners now are imagination, poetry, the people. Hence the rapid and innumerable changes undergone by this style of architecture that counts only three centuries of existence, so striking in contrast to the stagnant immobility of Roman architecture that had lasted for six or seven. Art, however, advances with giant strides. The genius and originality of the people do the work formerly undertaken by the bishops. Every generation as it passes adds a line to the book, it erases the ancient Roman hieroglyphics on the frontispieces of the cathedrals, and it is as much as dogma can do to pierce here and there through the new symbols that overlie it. The skeleton of religion is hardly to be guessed at under the popular garment. No idea can be had of the licence which the architects now allowed themselves even in regard to the church. Here we see capitals intertwined with figures of monks and nuns in disgraceful association, as in the Salle des Cheminées of the Palais de Justice in Paris, and here Noah's misadventure sculptured literally on the main porch at Bourges. Or it is a convivial monk with donkey's ears, a drinking-glass in his hand, laughing in the face of the whole community, as in the lavatory of the Abbey de Bocherville. The licence granted in those days to the writing in stone may be compared to the liberty of the press at the present time. It was the liberty of architecture.

And it was carried to great lengths. Sometimes a porch, or a façade, or an entire church lacked all trace of religion in its symbolism; at times this was even hostile to the church. We find such seditious pages from the hand of Guillaume de Paris in the thirteenth century, and of Nicolas Flamel in the fifteenth. Saint Jacques de la Boucherie was, from roof to floor, an opposition church.

In this way only was thought free in those days, nor could it find full expression except in these books under the form of buildings. Under the form of manuscript, had any one been imprudent enough to run the risk, it would have been publicly burnt by the executioner. The thought-inscribed portal of the church would have assisted at the execution of free thought under another guise. Having therefore no outlet but that of architecture, thought from all sides precipitated itself in this direction. Hence the prodigious number of cathedrals all over Europe, almost incredible even after verifying it. All the material and intellectual forces of society converged to the same point—architecture. Thus art, under pretext of raising churches to God, developed along magnificent lines.

In those days if a man was born a poet he turned architect. Genius scattered among the masses, kept down on all sides by feudality, as under a *testudo* of brazen shields, and finding no other point of issue, escaped by way of architecture, and its Iliads took the form of cathedrals. All the other arts became obedient, and submitted to its authority. They were the artisans of the great work. The architect, the poet, the master summed up in his own person the sculpture that ornamented his façades, the painting that illuminated his windows, the music that set his bells ringing and breathed through his organ. Even poor poetry, properly so called, that continued obstinately to vegetate in manuscripts, was obliged, in order to be known, to insert itself in the building in the shape of hymn or *prose*; the same part, after all, which was played by the tragedies of Æschylus at the religious festivals of Greece, and by the Genesis in the temple of Solomon.

Architecture was, therefore, up to the time of Gutenberg, the chief and universal mode of writing. The Middle Ages wrote the last page of this granite volume, which had been begun in the East, and continued by ancient Greece and Rome. Moreover, the phenomenon we have mentioned of a popular architecture succeeding to an architecture of caste in the Middle Ages, reappears with every analogous movement of human intelligence at other critical epochs of history. To sum up a law which would require volumes for its development; in the East, the cradle of the world, after Hindoo architecture came the Phœnician, the opulent mother of Arabian architecture; in later antiquity, Egyptian architecture, of which the Etruscan style and the Cyclopean monuments were but variants, was followed by Greek architecture, the Roman being but a continuation of this over-weighted with the Carthaginian dome; in modern times Roman architecture was succeeded by the Gothic, and if we separate these three series we shall find on the three elder sisters, the Hindoo, Egyptian, and Roman architectures, the same symbolic creed — theocracy, caste, unity, dogma, myth, God; while the three younger sisters, Phœnician, Greek, and Gothic architecture, whatever variety may be inherent in their style, bear a similar significance—liberty, the people, man.

Under whatever name he appears—Brahmin, Magian, or Pope, in Hindoo, Egyptian, or Roman edifices, one is perpetually conscious of the priest and nothing but the priest. It is not so with the architecture of the masses. It is less rich and less saintly. In the Phœnician we recognise the merchant; in the Greek, the republican; in the Gothic, the citizen.

The general characteristics of all theocratic architecture are immutability, dread of progress, preservation of tradition, consecration of primitive types, and the continual adaptation of all human and natural forms to the incomprehensible caprices of symbolism. They are obscure books that the initiated alone know how to decipher. Moreover, every outline, every deformity even, has a meaning which renders it inviolable. Do not ask of the Hindoo, Egyptian, and Roman masons to correct their drawing or amend their statuary. Every attempt at improvement is to them an act of impiety. The rigidity of dogma appears diffused over the stones of these buildings like a second petrification. The general characteristics of popular architecture are, on the contrary, variety, progress, originality, opulence, perpetual motion. They are sufficiently detached from religion to give thought to their beauty, and to cherish it, and to make continual efforts towards improving their rich garment of statuary and arabesques. They belong to their age. There is a feeling of humanity about them mingled with the divine symbolism which still inspires the workman's hand. And so we have edifices that appeal to every soul, intelligence, and imagination, symbolical still, but as easy to understand as nature. Between theocratic architecture and this there is the difference between sacred language and the vulgar tongue, between hieroglyphics and art, between Solomon and Pheidias.

Omitting the detailing of a thousand proofs, and a thousand objections to what has been said, we may sum the matter up as follows:—That architecture, up to the fifteenth century, was the chief register of humanity; that during this interval, no thought of any complexity appeared in the world that was not built into an edifice; that every popular idea, as well as every religious commandment, had its monument; that human nature, in short, had no thought of importance that it did not write in stone. And why? because every idea, whether religious or philosophic, is concerned in being perpetuated. The idea that has stirred the emotions of one generation desires to affect others, and to leave its trace behind. And the immortality of the manuscript, how precarious it is! An edifice is a book of very different solidity, durable and resisting. To destroy the written word, we only want a torch and a Turk. To demolish the constructed word requires a social revolution, or a terrestrial upheaval. The barbarians passed over the coliseum, the deluge perhaps over the Pyramids.

In the fifteenth century, everything underwent a change. Humanity discovered a means of perpetuating thought more lasting and durable than architecture, and even simpler and easier. Architecture was dethroned. To the stone letters of Orpheus are to succeed Gutenberg's letters of lead.

The book will destroy the building!

The invention of printing is the greatest event in history. It was the supreme revolution. It meant the complete renovation of humanity's mode of expression, the discarding by human thought of one form to reclothe itself in another, the complete and final casting of the skin of that symbolic serpent, which, since Adam, had served as the representation of intellect.

In the form of print, thought becomes more imperishable than ever; it is winged, intangible, indestructible. It mingles with the air. In the days of architecture it transformed itself into a mass of stone, and took forcible possession of an age and place. Now it is turned into a flock of birds, winging its way in all directions, and occupying at the same time every corner of air and space.

Who will not acknowledge that in this way thought has become more indelible? As it was once immovable it is now long-lived; it has passed from durability to immortality. A solid mass may be demolished, but what can extirpate ubiquity? Let a flood arise, the birds will still be flying in the air long after the mountain has disappeared beneath the waters; if but a single arch floats above the surface of the destroying deluge, they will perch upon it, swim along with it, look on with it at the subsiding of the waters, and the new world which arises from the chaos will awaken to see, hovering above it, winged and alive, the thought of the world that has been engulfed.

And if we see that this method of expression is not only the most preservative, but at the same time the simplest, most convenient, and most practicable, and further, take into account that it carries with it no heavy luggage and requires no cumbrous paraphernalia; if, again, we compare the thought that, in order to translate itself into stone, has to set four or five other arts at work, and needs tons of money, a whole mountain of stone, a whole forest of beams, a whole nation of workpeople; if, I repeat, we compare this thought with the thought that finds its medium of expression in a book, for which a little paper and a little ink and a pen are sufficient, can we be surprised that the human intellect forsook architecture for printing? If you suddenly cut a canal through the original bed of a river below its level, the river will forsake its bed.

From the moment, therefore, that printing was discovered, architecture gradually lost its vitality, declined, and became denuded. Do we not feel the waters slowly sinking, the sap of life failing, the thought of the time and of the people withdrawing from it? The change was hardly perceptible in the fifteenth century, the press as yet was feeble, and at the most only drew off some of the superfluous life from architecture, which was still a power. In the sixteenth century, however, architecture begins to show signs of its disease; it no longer represents the essential tone of society; it adopts a degraded classic style; its Gallic, European, and native art now becomes Greek and Roman, a mixture of ancient and modern, pseudo-antique. To this decadence we give the name of Renaissance. A magnificent decadence, nevertheless, for the ancient Gothic genius, the sun that sank behind the gigantic press of Mainz, still shed a few last rays on the hybrid conglomeration of Roman arcades and Corinthian columns.

It was this sinking sun which men mistook for the dawn.

Architecture, having fallen to the level of the other arts, and being no longer looked upon as the one all-embracing, sovereign, and enslaving art, lost its power of retaining others in its service. These, therefore, rebelled, threw off the yoke of architecture, and went every one its own way. Each of them benefited by this divorce. Everything grows grander in isolation. Carving became sculpture; imagery, painting; the canon, music. It was like the dismemberment of an empire on the death of its Alexander—each province making itself a kingdom.

And so we have Raphael, Michael Angelo, Jean Goujon, Palestrina—these glories of the resplendent sixteenth century.

With the arts, thought also threw off its shackles. The heresiarchs of the Middle Ages had already made large inroads on Catholicism. The sixteenth century shattered the unity of the Church. Before the advent of printing, reform was only a schism; printing made it a revolution. Take away the press, and heresy grows enervated. Whether fatal or providential, the fact remains that Gutenberg was the forerunner of Luther.

When the sun of the Middle Ages had finally set, when Gothic genius had faded for ever from the horizon of art, architecture grew more colourless and lifeless, gradually sinking into oblivion. That gnawing canker-fly, the printed book, sucks the life-blood out of the great stone pile. Its leaves fall, it grows visibly barer. It has grown mean, poor, worthless. It expresses nothing, not even the memory of the art of a former day. Architecture left to itself, forsaken by the other arts since human thought has abandoned it, calls in artisans instead of artists to its aid. Plain glass replaces the coloured windows; the stone-cutter takes the place of the sculptor. Farewell to vigour, originality, life, and intellect. It drags itself along, pitiable beggar of the studios, from one model to another. Michael Angelo, who could, even in the sixteenth century, detect its moribund condition, had one last desperate idea. This Titan of art heaped Pantheon on Parthenon, and gave Rome its St. Peter's—a mighty work which deserved to remain unique, the last original inspiration of architecture, the signature of a colossal artist at the foot of the gigantic register of stone which was now closed. Michael Angelo dead, what did this miserable architecture that had outlived itself and lingered only as a spectral shadow do then? It took St. Peter's, copied, and parodied it. It was a mania, and a deplorable one. Every age has its St. Peter; the seventeenth the Val-de-Grace, the eighteenth Sainte-Geneviève. Every country has its St. Peter. London has one, and St. Petersburg. Paris has two or three. A worthless legacy of a decrepit art fallen into a second childhood before its death.

If we turn from characteristic monuments, such as those of which we have been speaking, and examine more closely the general art of the period extending from the sixteenth to the eighteenth, we notice the same phenomena of decline and decay.

From the time of Francis II., the architectural form of the edifice is lost sight of more and more, and the geometrical form becomes prominent, like the bony structure of an emaciated invalid. The beautiful lines of art give place to the inexorable lines of geometry. An edifice is no longer an edifice, it is a polyhedron. Architecture strives, however, to conceal its nudity. Here is the Greek pediment inscribing itself in the Roman pediment, and the Roman doing the same by the Greek. Everywhere we see the Pantheon combined with the Parthenon, St. Peter's at Rome. See, for instance, the brick houses of Henry IV.'s time with their stone cornerpieces; the Place Royale, the Place Dauphine. And then again the churches of Louis XIII.'s time, heavy, squat, surbased, thick-set, with a dome like a hump on the top. Or the Mazarin architecture, the degraded Italian pistaccio of the four nations. See further the palaces of Louis XIV., long court barracks, stiff, cold, and dull. Then we come to Louis XV., wth the chicory and vermicelli, and all the warts and fungi which disfigure this old, decaying, toothless, and coquettish architecture. The evil has increased by geometrical progression during the period that has elapsed between Francis II. and Louis XV. Art has hardly any skin left on its bones. It is dying a miserable death.

Meanwhile, what has become of printing? All the life slowly drained from architecture has been absorbed by it. As architecture sinks, printing rises and flourishes. The capital of forces, which human thought had hitherto spent on edifices, it henceforth spends on books. And so with the sixteenth century begins the struggle between the printing-press, which stood now on a level with its opponent, and architecture, and the latter falls. In the seventeenth century the printing-press has attained to such sovereignty and triumph, and is so assured of her victory that she can treat the world to a grand century of literature. In the eighteenth, after a long season of repose at Louis XIV.'s court, it once more seizes Luther's old sword, puts it in Voltaire's hand, and rushes tumultuously to the attack of the same old Europe whose architectural expression it had already destroyed. By the close of the eighteenth century it had annihilated everything. The work of reconstruction will be its task in the nineteenth.

And now we may pause to ask which of these two arts have actually represented human thought during the last three centuries? Which has faithfully transcribed it? Which has given expression, not only to literary and scholastic vagaries, but to the whole vast, profound, universal spirit of life? Which of the two, without break or intermission, has superposed itself on the human race—that monster of a thousand feet, for ever pressing forward?

Architecture or Printing?

Printing. Do not let us deceive ourselves. Architecture is dead, dead beyond recall, slain by the printed book, slain because it was less durable, slain because it cost too much. Every cathedral represents a milliard. Think of the sums it would take to rewrite that book of stone, to rebuild so that the earth might swarm again with its millions of edifices, to return to those ages when the mass of monuments was such that, as an eye-witness writes, "One might think that the earth had shaken off its old garments in order to clothe itself in a white vesture of churches." *Erat enim ut si mundus, ipse excutiendo semet, rejecta octustate, candidam ecclesiarum vestem indueret.* (Glaber Radulphus.)

A book is so soon finished, costs so little, and can travel so far! What wonder that human thought flows readily along this channel? Not that architecture will be henceforth incapable of producing a fine work now and then, an isolated masterpiece. No doubt from time to time it will be still possible, under the reign of printing, to have a column of molten cannon set up by a whole army, as under that of architecture we had Iliads and Romanceros, the Mahabâhrata and the Nibelungen, composed by a whole people from mingled stores of rhapsodies. The splendid chance of an architect of genius suddenly appearing in the twentieth century might occur, as that of Dante in the thirteenth. But architecture can never again be the art *par excellence,* social, collective, supreme. The great poem, the great edifice, the great work of humanity will not be a matter of building but of printing.

Moreover, if architecture should by chance undergo revival, it will not again have undivided power. It will have to submit to the law which it gave itself to literature. The position of the two arts will be reversed. During the architectural period, poems, which were rare it is true, resembled monuments. In India, Vyasa is as multifarious, strange, and impenetrable as a pagoda. In Egypt, poetry, like the buildings, is majestic and composed in outline; in ancient Greece, it has beauty, serenity, calm; in Christian Europe, religious majesty, homely simplicity, the rich and luxuriant vegetation of an age of renewal. The Bible may be compared to the Pyramids, the Iliad to the Parthenon, Homer to Pheidias. Dante, in the thirteenth century, is the last Romanesque church; Shakespeare, in the sixteenth, the last Gothic cathedral.

To sum up this unavoidably brief and imperfect sketch—the human race has had two books, two registers, two testaments—architecture and printing, the Bible of stone and the Bible of paper. As we contemplate these two Bibles, lying open for us through the centuries, we may be allowed perhaps to regret the visible majesty of the granite writing, those colossal alphabets composed of colonnades, pylons, and obelisques, those, as it were, human mountains which have covered the face of the earth from ages past, from the pyramid to the steeple, from Cheops to Strasburg. The past should be studied on these marble pages; as we turn the leaves of the architectural book we cannot cease to admire, but for all that we must not deny the grandeur of the edifice erected in its turn by printing. And this edifice is immense. Some maker of statistics, I do not know who, has calculated that if all the books that have been issued from the press since Gutenberg were placed one above the other, they would reach to the moon; but it is not of this kind of grandeur we wish to speak. And yet if we try to form a mental image of the whole product of printing up to our own time, does not it seem to us like an enormous construction, based on the whole world, at which humanity labours without relaxation, and of which the gigantic summit is lost in the dark mists of futurity? It is the ant-hill of intellect. The hive where all fancy and imagination, those golden bees, store up their honey. The edifice rises in a thousand stories. Within, it is intersected with obscure caves of science, opening here and there upon its stairway. The eye may luxuriate in the arabesques, rose-windows, and lace-work on its outer walls. Every individual work, however fantastic and isolated it may appear, has its niche in that building. The result of the whole is harmony. From the cathedral of Shakespeare to the mosque of Byron, a thousand turrets cluster promiscuously about this metropolis of universal thought. At its base, certain old titles of humanity have been rewritten which architecture had failed to register. To the left of the entrance a seal has been placed in the ancient white marble bas-relief of Homer, to the right the polyglot Bible rears its seven heads, and a little farther on the hydra of romance is seen with other hybrid forms, the Vedas and the Nibelungen. Moreover, the prodigious edifice remains still unfinished. That gigantic machine, the printing-press, is for ever pumping in all the intellectual sap of society, and for ever vomiting fresh materials for its work. The whole human race is at work on the scaffolding. Every mind is a mason. The humblest stops his hole or lays his brick. Rétif de la Bretonne brings his hod of cement. Every day a fresh course is laid. Independent of the original and separate contributions of the several writers, there are collective supplies. The eighteenth century provides the Encyclopædia, the Revolution its Moniteur. It is, in fact, a construction that gathers bulk and height from infinity of spirals; here also is there confusion of tongues, incessant labour, indefatigable industry, a frantic concourse of struggling humanity; and here, too, the promised refuge for the human intellect against another deluge, another submersive inroad of barbarians. It is the second Tower of Babel of the human race.

BOOK VI

CHAPTER I

AN IMPARTIAL VIEW OF THE OLD MAGISTRACY

A RIGHT enviable personage, in the year of grace 1482, was *noble homme* Robert d'Estouteville, Knight, Sieur of Beyne, Baron of Ivry and St. Andry in Marche, councillor and chamberlain to the King, and keeper of the provostry of Paris. Already it was nearly seventeen years since he had received from King Louis, on the 7th of November 1465, the year of the comet,[1] that fine place of Provost of Paris, which was regarded rather as a *seigneurie* than as an office. *Dignitas,* says Joannes Lœmnœus, *quæ cum non exiguâ potestate politiam concernente, atque prærogativis multis et juribus conjuncta est.* It was a thing quite marvellous that in the year '82 there should be a gentleman holding the king's commission, whose letters of institution were dated as far back as the time of the marriage of Louis XI.'s natural daughter with Monsieur the Bastard of Bourbon. On the same day that Robert d'Estouteville had taken the place of Jacques de Villiers in the provostry of Paris, Maître Jean Dauvet succeeded Messire Hélye de Thorrettes in the first presidency of the court of Parliament, Jean Jouvenal des Ursins supplanted Pierre de Morvilliers in the office of Chancellor of France, and Regnault des Dormans relieved Pierre Puy of the post of Master of Requests-in-ordinary to the King's household. Now, over how many heads had the presidency, the chancellorship, and the mastership travelled since Robert d'Estouteville had held the provostry of Paris? It had been "granted into his keeping," said the letters patent; and certainly he kept it well. He had clung to it, incorporated himself, identified himself with it so thoroughly, that he had escaped that rage for changes which possessed Louis XI., a distrustful, parsimonious, and laborious king, bent upon maintaining, by frequent appointments and dismissals, the elasticity of his power. Nay, more—the worthy chevalier had procured the reversion of his office for

[1] This comet, against which Pope Calixtus ordered public prayers, is the same which is to reappear in 1835.

his son; and already, for two years, had the name of *noble homme* Jacques d'Estouteville, Esquire, figured at full length beside his own at the head of the register of the ordinary of the provostry of Paris—a rare, assuredly, and signal favour! True it is that Robert d'Estouteville was a good soldier; that he had loyally lifted his pennon against "the league of the public weal;" and that he had made a present to the Queen, on the day of her entry into Paris in the year 14—, of a very wonderful stag, all made of confectionery. And, moreover, he had a good friend in Messire Tristan l'Hermite, provost-marshal of the King's household. So that Messire Robert enjoyed a very comfortable and agreeable existence. First of all, he had a very good salary, to which were attached, depending like so many additional bunches from his vine, the revenues of the registries, civil and criminal, of the provostry; then the revenues of the Auditoires d'Embas, or inferior courts, of the Châtelet; besides some little toll from the bridges of Mante and Corbeil, and the profits of the *tru* on the *esgrin* of Paris, and on the measures of firewood and the metres of salt. Add to all this the pleasure of displaying, in his official rides through the town, in contrast with the gowns, half red and half tawny, of the échevins and the *quarteniers*, his fine military dress, which you may still admire sculptured upon his tomb at the Abbey of Valmont in Normandy, as you may his richly-embossed morion at Montlhéry. And then, was it nothing to have all supremacy over the sergeants of the *douzaine*, the keeper and the watcher of the Châtelet (*auditores Castelleti*), the sixteen commissioners of the sixteen quarters of the city, the jailer of the Châtelet, the four enfeoffed sergeants, the hundred and twenty mounted sergeants, the hundred and twenty sergeants of the wands, and the knight of the watch, with his men of the watch, the under-watch, the counter-watch, and the rear-watch? Was it nothing to exercise high and low justice, the right of turning, hanging, and drawing, besides the jurisdiction over minor offences in the first resort (*in prima instantia*, as the charters have it) over that viscounty of Paris, to which were so gloriously appended seven noble bailiwicks? Can anything be imagined more gratifying than to pass judgment and sentence, as Messire Robert d'Estouteville daily did in the Grand Châtelet, under the wide, depressed Gothic arches of Philip-Augustus; and to go, as was his wont, every evening to that charming house situated in the Rue Galilée, within the precincts of the Palais-Royal, which he held in right of his wife, Madame Ambroise de

Loré, to repose from the fatigue of having sent some poor devil to pass his night in " that small cage in the Rue de l'Escorcherie, which the provosts and échevins of Paris were wont to make their prison, the dimensions of the same being eleven feet in length, seven feet four inches in width, and eleven feet in height?"[1]

And not only had Messire Robert d'Estouteville his particular justice as provost and viscount of Paris, but also he had his share, both by presence and action, in the *grande justice* of the King. There was no head of any elevated rank but had passed through his hands before it came into those of the executioner. It was he who had gone to the Bastille St. Antoine to fetch Monsieur de Nemours from thence to the Halles; and to the same place to carry from thence to the Grève Monsieur de St. Pol, who grumbled and complained, to the great joy of Monsieur the Provost, who was no friend to Monsieur the Constable.

Here assuredly was more than enough to make a man's life illustrious and happy, and to earn some day a notable page in that interesting history of the provosts of Paris, from which we learn that Oudard de Villeneuve had a house in the Rue des Boucheries, that Guillaume de Hangest bought the great and the little Savoie, that Guillaume Thiboust gave his houses in the Rue Clopin to the nuns of Ste. Geneviève, that Hugues Aubriot lived in the Hôtel du Porc-Epic—with other facts of the like importance.

And yet, with all these reasons for taking life patiently and cheerfully, Messire Robert d'Estouteville had awoken on the morning of the 7th January 1482 very sulky—quite, indeed, in a *massacring* humour—though for what cause he himself could not well have told. Was it because the sky was dingy? or because the buckle of his old Montlhéry sword-belt was ill fastened, and girded too militarily his provost-beseeming portliness? or because he had seen the army of ribalds marching through the street, four by four, under his window, jeering at him as they passed by, in doublets without shirts, under hats with their crowns out, and scrip and bottle at their sides? Was it a vague presentiment of the three hundred and seventy livres sixteen sols eight deniers which the future king, Charles VIII., was to deduct the following year from the revenues of the provostry? Among these reasons the reader is at liberty to choose; for our own parts, we are much inclined to believe that he was in an ill humour simply because he was in an ill humour.

[1] Compte du domaine, 1383.

Besides, it was the day after a holiday—a day of disgust for everybody, and especially for the magistrate whose business it was to sweep away all the filth, whether in the literal or the figurative sense of the word, that a holiday accumulated in Paris. And then he was to hold a sitting in the Grand Châtelet; and the reader will probably have remarked that judges in general contrive matters so that their day of sitting shall also be their day of ill-humour, in order that they may always have some one upon whom to vent it conveniently, in the name of the king and the law.

The magisterial operations, however, had commenced without him. His deputies, *au civil, au criminel,* and *au particulier* were acting for him, according to custom; and as early as eight o'clock in the morning some scores of townspeople, men and women, crowded together in a dark corner of the Auditoire d'Embas of the Châtelet, between the wall and a strong barrier of oak, were blissfully attending at the varied and exhilarating spectacle of the administration of civil and criminal justice by Maître Florian Barbedienne, auditor at the Châtelet, deputy of Monsieur the Provost—a little pell-mell, to be sure, and altogether at random.

The room was small, low, and vaulted. At the farther end was a table, figured over with fleur-de-lis, with a great arm-chair of carved oak for the provost, which was empty, and on the left hand of it a stool for the auditor, Maître Florian. Below sat the registrar, scribbling away. In front were the people; and before the door, and before the table, were a number of sergeants of the provostry in their violet hacquetons with white crosses upon them. Two sergeants of the Parloir-aux-Bourgeois, or Common-hall, in jackets half red and half blue, stood sentry before a low closed door, which was visible at the other end, behind the table. One solitary pointed window, straitly encased in the massive wall, threw a few pale January rays upon two grotesque countenances—that of the fantastic demon carved upon the keystone of the vaulted ceiling, and that of the judge, seated at the extremity of the chamber, upon the fleur-de-lis.

Indeed, figure to yourself, at the prevotal table, between two bundles of cases—leaning upon his elbows, with his foot upon the tail of his gown of plain brown cloth, and his face in its lining of white lambskin, with which his brows seemed to be of a piece—red-faced—harsh-looking—winking—carrying majestically the load of flesh upon his cheeks, which met from either side under his chin—Maître Florian Barbedienne, auditor at the Châtelet.

Now the auditor was deaf—a slight defect for an auditor; and Maître Florian did not the less decide without appeal, and quite competently. It is certainly quite sufficient that a judge should appear to listen; and the venerable auditor the better fulfilled this condition, the only one essential to the good administration of justice, as his attention could not possibly be distracted by any noise.

However, there was among the audience a merciless censor of his deeds and gestures, in the person of our friend Jehan Frollo du Moulin, the little scholar of the day before—that stroller who was sure to be met with everywhere in Paris, except before the professor's chair.

"Look," said he to his companion Robin Poussepain, who was tittering beside him while he commented on the scenes that were passing before them, "there's Jehanneton du Buisson, the pretty girl at the Cagnard-au-Marché-Neuf! On my soul, he's condemning her—the old fellow! Then he's no more eyes than ears! Fifteen sous four deniers parisis for wearing two strings of beads—that's rather dear. *Lex duri carminis*. Who's that? Robin Chief-de-Ville, hauberk-maker, for being passed and admitted a master in the said art and mystery. It's his entrance-money. Ah, what! two gentlemen among these rascals—Aiglet de Soins, Hutin de Mailly—two esquires!—*Corpus Christi!*—Oh, they've been playing at dice. When shall we see our rector here, I wonder? Fined a hundred livres parisis to the King! Barbedienne hits like a deaf man as he is! May I be my brother the archdeacon if that shall hinder me from playing by day, playing by night, living at play, dying at play, and staking my soul when I've lost my shirt! Holy Virgin! what lots of girls!—one after another, my lambs. Ambroise Lécuyère! Isabeau-la-Paynette! Berarde Gironin!—I know them all, *par Dieu!* Fine them! fine them! We'll teach you to wear gilt belts! Ten sols parisis apiece, you coquettes! Oh, the old muzzle of a judge, deaf and doting! O Florian the lubber! O Barbedienne the dolt! There you see him at table—he dines off the pleader—he dines off the case—he eats—he chews—he swallows—he fills himself!—Fines, estrays, dues, expenses, costs, wages, damages, torture, jail and stocks, are to him Christmas camichons and midsummer marchpanes. Look at him, the pig! Go on. Good again!—another amorous lady—Thibaude-la-Thibaude, I declare—for going out of the

Rue Glatigny. What's this youth? Gieffroy Mabonne, gendarme bearing the crossbow—he's been profaning the name of the Father. A fine for La Thibaude! a fine for Gieffroy! a fine for them both! The old deaf boy! he must have jumbled the two things together. Ten to one but he makes the girl pay for the oath and the gendarme for the amour! Attention, Robin Poussepain! What are they bringing in now? Here are plenty of sergeants, by Jupiter—all the hounds of the pack. This must be the grand piece of game of all—a wild boar at least! It is one, Robin—it is one, and a fine one too! *Hercle!* it's our prince of yesterday—our fools' pope—our ringer—our one-eye—our hunchback—our grin of grins! It's Quasimodo!"

It was he indeed. It was Quasimodo, bound, girded, hooped, pinioned, and well guarded. The detachment of sergeants that surrounded him were accompanied by the *chevalier du guet*, or knight of the watch, in person, bearing the arms of France embroidered on his breast, and those of the town of Paris on his back. However, there was nothing in Quasimodo, his deformity excepted, to justify all this display of halberts and arquebusses. He was gloomy, silent, and tranquil—his one eye only just throwing, from time to time, a sullen and resentful glance upon the bonds that covered him. He cast the same look around him; but it seemed so dull and sleepy that the women pointed him out to each other with their fingers in derision only.

Meanwhile Maître Florian, the auditor, turned over attentively the leaves of the written charge drawn up against Quasimodo and presented to him by the registrar, and, after taking that glance, appeared to be meditating for a minute or two. Owing to this precaution, which he was always careful to take at the moment of proceeding to an interrogatory, he knew beforehand the name, quality, and offence of the accused; made premeditated replies to answers foreseen; and so contrived to find his way through all the sinuosities of the interrogatory without too much betraying his deafness. The written charge was to him as the dog to the blind man. If it so happened that his infirmity discovered itself here and there by some incoherent apostrophe or unintelligible question, it passed with some for profundity, with others for imbecility. In either case the honour of the magistracy did not suffer; for a judge had better be considered either imbecile or profound than deaf. So he took great care to disguise his deafness from the observation of all; and he commonly succeeded so well that he had come at last even to deceive himself about the matter—a species of deception, indeed, which is not so difficult as it may be thought: all hunchbacks walk with head erect, all stammerers are given to speechifying, and the deaf always talk in a whisper. For his part, the utmost admission that he made to himself on this point was that his hearing was not quite so quick as some people's; it was the only concession in this respect that he could bring himself to make to public opinion, in his moments of candour and examination of conscience.

Having, then, well ruminated on the affair of Quasimodo, he threw back his head and half closed his eyes, by way of greater majesty and impartiality; so that at that moment he was blind as well as deaf—a double condition, without which no judge is perfect. It was in this magisterial attitude that he commenced the interrogatory.

"Your name?"

Now here was a case which had not been "foreseen by the law," that of one deaf man interrogated by another.

Quasimodo, receiving no intimation of the question thus addressed to him, continued to look fixedly at the judge without making any answer. The deaf judge, on the other hand, receiving no intimation of the deafness of the accused, thought that he had answered, as the prisoners generally did, and continued, with his mechanical and stupid right-forwardness,—

"Well, your age?"

Quasimodo made no more answer to this question than to the preceding one; but the judge, thinking it replied to, went on,—

"Now, your calling?"

The culprit was still silent. The bystanders, however, were beginning to whisper and to look at each other.

"Enough!" added the imperturbable auditor when he supposed that the accused had consummated his third answer. "You stand charged before us—*primo,* with nocturnal disturbance; *secundo,* with dishonest violence upon the person of a light woman—*in prejudicium meretricis; tertio,* of rebellion and disloyalty towards our lord the King's archers. Explain yourself on all these points.—Registrar, have you taken down what the prisoner has said so far?"

At this unlucky question a burst of laughter was heard, caught by the audience from the registrar—so violent, so uncontrollable, so contagious, so universal, that neither of the deaf men could help perceiving it. Quasimodo turned round, shrugging up his hump in disdain; while Maître Florian, astonished like himself, and supposing that the laughter of the spectators had been excited by some irreverent reply from the accused, rendered visible to him by that shrug, apostrophised him indignantly.

"Fellow," said he, "you gave me an answer then that deserves the halter. Know you to whom you are speaking?"

This sally was not at all calculated to extinguish the explosion of the general merriment. It seemed to all present so incongruous and left-handed that the wild laugh caught even the sergeants of the Parloir-aux-Bourgeois, a sort of serving-men carrying pikes, with whom stupidity was part of their uniform. Quasimodo alone preserved his gravity—for the very good reason that he understood nothing at all of what was passing around him. The judge, growing more and more angry, thought himself bound to go on in the same tone, hoping thereby to strike a terror into the accused, which would react upon the bystanders, and bring them back to a proper sense of respect,—

"So it seems, then, master, perverse and riotous as you are, that you presume to be impertinent to the auditor of the Châtelet—to the magistrate entrusted with the popular police of Paris—charged to make search into all crimes, offences, and bad courses—to control all trades and interdict monopolies—to repair the pavements—to prevent forestalling and regrating of poultry and wild fowl—to superintend the measuring of firewood and other sorts of wood—to cleanse the town of mud, and the air of contagious distempers—in a word, to be doing continually the work of the public without fee or reward, or expectation of any. Know you that my name is Florian Barbedienne, Monsieur the Provost's own proper deputy, and moreover commissioner, inquisitor, controllor, and examiner, with equal power in provostry, bailiwork, conservatorship, and presidial court?"

There is no reason why a deaf man talking to a deaf man should ever stop. God only knows where and when Maître Florian would have come to anchor, launched thus in full career upon the main ocean of eloquence, had not the low door behind him opened all at once for the entrance of Monsieur the Provost in person. At this entrance Maître Florian did not stop short; but turning half round upon his heel, and suddenly aiming at the provost the harangue with which the moment before he had been battering Quasimodo, "Monsieur," said he, "I have to request such penalty as it shall please you, upon the accused here present, for flagrant and aggravating contempt of court."

Then he sat down again, quite out of breath, wiping away the big drops that fell from his forehead and moistened, like tears, the parchments spread out before him. Messire Robert d'Estouteville knitted his brow, and made a motion to Quasimodo to attend, in a manner so imperious and significant that the deaf prisoner in some degree understood it.

The provost addressed him with severity: "Rascal, what hast thou done to be brought hither?"

The poor devil, supposing that the provost was asking him his name, now broke the silence which he habitually kept, and answered in a hoarse and guttural voice, "Quasimodo."

The answer so little corresponded to the question that the loud laugh again began to go round; and Messire Robert exclaimed, all reddening with anger, "What! you arrant rogue, you jest at me too, do you?"

"Ringer at Notre-Dame," answered Quasimodo, thinking that this time he was commanded to state to the judge who he was.

"Ringer!" returned the provost, who, as we have already said, had got up that morning in so bad a humour that his fury needed not to be kindled by such unaccountable answers —"Ringer, indeed! I'll make them ring a peal of rods on thy back through every street in Paris! Dost thou hear, rascal?"

"If it's my age you want to know," said Quasimodo, "I believe I shall be twenty next Martinmas."

This was rather too strong. The provost could endure it no longer.

"Ha! so you jeer at the provostry, you wretch!—Messieurs the sergeants of the wand, you'll take this fellow to the pillory in the Grève, and there flog him and turn him for an hour. He shall pay for his impudence, *tête-Dieu!* And I order that his present sentence be proclaimed by four sworn trumpeters in the seven castellanies of the viscounty of Paris."

The registrar set about drawing up the sentence forthwith.

"*Ventre-Dieu!* but that's a good sentence," cried the little scholar, Jehan Frollo du Moulin, from his corner.

The provost turned round, and again fixed his eyes, all flashing, upon Quasimodo. "I believe the fellow said, *Ventre-Dieu!*—Registrar, add a fine of twelve deniers parisis for swearing; and let one half of it go towards the repairs of St. Eustache's church—I've a particular devotion for St. Eustache."

In a few minutes the judgment was drawn out. The tenor of it was simple and brief. The custumal of the provostry and viscounty of Paris had not yet been elaborated by the president, Thibaut Baillet, and Roger Barmue, king's advocate; it was not yet obscured by that deep forest of chicanery and circumlocution which the two jurisconsults placed in it at the commencement of the sixteenth century. All was clear, expeditive, explicit, going direct to the point; and straight you saw before you, at the end of every path, without any ticket about it or bend in the way to it, the wheel, the gibbet, or the pillory. You at least knew whither you were going.

The registrar presented the sentence to the provost, who affixed his seal to it, and then went away, to continue his round at the several *auditoires*, in a temper of mind which seemed destined that day to fill every jail in Paris. Jehan Frollo and Robin Poussepain were laughing in their sleeves; while Quasimodo looked upon the whole with an air of indifference and astonishment.

However, the registrar, at the moment that Maître Florian Barbedienne was in his turn reading over the judgment previous to signing it, felt himself moved with pity for the poor devil under condemnation; and in the hope of obtaining some mitigation of penalty, he approached the auditor's ear as close as he could, and said to him, pointing to Quasimodo, "That man is deaf."

He hoped that a sense of their common infirmity would awaken some interest for the condemned in the breast of Maître Florian. But in the first place, as we have already observed, Maître Florian did not care to have his deafness remarked; and in the next place, his ear was so obtuse that he did not distinguish a single word of what the registrar said to him: nevertheless, choosing to seem as if he heard, he replied, "Ha, ha! that makes a difference. I didn't know that. In that case, let him have an hour more on the pillory." And he signed the sentence with this modification.

"Well done!" said Robin Poussepain, who still had a grudge against Quasimodo; "that'll teach him to handle folks so roughly."

CHAPTER II

THE RAT-HOLE

THE reader will now accompany us back to the Place de Grève, which we quitted yesterday with Gringoire, to follow La Esmeralda.

It is ten in the morning. We find everything denoting the day after a holiday. The ground is covered with shreds, ribbons, trimmings, feathers dropped from the plumes, drops of wax from the torchlights, and fragments from the public banquet. A good many of the townspeople are sauntering about—turning over with their feet the extinguished brands of the bonfire—bursting into rapture before the Maison-aux-Piliers, at the recollection of the fine hangings exhibited there the day before, and now contemplating the nails that fastened them, the only remnant of the ravishing spectacle. The vendors of beer and cider are rolling about their barrels among the several groups. On the other hand, some individuals are going this way and some that, evidently on business. The tradespeople are talking and calling to one another from their shop doors. The holiday, the ambassadors, Coppenole, the Fools' Pope, are in every one's mouth: they seem to be striving who shall make the smartest comments and laugh the most. Meanwhile, however, four sergeants on horseback, who have just now posted themselves at the four sides of the pillory, have already concentrated around them a good part of the *populaire* that had been scattered over the Place, which crowd are condemning themselves to stand wearisomely waiting, in expectation of witnessing the punishment of some criminal.

If the reader will now, after contemplating this stirring and clamorous scene which is enacting upon every point of the square, turn his eyes towards that ancient house of demi-Romanish architecture, of the Tour-Roland, which stands at the western corner next the quay, he may remark, at the angle of its front, a large public breviary richly illuminated, protected from the rain by a small penthouse, and from thieves by a grating, which, however, allows the passengers to turn over its leaves. Close by this breviary is a narrow, pointed window-hole, guarded by two iron bars placed crosswise, and looking towards the square—the only aperture by which a little air and light are admitted into a small cell without a door, constructed on the level of the ground, in the thickness of the wall of the old mansion, and filled with a stillness the more profound, a silence the more dead, inasmuch as a public square, the most populous and the noisiest in Paris, is swarming and clamouring around.

This cell had been famous in Paris for three centuries, since Madame Rolande, of Roland's Tower, in mourning for her father, who died in the crusades, had caused it to be hollowed out of the wall of her own house, to shut herself up in it for ever, keeping of all her palace only this wretched nook, the door of which was walled up, and the window open to the elements, in winter as in summer—giving all the rest to God and to the poor. The desolate lady had, in fact, awaited death for twenty years in that anticipated tomb, praying day and night for the soul of her father, sleeping in ashes, without even a stone for her pillow, clad in black sackcloth, and living only upon such bread and water as the pity of the passersby deposited upon the edge of her window-place—thus receiving charity after she had given it. At her death—at the moment of her passing into the other sepulchre—she had bequeathed this one in perpetuity to women in affliction, mothers, widows, or maidens, who should have many prayers to offer up for others or for themselves, and should choose to bury themselves alive in the greatness of their grief or their penitence. The poor of her time had honoured her funeral with tears and benedictions; but to their great regret the poor maiden had been unable, for want of patronage, to obtain the honours of canonisation. Such of them as were a little given to impiety had hoped that the thing would be done more easily in heaven than at Rome, and had actually presumed to offer up their prayers for the deceased to God himself, in default of the Pope. Most of them, however, had contented themselves with holding Rolande's memory sacred, and converting the rags she left behind her into relics. The town of Paris, too, had founded, in pursuance of the lady's intention, a public breviary, which had been permanently fixed near to the window of the cell, in order that the passengers might stop at it now and then, if only to pray; that prayer might make them think of almsgiving; and that the poor female recluses inheriting the stony cave of Madame Rolande might not absolutely die of famine and neglect.

Nor was it very rarely that these sort of tombs were to be found in the towns of the Middle Ages. There was not unfrequently to be met with, in the most frequented street, in the most crowded and noisy market-place, in the very midst—under the horses' feet and the wagon wheels, as it were—a cave—a well—a walled and grated cabin—at the bottom of which was praying, day and night, a human being, voluntarily devoted to some everlasting lamentation or some great expiation. And all the reflections that this strange spectacle would awaken in us of the present day—that horrid cell, a sort of intermediate link between the dwelling-house and the tomb, between the city and the cemetery—that living being cut off from the communion of mankind, and thenceforth numbered with the dead—that lamp consuming its last drop of oil in the darkness—that remnant of life already wavering in the grave—that breath, that voice, that everlasting prayer encased in stone—that face for ever turned towards the other world—that eye already illumined by another sun—that ear inclined intently to the walls of the sepulchre—that soul a prisoner in that body—that body a prisoner in that dungeon—and under that double envelope of flesh and granite the murmuring of that soul in pain—nothing of all that struck upon the apprehension of the multitude. The piety of that age, little reasoning and little refined, did not find in an act of religion so many different points of view. It took things in the gross—honouring, venerating, and upon occasion making, the sacrifice; but not analysing the sufferings attending it, nor feeling any depth of pity for them. It brought some pittance, from time to time, to the wretched penitent; looked through the hole to see if he were yet living; knew not his name; scarcely knew how many years it was since he had begun to die; and to the stranger who questioned them respecting the living skeleton rotting in that cave the neighbours would simply answer, "It's the recluse."

Thus it was that everything was then seen—unmetaphysically—without exaggeration—through no magnifying-glass, but with the naked eye. The microscope was not yet invented for objects of mind any more than for those of matter.

However, little wonder or speculation as they excited, the instances of this sort of seclusion in the heart of towns were, as we have already observed, in reality frequent. In Paris itself there were a considerable number of those cells of penitence and prayer, and nearly all of them were occupied. It is true that the clergy were rather solicitous that they should not be left empty, as that implied lukewarmness in the faithful; and that lepers were put into them when penitents were not to be had. Besides the *logette*, or cell already described at the Grève, there were one at Montfaucon, one at the charnel-house of the Holy

Innocents, another we hardly recollect where—at the *logis Clichon,* we believe—and others at many different spots, where, in default of monuments, their memory is perpetuated by tradition. The University too had its share of them. On the Montagne Ste. Geneviève a sort of Job of the Middle Ages sang for thirty years the seven penitential psalms, upon a dungheap at the bottom of a cistern, beginning again immediately each time that he came to the end—singing louder in the night-time, *magna voce per umbras ;* and the antiquary still fancies that he hears his voice as he enters the Rue du Puits-qui-parle, or street of the talking well.

To confine ourselves here to the den in Roland's Tower, we are bound to declare that it had scarcely ever lain idle for want of a tenant. Since Madame Rolande's death it had rarely been vacant even for a year or two. Many a woman had come and wept their until death over the memory of her parent, her lover, or her failings. The mischievousness of the Parisians, which meddles with everything, even with those things which concern them the least, used to pretend that among the number there had been very few widows.

After the manner of the period, a Latin legend, inscribed upon the wall, indicated to the lettered passenger the pious purpose of the cell. This usage continued until the middle of the sixteenth century, of placing a brief explanatory motto above the entrance of a building. Thus in France we still read, over the wicket of the prison belonging to the seigneurial mansion of Tourville, *Sileto et spera ;* in Ireland, under the escutcheon placed above the great gateway of Fortescue Castle, *Forte scutum, salus ducum ;* and in England, over the principal entrance of the hospitable mansion of the Earls Cowper, *Tuum est.* Every edifice was then, as it were, a thought.

As there was no door to the walled-up cell of the Tour-Roland, there had been engraven, in great Roman capitals, over the window, these two words of invitation to prayer,—

TU, ORA.

Whence it was that the people, whose straightforward good sense sees not so many subtleties in things, but readily translates *Ludovico Magno* into *Porte Saint-Denis,* had given to this dark, damp, dismal cavity the name of *Trou-aux-Rats* [1]—an explanation less sublime, perhaps, than the other, but, on the other hand, more picturesque.

[1] Signifying *rat-hole,* and pronounced *troo-o-rah*—a very credible vul garisation of the French mode of pronouncing the Latin *Tu, ora.*

CHAPTER III

THE STORY OF A WHEATEN CAKE

At the period at which the principal events of this history occurred, the cell of the Tour-Roland was occupied. If the reader desires to know by whom, he has only to listen to the conversation of three fair gossips, who, at the moment that we have called his attention to the Trou-aux-Rats, were directing their steps precisely to the same spot, going up the river side from the Châtelet towards the Grève.

Two of these women were attired after the manner of the good *bourgeoises* of Paris. The fine white gorget; the petticoat of tiretaine, with red and blue stripes; the white knitted stockings, worked in colours at the ankles, and drawn tight upon the leg; the square-toed shoes of brown leather with black soles; and especially their head-dress—that sort of tinsel-covered horn, loaded with ribbons and lace, which is still worn by the *Champenoises*, or women of Champagne, in common with the grenadiers of the Russian imperial guard—announced that they belonged to that class of rich tradeswomen who hold the medium between what Parisian lackeys call a woman and what they call a lady. They wore neither rings nor golden crosses; but it was easy to perceive that this was owing not to their poverty, but simply to their apprehension of the fine incurred by so doing. Their companion was decked out nearly in the same manner; but there were, in her *mise* and her *tournure*—that is to say (as nearly as we can render these niceties of the French language into our more downright English tongue), in the arrangement of her dress and in her carriage—that certain something which indicates the wife of a *notaire de province*, or country attorney. It was evident, from the shortness of her waist, that she had not been long at Paris; to which were to be added a *gorgèrette pelissée, knots of ribbon* upon her shoes, her skirt striped across instead of downwards, and fifty other enormities revolting to *le bon goût*.

The two first walked with the step peculiar to Parisian women showing Paris to ladies from the country; and the provincial one held by the hand a big chubby boy, who carried in his hand a large thin cake—and we are sorry to be obliged to add that, owing to the severity of the season, his tongue was performing the office of his pocket-handkerchief. The boy made his mother drag him along, ***non passibus æquis***, as Virgil says, and stumbling every moment, to her great outcrying. It is true that he looked more at the cake than upon the ground. Some grave reason, no doubt, prevented him from setting his teeth in it (in the cake), for he contented himself with looking at it affectionately. But the mother ought surely to have taken charge of the cake herself; it was cruel thus to make a Tantalus of the lad.

Meanwhile the three *damoiselles* (for the epithet of dame or lady was then reserved for women of the *noblesse*) were all talking at once,—

"Let us make haste, Damoiselle Mahiette," said the youngest of the three, who was also the fattest, to the provincial. "I'm very much afraid we shall get there too late; they told us at the Châtelet that they were going to carry him to the pillory directly."

"Ah, bah! what are you talking about, Damoiselle Oudarde Musnier?" interrupted the other Parisian lady. "He'll be two hours on the pillory. We've time enough.—My dear Mahiette, did you ever see anybody pilloried?"

"Yes," said the provincial, "I have at Reims."

"Ah, bah! what's that? What's your pillory at Reims! A paltry cage, where they turn nothing but clowns. That's a great thing, to be sure!"

"What clowns!" said Mahiette. "Clowns in the Cloth Market at Reims! We've had very fine criminals there, I can tell you—that had killed both father and mother. Clowns indeed! What do you take us for, Gervaise?"

It is certain that the country dame was on the point of being in a passion for the honour of her pillory. Fortunately, the discreet Damoiselle Oudarde Musnier gave a timely turn to the conversation.

"By-the-by, Damoiselle Mahiette, what say you to our Flemish ambassadors? Have you any so fine at Reims?"

"I must acknowledge," answered Mahiette, "that it's only at Paris one can see such Flemings as those."

"Did you see, among the embassy, that great ambassador that's a hosier?" asked Oudarde.

"Yes," said Mahiette; "he looks like a very Saturn!"

"And that fat one, with a face looking like a naked paunch? And that little one with little eyes, and red eyelids all jagged and bearded like the head of a thistle?"

"It's their horses that are fine to see," said Oudarde, "all dressed as they are, after their country fashion."

"Ah, my dear!" interrupted the provincial Mahiette, assuming in her turn an air of superiority, "what would you say, then, if you'd seen, in '61, at the coronation at Reims, one-and-twenty years ago, the horses of the princes and all the King's company? There were housings and caparisons of all sorts—some of Damascus cloth, fine cloth of gold, trimmed with sables; some of velvet, trimmed with ermine; some all loaded with gold-work and great gold and silver fringe. And then, the money that it all cost; and the beautiful boys, the pages, that were upon them!"

"But, for all that," replied Damoiselle Oudarde dryly, "the Flemings have very fine horses; and yesterday they'd a splendid supper given them by Monsieur the Provost-merchant at the Hôtel-de-Ville, where they served up sweetmeats, hippocrass, spices, and such like singularities."

"What are you talking of, my dear neighbour?" said Gervaise. "It was at the Lord Cardinal's, at the Petit-Bourbon, that the Flemings supped."

"No, no; it was at the Hôtel-de-Ville."

"Yes, yes; I tell you it was at the Petit-Bourbon."

"So surely was it at the Hôtel-de-Ville," returned Oudarde sharply, "that Doctor Scourable made them a Latin speech, and they were very well pleased with it. It was my husband that told me so, and he's one of the sworn booksellers."

"So surely was it at the Petit-Bourbon," rejoined Gervaise no less warmly, "that I'll just tell you what my Lord Cardinal's attorney made them a present of — twelve double quarts of hippocrass, white, claret, and vermilion; four-and-twenty cases of gilt double Lyons marchpane; four-and-twenty wax torches of two pounds a-piece; and six demi-queues of Baune wine, white and claret, the best that could be found. I hope that's proof enough. I had it from my husband, who's *cinquantenier* at the Parloir-aux-Bourgeois, and who was making a comparison this morning between the Flemish ambassadors and those of Prester John and the Emperor of Trebizond, that came to Paris from Mesopotamia, in the last king's time, and that had rings in their ears."

"So true is it that they supped at the Hôtel-de-Ville," replied Oudarde, not a whit moved by all this display, "that never was there seen so fine a show of meat and sugar-plums."

"I tell you that they were waited on by Le Sec, town-sergeant, at the Hôtel du Petit-Bourbon, and that's what has deceived you."

"At the Hôtel-de-Ville, I tell you!"

"At the Petit-Bourbon, my dear; for they'd illuminated the word *Espérance* that's written over the great doorway with magical glasses."

"At the Hôtel-de-Ville! at the Hôtel-de-Ville! for Husson-le-Voir was playing the flute to them."

"I tell you no."

"I tell you yes."

"I tell you no."

The good plump Oudarde was preparing to reply, and the quarrel would perhaps have gone on to the pulling of caps, if Mahiette had not all at once exclaimed, "Look at those people there, gathered together at the end of the bridge. There's something amongst them that they're all looking at."

"I do indeed hear a tambourining," said Gervaise; "I think it's little Smeralda doing her mummeries with her goat. Make haste, Mahiette; double your pace, and pull your boy along. You're come here to see all the curiosities of Paris. Yesterday you saw the Flemings—to-day you must see the little gipsy."

"The gipsy!" said Mahiette, turning sharply round, and forcibly grasping her son's arm. "God preserve me from her. She'd steal my child.—Come alone, Eustache!"

And she set off running along the quay towards the Grève, until she had left the bridge far enough behind her. The boy, too, whom she was dragging along, stumbled and fell upon his knees, and she herself was out of breath. Oudarde and Gervaise now came up with her.

"That gipsy steal your child!" said Gervaise, "that's an odd fancy of yours!"

Mahiette shook her head thoughtfully.

"It's curious enough," observed Oudarde, "that the Sachette has the same notion about the Egyptian women."

"What's the Sachette?" inquired Mahiette.

"Why," said Oudarde, "it's Sister Gudule."

"And who's Sister Gudule?" returned Mahiette.

"You must be very knowing—with your Reims—not to know that!" answered Oudarde, looking wise. "It's the recluse of the Trou-aux-Rats."

"What!" exclaimed Mahiette; "that poor woman that we're carrying this cake to?"

Oudarde nodded affirmatively. "Precisely," said she. "You'll see her directly, at her window-place, on the Grève. She looks as you do upon those vagabonds of Egypt that go about tambourining and fortune-telling. Nobody knows what has given her this horror of zingari and Egyptians. But what makes *you* run away so, Mahiette, at the very sight of them?"

"Oh!" said Mahiette, taking in both hands the chubby head of her boy, "I wouldn't have that happen to me which happened to Pâquette-la-Chantefleurie!"

"Ha, now you're going to tell us a story, my good Mahiette," said Gervaise, taking her arm.

"I'm quite willing," answered Mahiette; "but you must be very knowing—with your Paris—not to know that. I must tell you, then—but we needn't stand still to go through our story—that Pâquette-la-Chantefleurie was a pretty girl of eighteen when I was one too—that is to say, eighteen years ago; and that it's her own fault if she's not now, as I am, a good fat fresh-looking mother of six-and-thirty, with a husband and a boy; but, alack! from the time that she was fourteen years old, it was too late. I must tell you, then, that she was the daughter of Guybertaut, a boat-minstrel at Reims—the same who had played before King Charles VII. at his coronation, when he went down our river Vesle from Sillery to Muison, and Madame la Pucelle was in the boat. The old father died while Pâquette was quite a child, so that she had only her mother left, who was sister to Monsieur Matthieu Pradon, a master brazier and tinman at Paris, Rue Parin-Garlin, who died last year. You see that she was of some family. The mother was a good simple woman unfortunately, and taught Pâquette nothing but a little needlework and toymaking, which did not hinder the little girl from growing very tall and remaining very poor. They lived both of them at Reims, by the river side—Rue de Folle-Peine; mark that, for I believe that's what brought misfortune to Pâquette. In '61, the year of the coronation of our King Louis XI., whom God preserve! Pâquette was so gay and so pretty that everywhere they called her nothing but La Chantefleurie. Poor girl! she'd pretty teeth, and she was fond of laughing to show them. Now a girl that's fond of laughing is on the way to cry—fine teeth are the ruin of fine eyes; so she was La Chantefleurie. She and her mother got their bread hardly—they were fallen very low since the death of the musician—their needlework brought them hardly above six deniers a week, which is not quite two *liards à l'aigle*. Where was the time when the father Guybertaut used to get twelve sols parisis, at a single coronation, for a song! One winter—it was in that same year '61—when the two women had neither logs nor fagots, and it was very cold—that gave such beautiful colours to La Chantefleurie that the men would call after her 'Pâquette'—that some of them called her 'Pâquerette'—and that she was ruined.—Eustache, let me see you bite the cake, if you dare.—We saw directly that she was ruined, one Sunday she came to church with a gold cross on her neck. At fifteen!—only think of that! At first it was the young Viscount de Cormontreuil, who has his bell-tower three-quarters of a league from Reims; then, Messire Henri de Triancourt the king's master of the horse; then going down lower, Chiart de Beaulion, sergeant-at-arms; then, lower still, Guery Aubergeon, king's carver; then Macé de Frépus, Monsieur the Dauphin's barber; then Thévenin le Moine, the king's first cook; then, still going on, from one to another, from the younger to the older, and from more noble to less noble, she came to Guillaume Racine, viol-player—and to Thierry-de-Mer, lampmaker. Then poor Chantefleurie—she was all things to all men; she was come to the last sou of her piece of gold. What think you, mesdamoiselles? At the coronation, in the same year '61, it was she that made the bed for the king of the ribalds! In the same year——"

Mahiette sighed, and wiped away a tear that had started to her eyes.

"Here's a story," said Gervaise, "that's not very uncommon; and I find nothing in all that neither about gipsies nor children."

"Patience!" resumed Mahiette; "as for a child, there's one coming for you. In '66—it'll be sixteen years ago this month—on St. Paul's day, Pâquette was brought to bed of a little girl. Unfortunate creature! she was in great joy at it; she'd long been wishing to have a child. Her mother, poor simple woman, who'd never known how to do anything but shut her eyes—her mother was dead. Pâquette had nothing in the world left to love, nor anything that loved her. For five years past, since she had gone astray, poor Chantefleurie had been a wretched creature. She was lone—lone in this world; pointed at, shouted after, through the streets; beaten by the sergeants, laughed at by the little ragged boys. And then she had seen her twentieth year—and twenty is old age for your amorous women. Her way of life was beginning to bring her no more than her needlework had brought formerly. For every wrinkle that came, a crown less found its way into her pocket; she was beginning again to find the winter severe—again was wood growing scarce in her fireplace, and bread in her cupboard. She couldn't work now; for in giving way to pleasure she'd given way to idleness; and she suffered much more than formerly, because while giving way to idleness she'd given way to pleasure. At least that's the way that Monsieur the Curé of St. Remy explains how it is that these sort of women feel more cold and hunger than other poor females do, as they get old——"

"Yes," interrupted Gervaise—"but the gipsies?"

"Do wait a moment, Gervaise!" said Oudarde, whose attention was less impatient; "what should we have at the end if everything was at the beginning?—Pray, Mahiette, go on. That poor Chantefleurie——"

Mahiette continued,—

"Well, then, she was very sorrowful, very wretched, and furrowed her cheeks with her tears. But in her shame, her infamy, and her abandonment, she thought she should be less ashamed, less infamous, and less abandoned, if there were something in the world or somebody that she could love and that could love her. She knew it must be a child, because only a child could be innocent enough for that. She was aware of this after trying to love a thief, the only sort of man that could have anything to say to her; but in a little time she had found out that the thief despised her. Those women of love must have a lover or a child to fill up their hearts, else they are very unhappy. As she could not have a lover, all her wishes turned towards having a child; and as she had all along been pious, she prayed to God everlastingly to send her one. So God took pity on her, and gave her a little girl. I cannot tell you what was her joy; it was a fury of tears, kisses, and caresses. She suckled the child herself; she made it swaddling-clothes out of her coverlet, the only one she had upon her bed; and now she felt neither cold nor hunger. Her beauty came again—an old maid makes a young mother—so poor Chantefleurie came into fashion again, and once more had visitors. And out of all those horrors she made baby clothes—lace robes and little satin caps—without so much as thinking of buying herself another coverlet.—Master Eustache, I've told you once not to bite of the cake.—Sure enough it is that little Agnès—that was the child's name, its Christian name, for as for a surname, it was long since La Chantefleurie had lost hers!—certain it is that the little thing was more wrapped about with ribbons and embroidery than a dauphiness of Dauphiny. Amongst other things, she'd a pair of little shoes that it's certain King Louis himself never had the like. Her mother had stitched them and embroidered them herself; she'd spent upon them all the art of a seamstress and all the passequilles of a Holy Virgin's gown. Indeed, they were the two prettiest little rose-coloured shoes that ever were seen. They were not longer than my thumb at the most; and unless you saw the infant's little feet come out of them, you could hardly have believed that they had ever gone in. To be sure, the little feet were so little, so pretty, so rosy—rosier than the satin of the shoes!—When you have children, Oudarde, you'll know that nothing's so pretty as those little feet and those little hands——"

"I wish for nothing better," said Oudarde, sighing; "but I must wait the good pleasure of Monsieur Andry Musnier."

"And then," resumed Mahiette, "Pâquette's infant had not pretty feet only. I saw her when she was only four months old; she was a perfect little love. She had eyes larger than her mouth, and such charming fine black hair, that was curling already. She'd have made a brave brunette at sixteen! Her mother grew fonder and fonder of her every day. She hugged her, kissed her, tickled her, washed her, dressed her out, devoured her. She thanked God for giving her this baby. In fact, it quite turned her head. Its pretty rosy feet especially—there was wondering without end—a very intoxication of joy. She was always pressing her lips to them—always admiring their littleness. She would put them into the little shoes, take them out again, admire them, wonder at them, hold them up to the light, pity them while she was teaching them to step one before the other upon her bed, and would gladly have passed her life upon her knees, covering and uncovering those little feet, as if they'd been the feet of an infant Jesus."

"The tale's all very fine and very good," said Gervaise in a half whisper, "but what is there about gipsies in all that?"

"You shall hear," replied Mahiette. "One day there came to Reims a very odd sort of gentry. They were beggars and truands, strolling about the country, led by their duke and their counts. Their faces were tawny, their hair all curly, and they'd rings of silver in their ears. The women were still uglier than the men. Their faces were darker, and always uncovered; they wore a sorry roquet about their body, an old piece of linen cloth interwoven with cords bound upon their shoulder, and their hair hanging like a horse's tail. The children that scrambled about their legs would have frightened as many monkeys. An excommunicated gang! They were all come in a straight line from lower Egypt to Reims, through Poland. The Pope had confessed them, it was said, and had set them for a penance to go through the world for seven years together without sleeping in a bed; and so they called themselves penitents, and smelt horribly. It seems they'd formerly been Saracens; and that's why they believed in Jupiter, and demanded ten livres tournois from all archbishops, bishops, and abbots, that carried crosier and mitre. It was a bull of the Pope that gave them that. They came to Reims to tell fortunes in the name of the King of Algeirs and the Emperor of Germany. You may suppose that was quite enough for them to be forbidden to enter the town. Then the whole gang encamped of their own accord near the Brain Gate, upon that mound where there's a windmill, close by the old chalk-pits. Then none of the folks in Reims could rest till they'd been to see them. They looked into your hand, and told you wonderful prophecies; they were bold enough to have foretold to Judas himself that he should be pope. At the same time there were shocking stories told about them—of child-stealing, purse-cutting, and eating of human flesh. The wise folks said to the foolish ones, 'Don't go!' and then went themselves by stealth. It was quite a rage. The fact is, that they said things enough to astonish a cardinal. Mothers made a great fuss with their children after the gipsy women had read in their hands all sorts of miracles, written in Turkish and Pagan. One of them had got an emperor, another a pope, another a captain. Poor Chantefleurie was taken with curiosity: she'd a mind to know what *she* had got, and whether her pretty little Agnès wasn't some day to be Empress of Armenia, or something. So she carried her to the gipsies; and the gipsy women admired the child, fondled it, kissed it with their black mouths, and wondered over its little hand—alas! to the great joy of its mother. Above all things, they were delighted with the pretty feet and the pretty shoes. The child was not yet a year old. She was already beginning to splutter—laughed at her mother like a little mad thing, was so fat and plump, and had a thousand little gestures of the angels in Paradise. She was very much frightened at the gipsy women, and cried. But her mother kissed her the harder, and went away delighted at the good fortune which the conjuring women had told her Agnes. She was to be a beauty, a virtue, a queen. So the mother went back to her garret in the Rue Folle-Peine, quite proud to carry with her a queen. The next day she seized a moment when the child was sleeping upon her bed (for she always had it to sleep with herself), pulled the door to softly, and left it ajar, for fear of disturbing the infant, and ran to relate to one of her neighbours in the Rue de la Séchesserie that the day was to come when her daughter Agnès was to be waited on at the table by the King of England and the Archduke of Ethiopia, and a hundred other marvels. When she came back, hearing no cry as she went up the staircase, she said to herself, 'Good—the child's asleep still.' She found her door more open than she had left it; the poor mother, however, went in and ran to the bed. The child was not there; the place was empty. Nothing was left of the baby but one of its pretty shoes. She rushed out of the room, flew downstairs, and began to beat the walls with her head, crying out, 'My child! my child! who has taken my child?' The street was solitary—the house stood alone—nobody could tell her anything about it; she went through the town—she sought through every street—ran up and down the whole day, wild, mad, terrible, peeping at the doors and windows like a wild beast that has lost its little ones. She was panting, dishevelled, frightful to look upon, and in her eyes there was a fire that dried her tears. She stopped the people that she met, and cried, 'My girl! my girl! my pretty little girl! He that will restore me my girl, I will be his servant—the servant of his dog, and he shall eat my heart if he likes.' She met Monsieur the Curé of St. Remy, and said to him, 'Monsieur le Curé, I'll dig the ground with my nails—but do give me back my child!' It was heartrending, Oudarde; and I saw a very hard-hearted man, Maître Ponce Lacabre, the attorney, that shed tears. Ah! the poor mother! At night she went back to her garret. While she was away one of her neighbours had seen two gispy women steal up to it with a bundle in their arms; then go down again, after shutting the door, and make haste away. After they were gone a sort of crying of a child was heard in Pâquette's room. The mother laughed aloud, flew up the staircase as if she'd had wings, burst in her door as if it was a cannon going off, and entered the room. A frightful thing to tell, Oudarde!—instead of her sweet little Agnès, so fresh and rosy, who was a gift from God, there was a sort of little monster, hideous, shapeless, one-eyed, with its limbs all awry, crawling and squalling upon the floor. She turned away her eyes with horror. 'Oh!' said she, 'can the witches have changed my girl into that frightful animal?' They carried the little clump-foot as quick as possible out of her sight. He'd have driven her mad. It was a monstrous child of some gipsy woman given to the devil. It was a boy, that seemed to be about four years old, and spoke a language that was not a human tongue—they were words that are quite impossible. La Chantefleurie had thrown herself upon the little shoe—all that was left her of all that she had loved. There she remained so long, motionless, speechless, breathless, that they thought she was dead. All at once her whole body trembled; she covered her relic with frantic kisses, and sobbed violently, as if her heart had burst. I assure you that we all wept with her. She said, 'O my little girl! my pretty little girl! where art thou?' and she said it in a tone that went to the bottom of your heart. I weep yet when I think of it. Our children, you see, are the very marrow of our bones.—My poor Eustache, thou art so handsome!—If you did but know how clever he is! Yesterday he said to me, 'I'll be a gendarme.' —O my Eustache, if I were to lose thee!—La Chantefleurie got up all on a sudden, and went running through Reims, crying out, 'To the gipsies' camp! to the gipsies' camp! Sergeants, to burn the witches!' The gipsies were gone; it was dark night, so that they couldn't pursue them. The next day, two leagues from Reims, on a heath between Gueux and Tilloy, they found the remains of a great fire, some ribbons that had belonged to Pâquette's child, some drops of blood, and some goat's dung. The night that was just gone over was a Saturday night. Nobody doubted but the gipsies had kept their Sabbath upon that heath, and had devoured the baby in company with Beelzebub, as is done among the Mohammedans. When La Chantefleurie heard of these horrible things, she shed no tears; she moved her lips, as if to speak, but could not. The next day her hair was grey; and the next but one she had disappeared."

"A dreadful story, indeed!" said Oudarde; "enough to draw tears from a Burgundian!"

"I don't wonder now," added Gervaise, "that the fear of the gipsies should haunt you so."

"And you have done the better," resumed Oudarde, "in running away just now with your Eustache, seeing that these too are gipsies from Poland."

"No," said Gervaise; "it's said they're come from Spain and Catalonia."

"Catalonia! well, that may be," answered Oudarde. "Polonia, Catalonia, Valonia—I always confound those three provinces. The sure thing is they *are* gipsies."

"And it's certain," added Gervaise, "that they've teeth long enough to eat little children. And I shouldn't be surprised if La Smeralda herself eats a little in that way too, for all that she screws up her mouth so. That white goat of hers has got too many mischievous tricks for there not to be some wickedness behind."

Mahiette was walking on in silence. She was absorbed in that species of musing which is, as it were, a prolongation of a mournful story, and which does not stop until it has communicated the thrilling, from vibration to vibration, to the last fibre of the heart. Gervaise, however, addressed her. "And so it was never known what became of La Chantefleurie?" Mahiette made no answer. Gervaise repeated her question, at the same time shaking her by the arm and calling her by her name. Mahiette seemed to awake from her reverie.

"What became of La Chantefleurie?" said she, mechanically repeating the words whose impression was yet fresh in her ear. Then making an effort to bring her attention to the sense of those words, "Ah!" said she emphatically, "it was never known." And after a pause she added,—

"Some said they had seen her go out of Reims, in the dusk of the evening, at the Porte Fléchembault; others, at daybreak, by the old Porte Basée. A poor man found her gold cross hung upon the stone cross in the close where the fair is held. It was that trinket that had ruined her in '61. It was a gift from the handsome Viscount de Cormontreuil, her first lover. Pâquette would never part with it, even in her greatest wretchedness; she clung to it as if it had been her life. So that when we saw this cross abandoned we all thought she was dead. However, there were some people, at the Cabaret-les-Vautes, who said they'd seen her go by on the Paris road, walking barefoot over the stones. But then she must have gone out at the Porte de Vesle—and all those things don't agree. Or rather, I'm inclined to think that she did indeed go out by the gate of the Vesle, but that she went out of this world."

"I don't understand you," said Gervaise.

"The Vesle," answered Mahiette with a melancholy smile, "is the river."

"Poor Chantefleurie!" said Oudarde, shuddering; "what—*drowned?*"

"Drowned," replied Mahiette. "And who would have foretold to the good father, Guybertaut, when he was passing down the stream under the Tinqueux bridge, singing in his boat, that his dear little Pâquette should one day pass under that same bridge, but with neither song nor boat!"

"And the little shoe?" inquired Gervaise.

"Disappeared with the mother," answered Mahiette.

"Poor little shoe!" said Oudarde.

Oudarde, a woman of full habit and tender fibre, would have been quite content to sigh along with Mahiette. But Gervaise, more curious, had not yet got to the end of her questions.

"And the monster," said she all at once to Mahiette.

"What monster?" asked the other.

"Why, the little gipsy monster that the witches left at La Chantefleurie's in exchange for her daughter. What did you do with it? I hope you drowned it too."

"No," answered Mahiette, "we did not."

"What?—burned it then? I' faith, that was a better way of disposing of a witch's child."

"We did neither the one nor the other, Gervaise. Monsieur the Archbishop took an interest in the child of Egypt: he exorcised it, blessed it, carefully took the devil out of its body, and sent it to Paris to be exposed upon the wooden bed at Notre-Dame as a foundling."

"Those bishops!" muttered Gervaise; "because they're learned, forsooth, they can never do anything like other folks. Only consider, Oudarde—to think of putting the devil among the foundlings! for it's quite certain that little monster *was* the devil. Well, Mahiette, and what did they do with it at Paris? I'll answer for it that not one charitable person would take it."

"I don't know indeed," answered the good lady of Reims. "It was just at that time that my husband bought the tabellionage of Beru, two leagues from the town; and we thought no more of all that story, for you must know that just in front of Beru there are the two mounds of Cernay, that take the towers of Reims Cathedral out of your sight."

While talking thus the three worthy bourgeoises had arrived at the Place de Grève. In the preoccupation of their minds they had passed by the public breviary of the Tour-Roland without observing it, and were proceeding mechanically towards the pillory, around which the crowd was every moment increasing. It is probable that the sight, which at that moment drew every eye towards it, would have made them completely forget the Trou-aux-Rats and the station they had intended to perform there, had not the big Eustache of six years old, whom Mahiette held by the hand, suddenly reminded them of the object of it. "Mother," said he, as if some instinct apprised him that they had left the Trou-aux-Rats behind them, "*now* may I eat the cake?"

Had Eustache been more adroit—that is to say, less greedy—he would have waited a little longer; and not until they had reached home in the university at Maître Andry Musnier's in the Rue Madame-la-Valence, when the two channels of the Seine and the five bridges of the city would have been between the cake and the Trou-aux-Rats, would he have hazarded that timid question, "Mother, now may I eat the cake?"

This same question, imprudent at the moment at which Eustache made it, aroused Mahiette's attention.

"By-the-bye," exclaimed she, "we were forgetting the recluse! Show me this Trou-aux-Rats of yours, that I may carry her her cake."

"To be sure," said Oudarde; "it'll be a charity."

This was not the thing for Eustache. "Let me have my cake!" said he, rubbing first one of his ears upon his shoulder and then the other—the sign in such cases of supreme dissatisfaction.

The three women retraced their steps; and when they had nearly reached the house of the Tour-Roland, Oudarde said to the other two, "We must not all three look into the hole at once, lest we should frighten the Sachette. Do you two make as if you were reading *Dominus* in the breviary, while I peep in at the window-hole. The Sachette knows me a little. I'll let you know when you may come."

She went by herself to the window-place. The moment that she looked in, profound pity depicted itself in all her features—her cheerful, open countenance changing its expression and its hue as suddenly as if it had passed out of a gleam of sunshine into one of moonlight; her eye moistened, and her mouth took that contraction which is the forerunner of weeping. A moment after she laid her finger on her lip, and beckoned to Mahiette to come and look.

Mahiette came, tremulous, silent, and stepping on the points of her toes, like one approaching a deathbed.

It was, in truth, a sorrowful sight that presented itself to the eyes of the two women, while they looked without stirring or drawing their breath, through the grated window of the Trou-aux-Rats.

The cell was of small dimensions, wider than it was deep, with a Gothic vaulted ceiling, and looking internally much in the shape of the inner part of a bishop's mitre. Upon the bare flagstones that formed its floor, in one corner, a woman was seated, or rather squatted down. Her chin was resting on her knees, with her arms, crossed before her, pressed close against her chest. Thus, gathered up as it were into a heap, clad in a brown sackcloth which wrapped her all round in large folds, with her long grey hair turned upon her forehead and hanging over her face, and down by her legs, to her feet, she presented at first sight only a strange form, projected on the dark background of the cell—a sort of dusky triangle, which the daylight from the window-place crudely distinguished into two tints, the one light, the other dark. It was one of those spectres, half light, half shade, such as are seen in dreams, and in the extraordinary work of Goya—pale, motionless, dismal, squatting on a tomb, or reared against the grating of a dungeon. It was neither woman nor man, nor living being, nor definite form; it was a figure—a sort of vision, in which the real and the fanciful were intermingled like light and shadow. Beneath her hair, that fell all about it to the ground, scarcely could you distinguish a severe and attenuated profile; scarcely did there peep from under the hem of her flowing gown the extremity of a naked foot, contracted upon the rigid and frozen pavement. The little of human form that was discernible under that mourning envelope made you shudder.

This figure, which looked as if it had been fixed in the floor, seemed to have neither motion, thought, nor breath. In that covering of thin brown linen—in January—lying upon a pavement of granite—without fire—in the darkness of a dungeon, the oblique loophole of which admitted only the north-east wind, and never the sun—she seemed not to suffer, not even to feel. You would have thought that she had turned to stone with the dungeon, to ice with the season. Her hands were clasped, her eyes were fixed. At the first glance you took her for a spectre; at the second, for a statue.

However, at intervals, her blue lips half opened with a breath, and trembled, but as deadly and mechanically as leaves parted by the wind. And from those dull, stony eyes there proceeded a look, ineffable, profound, lugubrious, imperturbable, constantly fixed upon one angle of the cell, which could not be seen from the outside—a look which seemed to concentrate all the gloomy thoughts of that suffering spirit upon some mysterious object.

Such was the creature who from her tenement was called

the *recluse,* and from her coarse linen or sacking garment the *Sachette.*

The three women (for Gervaise had come up to Mahiette and Oudarde) were looking through the window-place. Their heads intercepted the feeble light of the dungeon, apparently without at all calling the wretched creature's attention in that direction. "Let us not disturb her," whispered Oudarde; "she's in her ecstasy—she's praying."

Meanwhile Mahiette was gazing with a constantly increasing anxiety upon that wan, withered, dishevelled head, and her eyes filled with tears. "That would be very singular!" muttered she.

She passed her head through the bars of the window, and succeeded in obtaining a glance into that angle of the cell upon which the unfortunate woman's look was immovably fixed. When she drew her head out again her face was covered with tears.

"What is that woman's name?" said she to Oudarde.

Oudarde answered, "We call her Sister Gudule."

"And I," returned Mahiette, "call her Pâquette-la-Chantefleurie."

Then laying her finger upon her lip, she made a sign to the amazed Oudarde to put her head through the bars as she had done, and to look.

Oudarde looked, and saw, in that corner upon which the eye of the recluse was fixed in that gloomy absorption, a little shoe of rose-coloured satin, decorated all over with gold and silver spangles.

Gervaise looked after Oudarde; and then the three women, gazing upon the unhappy mother, began to weep.

However, neither their looks nor their weeping had disturbed the recluse. Her hands remained clasped, her lips mute, her eyes fixed, and to any one who knew her story that gaze of hers upon that little shoe was heartrending.

The three women had not uttered a word; they dared not speak, even in a whisper. That deep silence, that deep grief, that deep forgetfulness in which every object had disappeared save one, had upon them the effect of a high altar at Easter or Christmas. They kept silence; they collected themselves; they were ready to kneel. They felt as if they had just entered a church on the Saturday in Passion week.

At length Gervaise, the most curious of the three, and therefore the least sensitive, tried to make the recluse speak, by calling to her, "Sister! Sister Gudule!"

She repeated this call to the third time, raising her voice higher every time. The recluse did not stir; there was not a word, not a look, not a sigh, not a sign of life.

Now Oudarde herself, in a softer and kinder tone, said to her, "Sister—holy Sister Gudule!" There was the same silence, the same immobility.

"An odd woman!" exclaimed Gervaise, "that wouldn't start at a bombard."

"Perhaps she's deaf," said Oudarde with a sigh.

"Perhaps blind," added Gervaise.

"Perhaps dead!" observed Mahiette.

It is certain that if the soul had not yet quitted that inert, torpid, lethargic body, it had at least retired within it, and hidden itself in depths to which the perceptions of the external organs did not penetrate.

"We shall be obliged, then," said Oudarde, "to leave the cake lying upon the window-case; and some lad or other will take it. What can we do to rouse her!"

Eustache, whose attention had until that moment been diverted by a little carriage drawn by a great dog, which had just passed them, all at once observed that his three conductresses were looking at something through the hole in the wall; and his own curiosity being thus excited, he mounted upon a curbstone, sprang up on his toes, and put his great rosy face to the opening, crying out, "Mother, let *me* see too."

At the sound of this voice of a child, clear, fresh, and sonorous, the recluse started. She turned her head with the dry and sudden motion of a steel spring; her two long, fleshless hands threw aside her hair upon her forehead; and she fixed upon the child a look of astonishment, bitterness, and despair. That look was but a flash. "O my God," exclaimed she all at once, hiding her head between her knees—and it seemed as if her hoarse voice tore her breast in passing—"at least don't show me those of others!"

"Good-day, madame," said the boy gravely.

This shock, however, had, as it were, awakened the recluse. A long shiver ran over her whole body, from head to foot; her teeth chattered; she half raised her head, and said, pressing her elbows against her hips, and taking her feet in her hands, as if to restore their warmth, "Oh, the severe cold!"

"Poor woman!" said Oudarde with deep pity, "will you have a little fire?"

She shook her head in token of refusal.

"Well," resumed Oudarde, offering her a flask, "here is some hippocrass that will warm you. Drink."

She shook her head again, looking steadfastly at Oudarde, and answered, "Some water!"

Oudarde insisted: "No, sister; that's not a January beverage. You must drink a little hippocrass, and eat this cake leavened with maize that we've baked for you."

She rejected the cake, which Mahiette offered her, and said, "Some black bread!"

"Here!" said Gervaise, seized with charity in her turn, and taking off her woollen roquet—"here's a cloak rather warmer than yours; put this over your shoulders."

She refused the cloak as she had done the liquor and the cake, at the same time answering, "A sack!"

"But at all events," resumed the kind Oudarde, "you must be aware, I should think, that yesterday was a holiday."

"I am aware of it," said the recluse. "For two days past I have had no water in my pitcher."

She added after a pause, "It's a holiday, and they forget me: they do well. Why should the world think of me, who think not of it? Cold ashes are fitting to a dead coal."

And then, as if fatigued with having said so much, she let her head drop upon her knees again. The simple and charitable Oudarde, thinking that she was to understand from these last words that the poor woman was still complaining of the cold, answered her with simplicity, "Then will you have a little fire?"

"Fire!" said the Sachette in a strange tone; "and will you make a little, too, for the poor little one that has been under ground these fifteen years?"

All her limbs trembled, her speech vibrated, her eyes shone. She had risen up on her knees; she suddenly stretched out her white meagre hand towards the child, which was gazing at her with an astonished look. "Take away that child!" she cried; "the gipsy woman's coming by!"

Then she fell with her face to the ground, and her forehead struck the floor with the noise of a stone upon a stone. The three women thought she was dead. A minute afterwards she stirred, and they saw her crawl upon her hands and knees into the corner that contained the little shoe. Then they did not venture to look; they saw her no longer, but they heard a thousand kisses and sighs, intermingled with afflicting exclamations, and with dull strokes, like those of a head knocking against a wall; then, after one of these strokes, so violent that it startled them all three, all was silent.

"Has she killed herself, I wonder?" said Gervaise, venturing to put her head between the bars. "Sister! Sister Gudule!"

"Sister Gudule!" repeated Oudarde.

"Ah, my God, she doesn't stir!" resumed Gervaise. "Is she dead, think you?—Gudule! Gudule!"

Mahiette, whose utterance had been choked until then, now made an effort. "Wait a moment," said she; and then, putting her head to the window, "Pâquette!" she cried, "Pâquette-la-Chantefleurie!"

A child that should blow unsuspectedly upon the ill-lighted match of a petard, and make it explode in his face, would not be more frightened than Mahiette was at the effect of this name thus suddenly breathed into the cell of Sister Gudule.

The recluse was agitated in every limb; she rose erect upon her naked feet, and flew to the loophole with eyes so flaming that Mahiette and Oudarde, their companion and the child, all retreated as far as the parapet of the quay.

Meanwhile the sinister visage of the recluse appeared close to the window-grate. "Oh, oh," she cried with a frightful laugh "it's the gipsy woman that calls me!"

At that moment a scene which was passing at the pillory arrested her haggard eye. Her forehead wrinkled with horror; she stretched out of her den her two skeleton arms, and cried out with a voice that rattled in her throat, "So it's thou again, daughter of Egypt; it's thou that call'st me, thou child-stealer! Well—cursed be thou! cursed, cursed, cursed——"

CHAPTER IV

A TEAR FOR A DROP OF WATER

THE concluding words of the foregoing chapter may be described as the point of junction of two scenes which, until that moment, had been simultaneously developing themselves, each upon its particular stage—the one, that which has just been related, at the Trou-aux-Rats; the other, now to be described, at the pillory. The former had been witnessed only by the three women with whom the reader has just now been made acquainted; the latter had had for spectators the whole crowd which we have seen collect a little while before upon the Place de Grève, around the pillory and the gibbet.

This crowd, whom the sight of the four sergeants posted from nine o'clock in the morning at the four corners of the pillory led to expect a penal exhibition of some kind—not, certainly, a hanging, but a flogging, a cutting off of ears, or something in this way—this crowd, we say, had so rapidly increased that the four sergeants, finding themselves too closely invested, had more than once been under the necessity of forcing it back by the application of their whitleather whips and their horses' cruppers.

The populace, however, well drilled to the waiting for this sort of spectacle, showed themselves tolerably patient. They amused themselves with looking at the pillory—a very simple sort of structure, in truth, consisting of a cubical mass of stone-work, some ten feet high, and hollowed internally. A very steep flight of steps, of unhewn stone, called by distinction the *échelle*, gave access to the upper platform, upon which was to be seen a plain horizontal wheel made of oak wood. The custom was to bind the sufferer upon this wheel, on his knees, with his arms pinioned. An upright shaft of timber, set in motion by a capstan concealed within the interior of the small edifice, made the wheel revolve horizontally and uniformly, thus presenting the face of the culprit successively to every point of the Place. This was called *turning* the criminal.

It is clear that the pillory of the Grève was far from possessing all the attractions of the pillory of the Halles. There was nothing architectural, nothing monumental. There was no iron-cross roof, no octagonal lantern; there were no slender *colonnettes* opening out against the border of the roof into capitals of foliage and flowers, no monster-headed gutters, no carved woodwork, no bold and delicate sculpture. The spectator was obliged to content himself with those four faces of rough stone, surmounted by two side-walls or parapets of stone still rougher, with a sorry stone gibbet, meagre and bare, standing beside them. The entertainment would have been pitiful enough for amateurs of Gothic architecture. But it is certain that none could be less curious in this way than the good cockneys of the Middle Ages, and that they took but little interest in the beauty of a pillory.

At last the culprit arrived, fastened at the tail of a cart, and as soon as he was hoisted upon the platform, so that he could be seen from every point of the Place, bound with cords and straps, upon the wheel of the pillory, a prodigious hooting, mingled with laughter and acclamations, burst from the assemblage in the square. They had recognised Quasimodo.

As regarded himself, the turn of affairs was somewhat striking—to be pilloried in that same square in which, the day before, he had been saluted and proclaimed pope and prince of the fools, in the train of the Duke of Egypt, the King of Tunis, and the Emperor of Galilee. Certain it is, however, that there was not one mind among the crowd—not even his own, though himself in turn the triumphant and the sufferer—that clearly drew this parallel. Gringoire and his philosophy were absent from this spectacle.

Anon, Michel Noiret, one of their lord the king's sworn trumpeters, after having silence cried to the *manans*, made proclamation of the sentence, pursuant to the ordinance and command of Monsieur the Provost. He then fell back behind the cart, with his men in their hacqueton uniform.

Quasimodo, quite passive, did not so much as knit his brow. All resistance was rendered impossible to him by what was then called, in the style of the *chancellerie criminelle*, " the vehemence and firmness of his bonds "—that is to say, that the small straps, and chains probably entered his flesh. " This, by-the-by," observes our author, " is a tradition which is not yet lost; the *menottes* or manacles still happily preserving it amongst ourselves, a people civilised, mild, and humane (the bagnio and the guillotine between parentheses)."

Quasimodo had let them lead him, thrust him, carry him along, hoist him up, bind and rebind him. Nothing was distinguishable in his countenance but the astonishment of a savage or an idiot. He was known to be deaf—he might have been taken to be blind.

They set him upon his knees on the circular plank, and stripped him to the waist; he made not the least resistance. They bound him down under a fresh system of straps and buckles; he let them buckle and strap him. Only from time to time he breathed heavily, like a calf when its head hangs tossing about over the side of the butcher's cart.

"The dolt!" said Jehan Frollo du Moulin to his friend Robin Poussepain (for the two scholars had followed the sufferer, as in duty bound), "he understands no more about it than a cockchafer shut in a box."

There was a wild laugh among the crowd when they saw, stripped naked to their view, Quasimodo's hump, his camel breast, his brawny and hairy shoulders. During all this merriment a man in the town livery, short and thick-set, ascended the platform, and placed himself by the culprit. His name was quickly circulated among the spectators; it was Maître Pierrat Torterue, sworn torturer at the Châtelet.

He commenced his operations by depositing on one corner of the pillory a black hour-glass, the upper cup of which was filled with red sand, which was filtering through into the lower recipient. Then he took off his parti-coloured doublet; and there was seen dangling from his right hand a whip with long slender white lashes, shining, knotted, and armed with points of metal. With his left hand he carelessly turned up his shirt-sleeve about his right arm as high as the armpit.

Meanwhile, Jehan Frollo cried out, lifting his light-haired, curly head above the crowd (for he had mounted for that purpose on the shoulders of Robin Poussepain), "Come and see, messieurs —mesdames! They're going peremptorily to flog Maître Quasimodo, ringer to my brother Monsieur the Archdeacon of Joas—a fellow of Oriental architecture, with his back like a dome, and his legs like twisted columns!"

And the people laughed, especially the boys and girls.

At last the torturer stamped with his foot. The wheel began to turn; Quasimodo staggered under his bonds. And the amazement that was suddenly depicted upon his deformed visage redoubled the bursts of laughter all around.

All at once, at the moment when the wheel in its rotation presented to Maître Pierrat Quasimodo's mountainous back, Maître Pierrat lifted his arm, the small lashes whistled sharply in the air like a handful of vipers, and fell with fury upon the poor wretch's shoulders.

Quasimodo made a spring, as if starting from his sleep. He now began to understand. He twisted himself about in his toils. A violent contraction, expressive of surprise and pain, discomposed the muscles of his face; but he breathed not a sigh. Only he turned back his head, first on the right side, then on the left, balancing it backwards and forwards, like a bull stung in the flank by a gadfly.

A second stroke followed the first, then a third, then another, and another; and so on, without ceasing, the wheel continuing to turn, and the lashes to descend upon the sufferer. Soon the blood began to flow; it was seen trickling in a thousand streaks over the dark shoulders of the hunchback; and the keen lashes, as they whistled through the air, scattered it in drops among the multitude.

Quasimodo had resumed, in appearance at least, his former passiveness. At first he had striven, silently and without any great external shock, to burst his bonds. His eye had been seen to kindle, his muscles to contract, his limbs to gather themselves up, and the straps and chains to be strained to their utmost tension. The effort was powerful, prodigious, desperate; but the old binders of the provostry resisted. They cracked, but that was all. Quasimodo sank exhausted, and on his countenance stupefaction was succeeded by an expression of bitter and deep discouragement. He closed his only eye, dropped his head upon his breast, and seemed as if he was dead.

Thenceforward he stirred not at all. Nothing could wring any motion from him—neither his blood, which continued to flow; nor the strokes of the whip, which fell with redoubled fury; nor the violence of the torturer, who worked himself up into a sort of intoxication; nor the keen whistling of the horrid lashes.

At length, an usher of the Châtelet, clothed in black, mounted on a black horse, and stationed at the side of the *échelle* from the commencement of the punishment, pointed, with his ebony wand, to the hour-glass. The torturer held his hand, the wheel stopped, and Quasimodo's eye slowly reopened.

The flagellation was finished. Two assistants of the sworn torturer washed the bleeding shoulders of the sufferer, rubbed them with some kind of unguent, which immediately closed the wounds, and threw over his back a sort of yellow cloth cut in the form of a chasuble. Meanwhile, Pierrat Torterue was letting the blood that soaked the lashes of his scourge drain from them in drops upon the ground.

However, all was not yet over for poor Quasimodo. He had still to undergo that hour on the pillory which Maître Florian Barbedienne had so judiciously added to the sentence of Messire Robert d'Estouteville, all to the greater glory of the old *jeu de mots*, physiological and psychological, of Jean de Cumène—*surdus absurdus*.

So they turned the hour-glass, and left the hunchback bound down upon the wheel, that justice might be perpetrated to the end.

The people, in the inferior sense of the word, have hitherto been, in society, especially in the Middle Ages, what the child is in a family. So long as they remain in that state of primitive ignorance, of moral and intellectual nonage, it may be said of them as has been said of childhood—"that age is a stranger to pity." We have already shown that Quasimodo was generally hated—for more than one good reason, it is true. There was hardly a spectator among that crowd but either had or thought he had some cause of complaint against the mischievous hunchback of Notre-Dame. All had rejoiced to see him make his appearance on the pillory; and the severe punishment he had just undergone, and the piteous plight in which it had left him, so far from softening the hearts of the populace, had but rendered their hatred the more malicious by furnishing it with matter for merriment.

And accordingly, the "public vengeance" being satisfied—the *vindicte publique*, as it is still called in the legal jargon of our neighbours—a thousand private revenges had now their turn. Here, as in the Grand' Salle, it was the women that broke forth with the greatest violence. They all bore malice against him—some for his mischievousness, others for his ugliness. The latter were the most curious of the two.

"O thou phiz of Anti-Christ," exclaimed one.

"Thou broomstick-rider!" cried another.

"What a fine tragical grin!" bawled a third—"and one that would have made him fools' pope if to-day had been yesterday."

"Good!" chimed in an old woman. "This is the pillory grin; when is he to give us the gallows grin?"

"When art thou to have thy big bell clapped upon thy head a hundred feet under ground, thou cursed ringer?" shouted one.

"And yet it's this devil that rings the Angelus!"

"O the deaf as a post! the one-eye! the hunchback! the monster!"

"He's a face to make a woman miscarry, better than any medicines or pharmacies!"

And the two scholars, Jehan du Moulin and Robin Poussepain, sang out as loud as they could bawl the burden of an old popular song,—

A halter for the gallows rogue!
A fagot for the witch!

A thousand other pieces of abuse were showered upon him, and hootings, and imprecations, and bursts of laughter, and here and there a stone.

Quasimodo was deaf, but he saw clearly; and the public fury was not less forcibly expressed in the countenances of the people than by their words. Besides, the stones that struck him explained the bursts of laughter.

At first he bore it all very well. But by degrees the patience which had braced up its fibres under the lash of the torturer relaxed and gave way under these insect stings. The Austrian bull that has borne unmoved the attacks of the *picador* is irritated by the dogs and the *banderillas*.

First, he cast slowly around a look of menace upon the crowd. But, bound hand and foot as he was, his look had no power to chase away the flies that gnawed his wound. Then he shook himself in his toils; and his furious efforts made the old wheel of the pillory creak upon its timbers—all which but increased the derision and the hooting.

Then the poor wretch, finding himself unable to burst his wild beast's chain, once more became quiet; only, at intervals, a sigh of rage heaved all the cavities of his breast. In his face there was neither shame nor blush. He was too far from the state of society and too near the state of nature to know what shame was. Besides, at that pitch of deformity, is infamy a thing that can be felt? But resentment, hatred, and despair were slowly spreading over that hideous visage a cloud that grew more and more gloomy, more and more charged with an electricity which shone in a thousand flashes from the eye of the cyclop.

However, that cloud was dissipated for a moment at the appearance of a mule which passed through the crowd, carrying a priest on its back. From the first moment that he perceived that priest and that mule approaching, the poor sufferer's countenance became milder. The fury which had contracted it was succeeded by a strange smile, full of a softness, a gentleness, a tenderness inexpressible. As the priest came nearer, this smile became plainer, more distinct, more radiant. It was as if the unfortunate creature was hailing the coming of a saviour. However, the moment that the mule had come near enough to the pillory for its rider to recognise the sufferer, the priest cast down his eyes, turned round abruptly, and spurred away his steed, as if in haste to escape humiliating appeals, and not at all anxious to be saluted and recognised by a poor devil in such a situation.

This priest was the Archdeacon Dom Claude Frollo, who, albeit he stood in much the same relation to Quasimodo as the knight of La Mancha did to his squire, was, in some respects, no more a Don Quixote than, in some others, Quasimodo was a Sancho Panza. And yet Sancho's blanket-tossing, from which the knight would have encountered any disgrace to have delivered him, was a mere trifle compared to this infliction undergone by the Archdeacon's devoted servant.

And now the cloud fell darker than ever upon the face of Quasimodo. The smile was still mingled with it for a time; but it was bitter, disheartened, and profoundly sad.

The time was going on. He had been there for at least an hour and a half, lacerated, abused, mocked, and almost stoned to death. All at once he made another struggle in his chains, with redoubled despèration that shook the whole wood-work upon which he was fixed; and, breaking the silence which until then he had obstinately kept, he cried out in a hoarse and furious voice, which was more like a dog's howl than a human shout, and which drowned the noise of the hooting, "Some drink!"

This exclamation of distress, far from exciting compassion, was an additional amusement to the good Parisian populace that surrounded the pillory, and who, it must be admitted, taken on the whole and as a multitude, were then scarcely less cruel and brutal than that horrible tribe of the Truands, to which we have already introduced the reader, and which, indeed, was itself neither more nor less than the lowest stratum of the people. Not a voice was raised around the unhappy sufferer, except in mockery of his thirst. It is certain that at that moment his appearance was yet more grotesque and repulsive than it was pitiable, with his reddened and trickling face, his bewildered eye, his mouth foaming with rage and suffering, and his tongue half hanging out. We must observe, too, that had there even been among the multitude any good charitable soul of a townsman or townswoman who should have been tempted to carry a glass of water to that miserable creature in pain, there reigned around the ignominious steps of the pillory so strong an air of infamy in the prejudices of the time, as would have sufficed to repel the good Samaritan.

At the end of a few minutes more Quasimodo cast around him a look of despair upon the crowd, and repeated, in a voice yet more heartrending, "Some drink!" And again they all laughed.

"Drink this!" cried Robin Poussepain, throwing in his face a sponge soaked in the kennel. "Here, you deaf scoundrel—I'm your debtor!"

A woman threw a stone at his head, saying, "That'll teach thee to wake us in the night with thy cursed ringing!"

"Well, my lad!" bawled a cripple, trying at the same time to reach him with his crutch, "wilt thou cast spells at us again from the top of the towers of Notre-Dame?"

"Here's a porringer to drink out of," said one man, hurling a broken pitcher at his breast. "It's thou that, with only passing before her, made my wife be brought to bed of a child with two heads!"

"And my cat of a kitten with six legs!" screamed an old woman as she flung a tile at him.

"Some drink!" repeated Quasimodo for the third time, panting. At that moment he saw the populace making way for some one, and a young girl fantastically dressed issued from the crowd. She was accompanied by a little white she-goat with gilt horns, and carried a small tambourine in her hand.

Quasimodo's eye sparkled. It was the gipsy girl whom he had attempted to carry off the night before, for which piece of presumption he had some confused notion that they were chastising him at that very moment—which, however, was by no means the case, seeing that he was punished only for the misfortune of being deaf and having a deaf judge. He doubted not that she too was come to take her revenge, and to aim her blow at him like all the rest of them.

In fact, he beheld her rapidly ascend the steps. He was choking with rage and vexation. He wished that he could have crumbled the pillory to atoms; and if the flash of his eye could have destroyed, the gipsy would have been reduced to ashes before she could have reached the platform. Without uttering a word, she approached the sufferer, who was vainly writhing about to escape her; and then, unfastening a gourd-bottle from her belt, she held it out to the poor wretch's parched lips.

Then from that eye, hitherto so dry and burning, was seen to roll a big tear, which fell slowly down that deformed visage so long contracted by despair. Perhaps it was the first that the unfortunate creature had ever shed.

Meanwhile he forgot to drink. The gipsy made her little accustomed grimace with impatience, and held up, smiling, the neck of the gourd to the jagged mouth of Quasimodo. He drank long draughts, for his thirst was burning.

When he had done, the poor wretch put out his black lips, undoubtedly to kiss the fair hand which had just relieved him; but the girl, who, remembering the violent attempt of the preceding night, was perhaps not without some mistrust, drew back her hand with the frightened look of a child afraid of being bitten by some animal.

Then the poor deaf creature fixed upon her a look reproachful and inexpressibly sad.

It would anywhere have been a touching spectacle to see that beautiful girl, so fresh, so pure, so charming, and at the same time so weak, thus piously hastening to the relief of so much wretchedness, deformity, and malice; but on a pillory the spectacle was sublime. The people themselves were struck by it, and clapped their hands, shouting, "Noël! Noël!"

It was at that moment that the recluse, through the loophole of her cell, observed the gipsy girl upon the steps of the pillory, and cast at her the dismal imprecation, "Cursed be thou, daughter of Egypt! cursed! cursed!"

CHAPTER V

END OF THE STORY OF THE CAKE

La Esmeralda turned pale, and descended from the pillory, tottering; the voice of the recluse pursued her still. "Come down, come down, Egyptian thief! thou shalt go up there again!"

"The Sachette's in her crotchets," said the people, muttering; but that was all they did, for this sort of women were feared, and that made them sacred. Nobody in those days was willing to attack any one that prayed day and night.

The hour had now arrived for carrying back Quasimodo; they unfastened him from the pillory, and the crowd dispersed.

Near the Grand Pont, Mahiette, who was going away with her two companions, suddenly stopped short. "By-the-bye, Eustache," said she, "what have you done with the cake?"

"Mother," said the boy, "while you were talking to that lady in the hole, there was a great dog came and bit of my cake, and then I bit of it too."

"What, sir!" cried she, "have you eaten it all?"

"Mother, it was the dog. I told him so; but he wouldn't listen to me. Then I bit a piece too—that's all."

"It's a shocking boy," said the mother, smiling and chiding at the same time.—"What do you think, Oudarde?—already he eats by himself all the cherries that grow upon the tree in our croft at Charlerange. So his grandfather says he'll be a captain.—Let me catch you at it again, Master Eustache. Get along, you greedy fellow!"

BOOK VII

CHAPTER I

OF THE DANGER OF CONFIDING IN A GOAT

SEVERAL weeks had elapsed. It was now the early part of the month of March. The sun, which Dubartas, that classic ancestor of periphrasis, had not yet named "the grand duke of the candles," was not therefore the less cheerful and radiant. It was one of those days of the early spring which are so mild and beautiful that all Paris turns out into the squares and promenades, to enjoy them as if they were holidays. On those days of clearness, warmth, and serenity there is one hour in particular at which you should go and admire the portal of Notre-Dame. It is that moment when the sun, already declining towards his setting, darts his rays almost directly upon the front of the cathedral. Becoming more and more horizontal, they gradually retire from the pavement of the Place, and mount up the perpendicular face of the structure, streaming full upon the thousand rotundities of its sculpture, while the great round central window flames like a cyclop's eye lit up by the reverberations of the forge.

At this hour it was that, opposite to the front of the lofty cathedral, reddened by the setting sun, upon the stone balcony constructed over the porch of a rich-looking Gothic house, at the angle formed by the Place with the Rue du Parvis, some handsome girls were laughing and talking together with all manner of grace and sportiveness. By the length of the veil which fell from the top of their pointed coif, all scrolled with pearls, down to their heels—by the fineness of the worked chemisette which covered their shoulders, revealing, according to the engaging fashion of that time, the swell of their fair virgin bosoms—by the richness of their under-petticoat, yet more costly than the upper skirt (admirable refinement!)—by the gauze, the silk, and the velvet with which the whole was loaded—and, above all, by the whiteness of their hands—it was easy to divine that they were noble and wealthy heiresses.

They were, in fact, Damoiselle Fleur-de-Lys de Gondelaurier and her companions, Diane de Christeuil, Amelotte de Montmichel, Colombe de Gaillefontaine, and the little De Champchevrier, all girls of family, assembled at that moment at the mansion of the lady widow De Gondelaurier, on account of Monseigneur de Beaujeau and Madame his wife, who were to come to Paris in April, to choose *accompagneresses d'honneur*, or maids of honour, to accompany the Dauphiness Marguerite, on the occasion of her reception in Picardy, at the hands of the Flemings, on her way to the court of France. Now all the *hobereaux* or gentry for thirty leagues round were seeking this honour for their daughters, and a good many of them had already brought or sent them to Paris. The young ladies in question had been entrusted by their parents to the discreet and reverent keeping of Madame Aloïse de Gondelaurier, widow of a *ci-devant* master of the king's crossbowmen, now living in retirement, with her only daughter, at her house in the Place du Parvis-Notre-Dame, at Paris.

The balcony at which these young ladies were amusing themselves opened into an apartment richly hung with fawn-coloured Flanders leather printed with golden foliage. The beams that ran across the ceiling diverted the eye with a thousand fantastic carvings, painted and gilt. Splendid enamels were glittering here and there upon the lids of cabinets curiously carved; and a boar's head in china crowned a magnificent sideboard, the two steps of which announced that the mistress of the house was the wife or widow of a knight banneret. At the upper end of the room, beside a lofty chimney-piece, covered with emblazonry from top to bottom, was seated, in a rich fauteuil of red velvet, the lady of Gondelaurier, whose fifty-five years of age were no less distinctly written on her dress than on her face. Beside her a young man was standing, of very imposing mien, though partaking somewhat of vanity and bravado—one of those fine fellows whom all women agree to admire, although their physiognomy is precisely that which makes grave and discerning men shake their heads. This young cavalier wore the brilliant uniform of a captain of archers of the *ordonnance du roi* or household troops—which uniform too closely resembled the costume of Jupiter, which the reader has already had an opportunity of admiring in the first chapter of this history, for us to weary him with a second description of it.

The young ladies were seated, part in the room, part in the balcony—the former on cushions of Utrecht velvet with gold corner-plates, the latter on oak stools carved in flowers and figures. Each of them held in her lap part of a large piece of tapestry, on which they were all at work, while one long end of it lay on the matting which covered the floor.

They were talking among themselves in that whispering voice and with those half-stifled laughs so common in an assembly of young girls when there is a young man among them. The young man himself, whose presence had the effect of bringing into play all this feminine vanity, appeared, on his part, to care very little about it; and whilst the lovely girls were vying with each other in endeavouring to attract his attention, he was specially occupied in polishing, with his doeskin glove, the buckle of his sword-belt.

From time to time the old lady addressed him in a low voice, and he answered as well as he was able, with a sort of awkward and constrained politeness. From the smiles and significant gestures of Madame Aloïse, as well as the glances which she threw towards her daughter Fleur-de-Lys as she spoke low to the captain, it was evident that the subject of their conversation was some previous betrothing, some marriage doubtless about to take place between the young man and Fleur-de-Lys. And from the cold, embarrassed air of the officer, it was easy to see that, so far at least as he was concerned, love had no longer any part in the matter. His whole demeanour conveyed an idea of constraint and ennui, which a modern French subaltern on garrison duty would admirably render by the exclamation, *Quelle chienne de corvée!*

The good lady, infatuated, like any other silly mother, with her daughter's charms, did not perceive the officer's want of enthusiasm, but exerted herself strenuously to point out in a whisper the infinite grace with which Fleur-de-Lys used her needle or wound her silk.

"Do look now, *petit cousin,*" said she, pulling him by the sleeve towards her, and speaking in his ear. "Look at her! See, now she stoops."

"Yes, indeed," answered the young man, and fell back into his cold, abstracted silence.

Shortly after he had to lean again on Dame Aloïse saying to him, "Did you ever see a more charming, lightsome face than that of your betrothed? Can anything be more fair or more lovely? Are not those hands perfect? and that neck—does it not assume every graceful curve of a swan's? How I envy you at times! and how happy you are in being a man, wicked rogue that you are! Is not my Fleur-de-Lys adorably beautiful? and are you not passionately in love with her?"

"Assuredly," answered he, thinking all the time of something else.

"Speak to her, then," said Madame Aloïse, abruptly pushing him by the shoulder—"say something to her; you're grown quite timid."

We can assure our readers that timidity was neither a virtue nor a defect of the captain's. He endeavoured, however, to do as he was bid.

"*Belle cousine,*" said he, approaching Fleur-de-Lys, "what is the subject of this tapestry you are so busy with?"

"*Beau cousin,*" answered Fleur-de-Lys in a pettish tone, "I have already told you three times. It is the grotto of Neptunus."

It was evident that Fleur-de-Lys saw more clearly than her mother through the cold, absent manner of her captain. He felt the necessity of entering into conversation.

"And for what is all this fine Neptune work intended?" asked he.

"For the Abbey of Saint-Antoine-des-Champs," said Fleur-de-Lys, without raising her eyes.

The captain took up a corner of the tapestry. "And pray, *ma belle cousine,* who is that big gendarme fellow there disguised as a fish, and blowing his trumpet till his cheeks are bursting?"

"That is Trito," answered she.

There was still a degree of pettishness in the tone of the few words uttered by Fleur-de-Lys. The young man understood that it was indispensable he should whisper in her ear some pretty nothing, some gallant compliment or other, no matter what. He accordingly leaned over, but his imagination could furnish nothing more tender or familiar than this: "Why does your mother always wear that petticoat with her arms worked upon it, like our great-grandmothers of Charles VII.'s time? Pray tell her, *belle cousine,* that it's not the fashion of the present day, and that, all emblazoned in that way, her dress makes her look like a walking mantelpiece. 'Pon honour, no one sits under their banner in that way now, I assure you."

Fleur-de-Lys raised her fine eyes towards his reproachfully. "Is that all you have to assure me of?" said she in a low voice.

Meanwhile the good Dame Aloïse, delighted to see them thus leaning over and whispering to each other, exclaimed, playing all the while with the clasps of her prayer-book, "Touching picture of love!"

The captain, more and more at a loss, passed to the subject of the tapestry again. "It is really a beautiful piece of work!" he cried.

At this juncture Colombe de Gaillefontaine, another beautiful white-skinned blonde, dressed up to the neck in blue damask, ventured to put in a word, addressed to Fleur-de-Lys, but in the hope that the handsome captain would answer her: "My dear Gondelaurier, did you ever see the tapestry at the Hôtel de la Roche-Guyon?"

"Is that the hôtel where the garden is belonging to the *Lingère* of the Louvre?" asked Diane de Christeuil, laughing; for having fine teeth, she laughed on all occasions.

"And where that big old tower is, part of the ancient wall of Paris?" added Amelotte de Montmichel, a pretty curly-headed, fresh-looking brunette, who had a habit of sighing, just as the other laughed, without knowing why.

"My dear Colombe," said Dame Aloïse, "are you speaking of the hôtel which belonged to Monsieur de Bacqueville in the reign of Charles VI.? There is indeed magnificent tapestry there of the high warp."

"Charles VI.! King Charles VI.!" muttered the young captain, curling his moustaches. "*Mon Dieu!* what a memory the good lady has for everything old!"

Madame de Gondelaurier continued, "Superb tapestry indeed! so superior that it is considered unrivalled!"

At that moment Bérangère de Champchevrier, an airy little creature of seven years of age, who was looking into the square through the trifoliated ornaments of the balcony, cried out, "Oh, do look, dear godmamma Fleur-de-Lys, at that pretty dancing-girl who is dancing in the street, and playing the tambourine in the midst of those common people!"

The sonorous vibration of a tambourine was, in fact, heard by the party. "Some gipsy girl from Bohemia," said Fleur-de-Lys, turning her head carelessly towards the square.

"Let us see! let us see!" cried her lively companions; and they all ran to the front of the balcony, while Fleur-de-Lys, musing over the coldness of her affianced lover, followed them slowly; and the latter, relieved by this incident, which cut short an embarrassed conversation, returned to the farther end of the room with the satisfied air of a soldier relieved from duty. And yet no unpleasing service was that of the lovely Fleur-de-

Lys, and such it had appeared to him formerly; but the captain had by degrees become dissipated, and the prospect of an approaching marriage grew more and more repulsive to him every day. Besides, he was of a fickle disposition, and, if one may say so, of rather vulgar tastes. Although of very noble birth, he had contracted, under his officer's accoutrements, more than one habit of the common soldier. He delighted in the tavern and its accompaniments, and was never at his ease but amidst gross language, military gallantries, easy beauties, and as easy successes. He had, notwithstanding, received from his family some education and some politeness of manner; but he had too early been a rover, and too early kept garrison, and each day the polish of the gentleman became more and more worn away under the friction of the gendarme's baldric. Though still continuing to visit her occasionally, through some small remnant of common respect, he felt doubly constrained with Fleur-de-Lys: first, because, by dint of dividing his love among so many different objects, he had very little left for her; and next, because, surrounded by a number of fine women of stiff, decorous, and formal manners, he was constantly in fear lest his lips, accustomed to the language of oaths, should inadvertently break through their bounds, and let slip some unfortunate tavern slang or other. The effect may be imagined!

And yet with all this were mingled great pretensions to elegance, taste in dress, and noble bearing. Let these things be reconciled as they may, our office is simply that of the historian.

He had been for some minutes thinking of something or of nothing, leaning in silence against the carved mantelpiece, when Fleur-de-Lys, turning suddenly round, addressed him; for after all the poor girl only pouted in self-defence,—

"*Beau cousin*, did you not tell us of a little gipsy girl whom you saved from a parcel of thieves about a month ago, as you were going the counter-watch at night?"

"I believe I did, *belle cousine*," said the captain.

"Well," rejoined she, "perhaps it is that very gipsy girl who is now dancing in the Parvis. Come and see if you recognise her, *beau cousin Phœbus*."

A secret desire of reconciliation was perceptible in the gentle invitation she gave him to draw near her, and in the care she took to call him by his name. Captain Phœbus de Chateaupers (for it is he whom the reader has had before him from the beginning of this chapter) with tardy steps approached the balcony.

"Look," said Fleur-de-Lys tenderly, placing her hand on his arm—"look at that little girl, dancing there in the ring. Is that your gipsy girl?"

Phœbus looked and said, "Yes; I know her by her goat."

"Ah! so there is—a pretty little goat!" said Amelotte, clasping her hands with delight.

"Are its horns really gold?" asked little Bérangère.

Without moving from her fauteuil Dame Aloïse inquired, "Is it one of those gipsy girls that arrived last year by the Porte Gibard?"

"My dear mother," said Fleur-de-Lys gently, "that gate is now called Porte d'Enfer."

Mademoiselle de Gondelaurier knew how much the captain's notions were shocked by her mother's antiquated modes of speech. Indeed, he was already on the titter, and began to mutter between his teeth, "Porte Gibard! Porte Gibard! That's to make way for King Charles VI."

"Godmamma," exclaimed Bérangère, whose eyes, incessantly in motion, were suddenly raised towards the top of the towers of Notre-Dame, "who is that black man up there?"

All the girls raised their eyes. A man, in fact, was leaning with his elbows upon the topmost balustrade of the northern tower, which looked towards the Grève. It was the figure of a priest; and they could clearly discern both his costume and his face, which was resting on his two hands. Otherwise he was as motionless as a statue; his steady gaze seemed riveted to the Place. There was in it something of the immobility of the kite when it has just discovered a nest of sparrows, and is looking down upon it.

"It is Monsieur the Archdeacon of Joas," said Fleur-de-Lys.

"You've good eyes if you know him at that distance," observed La Gaillefontaine.

"How he looks at the little dancing-girl!" remarked Diane de Christeuil.

"Let the gipsy girl beware," said Fleur-de-Lys, "for he loves not Egypt."

"It's a great pity that man looks at her so," said Amelotte de Montmichel, "for she dances delightfully."

"*Beau cousin Phœbus*," said Fleur-de-Lys suddenly, "since you know this little gipsy girl, beckon to her to come up. It will be an amusement for us."

"Oh yes!" cried all her companions, clapping their hands.

"It's really not worth while," answered Phœbus: "she has

forgotten me, I dare say; and I don't so much as know her name. However, since you wish it, ladies, I will see." And leaning over the balustrade of the balcony, he began to call out, "Little girl!"

The dancing-girl was not at that moment playing her tambourine, and turning her head towards the point from whence she heard herself called, her brilliant eyes rested on Phœbus, and she stopped short suddenly.

"Little girl!" repeated the captain, and he beckoned to her to come in.

The young girl looked at him again, then blushed, as if a flame had risen to her cheeks; and taking her tambourine under her arm, she made her way through the midst of the gaping spectators towards the door of the house where Phœbus was, with slow and tottering steps, and with the troubled air of a bird yielding to the fascination of a serpent.

A moment or two after the tapestry hanging at the entrance was raised, and the gipsy girl made her appearance on the threshold of the room, blushing, confused, and out of breath, her large eyes cast down, and not daring to advance a step farther.

Bérangère clapped her hands.

Meanwhile the dancing-girl remained motionless at the entrance of the apartment. Her appearance had produced on this group of young women a singular effect. It is certain that a vague and undefined desire of pleasing the handsome officer at once animated the whole party; that the splendid uniform was the object at which all their coquetry was aimed; and that, from the time of his being present, there had arisen among them a certain tacit, covert rivalry, scarcely acknowledged to themselves, but which did not the less constantly display itself in all their gestures and remarks. Nevertheless, as they all possessed nearly the same degree of beauty, they contended with equal arms, and each might reasonably hope for victory. The arrival of the gipsy girl suddenly destroyed this equilibrium. Her beauty was of so rare a cast that the moment she entered the apartment she seemed to shed around it a sort of light peculiar to herself. Within this enclosed chamber, surrounded by its dusky hangings and wainscotings, she was incomparably more beautiful and radiant than in the public square. She was as the torch suddenly brought from the midday light into the shade. The noble damsels were dazzled by it in spite of themselves. Each felt that her beauty had in some degree suffered; and in consequence their line of battle (if we may be allowed the expression) was changed immediately, without a single word being uttered by any of them. But they understood each other perfectly. The instincts of women comprehend and correspond with each other more quickly than the understandings of men. An enemy had arrived in the midst of them: all felt it—all rallied. One drop of wine is sufficient to tinge a whole glass of water; and to diffuse a certain degree of ill-temper throughout a company of pretty women, it is only necessary for one still prettier to make her appearance—especially when there is but one man in the way. Thus the gipsy girl's reception proved mightily freezing. They eyed her from head to foot, then looked at each other; and that was enough—all was understood. Meanwhile the young girl, waiting for them to speak to her, was so much affected that she dared not raise her eyelids.

The captain was the first to break silence. "'Pon honour," said he, with his tone of brainless assurance, "here's a charming creature! What do you think of her, *belle cousine?*"

This observation, which a more delicate admirer would at least have made in an undertone, did not tend to dissipate the feminine jealousies which were on the alert in the presence of the gipsy girl.

Fleur-de-Lys answered the captain with a simpering affectation of contempt, "Ah, not amiss."

The others whispered together.

At length Madame Aloïse, who was not the less jealous for being so on her daughter's account, addressed the dancing-girl,—

"Come hither, little girl," said she.

"Come hither, little girl," repeated, with comic dignity, little Bérangère, who would have stood about as high as her hip.

The gipsy girl advanced towards the noble lady.

"My pretty girl," said Phœbus significantly, likewise advancing a few paces towards her, "I don't know whether I have the supreme felicity of being remembered by you."

She interrupted him by saying, with a look and smile of infinite sweetness, "Oh yes."

"She has a good memory," observed Fleur-de-Lys.

"So," resumed Phœbus, "you contrived to make your escape in a hurry the other evening. Did I frighten you?"

"Oh no," said the gipsy girl. There was in the accent with which this "Oh no," following immediately the "Oh yes," was pronounced an indescribable something which stung poor Fleur-de-Lys.

"You left me in your stead, my fair one," continued the captain, whose tongue became unloosed while speaking to a girl out of the street, "a rare grim-faced fellow, humpbacked and one-eyed, the ringer of the bishop's bells, I believe. They tell me he's an archdeacon's bastard and a devil by birth. He has a pretty name, too; they call him Quatre-Temps,[1] Pâques-Fleuries,[2] Mardi-Gras,[3] I don't know what—a bell-ringing holiday-name, in short. And so he thought fit to carry you off, as if you were made for such fellows as beadles! That is going a little too far. What the deuce could that screech-owl want with you, eh?"

"I don't know," answered she.

"Only imagine his insolence! a bell-ringer to carry off a girl like a viscount! a clown poaching the game of gentlemen! A rare piece of assurance, truly! But he paid pretty dear for it. Maître Pierrat Torterue is as rough a groom as ever curried a rascal! and your ringer's hide—if that will please you—got a thorough dressing at his hands, I warrant you."

"Poor man!" said the gipsy girl, the scene of the pillory brought back to her remembrance by these words.

The captain burst out laughing. "*Corne-de-bœuf!* your pity's about as well placed as a feather in a pig's tail. May I have a belly like a pope if——" He stopped suddenly short. "Pardon me, ladies; I fear I was about to let slip some nonsense or other."

"Fie, monsieur!" said La Gaillefontaine.

"He speaks to this creature in her own language," added Fleur-de-Lys in an undertone, her vexation increasing every moment. This vexation was not diminished by seeing the captain, delighted with the gipsy girl, and above all with himself, turn round on his heel and repeat with naïve and soldier-like gallantry, "A lovely girl, upon my soul!"

"Very barbarously dressed!" said Diane de Christeuil, laughing to show her fine teeth.

This remark was like a flash of light for the others. It gave to view the gipsy's assailable point; having nothing to find fault with in her person, they all fell upon her dress.

"It's very true," said La Montmichel.—"Pray, little girl, where did you learn to run about the streets in that way, without either neckerchief or tucker?"

[1] *Quatre-Temps.*—Ember Week.
[2] *Pâques-Fleuries.*—Palm Sunday.
[3] *Mardi-Gras.*—Shrove Tuesday.

"What a dreadful short petticoat!" added La Gaillefontaine.

"You'll get yourself taken up, child, by the sergeants of the *douzaine*, for your gilt belt," continued Fleur-de-Lys harshly.

"Little girl, little girl," resumed Christeuil, with an unmerciful smile, "if you had the decency to wear sleeves on your arms they would not get so sunburnt."

It was a sight worthy a more intelligent spectator than Phœbus to watch how those fine girls, with their envenomed and angry tongues, turned, glided, and wound, as it were, around the street dancer. They were at once cruel and courteous; they searched and pried maliciously into every part of her poor, wild dress of spangles and tinsel. Then followed the laugh, the ironical jest, humiliations without end. Sarcasms, haughty condescensions, and evil looks were poured upon the gipsy girl. One might have fancied them some of those young Roman ladies that used to amuse themselves with thrusting golden pins into the bosom of some beautiful slave; or have likened them to elegant greyhounds, turning, wheeling, with distended nostrils and eager eyes, around some poor hind of the forest whom nothing but their master's eye prevents them from devouring.

And what, in fact, was a poor dancing-girl of the public square to those high-born maidens? They did not seem so much as to recognise her presence; but spoke of her, before her, and to herself, aloud, as of something pretty enough, perhaps, but at the same time loathsome and abject.

The gipsy girl was not insensible to these petty stings. From time to time a glow of shame or a flash of anger inflamed her eyes or cheeks—a disdainful exclamation seemed to hover on her lips—she made contemptuously the little grimace with which the reader is already familiar—but remained motionless, her eyes fixed, with a sweet, resigned, and melancholy expression, upon Phœbus. In this look, too, were mingled delight and tenderness. It seemed as if she restrained herself for fear of being driven away.

As for Phœbus himself, he laughed, and took the gipsy girl's part, with a mixture of pity and impertinence. "Let them talk, little one," repeated he, jingling his gold spurs. "Doubtless your dress is a little wild and extravagant; but in a charming girl like you what does that signify?"

"*Mon Dieu!*" exclaimed the blonde Gaillefontaine, drawing up her swan-like neck with a bitter smile, "I see that messieurs the king's archers take fire easily at bright gipsy eyes."

"And why not?" said Phœbus.

At this rejoinder, uttered carelessly by the captain, like a stone thrown at random, the fall of which one does not so much as turn to watch, Colombe began to laugh, as did Amelotte, Diane, and Fleur-de-Lys, while a tear rose at the same time to the eyes of the latter.

The gipsy girl, who had cast her eyes on the ground as Colombe and Gaillefontaine spoke, raised them, all beaming with joy and pride, and fixed them again on Phœbus. She looked angelic at that moment.

The old lady, who observed this scene, felt herself piqued without well understanding why.

"Holy Virgin!" cried she suddenly, "what's that about my legs? Ah, the nasty animal!"

It was the goat, which had just arrived in search of its mistress, and which, in hurrying towards her, had got itself entangled by the horns in the pile of stuff which the noble lady's ample habiliments heaped around her whenever she was seated. This made a diversion. The gipsy girl, without saying a word, disentangled the little creature's horns.

"Oh, here's the pretty little goat with the golden feet," cried Bérangère, jumping with joy.

The gipsy girl squatted on her knees, and pressed her cheek against the fondling head of the goat, as if to beg its pardon for having left it behind.

Meanwhile Diane bent over and whispered in Colombe's ear. "Ah, *mon Dieu!* how is it I didn't think of it before! It's the gipsy girl with the goat. They say she's a sorceress, and that her goat performs very miraculous tricks."

"Well," said Colombe, "let the goat amuse us now in its turn, and perform us a miracle."

Diane and Colombe eagerly addressed the gipsy girl, "Little girl, do let your goat perform a miracle."

"I don't know what you mean," said the dancing-girl.

"Why, a miracle—a conjuring trick—a feat of witchcraft."

"I do not understand," she replied. And she turned to caressing the pretty animal again, repeating, "Djali! Djali!"

At that moment Fleur-de-Lys remarked a little embroidered leathern bag hanging about the goat's neck. "What's that?" asked she of the gipsy girl.

The girl raised her large eyes towards her, and answered gravely, "That's my secret."

"I should like to know your secret," thought Fleur-de-Lys.

Meanwhile the noble dame had risen angrily. "Come, come,

gipsy girl; if neither you nor your goat have anything to dance to us, what do you here?"

The gipsy girl, without answering, directed her steps slowly towards the door. But the nearer she approached it the slower was her pace. An irresistible magnet seemed to arrest her steps. Suddenly she turned, her eyes moistened with tears, towards Phœbus, and stood still.

"*Vrai Dieu!*" cried the captain, "you shall not go away thus. Come back, and dance us something or other. By-the-bye, sweet love, what's your name?"

"La Esmeralda," said the dancing-girl, without taking her eyes off him.

At this strange name the girls burst forth into an extravagant laugh.

"A formidable name, indeed, for a young lady," said Diane.

"You see, plain enough," remarked Amelotte, "that she's an enchantress."

"My dear," cried Dame Aloise seriously, "your parents never found that name for you in the baptismal font."

Meanwhile, Bérangère, without any one's observing it, had a few minutes before enticed the goat into a corner of the room with a piece of sweet cake. In an instant they had become good friends, and the curious child had untied the little bag which hung at the goat's neck, had opened it, and spread its contents on the matting; it was an alphabet, each letter of which was inscribed separately on a small tablet of wood. No sooner were these toys displayed on the matting than the child saw, with surprise, the goat (one of whose miracles doubtless it was) draw towards her with her golden paw certain letters, and arrange them, by pushing them about gently, in a particular order. In a minute they formed a word which the goat seemed practised in composing, so little was she at a loss in forming it; and Bérangère suddenly cried out, clasping her hands with admiration,—

"Godmamma Fleur-de-Lys, do see what the goat has been doing!"

Fleur-de-Lys ran to look, and started at the sight. The letters arranged on the floor formed, in the Gothic characters of the time, the word

Phœbus.

"Did the goat write that?" asked she, with a faltering voice.

"Yes, godmamma," answered Bérangère. It was impossible to doubt it, for the child could not spell.

"Here's the secret!" thought Fleur-de-Lys. Meanwhile, at the child's exclamation, they had all hurried forward to look—the lady mother, the young ladies, the gipsy, and the officer.

The gipsy girl saw the blunder the goat had committed. She turned red, then pale, and began to tremble like a guilty thing before the captain, who looked at her with a smile of satisfaction and astonishment.

"*Phœbus!*" whispered the girls in amazement; "that's the captain's name!"

"You have a wonderful memory," said Fleur-de-Lys to the petrified gipsy girl. Then bursting into sobs: "Oh!" stammered she sorrowfully, hiding her face between her two fair hands, "she is a sorceress!" while she heard a voice yet more bitter whisper from her inmost heart, "she is a rival!" And therewith she fainted away.

"My child! my child!" cried the terrified mother. "Begone, you diabolical gipsy!"

La Esmeralda gathered together in a trice the unlucky letters, made a sign to Djali, and quitted the room at one door as Fleur-de-Lys was being carried out at the other.

Captain Phœbus, left alone, hesitated a moment between the two doors, then followed the gipsy girl.

CHAPTER II

SHOWING THAT A PRIEST AND A PHILOSOPHER ARE TWO DIFFERENT MEN

THE priest whom the young ladies had observed on the top of the northern tower, leaning over towards the square, and so attentive to the gipsy girl's dancing, was in fact the Archdeacon Claude Frollo.

Our readers have not forgotten the mysterious cell which the archdeacon had appropriated to himself in this tower. By the way, we do not know whether it is not the same, the interior of which may be seen to this day, through a small square window, opening towards the east, at about the height of a man from the floor, upon the platform from which the towers spring; a mere dog-hole now, naked, empty, and falling to decay; the ill-plastered walls of which are, even at this time, decorated here and there with a parcel of sorry yellow engravings representing cathedral fronts. We presume that this hole is jointly inhabited by bats and spiders, and that consequently a double war of extermination is carried on there against the flies.

Every day, an hour before sunset, the archdeacon ascended the staircase of the tower, and shut himself up in this cell, where he sometimes passed whole nights. On this day, just as he had reached the low door of his little nook and was putting into the lock the small key with its intricate wards which he always carried about him in the *escarcelle* or large purse suspended at his side, the sound of a tambourine and castanets reached his ears. This sound proceeded from the Place du Parvis. The cell, as we have already said, had but one window, looking upon the back of the church. Claude Frollo had hastily withdrawn the key, and in an instant was on the summit of the tower, in that gloomy, thoughtful attitude in which the young ladies had first seen him.

There he was, grave, motionless, absorbed in one look, one thought. All Paris lay at his feet, with her thousand spires and her circular horizon of softly-swelling hills; with her river winding under her bridges, and her people flowing to and fro through her streets; with the cloud of her smoke; with her hilly chain of roofs pressing round Notre-Dame with redoubled folds: yet in all that city the archdeacon saw but one spot on its pavement, the Place du Parvis; in all that crowd but one figure, that of the gipsy girl.

It would have been difficult to say what was the nature of that look, or whence arose the flame that issued from it. It was a fixed gaze, and yet full of trouble and tumult. And from the profound stillness of his whole body, only just agitated at intervals by an involuntary shiver, like a tree shaken by the wind, his stiffened elbows, more marble than the balustrade on which they leaned, and the petrified smile which contracted his countenance, one might have said that no part of Claude Frollo was alive but his eyes.

The gipsy girl was dancing, twirling her tambourine on the point of her finger, and throwing it aloft in the air as she danced the Provençal sarabands: agile, light, joyous, and unconscious of the formidable gaze which lighted directly on her head.

The crowd swarmed around her; occasionally a man, tricked out in a red and yellow *casaque* or long loose coat, went round to make the people keep the ring; then returned to seat himself in a chair, a few steps off the dancer, and took the head of the goat upon his knees. This man appeared to be the companion of the gipsy girl. Claude Frollo, from the elevated spot on which he stood, could not distinguish his features.

No sooner had the archdeacon perceived this unknown than his attention seemed to be divided between him and the dancer, and his countenance became more and more sombre. Suddenly he drew himself up, and a trembling ran through his whole frame. "Who's that man?" muttered he to himself. "I've always seen her alone before."

He then disappeared under the winding vault of the spiral staircase and once more descended. Passing before the door of the bell-room, which was partly open, he saw something which struck him: it was Quasimodo, who, leaning towards an opening in those great slate eaves which resemble enormous projecting blinds, was likewise looking earnestly into the square. He was engaged in such profound contemplation that he did not observe his adoptive father passing by. His wild eye had in it a singular expression; it was a look at once tender and fascinated. "That's strange!" murmured Claude. "Is it at the gipsy girl that he's looking so?" He proceeded to descend. In a few minutes the moody archdeacon entered the square by the door at the bottom of the tower.

"What's become of the gipsy girl?" said he, mingling with the group of spectators which the sound of the tambourine had collected together.

"I don't know," answered one of those nearest him; "she's just disappeared. I think she's gone to dance some fandango or other in the house opposite, whither they called her."

In the place of the gipsy girl, on that same carpet, the arabesques of which but the moment before seemed to vanish beneath the no less fantastic figures of her dance, the archdeacon saw no one but the red and yellow man, who, in order to gain a few testons in his turn, was parading round the circle, his elbows on his hips, his head thrown back, his face all red, his neck stretched out, with a chair between his teeth. On this chair he had fastened a cat, which a woman of the neighbourhood had lent him, and which was swearing with terror.

"*Notre-Dame!*" cried the archdeacon, just as the mountebank, the perspiration rolling off his face, was passing before him with his pyramid of chair and cat; "what does Maître Pierre Gringoire do there?"

The harsh voice of the archdeacon struck the poor devil with such commotion that he lost his equilibrium, and down fell the whole edifice, chair and cat and all, pell-mell upon the heads of the bystanders, in the midst of inextinguishable hootings.

It is probable that Maître Pierre Gringoire (for he indeed it was) would have had a fine account to settle with the cat's proprietor, and all the bruised and scratched faces around him, if he had not hastily availed himself of the tumult to take refuge in the church, whither Claude Frollo beckoned him to follow.

The cathedral was already dark and solitary; the transepts were in thick darkness; and the lamps of the chapels were beginning to twinkle, so black had the vaulted roofs become. The great central window of the front alone, whose thousand tints were steeped in one horizontal stream of the sun's declining rays, glistened in the shade like a mass of diamonds, and cast against the other extremity of the nave its dazzling many-coloured image.

When they had proceeded a few steps Dom Claude, leaning his back against a pillar, looked steadfastly at Gringoire. This look was not the one which Gringoire had apprehended in his shame at being surprised by so grave and learned a personage in his merry-andrew costume. There was in the priest's glance neither scoff nor irony; it was serious, calm, and searching. The archdeacon was the first to break silence.

" Come, Maître Pierre," said he, " you have many things to explain to me. And first, how is it that I have not seen you for the last two months, and that I meet with you again in the public street, in rare guise i' faith, half red, half yellow, like a Caudebec apple? "

" Messire, a most marvellous gear is it indeed," said Gringoire piteously, " and behold me about as comfortable in it as a cat with a calabash clapped on her head. Most hard is it, too, I acknowledge, that I should subject those gentlemen, the sergeants of the watch, to the risk of beating, under this casaque, the humerus of a Pythagorean philosopher. But what would you, my reverend master? The fault is all in my old coat, which basely forsook me in the depth of winter, under pretence that it was falling in tatters, and that it was under the necessity of reposing itself in the ragman's pack. What was to be done? Civilisation has not yet arrived at such a pitch that one may go quite naked, as old Diogenes could have wished. Add to this, that the wind blew very cold, and the month of January is not the time to attempt successfully that new step in refinement. This casaque offered itself; I took it, and left off my old black souquenille, which, for an hermetic philosopher like myself, was far from being hermetically closed. Behold me, then, in my buffoon's habit, like Saint Genest. What would you have?—it's an eclipse—Apollo, you know, tended the flocks of Admetus."

"It's a fine trade you've taken up!" replied the priest.

"I confess, my master, that it's better to philosophise and poetise—to blow a flame in the furnace, or receive one from heaven—than to be carrying cats in triumph. And that's why, when you addressed me, I felt as silly as an ass before a roasting-jack. But what was to be done, messire?—one must eat every day; and the finest Alexandrine verses, to an empty stomach, are not to be compared to a piece of Brie cheese. Now, I composed for the Lady Margaret of Flanders that famous epithalamium, you know; and the town has not paid me for it, pretending that it was not excellent; as if, for four écus, one could write a tragedy of Sophocles. Well, you see I was near dying of hunger. Fortunately for me, I am rather strong in the jaw; so I said to my jaw, 'Perform some feats of strength and equilibrium—find food for thyself—*Ale te ipsam.*' A parcel of vagabonds, who are become my good friends, taught me twenty different sorts of Herculean tricks; and now I feed my teeth every night with the bread they have earned in the day in the sweat of my brow. After all, *concedo,* I concede that it is but a sorry employ of my intellectual faculties, and that man is not formed to pass his life in tambourining and biting chairs. But, reverend master, it is not enough to pass one's life; one must do something to keep one's self alive."

Dom Claude listened in silence. All at once his sunken eye assumed an expression so sagacious and penetrating that Gringoire felt as if searched to his inmost soul by that look.

"Very well, Maître Pierre; but how is it that you are now in company with that dancing-girl of Egypt?"

"Why, just," said Gringoire, "because she is my wife and I am her husband."

The priest's dark eye took fire. "And hast thou done that, miserable man?" he cried, furiously grasping Gringoire's arm; "and hast thou been so abandoned of God as to lay thy hand upon that girl?"

"By my chance of paradise, monseigneur," answered Gringoire, trembling in every limb, "I swear to you that I have never touched her, if that be what disturbs you so."

"But what speak you, then, of husband and wife?" said the priest.

Gringoire eagerly related to him, as succinctly as possible, what the reader is already acquainted with—his adventure of the Cour des Miracles, and his broken pitcher marriage—which marriage appeared, as yet, to have had no result whatever, the gipsy girl contriving to leave him every night, as she had done on the first, in single blessedness. "It's a bore," said he; "but that comes of my having had the misfortune to marry a maid."

"What do you mean?" inquired the archdeacon, whom this account had gradually appeased.

"It's very difficult to explain," answered the poet. "It's a superstition. My wife, as an old thief that's called amongst us the Duke of Egypt has told me, is a foundling—or a lostling—which is the same thing. She wears about her neck an amulet, which they declare will some day make her find her parents again, but would lose its virtue if the girl lost hers. Whence it follows that we both of us remain quite virtuous."

"So," resumed Claude, whose brow was now clearing apace, "you believe, Maître Pierre, that this creature has not been approached by any man."

"Why, Dom Claude, what would you have a man do with a superstition? She has got that in her head. I do indeed believe it to be rarity enough to find such a nunnish prudery keeping its wildness amidst all those gipsy girls so easily tamed; but she has three things to protect her—the Duke of Egypt, who has taken her under his safeguard, reckoning, perhaps, that he shall sell her to some jolly abbot or other; her whole tribe, who hold her in singular veneration, like an Our Lady; and a certain pretty little poniard, which the jade always carries about her in spite of the provost's ordinances, and which darts forth in her hand when you press her waist. It's a fierce wasp, I can tell you."

The archdeacon pressed Gringoire with questions.

La Esmeralda was, in Gringoire's opinion, a creature inoffensive, charming, and pretty—allowance being made for a certain little grimace which was peculiar to herself—a girl artless and impassioned, ignorant of everything and enthusiastic about everything—fond, above all things, of dancing, of bustle, of the open air—a sort of bee of a woman, with invisible wings to her feet, and living in a continual whirl. She owed this nature to the wandering life she had always led. Gringoire had contrived to ascertain that while quite a child she had gone all through

Spain and Catalonia to Sicily; he thought, too, that the caravan of zingari to which she belonged had carried her into the kingdom of Algiers—a country situated in Achaia—which Achaia was adjoining, on one side to Lesser Albania and Greece, on the other to the sea of the Sicilies, which was the way to Constantinople. The Bohemians, said Gringoire, were vassals to the King of Algiers in his capacity of chief of the nation of the white Moors. Certain it was that La Esmeralda had come into France while yet quite young by way of Hungary. From all those countries the girl had brought with her fragments of fantastic jargons, foreign songs and ideas, which made her language almost as motley as her half Parisian half African costume. However, the people of the quarters which she frequented loved her for her gaiety, her gracefulness, her lively step, her dances, and her songs. In all the town, she believed herself to be hated by two persons only, of whom she often spoke with dread—the Sachette of the Tour-Roland, a miserable recluse, that bore a strange malice against gipsy women, and was in the habit of heaping curses upon the poor dancing-girl every time she passed before her loophole; and a priest, who never met her without casting upon her looks and words that affrighted her. The mention of this latter circumstance visibly disturbed the archdeacon, but without Gringoire's much attending to his perturbation, the two months that had elapsed having been quite sufficient to make the poet forget the singular particulars of that evening when he had first met with the gipsy girl, and the apparent presence of the archdeacon on that occasion. For the rest, the little dancer, he said, feared nothing; she did not tell fortunes, and so was secure from those prosecutions for magic that were so frequently instituted against the gipsy women. And then Gringoire was as a brother to her, if not as a husband. After all, the philosopher very patiently endured this kind of Platonic marriage. At all events, there were food and lodging for him: each morning he set out from the truandry, most frequently in company with the gipsy girl; he helped her to make in the crossways her gathering of *targes* and *petits-blancs*; each evening he returned with her under the same roof, let her bolt herself in her own little chamber, and slept the sleep of the just—a very agreeable existence on the whole, said he, and very favourable to reverie. And then, in his heart and conscience, the philosopher was not quite sure that he was desperately in love with the gipsy girl. He loved her goat almost as much. It was a charming animal, gentle, intelligent, clever, and knowing. Nothing was more common in the middle ages than these knowing animals; at which the people mightily wondered, and which frequently brought their instructors to the stake. However, the sorceries of the goat with the gilded feet were very harmlesss tricks indeed. Gringoire explained them to the archdeacon, whom these particulars seemed strongly to interest. In most cases it was sufficient to present the tambourine to the animal in such or such a manner to obtain from it the action desired. It had been trained to that by its mistress, who had so singular a talent for that species of tuition that two months had been sufficient for her to teach the goat to compose, with movable letters, the word *Phœbus*.

" *Phœbus!*" said the priest. " Why *Phœbus?*"

" I don't know," replied Gringoire. " Perhaps it's a word that she thinks endowed with some magical and secret virtue. She often repeats it in an undertone when she thinks she's by herself."

" Are you sure," rejoined Claude, with his penetrating look, " that it's *only* a word, and that it's not a *name?*"

" Name of whom?" said the poet.

" How should I know?" said the priest.

" This is what I imagine, messire. These gipsies are something of Guebres, and worship the sun—whence this *Phœbus*."

" That does not seem so clear to me as it does to you, Maître Pierre."

" Well, it's no matter to me. Let her mutter her Phœbus to her heart's content. It's a sure thing that Djali loves me already almost as much as she does."

" Who's Djali?"

" It's the goat."

The archdeacon placed his hand under his chin, and seemed ruminating for a moment. All at once he turned round abruptly to Gringoire,—

" And you swear to me that you have not touched her?"

" Touched what?" said Gringoire. " The goat?"

" No; that woman."

" My wife? I swear to you I have not."

" And yet you are often alone with her."

" Every night, for a full hour."

Dom Claude knit his brows. " Oh, oh," said he, " *Solus cum solâ non cogitabuntur orare Pater Noster*."

" Upon my soul, I might say the *Pater*, and the *Ave Maria*, and the *Credo in Deum patrem omnipotentum,* without her taking any more notice of me than a hen does of a church."

"Swear to me by thy mother's womb," repeated the archdeacon, with vehemence, "that thou hast not so much as touched that creature with thy finger's end."

"I could swear it, too, by my father's head," answered the poet. "But, my reverend master, just permit me to ask you a single question."

"Speak, sir."

"What does that signify to you?"

The pale countenance of the archdeacon reddened like the cheek of a girl. He kept silence for a moment, then answered with visible embarrassment, "Harken, Maître Pierre Gringoire. You are not yet damned, that I know of. I feel interested for you, and wish you well. Now, the slightest contact with that gipsy girl of the demon would make you a vassal of Satan. You know it's always the body that ruins the soul. Woe to you if you approach that woman! That's all I have to say."

"I tried once," said Gringoire, scratching his ear; "it was the first day, but I only got myself stung."

"And had you that audacity, Maître Pierre?" and the priest's brow darkened again.

"Another time," continued the poet, smiling, "before I went to bed, I looked through her keyhole, and indeed I saw the most delicious damsel in her shift that ever stepped upon a bedside with her naked foot."

"Go to the devil with you!" cried the priest, with a terrible look; and pushing the amazed Gringoire by the shoulders, he plunged with hasty strides under the darkest arches of the cathedral.

CHAPTER III

THE BELLS

SINCE the morning of his being pilloried, the inhabitants in the neighbourhood of Notre-Dame thought they perceived that Quasimodo's bell-ringing ardour had remarkably abated. Before that time the bells were going on all occasions: long matin chimes which lasted from Primes to Complins; peals of the great bell for high mass; rich gamuts running up and down the small bells for a wedding or a christening, and mingling in the air like a rich embroidery of all sorts of delightful sounds. The old church, all vibrating and sonorous, was in a perpetual joyous whirl of bells. Some spirit of noise and whim appeared to be sending forth a never-ending carol through those brazen lips. Now, that spirit seemed to have departed. The cathedral seemed to have grown wilfully sullen and silent. The holidays and interments had their simple accompaniment, bare and unadorned—just what the ritual demanded, and nothing more: of the double sound proceeding from a church, that of the organ within and the bells without, the organ only was heard. It seemed as if there was no longer any musician in the steeples. Nevertheless, Quasimodo was still there. What had come to him then? Was it that the shame and desperation of the pillory scene still lingered about his heart, that the lashes of the torturer were ever present to his mind, and that his grief at such treatment had extinguished all feeling in him, even to his passion for the bells? Or was it rather that Marie had a rival in the heart of the ringer of Notre-Dame, and that the great bell and her fourteen sisters were neglected for something more beautiful and pleasing?

It happened that in the year of our Lord 1482 the Annunciation fell on Tuesday, the 25th of March. On that day the air was so pure and light that Quasimodo felt a little returning affection for his bells. He accordingly ascended the northern tower, whilst the beadle below threw wide the large doors of the church, which were formed at that time of enormous panels of strong wood, covered with leather, bordered with iron nails gilt, and encased with sculpture "very skilfully wrought."

Arrived in the high cage of the bells, Quasimodo fixed his eye for some time, with a sorrowful shake of the head, on his six songstresses, as if he sighed to think that something strange had intruded into his heart between himself and them. But when he had set them going—when he felt the whole cluster of bells moving under his hand—when he saw, for he did not hear it, the palpitating octave ascending and descending in the sonorous diapason like a bird hopping from branch to branch—when the demon of music, that demon who shakes a sparkling bundle of stretti, trills, and arpeggios, had taken possession of the poor deaf creature—then he became happy again; he forgot everything, and the dilation of his heart expanded on his countenance.

He went to and fro, clapping his hands; he ran from one rope to another, animating the six songsters by his voice and his gestures, like a leader of the band spurring on scientific musicians.

"Come, come, Gabrielle," said he, "pour forth all your sound into the square; it's a holiday. Thibauld, none of your idleness. What! you are lagging! Get on with you. Are you grown rusty, lazybones? That's it!—quick! quick!—don't let the clapper be seen. Make them all as deaf as I am. Bravo, Thibauld!—Go it, Guillaume! Guillaume, you are the biggest, and Pasquier's the least, and Pasquier goes best. I'll lay anything that those who can hear, hear him better than you. Well done, Gabrielle—harder, harder! Hey! you there, The Sparrows, what are you both about? I don't see you make the least noise. What's the meaning of those brazen beaks of yours, that seem to be gaping when they ought to be singing? Come, work away!—it's the Annunciation. There's a fine sunshine, and we'll have a merry peal. Poor Guillaume. What! are you out of breath, my old fellow?"

He was fully occupied in goading on his bells, which were all six leaping one against another as in rivalry, and shaking their shining backs, like a noisy team of Spanish mules urged forward by the apostrophisings of the driver.

All at once, happening to cast his eye between the large slate scales which cover at a certain height the perpendicular wall of the steeple, he saw in the square a young girl fantastically dressed, who had stopped, and was laying down a carpet on which a little goat came and placed itself, and around whom a group of spectators was gathering. This view suddenly changed the course of his ideas and cooled his musical enthusiasm. He stopped, turned his back to the bells, and squatted behind the slate eaves, fixing on the dancer that thoughtful, tender, and softened look which had already astonished the archdeacon. Meanwhile the forgotten bells all at once became utterly silent, to the great disappointment of the amateurs of ringing, who were listening to the peal in good earnest from off the Pont-au-Change, and who went away as confounded as a dog that has had a bone offered him and a stone given him instead.

CHAPTER IV

ΑΝΆΓΚΗ

It happened one fine morning in this same month of March—we believe it was on Saturday the 29th, St. Eustache's Day—that our young college friend, Jehan Frollo du Moulin, perceived, as he was dressing himself, that his breeches, containing his purse, emitted no metallic sound. "Poor purse!" said he, drawing it out of his fob. "What! not the smallest parisis! How cruelly have dice, Venus, and pots of beer disembowelled thee! Behold thee empty, wrinkled, and flabby. Thou art like the neck of a fury! I would ask you, now, Messer Cicero and Messer Seneca, whose dog's-eared tomes I see there scattered upon the floor, of what use it is for me to know better than a governor of the mint, or a Jew of the Pont-aux-Changeurs, that a gold *écu à la couronne* is worth thirty-five *unzains* at twenty-five sous eight deniers parisis each! and that an *écu au croissant* is worth thirty-six unzains at twenty-six sous six deniers tournois apiece; if I've not one miserable black liard to risk upon the double-six! O Consul Cicero! this is not a calamity from which one can extricate one's self by a periphrasis—by *quemadmodums* and *verumenimveros!*"

He dressed himself with a sad heart. A thought came into his head as he was lacing his boots, which he at first repelled; it returned, however, and he put on his waistcoat wrong side outwards, an evident sign of a violent internal struggle. At length he threw his cap vehemently on the ground and exclaimed, "Be it so! Come what may, I'll go to my brother! I shall get a sermon, I know, but I shall get an écu as well."

He then put on hastily his fur-trimmed casaque, picked up his cap, and rushed out like a madman.

He turned down the Rue de la Harpe towards the City. Passing the Rue de la Huchette, the odour from those admirable spits, which were there incessantly going, saluted his olfactory organs, and he cast an amorous look towards that Cyclopean cookery which one day extorted from the cordelier Calatagirone the pathetic exclamation, *Veramente, queste rotisserie sono cosa stupenda?* But Jehan had not wherewithal to buy a breakfast; and he passed, with a profound sigh, through the gate of the Petit-Châtelet, that enormous double trefoil of massive towers which guarded the entrance to the City. He did not so much as give himself time to throw, as was usual, a stone in passing at the miserable statue of that Perinet Leclerc, who had given up the Paris of Charles VI. to the English, a crime which his effigy, the face all battered with stones and soiled with mud, expiated during three centuries, as in an everlasting pillory, at the corner of the streets De la Harpe and De Bussy.

Having crossed the Petit-Pont, and strided down the Rue Neuve-Sainte-Geneviève, Jehan de Molendino found himself in front of Notre-Dame. Then all his indecision returned, and he walked about for some moments around the statue of M. le Gris, repeating to himself with anguish. "The sermon is certain enough; the écu is doubtful."

He stopped a beadle who was coming out from the cloisters—"Where's monsieur the Archdeacon of Joas?"

"I believe he's in his hiding-place in the tower," said the beadle; "and I advise you not to disturb him unless you come from some one like the Pope or the King himself."

Jehan clapped his hands. "*Bédiable!* this is a prime opportunity for seeing the famous sorcery-box!"

Decided by this reflection, he advanced resolutely through the little dark doorway, and began to ascend the winding staircase of St. Gilles, which leads to the upper stories of the tower.

"I shall see!" said he as he proceeded. "By the corbignolles of the Holy Virgin! it must be a curious concern that cell which my reverend brother keeps so snugly to himself! They say he lights up hell's own fires there, and cooks at them the philosopher's stone. Egad! I care as little for the philosopher's stone as for a pebble; and I'd rather find over his furnace an omelet of Easter eggs fried in lard, than the biggest philosopher's stone in the world."

Arrived at the gallery of the *colonnettes*, he took breath a moment, swearing against the interminable staircase by we know not how many million cart-loads of devils; he then continued his ascent by the narrow door of the northern tower, now closed to the public. In a few moments after, having passed by the cage of the bells, he came to a small landing contrived in a recess on one side, and, under the arched roof, a low pointed door; whilst a loophole opposite, in the circular wall of the staircase, enabled him to discern its enormous lock and strong iron bars. Persons in our day desirous of visiting this door might recently know it by this inscription, in white letters on the black wall: J'ADORE CORALIE. 1823. *Signé Ugène.* This diplomatic *Signé* is in the original.

"Whew!" said the scholar; "here it is doubtless." The key was in the lock. The door was close by him; he pushed it gently and put his head in at the opening.

The reader must have seen some of those admirable sketches by Rembrandt—who in some respects may be truly styled the Shakespeare of painting. Amongst so many wonderful engravings there is one in particular, an etching, representing, as is supposed, Doctor Faustus, which it is impossible to look at without astonishment. It represents a gloomy cell; in the middle is a table, loaded with hideous objects—death's-heads, spheres, alembics, compasses, hieroglyphic parchments. The doctor is before this table, dressed in his wide greatcoat, his head covered with a fur cap which reaches to his eyebrows. Only half of his body is seen. He has partly risen from his immense fauteuil, his bent knuckles are resting on the table, and he is gazing with curiosity and terror at a luminous circle, formed of magic letters, which are shining on the wall in the background like the solar spectrum in the camera obscura. This cabalistic sun seems to tremble before the eye, and fills the dim cell with its mysterious radiancy. It is at once horrible and beautiful.

Something very similar to Faust's cell presented itself to the view of Jehan when he ventured his head within the half-open door. It was a similar gloomy, dim-lighted nook. There were also a large fauteuil and a large table; compasses; alembics; skeletons of animals suspended from the ceiling; a sphere rolling on the floor; *hippocephales* promiscuously with *boccals* in which were quivering leaves of gold; death's-heads lying on sheets of vellum streaked all over with figures and characters; thick manuscripts piled up, all open, without any pity for the cracking corners of the parchment—in short, all the rubbish of science, dust and cobwebs covering the whole heap; but there was no circle of luminous letters, no doctor in ecstasy contemplating the flaming vision as the eagle gazes at the sun.

Nevertheless the cell was not solitary. A man was seated in the fauteuil and leaning over the table. Jehan, to whom his back was turned, could only see his shoulders and the back of his head; but he had no difficulty in recognising that bald head, on which nature had bestowed an everlasting tonsure, as if to mark, by this external sign, the irresistible clerical vocation of the archdeacon.

Jehan accordingly recognised his brother; but the door had been opened so gently that Dom Claude was not aware of his presence. The curious scholar availed himself of the opportunity to examine the cell for a few moments at his leisure. A large furnace, which he had not remarked at his first glance, was to the left of the fauteuil, under the small window. The ray of light which penetrated through this opening made its way through the circular web of a spider, who had tastefully traced her delicate *rosace* in the point of the window, and in the centre of it the insect architect remained motionless, like the nave of this lace wheel. On the furnace were heaped in disorder all sorts of vessels—stone bottles, glass retorts, coal mattresses. Jehan observed with a sigh that there was neither frying-pan nor saucepan. "The kitchen apparatus is all cold!" thought he.

In fact, there was no fire in the furnace, and it seemed as if none had been lighted there for a long time. A glass mask which Jehan remarked among the utensils of the alchemist, and which, doubtless, was used to protect the archdeacon's face when he was elaborating any formidable substance, lay in a corner, covered with dust, as if quite forgotten. By its side lay a pair of bellows, equally dusty, the upper side of which bore this motto incrusted in letters of copper: *Spira, spera!*

A great number of other mottoes were, according to the fashion of the hermetic philosophers, written upon the walls—some traced in ink, others engraved with a metallic point. Moreover, there were Gothic characters, Hebrew characters, Greek and Roman characters, pell-mell together; inscriptions overflowing at random, one upon the other, the more recent effacing the more ancient, and all entangled with each other, like the branches of a thicket, or pikes in a mêlée. It was, in fact, a strangely confused mingling of all human reveries, all human science. Here and there one shone out above the rest like a banner amid the lances' heads, but for the most part they consisted of some brief Latin or Greek motto, after the ingenious fashion of the Middle Ages—as thus: *Undè? indè? Homo homini monstrum! Astra, castra, nemen, numen.* Μέγα βιζλίον, μέγα χαχνό. *Sapere aude. Fiat ubi vult,* etc. Sometimes a word apparently devoid of all meaning, as Ἀναγχοφαγία—which perhaps concealed some bitter allusion to the régime of the cloister; and sometimes it was a simple maxim of clerical discipline, set forth in a regular hexameter,—

"Cælestem dominum, terrestrem dicito domnum."

There were also scattered throughout pieces of Hebrew conjuration, about which Jehan, who was nothing of a conjurer, and not even much of a Grecian, understood nothing; and the whole was crossed about in all directions with stars, figures of men or animals, and triangles intersecting each other; which contributed in no small degree to liken the daubed wall of the cell to a sheet of paper over which a monkey has been dragging about a pen full of ink.

The *tout ensemble* of the retreat, in short, presented a general aspect of neglect and ruin; and the sorry condition of the utensils led to the supposition that their master had long been diverted from his labours by pursuits of some other kind.

This master, however, leaning over a vast manuscript, adorned with singular paintings, appeared to be tormented by some idea which constantly mingled itself with his meditations; so at least Jehan thought, as he heard him exclaim, with the musing intermissions of a waking dreamer who thinks aloud,—

"Yes—so Manou said and Zoroaster taught—the sun is born of fire, the moon of the sun. Fire is the soul of the universe; its elementary atoms are diffused and in constant flow throughout the world, by an infinite number of channels. At the points where these currents cross each other in the heavens they produce light; at their points of intersection in the earth they produce gold. Light—gold, the same thing; fire in its concrete state; the difference between the visible and the palpable, the fluid and the solid, in the same substance—between vapour and ice—nothing more. These are not chimeras; it is the general law of nature. But how to extract from science the secret of this general law? What—this light which bathes my hand is gold! These same atoms dilated according to a certain law, it is only necessary to condense them according to a certain other law. How is it to be done? Some have thought of burying a ray of the sun. Averroës—yes, it is Averroës—Averroës buried one under the first pillar to the left of the sanctuary of the Koran, in the grand mosque of Cordova; but the vault was not to be opened, to see whether the operation had succeeded, under eight thousand years."

"The devil!" said Jehan to himself, "that's a long time to wait for an écu."

"Others have thought," continued the archdeacon, musing, "that it would be better to operate upon a ray of Sirius. But it is difficult to get this ray pure, on account of the simultaneous presence of other stars, whose rays mingle with it. Flamel considers that it is more simple to operate on terrestrial fire. Flamel! there's predestination in the name! *Flamma!* Yes —fire. That is all. The diamond is in charcoal—gold in fire. But how to extract it? Magistri affirms that there are certain names of women which possess so sweet and mysterious a charm that it is sufficient to pronounce them during the operation. Let us hear what Manou says about it: 'Where women are honoured, the divinities are complacent; where they are despised, it is useless to pray to God. The lips of a woman are constantly pure; they are as running waters, as rays of the sun. A woman's name should be pleasing, soft, and fanciful, should end with a long vowel, and resemble words of benediction." Yes, indeed the sage is right: *Maria—Sophia—Esmeral* . . . Damnation! Ever that thought!"

And he closed the book with violence.

He passed his hand across his forehead, as if to chase some idea which haunted him; then he took from off the table a nail and a small hammer, the handle of which was ingeniously painted in cabalistic characters.

"For some time," said he with a bitter smile, "I have failed in all my experiments; one idea possesses me, and scorches my brain like a seal of fire. I have not so much as been able to discover the secret of Cassiodorus, whose lamp burned without wick or oil—a thing simple enough nevertheless."

"A plague upon it!" said Jehan through his teeth.

"One single miserable thought, then," continued the priest, "suffices to render a man weak and beside himself! Oh, how Claude Pernelle would laugh at me—she who could not for a moment turn aside Nicolas Flamel from his pursuit of the great work! What! I hold in my hand the magic hammer of Ezekiel. At each blow which from the depth of his cell the formidable rabbi struck upon this nail with this hammer, that one amongst his enemies whom he had condemned, even were he two thousand leagues off, sank a cubit's depth into the earth, which swallowed him up. The King of France himself, for having one evening inadvertently struck against the door of the thaumaturgus, sank up to the knees in his pavement of Paris. This happened three centuries ago. Well! I have the hammer and the nail, and yet these implements are no more formidable in my hands than a punching-tool in the hands of a smith. And yet it is only necessary to discover the magic word which Ezekiel pronounced as he struck upon the nail."

"What nonsense!" thought Jehan.

"Come, let us try," resumed the archdeacon eagerly. "If I succeed, I shall see the blue spark fly out of the head of the nail. *Emen-Hetan! Emen-Hetan!* That's not it. *Sigeani! Sigeani!* May this nail open the grave for whosoever bears the name of Phœbus! . . . A curse upon it! still—again—eternally the same idea!"

And he threw aside the hammer angrily. He then sank so low into his fauteuil and upon the table, that Jehan lost sight of him behind the high back of his chair. For some minutes he could see nothing but his convulsed hand clenched over a book. All at once Dom Claude arose, took a pair of compasses, and engraved in silence on the wall, in capital letters, this Greek word,—

'ANÁΓKH

"My brother's a fool," said Jehan to himself. "It would have been much more simple to have written *fatum*: everybody's not obliged to know Greek."

The archdeacon reseated himself in his fauteuil, and leaned his head on his two hands, like a sick person whose temples are heavy and burning.

The scholar viewed his brother with surprise. He, for his part, knew not—he, whose heart was as light as air—he, who observed no law in the world but the good old law of nature—he, who allowed his passions to flow according to their natural tendency, and in whom the lake of strong emotions was always dry, by so many fresh drains did he let it off daily—he knew not with what fury that sea of the human passions ferments and boils when it is refused all egress—how it gathers strength, swells, and overflows—how it wears away the heart—how it breaks forth in inward sobs and stifled convulsions, until it has rent away its dikes and even burst its bed. The austere and icy exterior of Claude Frollo, that cold surface of rugged and inaccessible virtue, had always deceived Jehan. The merry scholar never dreamed of the boiling, furious, and deep lava beneath the snowy brow of Etna.

We do not know if any sudden perception of this kind crossed the mind of Jehan; but giddy-brained as he was, he understood that he had seen what he should not have seen—that he had surprised the soul of his elder brother in one of its most secret flames—and that he must not let Claude discover it. Perceiving that the archdeacon had fallen again into his previous immobility, he withdrew his head very softly, and made a slight noise of steps behind the door, as of some one arriving and giving notice of their approach.

"Come in!" cried the archdeacon from the interior of his cell. "I was expecting you; I left the key in the door purposely. Come in, Maître Jacques."

The scholar entered boldly. The archdeacon, whom such a visit embarassed extremely in such a place, shook in his fauteuil. "What! is it you, Jehan?"

"Still a J," said the scholar, with his ruddy, saucy, and joyous face.

The countenance of Dom Claude had recovered its severe expression. "What are you doing here?"

"Brother," answered the scholar, endeavouring to attain a decent, serious, and modest demeanour; twirling his cap in his hands with an air of innocence, "I came to ask——"

"What?"

"A moral lesson, of which I have great need." Jehan dared not add aloud, "And a little money, of which I have still greater need." This last member of the sentence remained unuttered.

"Sir," said the archdeacon coldly, "I am very much displeased with you."

"Alas!" sighed the scholar.

Dom Claude described a quarter of a circle with his fauteuil, and looked at Jehan earnestly. "I am very glad to see you."

This was a formidable exordium. Jehan prepared for a rough encounter.

"Jehan, I hear every day sad complaints of you. What was that scuffle about in which you beat and bruised with a stick a certain little viscount, Albert de Ramonchamp?"

"Oh," said Jehan, "a grand affair that! all about a good-for-nothing page that amused himself with splashing the scholars by galloping his horse through the mud."

"And what's this affair of Mahiette Fargel's, whose gown you have torn? *Tunicam dechiraverunt*, says the charge."

"Pshaw! a sorry Montaigu *cappette*. Isn't that it?"

"The accusation says *tunicam*, not *cappettam*. Do you understand Latin?"

Jehan made no answer.

"Yes," continued the priest, shaking his head; "see what study and letters are come to now! The Latin tongue is scarcely understood; the Syriac unknown; the Greek so odious that it is not considered ignorance in the most learned to skip a Greek word without reading it, and to say, *Græcum est, non legitur.*"

The scholar raised his eyes boldly. "Brother, shall I tell you in good French the meaning of that Greek word on the wall?"

"What word?"

"'ΑΝΑΓΚΗ."

A slight blush spread itself over the mottled cheeks of the archdeacon, like a puff of smoke announcing externally the secret commotions of a volcano. The scholar scarcely remarked it.

"Well, Jehan," stammered out the elder brother with difficulty, "what does the word mean?"

"Fate."

Dom Claude turned pale again, and the scholar continued carelessly: "And that word underneath, engraved by the same hand, Αναγνεία, signifies impurity. You see I know my Greek."

The archdeacon remained silent. This Greek lesson had set him musing. Master Jehan, who had all the finesse of a spoiled child, judged the moment favourable for venturing his request. So, assuming a particularly soft accent, he began,—

"My dear brother, do you hate me so, then, as to look grim at me on account of a few poor scuffles and fisticuffs, dealt, all in fair play, amongst a pack of boys and marmosets, *quibusdam marmosetis?* You see I know my Latin, brother Claude."

But all this fawning hypocrisy had not its accustomed effect on the severe elder brother. Cerberus did not snap at the honey-cake. The archdeacon's brow unfolded not a single wrinkle. "What is it you're aiming at?" said he in a sharp tone.

"Well, then, the case is this," answered Jehan bravely: "I want money."

At this audacious declaration the archdeacon's physiognomy completely assumed the pedagogic and paternal expression.

"You know, M. Jehan, that our fief of Tirechappe only brings in, including both the quit-rents and the rents of the twenty-one houses, thirty-nine livres eleven sous six deniers parisis. It's half as much again as in the times of the brothers Paclet; but it is not much."

"I want money," said Jehan stoically.

"You know that the official decided that our twenty-one houses were held in full fee of the bishopric, and that we could only redeem this homage by paying to his reverence the bishop two marks of silver gilt at six livres parisis each. Now I have not yet been able to get together these two marks; you know it well."

"I know that I want money," repeated Jehan for the third time.

"And what do you want it for?" At this question a ray of hope shone in the eyes of Jehan. He put on his demure, modest look.

"Hark you, my dear brother Claude, I do not come to you with any bad intention. I am not going to show off at taverns with your unzains, or to parade the streets of Paris in gold brocade trappings, with my lackey—*cum meo laquasio*. No, brother; it's for a good work."

"What good work?" asked Claude, a little surprised.

"Two of my friends wish to purchase some childbed linen for a poor Haudriette widow. It's a charity. It will cost three florins, and I wish to subscribe to it."

"What are the names of your two friends?"

"Pierre l'Assommeur and Baptiste Croque-Oison."

"Humph!" said the archdeacon; "they are names that go about as fitly to a good work as a bombard would upon a high altar."[1]

It is certain that Jehan had very ill chosen the names of his two friends. He felt it when too late.

"And then," continued the shrewd Claude, "what sort of childbed linen is it to cost three florins, and that for the child of a Haudriette widow? And how long is it since Haudriette widows have begun to have brats in swaddling clothes?"

Jehan broke the ice once more.

"Well, then, I want some money to go and see Isabeau-la-Thierrye this evening, at the Val d'Amour."

"Vile libertine!" exclaimed the priest.

"Αναγνεία!" said Jehan.

This quotation, which the scholar borrowed, perhaps mischievously, from the wall of the cell, had a singular effect upon the priest. He bit his lip, and his anger was lost amidst his confusion.

"Away with you," said he to Jehan; "I am expecting some one."

The scholar tried one more effort. "Brother Claude, give me at least one little parisis, to buy food."

[1] These two names are equivalent in English to *Peter the Knocker-Down* and *Baptist Filch-Gosling*.

"How far have you got with the decretals of Gratian?" asked Dom Claude.

"I've lost my copy-books."

"Where are you with the Latin classics?"

"Somebody has stolen my copy of Horatius."

"And whereabouts with Aristoteles?"

"'Faith, brother, what is the name of that father of the church who says the errors of heretics have ever found shelter amid the thickets of Aristotle's metaphysics? A fig for Aristotle! I'll never mangle my religion with his metaphysics."

"Young man," continued the archdeacon, "at the last entry of the King there was a gentleman named Philippe de Comines, who had embroidered on his horse's housings this motto of his, which I advise you to ponder over: *Qui non laborat, non manducet.*"

The scholar remained a moment silent, his finger in his ear, his eyes bent upon the ground, and his countenance chagrined. Suddenly he turned towards Claude with the lively quickness of a wag-tail.

"So, my good brother, you refuse me a sou parisis, to buy me a crust at a talmellier's?"

"*Qui non laborat, non manducet.*"

At this answer of the inflexible archdeacon Jehan hid his head between his hands, like a woman sobbing, and exclaimed, with an expression of despair, "O *τοτοτοτο-τοι*!"

"What does all this mean, sir?" asked Claude, surprised at this freak.

"Well, what!" said the scholar; and he raised towards Claude his saucy eyes, into which he had been thrusting his fists, to make them look as if they were red with tears. "It's Greek—it's an anapest of Æschylus which is admirably expressive of grief."

And here he burst out into a fit of laughter so ludicrous and so violent that the archdeacon could not help smiling. It was, in fact, Claude's fault: why had he so spoiled this boy?

"O dear brother Claude," continued Jehan, emboldened by this smile, "look at my wornout boots. Can any buskin in the world be more tragic than a boot with its poor sole hanging out its tongue so?"

The archdeacon had quickly recovered his former severity. "I will send you some new boots, but no money."

"Only one poor little parisis, brother," persisted the suppliant Jehan. "I'll learn Gratian by heart—I'll believe well in God

—I'll be a perfect Pythagoras of science and virtue! Only one little parisis, for pity's sake! Would you have me devoured by famine, which stands staring me in the face with its gaping jaws, blacker, deeper, and more noisome than Tartarus or a monk's nose?"

Dom Claude shook his wrinkled head. "*Qui non laborat . . .*"

Jehan did not let him finish.

"Well," cried he, "to the devil then! huzza! I'll go to the tavern—I'll fight—I'll go and see the girls—and there shall be the devil to pay."

So saying, he threw his cap against a wall and snapped his fingers like castanets.

The archdeacon looked at him seriously. "Jehan," said he, "you have no soul."

"In that case, according to Epicurus, I want a something, made of another something, which is without a name."

"Jehan, you must think seriously of amending your life."

"Oh yes," cried the scholar, looking alternately at his brother and at the alembics on the furnace, "everything's atwist here, I see—ideas as well as bottles."

"Jehan, you are on the downward road: do you know whither you are going?"

"To the public-house," said Jehan.

"The public-house leads to the pillory."

"It's only another sort of lantern; and with that, perhaps, Diogenes would have found his man."

"The pillory leads to the gibbet."

"The gibbet is a balance, with a man at one end and the whole world at the other. It's fine to be the man."

"The gibbet leads to hell."

"That's a rousing fire."

"Jehan, Jehan! all this will have a bad end."

"It'll have had a good beginning."

At this moment the noise of footsteps was heard on the staircase.

"Silence!" said the archdeacon, putting his finger on his lips; "here's Maître Jacques. Hark you, Jehan," added he in a low voice, "beware of ever speaking of what you have seen and heard here. Hide yourself quickly under this furnace, and do not breathe."

The scholar skulked under the furnace, and just then a happy thought struck him.

"Apropos, brother Claude—a florin for not breathing!"

"Silence! I promise it you."

"You must give it me."

"Take it, then!" said the archdeacon, throwing him his purse angrily. Jehan crept under the furnace, and the door opened.

CHAPTER V

THE TWO MEN IN BLACK

THE person who now entered wore a black gown and a doleful mien. What at the first glance struck our friend Jehan (who, as may well be supposed, so placed himself in his corner as to be able to see and hear all at his good pleasure) was the perfect sadness both of the garment and the visage of this newcomer. There was, nevertheless, a certain meekness diffused over that countenance; but it was the meekness of a cat or of a judge—a sort of affected gentleness. He was very grey and wrinkled, was approaching his sixtieth year, had twinkling eyes, white eyebrows, a hanging lip, and large hands. When Jehan saw that it was nothing more—that is to say, to all appearance only a physician or a magistrate—and that this man's nose was very far from his mouth, a sign of stupidity, he ensconced himself in his hole, desperate at having to remain, he knew not how long, in such an uneasy posture and in such bad company.

The archdeacon in the meanwhile had not so much as risen to receive this personage. He motioned to him to be seated on a stool near the door; and after a few moments' silence, during which he seemed to be carrying on some previous meditation, he said to him with a patronising air, "Good-day to you, Maître Jacques."

"Your servant, maître," answered the man in black.

There was, in the two ways of pronouncing, on the one side, this Maître Jacques, and on the other this maître by distinction, the difference between *monseigneur* and *monsieur*, between *domine* and *domne*. It was evidently the meeting of the doctor and the disciple.

"Well," resumed the archdeacon, after another silence, which Maître Jacques did not care to disturb, "how do you succeed?"

"Alas, maître," said the other with a sorrowful smile, "I

keep on blowing. As many cinders as I like, but not a spark of gold."

Dom Claude betrayed signs of impatience.

"I am not speaking to you of that, Maître Jacques Charmolue, but of the suit against your magician—Marc Cenaine I think you call him—the butler of the Court of Accompts. Does he confess his sorcery? Has the torture succeeded?"

"Alas, no!" answered Maître Jacques, still with his sad smile; "we have not that consolation. That man's a prefect stone; we might boil him in the Marché-aux-Pourceaux before he would say anything. However, we spare no pains to get at the truth. He has already every joint dislocated; we put all our irons on the fire, as says the old comic writer Plautus,—

> 'Advorsum stimulos, laminas, crucesque, compedesque,
> Nervos, catenas, carceres, numellas, pedicas, boias.'

But all to no purpose—that man's terrible—I quite lose my labour with him."

"You have found nothing fresh in his house?"

"Yes, yes," said Maître Jacques, feeling in his pouch—"this parchment. There are words in it which we do not understand. And yet monsieur the criminal advocate, Philippe Lheulier, knows a little Hebrew, which he learned in that affair of the Jews of the Rue Kantersten at Brussels."

So saying, Maître Jacques unrolled a parchment. "Give it me," said the archdeacon. And casting his eyes over the scroll, "Pure magic, Maître Jacques!" cried he. "*Emen Hetan!*—that's the cry of the witches when they arrive at their sabbath. *Per ipsum, et cum ipso, et in ipso!*—that's the command which chains the devil down in hell again. *Hax, pax, max!*—that has to do with medicine—a spell against the bite of a mad dog. Maître Jacques, you are King's attorney in the ecclesiastical court; this parchment is abominable."

"We'll put the man to the torture again. Here's something else," added Maître Jacques, rummaging again in his bag, "which we found at Marc Cenaine's."

It was a vessel of the same family as those which covered the furnace of Dom Claude. "Ah," said the archdeacon, "an alchemist's crucible!"

"I confess to you," replied Maître Jacques, with his timid and constrained smile, "that I have tried it over the furnace, but I have succeeded no better with it than with my own."

The archdeacon set about examining the vessel. "What

has he engraved on his crucible? *Och! och!*—a word to drive away fleas! This Marc Cenaine's an ignoramus. I can easily believe you'll not make gold with this; it will do to put in your alcove in the summer, and that's all."

"Since we are on the subject of errors," said the King's attorney, "I have just been studying, before I came up, the figures on the portal below. Is your reverence quite sure that it's the opening of the book of natural philosophy that's represented there on the side towards the Hôtel-Dieu, and that, among the seven naked figures at the feet of our Lady, that which has wings at his heels is Mercurius?"

"Yes," answered the priest; "so Augustin Nypho writes—that Italian doctor who had a bearded demon which taught him everything. But we will go down, and I will explain it to you from the text."

"Thank you, maître," said Charmolue, bending to the ground. "By-the-bye, I had forgotten. When do you wish me to apprehend the little sorceress?"

"What sorceress?"

"That gipsy girl, you know, that comes and dances every day on the Parvis in spite of the official's prohibition. She has a goat with devil's horns, which is possessed: it reads and writes, understands mathematics like Picatrix, and would be enough to hang all Bohemia. The prosecution is quite ready, and will soon be got through, take my word for it. She's a pretty creature, upon my soul, that dancing girl—the finest black eyes—two Egyptian carbuncles! When shall we begin?"

The archdeacon was excessively pale.

"I will let you know," stammered he in a voice scarcely articulate. He added with an effort, "Look you to Marc Cenaine."

"Never fear," said Charmolue, smiling; "when I get back I'll have him buckled on the bed of leather again. But he's a devil of a man: he tires out Pierrat Torterue himself, who has larger hands than I have. As says the excellent Plautus,—

'Nudus vinctus, centum pondo, es quando pendes per pedes.'"

"The torture with the roller is the most effectual; we shall try it."

Dom Claude seemed sunk in gloomy abstraction. He turned towards Charmolue. "Maître Pierrat . . . Maître Jacques, I mean—look to Mark Cenaine."

"Yes, yes, Dom Claude. Poor man! he'll have suffered like

Mummol. But what an idea, for a butler of the Court of Accompts, who must know the text of Charlemagne, *Stryga vel masca*, to attend the witches' sabbath! As to the little one—Smelarda, as they call her—I'll wait your orders. Ah! as we pass under the portal you'll explain to me that gardener painted in relief that you see on entering the church—the Sower, is it not? Eh, maître, what are you thinking about?"

Dom Claude, lost in his own thoughts, heard him not. Charmolue, following the direction of his eyes, saw that they had fixed themselves mechanically on the large spider's web which hung like a drapery over the small window. At that moment a giddy fly, courting the March sun, threw itself across the net, and got entangled in it. At the shaking of the web the enormous spider made a sudden movement from out his central cell; then at one bound rushed upon the fly, which he bent double with his fore feelers, whilst with his hideous trunk he scooped out its head. "Poor fly!" said the King's attorney in the ecclesiastical court, and he raised his hand to save it. The archdeacon, as if starting out of his sleep, held back his arm with convulsive violence.

"Maître Jacques," cried he, "let fate do its work!"

The King's attorney turned round quite scared. He felt as if his arm was grasped with iron pincers. The eye of the priest was motionless, haggard, glaring, and remained fixed on the little horrible group of the spider and the fly.

"Ah, yes!" continued the priest, in a voice which seemed to issue from the bottom of his heart; "there is a symbol of the whole! She flies—she is joyous—she emerges into life—she courts the spring, the open air, liberty—oh yes! but she strikes against the fatal net-work—the spider issues from it, the hideous spider! Poor dancer! poor predestined fly! Maître Jacques, leave it alone—'tis fate! Alas, Claude, thou art the spider! Claude, thou art the fly too! Thou didst hasten forward in search of knowledge, of the light, the sun—thy only care was to reach the pure air, the broad day-beams of eternal truth; but rushing towards the dazzling loophole which opens on another world—a world of brightness, of intellect, of science—infatuated fly! insensate sage! thou didst not see the subtle spider's web by destiny suspended between the light and thee—thou didst madly dash thyself against it, wretched maniac—and now thou dost struggle, with crushed head and mangled wings, between the iron antennæ of Fate! Maître Jacques, Maître Jacques, let the spider work on!"

"I assure you," said Charmolue, who looked at him without understanding him, "that I will not touch it. But let go my arm, maître, for pity's sake! You have a hand of iron."

The archdeacon heard him not. "O madman!" continued he, without taking his eyes off the window. "And even couldst thou have broken through that formidable web with thy gnat-like wings, thoughtst thou to have attained the light? Alas! that glass beyond—that transparent obstacle—that wall of crystal harder than brass—which separates all philosophy from the truth—how couldst thou have passed beyond it? Oh, vanity of science, how many sages have come fluttering from afar, to dash their heads against thee! How many clashing systems buzz vainly about that everlasting barrier!"

He was silent. These last ideas, which had insensibly called off his thoughts from himself to science, appeared to have calmed him, and Jacques Charmolue completely brought him back to a sense of reality by addressing to him this question: "Come, come, maître, when will you help me to make gold? I long to succeed."

The archdeacon shook his head with a bitter smile. "Maître Jacques, read Michael Psellus: *Dialogus de energiâ et operatione dæmonum*. What we are doing is not quite innocent."

"Speak lower, maître; I have my doubts," said Charmolue. "But one may surely practise a little hermetic philosophy when one's only a poor King's attorney in the ecclesiastical court, at thirty crowns tournois a year. Only, let us speak low."

At that moment the noise of jaws in the art of mastication, issuing from under the furnace, struck the anxious ear of Charmolue.

"What's that?" asked he.

It was the scholar, who, very tired and uneasy in his hiding-place, had just discovered a stale crust and a corner of mouldy cheese, and had begun to eat both, without any ceremony, by way of consolation and breakfast. As he was very hungry, he made a great noise, laying strong emphasis on each mouthful, and this it was that had roused and alarmed the King's attorney.

"It's a cat of mine," said the archdeacon quickly, "feasting herself below there upon some mouse or other."

This explanation satisfied Charmolue. "Why, indeed, maître," answered he with a respectful smile, "all great philosophers have had some familiar animal. You know what Servius says—*Nullus enim locus sine genio est*."

Meanwhile Dom Claude, fearing some new freak of Jehan's,

reminded his worthy disciple that they had some figures on the portal to study together; and they both quitted the cell, to the great relief of the scholar, who began seriously to fear that his knee would take the impression of his chin.

CHAPTER VI

THE EFFECT PRODUCED BY SEVEN OATHS UTTERED IN THE OPEN AIR

"*Te Deum laudamas!*" exclaimed Maître Jehan, issuing from his hole, "the two screech-owls are gone at last. *Och! och!—Hax! pax! max!*—fleas!—mad dogs!—the devil! I've had enough of their conversation! My head hums like a bell. Mouldy cheese into the bargain! Whew! let me get down and take the purse of my high and mighty brother, and convert all these coins into bottles."

He cast a look of tenderness and admiration into the interior of the precious *escarcelle;* adjusted his dress; rubbed his boots; dusted his poor furred sleeves, all white with ashes; whistled an air; pirouetted a movement; looked about the cell to see if there was anything else he could take; scraped up here and there from off the furnace some amulet in glassware by way of trinket to give to Isabeau-la-Thierrye; and, finally, opened the door which his brother had left unfastened as a last indulgence, and which he in his turn left open as a last piece of mischief; and descended the circular staircase skipping like a bird.

In the midst of the darkness of the spiral stairs he elbowed something, which moved out of the way with a growl; he presumed that it was Quasimodo, and his fancy was so tickled with the circumstance that he descended the rest of the stairs holding his sides with laughter, and was still laughing when he got out into the square.

He stamped his foot when he found himself on terra firma. "Oh," said he, "most honourable and excellent pavement of Paris! O cursed staircase—enough to wind the angels of Jacob's ladder! What was I thinking of to go and thrust myself into that stone gimlet which bores the sky, and all to eat bearded cheese and to see the steeples of Paris through a hole in the wall!"

He advanced a few steps, and perceived the two screech-owls—that is to say, Dom Claude and Maître Jacques Charmolue—busy contemplating some sculpture on the portal. He approached them on tiptoe, and heard the archdeacon say in a whisper to Charmolue, "It was Guillaume de Paris that had a Job engraven on that stone of lapis lazuli, gilt at the edges. By Job is meant the philosopher's stone, which must be tried and tortured to become perfect, as Raymond Lully says: *Sub conversatione formæ specificæ salva anima.*"

"It's all one to me," said Jehan; "I've got the purse."

At that moment he heard a powerful and sonorous voice behind him uttering a series of formidable oaths: "*Sang-Dieu! Ventre-Dieu! Bé-Dieu! Corps de Dieu! Nombril de Belzébuth! Nom d'un pape! Corne et tonnerre!*"

"My life for it," exclaimed Jehan; "that can be no other than my friend Captain Phœbus!"

This name of Phœbus reached the ears of the archdeacon just as he was explaining to the King's attorney the dragon concealing its tail in a bath from whence issue smoke and a king's head. Dom Claude started and stopped short, to the great astonishment of Charmolue, turned round, and saw his brother Jehan accosting a tall officer at the door of the Logis Gondelaurier.

It was, in fact, Captain Phœbus de Chateaupers. He was standing with his back against the corner of the house of his betrothed, and swearing like a Turk.

"I' faith, Captain Phœbus," said Jehan, taking him by the hand, "you swear with admirable unction."

"*Corne et tonnerre!*" answered the captain.

"*Corne et tonnerre* yourself!" replied the scholar. "How now, my brave fellow? What's the meaning of this overflow of fine language?"

"Your pardon, friend Jehan," cried Phœbus, shaking him by the hand; "a spurred horse can't stop on a sudden. Now I was swearing at full gallop. I've just left those silly women, and when I come away I've always my throat full of oaths, and if I don't spit them out I should choke, *corne et tonnerre!*"

"Will you come and have something to drink?" asked the scholar.

This proposal tranquillised the captain.

"I would with all my heart, but I've no money."

"I have though."

"Nonsense! let's see."

Jehan displayed the purse before the captain's eyes with dignity and simplicity. Meanwhile the archdeacon, having left Charmolue all aghast, had approached them, and stopped a few steps off, observing them both without their noticing him, so absorbed were they in the contemplation of the purse.

Phœbus exclaimed, " A purse in your pocket, Jehan! Why, it's the moon in a pail of water: one sees it, but it's not there—there's nothing but the reflection. Egad! Ill lay anything they're pebble stones."

Jehan answered coolly, " These are the pebbles with which I pave my fob."

And without adding another word he emptied the purse upon a *borne* or high curbstone that was near, with the air of a Roman saving his country.

" *Vrai Dieu!* " growled out Phœbus. " *Targes!—grands blancs!—petits blancs!—mailles* at two to a tournois!—deniers parisis!—and real eagle liards!—it's enough to stagger one! "

Jehan remained dignified and immovable. A few liards rolled into the dirt; the captain, in his enthusiasm, stopped to pick them up. Jehan withheld him. " Fie, Captain Phœbus de Chateaupers! "

Phœbus counted the money; and, turning with solemnity towards Jehan, " Do you know, Jehan," said he, " that there are twenty-three sous parisis here? Whom have you been clearing out last night in Rue Coupe-Gueule? "

Jehan threw back his fair and curly head, and said, half closing his eyes as if in scorn, " What if one has a brother an archdeacon and a simpleton! "

" *Corne de Dieu!* " cried Phœbus, " the worthy man."

" Let's go and drink," said Jehan.

" Where shall we go? " said Phœbus—" to the Pomme d'Eve? "

" No, captain; let's go to the Vieille Science. Une *vieille* qui *scie* une *anse*. That's a rebus, and I like a rebus."

" Deuce take the rebuses, Jehan! the wine's better at the Pomme d'Eve; and then, by the side of the door, there's a vine in the sun, that cheers me when I'm drinking."

" Very well, then, here goes for Eve and her apple," said the scholar, taking Phœbus by the arm. " By-the-bye, my dear captain, you said just now *Rue Coupe-Gueule*. That's speaking very incorrectly. We are no longer so barbarous; we say *Rue Coupe-Gorge*."

The two friends directed their steps towards the Pomme

d'Eve. It is hardly necessary to say that they first gathered up the money, and that the archdeacon followed them.

The archdeacon followed them with a haggard and gloomy countenance. Was that the Phœbus whose accursed name, since his interview with Gringoire, had mingled with all his thoughts? He did not know, but, at any rate, it was a Phœbus; and that magic name was a sufficient inducement for the archdeacon to follow the two thoughtless companions with a stealthy pace, listening to their words and observing their slightest gestures with anxious attention. However, nothing was easier than to hear all they said, so loud they talked, and so little did they care for the passers-by knowing their secrets. They talked of duels, girls, and pranks of all sorts.

At the turn of a street the sound of a tambourine struck upon their ears from a neighbouring crossway. Dom Claude heard the officer say to the scholar, "*Tonnerre!* let's quicken our steps."

"Why, Phœbus?"

"I'm afraid the gipsy will see me."

"What gipsy?"

"The little one with her goat."

"La Esmeralda?"

"That's it, Jehan. I always forget her devil of a name. Let's make haste; she'd recognise me, and I wouldn't have her accost me in the streets."

"Do you know her then, Phœbus?"

Here the archdeacon observed Phœbus chuckle, lean aside, and whisper something in Jehan's ear. Phœbus then burst out laughing, and tossed his head with a triumphant air.

"In very deed?" said Jehan.

"Upon my soul!" said Phœbus.

"This evening?"

"This evening!"

"Are you sure she'll come?"

"Are you a fool, Jehan? Does one ever doubt those sort of things?"

"Captain Phœbus, you're a happy gendarme."

The archdeacon overheard all this conversation. His teeth chattered; a visible shudder ran through his whole frame. He stopped a moment, leaned against a post like a drunken man, then followed the track of the two joyous boon companions.

Just as he came up to them again they had changed their

conversation; and he heard them singing, at the full stretch of their lungs, the burden of an old song,—

"The lads the dice that merrily throw
Merrily to the gallows go."

CHAPTER VII

THE SPECTRE MONK

The illustrious cabaret of the Pomme d'Eve was situated in the University, at the corner of the Rue de la Rondelle and the Rue du Bâtonnier. The principal room was on the ground floor, very large and very low, supported in the centre by a heavy wooden pillar, painted yellow. There were tables all around; shining pewter pots hung up against the wall; a constant abundance of drinkers, and girls in plenty; a large casement looking into the street; a vine at the door; and over the door, a creaking iron plate, with an apple and a woman painted upon it, rusted by the rain, and turning with the wind upon an iron pin. This sort of weathercock, looking towards the highway, was the sign of the house.

Night was falling; the street was dark; the cabaret, full of lighted candles, flamed afar like a forge in the darkness, and emitted the noise of glasses, of feasting, of oaths, of quarrels, all escaping through the broken panes. Through the mist which the heat of the room diffused over the long casement in front were seen a multitude of figures confusedly swarming; and now and then there burst forth a loud peal of laughter. The people going along the street upon their business passed by this tumultuous casement without casting their eyes that way. Only now and then some little tattered boy would spring up on his toes until he could just see in at the window, and shout into the cabaret the old bantering cry with which it was then the custom to follow drunkards, "*Aux Houls, saouls, saouls, saouls!*"

One man, however, was walking backwards and forwards imperturbably before the noisy tavern, looking towards it incessantly, and stepping no farther away from it than a pikeman from his sentry-box. He was cloaked up to the nose. He had just bought the cloak at a ready-made clothes-shop near to the Pomme d'Eve, doubtless to secure himself from the cold of a

March night—perhaps, also, to conceal his costume. From time to time he stopped before the dim lattice-headed casement, listening, looking, and beating with his foot.

At length the door of the cabaret opened, and for that he seemed to have been waiting. A pair of boon companions came out. The gleam of light that now issued through the doorway cast a glow for a moment on their jovial faces. The man in the cloak went and placed himself on the watch under a porch on the other side of the street.

"*Corne et tonnerre!*" said one of the two companions, "it's on the stroke of seven. It's the hour of my assignation."

"I tell you," said the other, speaking thick, "that I don't live in the Rue des Mauvaises Paroles—*indignus qui inter mala verba habitat.* I lodge in the Rue Jean-Pain-Mollet—*in vico Joannis-Pain-Mollet*—and you're a wry-brained fellow if you say the contrary. Everybody knows that he that gets once upon a bear's back is never afraid; but you've a nose for smelling out a dainty bit, like St. Jacques-de-l'Hôpital."

"Jehan, my friend, you're drunk," said his companion.

The other answered, staggering all the while. "It pleases you to say so, Phœbus; but it's proved that Plato had the profile of a hound."

Doubtless the reader has already recognised our two worthy friends, the captain and the scholar. It seems that the man who was watching them in the dark had recognised them too, for he followed with slow steps all the zigzags which the reeling scholar forced the captain to make, who, being a more seasoned drinker, had retained all his self-possession. By listening attentively the man in the cloak overheard the whole of the interesting conversation which follows.

"*Corbacque!* Try to walk straight, Monsieur the Bachelor; you know that I must leave you. It's seven o'clock, and I have to meet a woman."

"Leave me, then. I can see stars and squibs. You're like Dampmartin Castle, that's bursting with laughter."

"By my grandmother's warts, Jehan, but this is talking nonsense a little too hard. By-the-bye, Jehan, have you no money left?"

"Monsieur the Rector, it's no fault of mine. The *petite boucherie—parva boucheria*——"

"Jehan—friend Jehan—you know I've promised to meet that little girl at the end of the Pont St. Michel, that I can take her nowhere but to La Falourdel's, the old woman's on the bridge, and that I must pay for the room. The old white-whiskered jade won't give me credit. Jehan, I pray you, have we drunk all the contents of the curé's pouch?—haven't you a single parisis left?"

"The consciousness of having spent our other hours well is a just and savoury sauce to our table."

"*Ventre et boyaux!*—a truce with your gibberish. Tell me—the devil's own Jehan—have you any coin left? Give it me, *Bé-Dieu!* or I'll search you all over, though I should find you as lousy as Job and as scabby as Cæsar."

"Monsieur, the Rue Galiache is a street with the Rue de la Verrerie at one end of it and the Rue de la Tixeranderie at the other."

"Well—yes—my good friend Jehan—my poor comrade—the Rue Galiache—good—very good. But in Heaven's name come to your senses. I want but one sou parisis—and seven o'clock's the time."

"Silence around, and attention to the song:—

'When mice have every case devour'd,
The King of Arras shall be lord:
When the sea, so deep and wide,
Is frozen at Midsummer-tide,
Then all upon the ice you'll see
The Arras men their town shall flee.'"

"Well, scholar of Antichrist, the devil strangle thee!" exclaimed Phœbus; and he roughly pushed the intoxicated scholar, who reeled against the wall and fell down gently upon the pavement of Philip-Augustus. Through a remnant of that fraternal pity which never absolutely deserts the heart of a bottle-companion, Phœbus rolled Jehan with his foot upon one of those pillows of the poor man which Providence keeps ready against every curbstone and post in Paris, and which the rich scornfully stigmatise with the name of dungheaps. The captain reared up Jehan's head on an inclined plane of cabbage stalks, and forthwith the scholar began to snore a most magnificent bass. However, all malice had not entirely left the heart of the captain. "So much the worse for thee, if the devil's cart picks thee up as it goes by," said he to the poor sleeping clerk; and he went his way.

The man in the cloak, who had kept following him, stopped for a moment before the recumbent scholar, as if agitated by some feeling of indecision; then heaving a deep sigh, he went on also after the captain.

Like them, we will now leave Jehan sleeping under the benevolent eye of the fair starlight; and with the reader's permission we will track their steps.

On turning into the Rue St. André-des-Arcs, Captain Phœbus perceived that some one was following him. He saw, while accidentally casting round his eyes, a sort of shade creeping behind him along the walls. He stopped—it stopped; he went on—then the shade went on again also. This, however, gave him very little concern. "Ah, bah!" said he to himself—"it matters little; I've not a sou about me."

In front of the College d'Autun he made a halt. It was at that college that he had shuffled through what he was pleased to call his studies; and through a certain habit of a refractory schoolboy which still clung to him, he never passed before the front of that college without stopping to pay his compliments to the statue of Cardinal Pierre Bertrand, which stood on the right hand of the gateway. While passing, as usual, before the effigy of the Cardinal, and snuffing the wind, the street being there quite solitary, he saw the shadow approaching him slowly—so slowly that he had full time to observe that this same shade had a cloak and a hat. When it had come nearly up to him it stopped, and remained almost as motionless as the statue of Cardinal Bertrand itself. But it fixed upon Phœbus two steadfast eyes, full of that vague sort of light which issues in the night-time from the pupils of a cat.

The captain was brave, and would have cared very little for a robber with a rapier in his hand. But this walking statue, this petrified man, made his blood run cold. At that time there were certain strange rumours afloat about a spectre monk that ranged the streets of Paris in the night-time, and they recurred confusedly to his recollection. He stood confounded for a few minutes, then broke silence, at the same time endeavouring to laugh. "Sir," said he, "if you be a thief, as I hope is the case, you're just now for all the world like a heron attacking a walnut-shell. My dear fellow, I'm a ruined youth of family. Try your hand hard by here. In the chapel of this college there's some wood of the true cross, set in silver."

The hand of the shade came forth from under its cloak, and fell upon Phœbus's arm with the force of an eagle's grip, the shade at the same time opening his lips, and saying with emphasis, "Captain Phœbus de Chateaupers!"

"What the devil!" said Phœbus; "do you know my name?"

"I not only know your name," returned the man in the cloak with his sepulchral voice, "but I also know that you have an appointment to-night."

"Yes," answered Phœbus in amazement.

"At seven o'clock."

"In a quarter of an hour."

"At La Falourdel's."

"Exactly so."

"The old woman's on the Pont St. Michel."

"Yes—St. Michel-Archange, as the Paternoster says."

"Impious man!" muttered the spectre. "With a woman?"

"*Confiteor.*"

"Whose name is——"

"La Smeralda," said Phœbus with alacrity, all his carelessness having gradually returned to him.

At that name the grip of the spectre shook Phœbus's arm furiously. "Captain Phœbus de Chateaupers, you lie!"

Any one who could have seen at that moment the fiery countenance of the captain—the spring which he made backwards, so violent that it disengaged him from the iron clutch which had seized him—the haughty mien with which he laid his hand upon the hilt of his sword—and, in the presence of all that passionate anger, the sullen stillness of the man in the cloak—any one who could have seen all that would have been affrighted. There was somewhat of the combat of Don Juan and the statue.

"Christ and Satan!" cried the captain; "that's a word that seldom assails the ear of a Chateaupers. Thou durst not repeat it."

"You lie!" said the spectre coolly.

The captain ground his teeth. Spectre monk, phantom, superstitions—all were forgotten at that moment. He now saw nothing but a man and an insult. "Ha! ha! this goes well!" spluttered he in a voice choking with rage. He drew his sword; then, still stammering—for anger as well as fear makes a man tremble—"Hither!" said he, "directly! Come on! Swords! swords! Blood upon these stones!"

Meanwhile the other did not stir. When he saw his adversary on his guard and prepared to defend himself, "Captain Phœbus," said he, and his accent vibrated with bitterness, "you forget your assignation."

The angry fits of such men as Phœbus are like boiling milk, of which a drop of cold water allays the ebullition. These few words brought down the point of the sword which glittered in the captain's hand.

"Captain," continued the man, "to-morrow—the next day—a month hence—ten years hence—you'll find me quite ready to cut your throat. But first go to your assignation."

"Why, in truth," said Phœbus, as if seeking to capitulate with himself, "a sword and a girl are two charming things to meet in a rendezvous; but I don't see why I should miss one of them for the sake of the other, when I can have them both." And so saying he put up his sword.

"Go to your assignation," resumed the unknown.

"Monsieur," answered Phœbus with some embarrassment, "many thanks for your courtesy. It will, in fact, be time enough to-morrow to make slashes and buttonholes upon each other in Father Adam's doublet. I'm much obliged to you for giving me leave to pass one pleasant quarter of an hour more. I was indeed in hopes to have laid you quietly in the gutter, and still have arrived in time for the lady—the more so as it is debonair to make a woman wait for you a little on such an occasion. But you seem to me to be a fellow of mettle—so that the safest way is to put off our game till to-morrow. So now I go to my rendezvous. Seven o'clock's the time, as you know." Here Phœbus scratched his ear. "Ah, Corne-Dieu! I'd forgotten! I've not a sou to pay the hire of the garret; and the old hag will want to be paid beforehand—she won't trust me."

"Here is wherewith to pay."

Phœbus felt the cold hand of the unknown slip into his a large piece of money. He could not help taking the money and grasping the hand. "Vrai-Dieu!" he exclaimed, "but you're a good fellow!"

"One condition," said the stranger. "Prove to me that I've been wrong, and that you spoke the truth. Hide me in some corner whence I may see whether this woman be really she whose name you have uttered."

"Oh," answered Phœbus, "it's just the same to me. We shall take the St. Martha room. You can see to your heart's content from the kennel that's on one side of it."

"Come then," rejoined the shade.

"At your service," said the captain. "I know not indeed whether you be not Messer Diabolus *in propriâ personâ*. But let us be good friends to-night, and to-morrow I'll pay you all my debts of the purse and of the sword."

They went forward at a rapid pace, and in a few minutes the noise of the river below announced to them that they were upon the Pont St. Michel, then loaded with houses. "I'll first introduce you," said Phœbus; "then I'll go and fetch the lady, who was to wait for me near the Petit-Châtelet. His companion made no answer; since they had been walking side by side he had not uttered a word. Phœbus stopped against a low door, and gave it a rough jolt. A light made its appearance through the crevices of the door. "Who's there?" cried a toothless voice. "*Corps-Dieu! tête-Dieu! ventre-Dieu!*" answered the captain. The door opened immediately, and exhibited to the newcomers an old woman and an old lamp, both of them trembling. The old woman was bent double, clothed in tatters, her head shaking, wrapped in a duster by way of *coiffure*, and perforated by two small eyes; wrinkled all over—her hands, her face, her neck; her lips turning inward, underneath her gums; and all round her mouth she had tufts of white hair, giving her the whiskered and demure look of a cat. The interior of this dog-hole was in no less decay than herself. There were walls of chalk; black beams in the ceiling; a dismantled fireplace; cobwebs in every corner; in the middle, a tottering company of maimed stools and tables; a dirty child in the ash-heap; and at the back a staircase, or rather a wooden ladder, ascending to a trap-door in the ceiling. As he entered this den Phœbus's mysterious companion pulled his cloak up to his eyes. Meanwhile the captain, swearing all the while like a Saracen, lost no time in producing his *écu*, saying, as he presented it, "The St. Martha room."

The old woman received him like any grandee, and shut up the *écu* in a drawer. It was the piece which Phœbus had received from the man in the black cloak. While her back was turned, the little long-haired tattered boy that was playing among the ashes went slyly to the drawer, took out the *écu*, and put there instead of it a dry leaf which he had plucked from a fagot.

The old woman beckoned to the two gentlemen, as she called them, to follow her, and ascended the ladder before them. On reaching the upper story she set down her lamp upon a chest; and Phœbus, as one accustomed to the house, opened a side door, which was the entrance to a dark and out-of-the-way nook. "Go in there, my dear fellow," said he to his companion. The man in the cloak obeyed without answering a word; the door closed upon him; he heard Phœbus bolt it outside, and a moment afterwards go downstairs again with the old woman. The light had disappeared.

CHAPTER VIII

THE CONVENIENCE OF WINDOWS LOOKING OUT ON THE RIVER

CLAUDE FROLLO (for we presume that the reader, better informed than Phœbus, has seen in all this adventure no other spectre monk than the archdeacon himself) groped about for some moments in the dark corner in which the captain had bolted him up. It was one of those which builders sometimes reserve in the angle formed by the roof with the wall that supports it. The vertical section of this kennel, as Phœbus had so aptly termed it, would have been a triangle. It had neither window nor skylight, and the inclined plane of the roof prevented a man's standing up in it. Claude was therefore under the necessity of squatting down in the dust and the plaster that cracked underneath him; and at the same time his head was burning. In ferreting about him with his hands, he found upon the floor a piece of broken glass, which he applied to his forehead, and the coolness of which gave him some little relief.

What was passing at that moment in the dark soul of the archdeacon? He and God alone could tell.

According to what fatal order was he disposing in his thoughts La Esmeralda, Phœbus, Jacques Charmolue, his young brother, of whom he was so fond, abandoned by him in the mud, his archdeacon's cassock, his reputation perhaps, thus dragged to La Falourdel's—all those images, all those adventures? We know not, but it is certain that these ideas formed a horrible group in his mind.

He had been waiting for a quarter of an hour, and he felt as if he had grown older by fifty years. All at once he heard the wooden staircase creak as some one ascended. The trap-door opened again, and again a light made its appearance. In the worm-eaten door of his nook there was a slit of considerable width, to which he put his face, so that he could see all that passed in the adjoining chamber. First of all, the old woman with the cat's face issued through the trap-door with her lamp in her hand; then Phœbus, curling his moustaches; then a third person, that beautiful and graceful figure La Esmeralda. The priest saw her issue from below like a dazzling apparition. Claude trembled; a cloud spread itself over his eyes; his pulses beat violently; his brain was in a whirl; he no longer saw or heard anything.

When he came to himself again Phœbus and La Esmeralda were alone, seated upon the wooden chest beside the lamp, the light of which exhibited to the archdeacon those two youthful figures, and a wretched-looking couch at the farther end of the room.

Close to the couch there was a window, the casement of which, burst like a spider's web upon which the rain has beaten, showed through its broken meshes a small patch of sky, with the moon reposing upon a pillow of soft clouds.

The young girl was blushing, confused, palpitating. Her long drooping lashes shaded her glowing cheeks. The officer, to whom she dared not lift her eyes, was quite radiant. Mechanically, and with a charming air of unconsciousness, she was tracing incoherent lines with the end of her finger upon the wooden seat, and looking at the finger. Her foot was not visible, for the little goat was lying upon it.

The captain was very gallantly arrayed. Upon his neck and his wrists he had tufts of fancy trimming, a great elegancy of that day.

It was not without difficulty that Dom Claude could overhear their conversation, through the humming of the blood that was boiling in his temples.

A dull affair enough, the talk of a pair of lovers—a perpetual "I love you"—a musical strain, the repetition of which is very monotonous and very insipid to all indifferent hearers when it is not set off with a few *fioriture*. But Claude was no indifferent hearer.

"Oh," said the young girl, without lifting her eyes, "do not despise me, Monseigneur Phœbus! I feel that I am doing what is wrong."

"Despise you, my pretty girl!" returned the officer with an air of gallantry *supérieure et distinguée*—"despise you, *tête-Dieu!* and why should I?"

"For having followed you."

"On that score, my charmer, we don't at all agree. I ought not only to despise you, but to hate you."

The young girl looked at him in affright. "Hate me!" exclaimed she. "Why, what have I done?"

" For having taken so much soliciting."

" Alas," said she, " it is that I'm breaking a vow! . . . I shall never find my parents . . . the amulet will lose its virtue. . . . But what then? what occasion have I for father and mother now? "

So saying, she fixed upon the captain her large black eyes, moist with joy and tenderness.

" Deuce take me if I understand you! " cried Phœbus.

La Esmeralda remained silent for a moment; then a tear issued from her eyes, a sigh from her lips, and she said, " O monseigneur, I love you."

There was around the young girl such a perfume of chastity, such a charm of virtue, that Phœbus did not feel quite at his ease with her. These words, however, emboldened him. " You love me! " said he with transport, and he threw his arm round the gipsy girl's waist; he had only been waiting for that opportunity.

The priest beheld it, and thereupon he felt with his finger's end the point of a dagger which he bore concealed in his breast.

" Phœbus," continued the gipsy girl, gently disengaging her waist from the tenacious hands of the captain, " you are good—you are generous—you are handsome: you have saved me—me, who am but a poor girl lost in Bohemia. I had long dreamt of an officer that was to save my life. It was of you that I dreamt, before I knew you, my Phœbus. The officer in my dream had a fine uniform like you—a grand look—a sword. Your name is Phœbus—it's a fine name; I love your name—I love your sword. Do draw your sword, Phœbus, that I may see it."

" Child! " said the captain, and he unsheathed his rapier, smiling. The gipsy girl looked first at the hilt, then at the blade; examined with wonderful curiosity the cipher upon the guard; and kissed the sword, saying, " You are the sword of a brave man. I love my captain."

Again Phœbus availed himself of the opportunity to impress upon her beautiful neck, bent aside in the act of looking, a kiss which made the young girl draw herself up again all crimson, and made the priest grind his teeth in the dark.

" Phœbus," resumed the gipsy girl, " let me speak to you. Do just walk a little, that I may see you at your full height and hear the sound of your spurs. How handsome you are! "

The captain rose to comply, chiding her at the same time with a smile of satisfaction. " Really, now, are you such a child!

By-the-bye, my darling, have you seen me in my state hacqueton?"

"Alas, no!" answered she.

"Ha, that's the finest thing of all!"

Phœbus came and seated himself beside her again, but much nearer than before. He began—"Just listen, my dear——"

The gipsy girl gave him several little taps of her pretty hand upon the lips, with childish and graceful sportiveness. "No, no," said she; "I will not listen to you. Do you love me? I want you to tell we whether you love me."

"Whether I love you, sweet angel?" cried the captain, bending one knee to the floor. "My blood, my soul, my property—all are thine, all at thy disposal. I love thee, and have never loved any but thee."

The captain had so many times repeated this sentence on many a like occasion that he delivered it all in a breath, and without a single blunder. At this impassioned declaration the gipsy girl raised to the dingy ceiling which here held the place of heaven a look full of angelic happiness. "Oh," murmured she, "such is the moment at which one ought to die!" Phœbus found "the moment" convenient for snatching from her another kiss, which went to torture the wretched archdeacon in his corner.

"To die!" cried the amorous captain. "What are you talking about, my angel? It's the time to live—or Jupiter is but a blackguard. Die at the beginning of such a pleasant thing! *Corne-de-bœuf!* what a joke! Not so, indeed. Just listen, my dear Similar . . . Esmenarda. . . . Pardon me, but you've got a name so prodigiously Saracen that I can't run it off my tongue; I get entangled in it like a brier."

"*Mon Dieu!*" said the poor girl, "and I, now, used to think that name pretty for its singularity. But since it displeases you, I'm quite willing to call myself Goton."

"Ha! no crying about such a little matter, my charmer. It's a name that one must get used to—that's all. When once I know it by heart it'll come ready enough. So hark ye, my dear Similar. I adore you to a very passion; I love you so that really it's quite miraculous. I know a little girl that's dying with rage about it."

The jealous girl interrupted him. "Who's that?" said she.

"Oh, what does that signify to us?" said Phœbus. "Do you love me?"

"Oh!" said she.

"Well, then, that's enough. You shall see how I love you too. May the great devil Neptunus stick his pitchfork into me if I don't make you the happiest creature alive! We'll have a pretty little lodging somewhere or other. I'll make my archers parade under your windows—they're all on horseback, and cut out Captain Mignon's. There are billmen, crossbowmen, and culverinmen. I'll take you to the great masters of the Parisians at the Grange de Rully. It's very magnificent. Eighty thousand men under arms—thirty thousand white harnesses, *jaques* or *brigandines*—the sixty-seven banners of the trades—the standards of the parliament, of the Chamber of Accompts, of the *trésor des généraux*, of the *aides des monnaies*—the devil's own turnout, in short. And then I'll take you to see the lions of the Hôtel-du-Roi—that are wild beasts, you know. All the women are fond of that."

For some moments the young girl, absorbed in her pleasing reflections, had been musing to the sound of his voice, without attending to the meaning of his words.

"Oh, you'll be so happy!" continued the captain, at the same time gently unbuckling the gipsy's belt. "What are you doing?" said she sharply. This movement had aroused her from her reverie.

"Nothing at all," answered Phœbus. "I was only saying that you must put off all that wild street-running dress when you're with me."

"When I'm with you, my Phœbus!" said the young girl tenderly. And again she became pensive and silent.

The captain, emboldened by her gentleness, threw his arm round her waist without her making any resistance; then began softly to unlace the poor girl's *corsage,* and so violently displaced her *gorgerette* that the priest, all panting, saw issue from underneath the lawn the charming bare shoulder of the gipsy girl, round and dusky like the moon rising through a misty horizon.

The young girl let Phœbus have his way. She seemed unconscious of what he was doing. The captain's eye sparkled. All at once she turned round to him. "Phœbus," said she, with an expression of boundless love, "instruct me in your religion."

"My religion!" cried the captain, bursting into a laugh. "Instruct you in my religion! *Corne et tonnerre!* what do you want with my religion?"

"That we may be married," answered she. The captain's

face took a mingled expression of surprise, disdain, unconcern, and libidinous passion. "Ah, bah!" said he, "is there any marrying in the case?"

The gipsy girl turned pale, and her head dropped upon her breast. "My sweet love," said Phœbus tenderly, "what signifies all that nonsense? Marriage is a grand affair, to be sure. Shall we love one another any the worse for not having Latin gabbled to us in a priest's shop?" And while saying this in his softest tone he approached extremely near the gipsy girl; his fondling hands had resumed their position about that waist so slender and so pliant, and his eye kindled more and more.

Meanwhile Dom Claude observed everything from his hiding-place. Its door was made of puncheon ribs, quite decayed, leaving between them ample passage for his look of a bird of prey. It was, it must be owned, a trying spectacle for a brown-skinned, broad-shouldered priest, condemned until that moment to the austere virginity of the cloister. He felt extraordinary movements within him; and any one who could then have seen the wretched man's countenance close against the worm-eaten bars might have thought they saw a tiger's face looking out from his cage upon some jackal devouring a gazelle.

All at once, by a sudden movement, Phœbus snatched the gipsy's *gorgerette* completely off. The poor girl, who had remained pale and thoughtful, started up as if out of her sleep; she hastily drew back from the enterprising officer, and casting a look over her bare neck and shoulders, blushing, confused, and mute with shame, she crossed her two lovely arms upon her bosom to hide it. But for the flame that was glowing in her cheeks, to see her standing thus silent and motionless, one might have taken her for a statue of Modesty. Her eyes were bent upon the ground.

This action of the captain's had laid bare the mysterious amulet which she wore about her neck. "What's that?" said he, laying hold of this pretext for going up to the beautiful creature that he had just scared away from him.

"Touch it not," answered she warmly; "it's my guardian. It's that by which I shall find my family again, if I keep worthy. Oh, leave me, *monsieur le capitaine!*—My mother! my poor mother! where are you? Come to my help!—Do, Monsieur Phœbus, give me back my *gorgerette*."

Phœbus drew back, and said coldly, "O mademoiselle, how plainly do I see that you don't love me!"

"Not love him!" exclaimed the poor unfortunate girl, and at the same time she clung with an air of fondness to the captain, whom she made sit down beside her. "Not love you, my Phœbus! What is it you are saying, wicked man, to rend my heart? Oh, come—take me—take all—do what you will with me—I am yours. What is the amulet to me now? What is my mother to me now? You are my mother, since I love you. Phœbus, my beloved Phœbus, dost thou see me? 'Tis I. Look at me. 'Tis that little girl whom thou wilt not spurn from thee—who comes, who comes herself to seek thee. My soul, my life, my person—all are yours, my captain. Well, then, be it so—let us not marry—it is not thy wish; and besides, what am I but a wretched girl of the common way? while you, my Phœbus, are a gentleman. A fine thing it would be truly for a dancing-girl to marry an officer! I was mad to think of it. No, Phœbus, no; I will be your mistress—your amusement—your pleasure—when you will—a girl that will be yours and yours only. For that alone was I made—to be stained, despised, dishonoured; but what then? Loved! I shall be the proudest and the happiest of women. And when I shall grow old or ugly, Phœbus—when I shall no longer be fit to love you, monseigneur—you will still suffer me to serve you. Others will embroider scarfs for you; I, your servant, will take care of them. You will let me polish your spurs, brush your hacqueton, and dust your riding-boots. Will you not, my Phœbus, have that pity? And in the meantime, take me to yourself. Here, Phœbus—all belongs to you. Only love me. That is all we gipsy girls have occasion for—air and love."

So saying, she threw her arms round the officer's neck, raising her eyes to him suppliantly and smiling through her tears. Her delicate neck was chafed by the woollen-cloth doublet and its rough embroidery. The captain, quite intoxicated, pressed his glowing lips to those lovely African shoulders; and the young girl, her eyes cast upwards to the ceiling, was all trembling and palpitating under his kisses.

All at once, above the head of Phœbus she beheld another head—a strange, livid, convulsive countenance, with the look of a demoniac; and close by that face there was a hand holding a poniard. They were the face and the hand of the priest; he had contrived to make his way through the crazy door of his hiding-place, and there he was. Phœbus could not see him. The young girl remained motionless, frozen, dumb, under the influence of the frightful apparition—like a dove that should raise her head at the moment that the osprey is looking into her nest with his round, fearful eyes.

She was unable even to utter a cry. She saw the poniard descend upon Phœbus, and rise again all reeking. "*Malèdiction!*" exclaimed the captain, and he fell upon the floor.

She fainted. At the moment that her eyes closed and all sense was forsaken her, she thought she felt a touch of fire impressed upon her lips, a kiss more burning than the executioner's branding-iron.

When she recovered her senses, she found herself surrounded by soldiers of the watch; they were carrying off the captain weltering in his blood; the priest had disappeared; the window at the back of the chamber, looking upon the river, was wide open; they were picking up from the floor a cloak which they supposed to belong to the officer; and she heard them saying around her, "It's a witch has been poniarding a captain."

BOOK VIII

CHAPTER I

CHANGE OF A CROWN TO A DEAD LEAF

Gringoire and the whole Court of Miracles were in a state of mortal anxiety. For a whole month it was not known what had become of La Esmeralda, which sadly grieved the Duke of Egypt and his friends the Truands; nor what had become of her goat, which redoubled the grief of Gringoire. One evening the gipsy girl had disappeared, since which time she had held no communication with them. All search had been fruitless. Some teasing *sabouleux* told Gringoire they had met her that same evening in the neighbourhood of the Pont-Saint-Michel, walking off with an officer; but this husband *à la mode de Bohème* was an incredulous philosopher; and besides, he knew better than any one his wife's extreme purity; he had been enabled to judge how impregnable was the chastity resulting from the two combined virtues of the amulet and the gipsy herself, and he had mathematically calculated the resistance of this chastity multiplied into itself. On that score, at least, his mind was at ease.

Still he could not account for her sudden disappearance, which was a source of deep mortification to him. He would have grown thinner upon it if the thing had been possible. He had in consequence neglected everything, even to his literary tastes, even to his great work, *De figuris regularibus et irregularibus,* which he intended printing with the first money he should get. For he raved upon printing ever since he had seen the Diadascolon of Hughes de Saint Victor printed with the celebrated types of Vindelin of Spires.

One day, as he was passing sorrowfully before the Tournelle Criminelle, he observed a crowd at one of the doors of the Palais de Justice. "What's that all about?" asked he of a young man who was coming out.

"I don't know, monsieur," answered the young man. "They say there's a woman being tried for the murder of a gendarme. As there seems to be some witchcraft in the business, the bishop and the official have interposed in the cause; and my brother, who's Archdeacon of Joas, can think of nothing else. Now I wished to speak to him; but I have not been able to get near him for the crowd—which annoys me sadly, for I want money."

"Alas, monsieur," said Gringoire, "I would I could lend you some; but though my breeches are in holes, it's not from the weight of écus."

He dared not tell the young man that he knew his brother, the archdeacon, towards whom he had not ventured to return since the scene of the church—a neglect which embarrassed him much.

The scholar passed on, and Gringoire proceeded to follow the crowd which was ascending the staircase of the Grand' Chambre. To his mind there was nothing equal to the spectacle of a trial in a criminal court for dissipating melancholy—the judges are generally so delightfully stupid. The people with whom he had mingled were moving on and elbowing each other in silence. After a slow and tiresome pattering through a long, gloomy passage, which wound through the Palais like the intestinal canal of the old edifice, he arrived at a low door opening into a *salle* or great public room, which his tall figure permitted him to explore with his eyes over the waving heads of the multitude.

The hall was spacious and gloomy, which latter circumstance made it appear still more spacious. The day was declining; the long, pointed windows admitted only a few pale rays of light, which were extinguished before they reached the vaulted ceiling, an enormous trellis-work of carved wood, the thousand figures of which seemed to be moving about confusedly in the shade. There were already several candles lighted here and there upon the tables, and glimmering over the heads of the *greffiers* or registrars, buried amidst the bundles of papers. The lower end of the room was occupied by the crowd; on the right and left were gentlemen of the gown at tables; at the extremity, upon an *estrade* or raised platform, were a number of judges, the farther rows just vanishing in the darkness—motionless and sinister visages. The walls were strewed with numberless fleurs-de-lis. Over the judges might be vaguely distinguished a large figure of Christ; and in all directions pikes and halberds, the points of which were tipped with fire by the reflection of the candles.

"Monsieur," asked Gringoire of one of those next him,

"who are all those persons yonder, ranged like prelates in council?"

"Monsieur," said his neighbour, "they are the councillors of the Grand' Chambre on the right; and those on the left are the councillors of the inquests, the *maîtres* in black gowns and the *messires* in red ones."

"And there, above them," continued Gringoire, "who's that great red-faced fellow all in a perspiration?"

"That's Monsieur the President."

"And those sheep behind him?" proceeded Gringoire, who, as we have already said, loved not the magistracy, which was owing, perhaps, to the ill-will he bore the Palais de Justice ever since his dramatic misadventure.

"They are Messieurs the Masters of Requests of the King's Household."

"And before him, that wild boar?"

"That's the Registrar of the Court of Parliament."

"And to the right, that crocodile?"

"Maître Philippe Lheulier, King's Advocate Extraordinary."

"And to the left, that great black cat?"

"Maître Jacques Charmolue, King's Attorney in the Ecclesiastical Court, with the Gentlemen of the Officiality."

"Ah, well, monsieur," said Gringoire, "and what, pray, are all those good folks about?"

"They're trying some one."

"Trying whom? I see no prisoner."

"It's a woman, monsieur. You cannot see her. Her back is towards us, and she is concealed by the crowd. Look, there she is, amidst that group of partisans."

"Who is the woman?" asked Gringoire. "Do you know her name?"

"No, monsieur; I'm only just arrived. I suppose, however, that there's some sorcery in the matter, since the official's engaged on the trial."

"Now, then," said our philosopher, "we are going to see all these men of the gown play the part of cannibals. Well, one sight's as good as another."

"Do you not think, monsieur," observed his neighbour, "that Maître Jacques Charmolue looks very mild?"

"Humph!" answered Gringoire, "I'm rather distrustful of mildness with a pinched-up nose and thin lips."

Here the bystanders imposed silence on the two talkers. An important deposition was being heard.

"Messeigneurs," said, from the middle of the room, an old woman, whose face was so buried under her clothes that she might have been taken for a walking bundle of rags—"messeigneurs, the thing is as true as that I am La Falourdel, for forty years a housekeeper on the Pont St. Michel, and paying regularly my rent, dues, and quit-rents; my door opposite the house of Tassin Caillart the dyer, who lives on the side looking up the river. An old woman now! a pretty girl once, messeigneurs! A few days ago some one said to me, 'Don't spin too much of an evening, La Falourdel; the devil's fond of combing old women's distaffs with his horns. It's certain that the spectre monk that was last year about the Temple is now wandering about the City. Take care, La Falourdel, that he doesn't knock at your door.' One evening I was turning my wheel; some one knocks at my door. 'Who is it?' says I. Some one swears. I open the door. Two men come in; a man in black, with a handsome officer. One could see nothing of the black man but his eyes—two live coals. All the rest was cloak and hat. And so they say to me, 'The St. Martha room.' That's my upper room, messeigneurs—my best. They give me an écu. I lock the écu in my drawer, and I says, 'That will buy some tripe to-morrow at the slaughter-house De la Gloriette.' We go upstairs. When we'd got up, whilst I turned my back, the black man disappears. This astounds me a little. The officer, who was as handsome as a great lord, goes down with me. He leaves the house. In about time enough to spin a quarter of a skein he comes in again with a pretty young girl—quite a paragon, messeigneurs—that would have shone like the sun if she'd had her hair dressed. She had with her a goat, a great he-goat, black or white, I don't remember which. This sets me a-thinking. The girl—that doesn't concern me; but the goat! I don't like those animals with their beards and their horns—it's so like a man. Besides, it has a touch of the Sabbath. However, I said nothing. I had the écu. That's only fair, you know, my lord judge. I show the captain and the girl into the upstairs room, and leave them alone—that's to say, with the goat. I go down, and get to my spinning again. I must tell you that my house has a ground floor and a story above. It looks out at the back upon the river, like the other houses on the bridge, and the ground-floor window and the first-floor window open upon the water. Well, as I was saying, I had got to my spinning. I don't know why, but I was thinking about the spectre monk, which the goat had put into my head—and then the pretty girl was rather queerly tricked out. All at once I hear a cry overhead, and something fall on the floor, and the window open. I run to mine, which is underneath, and I see pass before my eyes a black heap, and it falls into the water. It was a phantom dressed like a priest. It was moonlight. I saw it quite plain. It was swimming toward the City. All in a tremble, I call the watch. The gentlemen of the *douzaine* come in; and at first, not knowing what was the matter, as they were merry, they began to beat me. I explained to them. We go upstairs, and what do we find? My poor room stained with blood, the captain stretched all his length with a dagger in his neck, the girl pretending to be dead, and the goat all in a fright. 'Pretty work!' says I; 'I shall have to wash the floor for a fortnight and more. It must be scraped. It'll be a terrible job.' They carry off the officer, poor young man, and the girl all in disorder. But stop. The worst of all is that the next day, when I was going to take the écu to buy my tripe, I found a withered leaf in its place."

The old woman ceased. A murmur of horror ran through the audience. "That phantom, that goat, all that savours of magic," said one of Gringoire's neighbours. "And that withered leaf!" added another. "No doubt," continued a third, "that it's some witch that's connected with the spectre monk to plunder officers." Gringoire himself was not far from considering this *ensemble* at once probable and terrific.

"Woman Falourdel," said Monsieur the President with majesty, "have you nothing further to say to the court?"

"No, monseigneur," answered the old woman, "unless it is that in the report my house has been called an old tumble-down, offensive hovel—which is most insulting language. The houses on the bridge are not very good-looking, because there are such numbers of people; but the butchers live there for all that, and they are rich men, married to pretty proper sort of women."

The magistrate who had reminded Gringoire of a crocodile rose. "Silence," said he. "I beg you, gentlemen, to bear in mind that a poniard was found on the accused. Woman Falourdel, have you brought the leaf into which the écu was changed that the demon gave you?"

"Yes, monseigneur," answered she; "I've found it. Here it is."

An usher of the court passed the withered leaf to the crocodile, who, with a doleful shake of the head, passed it to the president, who sent it on to the King's Attorney in the Ecclesiastical Court; so that it made the round of the room. "It's a beech leaf," said Maître Jacques Charmolue; "an additional proof of magic."

A councillor then began: "Witness, two men went upstairs in your house at the same time: the black man, whom you at first saw disappear, then swim across the Seine in priest's clothes; and the officer. Which of them gave you the crown?"

The old woman reflected a moment, and then said, "It was the officer."

A murmur ran through the crown.

"Ha," thought Gringoire, "that creates some doubt in my mind."

Meanwhile, Maître Philippe Lheulier, King's Advocate Extraordinary, again interposed. "I would remind you, gentlemen, that the murdered officer, in the deposition written at his bedside, while stating that a vague notion had crossed his mind, at the instant when the black man accosted him, that it might be the spectre monk, added that the phantom had eagerly pressed him to go and meet the prisoner, and on his (the captain's) observing that he was without money, he had given him the écu which the said officer had paid La Falourdel. Thus the écu is a coin from hell."

This concluding observation appeared to dissipate all the doubts both of Gringoire and the other sceptics among the auditory.

"Gentlemen, you have the bundle of documents," added the King's Advocate, seating himself; "you can consult the deposition of Phœbus de Chateaupers."

At that name the prisoner rose; her head was now above the crowd, and Gringoire, aghast, recognised La Esmeralda.

She was pale; her hair, formerly so gracefully braided and spangled with sequins, fell in disorder; her lips were blue; her hollow eyes were terrific. Alas!

"Phœbus!" said she wildly; "where is he? Oh, messeigneurs, before you kill me, for mercy's sake tell me if he yet lives!"

"Hold your tongue, woman," answered the president; "that's not our business."

"Oh, for pity's sake tell me if he is living," continued she, clasping her beautiful wasted hands; and her chains were heard as they brushed along her dress.

"Well," said the King's Advocate roughly, "he is dying. Does that content you?"

The wretched girl fell back on her seat, speechless, tearless, white as a form of wax.

The president leaned over to a man at his feet, who was dressed in a gilt cap and black gown, and had a chain round his neck and a wand in his hand. "Usher, bring in the second prisoner."

All eyes were now turned towards a small door, which opened, and, to the great trepidation of Gringoire, made way for a pretty she-goat with gilt feet and horns. The elegant animal stopped a moment on the threshold, stretching out her neck as if, perched on the point of a rock, she had before her a vast horizon. All at once she caught sight of the gipsy girl, and leaping over the table and a registrar's head, in two bounds she was at her knees. She then rolled herself gracefully over her mistress's feet, begging for a word or a caress; but the prisoner remained motionless, and even poor Djali herself obtained not a look.

"Ay, ay, that's the horrid beast," said the old Falourdel, "and well I know them both again."

Jacques Charmolue interposed. "If you please, gentlemen, we will proceed to the examination of the goat."

The goat was, in fact, the second prisoner. Nothing was more common in those times than a charge of sorcery brought against an animal. Amongst others, in the Provostry Accompts for 1466, may be seen a curious detail of the expenses of the proceedings against Gillet Soulart and his sow, executed "for their demerits" at Corbeil. Everything is there—the cost of the pit to put the sow in; the five hundred bundles of wood from the wharf of Morsant; the three pints of wine and the bread, the sufferer's last repast, shared in a brotherly manner by the executioner; and even the eleven days' custody and feed of the sow, at eight deniers parisis per day. Sometimes they went farther even than animals. The capitularies of Charlemagne and Louis le Débonnaire impose severe penalties on the fiery phantoms which might think fit to appear in the air.

Meanwhile the King's Attorney in the Ecclesiastical Court had exclaimed, "If the demon which possesses this goat, and which has resisted all exorcisms, persist in his sorceries—if he astound the court with them—we forewarn him that we shall be obliged to have recourse against him to the gibbet or the stake."

Gringoire was all in a cold perspiration. Charmolue took up from a table the gipsy girl's tambourine, and presenting it in a certain manner to the goat, he asked her, "What's o'clock?"

The goat looked at him with a sagacious eye, raised her gilt foot, and struck it seven times. It was indeed seven o'clock. A movement of terror ran through the crowd. Gringoire could bear it no longer.

"She'll be her own ruin," cried he aloud; "you see she does not know what she's about!"

"Silence, you people at the end of the room!" said the usher sharply.

Jacques Charmolue, by means of the same manœuvres with the tambourine, made the goat perform several other tricks—about the day of the month, the month of the year, etc.—which the reader has already witnessed. And by an optical illusion peculiar to judicial proceedings, those same spectators who, perhaps, had more than once applauded in the public streets the innocent performances of Djali, were terrified at them under the roof of the Palais de Justice. The goat was indisputably the devil.

It was still worse when, the King's Attorney having emptied on the floor a certain leathern bag full of movable letters, which Djali had about her neck, they saw the goat pick out with her foot from among the scattered alphabet the fatal name Phœbus. The sorcery of which the captain had been the victim seemed unanswerably proved; and in the eyes of all the gipsy girl, that charming dancer, who had so often dazzled the passers-by with her airy grace, was neither more nor less than a frightful witch.

She on her part gave no signs of life—neither the graceful evolutions of Djali, nor the threatenings of the men of law, nor the stifled imprecations of the auditory—nothing now reached her apprehension.

She could only be roused by a sergeant shaking her pitilessly, and the president raising his voice with solemnity. "Girl, you are of Bohemian race, given to sorcery. You, with your accomplice, the enchanted goat, implicated in the charge, did, on the night of the 29th of March last, wound and poniard, in concert with the powers of darkness, by the aid of charms, and spells, a captain of the king's archers, Phœbus de Chateaupers by name. Do you persist in denying it?"

"Horrible!" cried the young girl, hiding her face with her hands. "My Phœbus! Oh, it's hellish!"

"Do you persist in denying it?" asked the president coolly.

"Do I deny it?" said she in a terrible accent; and she rose and her eye flashed.

The president continued straightforwardly, "Then how do you explain the facts laid to your charge?"

She answered in a broken voice, "I've already said I don't know. It's a priest—a priest that I do not know—an infernal priest that pursues me!"

"Just so," replied the judge; "the spectre monk!"

"O gentlemen, have pity upon me! I'm only a poor girl——"

"Of Egypt," said the judge.

Maître Jacques Charmolue commenced with mildness, "Seeing the painful obstinacy of the accused, I demand the application of the torture."

"Granted," said the president.

A shudder ran through the whole frame of the unhappy girl. She rose, however, at the order of the partisan men, and walked with a tolerably firm step, preceded by Charmolue and the priests of the officiality, between two rows of halberds, towards a false door, which suddenly opened and shut again upon her, having the effect upon Gringoire of a mouth gaping to devour her.

When she disappeared a plaintive bleating was heard. It was the little goat crying.

The sitting of the court was suspended. A councillor having observed that gentlemen were fatigued, and that it would be long to wait for the conclusion of the torture, the president answered that a magistrate must sacrifice himself to his duty.

"What a troublesome, vexatious jade!" said an old judge, "to make one give her the torture when one has not supped!"

CHAPTER II

SEQUEL OF THE CROWN CHANGED TO A DEAD LEAF

After ascending and descending several flights of steps as they proceeded through passages so gloomy that they were lighted with lamps at midday, La Esmeralda, still surrounded by her lugubrious attendants, was pushed forward by the sergeants of the Palais into a dismal chamber. This chamber, of a circular form, occupied the ground floor of one of those large towers which still in our day appear through the layer of recent edifices with which modern Paris has covered the ancient one. There were no windows to this vault, no other opening than the low overhanging entrance of an enormous iron door. Still it did not want for light; a furnace was contrived in the thickness of the wall; a large fire was lighted in it, which filled the vault with its crimson reflection, and stripped of every ray a miserable candle placed in a corner. The sort of portcullis which was used to enclose the furnace, being raised at the moment, only gave to view at the mouth of the flaming edifice, which glared upon the dark wall, the lower extremity of its bars, like a row of black, sharp teeth set at regular distances, which gave the furnace the appearance of one of those dragon's mouths which vomit forth flames in ancient legends. By the light which issued from it the prisoner saw all around the chamber frightful instruments of which she did not understand the use. In the middle lay a mattress of leather almost touching the ground, over which hung a leathern strap with a buckle, attached to a copper ring held in the teeth of a flat-nosed monster carved in the keystone of the vault. Pincers, nippers, large ploughshares were heaped inside the furnace, and were heating red-hot, promiscuously, upon the burning coals. The sanguine glow of the furnace only served to light up throughout the chamber an assemblage of horrible things.

This Tartarus was called simply *la chambre de la question.*

Upon the bed was seated, unconcernedly, Pierrat Torterue, the sworn torturer. His assistants, two square-faced gnomes, with leather aprons and tarpaulin coats, were turning about the irons on the coals.

In vain had the poor girl called up all her courage; on entering this room she was seized with horror.

The sergeants of the bailiff of the Palais were ranged on one side, the priests of the officiality on the other. A registrar, a table, and writing materials were in one corner. Maître Jacques Charmolue approached the gipsy girl with a very soft smile. "My dear child," said he, "you persist, then, in denying everything?"

"Yes," answered she in a dying voice.

"In that case," resumed Charmolue, "it will be our painful duty to question you more urgently than we should otherwise wish. Have the goodness to sit down on that bed. Maître Pierrat, make room for mademoiselle, and shut the door."

Pierrat rose with a growl. "If I shut the door," muttered he, "my fire will go out."

"Well, then, my good fellow," replied Charmolue, "leave it open."

Meanwhile La Esmeralda remained standing. That bed of leather, upon which so many poor wretches had writhed, scared her. Terror froze her very marrow; there she stood, bewildered and stupefied. At a sign from Charmolue the two assistants took her and seated her on the bed. They did not hurt her; but when those men touched her—when that leather touched her—she felt all her blood flow back to her heart. She cast a wandering look around the room. She fancied she saw moving and walking from all sides towards her, to crawl upon her body and pinch and bite her, all those monstrous implements of torture, which were, to the instruments of all kinds that she had hitherto seen, what bats, centipedes, and spiders are to birds and insects.

"Where is the physician?" asked Charmolue.

"Here," answered a black gown that she had not observed before.

She shuddered.

"Mademoiselle," resumed the fawning voice of the attorney of the ecclesiastical court, "for the third time, do you persist in denying the facts of which you are accused?"

This time she could only bend her head in token of assent—her voice failed her.

"You persist, then?" said Jacques Charmolue. "Then I'm extremely sorry, but I must fulfil the duty of my office."

"Monsieur the King's Attorney," said Pierrat gruffly, "what shall we begin with?"

Charmolue hesitated a moment, with the ambiguous grimace of a poet seeking a rhyme. "With the brodequin," said he at last.

The unhappy creature felt herself so completely abandoned of God and man that her head fell on her chest like a thing inert, which has no power within itself.

The torturer and the physician approached her both at once. The two assistants began rummaging in their hideous armoury. At the sound of those frightful irons the unfortunate girl started convulsively. "Oh!" murmured she, so low that no one heard her, "O my Phœbus!" She then sank again into her previous insensibility and petrified silence. This spectacle would have torn any heart but the hearts of judges. She resembled a poor sinful soul interrogated by Satan at the crimson wicket of hell. The miserable body about which was to cling that frightful swarm of saws, wheels, and chevalets—the being about to be handled so roughly by those grim executioners and torturing pincers—was, then, that soft, fair, and fragile creature—a poor grain of millet, which human justice was sending to be ground by the horrid millstones of torture.

Meanwhile the callous hands of Pierrat Torterue's assistants had brutally stripped that charming leg, that little foot, which had so often astonished the passers-by with their grace and beauty, in the streets of Paris. "It's a pity," growled out the torturer as he remarked the grace and delicacy of her form. If the archdeacon had been present he certainly would have remembered at that moment his symbol of the spider and the fly. Soon the unhappy girl saw approaching through the mist which was spreading over her eyes the brodequin or wooden boot; soon she saw her foot, encased between the iron-bound boards, disappear under the terrific apparatus. Then terror restored her strength. "Take that off," cried she angrily, starting up all dishevelled. "Mercy!"

She sprang from the bed to throw herself at the feet of the king's attorney; but her leg was caught in the heavy block of oak and ironwork, and she sank upon the brodequin more shattered than a bee with a heavy weight upon its wing.

At a sign from Charmolue they replaced her on the bed, and two coarse hands fastened round her small waist the leathern strap which hung from the ceiling.

"For the last time, do you confess the facts of the charge?" asked Charmolue with his imperturbable benignity.

"I am innocent," was the answer.

"Then, mademoiselle, how do you explain the circumstances brought against you?"

"Alas, monseigneur, I don't know."

"You deny, then?"

"All!"

"Proceed," said Charmolue to Pierrat.

Pierrat turned the screw, the brodequin tightened, and the wretched girl uttered one of those horrible cries which are without orthography in any human tongue. "Stop," said Charmolue to Pierrat.

"Do you confess?" said he to the gipsy girl.

"All!" cried the wretched girl. "I confess! I confess! Mercy!"

She had not calculated her strength in braving the torture.

Poor child! whose life hitherto had been so joyous, so pleasant, so sweet—the first pang of acute pain had overcome her.

"Humanity obliges me to tell you," observed the king's attorney, "that in confessing you have only to look for death."

"I hope so," said she. And she fell back on the bed of leather, dying, bent double, letting herself hang by the strap buckled round her waist.

"Come, come, my darling, hold up a bit," said Maître Pierrat, raising her. "You look like the gold sheep that hangs about Monsieur of Burgundy's neck."

Jacques Charmolue raised his voice,—

"Registrar, write down.—Young Bohemian girl, you confess your participation in the love-feasts, sabbaths, and sorceries of hell with wicked spirits, witches, and hobgoblins? Answer."

"Yes," said she, so low that the word was lost in a whisper.

"You confess having seen the ram which Beelzebub causes to appear in the clouds to assemble the sabbath, and which is only seen by sorcerers."

"Yes."

"You confess having adored the heads of Bophomet, those abominable idols of the Templars."

"Yes."

"Having held habitual intercourse with the devil, under the form of a familiar she-goat, included in the prosecution?"

"Yes."

"Lastly, you vow and confess having, with the assistance of the demon, and the phantom commonly called the spectre monk, on the night of the twenty-ninth of March last, murdered and assassinated a captain named Phœbus de Chateaupers?"

She raised her large fixed eyes towards the magistrate, and answered, as if mechanically, without effort or emotion, "Yes." It was evident her whole being was shaken.

"Write down, registrar," said Charmolue. And addressing himself to the torturers—"Let the prisoner be unbound and taken back into court."

When the brodequin was removed the attorney of the ecclesiastical court examined her foot, still paralysed with pain. "Come," said he, "there's not much harm done. You cried out in time. You could dance yet, my beauty!" He then turned towards his acolytes of the officiality. "At length justice is enlightened!—that's a relief, gentlemen! Mademoiselle will at least bear this testimony—that we have acted with all possible gentleness."

CHAPTER III

END OF THE CROWN CHANGED TO A DEAD LEAF

When, pale and limping, she re-entered the court a general hum of pleasure greeted her. On the part of the auditory it was that feeling of satisfied impatience which is experienced at the theatre at the expiration of the interval between the two last acts of a play, when the curtain is raised, and "the end," according to the French expression, "is about to begin." On the part of the judges it was the hope of soon getting their supper. The little goat, too, bleated with joy. She would have run to her mistress, but they had tied her to the bench.

Night had quite set in. The candles, whose number had not been increased, gave so little light that the walls of the spacious room could not be seen. Darkness enveloped every object in a sort of mist. A few apathetic judges' faces were just visible. Opposite to them, at the extremity of the long apartment, they could distinguish an ill-defined white point standing out amidst the gloomy background. It was the prisoner.

She had crawled to her place. When Charmolue had magisterially installed him in his, he sat down; then rose and said, without exhibiting too much of the self-complacency of success, "The accused has confessed all."

"Bohemian girl," continued the president, "you have confessed all your acts of sorcery, prostitution, and assassination upon Phœbus de Chateaupers?"

Her heart was full. She was heard sobbing amid the gloom. "Whatever you will," answered she feebly; "but make an end of me quickly."

"Monsieur the King's Attorney in the Ecclesiastical Court," said the president, "the chamber is ready to hear your requisitions."

Maître Charmolue exhibited a frightful scroll, and began to read over, with much gesticulation and the exaggerated emphasis of the bar, a Latin oration, in which all the evidence of the trial was drawn out in Ciceronian periphrases, flanked by quotations from Plautus, his favourite comic author. We regret that it is not in our power to present our readers with this extraordinary piece of eloquence. The orator delivered it with marvellous action. He had not concluded the exordium before the perspiration began to start from his forehead and his eyes from his head. All at once, in the middle of a finely-turned period, he broke off, and his countenance, which was generally mild enough, and, indeed, stupid enough, became terrible. "Gentlemen," cried he (this time in French, for it was not in the scroll), "Satan is so mixed up in this affair that, behold! he is present at our councils, and makes a mock of their majesty. Behold him!" So saying, he pointed to the little goat, which, seeing Charmolue gesticulating, thought it quite proper she should do the same, and had seated herself on her haunches, mimicking as well as she could, with her fore-feet and shaggy head, the pathetic action of the king's attorney in the ecclesiastical court. It was, if we remember right, one of her prettiest talents. This incident, this last proof, produced a great effect. They tied the goat's feet, and the king's attorney resumed the thread of his eloquence. It was a long thread indeed, but the peroration was admirable. The last sentence ran thus; we leave the reader's imagination to combine with it the hoarse voice and broken-winded gestures of Maître Charmolue: "*Ideò, domni, coram strygâ demonstratâ, crimine patente, intentione criminis existente, in nomine sanctæ ecclesiæ Nostræ-Dominæ Parisiensis quæ est in saisinâ habendi omnimodam altam et bassam justitiam in illâ hac intemeratâ Civitatis insulâ, tenore præsentium declaramus nos requirere, primo, aliquamdam pecuniariam indemnitatem; secundo, amendationem honorabilem ante portalium maximum Nostræ-Dominæ, ecclesiæ cathedralis; tertio, sententiam in virtute cujus ista stryga cum suâ capellâ, seu in trivio vulgariter dicto* la Grève, *seu in insulâ exeunte in fluvio Secanæ, juxtà pointam jardini regalis, executatæ sint!*"[1]

He put on his cap again, and reseated himself.

"*Eheu!*" muttered Gringoire, quite overwhelmed; "*bassa latinitas!*"

[1] It may be as well to attempt a translation for the reader of this delectable specimen of the barbarous Latin and the legal jargon of the Middle Ages:—

"Therefore, gentlemen, the witchcraft being proved, and the crime made manifest, as likewise the criminal intention, in the name of the holy church of Our Lady of Paris, which is seised of the right of all manner of justice, high and low, within this inviolate island of the City, we declare, by the tenor of these presents, that we require, firstly, some pecuniary compensation; secondly, penance before the great portal of the cathedral church of Our Lady; thirdly, a sentence, by virtue of which this witch, together with her she-goat, shall, either in the public square, commonly called La Grève, or on the island standing forth in the river Seine, adjacent to the point of the royal gardens, be executed."

Another man in a black gown then rose near the prisoner; it was her advocate or counsel. The fasting judges began to murmur.

"Mr. Advocate, be brief," said the president.

"Monsieur the President," answered the advocate, "since the defendant has confessed the crime, I have only one word to say to these gentlemen. I hold in my hand a passage of the Salic law: 'If a witch has eaten a man, and is convicted of it, she shall pay a fine of eight thousand deniers, which make two hundred sous of gold.' Let the chamber condemn my client to the fine."

"An abrogated clause," said the King's Advocate Extraordinary.

"*Nego,*" replied the prisoner's advocate.

"Take the votes," said a councillor; "the crime is manifest, and it is late."

The votes were taken without going out of court. The judges voted by the lifting of their caps—they were in haste. Their hooded heads were seen uncovering one after another in the shade at the lugubrious question addressed to them in a low voice by the president. The poor prisoner seemed to be looking at them, but her bewildered eye no longer saw anything.

Then the registrar began to write; then he handed to the president a long scroll of parchment. Then the unhappy girl heard the people stirring, the pikes clashing, and a freezing voice saying,—

"Bohemian girl, on such day as it please our lord the King, at the hour of noon, you shall be taken in a tumbrel, in your shift, bare-footed, with a rope round your neck, before the great portal of Notre-Dame; and there you shall do penance with a wax torch of two pounds weight in your hand, and from thence you shall be taken to the Place de Grève, where you shall be hanged and strangled on the town gibbet, and your goat likewise; and shall pay to the official three lions of gold, in reparation of the crimes by you committed and confessed, of sorcery, magic, prostitution, and murder, upon the person of Monsieur Phœbus de Chateaupers. So God have mercy on your soul!"

"Oh, it's a dream!" murmured she; and she felt rude hands bearing her away.

CHAPTER IV

LASCIATE OGNI SPERANZA

In the Middle Ages, when an edifice was complete, there was almost as much of it within the ground as above it. Except, indeed, it was built upon piles, like Notre-Dame, a palace, a fortress, or a church, had always a double bottom. In the cathedrals it was, as it were, another cathedral, subterraneous, low, dark, mysterious, blind, and dumb, under the aisles of the building above, all flooded with light and resounding night and day with the music of bells and organs. Sometimes it was a sepulchre. In the palaces and the bastilles it was a prison—sometimes a sepulchre too—and sometimes it was both together. Those mighty masses of masonry, of which we have explained elsewhere the mode of formation and vegetation, had not foundations merely—they might be said to have roots, branching out under ground in chambers, galleries, and staircases, like the structure above. Thus all of them, churches, palaces, and bastilles, stood half within the earth. The subterraneous vaults of an edifice formed another edifice, in which you descended instead of ascending; and the underground stories of which extended downwards beneath the pile of external stories of the structure, like those inverted forests and mountains which are seen in the liquid mirror of a lake, underneath the forests and mountains on its borders.

At the Bastille St. Antoine, at the Palais de Justice of Paris, and at the Louvre, these subterraneous edifices were prisons. The stories of these prisons, as they went deeper into the ground, grew narrower and darker. They formed so many zones, presenting, as by a graduated scale, deeper and deeper shades of horror. Dante could find nothing better for the construction of his hell. These dungeon funnels usually terminated in a low hollow, shaped like the bottom of a tub, in which Dante has placed his Satan, and in which society placed the criminal condemned to death. When once a miserable human existence was there interred—then farewell light, air, life, *ogni speranza*—it never went out again but to the gibbet or the stake. Sometimes it rotted there—and human justice called that forgetting. Between mankind and himself the condemned felt weighing upon his head an accumulation of stones and jailers, and the whole prison together, the massive bastille, was now but one enormous complicated lock that barred him out of the living world.

It was one of those low damp holes, in the *oubliettes* excavated by St. Louis in the *in pace* of the Tournelle, that—for fear of her escaping, no doubt—they had deposited La Esmeralda condemned to the gibbet, with the colossal Palais de Justice over her head—a poor fly that could not have stirred the smallest of its stones.

Assuredly, Providence and society had here been alike unjust; such a profusion of misfortune and of torture was not necessary to shatter so fragile a creature.

She was there lost in darkness, buried, walled up. Any one that could have seen her in that state, after having seen her laughing and dancing in the sunshine, would have shuddered. Chill as night—chill as death—no longer a breath of air in her locks—no longer a human voice in her ear—no longer a glimpse of daylight in her eyes—broken in two, as it were—crushed with chains—bent double beside a pitcher and a loaf of bread, upon a little straw, in the pool of water that formed itself under her from the oozings of the dungeon—without motion—almost without breath—she was now scarcely sensible even to suffering. Phœbus—the sunshine—noonday—the open air—the streets of Paris—her dancing amid the applauses of the spectators—her soft prattlings of love with the officer; and then the priest—the old woman—the poniard—blood—the torture—the gibbet; all that was indeed still floating in her mind—now as a harmonious and golden vision, then as a frightful nightmare; but her apprehension of it all was now but that of a vaguely horrible struggle involved in darkness, or of a distant music that was still playing above ground, but was no longer audible at the depth to which the unfortunate girl had fallen. Since she had been there she neither waked nor slept; in that misery—in that dungeon—she could no more distinguish waking from sleeping, dreams from reality, than she could the day from the night. All was mingled, broken, floating, confusedly scattered in her thoughts. She no longer felt, no longer knew, no longer thought—at most, she only dreamed. Never had living creature been plunged more deeply into annihilation.

Thus benumbed, frozen, petrified, scarcely had she remarked, at two or three different times, the noise of a trap-door which had opened somewhere above her, without even admitting a ray of light, and through which the hand of some one had thrown her a crust of black bread. Yet this was her only remaining communication with mankind—the periodical visit of the jailer. One thing alone still mechanically occupied her ear: over her head the damp filtered through the mouldy stones of the vault, and at regular intervals drop after drop, thus collected, fell into the pool of water beside her with a splashing to which, in her stupor, she involuntarily listened.

That drop of water falling into that pool was the only movement still perceptible about her—her only clock to mark the time—the only noise that reached her, of all the noise that is made upon the earth; except, indeed, that she also felt from time to time, in that sink of mire and darkness, something cold passing here and there over her foot or her arm, and making her shiver.

How long had she been there? She knew not. She had some recollection of a sentence of death pronounced somewhere upon some one, that then they had carried herself away, and that she had awoke in darkness and silence, freezing. She had crawled along upon her hands; then she had felt iron rings cutting her ankles, and chains had clanked. She had discovered that all around her was wall—that underneath her were flag-stones covered with wet, and a bundle of straw; but there was neither lamp nor ventilator. Then she had seated herself upon that straw; and sometimes, for a change of posture, upon the lowest step of a stone flight which there was in her dungeon. At one moment she had endeavoured to count the dark minutes which the drops of water measured to her ear; but soon that mournful employment of her sick brain had broken itself off, and left her in stupor again.

At length one day, or one night (for midnight and noon had the same hue in this sepulchre), she heard above her a louder noise than that which the turnkey generally made when he brought her her loaf of bread and pitcher of water. She raised her head, and saw a reddish light through the crevices of the sort of trap-door made in the vault of the *in pace*. At the same time the heavy iron creaked, the trap-door grated on its rusty hinges, turned back, and she saw a lantern, a hand, and the lower part of the bodies of two men, the door being too low for her to see the upper. The light affected her eyes so sensibly that she closed them.

When she reopened them the door was closed, the lantern was placed on a step of the staircase; a man, alone, was standing before her. A *cagoule* fell to his feet, a *caffardum* of the same colour concealed his face. Nothing was seen of his person, neither his face nor his hands. It was a long black winding-sheet standing on end, and under which something was perceived to move. She looked steadily for some minutes at this sort of spectre. Meanwhile neither of them spoke. They were like two statues confronting each other. Two things alone seemed to have life in the vault—the wick of the lantern, which crackled owing to the humidity of the atmosphere, and the drop of water from the roof, which broke this irregular crepitation by its monotonous plash, and made the reflection of the lantern tremble in concentric circles upon the oily water of the pool.

At length the prisoner broke silence. "Who are you?"

"A priest."

The word, the accent, the sound of the voice, made her start.

The priest continued in a hollow tone, "Are you prepared?"

"For what?"

"For death."

"Oh!" said she; "will it be soon?"

"To-morrow."

Her head, which she had raised joyfully, fell back again upon her bosom. "That's very long!" murmured she. "What could it signify to them if it had been to-day?"

"You are very wretched, then?" asked the priest, after a short silence.

"I'm very cold," answered she.

She took her feet between her hands—a habitual gesture with poor creatures extremely cold, and which we have already remarked in the recluse of the Tour-Roland—and her teeth chattered.

The priest's eyes appeared to be wandering from under his hood around the dungeon. "Without light!—without fire!—in the water! 'Tis horrible!"

"Yes," answered she, with the bewildered air which misery had given her. "The day is for every one—why do they give me nothing but night?"

"Do you know," resumed the priest after another silence, "why you are here?"

"I think I knew it once," said she, passing her thin fingers across her brow as if to assist her memory, "but I don't know now."

All at once she began to weep like a child. "I want to go away from here, monsieur. I'm cold—I'm afraid, and there are creatures crawling over me."

"Well, then, follow me."

So saying, the priest took her arm. The poor girl was frozen to her very vitals, and yet that hand felt cold to her.

"Oh!" murmured she, "it's the icy hand of death. Who are you?"

The priest raised his hood. She looked; it was that ominous visage which had so long pursued her—that demon's head that had appeared to her at La Falourdel's over the adored head of her Phœbus—that eye which she had the last time seen glaring by the side of a poniard.

This apparition, ever so fatal to her, and which had thus pushed her on from misfortune to misfortune, even to an ignominious death, roused her from her stupor. It seemed to her as if the sort of veil which had woven itself upon her memory was rent away. All the details of her dismal adventure, from the nocturnal scene at La Falourdel's to her condemnation at the Tournelle, were at once brought back to her mind, not vague and confused as hitherto, but distinct, decided, breathing, terrible. These recollections, almost obliterated by excess of suffering, were revived at the sight of the gloomy figure before her, as the approach of fire brings out afresh upon the white paper the invisible letters traced on it with sympathetic ink. It seemed as if all the wounds of her heart were at once reopened and bleeding.

"Ha!" cried she, her hands before her eyes and with a convulsive shiver, "it's the priest!"

She then let fall her unnerved arms, and remained sitting, her head cast down, her eyes fixed on the ground, speechless, and continuing to tremble.

The priest looked at her with the eye of a kite which has been long hovering from the upmost heaven around a poor lark cowering in the corn, and has been gradually and silently contracting the formidable circles of its flight, until it suddenly darts down like lightning upon its prey, and holds it panting between its talons.

She began to murmur in a low tone, "Finish! finish!—the last blow!" And her head sank between her shoulders, like a sheep awaiting the stroke of the butcher.

"You have a horror of me, then?" said he at length.

She did not answer.

"Have you a horror of me?" repeated he.

Her lips contracted as if she was smiling. "Yes," said she; "the executioner taunts the condemned! For months he pursues me—threatens me—terrifies me. But for him, my God, how happy I was! It is he that has cast me into this abyss! O heavens, it is he that killed—it is he that killed him —my Phœbus!" Here, bursting into sobs, and raising her eyes towards the priest, "O wretch!—who are you? What have I done to you? Do you hate me so, then? Alas! what have you against me?"

"I love thee!" cried the priest.

Her tears suddenly ceased; she looked at him with an idiotic air. He had fallen on his knees, and was looking her through with eyes of fire.

"Dost thou hear?—I love thee!" cried he again.

"What love!" said the wretched girl, shuddering.

He continued, "The love of the damned."

Both remained for some minutes silent, crushed under the weight of their emotions—he maddened—she stupefied.

"Listen," said the priest at length, and a strange calm came over him; "thou shalt know all. I am about to tell thee what hitherto I have scarcely dared tell myself, when secretly I have interrogated my conscience in those deep hours of the night when it has been so dark that it seemed as if God could no longer see me. Listen—before I met thee, young girl, I was happy——"

"And I too!" sighed she feebly.

"Interrupt me not. Yes—I was happy; at least I thought myself so. I was pure—my soul was filled with limpid light. No head ever rose more lofty or more radiant than mine. Priests consulted me upon chastity, doctors upon doctrine. Yes, science was everything to me; it was a sister—and a sister sufficed me. Not but that, with age, other ideas came across my mind. More than once my blood was roused by the passing of a female form. That force of sex and blood, which, foolish youth! I had thought stifled for ever, had more than once shaken convulsively the chain of the iron vows which bind me, miserable wretch, to the cold stones of the altar. But fasting, prayer, study, the macerations of the cloister, had again restored the soul's empire over the body. And then I avoided women. Besides, I had only to open a book for all the impure vapours of the brain to evaporate before the splendour of science. In a few minutes I saw flee before me the gross things of earth; and again I became tranquil, beguiled, and serene before the calm radiance of eternal truth. So long as the demon only sent to encounter me vague shadows of women, passing here and there before my eyes, in the church, in the streets, in the fields, and which were scarcely retraced in my dreams, I vanquished him easily. Alas! if victory stayed not with me, the fault is in God, who made not man and the demon of equal strength. Listen—one day——"

Here the priest stopped; and the prisoner heard issuing from his bosom sighs which seemed to rend him. He resumed,—

"One day I was leaning against the window of my cell. What book was I reading then? Oh! all that's confusion in my head. I was reading. The window overlooked a square. I hear the sound of a tambourine and music. Angry at being thus disturbed in my reverie, I look into the square. What I saw—there were others that saw it too—and yet it was not a spectacle for human eyes. There, in the middle of the pavement—it was noon—a burning sun—a creature was dancing—a creature so beautiful that God would have preferred her to the Virgin—would have chosen her for His mother—would have been born of her, if she had existed when He became man. Her eyes were black and splendid. Amidst her raven locks a few single hairs, through which the sunbeams shone, were glistening like threads of gold. Her feet were lost in the rapidity of their movement. Around her head, amongst her ebon tresses, were plates of metal, which sparkled in the sun and formed about her temples a diadem of stars. Her dress, thick-set with spangles, twinkled, all blue and studded with sparkles, like a summer's night. Her brown and pliant arms twined and untwined themselves about her waist like two silken scarfs. Her form was effulgent with beauty. Oh, the resplendent figure, which stood out like something luminous even in the sunlight itself! Alas! young girl, it was thou! Surprised, intoxicated, enchanted, I suffered myself to look. I looked at thee so long that all at once I shuddered with affright. I felt that fate was laying hold on me."

The priest, overcome, again ceased a moment; then continued,—

"Already half fascinated, I strove to cling to something that might break my fall. I recalled to mind the snares which Satan had already laid for me. The creature before me was of that preternatural beauty which can only be of heaven or hell. That was no mere girl made of a little of our clay, and feebly lighted within by the vacillating ray of a woman's soul. It was an angel, but of darkness—of flame, not of light. At the moment when thinking thus, I saw near thee a goat, a beast of the sabbath, which looked at me laughingly. The midday sun gilded its horns with fire. Then I caught a glimpse of the demon's snare, and I no longer doubted that thou camest from hell, and that thou camest for my perdition. I believe so."

Here the priest looked in the face of the prisoner, and added coolly,—

"I believe so still. Meanwhile the charm operated by degrees; thy dancing whirled in my brain; I felt the mysterious spell at work within me. All that should have kept awake fell asleep in my soul; and, like those who die in the snow, I found pleasure in yielding to that slumber. All at once thou didst begin to sing. What could I do, wretch that I was? Thy song was still more bewitching than thy dance. I would have fled—I felt it impossible. I was nailed, rooted to the ground. It seemed as if the marble flags had risen to my knees. I was obliged to stay to the end. My feet were ice—my brain was boiling. At length, thou didst perhaps take pity on me; thou didst cease to sing; thou didst disappear. The reflection of the dazzling vision, the reverberation of the enchanting music, vanished by degrees from my eyes and ears. Then I fell into the corner of the window, more stiff and helpless than a loosened statue. The vesper bell awoke me. I rose—I fled; but, alas! there was something within me fallen to rise no more—something come upon me from which I could not flee!"

He made another pause, and resumed: "Yes; from that day forward there was within me a man I knew not. I had recourse to all my remedies—the cloister—the altar—labour—books. Folly! Oh! how hollow does science sound when a head full of passions in despair strikes against it! Knowest thou, young girl, what I ever after saw between the book and me? It was thyself, thy shade, the image of the luminous apparition which had one day crossed the space before me. But that image no longer wore the same hue—it was gloomy, funereal, darksome—like the black circle that long hangs about the vision of the imprudent one who has been gazing steadfastly at the sun.

"Unable to get rid of it—constantly hearing thy voice warbling in my ears—constantly seeing thy feet dancing on my breviary—constantly feeling at night in my dreams thy form in contact with my own—I wished to see thee again—to touch thee—to know who thou wert—to see whether I should find thee indeed equal to the ideal image that had remained of thee—to dispel, perhaps, my dream with the reality. At all events, I hoped a fresh impression would efface the former one, and the former was become insupportable. I sought thee. I saw thee again. Misery! When I had seen thee twice, I wished to see thee a thousand times—I wished to see thee always! Then, how to stop short on that hellish declivity! Then I was no longer my own. The other end of the thread which the demon had tied about my pinions was fastened to his foot. I became vagrant and wandering like thyself—I waited for thee under porches—I spied thee out at the corners of streets—I watched thee from the top of my tower. Each evening I re-entered within myself more charmed, more desperate, more fascinated, more undone!

"I had learned who thou wast—a gipsy—a Bohemian—a gitana—a zingara. How could I doubt of the magic?—Listen. I hoped that a prosecution would rid me of the charm. A sorceress had bewitched Bruno of Asti; he had her burned, and was cured. I knew it. I wished to try the remedy. I first endeavoured to get thee prohibited the Parvis Notre-Dame, hoping to forget thee if thou camest no more. Thou heededest it not. Thou camest again. Then arose the idea of carrying thee off. One night I attempted it. There were two of us. Already we laid hold on thee, when that wretched officer came upon us. He delivered thee. Thus was he the beginning of thy misfortunes, of mine, and of his own. At length, not knowing what to do or what was to become of me, I denounced thee to the official. I thought I should be cured like Bruno of Asti. I thought also, confusedly, that a prosecution would place thee at my disposal—that in a prison I should hold thee, I should have thee—that there thou couldst not escape me—that thou hadst possessed me long enough for me to possess thee in my turn. When one does evil one should do it thoroughly. 'Tis madness to stop midway in the monstrous! The extremity of crime has its delirium of joy. A priest and a witch may mingle in its ecstasies upon the straw of a dungeon floor!

"So I denounced thee. 'Twas then that I used to terrify thee whenever I met thee. The plot which I was weaving against thee, the storm which I was brewing over thy head, burst from me in muttered threats and lightning glances. Still, however, I hesitated. My project had its appalling points of view, which made me shrink back.

"Perhaps might I have renounced it—perhaps might my hideous thought have withered in my brain without bearing any fruit. I thought it would always depend upon myself either to follow up or set aside this prosecution. But every evil thought is inexorable, and will become an act; and there where I thought myself all-powerful, fate was more powerful than I. Alas! alas! 'tis fate has laid hold on thee, and cast thee amid the terrible machinery of the engine I had darkly constructed! Listen—I have almost done.

"One day—it was another day of sunshine—I see pass before me a man who pronounces thy name and laughs; he carries profligacy in his eyes. Damnation! I followed. Thou knowest the rest."

He was silent. The young girl could only find one word to utter—"O my Phœbus."

"No more of that name!" said the priest, seizing her arm with violence. "Pronounce not that name! Oh! wretched that we are, 'tis that name has undone us! or rather, we have undone one another, all through the inexplicable play of fate! Thou art suffering, art thou not? thou art cold; darkness blinds thee; the dungeon wraps thee round; but perhaps hast thou still some light yet shining within thee—were it only thy childish love for that empty being that was trifling with thy heart!—whilst I—I bear the dungeon within me—within me is the winter, the ice, the despair; I have the darkness in my soul. Know'st thou all that I have suffered? I was present at thy trial. I was seated on the bench of the official. Yes—under one of those priestly hoods were the contortions of a damned spirit. When thou wast brought in I was there; when thou wast interrogated I was there. The den of wolves! 'Twas my own crime, 'twas my own gibbet, they were slowly constructing over thy head! At each deposition, at each proof, at each pleading, I was there. I could count each one of thy steps in the way of sorrow. I was there, too, when that wild beast. . . . Oh! I had not foreseen the torture! Listen. I followed thee into the chamber of anguish. I saw thee undressed and half naked under the vile hands of the torturer. I saw thy foot—that foot, to have imprinted a kiss on which and to have died, I would have given an empire—that foot, to have had my head crushed under which I should have felt so much ecstasy—that foot I saw put into the horrible brodequin—that brodequin which makes the limb of a living being all one bloody clod! O miserable wretch!—whilst I was looking on, with a poniard I had under my gown I was lacerating my breast. At the cry thou utteredst, I plunged it in my flesh; at a second cry, it would have entered my heart. Look—I think the wound is bleeding still."

He opened his cassock. His chest was indeed torn as if by a tiger's claws; and in his side was a large ill-closed wound.

The prisoner shrunk back with horror.

"Oh!" said the priest, "young girl, take pity on me! Thou thinkest thyself miserable. Alas! alas! thou knowest not what misery is. Oh! to love a woman—to be a priest—to be hated—to love with all the powers of one's soul—to feel that one would give for the least of her smiles one's blood, one's vitals, one's fame, one's salvation, immortality, and eternity, this life and that which is to come—to regret one is not a king, a genius, an emperor, an archangel, God, that one might place a greater slave under her feet—to clasp her day and night in one's dream, in one's thoughts; and to see her in love with the trappings of a soldier, and have nothing to offer her but a priest's poor cassock, at which she will feel fear and disgust! To be present, with one's jealousy and one's rage, while she lavishes on a wretched imbecile fanfaron those treasures of love and beauty! To behold that form which maddens you, that voluptuous bosom, that flesh panting and blushing under the kisses of another! O heavens! to love her foot, her arm, her shoulder—to think of her blue veins, of her brown skin, till one writhes for nights together on the pavement of one's cell, and to see all those caresses one has dreamed of end in her torture—to have succeeded only in laying her on the bed of leather! Oh, these are the true pincers heated at the fires of hell! Oh, blessed is he that is sawn asunder between two boards, or torn to pieces by four horses! Knowest thou what that torture is, endured through long nights, from boiling arteries, a breaking heart, a bursting head, and teeth-gnawed hands—fell tormentors which are unceasingly turning you, as on a burning gridiron, over a thought of love, jealousy, and despair? Young girl, mercy! A truce for a moment! A few ashes on this living coal! Wipe away, I conjure thee, the perspiration that streams in large drops from my brow! Child, torture me with one hand, but caress me with the other! Have pity, young girl! have pity on me!"

The priest rolled himself on the wet floor and beat his head against the angles of the stone steps. The young girl listened to him, looked at him. When he ceased, exhausted, and panting, she repeated in an undertone, "O my Phœbus!"

The priest crept towards her on his knees. "I implore thee."

cried he, "if thou hast any bowels of compassion, repulse me not! Oh, I am a wretch! When thou utterest that name, unhappy girl, it is as if thou wert grinding between thy teeth every fibre of my heart. Mercy! If thou comest from hell, I go thither with thee. I have done enough for that. The hell where thou art shall be my paradise; the sight of thee is more to be desired than that of God! Oh, say, wilt thou none of me, then? I should have thought the very mountains would have been removed before a woman would have repulsed such a love. Oh, if thou wouldst! . . . Oh, how happy could we be! We would fly—I would contrive thy escape—we would go somewhere—we would seek that spot on the earth where the sun is the brightest, the trees most luxuriant, the sky the bluest. We would love each other—our two souls should be poured out into each other—and each of us should have an inextinguishable thirst for the other, which we would quench incessantly and in common at that inexhaustible fountain of love!"

She interrupted him with a horrible and thrilling laugh. "Look, father! you have blood upon your fingers!"

The priest remained for some moments as if petrified, his eyes fixed on his hand.

"Yes—'tis well," continued he at length, with singular calmness; "insult me, taunt me, overwhelm me with scorn, but come, come away. Let us hasten. 'Tis to be to-morrow, I tell thee. The gibbet of the Grève, thou knowest? It still awaits thee. 'Tis horrible—to see thee carried in that cart! Oh, mercy! Never did I feel as now I do how much I love thee. Oh, follow me! Thou shalt take time to love me after I have saved thee. Thou shalt hate me as long as thou wilt. But come. To-morrow! to-morrow!—the gibbet! thy execution! Oh, save thyself!—spare me!"

He took her arm—he was wild—he offered to drag her away.

She fixed on him a steady gaze. "What's become of Phœbus?"

"Ah!" said the priest, letting go her arm; "you have no pity."

"What's become of Phœbus?" repeated she coldly.

"He's dead!" cried the priest.

"Dead!" said she, still frozen and motionless. "Then why do you talk to me of living?"

He was not listening to her. "Oh yes," said he, as if speaking to himself, "he must be dead enough. The blade entered deep. I think I reached his heart with the point. Oh, my very soul was in that dagger's point."

The young girl rushed upon him like a furious tigress, and pushed him against the flight of steps with supernatural strength. "Begone, monster! begone, murderer! leave me to die! May the blood of both of us be an everlasting stain upon thy forehead! Be thine, priest? Never, never! Nothing shall unite us—not hell itself! Begone, accursed! Never!"

The priest had stumbled against the stairs. He silently disengaged his feet from the folds of his gown, took up his lantern, and began slowly to ascend the steps leading to the door; he reopened that door and went out. All at once the young girl saw his head reappear; its expression was terrible; and he cried out, hoarse with rage and despair, "I tell thee he's dead!"

She fell with her face to the floor; and no other sound was now to be heard in the dungeon save the trickling of the drop of water which ruffled the surface of the pool in the darkness.

CHAPTER V

THE MOTHER

We doubt whether there be anything in the world more gladdening to the heart of a mother than the ideas awakened by the sight of her infant's little shoe; above all, when it is the holiday, the Sunday, the christening shoe, the shoe embroidered to the very sole—a shoe in which the child has not yet taken one step. That shoe, so tiny, has such a charm in it—'tis so impossible for it to walk—that it is to the mother as if she saw her child. She smiles at it; she kisses it; she talks to it; she asks herself, Can it really be that there's a foot so small? And should the child be absent, the little shoe suffices to bring back to her view the soft and fragile creature. She thinks she sees it—sees it all—living, joyous, with its delicate hands, its round head, its pure lips, its clear eyes with their whites so blue. If it be winter, there it is, crawling on the carpet, climbing laboriously up a stool; and the mother trembles lest it should go near the fire. If it be summer, it creeps about the yard, the garden—plucks up the grass from between the stones—gazes with heartless wonder, and without fear, at the great dogs, the great horses—plays with the shell-work, the flowers, and makes the gardener scold when he finds the gravel on the beds and the mould in the walks. Everything smiles, everything is bright, everything plays around it, like itself—even to the zephyr and the sunbeam, which sport in rivalry amidst its wanton curls. The shoe brings all this home to the mother, and her heart melts before it as wax before the fire.

But when the child is lost, those thousand images of joy, of delight, of tenderness which swarmed around the little shoe become so many sources of horror. The pretty little embroidered shoe is now only an instrument of torture, wearing away incessantly the heart of the mother. It is still the same chord which vibrates, the fibre the most sensitive, the most profound; but instead of its being touched by an angel, it is now wrenched by a demon.

One morning, as the May sun was rising on one of those dark-blue skies in which Garofolo loves to place his descents from the cross, the recluse heard a noise of wheels, of horses, and the clanking of irons in the Place de Grève. She was but little roused by it, fastened her hair over her ears to deaden the sound, and on her knees resumed her contemplation of the inanimate object which she had been thus adoring for fifteen years. That little shoe, we have already said, was to her the universe. Her thoughts were locked up in it, and were never to quit it until death. What bitter imprecations she had breathed to heaven, what heartrending complaints, what prayers and sobs about this charming, rosy, satin toy, the gloomy cave of the Tour-Roland only knew! Never was more despair lavished upon a thing more charming or more graceful. That morning it seemed as if her grief was venting itself still more violently than usual; and she was heard from without lamenting in a loud and monotonous voice that went to the heart.

"O my child," said she, "my child, my poor dear little babe, I shall see thee, then, no more!—all's over then! It seems to me always as if it was done but yesterday. My God! my God! to take her from me so soon; it would have been better not to have given her to me! You do not know, then, that our children are of our own bowels, and that a mother that has lost a child believes no longer in God? Ah, wretched that I am, to have gone out that day! Lord, Lord! to take her from me so! You never saw me with her, then—when I warmed her all joyous at my fire—when she laughed at me as I gave her suck—when I made her little feet creep up my bosom to my lips? Oh, if you had but seen that, my God, you would have had pity on my joy—you would not have taken from me the only thing I had left to love! Was I such a wretched creature, then, Lord, that you could not look at me before you condemned me? Alas! alas! there's the shoe; but the foot, where is it? Where is the rest? where is the child?—My babe; my babe! what have they done with thee?—Lord, give her back to me! For fifteen years have I worn my knees in praying to Thee, my God! Is not that enough? Give her back to me for one day, one hour, one minute—but one minute, Lord—and then cast me to the evil one for ever! Oh, if I knew where lay but the hem of your garment, I would cling to it with both hands, and you would be obliged to give me my child! Her pretty little shoe—have you no pity on it, Lord? Can you condemn a poor mother to this fifteen years' torture? Good Virgin! good Virgin of heaven! my own infant Jesus—they have taken it from me—they have stolen it—they have eaten it on the wild heath—they have drunk its blood—they have gnawed its bones! Good Virgin, have pity on me! My girl! I must have my girl! What care I that she's in heaven? I'll none of your angel; I want my child! I am the lioness; I want my whelp! Oh, I'll writhe upon the ground—I'll dash my forehead against the stones—I'll damn myself, and curse you, Lord, if you keep from me my child! You see how my arms are gnawed all over, Lord? Has the good God no pity? Oh, give me only black bread and salt, only let me have my child to warm me like a sun! Alas! Lord God, I am only a vile sinner; but my child made me pious. I was full of religion for her sake, and I saw you through her smile as through an opening of heaven. Oh, let me only once, once again, one little once, put this shoe on her pretty little rosy foot, and I will die, good Virgin, blessing you! Ah, fifteen years! She would be grown up now! Unhappy child! What! is it true, then, I shall never see her more, not even in heaven? for I shall never go there. Oh, what misery to have to say, 'There is her shoe, and that is all'!"

The wretched woman had thrown herself on this shoe, for so many years her consolation and despair; and her heart was rent with sobs as at the first day—for to a mother that has lost her child it is always the first day—that grief never grows old. In vain may the mourning garments wear out and lose their dye: the heart remains dark as at first!

At that moment some fresh and joyous children's voices passed before the cell. Whenever any children met her eye or ear, the poor mother used to rush into the darkest corner of her sepulchre, and seemed as if she would plunge her head into the stone that she might not hear them. This time, on the contrary, she started up, and listened eagerly. One of the little boys had just said, "They're going to hang a gipsy woman to-day."

With a sudden bound, like that of the spider which we have seen rush upon a fly at the shaking of her web, she ran to her loophole, which looked out, as the reader is aware, upon the Place de Grève. There, indeed, was a ladder reared up against the permanent gibbet, and the hangman's assistant was busy in adjusting the chains rusted by the rain. Some people were standing around.

The smiling group of children was already far off. The Sachette sought with her eyes some passer-by whom she might interrogate. Close to her cell she caught sight of a priest, who seemed to be reading in the public breviary, but whose mind was much less occupied with the lattice-guarded volume than with the gibbet, towards which he cast from time to time a stern and gloomy look. She recognised Monsieur the Archdeacon of Joas, a holy man.

"Father," asked she, "who's going to be hanged there?"

The priest looked at her without answering. She repeated her question, and then he said, "I don't know."

"There were some children here just now who said it was a gipsy woman," continued the recluse.

"I believe it is," said the priest.

Then Pâquette-la-Chantefleurie burst into a hyena laugh.

"Sister," said the archdeacon, "you hate the gipsy women heartily, then?"

"Hate them!" cried the recluse. "They are witches—child-stealers! They devoured my little girl—my child—my only child! I have no heart left—they have devoured it."

She was frightful. The priest looked at her coldly.

"There's one of them that I hate above all, and that I've cursed," resumed she—"a young one, who's the age my girl would be if her mother had not eaten my girl. Every time that young viper passes before my cell she makes my blood boil."

"Well, sister, be joyful now," said the priest, as icy cold as a sepulchral statue; "that's the one you are going to see die."

His head fell upon his breast, and he withdrew slowly.

The recluse writhed her arms with joy. "I had foretold it to her that she should go up there again. Thank you, priest," cried she; and then she began to pace with rapid steps before the bars of her window-place, her hair dishevelled, her eye glaring, striking her shoulder against the wall with the wild air of a caged she-wolf that has long been hungry and feels that the hour of her repast is approaching.

CHAPTER VI

THREE MEN'S HEARTS OF DIFFERENT STAMP

PHŒBUS, however, was not dead. Men of his description are not easily killed. When Maître Philippe Lheulier, King's Advocate Extraordinary, had said to the poor Esmeralda, "He's dying," it was by mistake or in jest. When the archdeacon had repeated to the condemned, "He is dead," the fact was that he knew nothing about the matter, but that he believed so, that he calculated it must be so, and fully hoped it was so. He could ill have brooked the giving to the woman he was in love with any good news of his rival. "Any man in his place," our author ingenuously remarks, "would have done likewise."

Not, indeed, that Phœbus's wound had not been serious, but it had been less so than the archdeacon flattered himself. The surgeon — the *maître-myrrhe*, as he was then called—to whose residence the soldiers of the watch had conveyed him in the first instance, had for a week been in fear for his life, and had even told him so in Latin. However, the vigour of a youthful constitution had triumphed; and as often happens, notwithstanding prognostics and diagnostics, Nature amused herself with saving the patient in spite of the physician. It was while he was yet lying upon the sick-bed of the son of Esculapius that he underwent the first interrogatories of Philippe Lheulier and the official's *enquêteurs* or inquest men, which he had found especially wearisome. And so one fine morning, feeling himself better, he had left his gold spurs in payment to the man of medicine, and had taken himself off. This, however, had by no means impeded the framing of the indictment and preparation of the evidence. The justice of that time was very little anxious about clearness and precision in the proceedings against a criminal. Provided only that the accused got hanged, that was sufficient. And then the judges had quite proof enough against La Esmeralda: they had believed Phœbus to be dead, and that was decisive.

Phœbus himself had fled to no great distance. He had merely, and very naturally, gone to join his company, then on garrison duty at Queue-en-Brie, in the Isle of France, a few stages from Paris.

After all, he felt that it would be by no means agreeable for him to appear personally in that trial. He had a vague impression that he should look rather ridiculous in it. In fact, he did not very well know what to think of the whole affair. Superstitious without devotion, like every soldier who is nothing more than a soldier, when he questioned himself upon the particulars of that adventure, he was not altogether without his suspicions respecting the little goat—the odd circumstances under which he had first met with La Esmeralda—the manner, no less strange, in which she had seemed to betray to him the secret of her passion—her being a gipsy—and last, but not least, the spectre monk. In all those incidents he thought he could discern much more magic than love—probably a sorceress—perhaps the devil—a sort of drama, in short, or, to speak the language of that day, a mystery—very disagreeable, indeed—in which he played a very awkward part, that of the personage beaten and laughed at. The captain felt abashed at this; he experienced that species of shame which Lafontaine has so admirably defined,—

> "As ashamed as a fox would be caught by a hen."

Besides, he hoped the affair would not be rumoured about—that, himself being absent, his name would hardly be pronounced in connection with it, or, at any rate, would not be heard beyond the courtroom of the Tournelle. Nor was he mistaken in that respect. There was not then any *Gazette des Tribunaux*, and as hardly a week passed in which there was not some coiner boiled to death, some witch hanged, or some heretic burned at some one of the innumerable justices of Paris, people were so much accustomed to see at every cross-way the old feudal Themis, with her arms bare and her sleeves turned up, at work at her gibbets, her *échelles*, and her pillories, that scarcely any notice was taken of the matter. The *beau monde* of that age hardly knew the name of the sufferer that passed by at the corner of the street, and at most it was only the populace that regaled themselves with that unsavoury viand. An execution was one of the incidents habitually met with in the public way, like the *braisière* of the *talmellier* or the slaughter-house of the *écorcheur*. The executioner was but a sort of butcher rather more versed in his trade than ordinary.

Phœbus, therefore, very soon set his mind at rest with respect to the enchantress Esmeralda, or Similar as he called her, the stab he had received from the gipsy girl or from the spectre monk (it mattered little to him which), and the issue of the trial. But no sooner was his heart vacant on that side than the image of Fleur-de-Lys returned to it; for the heart of Captain Phœbus, like the natural philosophy of that day, abhorred a vacuum.

Moreover, he found it very dull staying at Queue-en-Brie, a village of farriers and milk-women with chapped hands—a long string of mean houses and hovels, bordering the highway on both sides for half a league—a tail, in short, as its name imports.

Fleur-de-Lys was his last flame but one—a pretty girl—a charming portion—and so one fine morning, being quite cured of his wound, and fairly presuming that after two months had elapsed the affair of the gipsy girl must be over and forgotten, the amorous cavalier arrived, prancing in full feather, at the door of the Logis Gondelaurier.

He paid no attention to a very numerous crowd that was collecting in the Place du Parvis, before the entrance of Notre-Dame. He recollected that it was the month of May—he supposed that there was some procession, some Whitsuntide or other holiday exhibition—fastened his horse's bridle to the ring at the porch, and gaily ascended the staircase in search of his fair betrothed. He found her and her mother alone.

Fleur-de-Lys had still weighing upon her heart the scene of the sorceress, with her goat and its cursed alphabet, and the lengthened absence of Phœbus. Nevertheless, when she saw her captain enter, she thought he looked so well, and wore so fresh a hacqueton, so shining a baldric, and so impassioned an air, that she blushed with pleasure. The noble damoiselle herself was more charming than ever. Her magnificent fair locks were braided to perfection; she was clad all in that heavenly blue which so well becomes a fair complexion (a piece of coquetry which she had learned from her acquaintance Colombe), and her eyes were steeped in that amorous languor which becomes it better still.

Phœbus, who had seen no description of beauty since he quitted the country wenches of Queue-en-Brie, was absolutely intoxicated with the sight of Fleur-de-Lys; which rendered our officer's manner so gallant and assiduous that his peace was made immediately. Madame de Gondelaurier herself, still maternally seated in her great fauteuil, had not resolution to scold him. As for Fleur-de-Lys's reproaches, they died away in tender cooings.

The young lady was seated near the window, still embroidering her grotto of Neptunus. The captain stood leaning over the back of her chair, while she murmured to him her gentle upbraidings.

"Where have you been for full two months past, you wicked man?"

"I swear," answered Phœbus, a little embarrassed by the question, "that you are beautiful enough to make an archbishop dream."

She could not help smiling. "Very good, very good, monsieur. But leave my beauty alone and answer me. Fine beauty to be sure."

"Well, my dear cousin, I was recalled to keep garrison."

"And where was that, if you please? and why did you not come and bid me adieu?"

"It was at Queue-en-Brie."

Phœbus was delighted that the first question had helped him to elude the second.

"But that's quite near, monsieur. How happened it that you did not come once to see me?"

Here Phœbus was very seriously perplexed. "Because . . . the service . . . and besides, my charming cousin, I've been unwell."

"Unwell?" exclaimed she in alarm.

"Yes; wounded."

"Wounded!"

The poor girl was quite overcome.

"Oh, don't be frightened about that," said Phœbus carelessly; "it's nothing at all. A quarrel—a crossing of swords—what does that signify to you, my dear?"

"What does that signify to me!" exclaimed Fleur-de-Lys, lifting her beautiful eyes filled with tears. "Oh, you don't think what you say. What was that crossing of swords? I want to know all about it."

"Well, my fair one, I've had a quarrel with Mahé Fédy, you know, the lieutenant of St. Germain-en-Laye; and each of us has ripped open a few inches of the other's skin—that's all."

The lying captain was well aware that an affair of honour always sets a man off to advantage in the eyes of a woman.

And, in fact, Fleur-de-Lys looked him in the face with mingled sensations of fear, pleasure, and admiration. However, she did not yet feel completely reassured.

"So that you are but perfectly cured, my Phœbus!" said she. "I don't know your Mahé Fédy, but he must be a vile fellow. And what was this quarrel about?"

Here Phœbus, whose imagination was not over-creative, began to be rather at a loss how to dispose conveniently of his prowess.

"Oh, I don't know . . . a mere nothing at all . . . a horse . . . a word dropped. *Belle cousine*," said he, by way of turning the conversation, "what's that noise about in the Parvis?" He went to the window. "O *mon Dieu! belle cousine*, there's a great crowd in the Place."

"I don't know," said Fleur-de-Lys; "it seems there's a witch going to do penance this morning before the church on her way to be hanged."

So absolutely did the captain believe the affair of La Esmeralda to be terminated that he was little affected by these words of Fleur-de-Lys. Nevertheless he asked her one or two questions.

"What's the witch's name?"

"I don't know," she answered.

"And what do they say she's done?"

Again she shrugged her white shoulders and replied, "I don't know."

"O *mon Dieu Jésus!*" exclaimed her mother, "there are so many sorcerers nowadays that I dare say they burn them without knowing their names. It would be of no more use than to try to know the name of every cloud in the sky. But, after all, we may make ourselves easy—God above keeps His register." Here the venerable dame rose and went to the window. "Seigneur!" she cried, "you're right, Phœbus: there is indeed a great crowd of the *populaire*. There they are, blessed be God! even up to the housetops! Do you know, Phœbus, that reminds me of my young days—the entry of King Charles VII.—when there was such a concourse too; I don't recollect what year it was. When I talk to you about that now, it sounds to you (doesn't it?) like something old, and to me like something young. Oh, there was a far finer crowd of people than there is now. There were some even upon the machicolations of the Porte St. Antoine. The King had the Queen on a pillion behind him; and after their highnesses came all the ladies, mounted behind the seigneurs. I remember there was much laughing; for by the side of Amanyon de Garlande, who was very short, there was the Sire Matefelon, a knight of giant stature, who had killed heaps of English. It was very fine indeed: a procession of all the gentlemen of France, with their oriflammes waving red before you. There were those of the pennon and those of the banner. Let me see—there was the Sire de Calan, with his pennon; Jean de Chateaumorant, with his banner; the Sire de Coucy, with his banner—and a richer one, too, than any of the others, except the Duke of Bourbon's. Alas! how melancholy to think that all that has existed, and that all has passed away!"

The two lovers were inattentive to the reminiscences of the venerable dowager. Phœbus had returned to lean over the back of the chair of his betrothed—a charming situation, from which his libertine glance could invade all the openings of Fleur-de-Lys's *collerette*, which yawned so conveniently, revealed to him so many exquisite things, and led him to divine so many others, that Phœbus, quite ravished with that satiny-glowing skin, said to himself, "How can a man love any but a fair beauty?" They both remained silent. The young lady lifted up to him from time to time her eyes full of gentleness and delight, and their hair mingled in the beams of the vernal sun.

"Phœbus," said Fleur-de-Lys all at once, in a whisper, "we are to be married in three months. Swear to me that you have never loved any woman but myself."

"I swear it, fair angel!" answered he; and to convince Fleur-de-Lys, an impassioned look was added to the sincere tone of his voice. Perhaps, indeed, at that moment he himself believed what he was saying.

Meanwhile the good mother, delighted to see the two *fiancés* on such excellent terms with each other, had quitted the apartment to attend to some household matter. Phœbus remarked it, and the being left thus alone so much emboldened the adventurous captain that some very strange ideas entered his brain. Fleur-de-Lys loved him—he was engaged to her—they were alone—his old inclination for her had revived, not in all its freshness indeed, but in all its ardour. After all, there could be no great crime. We know not exactly whether all these thoughts actually crossed his mind, but this is certain, that Fleur-de-Lys was all at once alarmed at the expression of his countenance. She looked around her, and saw that her mother was gone.

"*Mon Dieu!*" said she, blushing and uneasy, "I'm very hot."

"I think, indeed," returned Phœbus, "it must be almost noon. The sun becomes annoying; there's no remedy but to draw the curtains."

"No, no!" cried the poor girl; "on the contrary, I've occasion for air."

And like a hind that scents the breath of the approaching pack, she rose, hurried to the window, opened it, and rushed upon the balcony.

Phœbus, little gratified at this movement, followed her thither.

The Place du Parvis Notre-Dame, upon which, as the reader is aware, the balcony looked, presented at that moment an odd and dismal spectacle, which suddenly altered the nature of the timid Fleur-de-Lys's alarm.

An immense crowd of people, extending into all the adjacent streets, covered the Place properly so called. The low wall enclosing the Parvis itself would not have sufficed to keep that interior space clear, but that it was lined by dense ranks of the sergeants of the Onze-vingts and of hackbuteers, culverin in hand. Owing, however, to this grove of pikes and arquebuses the Parvis was empty. Its entrance was guarded by a body of the bishop's own halberdiers. The great doors of the church were shut, thus contrasting with the numberless windows round the Place, which, being all open up to the very gables, exhibited thousands of heads piled in heaps, something like the balls in a park of artillery.

The surface of the multitude was dingy and dirty-looking. The sight which they were waiting to see was evidently one of those whose privilege it is to bring out and call together all that is most unclean in the population of a city. Nothing could be more hideous than the murmur that rose from that swarm of yellow caps and dirty heads. In this crowd there were fewer shouts than peals of laughter, fewer men than women.

From time to time some shrill voice pierced through the general hum.

"I say, Mahiet Baliffre, are they going to hang her there?"

"You simpleton! this is to be the penance in her shift. God Almighty's going to cough Latin in her face. That's always done here at noon. If it's the gallows you want, you must go to the Grève."

"I'll go there after."

" Do just tell me, La Boucanbry, is it true that she's refused to have a confessor? "

" It seems it is, La Bechaigne."

" Oh, the pagan! "

. . . .

" Sir, it's the custom. The bailiff of the Palais is bound to deliver the malefactor, ready sentenced, for execution: if it's a layman, to the Provost of Paris; if it's a clerk, to the official of the bishopric."

" Thank you, sir."

. . . .

" O my God! " said Fleur-de-Lys—" the poor creature! "

This thought filled with sadness the look which she cast over the populace. The captain, whose attention was much more occupied by herself than by that congregation of the rabble, was amorously fingering her waist behind. She turned round with a look half smiling and half entreating. " Now, do leave me alone, Phœbus. If my mother were to come in, she would see your hand."

At that moment the clock of Notre-Dame slowly struck twelve. A murmur of satisfaction burst from the crowd. The last vibration of the twelfth stroke had hardly expired on the ear when the heads of the multitude were all set in motion like the waves before a sudden gale, and an immense shout rose at once, from the ground, from the windows, and from the roofs, of " Here she comes! "

Fleur-de-Lys put her hands before her eyes, that she might not see.

" My charmer," said Phœbus, " will you go in? "

" No," answered she; and those eyes which she had just closed through fear she opened again through curiosity.

A tumbrel drawn by a strong Norman horse, and quite surrounded by horsemen in the violet uniform with the white crosses, had just entered the Place from the Rue Saint-Pierre-aux-Bœufs. The sergeants of the watch made way for it through the multitude by a vigorous use of their whitleather *boullayes*. By the side of the tumbrel rode some officers of justice and of police, distinguishable by their black costume and their awkwardness on horseback. Maître Jacques Charmolue paraded at their head. In the fatal cart a young girl was seated, with her hands tied behind her, and without any priest at her side. She was in her shift; her long black hair (for it was then the custom not to cut it until reaching the foot of the gibbet) fell unbound upon her neck and over her half-uncovered shoulders.

Across those dishevelled and undulating locks, more shining than a raven's plumage, was seen, twisted and knotted, a thick brown cord, which roughly chafed the poor girl's pretty, fragile neck, encircling it like an earthworm twined about a flower. Beneath that rope glittered a small amulet, ornamented with green glass, which no doubt she had been allowed to keep merely because it was thought not worth while to refuse it to one just going to die. The spectators up at the windows could discern at the bottom of the tumbrel her naked legs, which she strove to conceal under her as if through a last remaining instinct of her sex. At her feet was a little she-goat, with its limbs also bound. The condemned was holding together with her teeth her ill-tied chemise. It seemed as if she still suffered in her misery from being thus exposed almost naked before all eyes. Alas! it was not for shudderings like this that feminine modesty was designed.

"Jesus!" said Fleur-de-Lys sharply to the captain, "look there, *beau cousin*. It's that vile gipsy girl with the goat."

So saying, she turned round to Phœbus. His eyes were fixed upon the tumbrel, and he looked very pale.

"What gipsy girl with the goat?" said he, stammering.

"Why," rejoined Fleur-de-Lys, "don't you remember?"

Phœbus interrupted her. "I don't know what you mean."

He made one step to go in; but Fleur-de-Lys, whose jealousy, but lately so vehement, so strongly excited by that same gipsy girl, was now reawakened, cast at him a glance full of penetration and mistrust. At that moment she vaguely recollected having heard speak of a captain whose name had been mixed up in the trial of that sorceress.

"What's the matter with you?" said she to Phœbus; "one would think that woman had discomposed you."

Phœbus strove to force a titter. "Me!" said he; "not the least in the world. Me, indeed!"

"Stay, then," said she, in a commanding tone, "and let us see it out."

The unlucky captain had no choice but to remain. However, it encouraged him a little to see that the condemned kept her eyes fixed upon the bottom of the tumbrel. It was but too truly La Esmeralda. In this last stage of ignominy and misfortune she was still beautiful: her large black eyes looked larger for the sinking of her cheeks, and her livid profile was pure and sublime. She resembled what she had been just in the degree that one of Masaccio's Virgins resembles one of Raphael's—looking weaker, slenderer, thinner.

As for her mien, she seemed to be all tossing about, as it were —everything, except as far as modesty dictated, being left to chance, so thoroughly had her spirit been broken by stupor and despair. Her form redounded at every jolt of the tumbrel, like something dead or dislocated; her look was fixed and unconscious; a tear was still to be seen in her eye, but motionless, as if it had been frozen there.

Meanwhile the dismal cavalcade had traversed the crowd, amid shouts of rejoicing and attitudes of curiosity. Nevertheless, historical fidelity calls upon us to testify that on seeing her so beautiful and so overwhelmed with affliction, many were moved to pity, even among the most hard-hearted. The tumbrel had entered the Parvis, and had stopped before the central doorway of the church.

The escort drew up in line on either side. The crowd were now silent; and amid that silence, so solemn and anxious, each half of the great door turned, as if of itself, upon its hinges, which creaked like the sound of a fife. Then the deep interior of the church was seen in its whole extent, gloomy, hung with mourning, faintly lighted by a few wax tapers twinkling afar off upon the high altar, yawning like a cavern amidst the Place inundated with light. Quite at the farther end, in the shade of the chancel, was dimly distinguished a gigantic silver cross, gleaming against a piece of black drapery, which hung from the vaulted ceiling down to the floor. The nave was quite solitary; but the heads of some priests were seen confusedly stirring in the distant stalls of the choir, and at the moment that the great door opened there burst from the interior of the church a solemn and monotonous chant, which cast, as in successive puffs, upon the head of the condemned, fragments of dismal psalms:—

"... *Non timebo millia populi circumdantis me: exsurge, Domine; salvum me fac, Deus!*"[1]

"... *Salvum me fac, Deus, quoniam intraverunt aquæ usque ad animam meam.*"[2]

[1] ... I will not fear the thousands of the people gathered together about me: arise, O Lord; save me, O my God.

[2] ... Save me, O God, albeit the waters have entered in even unto my soul.

" . . . *Infixus sum in limo profundi, et non est substantia.*" [1]

At the same time another voice, isolated from the choir, gave out from the steps of the high altar this melancholy offertory:—

"*Qui verbum meum audit, et credit ei qui misit me, habet vitam æternam, et in judicium non venit; sed transit a morte in vitam.*" [2]

This chant, which some old men, lost to view in the darkness of the church, were thus pouring forth over that beautiful creature full of youth and life, wooed by the tepid airs of spring and wrapped in sunshine, was the mass for the dead.

The multitude listened in mute attention.

The unfortunate girl, quite bewildered, seemed to lose her view and her consciousness in the dark interior of the cathedral. Her pale lips moved as if uttering a prayer; and when the executioner's assistant approached to help her down from her tumbrel, he heard her repeat in a whisper the word Phœbus.

They untied her hands, and made her descend from the vehicle, accompanied by her goat, which they also unbound, and which bleated with joy to feel itself at liberty. They then made her walk barefoot over the pavement, to the bottom of the great steps of entrance—the rope that was passed round her neck trailing behind her, and looking like a serpent closely pursuing her.

Then there was a pause in the chant within the church. A great cross of gold and a file of wax tapers were seen beginning to move in the dark distance. The halberds of the motley-dressed yeomen of the bishop were heard to clang upon the floor; in a few minutes a long procession of priests in their chasubles, and deacons in their dalmatics, coming, psalm-singing, slowly along, developed itself to the view of the condemned and to that of the multitude. But her eye fixed itself upon the one who walked at their head, immediately after the cross-bearer. "Oh," said she to herself, in a low whisper, shuddering as she spoke, "'tis he again—the priest!"

It was, in fact, the archdeacon. On his left walked the sub-chanter; and on his right the precentor, carrying his staff of

[1] . . . Behold, I am set fast in the slime of the great deep, and there is no ground under my feet.

[2] . . . Whoso heareth my word, and believeth in him that sent me, hath life everlasting; he cometh not unto judgment, but from death he passeth unto life.

office. He advanced with his head thrown back, his eyes wide open and fixed, singing in a strong voice:—

"*De ventre inferi clamavi, et exaudisti vocem meam.*[1]

"*Et projecisti me in profundum in corde maris, et flumen circumdedit me.*" [2]

At the moment that he appeared in the broad daylight, under the high pointed doorway, wrapped in an ample silver cope, marked with a black cross, he was so pale that some among the crowd actually thought that one of the marble bishops kneeling on the tombstones in the choir had risen upon his feet, and was come to receive on the threshold of the grave her who was going to die.

She herself, no less pale, and statue-like, had scarcely perceived that they had put into her hand a heavy, lighted taper of yellow wax. She had not hearkened to the clamorous voice of the registrar reading over the fatal tenor of the *amende honorable;* only when they had told her to answer Amen she had answered "Amen!"

She was not brought back to some slight consciousness of life and strength until she saw the priest make a sign to her guards to retire, and himself advance towards her. But now she felt her blood boiling in her head, and a remaining spark of indignation was kindled in that spirit already benumbed and cold.

The archdeacon approached her slowly. Even in that her dire extremity she perceived him cast over her exposed form an eye sparkling with jealousy and lascivious desire. Then he said to her in a loud voice, "Young woman, have you asked pardon of God for your sins and your offences?" He leaned to her ear, and added (while the spectators supposed that he was receiving her last confession), "Will you have anything to say to me? I can save you yet."

She looked him steadfastly in the face, and said, "Begone, you demon, or I'll denounce you."

He smiled—a horrid smile. "They'll not believe you; you will but be adding a scandal to a crime. Answer me quickly: will you have anything to say to me?"

"What have you done with my Phœbus?" she returned.

"He's dead!" said the priest.

[1] Out of the bowels of the earth I have called unto thee, and thou hast heard my voice.

[2] And thou hast cast me out into the depths of the sea, and the waters have gone about me.

At that moment the wretched archdeacon raised his head mechanically, and saw, at the opposite side of the Place, on the balcony of the Logis Gondelaurier, the captain himself, standing close by Fleur-de-Lys. He staggered, passed his hand over his eyes, looked again, muttered a malediction, and every line of his face was violently contracted.

"Well, then, die thou!" said he, between his teeth; "no one shall have thee!" Then lifting his hand over the gipsy girl, he exclaimed in a sepulchral voice—"*I nunc anima anceps, et sit tibi Deus misericors.*" [1]

This was the awful formula with which it was the custom to close that gloomy ceremonial. It was the preconcerted signal given by the priest to the executioner.

Hereupon the people knelt down.

"*Kyrie Eleison!*" [2] said the priests, remaining under the great arched doorway.

"*Kyrie Eleison!*" repeated the multitude, with that murmuring noise which runs over a sea of heads, like the splashing of the waves of the sea itself when in agitation.

"Amen!" said the archdeacon.

He turned his back upon the condemned; his head fell upon his breast; his hands crossed themselves; he returned to his train of priests; and in a minute he was seen to disappear with the cross, the tapers, and the copes, under the dim arches of the cathedral; and his sonorous voice gradually died away in the choir, while chanting this verse of despair:—

"*Omnes gurgites tui et fluctus tui super me transierunt!*" [3]

At the same time the intermitted clang of the iron-covered butt-ends of the yeomen's pikes, dying away successively under the several intercolumniations of the nave, sounded like the hammer of a clock striking the last hour of the condemned.

Meanwhile the doors of Notre-Dame remained open, showing the interior of the church, empty, desolate, in mourning, torchless, and voiceless.

The condemned remained motionless on the spot where they had placed her, waiting to be disposed of. It was necessary for one of the sergeants of the wand to give information of the circumstance to Maître Charmolue, who during all this scene had set himself to study that bas-relief of the grand portal which represents, according to some, Abraham's sacrifice; according

[1] Go thy way now, lingering soul; and may God have mercy upon thee!
[2] Lord, have mercy upon us!
[3] All thy whirlpools, O Lord, and all thy waves have gone over me!

to others, the *magnum opus*, the grand alchemical operation—the sun being figured by the angel, the fire by the fagot, and the operator by Abraham.

They had much ado to draw him away from this contemplation; but at last he turned round, and at a sign which he made them two men dressed in yellow, the excutioner's assistants, approached the gipsy girl to tie her hands again.

The unfortunate girl, at the moment of reascending the fatal cart, and moving on towards her final scene, was seized, perhaps, by some last overwhelming clinging to life. She lifted her dry reddened eyes to heaven — to the sky — to the sun — to the silvery clouds, intermingled with patches of brilliant blue; then she cast them around her upon the ground, the people, the houses. All at once, while the man in yellow was pinioning her, she uttered a terrible cry, a cry of joy. At that balcony—over there—at the angle of the Place—she had distinguished his form—the form of him—her friend—her lord—Phœbus—that other apparition of her life! The judge had lied! the priest had lied! it was he indeed—she could not doubt it. He was there—living—beautiful—clad in his brilliant uniform, with the plume on his head and the sword by his side.

"Phœbus!" she cried—"my Phœbus!" and she would have stretched out to him her arms all trembling with love and delight; but they were bound.

Then she saw the captain knit his brows; a fine young woman, leaning upon his arm, looked at him with scornful lip and angry eye; then Phœbus uttered some words which did not reach her ear, and then he and the lady both hastily disappeared behind the casement of the balcony, which immediately closed.

"Phœbus!" cried the unfortunate girl, "can it be that thou believ'st it?"

A monstrous idea had just suggested itself to her. She recollected that she had been condemned for murder committed on the person of Phœbus de Chateaupers.

She had supported everything until now; but this last blow was too severe. She fell senseless upon the ground.

"Come," said Charmolue, "carry her into the cart, and let us finish."

No one had yet remarked, in the gallery of royal statues carved immediately above the arches of the portal, a strange-looking spectator, who until then had been observing all that passed with such absolute passiveness—a neck so intently stretched—a visage so deformed—that but for his habiliments, half red and half white, he might have been taken for one of the stone monsters through whose mouths the long gutters of the cathedral have disgorged themselves for six hundred years. No visible circumstance of all that had been transacted before the entrance of Notre-Dame since the hour of twelve had escaped this spectator. And at the very commencement, without any one's noticing the action, he had fastened firmly to one of the small columns of the gallery a strong knotted rope, the other end of which fell down below upon the top of the steps of entrance. This being done, he had set himself to look quietly on, only whistling from time to time when some blackbird flew by him. All at once, at the moment that the chief executioner's two assistants were preparing to execute Charmolue's phlegmatic order, he strided over the balustrade of the gallery, gripped the cord with his feet, his knees, and his hands; then he was seen to slide down over that part of the façade like a drop of rain gliding down a pane of glass—run up to the two sub-executioners with the speed of a cat just dropped from a housetop—knock them both down with a pair of enormous fists—carry off the gipsy girl with one hand, as a child does a doll—and leap at one bound into the church, lifting the girl above his head, and crying out with a formidable voice, "Sanctuary!"

This was done with such rapidity that had it been night the whole might have been seen by the glare of a single flash of lightning.

"Sanctuary! sanctuary!" repeated the crowd; and the clapping of ten thousand hands made Quasimodo's only eye sparkle with joy and pride.

This shock brought the condemned to her senses. She lifted her eyelids, looked at Quasimodo, then suddenly dropped them again, as if terrified at her deliverer.

Charmolue, the executioners, and the whole escort were confounded. The fact was that within the walls of Notre-Dame the condemned was inviolable. The cathedral was a recognised place of refuge; all temporal jurisdiction expired upon its threshold.

Quasimodo had stopped under the grand doorway. His broad feet seemed to rest as solidly upon the floor of the church as the heavy Roman pillars themselves. His great dishevelled head looked compressed between his shoulders, like that of the lion, which animal, in like manner, has a mane, but no neck. He held the young girl, all palpitating, suspended in his horny hands, like a piece of white drapery; but he bore her so cautiously that he seemed to be afraid of breaking or withering her. It was as if he felt that she was something delicate, exquisite, precious, made for other hands than his. At some moments he looked as if not daring to touch her even with his breath. Then all at once he would strain her closely in his arms to his angular breast—as if she were his only good—his treasure—as the mother of that child would have done. His gnome's eye, bent down upon her, poured over her a flood of tenderness, grief, and pity; and then again it was lifted up all flashing. Then the women laughed and wept—the crowd stamped their feet with enthusiasm—for at that moment Quasimodo had really a beauty of his own. Yes; that orphan, that foundling, that outcast, was fair to look upon. He felt himself august in his strength. He stood erect, looking full in the face that society from which he was banished, yet in which he was displaying so powerful an intervention—that human justice from which he had snatched its prey—all those tigers whose longing jaws he forced to remain empty—all those police agents, those judges, those executioners—all that force of the King which he, poor and helpless as he was, had broken with the force of God.

And then there was something affecting in that protection falling from a being so deformed upon one so unfortunate—in the circumstance of a poor girl condemned to death being saved by Quasimodo. It was the extremity of natural and that of social wretchedness meeting and assisting each other.

Meanwhile, after a few minutes' triumph, Quasimodo had suddenly plunged with his burden into the darksome interior of the church. The people, fond of any display of prowess, sought him with their eyes under the gloomy nave, regretting that he had so quickly withdrawn himself from their acclamations. All at once he was seen to reappear at one extremity of the gallery of the royal statues. He passed along it, running like a madman, lifting his conquest in his arms, and shouting "Sanctuary!" Fresh plaudits burst from the multitude. Having traversed the gallery, he plunged again into the interior of the church. A minute afterwards he appeared upon the upper platform, still bearing the gipsy in his arms, still running wildly along, still shouting "Sanctuary!" and the crowd still applauding. At last he made a third appearance on the summit of the tower of the great bell. From thence he seemed to show exultingly to the whole city the fair creature he had saved;

and his thundering voice, that voice which was heard so seldom, and which he never heard at all, thrice repeated with frantic vehemence, even in the very clouds, "Sanctuary! sanctuary! sanctuary!"

"Noël! Noël!" cried the people in their turn; and that multitudinous acclamation resounded upon the opposite shore of the Seine, to the astonishment of the crowd assembled in the Place de Grève, and of the recluse herself, who was still waiting with her eyes fixed upon the gibbet.

BOOK IX

CHAPTER I

FEVER

CLAUDE FROLLO was no longer in Notre-Dame when his adopted son thus abruptly cut the fatal knot in which the unhappy archdeacon had bound the gipsy girl and caught himself. On returning into the sacristy he had torn from his shoulders the alb, the cope, and the stole; thrown them all into the hands of the amazed verger; made his escape through the private door of the cloister; had ordered a wherryman of the Terrain to convey him to the left bank of the Seine; and plunged into the hilly streets of the University—going he knew not whither; meeting at every step parties of men and of women, pressing joyously towards the Pont St. Michel, in the hope that they should still "get there in time" to see the witch hanged—looking pale and wild—more troubled, more blinded, and more scared than some bird of night let fly and pursued by a troop of children in broad daylight. He knew not where he was—what he thought—what he dreamed. He went forward—walking—running—taking each street at random—making no selection of his route—only still urged on by that Grève, that horrible Grève, which he confusedly felt to be behind him.

In this manner he proceeded the whole length of the Montagne St. Geneviève, and at last issued out of the town by the Porte St. Victor. He continued his flight so long as, on turning round, he could see the towered enclosure of the University and the scattered houses of the faubourg; but when at last a ridge of ground had taken completely out of his view that hateful Paris—when he could imagine himself a hundred leagues from it—in the country, in a desert—he stopped, and felt as if he breathed more freely.

Then frightful ideas rushed upon his mind. He saw down clear into his soul, and shuddered. He thought of that unfortunate girl who had destroyed him and whom he had destroyed. He cast a haggard eye over the two winding paths, along which Fate had driven their separate destinies, to that point of intersection at which she had pitilessly shattered them against each other. He thought of the folly of everlasting vows—the emptiness of chastity, science, religion, virtue—the inutility of God. He took his fill of these bad thoughts, and while plunging deeper into them, he felt as if the fiend were laughing within him.

And while thus diving into his soul, when he saw how large a space nature had assigned in it to the passions, he smiled more bitterly still. He stirred up from the bottom of his heart all his hatred, all his wickedness; and he discovered, with the cool eye of a physician examining a patient, that this hatred, this wickedness, were but vitiated love—that love, the source of every virtue in man, turned to things horrible in the heart of a priest—and that a man constituted as he was, by making himself a priest made himself a demon. Then he laughed frightfully, and all at once he grew pale again in contemplating the worst side of his fatal passion—of that love, corroding, venomous, malignant, implacable, which had driven one of them to the gibbet, the other to hellfire—her to condemnation, him to damnation.

And then his laugh came again when he reflected that Phœbus was living—that the captain was alive, gay, and happy, had finer hacquetons than ever, and a new mistress, whom he brought to see the old one hanged. And he sneered at himself with redoubled bitterness when he reflected that, of the living beings whose death he had desired, the only one whom he did not really hate was the only one he had not failed to kill.

Then his thoughts wandered from the captain to the assembled multitude, and he was seized with a jealousy of a novel kind. He reflected that the people too—the whole people—had had before their eyes the woman whom he loved, exposed almost in a state of nudity. He writhed his arms with agony at the idea that that woman, but a glimpse of whose form caught by himself alone in the darkness would have been to him the very height of happiness, had been given thus, in broad daylight, at the very noontide, to the gaze of a whole multitude, clad as for a bridal night. He wept with rage over the thought that all those mysteries of love should be thus profaned, sullied, stripped, withered for ever. He wept with rage as he figured to himself how many impure looks that ill-attached vesture had gratified—that this lovely girl, this virgin lily, thus cup of purity and delight, which he could not have approached with his lips but in trembling, had been converted, as it were, into a public trough, at which the vilest of the Parisian populace—the thieves, the beggars, the lackeys—had come to drink in common of a pleasure shameless, impure, and depraved.

And then, when he sought to picture to his imagination the happiness which he might have found upon earth, had not she been a gipsy and he a priest, had Phœbus not existed, and had she but loved him—when he figured to himself that a life of serenity and love would have been possible for him too—that at that very moment there were happy couples to be found here and there upon the earth, whiling away the hours in sweet and devious converse, in orange-groves, on the side of rivulets, by the setting sun or under a starry sky—and that, had it been God's will, he might have formed with her one of those blissful couples—his heart melted in tenderness and despair.

Oh, she! still she! It was that fixed idea that haunted him incessantly—that tortured him—that gnawed his brain and corroded his heart. He did not regret—he did not repent; all that he had done he was ready to do again—he liked better to see her in the hands of the executioner than in the arms of the captain. But he was suffering—suffering so violently that at some moments he tore handfuls of hair from his head to see if it were not whitening.

There was one moment among the rest at which it entered his mind that perhaps at that very minute the hideous chain which he had seen in the morning was drawing its noose of iron about that neck so slender and so graceful. This thought brought the perspiration boiling through his pores.

There was another moment at which, in the midst of a diabolical laugh at himself, he pictured to his imagination at one and the same time La Esmeralda as he had seen her for the first time—lively, careless, joyous, gaily attired, dancing, winged, harmonious—and La Esmeralda at her last hour, in her scanty shift, with the rope about her neck, ascending slowly with her naked feet the sharp-cornered steps of the gibbet. He drew this picture to himself so vividly that he uttered a terrific cry.

While this hurricane of despair was overturning, breaking, tearing up, bending to the earth, uprooting all within him, he looked upon the face of nature around him. At his feet some fowls were stirring about among the bushes, pecking the scaly insects that were running in the sunshine. Over his head were some groups of dappled clouds, gliding over a deep blue sky. In the horizon the spire of St. Victor's Abbey shot up its obelisk of slate above the intervening ridge of ground. And the miller of the Butte Copeaux was whistling light-heartedly while he looked at the steady-turning sails of his mill. All those objects, instinct with a life active, organised, and tranquil, recurring around him in a thousand forms, were painful to him; and again he began to fly.

Thus he hurried on through the country until the evening. This flight of his from nature, from life, from himself, from man, from God, from everything, lasted the whole day. Sometimes he threw himself with his face to the ground, and tore up with his nails the young blades of corn. Sometimes he stopped in the solitary street of a village, and his thoughts were so insupportable that he would take his head between both his hands, as if to tear it from his shoulders and dash it on the stones.

Towards the hour of sunset he examined himself again, and found himself almost mad. The storm that had been raging within him ever since the moment that he had lost all hope and wish to save the gipsy girl had left him unconscious of a single sound idea, a single rational thought. His reason lay prostrate, almost utterly destroyed. Only two distinct images remained in his mind—La Esmeralda and the gallows; all beside was utter darkness. Those two images, appearing together, presented to him a frightful group; and the more he fixed upon them such power of attention and contemplation as remained to him, the more he saw them increase according to a fancied progression—the one in grace, in charm, in beauty, in light; the other in deformity and horror—until at last La Esmeralda appeared to him as a star, the gibbet as an enormous, fleshless arm.

It is remarkable that during all this torture he was visited by no serious thought of dying. So the wretched man was constituted; he clung to life—perhaps, indeed, he really saw hell in prospect.

Meanwhile the daylight was declining. The living spirit still existing within him began confusedly to think of return. He thought himself far from Paris; but on striving to ascertain its bearing, he discovered that he had only been travelling round the circuit of the University. The spire of St. Sulpice and the three lofty needles of St. Germain-des-Près shot up above the horizon on his right. He bent his steps in that direction. When he heard the "*Qui vive!*" of the abbot's men-at-arms around the embattled circumvallation of St. Germain's, he turned aside, took a path that lay before him, between the abbey mill and the Maladerie or lazaretto of the bourg, and in a few minutes found himself upon the border of the Pré-aux-Clercs. This Pré was celebrated for the tumults that arose in it night and day: it was a hydra to the poor monks of St. Germain's—*Quod monachis Sancti Germani Pratensis hydra fuit, clericis nova semper dissidiorum capita suscitantibus.* The archdeacon was afraid of meeting some one there; he dreaded to encounter any human face: he had avoided the University and the Bourg St. Germain, and he wished to enter the streets again at the latest hour possible. He passed along the side of the Pré-aux-Clercs, took the solitary path which lay between it and the Dieu-Neuf, and at length reached the waterside. There Dom Claude found a boatman, who for a few deniers parisis conveyed him up the Seine to the extremity of the island of the City, and landed him upon that uninhabited tongue of land on which the reader has already seen poor Gringoire musing, and which extended beyond the King's gardens, parallel to the islet of the Passeur-aux-Vaches.

The monotonous rocking of the boat and the dashing of the water had in some degree lulled the unhappy Claude. When the wherryman had taken his departure he remained standing in stupor upon the bank, looking straight before him, but perceiving objects only through such magnifying oscillations as made all a sort of phantasmagoria to him. The exhaustion of a violent grief will often produce this effect upon the mind.

The sun had set behind the lofty Tour de Nesle, and it was now the twilight hour. The sky was white, and so was the surface of the river. Between these two sheets of white the left bank of the Seine, upon which his eyes were fixed, projected its dark mass, which, gradually tapering away in the perspective, shot out into the grey horizon like a huge black spire. It was loaded with houses, of which nothing was distinguishable but the dark outline of the whole, boldly marked upon the clear light tint of the sky and the water. Here and there the windows were beginning to twinkle from the lights within. That immense black obelisk, thus isolated between the two white expanses of the sky and the river (at that place very broad), had a singular appearance to Dom Claude, similar to that which would be experienced by a man lying with his back to the ground at the foot of the steeple of Strasburg, and looking up at the enormous spire piercing into the sky above him in the dim twilight. Only there was this difference—that here Claude was erect, and the obelisk was horizontal; but as the river, by reflecting the sky, deepened indefinitely the abyss beneath him, the vast promontory seemed springing as boldly in the void as any cathedral spire, and the impression was the same. Here, indeed, the impression was in this respect stronger and more profound—that although it was indeed the steeple of Strasburg, it was the steeple of Strasburg two leagues high—something unexampled, gigantic, immeasurable—a structure such as no human eye had seen, except it were the tower of Babel. The chimneys of the houses, the battlements of the walls, the fantastically-cut gables of the roofs, the spire of the Augustines, the Tour de Nesle—all those projections which indented the profile of the colossal obelisk—added to the illusion by their odd resemblance to the outline of a florid and fanciful sculpture. Claude, in the state of hallucination in which he then was, thought he saw with his living eyes the very steeple of hell. The thousand lights scattered over the whole height of the fearful tower seemed to him to be so many openings of the vast internal furnace, while the voices and the noises that escaped from it were so many shrieks and groanings of the damned. Then he was terror-struck: he put his hands to his ears that he might hear no longer, turned his back that he might no longer see, and strode hastily away from the frightful vision. But the vision was in himself.

When he came into the streets again, the people, passing to and fro in the light of the shop fronts, appeared to him like an everlasting movement of spectres about him. He had strange noises in his ears, and extraordinary fancies disturbed his brain. He saw neither the houses, nor the pavement, nor the vehicles, nor the men and women, but a chaos of undefined objects merging one into another. At the corner of the Rue de la Barillerie there was a chandler's shop, which had the penthouse above its window, according to immemorial custom, garnished all round with tin hoops, from each of which was suspended a circle of wooden candles, clattering against each other in the wind with a noise like that of castanets. He thought he heard, rattling one against another in the dark, the bundle of skeletons at Montfaucon.

" Oh," muttered he, " the night wind drives them one against another, and mixes the rattle of their chains with the rattle of their bones! Perhaps she is there, in the midst of them."

Quite bewildered, he knew not whither he was going. After advancing a few steps farther, he found himself upon the Pont St. Michel. There was a light at a ground-floor window; he went up to it. Through the cracked panes he saw a dirty room, which awakened in his mind a confused recollection. In that room, ill lighted by a meagre lamp, there was a young man, fair and fresh-looking, with a joyous face, throwing his arms with boisterous laughter about a girl very immodestly attired; and near the lamp there was an old woman spinning and singing with a tremulous voice. As the young man's laughter was not heard at every instant, the old woman's song made its way in fragments to the ear of the priest; it was something unintelligible yet frightful:—

"Growl, Grève; bark, Grève!
Spin away, my distaff brave:
Let the hangman have his cord,
That whistles in the prison-yard
Growl, Grève; bark, Grève!

"Hemp, that makes the pretty rope,
Sow it widely, give it scope—
Better hemp than wheaten sheaves;
Thief there's none that ever thieves
The pretty rope, the hempen rope.

"Bark, Grève; growl, Grève!
To see the girl of pleasure brave
Dangling on the gibbet high,
Every window is an eye—
Bark, Grève; growl, Grève."

Hereupon the young man was laughing and caressing the girl. The old woman was La Falourdel, the girl was a girl of the town, and the young man was his brother Jehan.

He continued looking; this sight pleased him then as well as any other.

He saw Jehan go to a window at the farther end of the room, open it, look out upon the quay, where a thousand lighted windows were shining in the distance; and then he heard him say, as he shut the window again,—

"Upon my soul, but it's night already! The townsfolk are lighting their candles, and God Almighty His stars."

Then Jehan returned to the wench, and broke a bottle that stood by them on a table, exclaiming, "Empty already, *corbœuf!* and I've no more money.—Isabeau, my darling, I shall not be satisfied with Jupiter till he's changed your two white nipples into two black bottles, that I may suck Beaune wine from them day and night."

This fine piece of wit made the courtesan laugh; and Jehan took his departure.

Dom Claude had only just time to throw himself on the ground in order to escape being met, looked in the face, and recognised by his brother. Fortunately the street was dark, and the scholar was drunk. Nevertheless, he espied the archdeacon lying upon the pavement in the mud. "Oh, oh," said he, "here's one that's had a merry time of it to-day."

He pushed Dom Claude with his foot, the archdeacon holding his breath the while.

"Dead drunk!" resumed Jehan. "Bravo! he's full!—a very leech, dropped off a wine-cask. He's bald," added he, stooping over him; "it's an old man—*Fortunate senex!*"

Then Dom Claude heard him go away, saying, "It's all one. Reason's a fine thing; and my brother the archdeacon's a lucky fellow to be wise and have money!"

The archdeacon then got up again, and hurried straight to Notre-Dame, the big towers of which he could see rising in the dark over the houses.

At the moment that he arrived, all panting, at the Place du Parvis, he shrunk back, and dared not lift his eyes towards the fatal edifice. "Oh," whispered he to himself, "and can it really be that such a thing took place here to-day—this very morning?"

And now he ventured a glance at the church. Its front was dark; the sky behind was glittering with stars; the crescent moon, in her flight upwards from the horizon, had at that moment reached the summit of the right-hand tower, and seemed to have perched upon it, like a luminous bird, on the edge of the dark trifoliated balustrade.

The gate of the cloister was shut; but the archdeacon always had with him the key of the tower containing his laboratory, and he now made use of it to enter the church.

He found within it the darkness and the silence of a cavern. By the great shadows that fell from all sides in broad masses, he perceived that the hangings of the morning ceremony were not yet taken away. The great silver cross was glittering amid the darkness, sprinkled over with a number of glittering points, like the milky way of that sepulchral night. The long windows of the choir showed, above the black drapery, the upper extremities of their pointed arches, the stained glass of which, as shown by the moonlight, had only the doubtful colours of the night—a sort of violet, white, and blue, of a tint to be found nowhere else but on the faces of the dead. The archdeacon, on observing all round the choir those pale pointed window tops, thought he saw so many mitres of bishops gone to perdition. He closed his eyes, and when he opened them again he thought they were a circle of pale visages looking down upon him.

He began to flee away through the church. Then it seemed to him as if the church itself took life and motion—that each massive column became an enormous leg that beat the ground with its broad foot of stone, and that the gigantic cathedral had become a sort of prodigious elephant, breathing and walking along, with its pillars for legs, its two towers for trunks, and the immense black drapery for its caparison.

Thus his fever, or his madness, had arrived at such a pitch of intensity that the whole external world was become to the unhappy man a sort of apocalypse, visible, palpable, frightful.

For one moment he felt some relief. On plunging into the side aisles he perceived issuing from behind a group of pillars a reddish light; he rushed towards it as toward a star of salvation. It was the feeble lamp that lighted day and night the public breviary of Notre-Dame under its iron trellis-work. He cast his eye eagerly upon the sacred book, in the hope of finding there some sentence of consolation or encouragement. The volume was open at this passage of Job, over which he ran his burning eye: "And a spirit passed before my face; and I heard a little breath; and the hair of my flesh stood up."

On reading this dismal sentence his sensations were those of a blind man when he feels himself pricked by the staff he has picked up. His knees dropped under him, and he sank upon the pavement, thinking of her who had died that day. He felt so many monstrous fumes inundating his brain, that it seemed to him as if his head was become one of the chimneys of hell.

It appears that he remained long in this posture, thinking no more, but overwhelmed and passive under the power of the demon. At last some strength returned to him; he thought of going and taking refuge in the tower, near to his faithful Quasimodo. He rose, and as fear was upon him, he took the lamp of the breviary to light him. This was a sacrilege; but he was now beyond regarding so slight a consideration.

He climbed slowly up the staircase of the towers, filled with a secret dread, which was likely to be communicated even to the few passengers at that hour through the Place du Parvis, by the mysterious light of his lamp ascending so late at night from loophole to loophole, to the top of the steeple.

All at once he felt some coolness upon his face, and found himself under the doorway of the upper gallery. The air was cold; the sky was streaked with clouds, the broad white flakes of which drifted one upon another like river-ice breaking up after a frost. The crescent moon gleaming amid them looked now like some celestial vessel set fast among those icebergs of the air.

He cast his eyes downwards, and gazed for a moment through the curtain of slender columns that connects the towers—afar off—through a light veil of mist and smoke—upon the silent multitude of the roofs of Paris—pointed, innumerable, crowded, and small, like the waves of a tranquil sea in a summer's night. The moon cast a feeble light, which gave to earth and sky an ashy hue.

At that moment the cathedral clock lifted its harsh, broken voice. It struck twelve. The priest thought of noon; it was twelve o'clock come again. "Oh," whispered he to himself, "she must be cold now!"

Suddenly a puff of wind extinguished his lamp, and almost at the same time there appeared to him, at the opposite angle of the tower, a shade—a something white—a shape—a female form. He started. By the side of that female form was that of a little goat, that mingled its bleating with the last sounds of the clock.

He had resolution enough to look: it was she!

She was pale—she was sad. Her hair fell upon her shoulders as in the morning, but no rope was round her neck, no cord upon her hands: she was free—she was dead! She was clad in white, and over her head was thrown a great veil.

She came towards him slowly, looking up to heaven, the unearthly goat following her. He felt himself of stone—too stiff to fly. At each step that she came forward he made one backward, and that was all. In this manner he re-entered under the dark vault of the staircase. He froze at the idea that she perhaps was going to enter there too; had she done so he would have died of terror.

She arrived indeed before the staircase door, stopped there for some moments, looked steadfastly into the dark cavity; then, without appearing to perceive the priest there, she passed on. He thought she looked taller than when she was alive; he saw the moon through her white robe, and was near enough to hear her breathing.

When she had passed by he began to re-descend the staircase with the same slowness which he had observed in the spectre, thinking himself a spectre too—all haggard, his hair erect, the lamp still extinguished in his hand; and as he descended the spiral stairs, he distinctly heard a voice laughing and repeating in his ear, " And a spirit passed before my face; and I heard a little breath; and the hair of my flesh stood up."

CHAPTER II

HUNCH-BACKED, ONE-EYED, LAME

EVERY town in the Middle Ages, and down to the time of Louis XII. every town in France, had its places of sanctuary. These sanctuaries, amid the deluge of penal laws and barbarous jurisdictions that inundated the state, were a sort of islands rising above the level of human justice. Every criminal that landed upon any one of them was saved. In each *banlieue* there were almost as many of these places of refuge as there were of execution. It was the abuse of impunity beside the abuse of capital punishments—two bad things endeavouring to correct each other. The royal palaces, the mansions of the princes, and especially the churches, had right of sanctuary. Sometimes a whole town that happened to want repeopling was converted for the time into a place of refuge for criminals. Thus Louis XI. made all Paris a sanctuary in 1467.

When once he had set foot within the asylum the criminal's person was sacred; but it behoved him to beware how he quitted it again. But one step out of the sanctuary, and he fell back into the flood. The wheel, the gibbet, and the strappado kept close guard around the place of refuge, watching incessantly for their prey, like sharks about a ship. Thus individuals under condemnation have been known to grow grey, confined to a cloister, to the staircase of a palace, the grounds of an abbey, or the porch of a church. So far, the sanctuary itself was but a prison under another name. It now and then happened that a solemn decree of the parliament violated the asylum, and reconsigned the condemned to the hands of the executioner; but this was a rare occurrence. The parliaments stood in fear of the bishops; for when the two gowns, the spiritual and the secular, happened to chafe each other, the simar had the worst of it in its collision with the cassock. Occasionally, however, as in the case of the assassins of Petît-Jean, the Paris executioner, and in that of Emery Rousseau, who had murdered Jean Valleret, temporal justice overleaped the pretensions of the church, and went on to the execution of its sentences. But except by virtue of a decree of the parliament, woe to him that forcibly violated a place of sanctuary! It is well known what was the end of Robert de Clermont, Marshal of France, and Jean de Châlons, Marshal of Champagne; and yet it was all about one Perrin Marc, a money-changer's man and a wretched assassin. But the two marshals had forced the doors of St. Méry's church—there was the enormity.

Around the places of sanctuary there floated such an atmosphere of reverence that, according to tradition, it sometimes affected even animals. Aymoin relates that a stag, hunted by King Dagobert, having taken refuge at the tomb of St. Denis, the hounds stopped short, barking.

The churches had usually a cell prepared for the reception of the suppliants. In 1407 Nicolas Flamel caused to be built for them, over the vaulted roof of the church of St. Jacques-de-la-Boucherie, a chamber which cost him four livres six sols sixteen deniers parisis.

At Notre-Dame it was a cell constructed over one of the side aisles, under the buttresses, and looking towards the cloister, precisely at the spot where the wife of the *concierge,* or keeper of the towers, in 1831 had made herself a garden, which was to the hanging gardens of Babylon as a lettuce is to a palm tree, or as a porter's wife is to a Semiramis.

There it was that, after his frantic and triumphal course along the towers and galleries, Quasimodo had deposited La Esmeralda. So long as that course lasted the girl had remained almost without consciousness, having only a vague perception that she was ascending in the air—that she was floating, flying there—that something was carrying her upwards from the earth. From time to time she heard the bursting laugh, the loud voice of Quasimodo, at her ear; she half opened her eyes; and then she saw, confusedly beneath her, Paris, all chequered over with its thousand roofs of tile and slate, like a red and blue mosaic-work; and just above her head Quasimodo's frightful and joy-illumined face. Then her eyelids dropped again: she believed that all was over—that she had been executed while in her fainting fit; and that the deformed genius that had ruled her destiny had now laid hold of her spirit and was bearing it away. She dared not look at him, but resigned herself to his power.

But when the poor ringer, all dishevelled and panting, had

deposited her in the cell of refuge—when she felt his clumsy hands gently untying the cord that had cut into her arms—she felt that sort of shock which startles out of their sleep the passengers in a vessel that strikes the bottom in the middle of a dark night. So were her ideas awakened, and they returned to her one after another. She saw that she was in Notre-Dame; she remembered having been snatched from the hands of the executioner—that Phœbus was living, and Phœbus loved her no longer; and these two ideas, of which the latter shed so much bitterness over the former, presenting themselves jointly to the poor sufferer, she turned to Quasimodo, who kept standing before her, and whose countenance affrighted her, and said to him, "Why have you saved me?"

He looked at her anxiously, as if striving to divine what she was saying to him. She repeated her question. He then gave her another look of profound sadness, and hastened away, leaving her in astonishment.

In a few minutes he returned, carrying a bundle, which he threw down at her feet. It was some wearing apparel, which certain charitable women had deposited at the threshold of the church. Then she cast down her eyes over her own person, found herself almost naked, and blushed. Life was now returning to her.

Somewhat of this feeling of modest shame seemed to communicate itself to Quasimodo. He veiled his eye with his broad hand, and once more went away, but with tardy steps.

She dressed herself in haste. There were a white gown and a white veil; it was the habit of a novice of the Hôtel-Dieu.

She had scarcely finished her toilette before she saw Quasimodo return, carrying a basket under one arm and a mattress under the other. The basket contained a bottle, with some bread and other provisions. He set the basket on the ground, and said to her, "Eat." He spread out the mattress upon the flagstones, and said, "Sleep." It was his own meal, his own bed, that the poor ringer had been to fetch.

The gipsy girl raised her eyes to thank him, but could not articulate a word. The poor devil was, in truth, horrible to look upon. She cast down her eyes again, shuddering.

Then he said to her, "I frighten you; I'm very ugly—am not I? Don't look at me; only listen to me. In the daytime you'll stay here; at night you can walk about the whole church. But don't go out of the church either by day or night. You'd be ruined. They'd kill you—and I should die."

Affected at his words, she raised her head to answer him; but he had disappeared. She found herself alone, musing upon the singular sentences of this almost monstrous being, and struck by the tone of his voice, so hoarse and yet so gentle.

Then she examined her cell. It was a little room, some six feet square, with a small window and a door upon the gently inclined plane of the roofing of flat stones. A number of spout-ends in the figure of animals seemed bending around her, outside, and stretching out their necks to look at her through the little window. Over the verge of the roof she discerned a thousand chimney tops casting up before her the smoke from the multitudinous fires of Paris—a melancholy sight to the poor gipsy girl—a foundling—a convict capitally condemned—an unfortunate creature, with no country, no family, no home.

At the moment that the thought of her loneliness in the world was oppressing her more poignantly than ever, she felt a hairy, shaggy head gliding between her hands, upon her lap. She startled (for everything frightened her now) and looked down. It was the poor little goat, the nimble Djali, which had escaped after her at the moment that Quasimodo had scattered Charmolue's brigade, and had been lavishing its caresses at her feet for nearly an hour without obtaining so much as a single look. Its mistress inundated it with kisses. "O Djali," said she, "how I had forgotten thee! So thou still thinkest of me. Oh, thou art not ungrateful!" At the same time, as if some invisible hand had lifted the weight that had so long repressed her tears within her heart, she began to weep, and as the tears flowed she felt as if what was sharpest and bitterest in her grief was departing with them.

When evening came she thought the night so fine, the moonlight so soft, that she went quite round the high gallery that encircles the cathedral; and this little promenade gave her some relief, so calm did the earth seem to her viewed from that elevation.

CHAPTER III

DEAF

The next morning the poor gipsy girl perceived, on waking, that she had slept—a thing which astonished her, she had been so long unaccustomed to sleep. Some cheerful rays of the rising sun streamed through her window and fell upon her face. At the same time with the sun she saw at the window the unfortunate face of Quasimodo. Involuntarily her eyes closed again, but in vain—she still thought she saw, through her roseate eyelids, that gnome's visage, one-eyed and gap-toothed. Then, still keeping her eyes shut, she heard a rough voice saying very gently, "Don't be afraid. I'm your friend. I was come to look at you sleeping. That doesn't hurt you, does it, that I should come and see you asleep? What does it signify to you my being here when you have your eyes shut? Now I'm going away. There, I've put myself behind the wall; now you may open your eyes again."

There was something yet more plaintive than these words—it was the tone in which they were uttered. The gipsy girl, affected at them, opened her eyes. He had, in fact, gone away from the window. She went up to it, and saw the poor hunchback crouching in an angle of the wall, in a posture of sorrow and resignation. She made an effort to overcome the repugnance which she felt at the sight of him. "Come hither," said she softly. From the movement of her lips Quasimodo thought that she was bidding him go away. Then he rose up and retreated, limping, slow, hanging his head, not venturing to lift up to the young girl his despairing countenance. "Come hither, I say," cried she; but he continued to move away. Then she hurried out of the cell, ran after him, and laid hold of his arm. On feeling the pressure Quasimodo trembled in every limb. He lifted a suppliant eye; and finding that she was striving to draw him towards her, his whole face beamed with joy and tenderness. She tried to make him enter her cell, but he persisted in remaining on the threshold. "No, no," said he, "the owl goes not into the nest of the lark."

Then she gracefully squatted down upon her couch, with her goat asleep at her feet. Both parties remained motionless for a few minutes, absorbed in the contemplation—he of so much grace, she of so much ugliness. Every moment she discovered in Quasimodo some additional deformity. Her eye wandered over him, from his bow legs to his hump back, from his hump back to his one eye. She could not understand how a being so awkwardly fashioned could be in existence. Yet over the whole there was diffused an air of so much sadness and gentleness that she was beginning to be reconciled to it.

He was the first to break silence. " So you were telling me to come back."

She nodded affirmatively, and said, " Yes."

He understood the motion of her head. " Alas!" said he, as if hesitating to finish the sentence, " you see, I'm deaf."

" Poor man!" exclaimed the gipsy girl, with an expression of benevolent pity.

He smiled sorrowfully. " You thought that was all I wanted —didn't you? Yes, I'm deaf. That's the way I'm made. It's horrible, isn't it? You know, you're so beautiful."

In the poor creature's tone there was so deep a feeling of his wretchedness that she had not resolution to say a word. Besides, he would not have heard it. He continued,—

" Never did I see my ugliness as I do now. When I compare myself to you, I do indeed pity myself, poor unhappy monster that I am. You must think I look like a beast. Tell me, now. You, now, are a sunbeam—a dewdrop—a bird's song. But me —I'm something frightful—neither man nor brute—a sort of a thing that's harder, and more trod upon, and more unshapely, than a flint stone."

Then he laughed—a heartrending laugh. He went on,—

" Yes, I'm deaf; but you'll speak to me by gesture and signs. I've a master that talks to me that way. And then I shall know your will very quickly by seeing how your lips move and how you look."

" Well, then," said she, smiling, " tell me why you saved me."

He looked at her intently while she was speaking.

" Oh, I understand," he replied; " you ask me why it was I saved you. You've forgotten a poor wretch that tried to carry you off one night—a poor wretch that you brought relief to the very next day on their shameful pillory—a drop of water and a little pity. There was more than I can pay you back with all my life. You've forgotten that poor wretch—but he remembers."

She listened to him with deep emotion. A tear stood in the

poor ringer's eye, but it did not fall; he seemed to make it, as it were, a point of honour to contain it. "Just hear me," said he, when he was no longer afraid that this tear would escape him. "We've very high towers here—if a man were to fall from one, he'd be dead before he got to the ground; when you like me to fall in that way, you'll not so much as have to say a word—a glance of your eye will be enough."

Then he rose up from his leaning posture. This odd being, unhappy as the gipsy girl herself was, yet awakened some compassion in her breast. She motioned to him to remain.

"No, no," said he. "I mustn't stay too long; I'm not at my ease. It's all for pity that you don't turn away your eyes. I'm going somewhere, from whence I shall see you and you won't see me; that will be better."

He drew from his pocket a small metal whistle. "There," said he; "when you want me—when you wish me to come—when you'll not be too much horrified at the sight of me—you'll whistle with that. I can hear that noise."

He laid the whistle on the ground and went his way.

CHAPTER IV

EARTHENWARE AND CRYSTAL

DAY after day passed over, and tranquillity returned by degrees to the spirit of La Esmeralda. Excessive grief, like excessive joy, being violent in its nature, is of short duration. The human heart is incapable of remaining long in an extreme. The gipsy girl had suffered so much that astonishment at it was all that she now felt.

With the feeling of security hope had returned to her.

She was out of society, out of life; but she had a vague sense that perhaps it was not quite impossible for her to return to them. It was as if one of the dead should have in reserve a key to open the tomb.

She felt gradually departing from her mind the terrible images which had so long beset her. All the hideous phantoms, Pierrat Torterue, Jacques Charmolue, were vanishing from her—not excepting the priest himself.

And then Phœbus was living—she was sure of it—she had seen him. To her the fact of his being alive was everything.

After the series of fatal shocks which had overturned everything in her soul, she had found nothing still keeping its place there but one feeling, her love for the captain. For love is like a tree vegetating of itself, striking deep roots through all our being, and often continuing to grow greenly over a heart in ruins.

And inexplicable as it is, the blinder is this passion the more it is tenacious. It is never more firmly seated than when it is without a shadow of reason. Assuredly La Esmeralda could not think of the captain without feelings of bitterness. Assuredly it was dreadful that he, too, should have been deceived; that he should have believed such a thing possible; that he should have conceived of a stab with a poniard coming from her who would have given a thousand lives to save him. And yet he was not so excessively to blame; for had she not acknowledged the crime? had she not yielded, weak woman as she was, to the torture? All the fault was her own; she ought rather to have let them tear the nails from her feet than such an avowal from her lips. But, then, could she but see Phœbus once more, for a single minute, a word, a look, would suffice to undeceive him, to bring him back. She doubted it not. She also strove to account to herself for many singular things—for Phœbus's happening to be present on the day of the penance at the church door, and for his being with that young lady. It was his sister, no doubt—an explanation by no means plausible, but with which she contented herself, because she needed to believe that Phœbus still loved her, and her alone. Had he not sworn to her? And what stronger assurance did she need, all simple and credulous as she was? And besides, in the sequel of the affair, were not appearances much more strongly against herself than against him? So she waited and hoped.

We may add that the church itself—that vast edifice—wrapping her, as it were, on all sides, protecting her, saving her—was a sovereign tranquilliser. The solemn lines of its architecture—the religious attitude of all the objects by which the girl was surrounded—the pious and serene thoughts escaping, as it were, from every pore of those venerable stones—acted upon her unconsciously to herself. The structure had sounds, too, of such blessedness and such majesty that they soothed that suffering spirit. The monotonous chant of the performers of the service; the responses of the people to the priests, now inarticulate, now of thundering loudness; the harmonious trembling of the casements; the organ bursting forth like the voice of a hundred trumpets; the three steeples humming like hives of enormous bees—all that orchestra, over which bounded a gigantic gamut, ascending and descending incessantly, from the voice of a multitude to that of a bell—lulled her memory, her imagination, and her sorrow. The bells especially had this effect. It was as a powerful magnetism which those vast machines poured in large waves over her. Thus each successive sunrise found her less pale, more tranquillised, and breathing more freely. In proportion as her internal wounds healed, her grace and her beauty bloomed again on her countenance, but more collected and composed. Her former character also returned—something even of her gaiety, her pretty grimace, her fondness for her goat, her love of singing, her feminine bashfulness. She was careful to dress herself in the morning in the corner of her little chamber, lest some inhabitant of the neighbouring garrets should see her through the little window.

When her thinking of Phœbus allowed her leisure, the gipsy girl sometimes thought of Quasimodo. He was the only link, the only means of communication with mankind, with the living, that remained to her. Unfortunate creature! she was more out of the world than Quasimodo himself. She knew not what to make of the strange friend whom chance had given her. Often she reproached herself for not having a gratitude which could shut its eyes, but positively she could not reconcile herself to the sight of the poor ringer—he was too ugly.

She had left the whistle he had given her lying on the ground. This, however, did not prevent Quasimodo from reappearing from time to time during the first days. She strove hard to restrain herself from turning away with so strong an appearance of disgust when he came and brought her the basket of provisions or the pitcher of water; but he always perceived the smallest motion of that kind, and then he went away sorrowful.

Once he happened to come at the moment she was caressing Djali. He stood for a few moments pensively contemplating that graceful group of the goat and the gipsy, and then he said, shaking his heavy and ill-formed head, "My misfortune is that I'm still too much like a man; I wish I were a beast outright, like that goat."

She raised her eyes towards him with a look of astonishment. To this look he answered, "Oh, I well know why!" and went his way.

Another time he presented himself at the door of the cell (into which he never entered) at the moment when La Esmeralda was singing an old Spanish ballad, the words of which she did not understand, but which had dwelt in her ear because the gipsy women had lulled her to sleep with it when a child. At the sight of that shocking countenance appearing suddenly in the middle of her song the girl broke it off with an involuntary gesture of affright. The unfortunate ringer fell upon his knees on the threshold, and clasped with a suppliant look his great shapeless hands. "Oh," said he, with a sorrowful accent, "go on, I entreat you, and don't send me away." She was unwilling to pain him; and so, all trembling, she resumed her romance. Her fright, however, dissipated by degrees, and she abandoned herself wholly to the expression of the plaintive air that she was singing. He, the while, had remained upon his knees, with his hands clasped as in prayer—attentive, hardly drawing his breath, his look fixed upon the beaming eyes of the gipsy. It seemed as if he was reading her song in those eyes.

At another time, again, he came to her with a look of awkwardness and timidity. "Listen," said he, with an effort; "I have something to say to you." She made him a sign that she was listening. Then he began to sigh, half opened his lips, seemed for a moment to be on the point of speaking, then looked her in the face, made a negative motion with his head, and slowly withdrew, with his hand pressed to his forehead, leaving the gipsy girl in amazement.

Among the grotesque figures carved upon the wall there was one for which he had a particular affection, and with which he often seemed to be exchanging fraternal looks. On one occasion the gipsy heard him saying to it, "Oh, why am I not made of stone like thee?"

At length one morning La Esmeralda, having advanced to the verge of the roof, was looking into the Place, over the sharp ridge of the church of Saint-Jean-le-Rond. Quasimodo was present, behind her. He used so to place himself of his own accord, in order to spare the young girl as much as possible the disagreeableness of seeing him. Suddenly the gipsy started—a tear and a flash of joy shone at once in her eyes; she knelt down on the edge of the roof, and stretched out her arms in anguish towards the Place, crying out, "Phœbus! Oh come! come hither! one word! but one word, in Heaven's name! Phœbus! Phœbus!" Her voice, her face, her gesture, her whole figure, had the heartrending aspect of a shipwrecked mariner making the signal of distress to some gay vessel passing in the distant horizon in a gleam of sunshine. Quasimodo leaned over towards the Place, and saw that the object of this tender and agonising prayer was a young man, a captain, a handsome cavalier, all glittering in arms and gay attire, who was passing by caracoling in the square beneath, and saluting with his plume a fine young lady, smiling, at her balcony. The officer, however, did not hear the call of the unfortunate girl, for he was too far off.

But the poor deaf ringer heard it. A deep sigh heaved his breast; he turned round; his heart was swelled with all the tears which he restrained from flowing; his hands, clenched convulsively, struck against his head, and when he drew them away there came with each of them a handful of his rough red hair.

The gipsy girl was paying no attention to him. He said in an undertone, grinding his teeth, "Damnation! So that's how a man should be—he need only be handsome outside!"

Meanwhile she had remained upon her knees, crying out with extraordinary agitation, "Oh, there! he's getting off his horse. He's going into that house. Phœbus! Phœbus! He does not hear me. Phœbus! What a wicked woman that is to talk to him at the same time that I do. Phœbus! Phœbus!"

The deaf man had his eye upon her all the while. He understood this (to him) dumb show. The poor ringer's eye filled with tears, but he let not one of them fall. All at once he pulled her gently by the extremity of the sleeve. She turned round. He had assumed a tranquil air, and said to her, "Should you like me to go and fetch him?"

She uttered an exclamation of joy. "Oh yes, go! go!—run! —quick!—that captain—bring him to me, and I'll love you!" She clasped his knees. He could not help shaking his head sorrowfully. "I'll bring him to you," said he in a faint voice. Then he turned his head and strode hastily to the staircase, his heart bursting with sobs.

When he reached the Place he found only the fine horse fastened at the door of the Logis Gondelaurier; the captain had just entered. He looked up to the roof of the church—La Esmeralda was still there, at the same spot, in the same posture. He made her a melancholy sign of the head, then set his back against one of the posts of the porch of the mansion, determined to wait until the captain came out.

It was at the Logis Gondelaurier one of those gala days that precede a marriage; Quasimodo saw many people enter, and nobody come away. Now and then he looked up to the roof of the church, and he saw that the gipsy girl did not stir from her place any more than himself. There came a groom, who untied the horse, and led him to the stable of the mansion.

The whole day was passed in this manner: Quasimodo against the post; La Esmeralda upon the roof; and Phœbus, no doubt, at the feet of Fleur-de-Lys.

At length night came, a dark, moonless night. In vain did Quasimodo fix his eye upon La Esmeralda—she soon faded into something white glimmering in the twilight, then quite disappeared from his view. All had vanished, all was black. Quasimodo now saw the light shining through the windows from top to bottom of the front of the Logis Gondelaurier; he saw the other windows of the Place lit up one after another; one after another, too, he saw the light disappear from them, till every one was dark, for he remained the whole evening at his post. The officer did not come away. When the latest passengers had returned home—when all the windows of the other houses were darkened—Quasimodo remained entirely alone, entirely in the dark. There was not then any *luminaire* in the Parvis of Notre-Dame.

However, the windows of the Logis Gondelaurier remained lighted, even after midnight. Quasimodo, motionless and attentive, saw passing to and fro behind the many-coloured panes a multitude of lively dancing shadows. Had he not been deaf, in proportion as the murmur of slumbering Paris died away, he would have heard more and more distinctly from within the Logis Gondelaurier the sounds of an evening entertainment, of laughter, and of music.

About one in the morning the company began to depart. Quasimodo, wrapped in darkness, looked at them all as they passed under the flambeau-lighted porch, but none of them was the captain.

He was full of melancholy thoughts; now and then he looked up into the air, like one weary of waiting. Great black clouds, heavy, torn, riven, were hanging like ragged festoons of crape under the starry arch of night.

At one of those moments he suddenly saw the long folding window that opened upon the balcony, whose stone balustrade projected above him, mysteriously open. The light glazed door admitted two persons through it upon the balcony, then softly closed behind them. They were a male and a female figure. It was not without difficulty that Quasimodo, in the dark, could recognise in the man the handsome captain, in the woman the young lady whom he had seen in the morning bidding the officer welcome from the same balcony. The Place was perfectly dark; and a double crimson curtain, which had fallen behind the glass door at the moment it had closed, intercepted almost every ray of light from the apartment within.

The young man and woman, as far as our deaf spectator could judge without hearing a word of what they said, appeared to abandon themselves to a very tender *tête-à-tête*. The young lady seemed to have permitted the officer to encircle her waist with his arm, and was gently resisting a kiss.

Quasimodo witnessed from below this scene, the more attractive as it was not intended to be witnessed. He contemplated that happiness, that beauty, with feelings of bitterness. After all, nature was not altogether silent in the poor devil; and his nervous system, strangely distorted as it was, was yet susceptible of excitement like another man's. He thought of the wretched share which Providence had dealt him—that woman, that the pleasures of love, were destined everlastingly to pass under his eyes without his ever doing more than witness the felicity of others. But that which pained him most of all in this spectacle—that which mingled indignation with his chagrin—was to think what the gipsy girl would suffer were she to behold it. True it was that the night was very dark, that La Esmeralda, if she had remained at the same place, as he doubted not she had, was very far off, and that it was all that he himself could do to distinguish the lovers on the balcony. This consoled him.

Meanwhile the conversation above became more and more animated. The young lady seemed to be entreating the officer to solicit nothing more from her. All that Quasimodo could distinguish was the fair clasped hands, the mingled smiles and tears, and the uplifted eyes of the young woman, and the eyes of the captain fixed ardently upon her.

Fortunately for the young lady, whose resistance was growing weaker, the door of the balcony suddenly reopened, and an old lady made her appearance; whereupon the young one looked confused, the officer chagrined, and they all three went in again.

A minute afterwards a horse came prancing under the porch, and the brilliant officer, wrapped in his night cloak, passed rapidly before Quasimodo.

The ringer let him turn the corner of the street, and then ran after him, with his monkey nimbleness, shouting, "Ho, there, captain!"

The captain stopped his horse. "What does the rascal want

with me?" said he, espying in the dark that out-of-the-way figure running hobblingly towards him.

Meanwhile Quasimodo had come up to him and boldly taken his horse by the bridle, saying, "Follow me, captain; there's somebody here that wants to speak to you."

"*Corne-Mahom!*" grumbled Phœbus, "here's a villainous ragged bird, that I think I've seen somewhere before. Hullo, master! won't you leave hold of my bridle?"

"Captain," answered the deaf man, "aren't you asking me who it is?"

"I tell thee to let go my horse," returned Phœbus impatiently. "What does the fellow want, hanging at my charger's rein? Dost thou take my horse for a gallows?"

Quasimodo, so far from leaving hold of the horse's bridle, was preparing to make him turn round. Unable to explain to himself the captain's resistance, he hastily said to him, "Come along, captain; it's a woman that's waiting for you;" then with an effort he added, "a woman that loves you."

"A rare scoundrel!" said the captain, "that thinks me obliged to go after every woman that loves me, or says she does. And, then, if she is but like thee, thou owl-faced villain! Tell her that sent thee that I'm going to be married, and that she may go to the devil."

"Hark ye!" cried Quasimodo, thinking to overcome his hesitation with a single word. "Come along, monseigneur; it's the gipsy girl that you know of."

This word did in fact make a great impression upon Phœbus, but it was not that which the deaf man expected from it. It will be remembered that our gallant officer had retired from the balcony with Fleur-de-Lys a few minutes before Quasimodo delivered the penitent out of the hands of Charmolue. Since then, in all his visits at the Logis Gondelaurier, he had been very careful to avoid mentioning that young woman—the recollection of whom, after all, was painful to him; and Fleur-de-Lys, on her part, had not deemed it politic to tell him that the gipsy girl was living. So Phœbus believed poor Similar, as he called her, to have been dead for a month or two. To which we must add that the captain had been thinking for a few moments of the profound darkness of the night, the supernatural ugliness and sepulchral voice of the messenger; that it was past midnight; that the street was as solitary as it had been the evening that the spectre monk had accosted him; and that his horse snorted at the sight of Quasimodo.

"The gipsy girl!" cried he, almost in a fright. "How now! Art thou come from the other world?" and so saying he laid his hand upon his dagger-hilt.

"Quick! quick!" said the deaf man, striving to turn the horse round; "this way."

Phœbus struck him a violent blow in the chest with the point of his boot.

Quasimodo's eye sparkled. He made a movement to throw himself upon the captain. But checking himself he said, "Ah, how happy you are, to have some one that loves you!"

He laid strong emphasis upon the words "some one," and leaving hold of the horse's bridle he said, "Go your way."

Phœbus spurred off, swearing. Quasimodo watched him plunge into the dark shades of the street. "Oh," whispered the poor deaf creature to himself, "to refuse that!"

He returned into Notre-Dame, lighted his lamp, and went up the tower again. As he had supposed, the gipsy girl was still at the same spot. The moment she perceived him coming she ran to meet him. "Alone!" cried she, clasping her beautiful hands in agony.

"I could not find him again," said Quasimodo coolly.

"You should have waited for him all night," returned she passionately.

He observed her angry gesture, and understood the reproof. "I'll watch him better another time," said he, hanging down his head.

"Get you gone!" said she.

He left her. She was dissatisfied with him. He had preferred being chid by her to giving her greater affliction. He had kept all the grief to himself.

From that day forward the gipsy saw no more of him; he came no longer to her cell. Now and then, indeed, she caught a distant glimpse of the ringer's countenance looking mournfully upon her from the top of one of the towers, but as soon as she perceived him he constantly disappeared.

We must admit that she was little afflicted by the voluntary absence of the poor hunchback. At the bottom of her heart she felt obliged to him for it. Nor was Quasimodo himself under any delusion about the matter.

She saw him no more, but she felt the presence of a good genius about her. Her provisions were renewed by an invisible hand during her sleep. One morning she found against her window a cage of birds. Over her cell there was a piece of sculpture that frightened her. She had repeatedly testified this in Quasimodo's presence. One morning (for all these things were done in the night-time) she saw it no longer—it had been broken off. He who had climbed up to that piece of carving must have risked his life.

Sometimes, in the evening, she heard the voice of one concealed under the penthouse of the steeple singing, as if to lull her to sleep, a melancholy and fantastic song, without rhyme or rhythm, such as a deaf man might make.

Oh, look not at the face,
Young maid, look at the heart:
The heart of a fine young man is often deformed;
There are some hearts will hold no love a long while.

Young maid, the pine's not fair to see,
Not fair to see as the poplar is,
But it keeps its leaves in winter-time.
Alas! it's vain to talk of that—
What is not fair ought not to be—
Beauty will only beauty love—
April looks not on January.

Beauty is perfection,
Beauty can do all,
Beauty is the only thing that does not shine by halves.

The crow flies but by day;
The owl flies but by night;
The swan flies night and day.

On waking one morning she saw in her window two bunches of flowers; one of them in a glass vessel, very beautiful and brilliant, but cracked: it had let all the water escape, and the flowers it contained were faded. The other vessel was of earthenware, rude and common, but had kept all the water, so that its flowers remained fresh and blooming.

We know not whether she did it intentionally, but La Esmeralda took the faded nosegay and wore it all day in her bosom.

That day she did not hear the voice from the tower sing.

She felt little concern about it. She passed her days in caressing Djali, watching the door of the Logis Gondelaurier, talking low to herself about Phœbus, and crumbling her bread to the swallows.

And then she had altogether ceased to see or to hear Quasimodo. The poor ringer seemed to have departed from the church. One night, however, as she lay awake, thinking of her handsome captain, she heard a strong breathing near her cell.

She rose up affrighted, and saw by the moonlight a shapeless mass lying across the front of her door. It was Quasimodo sleeping there upon the stones.

CHAPTER V

THE KEY OF THE PORTE ROUGE

MEANWHILE public rumour had acquainted the archdeacon with the miraculous manner in which the gipsy girl had been saved. When he learnt this, he felt he knew not what. He had reconciled his mind to the thought of La Esmeralda's death, and so he had become calm: he had gone to the bottom of the greatest grief possible. The human heart (and Dom Claude had meditated upon these matters) cannot contain more than a certain quantity of despair. When the sponge is thoroughly soaked, the sea may pass over it without its imbibing one tear more.

Now, La Esmeralda being dead, the sponge was thoroughly soaked; all was over for Dom Claude upon this earth. But to feel that she was alive, and Phœbus too—that was the recommencement of torture, of pangs, of alternations, of life, and Dom Claude was weary of all that.

When this piece of intelligence reached him he shut himself up in his cloister cell. He appeared neither at the conferences of the chapter nor at the services in the church. He shut his door against every one, even against the bishop. He kept himself thus immured for several weeks. He was thought to be ill, and so indeed he was.

What was he doing, shut up thus? With what thoughts was the unfortunate man contending? Was he making a final struggle against his formidable passion? Was he combining some final plan of death for her and perdition for himself?

His Jehan, his cherished brother, his spoiled child, came once to his door, knocked, swore, entreated, announced himself ten times over—but Claude kept the door shut.

He passed whole days with his face close against the casement of his window. From that window, situated in the cloister, he could see the cell of La Esmeralda; he often saw herself, with her goat—sometimes with Quasimodo. He remarked the deaf wretch's assiduities, his obedience, his delicate and submissive behaviour to the gipsy girl. He recollected—for he had a good memory, and memory is the tormentor of the jealous—he recollected the singular look which the ringer had cast upon the dancing-girl on a certain evening. He asked himself what motive could have urged Quasimodo to save her. He was an eye-witness to a thousand little scenes that passed between the gipsy and the ringer; the action of which, as seen at that distance and commented on by his passion, he thought very tender. He had his misgivings with respect to feminine capriciousness. Then he felt confusedly arising within him a jealousy such as he had never anticipated—a jealousy that made him redden with shame and indignation. "As for the captain," thought he, "that might pass; but this one!" And the idea quite overpowered him.

His nights were dreadful. Since he had learned that the gipsy girl was alive, all those cold images of spectres and the grave which had beset him for a whole day had vanished from his spirit, and the flesh began again to torment him.

Each night his delirious imagination represented to him La Esmeralda in all the attitudes that had most strongly excited his passion. He beheld her leaning faint upon the poniarded captain—her eyes closed—her fair, naked neck crimsoned with the blood of Phœbus; at that moment of wild delight at which the archdeacon had imprinted on her pale lips that kiss of which the unfortunate girl, half dying as she was, had felt the burning pressure. Again, he beheld her, undressed by the savage hands of the torturers, letting them thrust, all naked, into the horrid iron-screwed boot her little foot, her round and delicate leg, her white and supple knee; and then she saw that ivory knee alone appearing, all below it being enveloped in Torterue's horrible apparatus. And again, he figured to himself the young girl, in her slight chemise, with the rope about her neck, with bare feet and uncovered shoulders, as he had seen her on the day of penance. These voluptuous images made him clench his hands, and sent a shiver through his nerves.

One night in particular they so cruelly inflamed his priestly virgin blood that he tore his pillow with his teeth, leaped out of bed, threw a surplice over his nightgown, and went out of his cell, with his lamp in his hand, half-naked, wild, with fire in his eyes.

He knew where to find the key of the Porte Rouge or Red Door, opening from the cloister into the church; and as the reader is aware, he always carried about him a key of the tower staircase.

That night La Esmeralda had fallen asleep in her little chamber, full of forgetfulness, of hope, and of flattering thoughts. She had been sleeping for some time, dreaming, as usual, of Phœbus, when she thought she heard some noise about her. Her sleep was light and airy—the sleep of a bird—the slightest thing awakened her. She opened her eyes. The night was very dark. Yet she discerned, at the little window, a face looking in upon her; there was a lamp, which cast its light upon this apparition. The moment that it perceived itself to be observed by La Esmeralda that face blew out the lamp. Nevertheless the young girl had caught a glimpse of its features—her eyelids dropped with terror. "Oh," said she in a faint voice, "the priest!"

All her past misfortune flashed upon her mind, and she fell back frozen with horror upon her bed.

A moment after, she felt a contact the whole length of her body, which made her shudder so violently that she started and sat up in bed wide awake and furious. The priest had glided up to her, and threw both his arms round her. She strove to cry out, but could not.

"Begone, monster! begone, murderer!" said she in a voice low and faltering with anger and dread.

"Mercy, mercy!" murmured the priest, pressing his burning lips to her shoulders.

She seized his bald head between her hands by its remaining hairs, and strove to repel his kisses as if he had been biting her.

"Mercy!" repeated the wretched man. "Didst thou but know what is my love for thee!—'tis fire—'tis molten lead—'tis a thousand daggers in my heart!"

And he held back both her arms with superhuman strength. Quite desperate, "Let me go," she cried, "or I'll spit in your face!"

He left hold. "Vilify me—strike me—be wicked—do what thou wilt," said he, "but oh, have mercy, and love me!"

Then she struck him with the fury of a child. She drew up her pretty hands to tear his face. "Begone, demon!"

"Love me, love me, for pity's sake!" cried the poor priest, answering her blows with his unwelcome caresses.

All at once she felt that he was overpowering her. "There must be an end of this," said he, grinding his teeth. She felt a lascivious hand wander over her. She made a last effort, and cried out, "Help me! help me! a vampire! a vampire!"

But nothing came. Only Djali was awake, and bleated with anguish.

"Silence!" said the panting priest.

Suddenly, in the midst of her struggling, the gipsy's hand came in contact with something cold and metallic—it was Quasimodo's whistle. She seized it with a convulsion of hope, put it to her lips, and blew with all her remaining strength. The whistle sounded clear, shrill, and piercing.

"What's that?" said the priest.

Almost at the same instant he felt himself dragged away by a vigorous arm. The cell was dark—he could not clearly distinguish who it was that held him thus; but he heard some one's teeth chattering with rage, and there was just light enough scattered in the darkness for him to see shining over his head a large cutlass blade.

The priest thought he could discern the form of Quasimodo. He supposed it could be no one else. He recollected having stumbled, in entering, against a bundle of something that was lying across the doorway outside. Yet as the newcomer uttered not a word he knew not what to think. He threw himself upon the arm that held the cutlass, crying out, "Quasimodo!" forgetting, at that moment of distress, that Quasimodo was deaf.

In a trice the priest was thrown upon the floor, and felt a knee of lead weighing upon his breast. By the angular impression of that knee he recognised Quasimodo. But what was he to do? how was he to make himself known to the other? Night made the deaf man blind.

He was lost. The young girl, pitiless as an enraged tigress, interfered not to save him. The cutlass was approaching his head—the moment was critical. Suddenly his adversary appeared seized with hesitation. "No blood upon her," said he, in an under voice. It was, in fact, the voice of Quasimodo.

Then the priest felt the great hand dragging him by the foot out of the cell—outside he was to die. Luckily for him, the moon had been risen for a few moments.

When they had crossed the threshold of the chamber its pale rays fell upon the features of the priest. Quasimodo looked in his face—a tremor came over him—he quitted his hold of the priest and shrunk back.

The gipsy girl, having come forward to the door of her cell, was surprised to see them suddenly change parts—for now it was the priest that threatened, and Quasimodo was the suppliant.

The priest, heaping gestures of anger and reproof upon the deaf man, motioned to him passionately to withdraw.

The deaf man cast down his eyes, then came and knelt before the gipsy girl's door. "Monseigneur," said he, in a tone of gravity and resignation, "afterwards you will do what you please—but kill me first."

So saying, he presented his cutlass to the priest; and the priest, who had lost all command of himself, was going to seize it. But the girl was quicker than he; she snatched the cutlass out of Quasimodo's hands, and burst into a frantic laugh. "Approach," said she to the priest.

She held the blade aloft. The priest hesitated. She would certainly have struck. "You dare not approach now, you coward," she resumed. Then she added, in a pitiless accent, and well knowing that it would be plunging a red-hot iron into the heart of the priest, "Ha! I know that Phœbus is not dead!"

The priest gave Quasimodo a kick which threw him down upon the stones, and then plunged back, all trembling with rage, under the vault of the staircase.

When he was gone Quasimodo picked up the whistle that had just saved the gipsy girl. "It was growing rusty," said he, as he gave it her; and then he left her to herself.

The young girl, quite overpowered by this violent scene, fell exhausted upon her couch, and began to weep and sob bitterly—again the horizon was growing dismal.

As for the priest, he had groped his way back into his cell.

'Twas done—Dom Claude was jealous of Quasimodo. He repeated pensively to himself his fatal sentence—"No one shall have her."

BOOK X

CHAPTER I

GRINGOIRE HAS SEVERAL GOOD IDEAS IN THE RUE DES BERNARDINS

FROM the time that Pierre Gringoire had seen the turn that all this affair was taking, and that hanging by the neck and other disagreeables were decidedly in store for the principal characters of this drama, he had felt no anxiety to take part in it. The Truands, amongst whom he had remained, considering, as he did, that, after all, they were the best company in Paris—the Truands had continued to feel interested for the gipsy girl. He thought that very natural in people who, like herself, had nothing but Charmolue and Torterue in prospect, and did not, like him, Gringoire, mount aloft in the regions of imagination between the wings of Pegasus. He had learned from their discourse that his bride of the broken pitcher had found refuge in Notre-Dame, and he was very glad of it. But he did not even feel tempted to go and see her there. He sometimes thought of the little goat, and that was all. In the daytime he performed feats of strength to get his bread; and at night he was elaborating a paper against the Bishop of Paris, for he remembered being drenched by his mill-wheels, and bore malice against him for it. He was also engaged in writing a commentary upon the fine work of Baudry-le-Rouge, Bishop of Noyon and Tournay, *De cupâ petrarum,* which had given him a violent inclination for architecture, a propensity which had supplanted in his breast his passion for hermetics, of which, too, it was but a natural consequence, seeing that there is an intimate connection between the hermetical philosophy and stonework. Gringoire had passed from the love of an idea to the love of the substance.

One day he had stopped near the church of Saint-Germain-l'Auxerrois, at the corner of a building called *Le For-l'Evêque,* which was opposite another called *Le For-le-Roi.* There was at this For-l'Evêque a beautiful chapel of the fourteenth century, the chancel of which was towards the street—Gringoire was examining devoutly its external sculpture. It was one of those moments of selfish, exclusive, and supreme enjoyment, in which the artist sees nothing in the world but his art, and the world itself in that art. All at once he felt a hand placed heavily on his shoulder; he turned round—it was his old friend, his old master, the archdeacon.

He was quite confounded. It was long since he had seen the archdeacon; and Dom Claude was one of those grave and ardent beings a meeting with whom always disturbs the equilibrium of a sceptical philosopher.

The archdeacon for some moments kept silence, during which Gringoire had leisure to observe him. He found Dom Claude much altered—pale as a winter morning; his eyes hollow, his hair almost white. The priest was the first to break this silence by saying in a calm but freezing tone, "How are you, Maître Pierre?"

"As to my health," answered Gringoire, "why, it's so so—I believe—on the whole, pretty good. I do not take too much of anything. You know, master, the secret of being well, according to Hippocrates—*id est: cibi, potus, somni, venus, omnia moderata sint.*"

"You have no care, then, Maître Pierre?" resumed the archdeacon, looking steadfastly at Gringoire.

"Faith, not I."

"And what are you doing now?"

"You see, master; I am examining the cutting of these stones, and the style in which this bas-relief is thrown out."

The priest began to smile, but with that bitter smile which raises only one of the extremities of the mouth. "And that amuses you?"

"It's paradise," exclaimed Gringoire. And leaning over the sculpture with the fascinated air of a demonstrator of living phenomena—"Now, for example, do you not think that that metamorphosis, in *baissetaille*, is executed with a great deal of skill, delicacy, and patience? Look at that small column—was ever capital entwined with leaves more graceful or more exquisitely touched by the chisel? Here are three alto-relievos by Jean Maillevin. They are not the finest specimens of that great genius. Nevertheless, the simplicity, the sweetness of those faces, the sportiveness of the attitudes and the draperies, and that undefinable charm which is mingled with all the imperfections, make the miniature figures so very light and delicate—perhaps even too much so. You do not find it interesting?"

"Oh yes," said the priest.

"And if you were to see the interior of the chapel!" continued the poet, with his loquacious enthusiasm. "Sculpture in all directions! It's as full as the heart of a cabbage! The style of the chancel is most heavenly, and so peculiar that I have never seen anything like it anywhere else."

Dom Claude interrupted him. "You are happy, then?"

Gringoire answered with vivacity,—

"Upon my honour, yes! At one time I loved women—then animals—now I love stones. They are quite as amusing as animals or women, and not so false."

The priest passed his hand across his forehead. It was a gesture habitual with him. "Indeed!"

"Hark you," said Gringoire, "one has one's enjoyments." He took the arm of the priest, who yielded to his guidance, and led him under the staircase turret of the For-l'Evêque. "There's a staircase!" he exclaimed. "Whenever I see it I am happy. That flight of steps is the most simple and the most uncommon in Paris—every step is hollowed underneath. Its beauty and simplicity consist in the circumstance of the steps, which are a foot broad or thereabouts, being interlaced, morticed, jointed, enchained, enchased, set one in the other, and biting into each other, in a way that's truly both substantial and pretty."

"And you desire nothing?" said the priest.

"No!"

"And you regret nothing?"

"Neither regret nor desire. I have arranged my mode of life."

"What man arranges," said Claude, "circumstances disarrange."

"I am a Pyrrhonean philosopher," answered Gringoire, "and I hold everything in equilibrium."

"And how do you earn your living?"

"I still write epopees and tragedies now and then; but what brings me in the most is that industrious talent of mine which you are aware of, master—carrying pyramids of chairs on my teeth."

"A low occupation for a philosopher."

"It's equilibrium, though," said Gringoire. "When one gets an idea in one's head, one finds it in everything."

"I know it," answered the archdeacon.

After a short silence the priest continued, "And yet you are poor enough?"

"Poor—yes; but not unhappy."

At that moment the sound of horses was heard, and our two interlocutors saw filing off at the end of a street a company of the king's archers, with their lances raised, and an officer at their head. The cavalcade was brilliant, and its march resounded on the pavement.

"How you look at that officer!" said Gringoire to the archdeacon.

"I think I know him," was the reply.

"How do you call him?"

"I believe," said Claude, "his name is Phœbus de Chateaupers."

"Phœbus! A curious sort of a name. There's Phœbus, too, Count of Foix. I recollect I knew a girl once who never swore by any other name."

"Come hither," said the priest. "I have something to say to you."

Since the passing of that troop a degree of agitation was perceptible through the frozen exterior of the archdeacon. He walked on. Gringoire followed him, accustomed to obey him, like all who had once approached that being so commanding. They reached in silence the Rue des Bernardins, which was pretty clear of people. Dom Claude stopped.

"What have you to say to me, master?" asked Gringoire.

"Do you not think," answered the archdeacon, with an air of profound reflection, "that the dress of those cavaliers whom we have just seen is handsomer than yours and mine?"

Gringoire shook his head. "No; 'faith, I like my red and yellow gonelle better than those iron and steel scales. A pleasant sort of thing to make a noise in going along, like an iron-wharf in an earthquake!"

"Then, Gringoire, you have never envied those fine fellows in their warlike hacquetons?"

"Envied what, monsieur the archdeacon?—their strength, their armour, their discipline? Give me rather philosophy and independence in rags. I would rather be the head of a fly than the tail of a lion."

"That's singular," said the musing priest. "A fine uniform is a fine thing nevertheless."

Gringoire, seeing him pensive, left him to go and admire the porch of a neighbouring house. He returned, clapping his hands. "If you were less occupied with the fine clothes of the soldiers, monsieur the archdeacon, I would beg you to go and see that doorway. I have always said that the Sieur Aubry's house has the finest entrance that ever was seen."

"Pierre Gringoire," said the archdeacon, "what have you done with that little gipsy dancing-girl?"

"La Esmeralda? You change the conversation very abruptly."

"Was she not your wife?"

"Yes, by dint of a broken pitcher. We were in for it for four years. By-the-bye," added Gringoire, looking at the archdeacon with a half-bantering air, "you think of her still, then?"

"And you—do you no longer think of her?"

"Not much—I have so many things!—My God, how pretty the little goat was!"

"Did not that Bohemian girl save your life?"

"Egad, that's true."

"Well, what became of her? What have you done with her?"

"I can't tell you. I believe they've hanged her."

"You believe?"

"I'm not sure. When I saw there was hanging in the case I kept out of the business."

"And that's all you know about her?"

"Stay. I was told she had taken refuge in Notre-Dame, and that she was there in safety—and I'm delighted at it—and I've not been able to find out whether the goat escaped with her—and that's all I know about the matter."

"I will tell you more about it," cried Dom Claude; and his voice, till then low, deliberate, and hollow, had become like thunder. "She has indeed taken refuge in Notre-Dame. But in three days justice will drag her again from thence, and she will be hanged at the Grève. There is a decree of the Parliament for it."

"That's a pity," said Gringoire.

The priest in a moment had become cool and calm again.

"And who the devil," continued the poet, "has taken the trouble to solicit a sentence of reintegration? Could they not leave the Parliament alone? Of what consequence can it be that a poor girl takes shelter under the buttresses of Notre-Dame among the swallows' nests?"

"There are Satans in the world," answered the archdeacon.

"That's a devilish bad piece of work," observed Gringoire.

The archdeacon resumed, after a short silence—"She saved your life, then?"

"Among my good friends the Truands. I was within an inch of being hanged. They would have been sorry for it now."

"Will you, then, do nothing for her?"

"I should rejoice to be of service, Dom Claude; but if I were to bring a bad piece of business about my ears!"

"What can it signify?"

"The deuce!—what can it signify! You are very kind, master. I have two great works begun."

The priest struck his forehead. In spite of his affected calmness, from time to time a violent gesture revealed his inward struggles.

"How is she to be saved?"

"Master," said Gringoire, "I will answer you—*Il padelt*—which means in the Turkish, 'God is our hope.'"

"How is she to be saved?" repeated Claude, ruminating.

Gringoire in his turn struck his forehead.

"Hark you, master. I have some imagination—I will find expedients for you. What if we were to entreat the king's mercy?"

"Mercy!—of Louis XI.!"

"Why not?"

"Go take from the tiger his bone!"

Gringoire began to rummage for other expedients.

"Well—stay—shall I address a memorial to the midwives, declaring that the girl is pregnant?"

At this the priest's sunken eyeballs glared.

"Pregnant! Fellow, do you know anything about it?"

Gringoire was terrified at his manner. He hastened to say, "Oh, not I. Our marriage was a regular *foris-maritagium.* I'm altogether out of it. But, at any rate, one should obtain a respite."

"Madness!—infamy!—hold thy peace!"

"You are wrong to be angry," muttered Gringoire. "One gets a respite—that does no harm to anybody, and it puts forty deniers parisis into the pockets of the midwives, who are poor women."

The priest heard him not. "She must go from thence nevertheless," murmured he. "The sentence is to be put in force within three days—otherwise, it would not be valid.—That Quasimodo! Women have very depraved tastes." He raised his voice—"Maître Pierre, I have well considered the matter. There is but one means of saving her."

"And what is it? For my part, I see none."

"Hark ye, Maître Pierre—remember that you owe your life to her. I will tell you candidly my idea. The church is watched day and night; no one is allowed to come out but those who have been seen to go in. Thus you can go in. You shall come, and I will take you to her. You will change clothes with her. She will take your doublet, and you will take her petticoat."

"So far so good," observed the philosopher; "and what then?"

"What then? Why, she will go out in your clothes, and you will remain in hers. You may get hanged, perhaps—but she will be saved."

Gringoire scratched his ear with a very serious air.

"Well," said he, "that's an idea would never have come into my head of itself."

At Dom Claude's unexpected proposal the open and benignant countenance of the poet had become instantaneously overcast, like a smiling Italian landscape when an unlucky gust of wind suddenly dashes a cloud across the sun.

"Well, Gringoire, what say you to the plan?"

"I say, master, that I shall not be hanged perhaps, but that I shall be hanged indubitably."

"That does not concern us."

"The plague!" said Gringoire.

"She saved your life. It's a debt you have to pay."

"There are many others I don't pay."

"Maître Pierre, it must absolutely be so."

The archdeacon spoke imperiously.

"Hark you, Dom Claude," answered the poet, in great consternation. "You cling to that idea, and you are wrong. I don't see why I should get myself hanged instead of another."

"What can you have to attach you so strongly to life?"

"Ah, a thousand reasons."

"What are they, pray?"

"What are they? The air—the sky—the morning—the evening—the moonlight—my good friends the Truands—our merry-makings with the old women—the fine architecture of Paris to study—three great books to write, one of them against the bishop and his mills—more than I can tell. Anaxagoras used to say he had come into the world to admire the sun. And then I have the felicity of passing the whole of my days, from morning till night, with a man of genius—no other than I myself—and that's very agreeable."

"Oh, thou head, fit only to make a rattle of!" muttered the archdeacon. "Speak, then—who preserved that life thou makest out to be so charming? To whom art thou indebted for the privilege of breathing that air, of seeing that sky, of being still able to amuse thy larklike spirit with trash and fooleries? Had it not been for her, where wouldst thou be? Thou wilt have her die, then?—she through whom thou livest. Thou wilt have her die—that creature so lovely, so sweet, so adorable—a creature necessary to the light of the world—more divine than divinity itself?—while thou, half sage, half fool, a mere sketch of something, a sort of vegetable which fancies it walks and thinks, wouldst continue to live with the life thou hast stolen from her, as useless as a taper at noon-day! Come, Gringoire, a little pity! Be generous in thy turn—she has set the example."

The priest was vehement. Gringoire listened to him at first with an air of indecision, then became moved, and concluded with making a tragical grimace which likened his wan countenance to that of a new-born child in a fit of the colic.

"You are very pathetic!" said he, wiping away a tear. "Well, I'll think of it. That's an odd idea of yours. After all," pursued he, after a moment's silence, "who knows?—perhaps they'll not hang me; there's many a slip between the cup and the lip. When they find me in that box so grotesquely muffled in cap and petticoat, perhaps they'll burst out laughing. And if they do hang me, what then? The rope—that's a death like any other. Or rather, it is not a death like any other. It's a death worthy of the sage who has been wavering all his life—a death which is neither fish nor flesh, like the mind of the true sceptic—a death fully marked with Pyrrhonism and hesitation—which holds the medium between heaven and earth —which leaves you in suspense. It's the death of a philosopher, and I was predestined to it, perhaps. 'Tis fine to die as one has lived."

The priest interrupted him. "Is it agreed?"

"What is death after all?" continued Gringoire heroically. "A disagreeable moment—a turnpike-gate—the passage from little to nothing. Some one having asked Cercidas of Megalopolis whether he could die willingly: 'Why should I not?' answered he; 'for after my death I shall see those great men, Pythagoras among the philosophers, Hecatæus among the historians, Homer among the poets, Olympus among the musicians.'"

The archdeacon held out his hand to him. "Then it's settled? You will come to-morrow?"

This gesture brought Gringoire back to reality.

"'Faith, no!" said he, with the tone of a man just awaking. "Be hanged! It's too absurd!—I will not."

"Fare you well, then;" and the archdeacon added between his teeth, "I shall find thee again."

"I don't wish that devil of a man to find me again so," thought Gringoire, and he ran after Dom Claude.

"Stay, monsieur the archdeacon," said he; "old friends should not fall out. You take an interest in that girl—my wife, I mean. That's all right. You have thought of a stratagem for getting her safe out of Notre-Dame; but your plan is extremely unpleasant for me, Gringoire. Now if I could suggest another myself! I beg to say a most luminous inspiration has just come over me. If I had an expedient for extricating her from her sorry plight without compromising my neck in the smallest degree with a slip knot, what would you say? Would not that suffice you? Is it absolutely necessary that I should be hanged to satisfy you?"

The priest was tearing the buttons from his cassock with impatience. "Thou everlasting stream of words! What is your plan?"

"Yes," continued Gringoire, talking to himself, and touching his nose with his forefinger in sign of deep cogitation, "that's it! The Truands are fine fellows. The tribe of Egypt love her. They will rise at the first word. Nothing easier. A bold stroke. By means of the disorder they will easily carry her off. To-morrow evening. Nothing would please them better."

"The means!—speak!" said the priest, shaking him.

Gringoire turned majestically towards him: "Let me alone—you see I am composing." He reflected again for a few seconds, then began to clap his hands at his thought, exclaiming, "Admirable!—certain success!"

"The means?" repeated Claude angrily.

Gringoire was radiant.

"Come hither," said he; "let me tell you in a whisper. It's a counter-plot that's really capital and that will get us all out of the scrape. Egad! you must allow I'm no simpleton."

He stopped short. "Ah, and the little goat—is she with the girl?"

"Yes—the devil take thee!"

"Why, they would have hanged her too, wouldn't they?"

"What's that to me?"

"Yes, they would have hanged her. They hanged a sow last month, sure enough. The executioner likes that—he eats the animal after. To think of hanging my pretty Djali! Poor little lamb!"

"A curse upon thee!" cried Dom Claude. "The hangman is thyself. What means of safety hast thou found, fellow? Wilt thou never be delivered of thy scheme?"

"Softly, master. You shall hear."

Gringoire leaned aside and spoke very low in the archdeacon's ear, casting an anxious look from one end of the street to the other, where, however, no one was passing. When he had done, Dom Claude took his hand and said coolly, "'Tis well. Till to-morrow, fare you well."

"Till to-morrow," repeated Gringoire; and while the archdeacon withdrew one way he went off the other, saying low to himself, "This is a grand affair, Monsieur Pierre Gringoire. Never mind; it's not to be said that because one's of little account one's to be frightened at a great undertaking. Biton carried a great bull on his shoulders—wagtails, linnets, and buntings cross the ocean."

CHAPTER II

TURN TRUAND

On re-entering the cloister the archdeacon found at the door of his cell his brother, Jehan du Moulin, who was waiting for him, and who had whiled away the tediousness of expectation by drawing on the wall with a piece of charcoal a profile of his elder brother, embellished with a nose of immoderate dimensions.

Dom Claude scarcely looked at his brother; he was full of other ruminations. That joyous, roguish countenance, the irradiation of which had so often cleared away the gloom from the physiognomy of the priest, had now no power to dissipate the mist which was each day gathering thicker and thicker over that corrupt, mephitic, and stagnant soul.

"Brother," said Jehan timidly, "I am come to see you."

The archdeacon did not so much as raise his eyes towards him. "Well?"

"Brother," continued the hypocrite, "you are so good to me, and give me such excellent advice, that I always come back to you."

"What next?"

"Alas! brother, you were very right when you used to say to me, 'Jehan, Jehan, *cessat doctorum doctrina, discipulorum disciplina*. Jehan, be prudent. Jehan, be studious. Jehan, do not go out of college at night without lawful occasion and leave of the master. Do not beat the Picards. *Noli, Joannes, verberare Picardos.* Do not grow old like an unlettered ass, *quasi asinus illiteratus*, amidst the litter of the schools. Jehan, go every evening to chapel, and sing an anthem with a verse and prayer to our lady the glorious Virgin Mary. Alas! how excellent was that advice!"

"And what then?"

"Brother, you see before you a guilty wretch, a criminal, a miscreant, a libertine, a monster! My dear brother, Jehan has treated your gracious counsels as dross and straw, fit only to be trampled under foot. Well am I chastised for it—and God Almighty is exceeding just. So long as I had money, I spent it in feasting, folly, and joviality. Oh, how grim-faced and vile to look back upon is that debauchery which appears so charming in prospect! Now I have not a single blanc left; I have sold my table-cloth, my shirt, and my towel. A merry life no longer—the bright taper is extinguished, and nothing is left me but its noisome snuff, which stinks under my nostrils. The girls mock at me. I drink water. I am tormented with remorse and creditors."

"Go on," said the archdeacon.

"Alas! dearest brother, I would fain lead a better life. I come to you full of contrition. I am penitent. I confess my faults. I beat my breast with heavy blows. You are very right to wish I should one day become a licentiate and sub-monitor of the Torchi College. I now feel a remarkable vocation for that office. But I have no ink left—I must buy some; I have no pens left—I must buy some; I have no paper left, no books left—I must buy some. I have great need of a little money for those purposes; and I come to you, brother, with my heart full of contrition."

"Is that all?"

"Yes," said the scholar; "a little money."

"I have none."

The scholar then said, with an air at once grave and decided.

"Well, brother, I am sorry to inform you that I have received from other quarters very advantageous offers and proposals. You will not give me any money? No? In that case I will turn Truand."

On pronouncing this monstrous word he assumed the part of an Ajax expecting to see the thunderbolt fall on his head.

The archdeacon said to him coolly, "Turn Truand, then."

Jehan made him a low bow, and redescended the cloister staircase whistling.

Just as he was passing through the court of the cloisters, under the window of his brother's cell, he heard that window open, raised his head, and saw the archdeacon's severe face looking through the opening. "Get thee to the devil!" said Dom Claude; "this is the last money thou shalt have of me."

So saying, the priest threw out a purse to Jehan, which raised a large bump on his forehead, and with which he set off, at once angry and pleased, like a dog that has been pelted with marrow bones.

CHAPTER III

VIVE LA JOIE

THE reader will not perhaps have forgotten that a part of the Court of Miracles was enclosed within the ancient wall of the town, a great number of the towers of which were beginning at that time to fall into decay. One of these towers had been converted into a place of entertainment by the Truands. There was a *cabaret* or public-house on the lowest floor, and the rest was carried on in the upper stories. This tower was the point the most alive, and consequently the most hideous, of the Truandry. It was a sort of monstrous hive, which was humming day and night. At night, when all the remainder of the rabble were asleep—when not a lighted window was to be seen in the dingy fronts of the houses in the square—when not a sound was heard to issue from its innumerable families, from those swarms of thieves, loose women, and stolen or bastard children—the joyous tower might always be distinguished by the noise which proceeded from it, by the crimson light which, gleaming at once from the air-holes, the windows, the crevices in the gaping walls, escaped, as it were, from every pore.

The cellar, then, formed the public-house. The descent to it was through a low door and down a steep staircase. Over the door there was, by way of sign, a marvellous daub representing new-coined sols and dead chickens, with this punning inscription underneath: *Aux sonneurs pour les trépassés*—that is, "The ringers for the dead."

One evening, at the moment when the curfew bell was ringing from all the steeples in Paris, the sergeants of the watch, had they been permitted to enter the formidable Court of Miracles, might have remarked that still greater tumult than usual was going on in the tavern of the Truands, that they were drinking deeper and swearing louder. Without, in the square, were a number of groups conversing in low tones, as if some great plot was hatching; and here and there a fellow, squatted down, was sharpening a sorry iron blade upon a stone.

Meanwhile, in the tavern itself, wine and gaming diverted the minds of the Truandry so powerfully from the ideas which had occupied them that evening, that it would have been difficult to have divined from the conversation of the drinkers what was the affair in agitation. Only they had a gayer appearance than usual, and between the legs of each of them was seen glittering some weapon or other—a pruning-hook, an axe, a large backsword, or the crook of an old hackbut.

The apartment, of a circular form, was very spacious; but the tables were so close together and the tipplers so numerous, that the whole contents of the tavern—men, women, benches, beer-jugs, the drinkers, the sleepers, the gamblers, the able-bodied, the crippled—seemed thrown pell-mell together with about as much order and arrangement as a heap of oyster-shells. A few greasy candles were burning upon the tables; but the grand luminary of the tavern, that which sustained in the pot-house the character of the chandelier in an opera-house, was the fire. That cellar was so damp that the fire was never allowed to go out in it even in the height of summer: an immense fireplace, with a carved mantelpiece, and thickset with heavy iron dogs and kitchen utensils, had in it, then, one of those large fires composed of wood and turf, which at night in a village street on the Continent cast so red a reflection through the windows of some forge upon the wall opposite. A large dog, gravely seated in the ashes, was turning before the glowing fuel a spit loaded with different sorts of meat.

In spite of the confusion, after the first glance, amid this multitude three principal groups might be distinguished, pressing around three several personages with whom the reader is already acquainted. One of these personages, fantastically bedizened with many an Oriental gaud, was Mathias Hungadi Spicali, Duke of Egypt and Bohemia. The old rogue was seated on a table, with his legs crossed and his finger in the air, exhibiting in a loud voice his skill in white and black magic to many a gaping face which surrounded him. Another set were gathering thick around our old friend, the valiant King of Tunis, armed to the teeth; and Clopin Trouillefou, with a very serious air and in a low voice, was superintending the ransacking of an enormous cask full of arms, staved wide before him, from which were issuing in profusion axes, swords, firelocks, coats of mail, lance and pike heads, crossbow bolts and arrows, like apples and grapes out of a cornucopia. Each one was taking something from the heap; one a morion, another a long rapier, and a third the cross-handled *misericorde* or small dagger. The children themselves were arming, and even the veriest cripples without either legs or thighs, all barbed and cuirassed, were moving about on their seats between the legs of the drinkers, like so many large beetles.

And lastly, a third audience, the most noisy, the most jovial, and the most numerous of all, were crowding the benches and tables from the midst of which a flute-like voice, haranguing and swearing, proceeded from under a heavy suit of armour, all complete from the casque to the spurs. The individual who had thus screwed himself up in full panoply was so lost under his warlike trappings that nothing was seen of his person but a red, impudent, turn-up nose, a lock of fair hair, red lips, and a pair of bold-looking eyes. His belt was full of daggers and poniards; a large sword hung by his side; a rusty cross-bow was on his left, and an immense wine-pot before him; besides a strapping wench, with her breast all open, seated on his right. All the mouths around him were laughing, swearing, and drinking.

Add to these twenty secondary groups; the waiters, male and female, running backwards and forwards with pitchers on their heads; the gamesters stooping over the *billes* (a rude sort of billiards), the *merèlles,* the dice, the *vachettes,* the exciting game of the *tringlett* (a kind of backgammon); quarrels in one corner—kisses in another—and some idea may then be formed of the whole collective scene; over which wavered the light of a great flaming fire, making a thousand grotesque and enormous shadows dance upon the tavern walls.

With respect to noise, the place might be likened to the interior of a bell in full peal.

The great dripping-pan before the fire, in which a shower of grease was crackling from the spit, filled up, with its unintermitted yelping, the intervals of those thousand dialogues which crossed each other in all directions from one side to another of the great circular room.

Amidst all this uproar there was, quite at one side of the tavern, upon the bench within the great open fireplace, a philosopher meditating with his feet in the ashes and his eye upon the burning brands. It was Pierre Gringoire.

"Come! quick! make haste! get under arms! we must march in an hour," said Clopin Trouillefou to his Argotiers.

A girl was humming an air,—

"Father and mother, good-night;
The latest up rake the fire."

Two card-players were disputing. "Knave," cried the reddest-faced of the two, shaking his fist at the other, "I'll mark thee. Thou might go and take Mistrigi's place in Messeigneur the King's own card-party."

"O Lord!" bawled one whom his nasal pronunciation showed to be a Norman, "we're all heaped together here like the saints at Caillouville."

"My lads," said the Duke of Egypt to his auditory, speaking in an affected, canting tone, "the witches of France go to the sabbath without ointment, broomstick, or anything to ride on, with a few magical words only. The witches of Italy have always a he-goat that waits for them at their door. All of them are bound to go out up the chimney."

The voice of the young fellow armed *cap-à-pie* was heard above the general hum. "Noël! Noël!" cried he; "so this is my first day in armour! A Truand! I'm a Truand, *ventre de Christ!* Fill my glass. Friends, my name is Jehan Frollo du Moulin, and I'm a gentleman. It's my opinion that if God were a gendarme he'd turn housebreaker. Brethren, we're going upon a noble expedition. We're of the valiant. Besiege the church—force the doors—bring away the pretty girl—save her from the judges—save her from the priests—dismantle the cloister—burn the bishop in his house—all that we shall do in less time than a burgomaster takes to eat a spoonful of soup. Our cause is just—we'll plunder Notre-Dame—and that's all about it. We'll hang up Quasimodo. Do you know Quasimodo, mesdemoiselles? Have you ever seen him work himself out of breath upon the big bell on a Whitsun holiday? *Corne du Père!* but it's very fine. You'd say it was a devil mounted upon a great gaping muzzle. Hark ye, my friends—I'm a Truand from the bottom of my heart—I'm an Argotier in my soul—I'm a Cagou born. I was very rich, and I've spent all I had. My mother wanted to make me an officer; my father, a subdeacon; my aunt, a councillor of the inquests; my grandmother, king's prothonotary; my great aunt, treasurer of the short robe: but I would make myself a Truand. I told my father so, and he spit his malediction in my face. I told my mother so, and she, poor old lady, began to cry and slobber like that log upon that iron dog there. Let's be merry! I'm a very Bicêtre in myself. Landlady, my dear, some more wine! I've got some money left yet. But mind, I'll have no more of that Surène wine—it hurts my throat. I'd as lief gargle myself, *cor-bœuf!* with a basket."

Meanwhile the company around applauded with boisterous laughter; and, finding that the tumult was redoubling around him, the scholar exclaimed, "Oh, what a glorious noise! *Populi debacchantis populosa debacchatio!*" Then he began to sing out, with an eye as if swimming in ecstasy, and the tone of a canon leading the vesper chant, "*Quæ cantica! Quæ organa! quæ cantilenæ! quæ melodiæ hic sine fine decantatur! Sonant melliflua hymnorum organa, suavissima angelorum melodia, cantica canticorum mira!*" . . . He stopped short. "Hey—you there—the devil's own barmaid!—let me have some supper."

There was a moment of something approaching to silence, during which the shrill voice of the Duke of Egypt was heard in its turn, instructing his Bohemians in the mysteries of the black art. "The weasel," said he, "goes by the name of Aduine; a fox is called Blue-foot, or the Wood-ranger; a wolf, Grey-foot, or Gilt-foot; a bear, the Old One, or the Grandfather. A gnome's cap makes one invisible, and makes one see invisible things. Whenever a toad is to be christened, it ought to be dressed in velvet, red or black, with a little bell at its neck and one at its feet. The godfather holds it by the head, and the godmother by the hinder parts. It's the demon Sidragasum that has the power of making girls dance naked."

"By the mass!" interrupted Jehan, "then I should like to be the demon Sidragasum!"

Meanwhile the Truands continued to arm, whispering to one another at the other side of the tavern.

"That poor Esmeralda!" exclaimed one of the gipsy men; "she's our sister; we must get her out of that place."

"So she's still at Notre-Dame, is she?" asked a Marcandier with a Jewish look.

"Yes, *pardieu!*" was the reply.

"Well, comrades," resumed the Marcandier, "to Notre-Dame, then! All the more, because there, in the chapel of Saints Féréol and Ferrution, there are two statues, the one of St. John the Baptist, the other of St. Anthony, of solid gold, weighing together seventeen gold marks and fifteen esterlins; and the pedestals, of silver gilt, weigh seventeen marks five ounces. I know it, for I'm a goldsmith."

Here they served up Jehan his supper. He called out, throwing himself back upon the bosom of the girl that sat by him, "By Saint-Voult-de-Lucques, called by the people Saint-Goguelu, now I'm perfectly happy. I see a blockhead there, straight before me, that's looking at me with a face as smooth as an archduke's. Here's another, at my left hand, with teeth so long that one can't see his chin. And then, I'm like the Maréchal de Gié at the siege of Pontoise—I've my right resting upon a *mamelon*. *Ventre-Mahom!* comrade! you look like a tennis-ball merchant—and you come and sit down by me! I'm noble, my friend—and trade's incompatible with nobility. Get thee away. Hollo! you there! don't fight. What! Baptiste Croque-Oison!—with a fine nose like thine—wilt thou go and risk it against that blockhead's great fists? You simpleton! *Non ciquam datum est habere nasum.* Truly, thou'rt divine, Jacqueline Rouge-Oreille!—its a pity thou hast no hair on thy head! Hollah! do you hear? My name's Jehan Frollo, and my brother's an archdeacon—the devil fly away with him! All that I tell you's the truth. By turning Truand I've jocundly given up one-half of a house situate in Paradise, which my brother had promised me—*dimidiam domum in paradiso;* those are the very words. I've a fief in the Rue Tirechappe—and all the women are in love with me—as true as it is, that Saint Eloi was an excellent goldsmith, and that the five trades of the good city of Paris are the tanners, the leather-dressers, the baldric-makers, the purse-makers, and the cordwainers; and that St. Lawrence was broiled over egg-shells. I swear to you, comrades,

For full twelve months I'll taste no wine
If this be any lie of mine.

My charmer, it's moonlight. Just look there, through that

air-hole, how the wind rumples those clouds—just as I do thy gorgerette. Girls, snuff the candles and the children. *Christ et Mahom!* what am I eating now, in the name of Jupiter? Hey, there, old jade! the hairs that are not to be found on thy wenches' heads we find in thy omelets. Do you hear, old woman? I like my omelets bald. The devil flatten thy nose! A fine tavern of Beelzebub is this—where the wenches comb themselves with the forks!"

And thereupon he broke his plate upon the floor, and began to sing out with all his might,—

> "Et je n'ai moi,
> Par la Sang-Dieu!
> Ni foi, ni loi,
> Ni feu, ni lieu,
> Ni roi,
> Ni Dieu!"

Meanwhile Clopin Trouillefou had finished his distribution of weapons. He went up to Gringoire, who seemed absorbed in profound reverie, with his feet against one of the iron dogs in the fireplace. "Friend Pierre," said the King of Tunis, "what the devil art thou thinking about?"

Gringoire turned round to him with a melancholy smile. "I'm fond of the fire, my dear seigneur—not for any such trivial reason as that the fire warms our feet or boils our soup, but because it throws out sparks. Sometimes I pass whole hours in looking at the sparks. I discover a thousand things in those stars that sprinkle the dark back of the chimney-place. Those stars themselves are worlds."

"*Tonnerre!* if I understand thee," said the Truand. "Dost thou know what o'clock it is?"

"I don't know," answered Gringoire.

Clopin then went up to the Duke of Egypt. "Comrade Mathias," said he, "this is not a good time we've hit upon. They say King Louis XI.'s at Paris."

"The more need to get our sister out of his clutches," answered the old gipsy.

"You speak like a man, Mathias," said the King of Tunis. "Besides, we shall do the thing well enough. There's no resistance to fear in the church. The canons are like so many hares, and we're in force. The Parliament's men will be finely balked when they come there for her to-morrow! *Boyaux du Pape!* I wouldn't have them hang the pretty girl!"

Clopin then went out of the cabaret.

Meantime Jehan was crying out in a voice hoarse with bawling. "I drink—I eat—I'm drunk—I'm Jupiter! Hey, you there, Pierre l'Assommeur, if you look at me in that way again, I'll fillip the dust off your nose!"

Gringoire, on the other hand, startled from his meditations, had set himself calmly to contemplate the passionate, clamorous scene around him, and muttered between his teeth, "*Luxuriosa res vinum et tumultuosa ebrietas.* Ah, what good reason have I to abstain from drinking! and how excellent is the saying of St. Benedict—*Vinum apostatare facit etiam sapientes!*"

At that moment Clopin re-entered, and cried out in a voice of thunder, "Midnight!"

At this word, which operated upon the Truands as the order to mount does upon a regiment halting, the whole of them, men, women, and children, rushed out of the tavern, with a great clatter of arms and iron implements.

The moon was now obscured by clouds, and the Court of Miracles was entirely dark. Not a single light was to be seen in it—but it was far from being solitary. There was discernible in it a great crowd of men and women talking to one another in a low voice. The hum of this multitude was to be heard; and all sorts of weapons were to be seen glittering in the darkness. Clopin mounted upon a large stone. "To your ranks, Argot!" cried he; "To your ranks, Egypt! To your ranks, Galilee!" Then there was a movement in the darkness. The immense multitude seemed to be forming in column. In a few minutes the King of Tunis again raised his voice: "Now, silence! to march through Paris. The password is *Petite flambe en baguenaud.* The torches must not be lighted till we get to Notre-Dame. March!"

And in ten minutes after, the horsemen of the night-watch were flying terrified before a long procession of men descending in darkness and silence towards the Pont-au-Change, through the winding streets that intersect in every direction the close-built neighbourhood of the Halles.

CHAPTER IV

AN UNLUCKY FRIEND

THAT same night, Quasimodo slept not. He had just gone his last round through the church. He had not remarked, at the moment when he was closing the doors, that the archdeacon had passed near him and had displayed a degree of ill-humour at seeing him bolt and padlock with care the enormous iron bars which gave to their large folds the solidity of a wall. Dom Claude appeared still more abstracted than usual. Moreover, since the nocturnal adventure of the cell he was constantly ill-treating Quasimodo; but in vain he used him harshly, even striking him sometimes; nothing could shake the submission, the patience, the devoted resignation of the faithful ringer. From the archdeacon he could endure anything—ill-language, menaces, blows, without murmuring a reproach, without uttering a complaint. At most he would follow Dom Claude anxiously with his eye, as he ascended the staircase of the towers; but the archdeacon had himself abstained from again appearing before the gipsy girl.

That night, then, Quasimodo, after casting one look towards his poor forsaken bells, Jacquelin, Marie, and Thibauld, ascended to the top of the northern tower; and there, placing his well-closed dark lantern on the leads, set himself to contemplate Paris. The night, as we have already said, was very dark. Paris, which, comparatively speaking, was not lighted at that period, presented to the eye a confused heap of black masses, intersected her and there by the silvery windings of the Seine. Not a light could Quasimodo see except from the window of a distant edifice, the vague and gloomy profile of which was distinguishable, rising above the roofs in the direction of the Porte St. Antoine. There, too, was some one wakeful.

While his only eye was thus hovering over that horizon of mist and darkness, the ringer felt within himself an inexpressible anxiety. For several days he had been upon the watch. He had seen constantly wandering around the church, men of sinister aspect, who never took off their eyes from the young girl's asylum. He feared lest some plot should be hatching against the unfortunate refugee. He fancied that she was an object of popular hatred as well as himself, and that something might probably very shortly happen. Thus he remained on his tower, on the lookout, *rêvant dans son rêvoir*, as Rabelais says, his eye by turns cast upon the cell and upon Paris, keeping safe watch like a trusty dog, with a thousand suspicions in his mind.

All at once, while he was reconnoitring the great city with that eye which nature, as if by way of compensation, had made so piercing that it almost supplied the deficiency of other organs in Quasimodo, it struck him that there was something unusual in the appearance of the outline of the quay of the Vieille Pelleterie—that there was some movement upon that point—that the line of the parapet which stood out black against the whiteness of the water was not straight and still like that of the other quays, but that it undulated before the eye like the waves of a river or the heads of a crowd in motion.

This appeared strange to him. He redoubled his attention. The movement seemed to be coming towards the city. No light was to be seen. It remained some time on the quay; then flowed off it by degrees, as if whatever was passing along was entering the interior of the island; then it ceased entirely, and the line of the quay became straight and motionless again.

Just as Quasimodo was exhausting himself in conjectures, it seemed to him that the movement was reappearing in the Rue du Parvis, which runs into the city perpendicularly to the front of Notre-Dame. In fine, notwithstanding the great darkness, he could see the head of a column issuing from that street, and in an instant a crowd spreading itself over the square, of which he could distinguish nothing further than that it was a crowd.

This spectacle was one of terror to Quasimodo. It is probable that that singular procession, which seemed so anxious to conceal itself in profound darkness, observed a silence no less profound. Still some sound must have escaped from it, were it only the pattering of feet. But even this noise did not reach our deaf hero; and that great multitude, of which he could scarcely see anything, from which he could hear nothing, and which, nevertheless, was walking and in agitation so near him, produced on him the effect of an assemblage of the dead, mute, impalpable, lost in vapour. He seemed to see advancing towards him a mist peopled with men—to see shades moving in the shade.

Then his fears returned: the idea of an attempt against the gipsy girl presented itself again to his mind. He had a vague feeling that he was about to find himself in a critical situation. In this crisis he held counsel with himself; and his reasoning was more just and prompt than might have been expected from a brain so ill-organised. Should he awaken the gipsy girl? assist her to escape? Which way? The streets were beset; behind the church was the river; there was no boat, no egress! There was but one measure to be taken—to meet death on the threshold of Notre-Dame; to resist at least until some assistance came, if any were to come, and not to disturb the sleep of La Esmeralda. The unhappy girl would be awake time enough to die. This resolution once taken, he proceeded to reconnoitre the enemy more calmly.

The crowd seemed to be increasing every moment in the Parvis. He concluded, however, that very little noise was made, since the windows of the street and the square remained closed. All at once a light shone out; and in an instant seven or eight lighted torches were waved above the heads, shaking their tufts of flame in the deep shade. Quasimodo then saw distinctly in commotion, in the Parvis, a frightful troop of men and women, in rags, armed with scythes, pikes, pruning-hooks, partisans; their thousand points all sparkling. Here and there, black pitchforks formed horns to those hideous visages. He had a confused recollection of that populace, and thought he recognised all the heads which, a few months before, had saluted him Pope of the Fools. A man holding a torch in one hand and a *boullaye* in the other, mounted a boundary-stone, and appeared to be haranguing. At the same time the strange army performed some evolutions, as if taking post around the church. Quasimodo took up his lantern, and descended to the platform between the towers, to observe more closely, and to deliberate on the means of defence.

Clopin Trouillefou, having arrived before the principal door of Notre-Dame, had, in fact, placed his troops in battle array. Although he did not anticipate any resistance, yet, like a prudent general, he wished to preserve such a degree of order as would, in case of need, enable him to face a sudden attack of the watch or the *onze-vingts*. He had accordingly drawn out his brigade in such a manner that, seen from on high and at a distance, it might have been taken for the Roman triangle of the battle of Ecnoma, the pig's head of Alexander, or the famous wedge of Gustavus Adolphus. The base of this triangle was formed along the back of the square, so as to bar the entrance to the Rue du Parvis; one of the sides looked towards the Hôtel-Dieu, the other towards the Rue Saint-Pierre-aux-Bœufs. Clopin Trouillefou had placed himself at the point, with the Duke of Egypt, our friend Jehan, and the boldest of the *sabouleux*

An enterprise such as the Truands were now attempting against Notre-Dame was no uncommon occurrence in the cities of the Middle Ages. What we in our day call police did not then exist. In populous towns, in capitals especially, there was no central power, sole and commanding all the rest. Feudality had constructed those great municipalities after a strange fashion. A city was an assemblage of innumerable seigneuries, which divided it into compartments of all forms and sizes. From thence arose a thousand contradictory establishments of police, or rather no police at all. In Paris, for example, independently of the hundred and forty-one lords claiming censive or manorial dues, there were twenty-five claiming justice and censive—from the Bishop of Paris, who had five hundred streets, to the Prior of Notre-Dame-des-Champs, who had only four. All these feudal justiciaries only recognised nominally the paramount authority of the King. All had right of highway-keeping. All were their own masters. Louis XI., that indefatigable workman who commenced on so large a scale the demolition of the feudal edifice, carried on by Richelieu and Louis XIV. to the advantage of the royalty, and completed in 1789 to the advantage of the people—Louis XI. had indeed striven to burst this network of seigneuries which covered Paris, by throwing violently athwart it two or three ordinances of general police. Thus in 1465 the inhabitants were ordered to light candles in their windows at nightfall, and to shut up their dogs, under pain of the halter. In the same year they were ordered to close the streets in an evening with iron chains, and forbidden to carry daggers or other offensive weapons in the streets at night. But in a short time all these attempts at municipal legislation fell into disuse. The townspeople allowed the candles at their windows to be extinguished by the wind, and their dogs to stray; the iron chains were only stretched across in case of siege; and the prohibition against carrying daggers brought about no other changes than that of the name of the Rue Coupe-gueule into Rue Coupe-gorge, which, to be sure, was a manifest improvement. The old framework of the feudal jurisdictions remained standing—an immense accumulation of bailiwicks and seigneuries, crossing one another in all directions throughout the city, straitening and entangling each other, interwoven with each other, and projecting one into another—a useless thicket of watches, under-watches, and counter-watches, through the midst of which the armed hand of brigandage, rapine, and sedition was constantly passing. Thus it was no unheard-of event, in this state of disorder, for a part of the populace to lay violent hands on a palace, a hôtel, or an ordinary mansion, in the quarters the most thickly inhabited. In most cases the neighbours did not interfere in the affair unless the pillage reached themselves. They stopped their ears against the report of the musketry, closed their shutters, barricaded their doors, and let the struggle exhaust itself with or without the watch; and the next day it would be quietly said in Paris, "Last night Etienne Barbette had his house forced," or "The Maréchal de Clermont was laid hold of," etc. Hence, not only the royal residences—the Louvre, the Palais, the Bastille, the Tournelles—but such as were simply seigneurial—the Petit-Bourbon, the Hôtel de Sens, the Hôtel d'Angoulême, etc.—had their battlemented walls and their machicolated gates. The churches were protected by their sanctity. Some of them, nevertheless, among which was Notre-Dame, were fortified. The Abbey of St. Germain-des-Près was castellated like a baronial mansion, and more weight of metal was to be found there in bombards than in bells. This fortress was still to be seen in 1610, but now barely the church remains.

To return to Notre-Dame.

When the first arrangements were completed—and we must say, to the honour of Truand discipline, that Clopin's orders were executed in silence and with admirable precision—the worthy leader mounted the parapet of the Parvis, and raised his hoarse and sullen voice, his face turned towards Notre-Dame, and shaking his torch, the light of which, agitated by the wind, and veiled at intervals by its own smoke, made the glowing front of the church by turns appear and disappear before the eye.

"Unto thee, Louis de Beaumont, Bishop of Paris, Councillor in the Court of Parliament, thus say I, Clopin Trouillefou, King of Tunis, Grand-Coësre, Prince of Argot, Bishop of the Fools: Our sister, falsely condemned for magic, has taken refuge in thy church. Thou art bound to give her shelter and safeguard. Now, the Court of Parliament wants to take her thence, and thou consentest to it; so that she would be hanged to-morrow at the Grève, if God and the Truands were not at hand. We come to thee, then, bishop. If thy church is sacred, our sister is so too; if our sister is not sacred, neither is thy church. Wherefore we summon thee to give us up the girl, if thou wilt save thy church; or we will take the girl, and will plunder the church. Which will be well and good. In witness whereof I here set up my standard. And so, God help thee, Bishop of Paris."

Quasimodo, unfortunately, could not hear these words, which were uttered with a sort of sullen, savage majesty. A Truand presented the standard to Clopin, who gravely planted it between two of the paving stones. It was a pitchfork, from the prongs of which hung, all bloody, a quarter of carrion meat.

This done, the King of Tunis turned about, and cast his eyes over his army, a ferocious multitude whose eyes glared almost as much as their pikes. After a moment's pause, "Forward, boys!" cried he. "To your work, Hutins."

Thirty stout men, square-limbed, and with picklock faces, stepped out from the ranks, with hammers, pincers, and iron crows on their shoulders. They advanced towards the principal door of the church, ascended the steps, and directly they were to be seen stooping down under the pointed arches of the portal, heaving at the door with pincers and levers. A crowd of Truands followed them, to assist or look on; so that the whole eleven steps were covered with them. The door, however, stood firm. "*Diable!* but she's hard and headstrong," said one. "She's old, and her gristles are tough," said another. "Courage, my friends!" cried Clopin. "I'll wager my head against a slipper that you'll have burst the door, brought away the girl, and undressed the great altar before there's one beadle of 'em all awake. There—I think the lock's going."

Clopin was interrupted by a frightful noise which at that moment resounded behind him. He turned round. An enormous beam had just fallen from on high, crushing a dozen of the Truands upon the church steps, and rebounding upon the pavement with the sound of a piece of artillery; breaking here and there the legs of others among the vagabond crowd, which shrunk away from it with cries of terror. In a trice the confined enclosure of the Parvis was empty. The Hutins, though protected by the deep, retiring arches of the doorway, abandoned the door, and Clopin himself fell back to a respectful distance from the church.

"Egad, I've had a narrow escape!" cried Jehan. "I felt the wind of it, *tête-bœuf!*—but Pierre the Knockerdown's knocked down at last."

The astonishment mingled with dread which fell upon the brigands with this unaccountable piece of timber is indescribable, They remained for some minutes gazing fixedly upwards, in greater consternation at this piece of wood than they would have been at twenty thousand King's archers. "Satan!" growled the Duke of Egypt, "but this smells of magic!"

"It's the moon that's been throwing this log at us," said Andry-le-Rouge.

"Why," remarked François Chanteprune, "you know, they say the moon's a friend of the Virgin's."

"*Milles papes!*" exclaimed Clopin, "you're all simpletons together." Yet he knew not how to account for the fall of the beam.

All this while nothing was distinguishable upon the grand front of the building, to the top of which the light from the torches did not reach. The ponderous beam lay in the middle of the Parvis, and groans were heard from the miserable wretches who had received its first shock and been almost cut in two upon the angles of the stone steps.

At last the King of Tunis, his first astonishment being over, hit upon an explanation which his comrades thought plausible. "*Gueule-Dieu!*" said he, "are the canons making a defence? If that be it, then, *A sac! à sac!*"

"*A sac!*" repeated the mob with a furious hurrah; and they made a general discharge of crossbows and hackbuts against the front of the church.

This report awoke the peaceful inhabitants of the neighbouring houses. Several window-shutters were seen to open, and nightcaps and hands holding candles appeared at the casements. "Fire at the windows!" cried Clopin. The windows were immediately shut again, and the poor citizens, who had scarcely had time to cast a bewildered look upon that scene of glare and tumult, went back trembling to their wives, asking themselves whether it was that the witches now held their sabbath in the Parvis Notre-Dame, or that they were assaulted by the Burgundians as in the year '64.

"*A sac!*" repeated the Argotiers; but they dared not approach. They looked first at the church and then at the marvellous beam. The beam lay perfectly still; the edifice kept its firm and solitary look: but something froze the courage of the Truands.

"To your work, Hutins!" cried Trouillefou. "Come, force the door."

Nobody advanced a step.

"*Barbe et ventre!*" said Clopin; "here are men afraid of a rafter!"

An old Hutin now addressed him. "Captain, it's not the rafter that we care about; it's the door—that's all overlaid with iron bars. The pincers can do nothing with it."

"What should you have, then, to burst it open with?" asked Clopin.

"Why, we should have a battering-ram."

The King of Tunis ran bravely up to the formidable piece of timber and set his foot upon it. "Here's one!" cried he; "the canons have sent it you." And making a mock reverence to the cathedral, "Thank you, canons," he added.

This bravado had great effect—the spell of the wonderful beam was broken. The Truands recovered courage; and soon the heavy timber, picked up like a feather by two hundred vigorous arms, was driven with fury against the great door which it had already been attempted to shake. Seen thus, by the sort of half-light which the few scattered torches of the Truands cast over the place, the long beam, borne along by that multitude of men rushing on with its extremity pointed against the church, looked like some monstrous animal, with innumerable legs, running, head foremost, to attack the stone giantess.

At the shock given by the beam the half-metal door sounded like an immense drum. It was not burst in; but the whole cathedral shook, and the deepest of its internal echoes were awakened. At the same moment a shower of great stones began to fall from the upper part of the front upon the assailants. "Diable!" cried Jehan, "are the towers shaking down their balustrades upon our heads?" But the impulse was given. The King of Tunis stuck to his text. It was decidedly the bishop making a defence. And so they only battered the door the more furiously, in spite of the stones that were fracturing their skulls right and left.

It must be remarked that these stones all fell one by one, but they followed one another close. The Argotiers always felt two of them at one and the same time, one against their legs, the other upon their heads. Nearly all of them took effect; and already the dead and wounded were thickly strewn, bleeding and panting under the feet of the assailants, who, now grown furious, filled up instantly and without intermission the places of the disabled. The long beam continued battering the door with periodical strokes, the stones to shower down, the door to groan, and the interior of the cathedral to reverberate.

Undoubtedly the reader has not yet to divine that this unexpected resistance which had exasperated the Truands proceeded from Quasimodo. Accident had unfortunately favoured our deaf hero's exertions.

When he had descended upon the platform between the towers his ideas were all in confusion. He ran to and fro along the gallery for some minutes like one insane—beholding from on high the compact mass of the Truands ready to rush against the church; imploring the powers celestial or infernal to save the gipsy girl. He once thought of ascending the southern steeple and sounding the tocsin; but then, before the loud voice of Marie could have uttered a single sound, would there not be interval enough for the door of the church to be forced ten times over? It was just the moment at which the Hutins were advancing towards it with their burglarious instruments. What was to be done?

All at once he recollected that some masons had been at work the whole day, repairing the wall, the woodwork, and the roofing of the southern tower. This was a beam of light to him. The wall was of stone; the roofing was of lead; and then there was the woodwork, so prodigious and so thick-clustering that it went by the name of the forest.

Quasimodo ran to this tower. The lower chambers of it were, in fact, full of materials. There were piles of building stone, sheets of lead rolled up, bundles of laths, strong beams already shaped by the saw, heaps of rubbish—in short, an arsenal complete.

Time pressed. The levers and the hammers were at work below. With a strength multiplied tenfold by the feeling of imminent danger, he lifted an end of one of the beams, the heaviest and longest of all. He managed to push it through one of the loopholes; then laying hold of it again outside the tower, he shoved it over the outer angle of the balustrade surrounding the platform, and let it fall into the abyss beneath.

The enormous beam, in this fall of a hundred and sixty feet, grazing the wall, breaking the sculptured figures, turned several times upon its centre, like one of the two cross arms of a windmill, going by itself. At length it reached the ground. A horrid cry arose; and the dark piece of timber rebounded upon the pavement, like a serpent rearing itself and darting.

Quasimodo saw the Truands scattered by the fall of the beam like ashes by the blowing of a child; and while they fixed their superstitious gaze upon the immense log fallen from the sky, and peppered the stone saints of the portal with a discharge of bolts and bullets, Quasimodo was silently piling up stones and rubbish, and even the masons' bags of tools, upon the verge of that balustrade from which he had already hurled the large timber.

And accordingly, as soon as they began to batter the great door, the shower of great stones began to fall, making them think that the church must be shaking itself to pieces upon their heads.

Any one who could have seen Quasimodo at that moment would have been affrighted. Independently of the missiles which he had piled up on the balustrade, he had got together a heap of stones upon the platform itself. As soon as the great stones heaped upon the external border were spent he had recourse to this latter heap. Then he stooped down, rose up, stooped, and rose again, with incredible agility. He thrust his great gnome's head over the balustrade; then there dropped an enormous stone—then another—then another. Now and then he followed some good big stone with his eye, and when he saw that it did good execution he ejaculated a "Hum!" of satisfaction.

The beggars, meanwhile, did not lose courage. Already above twenty times had the massive door which they were so furiously assailing shaken under the weight of their oaken battering-ram, multiplied by the strength of a hundred men. The panels cracked; the carving flew in splinters; the hinges, at each shock, danced upon their hooks; the planks were forced out of their places; the wood was falling in dust, bruised between the sheathings of iron. Fortunately for Quasimodo's defence, there was more iron than wood.

Nevertheless he felt that an impression was being made upon the great door. Each stroke of the battering-ram, notwithstanding that he did not hear it, awakened not only the echoes within the church, but a pang of apprehension in his heart. As he looked down upon the Truands, he beheld them, full of exultation and of rage, shaking their fists at the dark front of the edifice; and he coveted, for the gipsy girl and himself, the wings of the owls that were flocking away affrighted over his head. His shower of stones did not suffice to repel the assailants.

It was in this moment of anguish that he fixed his eyes a little below the balustrade from which he had been crushing the Argotiers, upon two long stone gutters which discharged themselves immediately over the grand doorway. The internal orifice of these gutters was in the floor of the platform. An idea occurred to him. He ran and fetched a fagot from the little lodge which he occupied as ringer; laid over the fagot a number of bundles of laths and rolls of lead—ammunition of which he had not yet made any use; and after placing this pile in the proper position as regarded the orifice of the gutters, he set fire to it with his lantern.

While he was thus employed, as the stones no longer fell, the Truands ceased looking up into the air. The brigands, panting like a pack of hounds baying the wild boar in his lair, were pressing tumultuously round the great door, all disfigured and shapeless from the strokes of the ram, but still erect. They waited in a sort of shuddering anxiety for the grand stroke of all—the stroke which was to burst it in. They were all striving to get nearest, in order to be the first, when it should open, to rush into that well-stored cathedral—a vast repository in which had been successfully accumulating the riches of three centuries. They reminded one another, with roars of exultation and greedy desire, of the fine silver crosses, the fine brocade cope, the fine silver gilt monuments—of all the magnificences of the choir—the dazzling holiday displays—the Christmas illuminations with torches—the Easter suns—all those splendid solemnities in which shrines, candlesticks, pixes, tabernacles, and reliquaries embossed the altars, as it were, with a covering of gold and jewels. Certain it is that at that flattering moment *cagoux* and *malingreux, archisuppôts* and *rifodés,* were all of them thinking much less about delivering the gipsy girl than about plundering Notre-Dame. Nay, we could even go so far as to believe that, with a good many of them, La Esmeralda was merely a pretext—if, indeed, thieves could have need of a pretext.

All at once, at the moment that they were crowding about the battering-ram for a final effort, each one holding in his breath and gathering up his muscles, so as to give full force to the decisive stroke, a howling more terrific yet than that which had burst forth and expired under the fall of the great beam arose from the midst of them. They who had not cried out, they who were still alive, looked, and saw two jets of melted lead falling from the top of the edifice into the thickest of the crowd. The waves of that human sea had shrunk under the boiling metal, which, at the two points where it fell, had made two black and reeking hollows in the crowd, like the effect of hot water thrown upon snow. There were to be seen dying wretches burned half to a cinder and moaning with agony. Around the two principal jets there were drops of that horrible rain falling scatteredly upon the assailants, and entering their skulls like fiery gimlet points.

The outcry was heartrending. They fled in disorder, throwing down the beam upon the dead bodies—the boldest of them as well as the most timid—and the Parvis was left empty for the second time.

All eyes were now cast upwards to the top of the church, and they beheld an extraordinary sight. On the topmost gallery, higher than the great central window, was a great flame ascending between the two steeples, with clouds of sparks—a great flame, irregular and furious, a portion of which, by the action of the wind, was at intervals enveloped in the smoke. Underneath that flame, underneath the trifoliated balustrade showing darkly upon its glare, two monster-headed gutters were vomiting incessantly that burning shower, the silver trickling of which shone out upon the darkness of the lower part of the grand front. As they approached the ground the two jets of liquid lead spread out into myriads of drops like water sprinkled from the small holes of a watering-pan. Above the flame the huge towers—of each of which two faces were to be seen in all their sharpness of outline, the one quite black, the other quite red—seemed huger still by all the immensity of shadow which they cast into the sky. Their innumerable sculptured demons and dragons assumed a formidable aspect. The restless, flickering light from the unaccountable flame made them seem as if they were moving. Some of the guivres seemed to be laughing; some of the gargouilles you might have fancied you heard yelping; there were salamanders puffing at the fire, tarasques sneezing in the smoke. And among those monsters thus awakened from their stony slumber by that unearthly flame, by that unwonted clamour, there was one walking about, and seen from time to time to pass before the blazing front of the pile like a bat before a torch.

Assuredly this strange beacon-light must have awakened the far woodcutter on the Bicêtre Hills, startled to see wavering upon his coppices the gigantic shadows of the towers of Notre-Dame.

The silence of terror now took place among the Truands, during which nothing was heard but the cries of alarm from the canons, shut up in their cloisters and more uneasy than the horses in a burning stable—the stealthy sound of windows opened quick and shut yet quicker—the stir in the interior of the houses and of the Hôtel-Dieu—the wind agitating the flame—the last groans of the dying—and the continued crackling of the shower of boiling lead upon the pavement.

Meanwhile the principal Truands, having retreated under the porch of the Logis Gondelaurier, were there holding a council of war. The Duke of Egypt, seated upon a boundary-stone, was contemplating with religious awe the phantasmagoric pile blazing two hundred feet aloft in the air. Clopin Trouillefou was gnawing his great fists with rage. "Not possible to get in!" muttered he to himself.

"An old elf of a church!" growled the old Bohemian, Mathias Hungadi Spicali.

"By the Pope's whiskers," added a grey-headed *narquois*, who had once been in actual service, "but there are two church gutters that spit molten lead at you better than the machicolles at Lectoure!"

"Do you see that demon going backwards and forwards before the fire?" cried the Duke of Egypt.

"Par-Dieu!" said Clopin, "it's the damned ringer—it's Quasimodo."

The Bohemian shook his head. "I tell you, no," said he: "it's the spirit Sabnac, the great marquis, the demon of fortification. Out of an armed soldier he's been making a lion's head. Sometimes he's mounted on a frightful horse. He turns men into stones, and builds towers of them. He commands fifty legions. It's he, sure enough. I know him again. Sometimes he has on a fine robe of gold, figured after the Turkish fashion."

"Where's Bellevigne-de-l'Etoile?" asked Clopin.

"He's dead," answered a female Truand.

Here Andry-le-Rouge observed, laughing idiotically, "Notre-Dame's finding work for the Hôtel-Dieu."

"Is there no way to force that door, then?" said the King of Tunis, stamping his foot.

Hereupon the Duke of Egypt pointed with a melancholy look to the two streams of boiling lead which streaked the dark front of the building, looking like two long phosphoric distaffs. "There have been churches known to defend themselves so," observed he, with a sigh. "St. Sophia's, at Constantinople—some forty years ago—threw down to the ground three times, one after another, the crescent of Mahound—just by shaking her domes, which are her heads. William of Paris, that built this here, was a magician."

"And are we to slink away pitifully, then, like so many

running footmen?" said Clopin. "What! leave our sister there, for those ugly hooded fellows of canons to hang to-morrow?"

"And the sacristy, where there are cartloads of gold?" said a Truand, with whose name we are sorry to say that we are not acquainted.

"Barbe-Mahom!" exclaimed Trouillefou.

"Let us try once more," rejoined the Truand.

Mathias Hungadi shook his head. "We shall not get in at the door," said he. "We must find out some seam in the old elf's armour—a hole—a false postern—a joint of some sort or other."

"Who's for it?" said Clopin. "I'll go at it again. By-the-bye, where's the little scholar Jehan, that had cased himself so?"

"He's dead, no doubt," answered some one, "for nobody hears him laugh."

The King of Tunis knit his brows. "So much the worse!" said he. "There was a stout heart under that iron case. And Maître Pierre Gringoire?"

"Captain Clopin," said Andry-le-Rouge, "he stole away before we'd got as far as the Pont-aux-Changeurs."

Clopin stamped with his foot. "Gueule-Dieu!" he cried; "that fellow pushed us into this business, and then leaves us here just in the thick of the job. A prating, nightcap-helmeted coward!"

"Captain Clopin," cried Andry-le-Rouge, looking up the Rue du Parvis, "here comes the little scholar."

"Blessed be Pluto!" said Clopin. "But what the devil is he pulling after him?"

It was in fact Jehan, coming up as quick as he found practicable under his ponderous knightly accoutrements, with a long ladder, which he was dragging stoutly over the pavement, more out of breath than an ant which has harnessed itself to a blade of grass twenty times its own length.

"Victory! Te Deum!" shouted the scholar. "Here's the ladder belonging to the unladers of St. Landry's wharf."

Clopin went up to him. "My lad," said he, "what are you going to do, corne-Dieu! with that ladder?"

"I have it," answered Jehan, panting. "I knew where it was—under the shed of the lieutenant's house. There's a girl there that I'm acquainted with that thinks me quite a Cupido for beauty. It was through her I tried to get the ladder; and now I have the ladder, Pasque-Mahom! The poor girl came out in her shift to let me in."

"Yes, yes," said Clopin; "but what do you want to do with this ladder?"

Jehan gave him a roguish, knowing look, and snapped his fingers. At that moment he was quite sublime. He had upon his head one of those overloaded helmets of the fifteenth century which affrighted the enemy with their monstrous-looking peaks. The one which he wore was jagged with no less than ten beaks of steel, so that Jehan might have contended for the formidable epithet of δεκεμβολος with the Homeric ship of Nestor.

"What do I want to do with it, august King of Tunis?" said he. "Do you see that row of statues there that look like blockheads over the three doorways?"

"Yes. Well?"

"It's the gallery of the kings of France."

"What's that to me?" said Clopin.

"Wait a bit. At the end of that gallery there's a door that's always on the latch. With this ladder I get up to it, and then I'm in the church."

"Let me get up first, my lad," said the other.

"No, comrade; the ladder's mine. Come along; you shall be the second."

"Beelzebub strangle thee!" said Clopin, turning sulky. "I'll not go after anybody."

"Then, Clopin, go look for a ladder."

And therewith Jehan set off again across the Place, dragging along his ladder, and shouting, "Follow me, boys!"

In an instant the ladder was reared up, and the top of it placed against the balustrade of the lower gallery, over one of the side doorways. The crowd of the Truands, raising great acclamations, pressed to the foot of it for the purpose of ascending. But Jehan maintained his right, and was the first that set foot on the steps of the ladder. The passage to be made was a long one. The gallery of the French kings is, at this day, about sixty feet from the ground; to which elevation was, at that period, added the height of the eleven steps of entrance. Jehan ascended slowly, much encumbered with his heavy armour, with one hand upon the ladder and the other grasping his crossbow. When he was half-way up he cast down a melancholy glance upon the poor dead Argotiers strewed upon the steps of the grand portal. "Alas!" said he, "here's a heap of dead worthy the fifth book of the *Iliad*." Then he continued his ascent. The Truands followed him. There was one upon each step of the ladder. To see that line of mailed backs thus rise undulating in the dark, one might have imagined it a serpent with steely scales, rearing itself up to assail the church, but that the whistling of Jehan, who formed its head, was not exactly the serpent-like sound requisite to complete the illusion.

The scholar at length reached the parapet of the gallery, and strode lightly over it, amid the applauses of the whole Truandry. Thus master of the citadel, he uttered a joyful shout, but stopped short all at once, confounded. He had just discovered, behind one of the royal statues, Quasimodo in concealment, his eye all flashing in the dark.

Before another of the besiegers had time to gain footing on the gallery the formidable hunchback sprang to the head of the ladder; took hold, without saying a word, of the ends of the two uprights with his two powerful hands; heaved them away from the edge of the balustrade; balanced for a moment, amid cries of anguish, the long bending ladder, covered with Truands from top to bottom; then suddenly, with superhuman strength, he threw back that cluster of men into the Place. For a moment or two the most resolute felt their hearts palpitate. The ladder, thus hurled backwards with all that living weight upon it, remained perpendicular for an instant, and its inclination seemed doubtful; then it wavered; then, suddenly describing a frightful arc of eighty feet radius, it came down upon the pavement, with its load of brigands, more swiftly than a drawbridge when its chains give way. There arose one vast imprecation; then all was still, and a few mutilated wretches were seen crawling out from under the heap of dead.

A mixed murmur of pain and resentment among the besiegers succeeded their shouts of triumph. Quasimodo, unmoved, his elbows resting upon the balustrade, was quietly looking on, with the mien of some old long-haired king looking out at his window.

Jehan Frollo, on the other hand, was in a critical situation. He found himself in the gallery with the redoubtable ringer—alone, separated from his companions by eighty feet of perpendicular wall. While Quasimodo was dealing with the ladder the scholar had run to the postern, which he expected to find on the latch. No such thing. The ringer, as he entered the gallery, had fastened it behind him. Jehan had then hidden himself behind one of the stone kings, not daring to draw breath, but fixing upon the monstrous hunchback a look of wild apprehension—like the man who, upon a time, making love to the wife of a menagerie-keeper, and going one evening to meet her in an assignation, scaled the wrong wall, and suddenly found himself *tête-à-tête* with a white bear.

For the first few moments the hunchback took no notice of him; but at length he turned his head and drew up his limbs, for the scholar had just caught his eye.

Jehan prepared for a rude encounter; but his deaf antagonist remained motionless. Only his face was turned towards the scholar, at whom he continued looking.

"Ho, ho!" said Jehan; "what dost thou look at me for with that one melancholy eye of thine?" And so saying, the young rogue was stealthily making ready his crossbow. "Quasimodo," he cried, "I'm going to change thy surname. They shall call thee the blind."

Jehan let fly the winged shaft, which whistled through the air, and struck its point into the left arm of the hunchback. This no more disturbed Quasimodo than a scratch would have done his stone neighbour, King Pharamound. He laid his hand upon the arrow, drew it out of his arm, and quietly broke it over his clumsy knee. Then he dropped, rather than threw, the two pieces on the ground. But he did not give Jehan time to discharge a second shaft. As soon as the arrow was broken, Quasimodo, breathing strongly through his nostrils, bounded like a grasshopper upon the scholar, whose armour this shock of his flattened against the wall.

Then, through that atmosphere in which wavered the light of the torches, was dimly seen a sight of terror.

Quasimodo had grasped in his left hand both the arms of Jehan, who made no struggle, so utterly did he give himself up for lost. With his right hand the hunchback took off, one after another, with ominous deliberateness, the several pieces of his armour, offensive and defensive—the sword, the daggers, the helmet, the breastplate, the arm-pieces—as if it had been a monkey peeling a walnut, Quasimodo dropped at his feet, piece after piece, the scholar's iron shell.

When the scholar found himself disarmed and uncased, feeble and naked, in those formidable hands, he did not offer to speak to his deaf enemy; but he fell to laughing audaciously in his face, and singing, with his careless assurance of a boy of sixteen, a popular air of the time:—

"Elle est bien habillée,
La ville de Cambrai
Marafin l'a pillée. . . ."

He had not time to finish. Quasimodo was now seen standing upon the parapet of the gallery, holding the scholar by the feet with one hand only, and swinging him round like a sling over the external abyss. Then a noise was heard like some box made of bone dashing against a wall; and something was seen falling, but it stopped a third part of the way down, being arrested in its descent by one of the architectural projections. It was a dead body, which remained suspended there, bent double, the loins broken and the skull empty.

A cry of horror arose from the Truands. "Revenge!" cried Clopin. "*A sac!*" answered the multitude. "Assault! assault!" Then there was a prodigious howling, mixed up of all languages, all dialects, and all tones of voice. The poor scholar's death inspired the crowd with a frantic ardour. They were seized with shame and resentment at having been so long kept in check before a church by a hunchback. Their rage found them ladders, multiplied their torches, and in a few minutes Quasimodo, in confusion and despair, saw a frightful swarm ascending from all sides to the assault of Notre-Dame. They who had not ladders had knotted ropes, and they who had not ropes climbed up by means of the projections of the sculpture. They hung at one another's tattered habiliments. There was no means of resisting this rising tide of frightful visages. Fury seemed to writhe in those ferocious countenances; their dirty foreheads were streaming with perspiration; their eyes flashed; and all those varieties of grimace and ugliness were besetting Quasimodo. It seemed as if some other church had sent her gorgons, her dogs, her *drées*, her demons, all her most fantastic sculptures, to assail Notre-Dame. It was a coat of living monsters covering the stone monsters of the façade.

Meanwhile a thousand torches had kindled in the Place. This disorderly scene, buried until then in thick obscurity, was wrapped in a sudden blaze of light. The Parvis was resplendent, and cast a radiance on the sky; while the pile that had been lighted on the high platform of the church still burned and illumined the city far around. The vast outline of the two towers, projected afar upon the roofs of Paris, threw amid that light a huge mass of shade. The whole town seemed now to be roused from its slumber. Distant tocsins were mournfully sounding; the Truands were howling, panting, swearing, climbing; and Quasimodo, powerless against so many enemies, trembling for the gipsy girl, seeing all those furious faces approaching nearer and nearer to his gallery, was imploring a miracle from heaven and writhing his arms in despair.

CHAPTER V

THE CLOSET WHERE MONSIEUR LOUIS DE FRANCE SAYS HIS PRAYERS

THE reader has probably not forgotten that Quasimodo, a moment or two before he perceived the nocturnal band of the Truands in motion, whilst looking over Paris from the top of his steeple, saw but one single remaining light, twinkling at a window in the topmost story of a lofty and gloomy building; close by the Porte St. Antoine. That building was the Bastille, and that twinkling light was Louis XI.'s candle.

Louis XI. had, in fact, been at Paris for the last two days. He was to set out again the next day but one for his citadel of Plessis, or Montilz-les-Tours. He seldom made his appearance in his good city of Paris; and when he did appear, it was during very short intervals, as he did not there feel himself surrounded by a sufficient abundance of pitfalls, gibbets, and Scottish archers.

He had come that day to sleep at the Bastille. His grand chamber at the Louvre, five toises square, with its grand chimney-piece loaded with twelve great beasts and thirteen great prophets, and his great bed, eleven feet by twelve, were little to his taste. He felt himself lost amidst all those grandeurs. This good, homely king preferred the Bastille with a chamber and a bed of humbler dimensions; and, besides, the Bastille was stronger than the Louvre.

It was, in fact, in France, like "the Tower" in England,[1]

[1] Lest any one should be disposed to consider the assimilation of the English Tower to the French Bastille as a forced one, we will just recall one or two facts by way of illustration.

And first of all, in their very names there is a remarkable affinity; the word *bastille*, in old French, originally meaning simply a building, though subsequently limited in its application to buildings of great strength; and La Bastille (anciently called La Bastille St. Antoine, to distinguish it from other bastilles) signifying consequently, "the building" *par excellence*. Just so, in England, "the Tower" was at first invariably called, by its Norman founders and possessors, *La Tour de Londres* (the Tower of London), to distinguish it from so many other strong towers in various parts of the kingdom, until its superior celebrity as a royal fortress and state prison acquired for it the name of "The Tower" by distinction.

So much for affinity of name. Now as for affinity of use. The Tower of London was originally constructed by William the Conqueror, "the foreign founder of our glorious constitution," to defend himself, his counsellors, and favourites against the English people—its very name, *Tour* or the grand seat and stronghold of the *ancien régime*—its dark battlements formed the very crest of that system of feudal oppression—of rule without right, falsely called government—which placed the lives, liberties, and properties of the vast majority of the nation at the mercy of a selfish and tyrannous court and aristocracy. No wonder, then, that that vast majority hailed its fall at last with rapturous exultation, as an earnest of the system's fall to rise no more. No wonder that they left not one stone of it upon another, but swept it utterly from the face of the earth, as something too boundlessly hateful and loathsome for even a trace of it to be preserved.

The chamber which Louis XI. reserved to himself in the famous state prison, notwithstanding its comparative smallness, was positively spacious, occupying the upper story of a secondary tower adhering to the donjon or great keep of the fortress. It was a circular apartment, hung with matting of shining straw, ceiled with wooden beams decorated with raised fleurs-de-lis of gilt metal, with coloured spaces between them, and wainscoted with rich carvings interspersed with rosettes of white metal, and painted of a fine light green made of orpiment and fine indigo.

There was but one window, a long pointed one, latticed with iron bars and brass wire, and still further darkened with fine glass painted with the arms of the king and queen, each pane of which had cost two-and-twenty sols.

There was but one entrance, a modern doorway under an overhanging circular arch, furnished inside with a piece of tapestry, and outside with one of those porches of Irish wood (*bois d'Irlande*), as it was called—frail structures of curious cabinet work, which were still to be seen abounding in old French mansions a hundred and fifty years ago. "Although they disfigure and encumber the places," says Sauval in despair, "yet our old gentlemen will not put them out of the way, but keep them in spite of everybody."

Tower, being at that time Norman and not English. It is needless to remark how many kings and courts it has since defended against the love of their subjects. Its existence as a fortress to overawe a great metropolis is bound up with that of the old regime. In France, the Bastille and the old regime are no more. In England, the Tower and the old regime are both of them yet standing—the Tower looking very strong, and the old regime thinking itself so. Nevertheless, judging from recent indications, the time may not be very far distant when it shall have to be decided whether our English Bastille shall be made the prison of men who, by being faithful to their country, may become "traitors" to the English aristocracy, or whether it shall be turned to some more innocent use than any it has yet been put to.

No description of ordinary furniture was to be seen in this chamber—neither benches, nor trestles, nor forms, nor common box stools, nor fine stools supported by pillars and counter-pillars at four sols apiece: there was only one easy armchair, a very magnificent one; the wood of it was painted with roses upon a red ground, and its seat was of red morocco, decorated with long silken fringe and with abundance of gold-headed nails. The soleness of this chair testified that one person alone was entitled to be seated in the chamber. By the chair, and close to the window, there was a table, the cover of which was figured with birds. On the table were a *gallemard* or standish, spotted with ink, some scrolls of parchment, some pens, and a *hanap* or large cup of silver chased. A little farther on were a *chauffe-doux*, and, for the purpose of prayer, a *prie-Dieu* or small pew of crimson velvet set off with golden bosses. And behind was a plain bed of yellow and pink damask, without any sort of tinsel decoration, having only an ordinary fringe. It was this same bed, famous for having borne the sleep or the sleeplessness of Louis XI., that was still to be beheld two hundred years back at the house of a counsellor of state, where it was seen by the aged Madame Pilou, celebrated in the great romance of *Cyrus* under the name of *Arricidie* and that of *La Morale Vivante*. Such was the chamber which was then popularly styled "the closet where Monsieur Louis of France says his prayers."

At the moment at which we have introduced the reader into it this closet was very dark. The curfew had rung an hour ago; it was dark night; and there was but one wavering wax-candle set upon the table to light five different persons variously grouped in the chamber.

The first upon whom the light fell was a seigneur splendidly attired in a doublet and hose of scarlet striped with silver, and a cloak with *mahoîtres*, or shoulder-pieces, of cloth of gold with black figures. This splendid costume, as the light played upon it, glittered flamingly at every fold. The man who wore it had upon his breast his arms embroidered in brilliant colours—*un chevron accompagné en pointe d'un daim passant*. The escutcheon was *accosté* on the right by an olive branch, and on the left by a stag's horn. This man wore in his girdle a rich dagger, the hilt of which, of silver gilt, was chased in the form of a helmet top, and surmounted by a count's coronet. His air was unprepossessing, his look haughty and stiff. At the first glance you saw arrogance in his face; at the second, cunning.

He was standing bareheaded, with a long written scroll in his hand, behind the easy chair, upon which was seated, with his body ungracefully bent double, his knees thrown one across the other, and his elbow resting on the table, a person in very indifferent habiliments. Imagine, indeed, upon the rich morocco seat, a pair of crooked joints, a pair of lean thighs poorly wrapped in a web of black worsted, a trunk wrapped in a loose coat of linsey-woolsey, the fur trimming of which had much more leather left than hair; and to crown the whole, an old greasy hat of the meanest black cloth, garnished all round with a band of small leaden figures. Such, together with a dirty skullcap, beneath which hardly a single hair was visible, was all that could be distinguished of the sitting personage. He kept his head so much bent down over his chest that nothing was visible of his face, thus thrown into shadow, except only the extremity of his nose, upon which a ray of light fell, and which, it was evident, must be a long one. The thinness of his wrinkled hand showed it to be an old man. It was Louis XI.

At some distance behind them were, talking in a low voice, two men habited after the Flemish fashion, who were not so completely lost in the darkness but that any one who had attended the performance of Gringoire's mystery could recognise in them two of the principal Flemish envoys, Guillaume Rym, the sagacious pensionary of Ghent, and Jacques Coppenole, the popular hosier. It will be recollected that these two men were concerned in the secret politics of Louis XI.

And quite behind all the rest, near the door, there was standing in the dark, motionless as a statue, a stout, brawny, thick-set man, in military accoutrements, with an emblazoned *casaque*, whose square face, with its prominent eyes, its immense cleft of a mouth, its ears concealed each under a great mat of hair, and with scarcely any forehead, seemed a sort of compound of the dog and the tiger.

All were uncovered except the King.

The seigneur standing by him was reading over to him a sort of long official paper, to which his Majesty seemed to be attentively listening; while the two Flemings were whispering to each other behind.

"*Croix-Dieu!*" muttered Coppenole, "I'm tired of standing. Is there never a chair here?"

Rym answered by a negative gesture, accompanied with a circumspect smile.

"*Croix-Dieu!*" resumed Coppenole, quite wretched at being

obliged thus to lower his voice, "I feel a mighty itching to sit myself down on the floor, with my legs across, hosier-like, as I do in my own shop."

"You had better beware of doing so, Maître Jacques," was the reply.

"Heyday! Maître Guillaume; so, then, here a man can be nohow but on his feet?"

"Or on his knees," said Rym.

At that moment the King raised his voice, and they ceased talking.

"Fifty sols for the gowns of our valets, and twelve livres for the mantles of the clerks of our crown! That's the way! Pour out gold by tons! Are you mad, Olivier?"

So saying, the old man had raised his head. The golden shells of the collar of St. Michel were now seen to glitter about his neck. The candle shone full upon his meagre and morose profile. He snatched the paper from the hands of the other.

"You're ruining us," cried he, casting his hollow eyes over the schedule. "What's all this? What need have we of so prodigious a household? Two chaplains at the rate of ten livres a month each, and a chapel clerk at a hundred sols! A valet-de-chambre at ninety livres a year! Four squires of the kitchen at a hundred and twenty livres a year each! A roaster, a potagier, a saucier, a chief cook, an armoury-keeper, two sumptermen, at the rate of ten livres a month each! Two turnspits at eight livres! A groom and his two helpers at four-and-twenty livres a month! A porter, a pastry-cook, a baker, two carters, each sixty livres a year! And the marshal of the forges a hundred and twenty livres! And the marshal of our exchequer chamber twelve hundred livres! And the controller five hundred! And God knows what besides! Why, it's absolutely monstrous! The wages of our domestics are laying France under pillage! All the treasure in the Louvre will melt away in such a blaze of expense! We shall have to sell our plate! And next year, if God and our Lady" (here he raised his hat from his head) "grant us life, we shall drink our ptisans out of a pewter pot!"

So saying, he cast his eye upon the silver goblet that was glittering on the table. He coughed, and continued,—

"Maître Olivier, princes who reign over great seigneuries, as kings and emperors, ought not to let sumptuousness be engendered in their households, for 'tis a fire that will spread from thence into their provinces. And so, Maître Olivier, set this down for certain—that the thing displeases us. What! *Pasque-Dieu!* until the year '79 it never exceeded thirty-six thousand livres; in '80 it rose to forty-three thousand six hundred and nineteen livres—I've the figures in my head; in '81 it came to sixty-six thousand six hundred and eighty; and this year, by the faith of my body, it will amount to eighty thousand livres! Doubled in four years! Monstrous!"

He stopped, quite out of breath; then resumed with vehemence, "I see none about me but people fattening upon my leanness. You suck money from me at every pore!"

All kept silence. It was one of those fits of passion which must be allowed to run its course. He continued,—

"It's just like that Latin memorial from the body of the French seigneurs, requesting us to re-establish what they call the great offices of the crown. Ha, messieurs! you tell us that we are no king to reign *dapifero nullo, buticulario nullo.* But we'll show you, *Pasque-Dieu!* whether we're a king or not."

Here he smiled in the consciousness of his power; his ill-humour was allayed by it, and he turned round to the Flemings:

"Look you, compère [1] Guillaume, the grand baker, the grand butler, the grand chamberlain, the grand seneschal are not so useful as the meanest valet. Bear this in mind, compère Coppenole—they're of no service whatever. Keeping themselves, thus useless, about the king, they put me in mind of the four evangelists that surround the face of the great clock of the Palais, and that Philippe Brille has just now been renovating. They're gilt, indeed, but they don't mark the hour, and the hand of the clock can do very well without them."

He remained thoughtful for a moment, and then added, shaking his aged head, "Ho, ho! by Our Lady, but I'm not Philippe Brille, and I'm not going to regild the great vassals. Proceed, Olivier."

[1] The English word gossip having been incorrectly used by the author of *Waverley*, in his romance of *Quentin Durward*, to render this old French expression of familiarity, it may be well to explain the impropriety in this place. Gossip is, indeed, synonymous with *compère* in two other senses, but not in that in which Louis XI. used it to his intimates. The English word, in its primitive sense of a baptismal sponsor, and its secondary sense of a hearer and teller of news, answers precisely to the French *compère* and *commère*. But the French *compère* has a third signification which has never belonged to the English gossip. In this third sense it is expressive of a broad familiarity, answering nearly to the English good fellow! In this sense it was used by Louis XI. to those habitually about him, to the least gossiping as well as to the most so, to the taciturn as well as to the talkative.

The person whom he designated by this name again took the sheet in his hands, and went on reading aloud:—

"... To Adam Tenon, keeper of the seals of the provostry of Paris, for the silver, workmanship, and engraving of the said seals, which have been made new, because the former ones, by reason of their being old and worn out, could no longer be used, twelve livres parisis.

"To Guillaume, his brother, the sum of four livres four sols parisis, for his trouble and cost in having fed and nourished the pigeons of the two pigeon-houses at the Hôtel des Tournelles during the months of January, February, and March of this year, for the which he has furnished seven sextiers of barley.

"To a cordelier, for confessing a criminal, four sols parisis."

The King listened in silence. From time to time he coughed; then he lifted the goblet to his lips, and swallowed a draught of its contents, at which he made a wry face.

"In this year have been made," continued the reader, "by judicial order, by sound of trumpet, through the streets of Paris, fifty-six several cries. Amount not made up.

"For search made in divers places, in Paris and elsewhere, after treasure said to have been concealed in the said places, but nothing has been found, forty-five livres parisis."

"Burying an écu to dig up a sou!" said the King.

"For putting in at the Hôtel des Tournelles six panes of white glass, at the place where the iron cage is, thirteen sols. For making and delivering, by the King's command, on the day of the musters, four escutcheons, bearing the arms of our said lord, and wreathed all round with chaplets of roses, six livres. For two new sleeves to the King's old doublet, twenty sols. For a box of grease to grease the King's boots, fifteen deniers. A new sty for keeping the King's black swine, thirty livres parisis. Divers partitions, planks, and trapdoors, for the safe keeping of the lions at the Hôtel St. Pol, twenty-two livres."

"Dear beasts, those!" said Louis XI. "But no matter; it's a fair piece of royal magnificence. There's a great red lion that I love for his pretty behaviour. Have you seen him, Maître Guillaume? Princes must have those wondrous animals. For dogs we kings should have lions, and for cats, tigers. The great befits a crown. In the time of the pagans of Jupiter, when the people offered up at the churches a hundred oxen and a hundred sheep, the emperors gave a hundred lions and a hundred eagles. That was very fierce and very noble. The kings of France have always those roarings about their throne. Nevertheless, this justice will be done me—to admit that I spend less money in that way than my predecessors, and that I have a more moderate stock of lions, bears, elephants, and leopards.—Go on, Maître Olivier; only we had a mind to say so much to our Flemish friends."

Guillaume Rym made a low bow, while Coppenole with his gruff countenance, looked much like one of the bears of whom his Majesty spoke. The King did not observe it—he had just then put the goblet to his lips, and was spitting out what remained in his mouth of the unsavoury beverage, saying, "Foh! the nauseous ptisan!" His reader continued:—

"For the food of a rogue and vagabond, kept for the last six months in the lock-up house of the Ecorcherie, until it should be known what was to be done with him, six livres four sols."

"What's that?" interrupted the King sharply. "Feeding what ought to be hanged! *Pasque-Dieu!* I'll not give a single sol towards such feeding. Olivier, you'll arrange that matter with Monsieur d'Estouteville; and this very night you'll make preparations for uniting this gentleman in holy matrimony to a gallows. Now, go on with your reading."

Olivier made a mark with his thumb-nail at the rogue and vagabond article, and went on:—

"To Henriette Cousin, executioner-in-chief at the justice of Paris, the sum of sixty sols parisis, to him adjudged by Monseigneur the Provost of Paris, for having bought, by order of the said lord the provost, a large, broad-bladed sword, to be used in executing and beheading persons judicially condemned for their delinquencies, and had it furnished with a scabbard and all other appurtenances; as also for repairing and putting in order the old sword, which had been splintered and jagged by executing justice upon Messire Louis of Luxemburg, as can be more fully made appear——"

Here the King interrupted him. "Enough," said he; "I shall give the order for that payment with all my heart. Those are expenses I make no account of. I have never grudged that money. Proceed."

"For making a great new cage——"

"Ha!" said the King, laying each hand upon an arm of his chair; "I knew I was come to this Bastille for something or other. Stop, Maître Olivier; I will see that cage myself. You shall read over to me the cost of it while I examine it. Messieurs the Flemings, you must come and see that—it's curious."

Then he rose, leaned upon the arm of his interlocutor, made a sign to the sort of mute who kept standing before the doorway to go before him, made another to the two Flemings to follow him, and went out of the chamber.

The royal train was recruited at the door by men-at-arms ponderous with steel, and slender pages carrying flambeaux. It proceeded for some time in the interior of the gloomy donjon, perforated by staircases and corridors even into the thickness of the walls. The captain of the Bastille walked at its head, and directed the opening of the successive narrow doors before the old, sickly, and stooping king, who coughed as he walked along.

At each doorway every one was obliged to stoop in order to pass except only the old man bent with age. "Hum!" said he between his gums, for he had no teeth left, "we're quite ready for the door of the sepulchre. A low door needs a stooping passenger."

At length, after making their way through the last door of all, so loaded with complicated locks that it took a quarter of an hour to open it, they entered a spacious and lofty chamber, of Gothic vaulting, in the centre of which was discernible, by the light of the torches, a great cubical mass of masonry, iron, and woodwork. The interior was hollow. It was one of those famous cages for state prisoners which were called familiarly *les fillettes du roi*. In its walls there were two or three small windows, so thickly latticed with massive iron bars as to leave no glass visible. The door consisted of a single large flat stone, like that of a tomb—one of those doors that serve for entrance only. The difference was that here the tenant was alive.

The King went and paced slowly round this small edifice, examining it carefully, while Maître Olivier, following him, read out his paper of expenses aloud:—

"For making a great new wooden cage, of heavy beams, joists, and rafters, measuring inside nine feet long by eight broad, and seven feet high between the planks, mortised and bolted with great iron bolts, which has been fixed in a certain chamber in one of the towers of the Bastille St. Antoine; in which said cage is put and kept, by command of our lord the King, a prisoner, that before inhabited an old, decayed, and worn-out cage. Used in making the said new cage, ninety-six horizontal beams and fifty-two perpendicular; ten joists, each three toises long. Employed, in squaring, planing, and fitting all the said woodwork in the yard of the Bastille, nineteen carpenters for twenty days——"

"Very fine heart of oak," said the King, rapping his knuckles against the timbers.

"Used in this cage," continued the other, "two hundred and twenty great iron bolts, nine feet and a half long, the rest of a medium length—together with the plates and nuts for fastening the said bolts—the said irons weighing altogether three thousand seven hundred and thirty-five pounds; besides eight heavy iron *equières* for fixing the said cage in its place, with the cramp-irons and nails, weighing altogether two hundred and eighteen pounds—without reckoning the iron for the trellis-work of the windows of the chamber in which the said cage has been placed, the iron bars of the door of the chamber, and other articles——"

"Here's a deal of iron," observed the King, "to restrain the levity of a spirit."

"The whole amounts to three hundred and seventeen livres five sols seven deniers."

"*Pasque-Dieu!*" cried the King.

At this oath, which was the favourite one of Louis XI., some one seemed to be roused in the interior of the cage. There was a noise of chains clanking upon its floor, and a feeble voice was heard, which seemed to issue from the tomb, exclaiming, "Sire, sire! mercy, mercy!" It could not be seen who uttered this exclamation.

"Three hundred and seventeen livres five sols seven deniers!" repeated Louis XI.

The voice of lamentation which had issued from the cage chilled the blood of all present, even that of Maître Olivier. The King alone looked as if he had not heard it. At his command, Maître Olivier resumed his reading, and his Majesty coolly continued his inspection of the cage.

". . . Besides the above, there has been paid to a mason for making the holes to fix the window-grates and the floor of the chamber containing the cage, because the other floor would not have been strong enough to support such cage by reason of its weight, twenty-seven livres fourteen sols parisis——"

Again the voice began to complain: "Mercy, sire! I assure you that it was Monsieur the Cardinal of Angers that committed the treason, and not I."

"The mason is a rough hand," said the King. "Proceed, Olivier."

Olivier continued: ". . . To a joiner for window-frames,

bedstead, close-stool, and other matters, twenty livres two sols parisis——"

The voice still continued: "Alas, sire! will you not listen to me? I protest it was not I that wrote that matter to Monseigneur of Guyenne; it was Monsieur the Cardinal Balue."

"The joiner charges high," observed the King. "Is that all?"

"No, sire. To a glazier for the window-glass of the said chamber, forty-six sols eight deniers parisis."

"Have mercy, sire!" cried the voice again. "Is it not enough that all my property has been given to my judges—my plate to Monsieur de Torcy, my library to Maître Pierre Doriolle, and my tapestry to the Governor of Rousillon? I am innocent. It is now fourteen years that I have been shivering in an iron cage. Have mercy, sire, and you will find it in heaven."

"Maître Olivier," said the King, "what is the sum total?"

"Three hundred and sixty-seven livres eight sols three deniers parisis."

"Our Lady!" exclaimed the King. "Here's a cage out of all reason!"

He snatched the account from the hands of Maître Olivier, and began to reckon it up himself upon his fingers, examining by turns the paper and the cage. Meanwhile the prisoner was heard sobbing within. The effect, in the darkness, was dismal in the extreme; and the faces of the bystanders turned pale as they looked at one another.

"Fourteen years, sire! It is fourteen years since April 1469. In the name of the holy mother of God, sire, hearken to me. All that time you have been enjoying the warmth of the sun; and shall I, wretched that I am, never again see the light? Mercy, sire! Be merciful! Clemency is a noble virtue in a king, that turns aside the stem of wrath. Does your Majesty think that at the hour of death it is a great satisfaction for a king to have left no offence unpunished? Besides, sire, it was not I that betrayed your Majesty; it was Monsieur of Angers. And I have a very heavy chain to my foot, with a huge ball of iron at the end of it, much heavier than is needful. Oh, sire, do have pity on me!"

"Olivier," said the King, shaking his head, "I observe that they put me down the bushel of plaster at twenty sols, though it's only worth twelve. You'll draw out this account afresh."

He turned his back on the cage, and began to move towards

the door of the chamber. The wretched prisoner judged, by the withdrawing of the torchlight and the noise, that the King was going away. "Sire, sire!" cried he in despair. The door closed again, and he no longer distinguished anything but the hoarse voice of the turnkey, humming in his ears a popular song of the day:—

"Maître Jehan Balue
Has lost out of view
His good bishoprics all:
Monsieur de Verdun
Cannot now boast of one;
They are gone, one and all."

The King reascended in silence to his closet, followed by the persons of his train, horror-struck at the last groanings of the condemned. All at once his Majesty turned round to the governor of the Bastille. "By-the-bye," said he, "was there not some one in that cage?"

"*Par-Dieu*, yes, sire," answered the governor, astounded at the question.

"And who, pray?"

"Monsieur the Bishop of Verdun."

The King knew that better than any one else, but this was a mania of his.

"Ha!" said he, with an air of simplicity, as if he was thinking of it for the first time; "Guillaume de Harancourt, the friend of Monsieur the Cardinal Balue. A good fellow of a bishop."

A few moments after, the door of the closet had reopened and then closed again upon the five persons whom the reader found there at the beginning of this chapter, and who had severally resumed their places, their postures, and their whispering conversation.

During the King's absence some dispatches had been laid upon the table, of which he himself broke the seal. Then he began to read them over diligently one after another; motioned to Maître Olivier, who seemed to act as his minister, to take up a pen; and, without communicating to him the contents of the dispatches, he began in a low voice to dictate to him the answers, which the latter wrote, very uncomfortably to himself, on his knees before the table.

Guillaume Rym was on the watch.

The King spoke so low that the Flemings could hear nothing at all of what he was dictating, except here and there a few isolated and scarcely intelligible fragments, as thus: " . . . To maintain the fertile places by commerce, the sterile ones by manufactures. . . . To show the English lords our four bombards—the Londres, the Brabant, the Bourg-en-Bresse, the St. Ome. . . . It is owing to artillery that war is now more judiciously carried on. . . . To our friend Monsieur de Bressuire. . . . The armies cannot be kept on foot without contributions. . . ." etc.

Once he spoke aloud: "*Pasque-Dieu!* Monsieur the King of Sicily seals his letters with yellow wax like a King of France! Perhaps we do wrong to permit him. My fair cousin of Burgundy gave no arms on a field *gules*. The greatness of a house is secured by maintaining the intergity of its prerogatives. Note that down, compère Olivier."

At another moment, "Oh, oh," said he, "the bold message! What is our friend the emperor demanding of us?" Then casting his eyes over the missive, interrupting his perusal here and there with brief interjections: "Certes, that Germany is so large and so powerful that it's hardly credible! But we don't forget the old proverb, 'The finest county is Flanders; the finest duchy, Milan; the finest kingdom, France.' Is it not so, Messieurs the Flemings?"

This time Coppenole bowed as well as Guillaume Rym. The hosier's patriotism was tickled.

The last dispatch of all made Louis XI. knit his brows. "What's that?" he exclaimed. "Complaints and petitions against our garrisons in Picardy!—Olivier, write with all speed to Monsieur the Marshal de Rouault. That discipline is relaxed. That the gendarmes of the ordonnance, the nobles, the free archers, the Swiss, do infinite mischief to the inhabitants. That the military, not content with what they find in the houses of the husbandmen, compel them, with heavy blows of staves or bills, to go and fetch from the town wine, fish, groceries, and other unreasonable articles. That the King knows all that. That we mean to protect our people from annoyance, theft, and pillage. That such is our will, by Our Lady. That furthermore, it does not please us that any musician, barber, or servant-at-arms should go clad like a prince, in velvet, silk, and gold rings. That such vanities are hateful to God. That we, who are gentlemen, content ourselves with a doublet made of cloth at sixteen sols the Paris ell. That messieurs the serving men of the army may very well come down to that price likewise. Order and command. To our friend, Monsieur de Rouault. Good."

He dictated this letter aloud, in a firm tone, and in short, abrupt sentences. At the moment of his finishing it the door opened and admitted a fresh person, who rushed, all aghast, into the chamber, crying, "Sire, sire, there's a sedition of the populace in Paris!"

The grave countenance of Louis XI. was contracted for a moment, but all that was visible in his emotion passed away like a flash. He contained himself, and said with a tone and look of quiet severity, "Compère Jacques, you enter very abruptly."

"Sire, sire, there is a revolt!" resumed compère Jacques, quite out of breath.

The King, who had risen from his seat, seized him roughly by the arm, and said in his ear, so as to be heard by no else one, with an expression of internal anger and an oblique glance at the Flemings, "Hold your tongue—or speak low."

The newcomer understood, and set himself to make to the King a very terrified narration, to which the latter listened calmly, while Guillaume Rym was calling Coppenole's attention to the face and dress of the news-bearer—his furred *capuce* or hood (*caputia fourrata*), his short èpitoge (*epitogia curta*), and his black velvet gown, which bespoke a president of the Court of Accompts.

No sooner had this person given the King some explanations than Louis XI. exclaimed, with a burst of laughter, "Nay, in sooth speak aloud, compère Coictier. What occasion have you to whisper so? Our Lady knows we have no secrets with our good Flemish friends."

"But, sire——"

"Speak up!" said the King.

Compère Coictier remained mute with surprise.

"Come, come," resumed the King, "speak out, sir. There's a commotion of the people in our good city of Paris?"

"Yes, sire."

"And which is directed, you say, against Monsieur the Bailiff of the Palais de Justice?"

"So it appears," said the compère, who still stammered out his words, quite confounded at the sudden and inexplicable change which had taken place in the mind of the King.

Louis XI. resumed: "Whereabouts did the watch meet with the mob?"

"Coming along from the great Truandry towards the Pont-aux-Changeurs, sire. I met it myself as I was coming hither in obedience to your Majesty's orders. I heard some of them crying, 'Down with the Bailiff of the Palais!'"

"And what grievances have they against the bailiff?"

"Ah," said compère Jacques, "that he is their seigneur."

"Is it really so?"

"Yes, sire. They are rascals from the Court of Miracles. They have long been complaining of the bailiff, whose vassals they are. They will not acknowledge him either as justiciary or as keeper of the highways."

"So, so," said the King, with a smile of satisfaction which he strove in vain to disguise.

"In all their petitions to the Parliament," continued compère Jacques, "they pretend that they have only two masters—your Majesty and their God, whom I believe to be the devil."

"Oh, oh!" said the King.

He rubbed his hands, laughed with that internal laugh which irradiates the countenance, and was quite unable to dissemble his joy, though he now and then strove to compose himself. None of those present could at all understand his hilarity—not even Maître Olivier. At length his Majesty remained silent for a moment, with a thoughtful but satisfied air.

All at once he asked, "Are they in force?"

"Yes, sire, that they certainly are," answered compère Jacques.

"How many?"

"At least six thousand."

The King could not help saying, "Good!" He went on, "Are they armed?"

"Yes, sire; with scythes, pikes, hackbuts, pickaxes—all sorts of most violent weapons."

The King seemed to be not at all disturbed by this awful detail. Compère Jacques thought proper to add, "Unless your Majesty sends speedy succour to the bailiff he is lost."

"We will send," said the King, with affected seriousness. "Good! Certainly we will send. Monsieur the Bailiff is our friend. Six thousand! They're determined rogues. Their boldness is marvellous, and deeply are we wroth at it. But we have few men about us to-night. It will be time enough to-morrow morning."

Compère Jacques could not help exclaiming, "Directly, sire! They'll have time to sack the bailiff's house twenty times over, violate the seigneurie, and hang the bailiff himself. For God's sake, sire, send before to-morrow morning."

The King looked him full in the face. "I have told you—to-morrow morning." It was one of those looks to which there is no reply.

After a pause Louis XI. again raised his voice. "My compère Jacques, you should know that. What was . . ." (he corrected himself)—"What is the bailiff's feudal jurisdiction?"

"Sire, the Bailiff of the Palais has the Rue de la Calandre, as far as the Rue de l'Herberie; the Place St. Michel, and the places commonly called Les Mureaux, situated near the church of Notre-Dame-des-Champs" [here the King lifted the brim of his hat], "which mansions amount to thirteen; besides the Court of Miracles, and the lazaretto called the Banlieue; and all the highway beginning at that lazaretto and ending at the Porte St. Jacques. Of those several places he is keeper of the ways—chief, mean, and inferior justiciary—full and entire lord."

"So ho!" said the King, scratching his left ear with his right hand, "that makes a good slice of my town! So Monsieur the Bailiff was king of all that, eh?"

This time he did not correct himself. He continued, ruminating and as if talking to himself, "Softly, Monsieur the Bailiff; you had a very pretty slice of our Paris in your clutches, truly!"

All at once he broke forth: "*Pasque-Dieu!* what are all these people that pretend to be highway-keepers, justiciaries, lords and masters, along with us—that have their toll-gate at the corner of every field, their justice and their *bourreau* at every crossway, amongst our people?—so that, as the Greek thought he had as many gods as he had springs of water, and the Persian as many as he saw stars, so the Frenchman reckons up as many kings as he sees gibbets. *Par-Dieu!* this thing is evil, and the confusion of it displeases me. I should like to be told, now, if it be God's pleasure that there should be at Paris any highway-keeper but the king—any justiciary but our Parliament—any emperor but ourself in this empire! By the faith of my soul, but the day must come when there shall be in France but one king, one lord, one judge, one headsman, as there is but one God in heaven!"

Here he lifted his cap again, and continued, still ruminating, and with the look and accent of a huntsman cheering on his pack: "Good, my people! Well done! Shatter those false seigneurs! Do your work. On, on! Pillage—hang—sack them! So you want to be kings, messeigneurs! On, my people, on!"

Here he suddenly stopped himself, bit his lip, as if to recall his half-wandering thoughts, fixing his piercing eye in turn upon each of the five persons around him; and then, all at once taking his hat between both hands, and looking steadfastly at it, he said, " Oh, I would burn thee if thou couldst know what I have in my head! "

Then once more casting around him the cautious, anxious look of a fox stealing back into his hole, " No matter," said he; " we will send succour to Monsieur the Bailiff. Unluckily, we have very few troops here at this moment, against such a number of the populace. We must wait till to-morrow. Order shall then be restored in the city, and all who are taken shall be hanged up forthwith."

" Apropos, sire," said compère Coictier, " I had forgotten that in my first perturbation. The watch have seized two stragglers belonging to the gang. If it be your Majesty's pleasure to see the men, they are here."

" If it be my pleasure! " exclaimed the King. " What, *Pasque-Dieu!* canst thou forget such a thing as that?—Run quick, Olivier—go and fetch them in."

Maître Olivier went out, and returned in a minute with the two prisoners surrounded by archers of the ordonnance. The first of the two had a great idiotic, drunken, and wonder-struck visage; he was clothed in tatters, and walked with one knee bent and the foot dragging along. The other had a pale, half-smiling countenance, with which the reader is already acquainted.

The King scrutinised them a moment without saying a word; then suddenly addressing the first of the two prisoners, " What is thy name? " he asked.

" Gieffroy Pincebourde."

" Thy trade? "

" A Truand."

" What wast thou going to do in that damnable sedition? "

The Truand looked at the King, swinging his arms the while with an air of sottish stupidity. His was one of those heads, of awkward conformation, in which the intellect is about as much at its ease as a light under an extinguisher.

" I don't know," said he. " They were going — and so I went."

" Were you not going outrageously to attack and plunder your lord the Bailiff of the Palais? "

" I know they were going to take something at somebody's —and that's all."

Here a soldier showed the King a pruning-hook which had

been found upon the Truand. "Dost thou know that weapon?" asked the King.

"Yes, it's my pruning-hook. I'm a vine-dresser."

"And dost thou know that man for thy comrade?" asked Louis XI., pointing to the other prisoner.

"No, I don't know him."

"Enough," said the King; and motioning with his finger to the silent person standing motionless by the door, whom we have already pointed out to the reader, "Compère Tristan," said he, "there's a man for you."

Tristan l'Hermite bowed to his Majesty, and then whispered an order to a couple of archers, who thereupon carried away the poor Truand.

Meanwhile the King had addressed the second prisoner, who was perspiring profusely. "Thy name?"

"Sire, it is Pierre Gringoire."

"Thy trade?"

"A philosopher, sire."

"How comes it, fellow, that thou hast the audacity to go and beset our friend Monsieur the Bailiff of the Palais? And what hast thou to say about this popular commotion?"

"Sire, I was not in it."

"Come, come, *paillard*,[1] wast thou not apprehended by the watch in that bad company?"

"No, sire; there's a mistake. It's a fatality. I write tragedies, sire. I implore your Majesty to hear me. I am a poet. It's the hard lot of men of my profession to be going about the streets at night. By mere chance I happened to be going by there this evening. They took me up without reason. I am quite innocent of this civil storm. Your Majesty saw that the Truand did not recognise me. I entreat your Majesty . . ."

"Hold your tongue," said the King, between two draughts of his ptisan—"you split our head."

Tristan l'Hermite stepped forward, and said, pointing to Gringoire, "Sire, may we hang that one too?" This was the first word he had uttered.

"Oh, why," answered the King carelessly, "I don't see any objections."

[1] Louis XI. was very fond of this word *paillard*, which, together with *Pasque-Dieu*, formed his chief stock of humour. Paillard signifies a man addicted to all kinds of low obscenity; and Louis was no less familiar with the name than he was, among so many others of the Lord's Anointed, with the thing. See *La Chronique Scandaleuse*, the right edition of which, the author of *Waverley* tells us, is reckoned so precious by collectors.

"But I see many," said Gringoire.

At this moment our philosopher's countenance was horribly livid. He saw, by the cool and indifferent manner of the King, that he had no resource but in something excessively pathetic; and he threw himself at the feet of Louis XI. with gestures of despair.

"Sire, your Majesty will vouchsafe to hear me. Sire, burst not in thunder upon so poor a thing as I am. God's great thunderbolts strike not the lowly plant. Sire, you are an august and most puissant monarch—have pity on a poor, honest man, as incapable of fanning the flame of revolt as an icicle of striking a spark. Most gracious sire, mildness is the virtue of a lion and of a king. Alas! severity does but exasperate: the fierce blasts of the north wind make not the traveller lay aside his cloak; but the sun, darting his rays by little and little, warms him so that at length he will gladly strip himself. Sire, you are the sun. I protest to you, my sovereign lord and master, that I am not a companion of Truands, thievish and disorderly. Rebellion and pillage go not in the train of Apollo; I am no man to go and rush into those clouds which burst in seditious clamour. I am a faithful vassal of your Majesty. The same jealousy which the husband has for the honour of his wife—the affection with which the son should requite his father's love—a good vassal should feel for the glory of his king. He should wear himself out for the upholding of his house and the promoting of his service. Any other passion that should possess him would be mere frenzy. Such, sire, are my maxims of state. Do not, then, judge me to be seditious and plundering because my garment is out at the elbows. If you show me mercy, sire, I will wear it out at the knees in praying for you morning and night. Alas! I am not extremely rich, it is true—indeed, I am rather poor; but I am not wicked for all that. It is no fault of mine. Everybody knows that great wealth is not to be acquired by the belles-lettres, and that the most accomplished writers have not always a great fire in winter-time. The gentlemen of the law take all the wheat to themselves, and leave nothing but the chaff for the other learned professions. There are forty most excellent proverbs about the philosopher's threadbare cloak. O sire, clemency is the only light that can enlighten the interior of a great soul. Clemency carries the torch before all the other virtues. Without her they are but blind, and seek God in the dark. Mercy, which is the same thing as clemency, produces loving subjects, who are the most powerful bodyguard of the prince. What can it signify to your Majesty, by whom all faces are dazzled, that there should be one poor man more upon earth?—a poor, innocent philosopher, creeping about in the darkness of calamity, with his empty fob lying flat upon his empty stomach. Besides, sire, I am a man of letters. Great kings add a jewel to their crown by patronising letters. Hercules did not disdain the title of Musagetes. Matthias Corvinus showed favour to Jean de Monroyal, the ornament of mathematics. Now, 'tis an ill way of patronising letters to hang up the lettered. What a stain to Alexander if he had had Aristoteles hanged! The act would not have been a small patch upon the face of his reputation to embellish it, but a virulent ulcer to disfigure it. Sire, I wrote a very appropriate epithalamium for Mademoiselle of Flanders and Monseigneur the most august Dauphin. That was not like a firebrand of rebellion. Your Majesty sees that I am no dunce—that I have studied excellently—and that I have much natural eloquence. Grant me mercy, sire. So doing, you will do an act grateful to Our Lady; and I assure you, sire, that I am very much frightened at the idea of being hanged."

So saying, the desolate Gringoire kissed the King's slippers; while Guillaume Rym whispered to Coppenole, "He does well to crawl upon the floor: kings are like the Jupiter of Crete—they hear only through their feet." And, quite inattentive to the Cretan Jupiter, the hosier answered with a heavy smile, and his eyes fixed upon Gringoire, "Ah, that's good! I could fancy I heard the Chancellor Hugonet asking me for mercy."

When Gringoire stopped at length quite out of breath, he raised his eyes, trembling, towards the King, who was scratching with his finger-nail a spot which he saw upon his breeches' knee, after which his Majesty took another draught from the goblet. But he uttered not a syllable—and this silence kept Gringoire in torture. At last the King looked at him. "Here's a terrible prater," said he. Then, turning to Tristan l'Hermite, "Pshaw! let him go."

Gringoire fell backwards upon his posteriors, quite thunderstruck with joy.

"Let him go!" grumbled Tristan. "Is it not your Majesty's pleasure that he should be caged for a little while?"

"Compère," returned Louis XI., "dost thou think it is for birds like this that we have cages made at three hundred and sixty-seven livres eight sols three deniers a-piece? Let him go directly, the paillard; and send him out with a drubbing."

"Oh," exclaimed Gringoire in ecstasy, "this is indeed a great King!"

Then, for fear of a countermand, he rushed towards the door, which Tristan opened for him with a very ill grace. The soldiers went out with him, driving him before them with hard blows of their fists, which Gringoire endured like a true stoic philosopher.

The good humour of the King, since the revolt against the bailiff had been announced to him, manifested itself in everything. This unusual clemency of his was no small sign of it. Tristan l'Hermite, in his corner, was looking as surly as a mastiff dog balked of his meal.

Meanwhile the King was gaily beating with his fingers upon his chair arm the Pont-Audemer march. Though a dissembling prince, he was much better able to conceal his sorrow than his rejoicing. These, his external manifestations of joy on the receipt of any good news, sometimes carried him great lengths; as, for instance, at the death of Charles the Rash of Burgundy, to that of vowing balustrades of silver to St. Martin of Tours; and on his accession to the throne to that of forgetting to give orders for his father's funeral.

"Ha, sire," suddenly exclaimed Jacques Coictier, "what has become of the sharp pains on account of which your Majesty sent for me?"

"Oh," said the King, "truly, my compère, I am suffering greatly. I've a singing in my ears, and teeth of fire raking my breast."

Coictier took the King's hand, and began to feel his pulse with a knowing look.

"Look there, Coppenole," whispered Rym. "There you see him between Coictier and Tristan. That's his whole court—a physician for himself, and a hangman for other people."

While feeling the King's pulse, Coictier was assuming a look of greater and greater alarm. Louis XI. looked at him with some anxiety; while the physician's countenance grew more and more dismal. The King's bad health was the only estate the good man had to cultivate, and accordingly he made the most of it.

"Oh, oh!" muttered he at last. "This is serious indeed."

"Is it not?" said the King, uneasy.

"*Pulsus creber, anhelans, crepitans, irregularis,*" continued the physician.

"*Pasque-Dieu!*" exclaimed his Majesty.

"This might carry a man off in less than three days."

"Our Lady!" cried the King. "And the remedy, compère?"

"I'm thinking of it, sire."

He made the King put out his tongue; shook his head; made a wry face; and in the midst of this grimacing, "*Par-Dieu*, sire," said he all of a sudden, "I must inform you that there is a receivership of episcopal revenues vacant, and that I have a nephew."

"I give the receivership to thy nephew, compère Jacques," answered the King; "but take this fire out of my breast."

"Since your Majesty is so gracious," resumed the physician, "I am sure you will not refuse to assist me a little in the building of my house in the Rue St. André-des-Arcs."

"Heu!" said the King.

"I'm at the end of my cash," said the doctor, "and it would really be a pity that the house should be left without a roof—not for the sake of the house itself, which is quite plain and homely, but for the sake of the paintings by Jehan Fourbault that adorn its wainscoting. There's a Diana flying in the air—so excellently done—so tender—so delicate—of an action so artless—her head so well dressed, and crowned with a crescent—her flesh so white—that she leads into temptation those who examine her too curiously. Then there's a Ceres, and she too is a very beautiful divinity. She's sitting upon corn-sheaves, and crowned with a goodly wreath of ears of corn intertwined with purple goat's-beard and other flowers. Never were seen more amorous eyes, rounder legs, a nobler air, or a more gracefully flowing skirt. She's one of the most innocent and most perfect beauties ever produced by the pencil."

"*Bourreau!*" grumbled Louis XI., "what art thou driving at?"

"I want a roof over these paintings, sire; and although it is but a trifle, I have no money left."

"What will thy roof cost?"

"Oh . . . why . . . a roof of copper, figured and gilt . . . not above two thousand livres."

"Ha, the assassin!" cried the King. "He never draws me a tooth but he makes a diamond of it."

"Am I to have my roof?" said Coictier.

"Yes—the devil take you! But cure me."

Jacques Coictier made a low bow, and said, "Sire, it is a repellant that will save you. We shall apply to your loins the grand defensive, composed of cerate, bole armoniac, white of eggs, oil, and vinegar. You will continue your ptisan—and we will answer for your Majesty's safety."

A lighted candle never attracts one gnat only. Maître Olivier, seeing the King in a liberal mood, and deeming the moment propitious, approached in his turn. "Sire."

"What next?" said Louis XI.

"Sire, your Majesty is aware that Maître Simon Radin is dead."

"Well?"

"He was king's councillor for the jurisdiction of the treasury."

"Well?"

"Sire, his place is vacant."

While thus speaking, Maître Olivier's haughty countenance had exchanged the arrogant for the fawning expression—the only alteration that ever takes place in the countenance of a courtier. The King looked him full in the face, and said dryly, "I understand."

His Majesty resumed: "Maître Olivier, Marshal de Boucicault used to say, 'There's no good gift but from a king; there's no good fishing but in the sea.' I see that you are of the Marshal's opinion. Now, hear this. We have a good memory. In the year '68 we made you groom of our chamber; in '69, castellan of the bridge of St. Cloud, with a salary of a hundred livres tournois—you wanted them parisis. In November '73, by letters given at Gergeaule, we appointed you keeper of the Bois de Vincennes, in lieu of Gilbert Acle, Esquire; in '75, warden of the forest of Rouvray-les-Saint-Cloud, in the place of Jacques Le Maire. In '78 we graciously settled upon you, by letters-patent sealed on extra label with green wax, an annuity of ten livres parisis, to you and your wife, upon the Place-aux-Marchands, situate at the Ecole St. Germain. In '79 we made you warden of the forest of Senart, in room of that poor Jehan Diaz; then captain of the castle of Loches; then governor of St. Quentin; then captain of the bridge of Meulan, of which you call yourself count. Out of the fine of five sols paid by every barber that shaves on a holiday you get three, and we get what you leave. We were pleased to change your name of Le Mauvais, which was too much like your countenance. In '74 we granted you, to the great displeasure of our nobility, armorial bearings of a thousand colours, that make you a breast like a peacock. *Pasque-Dieu!* have you not your fill? Is not the draught of fishes fine and miraculous enough? And are you not afraid lest a single salmon more should be enough to sink your boat? Pride will ruin you, my compère. Pride is ever followed close behind by ruin and shame. Think of that, and be silent."

These words, uttered in a tone of severity, brought back the chagrined physiognomy of Maître Olivier to its former insolent expression. "Good!" muttered he, almost aloud. "It's plain enough that the King's ill to-day, for he gives all to the physician."

Louis XI., far from taking offence at this piece of presumption, resumed with some mildness, "Stay—I forgot to add that I made you ambassador to Madame Marie at Ghent.—Yes, gentlemen," added the King, turning to the Flemings, "this man has been an ambassador.—There, my compère," continued he, again addressing Maître Olivier, "let us not fall out—we're old friends. It's getting very late. We've got through our work. Shave me."

Our readers have doubtless already recognised in Maître Olivier that terrible Figaro whom Providence, the great dramatist of all, so artfully mixed up in the long and sanguinary play of Louis XI.'s reign. We shall not here undertake to develop at full length that singular character. This barber to the King had three names. At court he was called politely Olivier-le-Daim, from the daim or stag upon his escutcheon; and among the people, Olivier-le-Diable, or the devil. But by his right name he was called Olivier-le-Mauvais, or the bad.

Olivier-le-Mauvais, then, stood motionless, looking sulkily at the King and enviously at Jacques Coictier. "Yes, yes—the physician!" muttered he.

"Well, yes—the physician!" resumed Louis XI. with singular good humour; "the physician has yet more influence than thyself. It's a matter of course. He has got our whole body in his hands, and thou dost but hold us by the chin. Come, come, my poor barber, there's nothing amiss. What wouldst thou say, and what would become of thy office, if I were a king like King Chilperic, whose way it was to hold his beard with one hand? Come, my compère, perform thy office, and shave me—go and fetch thy tools."

Olivier, seeing that the King had resolved to take the matter in jest, and that there was no means even of provoking him, went out grumbling to execute his commands. The King rose from his seat, went to the window, and suddenly opening it in extraordinary agitation—"Oh yes!" exclaimed he, clapping his hands; "there's a glare in the sky over the city. It's the bailiff burning; it cannot be anything else. Ha! my good people, so you help me, then, at last, to pull down the seigneuries!"

Then turning to the Flemings—"Gentlemen," said he, "come and see. Is not that a fire that glares so red?"

The two Gantois came forward to look.

"It is a great fire," said Guillaume Rym.

"Oh," added Coppenole, whose eyes all at once began to sparkle, "that reminds me of the burning of the house of the Seigneur d'Hymbercourt. There must be a stout revolt there."

"You think so, Maître Coppenole?" said the King; and he looked almost as much pleased as the hosier himself. "Don't you think it will be difficult to resist it?" he added.

"*Croix-Dieu!* sire, it may cost your Majesty many a company of good soldiers."

"Ha! cost me!—that's quite another thing," returned the King. "If I chose——"

The hosier rejoined boldly, "If that revolt be what I suppose, you would choose in vain, sire."

"Compère," said Louis XI., "two companies of my ordonnance, and the discharge of a serpentine, are quite sufficient to rout a mob of the common people."

The hosier, in spite of the signs that Guillaume Rym was making to him, seemed determined to contest the matter with the King. "Sire," said he, "the Swiss were common people too. Monsieur the Duke of Burgundy was a great gentleman, and made no account of that canaille. At the battle of Grandson, sire, he called out, 'Cannoneers, fire upon those villains!' and he swore by St. George. But the avoyer, Scharnactal, rushed upon the fine duke with his club and his people; and at the shock of the peasants, with their bull-hides, the shining Burgundian army was shattered like a pane of glass by a flintstone. Many a knight was killed there by those base churls; and Monsieur de Château-Guyon, the greatest lord in Burgundy, was found dead, with his great grey horse, in a little boggy field."

"Friend," returned the King, "you're talking of a battle; but here it's only a riot, and I can put an end to it with a single frown when I please." The other replied unconcernedly, "That may be, sire. In that case the people's hour is not yet come."

Guillaume Rym thought he must now interfere. "Maître Coppenole," said he, "you're talking to a mighty king."

"I know it," answered the hosier gravely.

"Let him go on, Monsieur Rym, my friend," said the King; "I like this plain speaking. My father, Charles VII., used to say that truth was sick. For my part I thought she was dead, and had found no confessor; but Maître Coppenole shows me I was mistaken."

Then clapping his nand familiarly upon Coppenole's shoulder, "You were saying, then, Maître Jacques——"

"I say, sire, that perhaps you are right—that the people's hour is not yet come with you."

Louis XI. looked at him with his penetrating eye. "And when will that hour come, Maître?"

"You will hear it strike."

"By what clock, pray?"

Coppenole, with his quiet and homely self-possession, motioned to the King to approach the window. "Hark you, sire," said he: "here there are a donjon, an alarm-bell, cannon, townspeople, soldiers. When the alarm-bell shall sound—when the cannon shall roar—when, with great clamour, the donjon walls shall be shattered—when townspeople and soldiers shall shout and kill each other—then the hour will strike."

The countenance of Louis XI. became gloomy and thoughtful. He remained silent for a moment, then tapping gently with his hand against the massive wall of the donjon, as if patting the crupper of a war-horse, "Ah no, no!" said he, "thou wilt not so easily be shattered, wilt thou, my good Bastille?"

Then, turning abruptly round to the bold Fleming, he said, "Have you ever seen a revolt, Maître Jacques?"

"I have made one," said the hosier.

"What do you do," said the King, "to make a revolt?"

"Oh," answered Coppenole, "it's not very hard to do. There are a hundred ways. First of all, there must be dissatisfaction in the town. That's nothing uncommon. And then, one must consider the character of the inhabitants. Those of Ghent are prone to revolt. They always like the son of the prince, but never the prince himself. Well, now, one morning, we'll suppose, somebody comes into my shop, and says, Father Coppenole, it's so and so—as that the Lady of Flanders wants to save her ministers—that the high bailiff is doubling the toll on vegetables—or what not—anything you like. Then I throw by my work, go out into the street, and cry, *A sac!* There's always some empty cask or other in the way. I get upon it, and say with a loud voice the first words that come into my head—what's uppermost in my heart—and when one belongs to the people, sire, one has always something upon one's heart. Then a crowd gets together—they shout—they ring the tocsin—the people get arms by disarming the soldiers—the market people join the rest—and then they go to work; and it will always be so, as long as there are seigneurs in the seigneuries, townspeople in the towns, and country people in the country."

"And against whom do you rebel thus?" asked the King. "Against your bailiffs? against your lords?"

"Sometimes. That's as it may happen. Against the Duke, too, sometimes."

Louis XI. returned to his seat, and said with a smile, "Ah! but here they have not yet got further than the bailiffs!"

At that moment Olivier-le-Daim re-entered, followed by two pages carrying the apparatus for dressing his Majesty; but what struck Louis XI. was to see him also accompanied by the Provost of Paris and the knight of the watch, who seemed both in consternation. There was consternation, too, in the look of the mortified barber; but there was satisfaction lurking under it. It was he that spoke first. "Sire, I ask pardon of your Majesty for the calamitous news I bring you."

The King, turning sharply round, grazed the mat upon the floor with the feet of his chair. "What's it about?" said he.

"Sire," returned Olivier, with the malicious look of a man rejoicing that he has to deal a violent blow, "it is not against the Bailiff of the Palais that this popular sedition is driving."

"Against whom, then?"

"Against you, sire."

The aged King rose upon his feet, and erect, like a young man. "Explain, Olivier, explain—and look well to thy head, my compère—for I swear to thee, by the cross of Saint Lô, that if thou speakest us false in this matter, the sword that cut Monsieur of Luxemburg's throat is not so dinted but it shall saw thine too!"

The oath was formidable. Louis XI. had never but twice in his life sworn by the cross of Saint Lô. Olivier opened his lips to reply. "Sire . . ."

"Down on your knees!" interrupted the King with violence. —"Tristan, keep your eye upon this man."

Olivier fell upon his knees, and said composedly, "Sire, a witch has been condemned to death by your court of parliament. She has taken refuge in Notre-Dame. The people want to take her from thence by main force. Monsieur the Provost and

Monsieur the Knight of the Watch, who are come straight from the spot, are here to contradict me if I speak not truth. It is Notre-Dame that the people are besieging."

"Ah, ah!" said the King, in an undertone, all pale and trembling with passion; "Notre-Dame! They are besieging Our Lady, my good mistress, in her own cathedral! Rise, Olivier. Thou art right—I give thee Simon Radin's office. Thou art right—it is me they're attacking. The witch is under the safeguard of the church—the church is under my safeguard—and I, who thought all the while that it was only the bailiff—'tis against myself!"

Then, invigorated by passion, he began to pace hurriedly to and fro. He laughed no longer—he was terrible. The fox was changed into a hyena. He seemed to be choking with rage—his lips moved without utterance—and his withered hands were clenched. All at once he raised his head; his hollow eye seemed full of light; and his voice burst forth like a clarion. "Upon them, Tristan! Fall upon the knaves! Go, Tristan, my friend! Kill! kill!"

When this paroxysm was over, he went once more to his seat, and said with cool and concentrated passion, "Here, Tristan! We have with us here in this Bastille the fifty lances of the Viscount de Gif, making three hundred horse—you'll take them. There's also Monsieur de Chateaupers's company of the archers of our ordonnance — you'll take them. You are provost-marshal, and have the men of your provostry—you'll take them. At the Hôtel St. Pol you'll find forty archers of Monsieur the Dauphin's new guard—you'll take them. And with the whole you'll make all speed to Notre-Dame.—Ha! messieurs the commons of Paris—so you presume to fly in the face of the crown of France, the sanctity of Our Lady, and the peace of this commonwealth!—Exterminate, Tristan! exterminate! and let not one escape except for Montfaucon!"

Tristan bowed. "'Tis well, sire."

He added after a pause, "And what shall I do with the witch?"

This question set the King ruminating. "Ha!" said he, "the witch!—Monsieur d'Estouteville, what did the people want to do with her?"

"Sire," answered the Provost of Paris, "I imagine that, as the people are come to drag her away from her sanctuary of Notre-Dame, it is her impunity that offends them, and they want to hang her."

The King seemed to reflect deeply; then, addressing himself to Tristan l'Hermite, he said, "Well, my compère, exterminate the people and hang the witch."

"Just so," whispered Rym to Coppenole. "Punish the people for wishing, and do what they wish."

"Enough, sire," answered Tristan. "If the witch be still in Notre-Dame, must we take her away in spite of the sanctuary?"

"*Pasque-Dieu!*—the sanctuary!" said the King, scratching his ear; "and yet that woman must be hanged."

Here, as if a thought had suddenly occurred to him, he knelt down before his chair, took off his hat, placed it upon the seat, and looking devoutly at one of the leaden figures with which it was loaded—"Oh," said he, clasping his hands, "Our Lady of Paris, my gracious patroness, pardon me. I will only do it this once. That criminal must be punished. I assure you, O Lady Virgin, my good mistress, that she is a witch, unworthy your kind protection. You know, Lady, that many very pious princes have trespassed upon the privileges of churches, for the glory of God and the necessity of the state. Saint Hugh, an English bishop, permitted King Edward to seize a magician in his church. My master, Saint Louis of France, transgressed for the like purpose in the church of Monsieur Saint Paul; as did also Monsieur Alphonse, King of Jerusalem, in the church of the Holy Sepulchre itself. Pardon me, then, for this once, Our Lady of Paris. I will never do so again; and I will give you a fine statue of silver like that which I gave last year to Our Lady of Ecouys. So be it."

He crossed himself, rose from his knees, put on his hat, and said to Tristan, "Make all speed, my compère. Take Monsieur de Chateaupers with you. You'll have the tocsin rung. You'll crush the populace. You'll hang the witch. That's settled. You yourself will defray all charges of the execution, and bring me in an account of them.—Come, Olivier, I shall not lie down to-night. Shave me."

Tristan l'Hermite bowed and departed. Then the King, motioning to Rym and Coppenole to retire: "God keep you, messieurs, my good Flemish friends!" said he. "Go and take a little rest. The night is fast wearing away; we are nearer the morning than the evening."

They both withdrew; and on reaching their apartments, to which they were conducted by the captain of the Bastille, Coppenole said to Guillaume Rym: "Humph! I've had enough of this coughing king. I've seen Charles of Burgundy drunk, but he was not so mischievous as Louis XI. sick."

"Maître Jacques," answered Rym with mock solemnity, "that is because a king finds less cruelty in his wine than in his barley-water!"

CHAPTER VI

THE PASSWORD

On quitting the Bastille, Gringoire ran down the Rue St. Antoine with the speed of a runaway horse. When he had reached the Porte Baudoyer, he walked straight up to the stone cross standing in the middle of the open space there, as if he could have discerned in the dark the figure of a man clothed and hooded in black, sitting upon the steps of the cross. "Is it you, master?" said Gringoire.

The person in black rose. "Death and passion! you drive me mad, Gringoire!" said he. "The man upon St. Gervais's tower has just been calling half-past one in the morning."

"Oh," returned Gringoire, "it's no fault of mine, but of the watch and of the King. I've had a narrow escape. Yet I always just miss being hanged; it's my predestination."

"You just miss everything," said the other. "But come along quick. Have you the password?"

"Only think, master. I've seen the King. I've just left him. He wears worsted breeches! It's an adventure, I can tell you."

"O thou spinner of words! What's thy adventure to me? Hast thou got the password of the Truands?"

"I've got it. Make yourself easy. It's *Petite flambé en baguenaud.*"

"Very well. Otherwise we should not have been able to make our way to the church. The Truands block up the streets. Fortunately, it seems, they've met with resistance. Perhaps we shall still get there in time."

"Yes, master; but how shall we get into Notre-Dame?"

"I have the key of the towers."

"And how shall we get out again?"

"There's a small door behind the cloister, which leads to the Terrain, and so to the water-side. I have taken possession of the key, and I moored a boat there this morning."

"I've had a nice miss of being hanged," repeated Gringoire.

"Ah—well—come along quick," said the other; and they both walked off at a great rate towards the city.

CHAPTER VII

CHATEAUPERS TO THE RESCUE

THE reader probably bears in his recollection the critical situation in which we left Quasimodo. The brave ringer, assailed on all sides, had lost, though not all courage, at least all hope of saving, not himself—he thought not of himself—but the gipsy girl. He ran wildly to and fro along the gallery. Notre-Dame was on the point of being carried by the Truands, when all at once a great galloping of horses filled the neighbouring streets, and, with a long file of torches and a dense column of horsemen, lances and bridles lowered, these furious sounds came rushing into the Place like a hurricane—"France! France! Cut down the knaves! Chateaupers to the rescue! Provostry! provostry!"

The Truands in terror faced about.

Quasimodo, though he heard nothing, saw the drawn swords, the flambeaus, the spearheads—all that cavalry, at the head of which he recognised Captain Phœbus. He saw the confusion of the Truands, the terror of some of them, the perturbation of the stoutest-hearted among them; and this unexpected succour so much revived his own energies that he hurled back from the church the most forward of the assailants, who were already striding over into the gallery.

It was, in fact, the King's troops that had just arrived.

The Truands bore themselves bravely and defended themselves desperately. Attacked in flank from the Rue Saint-Pierre-aux-Bœufs, and in the rear from the Rue du Parvis, pressed against Notre-Dame, which they were still assailing, and which Quasimodo was defending—at once besieging and besieged—they were in the singular situation which subsequently, at the famous siege of Turin in 1640, was that of Count Henri d'Harcourt, between Prince Thomas of Savoy, whom he was besieging, and the Marquis of Leganez, who was blockading him—*Taurinum obsessor idem et obsessus*, as his epitaph expresses it.

The *mêlée* was frightful. Wolves' flesh calls for dogs' teeth, as Father Matthieu phrases it. The King's horsemen, amidst whom Phœbus de Chateaupers bore himself valiantly, gave no quarter, and they who escaped the thrust of the lance fell by the edge of the sword. The Truands, ill-armed, foamed and bit with rage and despair. Men, women, and children threw themselves upon the cruppers and chests of the horses, and clung to them like cuts with their teeth and claws; others struck the archers in the face with their torches; and others, again, aimed their bill-hooks at the necks of the horsemen, striving to pull them down, and mangled such as fell. One of them was seen with a large glittering scythe, with which for a long time he mowed the legs of the horses. He was terrific: he went on, singing a song with a nasal intonation, taking long and sweeping strokes with his scythe. At each stroke he described around him a great circle of severed limbs. He advanced in this manner into the thickest of the cavalry, with the quiet slowness, the regular motion of the head and drawing of the breath of a harvestman putting the scythe into a field of corn. This was Clopin Trouillefou. He fell by the shot of an arquebus.

Meantime the windows had opened again. The neighbours, hearing the war-shouts of the King's men, had taken part in the affair, and from every story bullets were showered upon the Truands. The Parvis was filled with a thick smoke, which the flashing of the musketry streaked with fire. Through it were confusedly discernible the front of Notre-Dame, and the decrepit Hôtel-Dieu, with a few pale-faced invalids looking from the top of its roof checkered with skylights.

At last the Truands gave way. Exhaustion, want of good weapons, the terror struck into them by this surprise, the discharges of musketry from the windows, and the spirited charge of the King's troops, all combined to overpower them. They broke through the line of their assailants, and fled in all directions, leaving the Parvis covered with their dead.

When Quasimodo, who had not for a moment ceased fighting, beheld this rout, he fell upon his knees and lifted his hands to heaven. Then, intoxicated with joy, he mounted with the quickness of a bird up to that cell the approaches of which he had so intrepidly defended. He had now but one thought: it was to go and fall upon his knees before her whom he had saved for the second time.

When he entered the cell, however, he found it empty.

BOOK XI

CHAPTER I

THE LITTLE SHOE

At the moment when the Truands had assailed the church La Esmeralda was asleep. But soon the constantly increasing clamour about the edifice, and the plaintive bleating of her goat, which was awakened before herself, had chased away her slumber. She had then sat up in bed, listened, looked round her; and then, frightened at the light and the noise, she had hurried out of the cell, and gone to see what was the matter. The aspect of the Place; the strange vision that was moving in it; the disorder of that nocturnal assault; that hideous crowd leaping about like a cloud of frogs, half distinguishable in the darkness; the croaking of that hoarse multitude; the few red torches running backwards and forwards, passing and repassing one another in the dark, like those meteors of the night that play over the misty surface of a marsh—all together seemed to her like some mysterious battle commenced between the phantoms of a witches' sabbath and the stone monsters of the church. Imbued from her infancy with the superstitions which at that day possessed the minds of many of her tribe, the notion that first suggested itself to her was that she had come unawares upon the magic revels of the beings proper to the night. Then she ran back in terror to cower in her cell, and ask of her humble couch some less horrible vision.

By degrees, however, the first fumes of her terror had dispersed from her brain; and by the constantly increasing noise, together with other signs of reality, she had discovered that she was beset, not by spectres, but by human beings. Then her fear, though it had not increased, had changed its nature. She had thought of the possibility of a popular rising to drag her from her asylum. The idea of once more losing life, hope, Phœbus, who still was ever present to her hopes; her extreme helplessness; all flight barred; her abandonment; her solitariness—these and a thousand other cruel thoughts had quite overwhelmed her. She had fallen upon her knees, with her head upon her couch, and her hands clasped upon her head, full of anxiety and trepidation; and gipsy, idolatress, and heathen as she was, she had begun sobbing, to ask mercy of the God of the Christians, and to pray to Our Lady her hostess. "For," says our author, "whether one believes anything or nothing, there are moments in life when one is always of the religion of the temple nearest at hand."

She remained thus prostrate for a considerable time—trembling, indeed, yet more than she prayed, her blood running cold as the breath of that furious multitude approached nearer and nearer; ignorant of the nature of this popular storm—of what was in agitation, of what was doing, of what was intended—but feeling a presentiment of some dreadful result.

In the very midst of all this anguish she heart footsteps approaching her. She turned her head. Two men, one of whom carried a lantern, had just entered her cell. She uttered a feeble cry.

"Don't be afraid," said a voice to which she was not a stranger; "'tis I."

"'Tis who?" asked she.

"Pierre Gringoire."

This name encouraged her. She raised her eyes, and saw that it was indeed the poet. But close by him there was a dark figure, veiled from head to foot, the sight of which struck her dumb.

"Ah!" resumed Gringoire in a reproachful tone, "Djali had recognised me before you did."

The little goat, in fact, had not waited for Gringoire to announce himself. No sooner had he entered than she had begun to rub herself affectionately against his knees, covering the poet with caresses and with white hairs, for she was changing her coat. Gringoire returned her caresses with the greatest cordiality.

"Who is that with you?" whispered the gipsy girl.

"Make yourself easy," answered Gringoire; "it's a friend of mine."

Then the philosopher, setting his lantern on the floor, squatted down upon the stones, and exclaimed with enthusiasm, clasping Djali in his arms, "Oh, it's a charming animal!—more remarkable, to be sure, for beauty and cleanliness than for size; but clever, cunning, and lettered as a grammarian!—Let us see now, my Djali, if thou rememberest all thy pretty tricks.—How does Maître Jacques Charmolue go?"

The man in black did not let Gringoire finish. He came up to him, and pushed him forcibly by the shoulder. Gringoire got up again. "True," said he; "I'd forgotten that we're in haste. However, master, that's no reason for using folks so roughly.—My pretty dear," said he, addressing the gipsy girl, "your life's in danger, and Djali's too. They want to hang you again. We're your friends, and are come to save you. Follow us."

"Is that true?" exclaimed she, quite overcome.

"Yes, quite true. Come, quick!"

"I will," faltered she; "but why does not that friend of yours speak?"

"Ha!" said Gringoire; "that's because his father and mother were whimsical people, and made him of a silent disposition."

She was obliged to content herself with this explanation. Gringoire took her by the hand. His companion took up the lantern and walked first. Fear made the young girl quite passive; she let them lead her along. The goat skipped after them, so delighted to see Gringoire again that she made him stumble at almost every step, with thrusting her horns against his legs. "Such is life," said the philosopher, once that he was very near being laid prostrate; "it is often our best friends that occasion our fall!"

They rapidly descended the staircase of the towers, crossed the interior of the church, which was all dark and solitary, but resounded from the uproar without, thus offering a frightful contrast; and went out by the Porte Rouge into the cloisters. The cloisters themselves were deserted, the canons having taken refuge in the bishop's house, there to offer up their prayers in common. Only some terrified serving-men were skulking in the darkest corners. They proceeded towards the small door leading from that court to the Terrain. The man in black opened it with a key which he had about him. Our readers are aware that the Terrain was a slip of ground enclosed with walls on the side next the city, and belonging to the Chapter of Notre-Dame, which terminated the island eastward, behind the church. They found this enclosure perfectly solitary. Here, too, they found the tumult in the air sensibly diminished. The noise of the assault by the Truands reached their ears more confusedly and less clamorously. The cool breeze which follows the current of the river stirred the leaves of the only tree planted at the point of the Terrain with a noise which was now perceptible to them. Nevertheless they were still very near the danger. The buildings nearest to them were the bishop's palace and the church. There was evidently great confusion within the residence of the bishop. Its dark mass was tracked in all directions by lights hurrying from one window to another, just as after burning a piece of paper there remains a dark structure of ashes, over which bright sparks are running in a thousand fantastic courses. And close by it the huge towers of Notre-Dame, seen thus from behind, with the long nave over which they rear themselves, showing black upon the vast red light which glowed above the Parvis, looked like the gigantic uprights of some Cyclopean fire-grate.

What was visible of Paris seemed wavering on all sides in a sort of shadow mingled with light, resembling some of Rembrandt's backgrounds.

The man with the lantern walked straight to the projecting point of the Terrain, where, at the extreme verge of the water, were the decayed remains of a fence of stakes with laths nailed across, upon which a low vine spread out its few meagre branches like the fingers of an open hand. Behind this sort of lattice-work, in the shade which it cast, a small boat lay hidden. The man motioned to Gringoire and the young woman to enter it; and the goat jumped in after them. The man himself got in last of all. Then he cut the rope, pushed off from the shore with a long boathook, and laying hold of a pair of oars, he seated himself in the front, and rowed with all his might across the stream. The Seine is very rapid at that place, and he found considerable difficulty in clearing the point of the island.

Gringoire's first care on entering the boat was to place the goat upon his lap. He placed himself in the hinder part of the boat; and the young girl, whom the sight of the stranger filled with indescribable uneasiness, went and seated herself as close as possible to the poet.

When our philosopher felt the boat in motion he clapped his hands, and kissed Djali upon the forehead. "Oh," cried he, "now we are all four saved!" He added, with the look of a profound thinker, "We are indebted sometimes to fortune, sometimes to contrivance, for the happy issue of a great undertaking.

The boat was making its way slowly towards the right bank. The young girl watched the movements of the unknown with a secret terror. He had carefully turned off again the light of his dark lantern, and he was now discernible, like a spectre, at the head of the boat. His hood, which was constantly down, was a sort of mask over his face; and every time that in rowing he half opened his arms, upon which he had large black hanging sleeves, they looked like a pair of enormous bat's wings. But he had not yet breathed a single syllable. There was perfect stillness in the boat, excepting only the periodical splash of the oars, and the rippling of the water against the side of the skiff.

"Upon my soul!" exclaimed Gringoire all at once, "here we go, as gay and as merry as owlets! We're as silent as so many Pythagoreans or so many fish. *Pasque-Dieu!* my friends, I should like somebody to talk to me. The human voice is music to the human ear. That's not a saying of mine, but of Didymus of Alexandria; and a capital sentence it is. Certes, Didymus of Alexandria is no mean philosopher.—One word, my pretty dear; do just say one word to me, I beg. By-the-bye, you used to have a curious odd little mow of your own; do you make it still? You must know, my dear, that the Parliament has full jurisdiction over all places of sanctuary, and that you were in great peril in that little box of yours at Notre-Dame. Alas! the little bird the trochylus maketh its nest in the crocodile's mouth.—Master, here's the moon coming out again. So that they don't discover us! We're doing a laudable act in saving mademoiselle. And yet they'd hang us up in the King's name if they were to catch us. Alas! every human action has two handles. One man gets praised for what another gets blamed for; one man admires Cæsar and reproaches Catiline. Is it not so, master? What say you to this philosophy? I possess the philosophy of instinct, of nature, *ut apes geometriam*, as the bees do geometry. So nobody answers me.—What a plaguy humour you're both in! I'm obliged to talk all by myself. That's what we call in tragedy a monologue. *Pasque-Dieu!* I'd have you to know that I have just now seen King Louis XI., and that it's from him I've caught that oath. *Pasque-Dieu!* then they're still making a glorious howl in the city. He's a vile, mischievous old king. He's all wrapped about with furs. He still owes me the money for my epithalamium; and he has all but hanged me to-night, which would have been very awkward for me indeed. He's niggardly to men of merit. He should e'en read Salvain of Cologne's four books *adversus Avaritiam*. In sooth, he's a king very paltry in his dealings with men of letters, and that commits very barbarous cruelties. He's a sponge sucking up the money that's raised from the people. His savings are as the spleen, that grows big upon the pining of the other members. And so the complaints of the hardness of the times turn to murmurs against the prince. Under this mild and pious lord of ours the gibbets are overloaded with carcasses, the blocks stream with gore, the prisons are crammed to bursting. This King strips with one hand and hangs with the other. He's grand caterer to Dame Gabelle and Monseigneur Gibet. The high are stripped of their dignities, and the low are everlastingly loaded with fresh burdens. It's an exorbitant prince. I don't like this monarch.—What say you, master?"

The man in black let the loquacious poet run on. He was still struggling against the strong compressed current which separates the prow of the city from the stern of the Ile Notre-Dame, now called L'Ile Saint-Louis.

"By-the-bye, master," resumed Gringoire suddenly, "just as we reached the Parvis through the enraged Truands, did your reverence observe that poor little devil whose brains that deaf man of yours seemed in a fair way to knock out upon the balustrade of the gallery of royal statues? I'm shortsighted, and could not distinguish his features. Who might it be, think you?"

The unknown answered not a word. But he suddenly left off rowing, his arms dropped as if they had been broken, his head fell upon his breast, and La Esmeralda could hear him sighing convulsively. She started; she had heard sounds like those before.

The boat, left to itself, followed for some moments the impulse of the stream. But at length the man in black recovered himself, seized the oars again, and again set himself to row against the current. He doubled the point of the Ile Notre-Dame, and made for the landing-place at the Port-au-Foin or Hay-wharf.

"Ha!" said Gringoire, "over there is the Logis Barbeau. There, master—look—that group of black roofs, that make such odd angles; there, just underneath that heap of low, dirty, ragged clouds, where the moon is all crushed and spread about like the yolk of an egg when the shell's broken. It's a fine mansion. There's a chapel with a little vaulted roof, lined with enrichments excellently cut. You may discern the bell-turret above it very delicately perforated. There's also a pleasant garden, consisting of a pond, an aviary, an echo, a mill, a labyrinth, a wild-beast house, and plenty of thick-shaded walks very agreeable to Venus. And then there's a rogue of a tree which they call *le luxurieux*, because it once favoured the pleasures of a famous princess and a certain constable of France, a man of wit and gallantry. Alas! we poor philosophers are to a constable of France as a cabbage-plot or a radish-bed is to a grove of laurels. After all, what does it signify? Human life is a mixture of good and evil for the great as well as for us. Sorrow ever attends upon joy—the spondee upon the dactyl. Master, I must tell you that story about the Logis Barbeau; it ends tragically. It was in 1319, in the reign of Philip V., the longest of all the French kings. The moral of the story is that the temptations of the flesh are pernicious and malign. Let us not look too steadfastly upon our neighbour's wife, how much soever our senses may be taken with her beauty. Fornication is a very libertine thought; adultery is a prying into another man's pleasure . . . Eh, what! the noise grows louder!"

The tumult was, in fact, increasing around Notre-Dame. They listened, and could very distinctly hear shouts of victory. All at once a hundred flambeaus, the light of which glittered upon the helmets of men-at-arms, spread themselves over the church at all elevations—on the towers, on the galleries, under the buttresses. Those torches seemed to be carried in search of something, and soon those distant clamours reached distinctly the ears of the fugitives. "The gipsy!" they cried—"the witch! Death to the gipsy!"

The head of the unfortunate girl dropped upon her hands, and the unknown began to row with violence towards the bank. Meanwhile our philosopher was reflecting. He pressed the goat in his arms, and sidled away very gently from the gipsy girl, who kept pressing closer and closer up to him, as to her only remaining protection.

It is certain that Gringoire was in a cruel perplexity. He reflected that the goat too, *d'après la législation existante,* would be hanged if she were retaken; that it would be a great pity, poor Djali! that two condemned females thus clinging to him would be too much for him; and that his companion would be most happy to take charge of the gipsy girl. Yet a violent struggle was taking place in his mind, wherein, like the Jupiter of the *Iliad,* he placed in the balance alternately the gipsy girl and the goat; and he looked first at one of them, then at the other, his eyes moist with tears, and muttering between his teeth, "And yet I cannot save you both!"

The striking of the boat at length apprised them that they had reached the shore. The fearful acclamations were still resounding through the city. The unknown rose, came up to the gipsy girl, and offered to take her arm in order to help her out of the boat. She pushed him away from her, and laid hold of Gringoire's sleeve, when he in turn, being fully occupied with the goat, almost repulsed her. Then she jumped ashore by herself. She was in such perturbation that she knew not what she was doing nor whither she was going. She remained thus for a few moments, quite stupefied, watching the water as it flowed. When she recovered a little she found herself alone upon the landing-place with the unknown. It appears that Gringoire had availed himself of the moment of their going ashore to make off with the goat into the mass of houses of the Rue Grenier-sur-l'Eau.

The poor gipsy girl shuddered to find herself alone with that man. She strove to speak, to cry out, to call Gringoire; but her tongue refused its office, and no sound issued from her lips. All at once she felt the hand of the stranger placed upon her own; the hand was cold and strong. Her teeth chattered; she turned paler than the moonbeams that were shining upon her. The man said not a word. He began to walk up the river-side at a rapid pace towards the Place de Grève, holding her by the hand. At that moment she had a vague feeling of the irresistibleness of destiny. No muscular strength remained to her; she let him drag her along, running while he walked. The quay at that place was somewhat rising before them, and yet it seemed to her as if she was going down a declivity.

She looked on all sides, but not a passenger was to be seen; the quay was absolutely solitary. She heard no sound; she perceived no one stirring, except in the glaring and tumultuous city, from which she was separated only by an arm of the Seine, and from which her name reached her ear mingled with shouts of "Death!" The rest of Paris lay spread around her in great masses of shade.

Meanwhile the unknown was still dragging her on in the same silence and with the same rapidity. She had no recollection of any of the places through which she was passing. As they were going by a lighted window she made one effort, suddenly drew up, and cried out "Help!"

The master of the house opened the window, showed himself in his nightgown with the lamp in his hand, looked out between sleeping and waking on the quay, uttered some words which she did not hear, and closed his shutter again. It was the extinction of her last ray of hope.

The man in black uttered not a svllable. He held her fast,

and walked on yet quicker than before. She made no more resistance, but followed him like a thing utterly powerless.

Now and then, indeed, she gathered just strength enough to say, with a voice interrupted by the unevenness of the pavement and the rapidity of her motion, which had almost taken her breath, "Who are you? who are you?" But he made no answer.

In this manner, keeping constantly along the quay, they arrived at a square of considerable size. There was then a little moonlight. It was the Grève. A sort of black cross was discernible, standing in the middle of it: that was the gibbet. She observed all this, and then she knew where she was.

The man stopped, turned towards her, and lifted his hood.

"Oh," faltered she, almost petrified, "I knew it was he again!"

It was, in fact, the priest. He looked like the ghost of himself. It was an effect of the moonlight—a light by which one seems to see only the spectres of objects.

"Listen," said he; and she shuddered at the sound of that ill-omened voice, which it was long since she had heard. He continued, speaking with that short and gasping utterance which bespeaks deep internal heavings. "Listen. We are here. I have to talk to thee. This is the Grève. This is an extreme point. Fate gives up each of us to the other. I am going to dispose of thy life; thou, of my soul. Beyond this place and this night nothing is to be seen. Listen to me then; I'm going to tell thee. . . . First of all, don't talk to me of thy Phœbus." So saying, he paced backwards and forwards, like a man incapable of standing still, dragging her after him. "Talk not of him. Mark me: if thou utter his name, I know not what I shall do, but it will be something terrible!"

Then, like a body finding its centre of gravity again, he once more became motionless; but his words betrayed no less agitation. His voice grew lower and lower. "Don't turn thy head aside so. Hearken to me. 'Tis a serious matter. First of all, I'll tell thee what has happened. There will be no laughing about this, I assure thee. What was I saying? remind me. Ah! it is that there's a decree of the Parliament, delivering thee over to execution again. I've just now taken thee out of their hands. But there they are pursuing thee. Look."

He stretched out his arm towards the city, where, indeed, the search seemed to be eagerly continued. The clamour came nearer. The tower of the lieutenant's house, situated opposite to the Grève, was full of noise and lights; and soldiers were running over the quay opposite, with torches in their hands, shouting, "The gipsy woman! where is the gipsy woman? Death! death!"

"Thou seest plainly enough," resumed the priest, "that they're pursuing thee, and that I tell no falsehood. I love thee. Open not thy lips. Rather, speak not a word, if it be to tell me that thou hatest me. I'm determined not to hear that again. I've just now saved thee. First, let me finish. I can save thee quite. I've made all things ready. Thou hast only to will it. As thou wilt, I can do."

Here he violently checked himself. "No; that is not what I had to say."

And with hurried step—making her hurry too, for he never let go her arm—he went straight up to the gibbet, and pointing to it, "Choose between us," said he coolly.

She tore herself from his grasp, fell at the foot of the gibbet, and clasped that dismal supporter; then she half turned her beautiful head, and looked at the priest over her shoulder. She had the air of a Madonna at the foot of the cross. The priest had remained quite still, his finger still raised towards the gibbet, and his gesture unchanged, like a statue.

At length the gipsy girl said to him, "It is less horrible to me than you are."

Then he let his arm drop slowly, and cast his eyes upon the ground in deep dejection. "If these stones could speak," muttered he—"yes, they would say, Here is, indeed, an unhappy man!"

He resumed. The young girl, kneeling before the gibbet, enveloped in her long flowing hair, let him speak without interrupting him. His accent was now mild and plaintive, contrasting mournfully with the haughty harshness of his features.

"I love you! Oh, still 'tis very true I do! And is nothing, then, perceivable without of that fire which consumes my heart? Alas, young girl, night and day—yes, night and day—does that deserve no pity? 'Tis a love of the night and the day, I tell you—'tis a torture! Oh, I suffer too much, my poor child! 'Tis a thing worthy of compassion, I do assure you. You see that I speak gently to you. I would fain have you cease to abhor me. For, after all, when a man loves a woman 'tis not his fault. O my God! What! will you never forgive me then? will you hate me always?—and is it all over? That is what makes me wicked, do you see, and horrible to myself. You don't so much as look at me. You are thinking of something else, perhaps, while I talk to you as I stand shuddering on the brink of eternity to both of us! But of all things don't talk to me of the officer! What! I might throw myself at your feet! What! I might kiss, not your feet—you would not permit it—but the ground under your feet! What! I might sob like a child; I might heave from my breast, not words, but my very heart, to tell you that I love you! and yet all would be in vain—all! And yet there is nothing in your soul but what is kind and tender. You are all beaming with the loveliest gentleness—all sweet, all merciful, all charming! Alas, you have no malevolence but for me alone! Oh, what a fatality!"

He hid his face in his hands. The young girl heard him weeping. It was the first time. Standing thus erect, and convulsed by sobbing, he looked even more wretched and suppliant than on his knees. For a while he continued weeping.

"But come," he continued, as soon as these first tears were over; "I find no words. And yet I had well meditated what I had to say to you. Now I tremble and shiver—I stagger at the decisive moment—I feel that something transcendent wraps us round—and my voice falters. Oh, I shall fall to the ground if you do not take pity on me, pity on yourself! Do not condemn us both. If you did but know how much I love you! What a heart is mine! Oh, what desertion of all virtue! what desperate abandonment of myself! A doctor, I mock at science; a gentleman, I tarnish my name; a priest, I make my missal a pillow of desire—I spit in the face of my God! All that for thee, enchantress—to be more worthy of thy hell! and yet thou rejectest the reprobate! Oh, let me tell thee all—more still—something more horrible—oh, yet more horrible!"

As he uttered these last words his look became utterly bewildered. He was silent for a moment; then resumed, as if talking to himself, and in a strong voice, "Cain, what hast thou done with thy brother?"

He paused again, and then continued: "What have I done with him, Lord? I have taken him to myself—nourished him, brought him up, loved him, idolised him, and killed him! Yes, Lord, just now, before my eyes, have they dashed his head upon the stones of thine house; and it was because of me—because of this woman—because of her!"

His eye was haggard, his voice was sinking; he repeated several times over mechanically, at considerable intervals, like the last stroke of a clock prolonging its vibration, "Because of her—because of her." Then his tongue articulated no perceptible sound, though his lips continued to move. All at once he sank down, like something falling to pieces, and remained upon the ground with his head between his knees.

A slight movement of the young girl, drawing away her foot from under him, brought him to himself. He passed his hand slowly over his hollow cheeks, and looked for some moments in stupor at his fingers, which were wet. "What!" murmured he, "have I been weeping?"

And turning suddenly to the gipsy girl with inexpressible anguish: "Alas! you have beheld me weep unmoved. Child, dost thou know that these tears are tears of fire? And is it, then, so true, that from the man we hate nothing can move us? Thou wouldst see me die, and thou wouldst laugh the while. Oh, I wish not to see thee die! One word—one single word of forgiveness! Tell me not that thou lovest me—tell me only that thou art willing; that will suffice, and I will save thee. If not—— Oh, the time flies. I entreat thee, by all that is sacred, wait not until I am become of stone again, like this gibbet, which claims thee too. Think that I hold both our destinies in my hand, that I am maddened—'tis terrible—that I may let all go, and that there is beneath us, unhappy girl, a bottomless abyss, wherein my fall will pursue thine for all eternity. One word of kindness—say one word—but one word!"

She opened her lips to answer him. He threw himself on his knees before her, to receive with adoration the word, perhaps of relenting, which was about to fall from those lips. She said to him, "You are an assassin!"

The priest took her in his arms with fury, and laughed an abominable laugh. "Well—yes—an assassin," said he, "and I will have thee. Thou wilt not have me for thy slave; thou shalt have me for thy master. I will have thee! I have a den, whither I will drag thee. Thou shalt follow me; thou must follow me, or I deliver thee over. You must die, my fair one, or be mine—the priest's—the apostate's—the assassin's—this very night. Dost thou hear? Come! joy! Come! kiss me, silly girl! The grave—or my couch!"

His eyes were sparkling with rage and licentiousness, and his lascivious lips were covering the young girl's neck with scarlet. She struggled in his arms, and he kept loading her with furious kisses.

"Don't bite me, monster!" cried she. "Oh, the hateful,

poisonous monk! Leave me! I'll pull off thy vile grey hair and throw it by handfuls in thy face!"

He turned red, then pale, then left hold of her, and gazed upon her with a dismal look. She now thought herself victorious, and continued, "I tell thee I belong to my Phœbus—that it is Phœbus I love—that 'tis Phœbus who is handsome. Thou, priest, art old! thou art ugly! Get thee gone."

He uttered a violent cry, like some wretch under a branding-iron. "Die, then!" said he, grinding his teeth. She saw his frightful look, and offered to fly. But he seized her again, shook her, threw her upon the ground, and walked rapidly towards the angle of the Tour-Roland, dragging her after him by her beautiful hands.

When he had reached that corner of the square, he turned round to her, and said, "Once for all, wilt thou be mine?"

She answered him with emphasis, "No!"

Then he called out in a loud voice, "Gudule, Gudule! here's the gipsy woman!—take thy revenge!"

The young girl felt herself seized suddenly by the arm. She looked: it was a fleshless arm extended through a window-place in the wall, and grasping her with a hand of iron.

"Hold fast," said the priest; "it's the gipsy woman escaped. Don't let her go. I'm going to fetch the sergeants. Thou shalt see her hanged."

A guttural laugh from the interior of the wall made answer to these deadly words—"Ha, ha, ha!" The gipsy girl saw the priest hurry away towards the Pont Notre-Dame, in which direction a trampling of horses was heard.

The young girl had recognised the malicious recluse. Panting with terror, she strove to disengage herself. She twisted herself about; made several bounds in agony and despair; but the other held her with incredible strength. The lean, bony fingers that pinched her were clenched and met round her flesh; it seemed as if that hand were riveted to her arm. It was more than a chain—more than an iron ring: it was a pair of pincers, with life and understanding, issuing from the wall.

Quite exhausted, she fell back against the wall; and then the fear of death came over her. She thought of all the charms of life—of youth—of the sight of the heavens—of the aspect of nature—of love—of Phœbus—of all that was flying from her; and then of all that was approaching—of the priest betraying her—of the executioner that was coming—of the gibbet that was there. Then she felt terror mounting even to the roots of her hair; and she heard the dismal laugh of the recluse, saying low to her, "Ha, ha! thou'rt going to be hanged!"

She turned with a dying look towards the window of the cell, and she saw the wild countenance of the Sachette through the bars. "What have I done to you?" said she almost inarticulately.

The recluse made no answer, but began to mutter, in a singing, irritated, and mocking tone, "Daughter of Egypt! daughter of Egypt! daughter of Egypt!"

The unfortunate Esmeralda let her head drop under her long flowing hair, understanding that it was no human being she had here to deal with.

All at once the recluse exclaimed, as if the gispy's question had taken all that time to reach her apprehension, "What hast thou done to me, gipsy woman? Well—hark thee. I had a child—dost thou see?—I had a child—a child, I tell thee—a pretty little girl—my Agnès!" she continued wildly, kissing something in the dark. "Well, dost thou see, daughter of Egypt? They took my child from me—they stole my child—they ate my child. That is what thou hast done to me."

The young girl answered, like the lamb in the fable, "Alas! perhaps I was not then born."

"Oh yes," rejoined the recluse, "thou must have been born then. Thou wast one of them; she would have been of thy age. For fifteen years have I been here—fifteen years have I been suffering—fifteen years have I been knocking my head against these four walls. I tell thee, they were gipsy women that stole her from me—dost thou hear that?—and that ate her with their teeth. Hast thou a heart? Only think what it is to see one's child playing, sucking, sleeping; it's so innocent! Well, that's what they've taken from me, what they've killed. God Almighty knows it well. Now it's my turn: I'm going to eat some gipsy woman's flesh. Oh, how I would bite thee, if the bars didn't hinder me! My head's too big. Poor little thing—while she was asleep! And if they woke her with taking her away, in vain might she cry: I was not there!—Ha! you gipsy mothers, you ate my child; now come and look at yours."

Then she laughed, or ground her teeth—for the two things were alike in that frantic countenance. The day was beginning to dawn, dimly spreading over this scene an ashy tint, and the gibbet was growing more and more distinctly visible in the centre of the Place. On the other side, towards the Pont

Notre-Dame, the poor condemned girl thought she heard the noise of the horsemen approaching.

"Madame!" she cried, clasping her hands and falling upon her knees, dishevelled, wild, distracted with extremity of dread—"madame, have pity! They're coming! I've done nothing to you. Can you wish me to die in that horrible manner before your eyes? You pity me, I am sure. 'Tis too dreadful! Let me fly for my life—let me go, for mercy's sake! I wish not to die so."

"Give me back my child," said the recluse.

"Mercy, mercy!"

"Give me back my child."

"Let me go, in Heaven's name!"

"Give me back my child."

And now again the young girl sank exhausted, powerless, having already the glazy eye of one in the grave. "Alas!" faltered she, "you seek your child. I seek my parents."

"Give me back my little Agnès!" continued Gudule. "Know'st thou not where she is? Then die! I'll tell thee. I was once a girl of pleasure—I had a child—they took my child from me—it was the gipsy woman. Thou seest plain enough that thou must die. When the gipsy mother comes to ask for thee, I shall say to her, 'Mother, look at that gibbet.' Else, give me back my child. Dost thou know where she is, little girl? Here—let me show thee—here's her shoe, all that's left me of her. Dost thou know where the fellow to it is? If thou dost, tell me; and if it's only at the other end of the earth, I'll go thither on my knees to fetch it."

So saying, with her other arm extended through the window-place, she showed the gipsy girl the little embroidered shoe. There was already daylight enough to distinguish its shape and its colours.

The gipsy girl, starting, said, "Let me see that shoe. O heavens!" And at the same time, with the hand she had at liberty, she eagerly opened the little bag with green glass ornaments which she wore about her neck.

"Ha, there!" muttered Gudule; "rummage thy amulet of the foul fiend——" She suddenly stopped short—her whole frame trembled—and she cried, in a voice that came from her inmost heart, "My daughter!"

The gipsy girl had just taken out of the bag a little shoe exactly matching the other. To the little shoe was attached a slip of parchment, upon which was written this rude couplet,—

"When thou the like to this shalt see,
Thy mother'll stretch her arms to thee."

With lightning quickness the recluse had compared the two shoes, read the inscription on the parchment, and then put close to the window bars her face all beaming with a celestial joy, exclaiming, "My daughter! my daughter!"

"My mother!" answered the gipsy girl. Here description fails us.

The wall and the iron bars were between them. "Oh, the wall!" cried the recluse. "To see her, and not embrace her! Thy hand, thy hand!"

The young girl passed her arm through one of the openings. The recluse threw herself upon that hand, pressed her lips to it, and there she remained, absorbed in that kiss, giving no sign of animation, but a sob which heaved her sides from time to time. Meanwhile she was weeping in torrents, in the silence and the darkness, like rain falling in the night. The poor mother was pouring out in floods upon that adored hand that deep dark well of sorrow into which all her grief had filtered drop by drop for fifteen years.

All at once she rose up, threw her long grey hair from off her forehead, and without saying a word, strove with both hands, and with the fury of a lioness, to shake the bars of her window-hole. But the bars were not so to be shaken. She then went and fetched from one corner of her cell a large paving-stone which served her for a pillow, and hurled it against them with such violence that one of the bars broke, casting numberless sparks. A second stroke completed the bursting out of the old iron cross that barricaded the window-place. Then, exerting both hands, she managed to loosen and remove the rusty stumps of the bars. There are moments when the hands of a woman are possessed of superhuman strength.

The passage being thus cleared—and it was all done in less than a minute—she took her daughter by the middle, and drew her through into the cell. "Come," murmured she, "let me drag thee out of the abyss."

As soon as she had her daughter within the cell, she set her gently on the ground, then took her up again, and carrying her in her arms as if she were still only her little Agnès, she paced to and fro in her narrow lodge, intoxicated, frantic with joy, shouting, singing, kissing her daughter, talking to her, laughing aloud, melting into tears—all at once and all vehemently.

"My daughter! my daughter!" said she. "I have my

daughter! Here she is! God Almighty has given her back to me. Ha! you—come all of you; is there anybody there to see that I've got my daughter? Lord Jesus, how beautiful she is! You have made me wait fifteen years, O my God, but it was that you might give her back to me so beautiful. So gipsy women had not eaten her! Who said that they had? My little girl! my little girl! kiss me! Those good gipsy women!—I love the gipsy women! So, 'tis thou indeed! So it was that that made my heart leap every time thou didst go by. And I took that for hatred! Forgive me, my Agnès, forgive me. Thou thoughtest me very malicious, didst thou not? I love thee. Hast thou that little mark on thy neck yet? Let me see. She has it yet. Oh, thou art so handsome! It was I that gave you those large eyes, mademoiselle. Kiss me. I love thee. What matters it to me that other mothers have children? I can laugh at them now. They have only to come and look. Here is mine. Look at her neck, her eyes, her hair, her hand. Find me anything so handsome as that! Oh, I'll answer for it she'll have plenty of lovers. I've wept for fifteen years. All my beauty has gone away, and has come again in her. Kiss me."

She said a thousand other extravagant things to her, of which the accent in which they were uttered made all the beauty; disordered the poor girl's apparel, even till she made her blush; smoothed out her silken tresses with her hand; kissed her foot, her knee, her forehead, her eyelids; was enraptured with everything. The young girl was quite passive the while, only repeating at intervals, very low and with infinite sweetness, "My mother!"

"Look you, my little girl," resumed the recluse, constantly interrupting her words with kisses, "look you—I shall love you so dearly. We will go away from here. We shall be so happy. I've inherited something at Reims, in our country. You know Reims. Oh no, you don't know that—you were too little. If you did but know how pretty you were at four months old! Such little feet, that people came to see all the way from Epernay, which is five leagues off. We shall have a field and a house. Thou shalt sleep in my own bed. O my God, who would believe it? I have my daughter again."

"O my mother!" said the young girl, gathering strength at last to speak in her emotion, "the gipsy woman had told me so. There was a good gipsy woman among our people, that died last year, and that had always taken care of me like a foster-mother. It was she that had put this little bag on my neck. She used always to say to me, 'Little girl, take care of this trinket—it's a treasure—it will make thee find thy mother again. Thou wearest thy mother about thy neck.' She foretold it—the gipsy woman."

Again the Sachette clasped her daughter in her arms. "Come," said she, "let me kiss thee. Thou sayest that so prettily. When we get into the country we'll put the little shoes on the feet of an infant Jesus in a church. We owe as much to the good Holy Virgin. Mon Dieu! what a pretty voice thou hast! When thou wast talking to me just now it was like music.—Ah, my Lord God, so I have found my child again! But is it to be believed now—all that story? Surely nothing will kill one—or I should have died of joy."

And then she clapped her hands again, laughing, and exclaiming, "We shall be so happy!"

At that moment the cell resounded with a clattering of arms and a galloping of horses, which seemed to be issuing from the Pont Notre-Dame, and approaching nearer and nearer along the quay. The gipsy girl threw herself in agony into the arms of the Sachette. "Save me! save me! my mother!—they are coming!"

The recluse turned pale again. "O heaven!—what dost thou say? I'd forgotten. They're pursuing thee! Why, what hast thou done?"

"I don't know," answered the unfortunate girl, "but I'm condemned to die."

"To die!" exclaimed Gudule, tottering as if struck by a thunderbolt. "To die!" she repeated slowly, looking upon her daughter with her fixed eye.

"Yes, my mother," repeated the young girl with wild despair; "they want to kill me. They're coming to hang me. That gallows is for me. Save me, save me! They're here. Save me!"

The recluse remained for a few moments in petrified stillness, then shook her head doubtingly, then suddenly falling into a burst of laughter, but of that former frightful laughter which had now returned to her, "Oh, oh no!" said she; "it's a dream thou art telling me of. Ah, what! that I should have lost her; that that should have lasted fifteen years; and that then I should find her again, and *that* should last only a minute! That they should take her from me again, now that she's handsome—that she's grown up—that she talks to me—that she loves me—that now they should come and devour her before my own eyes, who am her mother! Oh no! such things cannot be; God Almighty permits nothing like that."

Now the cavalcade seemed to stop, and a voice at a distance was heard saying, "This way, Messire Tristan. The priest says we shall find her at the Trou-aux-Rats." The trampling of horses was then heard to recommence.

The recluse started up with a cry of despair. "Fly, fly, my child! I remember it well! Thou art right. 'Tis thy death! O horror—malediction! Fly!"

She put her head to the loophole, and drew it back again hastily. "Stay!" said she in an accent low, brief, and dismal, pressing convulsively the hand of the gipsy girl, who was already more dead than alive. "Stay, don't breathe. There are soldiers all about. You can't go out. There's too much daylight."

Her eyes were dry and burning. For a few moments she said nothing, only pacing hurriedly to and fro in the cell, and stopping now and then, plucking her grey hairs in frenzy from her head.

All at once she said, "They're coming near. I'll speak to them. Hide thee in that corner. They'll not see thee. I'll tell them that thou art run away—that I let thee go, i'faith."

She set down her daughter (for she had constantly been carrying her in her arms) in an angle of the cell which was not visible from without. She made her squat down; arranged all carefully, so that neither foot nor hand should project from out the shade; unbound her black hair, and spread it over her white gown, to mask it from view; and set before her her pitcher and her paving-stone—the only articles of furniture she had—imagining that that pitcher and that stone would conceal her. And when all was finished, finding herself more calm, she knelt down and prayed. As the dawn was only just breaking, there was still great darkness in the Trou-aux-Rats.

At that instant the voice of the priest—that infernal voice—passed very near the cell, crying, "This way, Captain Phœbus de Chateaupers!"

At that name, from that voice, La Esmeralda, squatted in her corner, made a movement. "Don't stir," said Gudule.

Scarcely had she said this before a tumultuous crowd of men, swords, and horses stopped around the cell. The mother, rising quick from her knees, went and posted herself before her loophole, to cover the aperture. She beheld a strong body of armed men, horse and foot, drawn up on the Grève. Their commander dismounted and walked up to her. "Old woman," said this man, whose features had an atrocious expression, "we're seeking a witch to hang her. We've been told that you had got her."

The poor mother, assuming as indifferent an air as she was able, replied, "I don't very well understand what you mean."

The other resumed, "*Tête-Dieu!* Then what sort of a tale was that wild, staring archdeacon telling us? Where is he?"

"Monseigneur," said a soldier, "he's disappeared."

"Come, come, old mad woman," resumed the commander; "don't tell me any lies. There was a witch given you to keep. What have you done with her?"

The recluse would not give a flat denial, for fear of awakening suspicion, but answered in a downright and surly tone, "If you're talking of a tall young girl that was given me to hold just now, I can tell you that she bit me, and I let her go. That's all. Leave me at rest."

The commander made a grimace of disappointment. "Let me have no lying, old spectre," he resumed once more, "My name's Tristan l'Hermite, and I'm the King's compère. Tristan l'Hermite. Dost thou hear?" he added, casting his eyes around the Place de Grève. "It's a name that has echoes here."

"If you were Satan l'Hermite," rejoined Gudule, gathering hope, "I should have nothing else to tell you, nor should I be afraid of you."

"*Tête-Dieu!*" said Tristan, "here's a commère. Ha! So the witch girl has got away! And which way is she gone?"

Gudule answered in a tone of unconcern, "By the Rue du Mouton, I believe."

Tristan turned his head and motioned to his men to make ready for resuming their march. The recluse took breath.

"Monseigneur," said an archer all at once, "just ask the old elf how it is that her window-bars are broken out so."

This question plunged the heart of the wretched mother in anguish again. Still she did not lose all presence of mind. "They were always so," stammered she.

"Pshaw!" returned the archer, "no longer ago than yesterday they made a fine black cross that it made one devout to look at."

Tristan cast an oblique glance at the recluse. "I think the commère's perplexed," said he.

The unfortunate woman felt that all depended upon keeping her self-possession; and so, though death was in her soul, she began to jeer at them. Mothers are equal to efforts like this.

"Bah!" said she, "that man is drunk. It's above a year since the back of a cart laden with stones ran against my window-place, and burst out the bars. I well remember how I scolded the driver."

"It's true," said another archer; "I was by when it happened."

There are always to be found, in all places, people who have seen everything. This unlooked-for testimony of the archer's revived the spirits of the recluse, who, in undergoing this interrogatory, was crossing an abyss upon the edge of a knife.

But she was doomed to a perpetual alternation of hope and alarm.

"If a cart had done that," resumed the first soldier, "the stumps of the bars must have been driven inward; but you see that they've been forced outwards."

"Ha, ha!" said Tristan to the soldier, "thou hast the nose of an inquisitor at the Châtelet. Answer what he says, old woman."

"*Mon Dieu!*" exclaimed she, reduced to the last extremity, and bursting into tears in spite of herself, "I assure you, monseigneur, that it was a cart that broke those bars. You hear—that man saw it. And besides, what has that to do with the gipsy girl you talk of?"

"Hum!" growled Tristan.

"*Diable!*" continued the soldier, flattered by the provost's commendation, "the iron looks quite fresh broken."

Tristan shook his head. She turned pale. "How long is it, do you say, since this cart affair?" he asked.

"A month—perhaps a fortnight, monseigneur. I don't recollect."

"At first she said above a year," observed the soldier.

"That looks queer," said the provost.

"Monseigneur," cried she, still standing close up to the loophole, and trembling lest suspicions should prompt them to put their heads through and look round the cell—"monseigneur, I do assure you it was a cart that broke this grating; I swear it to you by all the angels in paradise. If it was not done by a cart, I wish I may go to everlasting perdition, and I deny my God!"

"Thou art very hot in that oath of thine," said Tristan, with his inquisitorial glance.

The poor woman felt her assurance deserting her more and more. She was already making blunders, and had a terrible consciousness that she was saying what she should not have said.

And now another soldier came up, crying, "Monseigneur, the old elf lies. The witch has not run away by the Rue du Mouton: the chain of that street has been stretched across all night, and the chainkeeper has seen nobody go by."

Tristan, the expression of whose countenance was every moment growing more sinister, again interrogated the recluse. "What hast thou to say to that?"

Still she strove to bear up against this fresh incident. "That I don't know, monseigneur," she replied—"that I may have been mistaken. In fact, I think she went across the water."

"That's on the opposite side," said the provost. "And yet it's not very likely that she should have wanted to go into the city again, where they were making search for her. You lie, old woman."

"And besides," added the first soldier, "there's no boat, neither on this side the water nor the other."

"She might swim across," replied the recluse, defending her ground inch by inch.

"Do women swim?" said the soldier.

"*Tête-Dieu!* old woman, you lie! you lie!" replied Tristan angrily. "I've a good mind to leave the witch and take thee. A quarter of an hour's questioning will perhaps get the truth out of thy throat. Come—thou shalt go along with us."

She caught eagerly at these words. "Just as you please, monseigneur. Do as you say. The *question,* the *question.* I'm quite willing. Carry me with you. Quick! quick!—let us go directly." In the meantime, thought she, my daughter will make her escape.

"*Mort-Dieu!*" said the provost, "what an appetite for the chevalet! This mad woman's quite past my comprehension."

An old grey-headed sergeant of the watch now stepped out of the ranks, and addressing the provost, said, "Mad, in truth, monseigneur! If she's let the gipsy go, it's not her fault, for she's no liking for gipsy women. For fifteen years have I been on this duty; and every night I hear her cursing against those Bohemian dames with execrations without end. If the one we are seeking be, as I believe she is, the little dancing-girl with the goat, she detests her above all the rest."

Gudule made an effort and repeated, "Her above all the rest."

The unanimous testimony of the men of the watch confirmed to the provost what the old sergeant had said. Tristan l'Hermite, despairing of getting anything out of the recluse, turned his back upon her; and she, with inexpressible anxiety, watched him pace slowly back towards his horse. "Come," said he grumblingly, "forward! we must continue the search. I will not sleep until the gipsy woman be hanged."

Still he hesitated for a while before mounting his horse. Gudule was palpitating between life and death while she beheld him throwing around the Place that restless look of a hound that feels himself to be near the lair of the game and is reluctant to go away. At last he shook his head, and sprang into his saddle.

Gudule's heart, which had been so horribly compressed, now dilated; and she said in a whisper, casting a glance upon her daughter, at whom she had not ventured to look since the arrival of her pursuers, "Saved!"

The poor girl had remained all this time in her corner, without breathing or stirring, with the image of death staring in her face. No particular of the scene between Gudule and Tristan had escaped her, and each pang of her mother's had vibrated in her own heart. She had heard, as it were, each successive cracking of the threads which had held her suspended over the abyss. Oftentimes had she thought she perceived it breaking asunder; and it was only now that she was beginning to take breath and to feel the ground steady under her feet. At that moment she heard a man saying to the provost, "*Corbœuf!* Monsieur the Provost, it's not my business, who am a man-at-arms, to hang witches. The rabble rout of the populace is put down. I leave you to do your own work by yourself. You'll allow me to go back to my company, who are waiting for their captain." The voice, as the reader will probably have divined, was that of Phœbus de Chateaupers. What passed in the breast of the gipsy girl it is not easy to describe. So he was there—her friend—her protector—her support—her shelter—her Phœbus! She started up; and before her mother could prevent her, she had sprung to the loophole, crying out, "Phœbus!—hither, my Phœbus!"

Phœbus was no longer there. He had just galloped round the corner of the Rue de la Coutellerie. But Tristan was not yet gone away.

The recluse rushed upon her daughter with a roar of agony, and drew her violently back, her nails entering the flesh of the poor girl's neck; but the grasp of a tigress mother cannot be nicely cautious. It was too late, however. Tristan had observed.

"Ha, ha!" he cried, with a laugh that showed all his teeth, and made his face resemble the muzzle of a wolf, "two mice in the trap!"

"I suspected as much," said the soldier.

Tristan slapped him on the shoulder, saying, "Thou art a good cat. Come," he added, "where is Henriet Cousin?"

A man who had neither the dress nor the mien of the soldiers now stepped out of their ranks. He wore a suit half grey, half brown—his hair combed out flat—leathern sleeves—and carried a bundle of ropes in his hand. This man constantly attended upon Tristan, who constantly attended upon Louis XI.

"Friend," said Tristan l'Hermite, "I presume that this is the witch we were seeking. Thou wilt hang me that one. Hast thou thy ladder with thee?"

"There's one under the shed of the Maison-aux-Piliers," answered the man. "Is it at *that* justice *there* that we're to do the job?" continued he, pointing to the stone gibbet.

"Yes."

"So ho!" said the man with a loud laugh more brutal still than that of the provost, "we shall not have far to go!"

"Make haste," said Tristan, "and do thy laughing after."

Meanwhile, since the time that Tristan had observed her daughter, and all hope was lost, the recluse had not yet uttered a word. She had thrown the poor gipsy girl, half dead, into the corner of the cell, and resumed her post at the loophole, her two hands resting upon the bottom of the stone window-case, like the clutches of some animal. In that attitude she was seen throwing intrepidly over all those soldiers her look, which was become wild and frantic again. At the moment that Henriet Cousin approached the Place, she looked at him so savagely that he shrank back.

"Monseigneur," said he, turning back to the provost, "which must I take?"

"The young one."

"So much the better, for the old one seems none so easy to take."

"Poor little dancing-girl with the goat!" said the old sergeant of the watch.

Henriet Cousin again approached the window-place. The mother's eye made his own droop. He said very timidly, "Madame——"

She interrupted him in a voice very low but furious—"What do you want?"

"Not you," said he, "but the other."

"What other?"

"The young one."

She began to shake her head, crying, "There's nobody! there's nobody! there's nobody!"

"Yes, there is somebody; you know it well enough," returned the hangman. "Let me take the young one; I don't want to do you any harm."

She answered with a strange sneering expression, "Ha! you don't want to do me any harm!"

"Let me have the other, madame," said the man. "It's the will of Monsieur the Provost."

She replied, with a look of insanity, "There's nobody!"

"I tell you there *is*," rejoined the hangman. "We've all seen that there were two of you."

"You'd better look!" said the recluse with her strange sneer. "Thrust your head through the window."

The man observed the threatening nails of the mother, and did not venture.

"Make haste!" cried Tristan, who had just drawn up his troops in a circle about the Trou-aux-Rats, and had stationed himself on horseback near the gibbet.

Henriet once more went back to the provost quite perplexed. He had laid his ropes upon the ground, and with a sheepish look was turning about his hat in his hands. "Monseigneur," he asked, "how must I get in?"

"Through the door."

"There is none."

"Through the window, then."

"It's not wide enough."

"Widen it then," said Tristan angrily. "Hast thou no picks with thee?"

The mother, from the interior of the cave, was still steadfastly watching them. She had ceased to hope—she no longer knew what she wanted—except that she wanted them not to take from her her daughter.

Henriet Cousin went and fetched the box of tools of the *basses-œuvres* (that is, the implements for the use of the sub-executioners) from under the *hangar*, or long shed, of the Maison-aux-Piliers. He also brought out from the same place the double ladder, which he immediately set up against the gibbet. Five or six of the provost's men provided themselves with pickaxes and crowbars, and Tristan went up to the window of the cell.

"Old woman," said the provost in a tone of severity, "give us up that girl quietly."

She looked at him like one who does not understand.

"*Tête-Dieu!*" resumed Tristan; "what good can it do thee to hinder that witch from being hanged as it pleases the King?"

The wretched woman fell a-laughing with her wild laugh. "What good can it do me? She's my daughter!"

The tone in which this word was uttered produced a shudder in Henriet Cousin himself.

"I'm sorry for it," returned the provost; "but it's the King's pleasure."

She cried, laughing her terrific laugh with redoubled loudness, "What's thy King to me? I tell thee it's my daughter!"

"Make a way through the wall," said Tristan.

To make an opening sufficiently large it was only necessary to loosen one course of stone underneath the window-place. When the mother heard the picks and the levers sapping her fortress, she uttered a dreadful cry. Then she began to go with frightful quickness round and round her cell—a habit of a wild beast, which her long residence in that cage had given her. She no longer said anything, but her eyes were flaming. The soldiers felt their blood chilled to the very heart.

All at once she took up her paving-stone, laughed, and threw it with both hands at the workmen. The stone, ill thrown (for her hands were trembling), touched no one, but fell quite harmless at the feet of Tristan's horse. She gnashed her teeth.

Meanwhile, although the sun was not yet risen, it was become broad daylight, and a fine roseate tint beautified the old decayed chimneys of the Maison-aux-Piliers. It was the hour when the windows of the earliest risers in the great city opened cheerfully upon the roofs. A few rustics, a few fruitsellers, going to the Halles upon their asses, were beginning to cross the Grève, stopped for a moment before that group of soldiers gathered about the Trou-aux-Rats, gazed at it with looks of astonishment, and passed on.

The recluse had gone and seated herself close to her daughter, covering her with her own figure—her eyes fixed—listening to the poor girl, who stirred not, but was murmuring low her only word, "Phœbus! Phœbus!" In proportion as the work of the demolishers seemed to be advancing, the mother mechanically shrunk away, pressing the young girl closer and closer against the wall. All at once the recluse saw the course of stone (for she was on the watch, and had her eye constantly upon it) beginning to give way, and she heard the voice of Tristan encouraging the workmen. Then starting out of the sort of prostration into which her spirit had sunk for some minutes, she cried out—and as she spoke her voice now tore the ear like a saw, now faltered as if every species of malediction had crowded to her lips to burst forth at one and the same time—"Ho! ho! ho! but it's horrible! You are robbers! Are you really going to take my daughter from me? I tell you she's my daughter. O the cowards! O the hangman lackeys!—the miserable murdering suttlers! Help! help! fire! And will they take my child from me so? Who is it, then, that they call the good God of heaven?"

Then, addressing herself to Tristan with foaming mouth and haggard eyes, on all-fours and bristling like a panther, "You'd better come and take my daughter. Dost thou not understand that this woman tells thee it's her daughter? Dost thou know what it is to have a child, eh, thou he-wolf? Hast thou never lain with thy mate? Hast thou never had a cub by her? And if thou hast little ones, when they howl, is there nothing stirs within thee?"

"Down with the stones!" said Tristan; "they're quite loose now."

The crowbars now heaved up the heavy course of stone. It was, as we have said, the mother's last bulwark. She threw herself upon it—she would fain have held it in its place—she scratched the stones with her nails; but the heavy mass, put in motion by half a dozen men, escaped her grasp, and fell gently down to the ground along the iron levers.

The mother, seeing the breach effected, threw herself on the floor across the opening, barricading it with her body, writhing her arms, beating her head against the flagstones, and crying in a voice hoarse and nearly inarticulate with exhaustion, "Help! help!—fire! fire!"

"Now take the girl," said Tristan, still imperturbable.

The mother looked at the soldiers in so formidable a manner that they had more disposition to retreat than to advance.

"Now for it!" resumed the provost. "You, Henriet Cousin."

Nobody advanced a step.

The provost swore, "*Tête-Christ!* my fighting-men! Afraid of a woman!"

"Monseigneur," said Henriet, "do you call *that* a woman?"

"She has a lion's mane," said another.

"Come!" continued the provost. "The gap's large enough. Enter three abreast, as at the breach of Pontoise. Let's get done with it, *mort-Mahom!* The first that gives back I'll cleave him in two."

Placed thus between the provost and the mother, the soldiers hesitated a moment; then made up their minds, and went up to the Trou-aux-Rats.

When the recluse saw this she suddenly reared herself upon her knees, threw aside her hair from over her face, then dropped her lean, grazed hands upon her hips. Then big tears issued one by one from her eyes, coursing each other down her furrowed cheeks, like a stream down the bed that it has worn itself. At the same time she began to speak, but in a voice so suppliant, so gentle, so submissive, so heart-piercing, that more than one old *argousin*, among those who surrounded Tristan, wiped his eyes.

"Messeigneurs!" said she; "messieurs the sergeants! one word! There's a thing I must tell you. It's my daughter, do you see—my dear little daughter, that I had lost. Listen—it's quite a history. Consider that I'm very well acquainted with messieurs the sergeants. They were always good to me in those times when the little boys used to throw stones at me because I was a girl of pleasure. So you see—you'll leave me my child when you know all! I was a poor woman of the town. It was the gipsy women that stole her away from me—by the same token that I've kept her shoe these fifteen years. Look! here it is. She'd a foot like that. At Reims—La Chantefleurie—Rue Folle-Peine. Perhaps you know all that. It was I. In your youth—in those days—it was a merry time—and there were merry doings. You'll have pity on me, won't you, messeigneurs? The gipsy women stole her from me. They hid her from me for fifteen years. I thought she was dead. Only think, my good friends—I thought she was dead! I've passed fifteen years here—in this cave—without fire in the winter. It's hard, that! The poor dear little shoe! I cried so much that at last God Almighty heard me! This night He has given me back my daughter! It's a miracle of God Almighty's. She was not dead. You'll not take her from me—I'm sure you won't. If it were myself now, I can't say—but to take her, a child of sixteen! Let her have time to see the sun. What has she done to you? Nothing at all. Nor I neither. If you did but know now that I have but her—that I am old—that it's a blessing the Holy Virgin sends me! And then, you're all of you so good!

You didn't know it was my daughter—but you know now. Oh, I love her so! Monsieur the Grand Provost, I would rather have a stab in my side than a scratch upon her finger! It's you that look like a good seigneur! What I tell you now explains the thing to you, doesn't it? Oh, if you have had a mother, monseigneur! You are the commander, leave me my child. Only consider that I'm praying to you on my knees, as they pray to a Christ Jesus! I ask nothing of anybody. I am of Reims, messeigneurs—I've a little field there that was Mahiet Pradon's. I'm not a beggar. I want nothing—but I want to keep my child! God Almighty, who is Master of all, has not given her back to me for nothing! The King—you say, the King—it can't be any great pleasure to him that they should kill my little girl. Besides, it's my daughter—it's my daughter—mine—she's not the King's—she's not yours! I want to go away from here—we both want to go—and when two women are going along, mother and daughter, you let them go quietly! Let us go quietly! We belong to Reims. Oh, you're so good, messieurs the sergeants—I love you all! You'll not take my dear little one away from me—it's impossible! Is it not now quite impossible? My child! my child!"

We shall not attempt to give an idea of her gesture, her accent, the tears which she drank in while speaking, the clasping and the writhing of her hands, the agonising smiles, the swimming looks, the sighs, the moans, the miserable and piercing cries, which she mingled with those disordered, wild, and incoherent words. When she ceased, Tristan l'Hermite knit his brows—but it was to conceal a tear that was standing in his tiger's eye. However, he overcame this weakness, and said with brief utterance, "The King wills it."

Then he whispered in the ear of Henriet Cousin, "Get done quickly." It might be that the redoubtable provost felt his own heart failing him—even *his*.

The executioner and the sergeants entered the cell. The mother made no resistance; she only crept up to her daughter, and threw herself madly upon her. When the gipsy girl saw the soldiers approaching, the horror of death gave her strength again. "My mother!" cried she in a tone of indescribable distress. "O my mother! they are coming; defend me!" "Yes, my love, I am defending you!" answered the mother in a faint voice; and clasping her closely in her arms she covered her with kisses. To see them both thus upon the ground, the mother upon the daughter, was truly piteous.

Henriet Cousin took hold of the gipsy girl just below her beautiful shoulders. When she felt his hands touching her she cried, "Heuh!" and fainted. The executioner, from whose eye big tears were falling upon her drop by drop, offered to carry her away in his arms. He strove to unclasp the embrace of the mother, who had, as it were, drawn her hands in a knot about her daughter's waist; but the grasp which thus bound her to the person of her child was so powerful that he found it impossible to unloose it. Henriet Cousin then dragged the young girl out of the cell, and her mother after her. The eyes of the mother were closed as well as those of the daughter.

The sun was rising at that moment; and already there was a considerable collection of people upon the Place, looking from a distance to see what they were thus dragging along the ground towards the gibbet. For this was a way of the Provost Tristan's at executions—he had a rage for preventing the curious from coming near.

There was nobody at the windows. Only there were to be seen at a distance, on the top of that one of the towers of Notre-Dame which looks upon the Grève, two men, whose figures stood darkly out against the clear morning sky, and who seemed to be looking on.

Henriet Cousin stopped with what he was dragging along at the foot of the fatal ladder, and with troubled breath—such a pity did he think it—he passed the rope round the young girl's lovely neck. The unfortunate girl felt the horrible contact of the hempen cord. She raised her eyelids, and beheld the skeleton arm of the stone gibbet extended over her head. Then she shook herself, and cried in a loud and agonising voice, "No! no! I won't! I wont!" The mother, whose head was quite buried under her daughter's attire, said not a word; but a long shudder was seen to run through her whole frame, and she was heard multiplying her kisses upon the form of her child. The executioner seized that moment to unclasp, by a strong and sudden effort, the arms with which she held fast the condemned; and, whether from exhaustion or despair, they yielded. Then he took the young girl upon his shoulder, from whence her charming figure fell gracefully bending over his large head. And then he set his foot upon the ladder in order to ascend.

At that moment the mother, who had sunk upon the ground, quite opened her eyes. Without uttering any cry she started up with a terrific expression of countenance; then, like a beast rushing upon its prey, she threw herself upon the executioner's hand, and set her teeth in it. This was done with the quickness of lightning. The executioner howled with pain. They came to his relief, and with difficulty liberated his bleeding hand from the bite of the mother. She kept a profound silence. They pushed her away with brutal violence, and it was remarked that her head fell back heavily upon the ground. They raised her up—she fell back again. The fact was, that she was dead.

The executioner, who had kept his hold of the young girl, began again to ascend the ladder.

CHAPTER II

LA CREATURA BELLA BIANCO VESTITA

(*Dante*)

When Quasimodo saw that the cell was empty—that the gipsy girl was gone—that she had been carried off while he had been defending her—he grasped his hair with both hands, and stamped with surprise and grief; then he went running over the whole church, seeking his young Bohemian—bawling strange cries at every corner, strewing his red hair upon the pavement. It was just the moment when the King's archers were entering victorious into Notre-Dame, likewise in search of the gipsy girl. The poor deaf ringer assisted their search without in the least suspecting their fatal intentions; he thought that the enemies of the gipsy girl were the Truands. He himself showed Tristan l'Hermite the way into every possible nook of concealment—opened him the secret doors, the false backs of the altars, the inner sacristies. Had the unfortunate girl been still there, it would have been he himself that would have put her in their hands. When the irksomeness of seeking in vain had tired out Tristan, who was not to be tired out easily, Quasimodo continued the search by himself. Twenty times, a hundred times over, did he make the circuit of the church, from one end to the other, and from top to bottom—ascending—descending—running—calling—shouting—peeping—rummaging—ferreting—putting his head into every hole—thrusting a torch under every vault—desperate—mad—haggard and moaning as a beast that has lost his mate. At length, when he had made himself sure, quite sure, that she was gone—that all was over—that they had stolen her from him—he slowly reascended the tower staircase, that staircase which he had mounted so nimbly and triumphantly on the day that he had saved her. He now passed by the same spots, with drooping head, voiceless, tearless, and hardly drawing breath. The church had become solitary and silent again. The archers had quitted it to pursue the sorceress in the city. Quasimodo, left alone in that vast Notre-Dame, the moment before so besieged and so tumultuous, took his way once more towards the cell in which the gipsy girl had slept for so many weeks under his protection. As he approached it he could not help fancying to himself that perhaps on arriving he should find her there again. On reaching that bend of the gallery which looks upon the roof of the side aisle he could see the narrow receptacle, with its little window and its little door, lying close under one of the great buttresses, like a bird's nest under a bough. The poor fellow's heart failed him, and he leaned against a pillar to keep himself from falling. He figured to himself that perhaps she might have come back thither—that some good genius had no doubt brought her back—that that little nest was too quiet, too safe, and too charming for her not to be there—and he dared not advance a step farther, for fear of dispelling the illusion. "Yes," said he to himself, "she's sleeping, perhaps—or praying; I mustn't disturb her." At last he summoned up courage—approached on tiptoe—looked—entered. Empty! the cell was still empty! The unhappy man moved slowly round it, lifted up her couch, and looked underneath it, as if she could have been hidden between the mattress and the stones; then he shook his head, and stood stupefied. All at once he furiously stamped out his torchlight, and, without uttering a word or breathing a sigh, he rushed with all his force head foremost against the wall, and fell senseless upon the floor.

When his senses returned he threw himself upon the bed, rolling about, and frantically kissing the yet warm place where the young girl had slept; then he remained for some minutes motionless, as if he was expiring there; then he rose again, streaming with perspiration, panting, frenzied, and fell to beating the walls with his head, with the frightful regularity of the stroke of a clock and the resolution of a man determined to fracture his skull. At length he sank exhausted a second time. Then he crawled to the outside of the cell, and remained crouching in an attitude of astonishment in front of the door for a full hour, with his eye fixed upon the solitary dwelling-place, more gloomy and pensive than a mother seated between the cradle and the coffin of her departed child. He uttered not a word; only at intervals a violent sob agitated his whole frame, but it was a sobbing devoid of tears.

It seems to have been then that, striving to divine, amidst his desolate ruminations, who could have been the unexpected ravisher of the gipsy girl, he thought of the archdeacon. He recollected that Dom Claude alone had a key of the staircase leading to the cell. He remembered his nocturnal attempts upon La Esmeralda, the first of which he, Quasimodo, had aided; the second of which he had prevented. He called to mind a thousand various particulars, and soon he felt quite convinced that it was the archdeacon that had taken the gipsy girl from him. Yet such was his reverence for the priest—his gratitude, his devotedness, his love for that man, were so deeply rooted in his heart—that they resisted, even at this dire moment, the pangs of jealousy and despair.

He reflected that the archdeacon had done it, and that sanguinary, deadly resentment which he would have felt for it against any other individual was turned in the poor ringer's breast, the moment that Claude Frollo was concerned, simply into an increase of sorrow.

At the moment that his thoughts were thus fixing themselves upon the priest, while the buttresses were whitening in the daybreak, he beheld, on the upper story of Notre-Dame, at the angle formed by the external balustrade, which runs round the top of the chancel, a figure walking. The figure was coming towards him. He recognised it: it was that of the archdeacon. Claude was pacing along gravely and slowly. He did not look before him as he advanced, directing his steps towards the northern tower; his face was turned aside towards the right bank of the Seine, and he carried his head erect, as if striving to obtain a view of something over the roofs. The owl has often that oblique attitude, flying in one direction and looking in another. In this manner the priest passed above Quasimodo without seeing him.

The deaf spectator, whom this sudden apparition had confounded, saw the figure disappear through the door of the staircase of the northern tower, which, as the reader is aware, is the one commanding a view of the Hôtel-de-Ville. Quasimodo rose up and followed the archdeacon.

Quasimodo ascended the tower staircase to learn why the priest was ascending it; but the poor ringer knew not what he himself was going to do—what he was going to say—what he wanted. He was full of rage and full of dread. The archdeacon and the gipsy girl clashed together in his heart.

When he had reached the top of the tower, before issuing from the shade of the staircase upon the open platform he cautiously observed whereabouts the priest was. The priest had his back towards him. An open balustrade surrounds the platform of the steeple. The priest, whose eyes were bent upon the town, was leaning his breast upon that one of the four sides of the balustrade which looks upon the Pont Notre-Dame.

Quasimodo stole up behind him to see what he was looking at so; and the priest's attention was so completely absorbed elsewhere that he heard not the step of his deaf servant near him.

It is a magnificent and captivating spectacle, and at that day it was yet more so, to look down upon Paris from the summit of the towers of Notre-Dame in the fresh light of a summer dawn. The day in question might be one of the early ones of July. The sky was perfectly serene. A few lingering stars were fading away in different directions, and eastward there was one very brilliant, in the lightest part of the heavens. The sun was on the point of making his appearance. Paris was beginning to stir. A very white, pure light showed vividly to the eye the endless varieties of outline which its buildings presented on the east, while the giant shadows of the steeples traversed building after building from one end of the great city to the other. Already voices and noises were to be heard from several quarters of the town. Here was heard the stroke of a bell, there that of a hammer, and there again the complicated clatter of a dray in motion. Already the smoke from some of the chimneys was escaping scatteredly over all that surface of roofs, as if through the fissures of some vast sulphur work. The river, whose waters are rippled by the piers of so many bridges and the points of so many islands, was wavering in folds of silver. Around the town, outside the ramparts, the view was lost in a great circle of fleecy vapours, through which were indistinctly discernible the dim line of the plains and the graceful swelling of the heights. All sorts of floating sounds were scattered over that half-awakened region. And eastward the morning breeze was chasing across the sky a few light locks plucked from the fleecy mantle of the hills.

In the Parvis some good women, with their milk-pots in their hands, were pointing out to one another, in astonishment, the singularly shattered state of the great door of Notre-Dame, and the two congealed streams of lead all down the crevices of the front. It was all that remained of the tumult of the night before. The pile kindled by Quasimodo between the towers was extinct. Tristan had cleared the ground of the Place, and had the dead thrown into the Seine. Kings like Louis XI. take care to clean the pavements quick after a massacre.

Outside the balustrade of the tower, exactly underneath the point where the priest had stopped, was one of those fantastically carved stone gutters which diversify the exterior of Gothic buildings, and in a crevice of this gutter two pretty wallflowers in full bloom, shaken and vivified as it were by the breath of the morning, made sportive salutation to each other; while over the towers, far above in the sky, were heard the cheerful voices of early birds.

But the priest neither saw nor heard anything of all that. He was one of those men to whom there are neither mornings, nor birds, nor flowers. In all that immense horizon, spread around him with such diversity of aspect, his contemplation was concentrated upon one single point.

Quasimodo burned to ask him what he had done with the gipsy girl; but the archdeacon seemed at that moment to be rapt out of the world. He was evidently in one of those violent passages of existence when the earth itself might fall to ruin without our perceiving it.

With his eyes invariably fixed upon a certain spot, he remained motionless and silent; and in that silence and immobility there was something so formidable that the savage ringer shuddered at the contemplation, and dared not obtrude upon them. All that he did—and it was one way of interrogating the archdeacon—was to follow the direction of his vision, which thus guided the view of the unfortunate hunchback to the Place de Grève.

In this manner he discovered what the priest was looking at. The ladder was erected against the permanent gibbet. There were some people in the Place, and a number of soldiers. A man was dragging along the ground something white, to which something black was clinging. This man stopped at the foot of the gibbet. Here something took place which Quasimodo could not very distinctly see; not that his only eye had not preserved its long reach, but there was a body of soldiers in the way which prevented him from distinguishing all. Moreover, at that instant the sun appeared, and such a flood of light burst over the horizon that it seemed as if every point of Paris—spires, chimneys, and gables—were taking fire at once.

Meantime the man began to ascend the ladder. Then Quasimodo saw him distinctly again. He was carrying a female figure upon his shoulder—a young girl clad in white. There was a noose round the young girl's neck. Quasimodo recognised her. It was she!

The man arrived with his burden at the top of the ladder. There he arranged the noose. And now the priest, to have a better view, set himself on his knees upon the balustrade.

All at once the man pushed away the ladder with his heel, and Quasimodo, who for some moments had not drawn his breath, saw wavering at the end of the cord, about two toises above the ground, the form of the unfortunate girl, with that of the man squatted upon her shoulders. The cord made several turns upon itself, and Quasimodo beheld horrible convulsions agitating the frame of the gipsy girl. On the other hand, the priest, with outstretched neck and starting eyeballs, was contemplating that frightful group of the man and the girl—the spider and the fly!

At the moment when it looked the most horrible a demoniacal laugh—a laugh such as can come only from one who is no longer human—burst from the livid visage of the priest. Quasimodo did not hear that laugh, but he saw it. The ringer made a few steps backward from behind the archdeacon, and then, rushing furiously upon him, thrusting both his large hands against his back, he pushed Dom Claude over into the abyss towards which he had been leaning.

The priest cried out, "Damnation!" and fell.

The gutter-head over which he had been leaning arrested his fall. He clung to it with desperate grip; but at the moment that he was opening his lips to cry out again, he saw passing along the verge of the balustrade above him the formidable and avenging countenance of Quasimodo, and was silent.

Beneath him were the abyss—a fall of full two hundred feet—and the pavement. In this dreadful situation the archdeacon said not a word, breathed not a groan. Only he writhed upon the gutter, making incredible efforts to reascend; but his hands had no hold of the granite, his feet constantly slid away upon the blackened wall. They who have ascended to the top of the towers of Notre-Dame know that the stonework swells out immediately below the balustrade. It was on the re-entering angle of this ridge that the miserable archdeacon was exhausting his efforts. It was not with a wall merely perpendicular that he was striving, but with a wall that sloped away from under him.

Quasimodo would only have had to stretch out his hand to him to draw him from the gulf; but he did not so much as look at him. He was looking on the Grève—he was looking on the gibbet—he was looking on the gipsy girl. The poor deaf creature had leaned his elbows on the balustrade in the very place where the archdeacon had been the moment before; and there, keeping his eye fixed upon the only object of which at that moment he was conscious, he was mute and motionless as one struck by the thunderbolt, except that a long stream of tears was flowing from that eye which until then had never shed but one.

Meanwhile the archdeacon was panting; his bald forehead was streaming with perspiration; his nails were bleeding against the stones; he was grazing his knees against the wall. He could hear his cassock, which had caught hold of the gutter, tearing more and more at each jerk that he gave it; and to complete his misfortune, the gutter itself terminated in a leaden pipe, which he could feel slowly bending under the weight of his body. The wretched man was saying to himself that when his hands should be worn out with fatigue, when his cassock should be rent asunder, when that lead should be completely bent, he must of necessity fall, and terror froze his vitals. Now and then he looked down bewilderedly upon a sort of small table formed, some ten feet lower, by projections of sculpture; and he implored Heaven, from the bottom of his agonising soul, that he might be permitted to spend the remainder of his life upon that narrow space of two feet square, though it were to last a hundred years. Once he ventured to look down into the Place below him; but when he turned his head upwards again, it was with closing eyes and hair erect.

There was something frightful in the silence of these two men. While the archdeacon was agonising in that horrible manner but a few feet from him, Quasimodo was weeping and looking upon the Grève.

The archdeacon, finding that all his efforts to raise himself served only to warp the one feeble point of support that remained to him, had at length resolved to remain quite still. There he was—clasping the gutter—scarce drawing his breath —stirring not at all—without any other motion than that mechanical convulsion of the viscera which is felt in a dream when we fancy we are falling. His fixed eyes were wide open with a stare of pain and astonishment. Meanwhile he felt himself going by degrees: his fingers slipped upon the gutter; he felt more and more the weakness of his arms and the weight of his body; the bending piece of lead that supported him inclined more and more downwards. He saw beneath him, frightful to look upon, the sharp roof of the church of Saint-Jean-le-Rond, small as a card bent double. He looked, one after another, at the imperturbable sculptures of the tower, like him suspended over the precipice, but without terror for themselves or pity for him. All around him was of stone; before his eyes the gaping monsters; in the Place below, the pavement; over his head, Quasimodo weeping.

Down in the Parvis there were some groups of worthy starers, quietly striving to guess what madman it could be that was amusing himself after so strange a fashion. The priest could hear them saying, for their voices mounted up to him clear and shrill, "Why, he'll surely break his neck!"

Quasimodo was weeping.

At length the archdeacon, foaming with rage and dread, felt that all was unavailing. However, he gathered what strength he had remaining for one last effort. He drew himself up on the gutter, sprung from against the wall with both his knees, hung his hands in a cleft of the stonework, and succeeded, perhaps, in climbing up with one foot; but the force which he was obliged to use gave a sudden bend to the leaden beak that supported him, and the same effort rent his cassock asunder. Then finding everything under him give way—having only his benumbed and powerless hands by which to cling to anything—the unhappy man closed his eyes, left hold of the gutter, and fell.

Quasimodo looked at him falling.

A fall from such a height is seldom perpendicular. The archdeacon, launched through the void, fell at first with his head downwards and his arms extended; then he turned round several times. The wind carried him against the top of one of the houses, upon which the miserable man was first dashed. However, he was not dead when he reached it. The ringer could perceive him still make an effort to cling to the gable with his hands; but the slope was too quick, and he had no strength left. He glided rapidly down the roof, like a loosened tile, then dashed upon the pavement, and there he lay quite still.

Quasimodo then lifted his eye to look upon the gipsy girl, whose body, suspended from the gibbet, he beheld quivering afar, under its white robes, in the last struggles of death; then again he dropped it upon the archdeacon, stretched a shapeless mass at the foot of the tower, and he said with a sob that heaved his deep breast to the bottom, "Oh—all that I've ever loved!"

CHAPTER III

MARRIAGE OF PHŒBUS

TOWARDS the evening of that day, when the judicial officers of the bishop came and gathered up from the Parvis the shattered corpse of the archdeacon, Quasimodo had disappeared from Notre-Dame.

This circumstance gave rise to various rumours. It was thought unquestionable that the day had at length arrived when, according to their compact, Quasimodo—that is to say, the devil—had been to carry off Claude Frollo—that is to say, the sorcerer. It was presumed that he had shattered the body in taking the soul, as a monkey cracks the shell to get at the nut.

Therefore it was that the archdeacon was not interred in consecrated ground.

Louis XI. died soon after, in August 1483.

As for Pierre Gringoire, he not only succeeded in saving the goat, but succeeded also in tragedy. It appears that, after tasting of astrology, philosophy, architecture, hermetics—of every vanity, in short—he came back to tragedy, which some people think is the vainest of all. This he called *coming to a tragical end*. On the subject of his dramatic triumphs, in the Ordinary's accompts for 1483 we read as follows:—

"To Jehan Marchand and Pierre Gringoire, carpenter and composer, for making and composing the mystery done at the Châtelet of Paris, on the day of the entry of Monsieur the Legate; for duly ordering the characters, with dresses and habiliments, meet for the said mystery; and likewise, for making the wooden stages thereunto necessary, a hundred livres."

Phœbus de Chateaupers, as our author maliciously expresseth it, "also came to *a tragical end*; for he—married."

CHAPTER IV

MARRIAGE OF QUASIMODO

WE have already said that Quasimodo disappeared from Notre-Dame on the day of the death of the gipsy girl and the archdeacon. And, in fact, he was never seen again, nor was it known what had become of him.

In the night that followed the execution of La Esmeralda, the executioners had taken down her body from the gibbet, and, according to custom, had carried it away and deposited it in the great charnel-vault of Montfaucon.

Montfaucon, to use the words of the antiquarian Sauval, "was the most ancient and most superb gibbet in the kingdom." Between the faubourgs of the Temple and St. Martin, at the distance of about a hundred and sixty toises from the walls of Paris, and a few bowshots from the village of La Courtille, was to be seen, on the summit of an almost imperceptibly rising ground, sufficiently elevated to be visible for several leagues round, an edifice of a strange form, much resembling a druidical cromlech, and having, like the cromlech, its human sacrifices.

Imagine, based upon a mound of plaster, a great oblong mass of stonework, fifteen feet high, thirty wide, and forty long, with a door, an external railing, and an upper platform, and, standing upon the platform, sixteen enormous pillars of unhewn stone, thirty feet high, ranged in a colonnade round three of the four sides of the huge block supporting them, and connected at the top by heavy beams from which chains were hanging at short intervals; at each of those chains a bundle of skeletons; not far off, in the plain, a stone cross and two secondary gibbets, rising like shoots from the great central tree; and in the sky above the whole, a perpendicular flocking of carrion crows. Such was Montfaucon.

At the end of the fifteenth century, this formidable gibbet, which had stood since 1328, was already much dilapidated; the beams were decayed, the chains corroded with rust, the pillars green over with mould, the courses of hewn stone were all gaping at their joints, and the grass was growing upon that platform to which no foot reached. The structure showed a most horrible profile against the sky—especially at night, when the moonlight gleamed upon those whitened skulls, or when the breeze of evening brushed the chains and skeletons, making them rattle in the dark. The presence of this gibbet communicated a dismal character to its whole vicinity.

The mass of stonework that formed the base of the repulsive edifice was hollow. An immense cave had been constructed within it, the entrance of which was closed with an old battered iron grating, and into which were thrown, not only the human relics taken down from the chains of Montfaucon, but also the carcases of the sufferers at all the other permanent gibbets of Paris. To that deep charnel-house, wherein so many human remains, and the memories of so many crimes, have festered and been confounded together, many a great one of the earth, and many of the innocent, at one time or other, contributed their bones—from Enguerrand de Marigni, who had the first turn at Montfaucon, and who was one of the just, down to the Admiral de Coligni, who had the last, and was of the just also.

As for Quasimodo's mysterious disappearance, all that we have been able to ascertain respecting it is this:—

About a year and a half or two years after the events that conclude this history, when search was made in the cave of Montfaucon for the body of Olivier-le-Daim, who had been hanged two days before, and to whom Charles VIII., son and successor of Olivier's kind master, granted the favour of being interred at the church of St. Laurent in better company, there were found amongst all those hideous carcases two skeletons, the arms of one of which were thrown round the other. One of the two, that of a woman, had still about it some tattered fragments of a garment, apparently of a stuff that had once been white; and about its neck was a string of grains of adrezarach, together with a small silken bag, ornamented with green glass, which was open and empty. These articles had been of so little value that the executioner, doubtless, had not cared to take them. The other skeleton, which held this one close in its arms, was that of a man. It was remarked in the latter that the spine was crooked, the head compressed between the shoulder-blades, and that one leg was shorter than the other. It was also remarkable that there was no rupture of the vertebræ at the nape of the neck, whence it was evident that he had not been hanged. Hence it was inferred that the man must have come hither of himself and died here. When they strove to detach this skeleton from the one it was embracing, it fell to dust.